MW01128024

# The Long List Anthology

## More Stories from the Hugo Award Nomination List

Edited by David Steffen

THE LONG LIST ANTHOLOGY
edited by David Steffen
www.diabolicalplots.com

Copyright © 2015 David Steffen
Stories copyright © 2014 by the authors
All rights reserved.
Published by Diabolical Plots, L.L.C.

"Worldcon," "World Science Fiction Society," "WSFS," "World Science Fiction Society," "Hugo Award," the Hugo Award Logo, and the distinctive design of the Hugo Award trophy rocket are service marks of the World Science Fiction Society, an unincorporated literary society.

Cover art: "A City On Its Tentacles" by Galen Dara, first published in Lackington's with a story of the same name by Rose Lemberg in February 2014.
Cover layout by Pat R. Steiner

Layout: Polgarus Studio

ISBN: 1519131194
ISBN-13: 978-1519131195

*I dedicate this book to my family.*
*And to my friends and supporters in writing and fandom.*

# Contents

# Permissions

"The Breath of War" by Aliette de Bodard. Copyright © 2014 by Aliette de Bodard. First published in *Beneath Ceaseless Skies* #142. Reprinted by permission of the author.

"When It Ends, He Catches Her" by Eugie Foster. Copyright © 2014 by Eugie Foster. First published electronically in *Daily Science Fiction*, September 26. Reprinted by permission of the author's estate.

"Toad Words" by T. Kingfisher. Copyright © 2014 by T. Kingfisher. First published electronically on LiveJournal, June 26. Reprinted by permission of the author.

"Makeisha in Time" by Rachael K. Jones. Copyright © 2014 by Rachael K. Jones. First published electronically in *Crossed Genres 2.0* #20. Reprinted by permission of the author.

"Covenant" by Elizabeth Bear. Copyright © 2014 by Elizabeth Bear. First published in *Hieroglyph: Stories and Visions for a Better Future*, edited by Ed Finn and Kathryn Cramer. Reprinted by permission of the author.

"The Truth About Owls" by Amal El-Mohtar. Copyright © 2014 by Amal El-Mohtar. First published in *Kaleidoscope*, edited by Alisa Krasnostein and Julia Rios. Reprinted by permission of the author.

"A Kiss With Teeth" by Max Gladstone. Copyright © 2014 by Max Gladstone. First published electronically on *Tor.com*, October 29. Reprinted by permission of the author.

"The Vaporization Enthalpy of a Peculiar Pakistani Family" by Usman T. Malik. Copyright © 2014 by Usman T. Malik. First published in *Qualia*

*Nous*, edited by Michael Bailey. Reprinted by permission of the author.

"This Chance Planet" by Elizabeth Bear. Copyright © 2014 by Elizabeth Bear. First published electronically on *Tor.com*, October 22. Reprinted by permission of the author.

"Goodnight Stars" by Annie Bellet. Copyright © 2014 by Annie Bellet. First published in *The End is Now*, edited by John Joseph Adams and Hugh Howey. Reprinted by permission of the author.

"We are the Cloud" by Sam J. Miller. Copyright © 2014 by Sam J. Miller. First published electronically in *Lightspeed Magazine* #52 . Reprinted by permission of the author.

"The Magician and LaPlace's Demon" by Tom Crosshill. Copyright © 2014 by Tom Crosshill. First published electronically in *Clarkesworld* #99. Reprinted by permission of the author.

"Spring Festival: Happiness, Anger, Love, Sorrow" by Xia Jia, translated by Ken Liu. Copyright of English translation © 2014 by Xia Jia and Ken Liu. First published in Chinese in *Science Fiction World* in June 2013. First published in English electronically in *Clarkesworld* #96. Reprinted by permission of the author and translator.

"The Husband Stitch" by Carmen Maria Machado. Copyright © 2014 by Carmen Maria Machado. First published electronically in *Granta*, October 27. Reprinted by permission of the author.

"The Bonedrake's Penance" by Yoon Ha Lee. Copyright © 2014 by Yoon Ha Lee. First published electronically in *Beneath Ceaseless Skies* #143. Reprinted by permission of the author.

"The Devil in America" by Kai Ashante Wilson. Copyright © 2014 by Kai Ashante Wilson. First published on *Tor.com*, April 2. Reprinted by permission of the author.

"The Litany of Earth" by Ruthanna Emrys. Copyright © 2014 by Ruthanna Emrys. First published electronically on *Tor.com*, May 14. Reprinted by permission of the author.

"A Guide to the Fruits of Hawai'i" by Alaya Dawn Johnson. Copyright © 2014 by Alaya Dawn Johnson. First published in *The Magazine of Fantasy & Science Fiction*, July/August 2014. Reprinted by permission of the author.

"A Year and a Day in Old Theradane" by Scott Lynch. Copyright © 2014 by Scott Lynch. First published in *Rogues*, edited by George R. R. Martin and Gardner Dozois. Reprinted by permission of the author.

"The Regular" by Ken Liu. Copyright © 2014 by Ken Liu. First published in *Upgraded*, edited by Neil Clarke. Reprinted by permission of the author.

"Grand Jeté (The Great Leap)" by Rachel Swirsky. Copyright © 2014 by Rachel Swirsky. First published electronically in *Subterranean Press Magazine*, Summer 2014. Reprinted by permission of the author.

# Foreword

I've followed the Hugo Awards for years, and have found them the most compelling of the science fiction literary awards for a variety of reasons. One of those reasons is that anyone who pays for a Supporting membership for the year's WorldCon also has a the right to nominate for and vote for the Hugos. Another reason is the Hugo Packet, which is a package of many of the nominated works to give one place where a voter can catch up on many of the works before they place their final ballots. I pay for a Supporting membership every year for the packet, which makes a great recommended reading list. If that sounds like a great deal, it is, and you might want to consider supporting WSFS and the Hugo Awards with that Supporting membership and by voting.

Every year, after the Hugo Award Ceremony at WorldCon, WSFS publishes a longer list of works that were nominated by the Hugo voters. I use this list as a recommended reading list. too, but I have mused that it would be nice if that longer list were all in one place like the Hugo packet, for convenient reading.

I have decided over the years that if I say "Someone ought to do this thing." enough times, then maybe I also ought to say "And that someone should be me." It has worked out well for me in the past, and here I am again. I confirmed interest from enough of the authors on that longer list to make an anthology of respectable size. I ran a Kickstarter to gauge interest, and there was enough interest to fund not only the book and the ebook, but an audiobook version professionally produced by Skyboat Media as well.

I sincerely hope you enjoy these stories as much as I have, and if readers like what I've put together here I'd like to repeat the project next year.

—David Steffen, December 2015—

# The Breath Of War
## By Aliette de Bodard

Going into the mountains had never been easy. Even in Rechan's first adult years, when the war was slowly burning itself to smouldering embers, every Spring Festival had been a slow migration in armed vehicles, her aunts and uncles frequently stopping in every roadside shop, taking stock of what ambushes or roadblocks might lie ahead.

The war might be over—or almost so, the planet largely at peace, the spaceports disgorging a steady stream of Galactic and Rong visitors onto Voc—but the pace was just as frustratingly slow.

They'd made good time at first: coming out of the city early in the morning and becoming airborne at the first of the authorised takeoff points, the steady stream of soldiers repatriated from the front becoming smaller and smaller as they flew higher, like insects on the intense brown of the road; zigzagging on the trails, laughing with relief as they unpacked the fried dough Rechan had baked for lunch, almost forgetting that they weren't setting on an adventure but on something with far longer-reaching consequences.

And then the flyer's motor made a funny sound, and the entire vehicle lurched downwards with a sickening crunch that jolted Rechan against the wall. And before they knew it, they were stranded on a dusty little road halfway up the mountains, leaving Rechan's niece Akanlam bartering with a local herder for a repair point.

By the sounds of it, the bartering was not going well.

Rechan sat against a large rock outcropping, rubbing the curve of her belly for comfort; feeling the familiar heaviness, the weight of the baby's body in her womb like a promise. *You'll be fine*, she thought, over and over, a saying that had become her lifeline, no matter how much of a lie it might be. *You'll be fine*.

"We should be able to solve this," Mau said. The stonewoman's face was as impassive as ever. Her eyes didn't crinkle as she spoke, her mouth didn't quirk; there was only the slow, quiet sound of her breath.

"You think so?" Rechan shook her head, trying not to think of her dreams. It was so many years since she'd carved Sang—so many years since she'd gone into the mountains with little more than rations and carving tools—but, with the particular link that bound a woman to her breath-sibling, she could feel him every night: blurred images of him hovering over the plateaux, never venturing far from the place of his birth. A relief, because he was her only hope.

On Voc, it took a stoneman's breath to quicken a baby at birth—and not any stoneman's, but the mother's breath-sibling, the one she had carved on accession to adulthood and entrusted with her breath. Without Sang, her baby would be stillborn.

"We'll find a vehicle," Mau said.

Rechan watched her niece from a distance. The discussion was getting animated and Akanlam's hand gestures more and more frantic. "Help me up," she said to Mau.

The stonewoman winced. "You shouldn't—"

"I've spent a lifetime doing what I shouldn't," Rechan said; and after a while Mau held out a hand, which she used to haul herself up. The stonewoman's skin was *lamsinh*— the same almost otherworldly translucency, the same coolness as the stone; the fingers painstakingly carved with an amount of detail that hadn't been accessible to Rechan's generation. Mau was Akanlam's breath-sibling; and Akanlam had put into her carving the same intensity she always put in her art. Unlike most stonemen, nothing in her looked quite human, but there was a power and a flow in the least of Mau's features that made her seem to radiate energy, even when sitting still.

"What is going on here?" Rechan asked, as she got closer.

Akanlam looked up, her face red. "He says the nearest repair point is two days down."

Rechan took in the herder: craggy face, a reflection of the worn rocks around them; a spring in his step that told her he wasn't as old as he looked. "Good day, younger brother," she said.

"Good day, elder sister." The herder nodded to her. "I was telling the younger aunt here—you have to go down."

Rechan shook her head. "Going down isn't an option. We have to get to the plateaux."

The herder winced. "It's been many years since city folks came this way."

"I know," Rechan said, and waited for the herder to discourage her. She'd gotten used to that game. But, to her surprise, he didn't.

"Exhalation?" he asked. "There are simpler ways."

"I know," Rechan said. He'd mistaken Mau as her breath-sibling and not Akanlam's—an easy mistake to make, for in her late stage of pregnancy, having a breath-sibling at hand would be crucial. "But it's not exhalation. She's not my breath-sibling; she's *hers.*"

The herder looked from her to Mau and then back to Akanlam. "How far along are you?" he asked.

Too far along; that was the truth. She'd waited too long, hoping a solution would present itself; that she wouldn't need to go back into the mountains. A mistake; hope had never gotten her anywhere. "Eight months and a half," Rechan said, and heard the herder's sharp intake of breath. "My breath-sibling is in the mountains." Which was… true, in a way.

The herder grimaced again, and looked at the bulge of her belly. "I can radio the nearest village," he said, finally. "They might have an aircar, or something you can borrow, provided you return it."

Rechan nodded, forcing her lips upwards into a smile. "Perfect. Thank you, younger brother."

• • • •

The village didn't have an aircar, or a cart, or any contrivance Rechan could have used. They did have mules and goats, but in her advanced state of pregnancy she dared not risk a ride on an animal. So they radioed the next village, which promised to send their only aircar. Rechan thanked them, and hunkered with Akanlam down in the kitchen to help with the communal cooking. There was a wedding feast that night, and the community would need the travellers' hands as much, if not more, than their money.

Mau came by the kitchen later, having spent the afternoon gossiping with the village elders. "They say there's rebel activity on the plateaux," she said, handing Rechan a thin cutting knife.

"Hmm." Rechan took a critical look at the seafood toasts on the table.

Half of them looked slightly crooked; hopefully in the dim light the guests wouldn't mind too much.

"Herders don't take their beasts into the mountains, and especially not on the *lamsinh* plateaux. They say people go missing there. Crossfire, probably. They say on quiet nights you can hear the sounds of battle."

Rechan thought of her dreams—of Sang's savage thoughts, the thrill of the hunt, the release of the kill, permeating everything until she woke up sweating. What kind of being had he become, left to his own devices on the plateaux? "You're not trying to discourage me, are you?"

Mau shifted positions; the light caught her face, frozen into the serene enigmatic smile that had been Akanlam's as a child. "Ha. I've since long learnt how useless that is. No, I just thought you'd like to know exactly what we're going into."

"War," Akanlam said from her place at the stove, her voice dour. "The last remnants of it, anyway."

The Galactic delegation had arrived a couple of days earlier, to formalise the peace agreement between the government and the rebels; the spaceports were being renovated, the terminals and pagodas painstakingly rebuilt. "I guess," Rechan said. "It always comes back to the mountains, doesn't it?" She shifted positions, feeling the baby move within her, a weight as heavy as stone. "Legend says that's where we all came from."

"The prime colony ark?" Akanlam scoffed, chopping vegetables into small pieces. "That was debunked years ago."

A cheer went up outside. Rechan shifted, to see onto the plaza. A gathering of people in silk clothes, clustered around the lucky trio. She was young, even younger than Akanlam; wearing a red, tight-fitting tunic with golden embroidery, and beaming; and her groom even younger than her, making it hard to believe he had cleared adolescence. The breath-sibling was a distinguished, elderly gentleman in the robes of a scholar, who reminded Rechan of her own grandfather. He was standing next to the bride, smiling as widely as she was. The sunlight seemed to illuminate his translucent body from within: it had been a beautiful block of stone he'd been carved from, a white shade the colour of Old Earth porcelain; likely, so close to the plateaux they could pick their blocks themselves, rather than rely on what the traders brought them.

By their side was someone who had to be the bride's sister, carrying a very young infant in her arms. The baby's face was turned towards the couple, eyes wide open in an attempt to take everything in; and a little brother in fur clothes was prevented, with difficulty, from running up to the bride. The baby was three months, four months old, perhaps? With the pudgy fingers and the chubby cheeks—her own child would be like that one day, would look at her with the same wide-eyed wonder.

"Life goes on," Akanlam said, her face softening. "Always."

"Of course." That was why Rechan had gotten herself inseminated, against the family's wishes: she might have been a failure by their standards, thirty years old and unmarried—for who would want to marry someone without a breath-sibling? But, with the war over, it was time to think of the future; and she didn't want to die childless and alone, without any descendants to worship at her grave. She wanted a family, like the bride; like the bride's sister: children to hold in her arms, to raise as she had been raised, and a house filled with noise and laughter instead of the silence of the war, when every month had added new holos to the altar of the ancestors.

"I'll go present our respects," Akanlam said.

"You never had much taste for cooking," Mau pointed out, and Akanlam snorted.

"Elder Aunt cooks quite well," she said with a smile. "Better to leave everyone do what they excel at, no?"

"You impossible child," Rechan said as she so often did, with a little of her usual amusement. Akanlam was the niece with the closest quarters to her own; and she and Mau and Rechan often got together for dinners and after-work drinks—though none of them ever let Akanlam cook. As Mau had said: not only did she not have much taste for it, but left without supervision she'd burn a noodle soup to a charred mess before anyone could intervene. She did mix superb fruit chunks, though. "What are you going to do when you get married?"

"You're assuming I want to get married," Akanlam said, without missing a beat. "And even if I did, I'd stay with you. You're going to need help with raising those children of yours. How many did you say you wanted?"

"I'd be lucky to have one," Rechan said, finally. But she'd dreamt of a larger family; of the dozens brothers and sisters and cousins of her youth, before war carved a swathe through them—a horde of giggling children always ready to get into trouble. If she could find her breath-sibling again...

"And I'm old enough to do what I'm doing."

"Oh, I have no doubt. But it's still a job for two people. Or three." Akanlam smiled. "I'll see you outside."

After Akanlam had gone, Mau swung from her wooden stool and came to stand by Rechan. "Let me have a look."

Rechan almost said no, almost asked what the point was. But she knew; too many things could go wrong at this stage. It wasn't only birth without her stoneman that could kill her baby.

Mau's hands ran over the bulge of her belly, lingered on a point above her hips. "The head is here," she said, massaging it. "He's shifted positions. It's pointing downwards, into your birth canal. It's very large."

"I know," Rechan said. "My doctor said the same after the scan. Said I'd have difficulty with the birth." There were new systems; new scanners brought by the Galactics, to show a profusion of almost obscene details about the baby in her belly, down to every fine hair on its skin. But none of them had the abilities and experience of a stoneman.

"Mmm." Mau ran her hands downwards. "May I?" After a short examination, she looked up, and her face lay in shadow.

"What is it?" Rechan asked. What could she possibly have found?

"You're partly open," Mau said, finally. "You'll have to be careful, elder aunt, or you're going to enter labour early."

"I can't—" Rechan started, and then realised how ridiculous it would sound to Mau, who could do little more in the way of medical attention. "I have to get back to the plateaux."

Mau shook her head. "I didn't tell Akanlam—because you know this already—but the path gets impracticable by aircar after a while. You'll have to walk."

As she had, all those years ago. "You're right," Rechan said. "I did know." She braced herself for Mau to castigate her, to tell her she couldn't possibly think of taking a mountain trail in her state. But the stonewoman's face was expressionless, her hands quite still on Rechan's belly.

"You'll have to be careful," she repeated at last.

She couldn't read Mau at all. Perhaps it came from never having lived with a breath-sibling of her own. "You never told me why you came," Rechan said. "Akanlam—"

"—came because she's your niece, and because she knew it was important to you." Mau nodded. Was it Rechan's imagination, or was the baby stirring at her touch? Mau was Akanlam's breath-sibling, not hers. She could deliver the baby, but couldn't give it the breath that would quicken it—yet still, perhaps there was something all stonewomen shared, some vital portion of the planet's energy, a simmering, life-giving warmth, like that stone she'd touched all those years ago before she started her carving. "I came because I was curious. You're a legend in the family, you know."

Rechan snorted. "The one without a breath-sibling? That's hardly worth much of anything."

Mau turned, so that the light caught on the stone of her arms, throwing every vein of the rock into sharp relief. "But you do have a breath-sibling, don't you, elder aunt?"

How much did she know, or suspect? Rechan's official story had always been she couldn't remember, and perhaps that had been the truth, once upon a time, but now that they were in the mountains again—now that the sky lay above them like a spread cloth, and the air was sharp with the tang of smoke—memories were flooding back.

"I know the story," Mau said. "They measured you when you came back down, attached electrodes to your chest and listened to the voice of your heart. You had no breath left in you; even if they gave you *lamsinh*, you wouldn't have been able to bring a carving to life. You'd already given it to someone. Or something." Her gaze was shrewd.

So that was it, the reason she'd come with them: knowledge. Akanlam was happy with her art gallery and her shows; but of all the curious apathy she could show with life, none of it had gone into her breath-sibling. "You were curious," Rechan said.

Mau smiled, that odd expression that didn't reach her eyes. "You carved something in the mountains—came back covered in stone dust. What was it, elder aunt?"

• • • •

She remembered her last trip into the mountains as if it was yesterday: going barefoot in the morning, with a curt message left on her parents' comms unit. She'd taken the set of carving tools that had been given to her on her sixteenth birthday—the straight cutter, the piercer, the driller, and all that would be necessary for her exhalation ceremony. It was a beautiful set, given by Breath-Mother: the finest hardened glass, as translucent as the best *lamsinh* stone, and hardly weighed anything on her back. As she walked away through the sparse scattering of buildings on the edge of the city, she heard, in the distance, the rumble of bombs hitting the Eastern District— the smell of smoke, the distant wail of militia sirens—and turned her head westwards, towards the mountains.

The mountains, of course, weren't better—just further away from any hospital, Flesh-Mother and Father would say with a frown—more isolated, so that if you were captured no one would know where you were for days and days. They'd have a block of *lamsinh* brought to her for the exhalation; everyone did, paying militia and soldiers and the occasional daredevil to cart the life-sized stone into the city. She just had to wait, and she'd be safe.

Rechan could not wait.

She was young, and impatient; and tired of being cooped up for her own safety. She should have been off-planet by now, sent off to Third Aunt for a year's apprenticeship in the ship-yards; except that the previous summer all spaceport traffic had been halted when a bomb exploded in the marketplace; and the apprenticeship went to some other relative who wasn't from Voc, who didn't have to cope with bombs and battles and food shortages. By now—if it hadn't been for those stupid rebels—she could have had her hands in motor oil; could have climbed into pilots' cabins, running her hands on the instruments and imagining what it would be like, hanging suspended in the void of space with only the stars for company.

Life wasn't fair, and she certainly wasn't going to wait any longer to become an adult.

• • • •

There probably was a divinity somewhere watching over thoughtless adolescents; for Rechan had made it into the mountains, and to the plateaux, without any major trouble. She hitched a ride on a peddler's cart—so many things that could have gone wrong there, but the peddler was nice and friendly, and glad for the company—and then, when there no longer were villages or people, she walked. From time to time, she'd had to duck when a flyer banked over the path. At this height, it had to be rebels, and they'd kill her if they found her, as they had killed Second Uncle and Seventh Aunt, and Cousin Thinh and Cousin Anh; all the absences like gaping wounds in the fabric of family life. Demons take the rebels, all of them; how much simpler would life would be if none of them were here.

And then she stood on the plateaux—her feet hurting, her bag digging into the small of her back, her breath coming in fiery gasps—and it didn't matter, any of it, because there was the stone.

She'd only seen the blocks the traders brought down. The one for her cousin's exhalation had been roughly the size of a woman; of course, with *lamsinh* at such a dear price, people would buy only what was necessary. But here were no such constraints. The stone towered over her, cliffs as tall as the Temple of Mercy, broken bits and pieces ranging from the size of a skyscraper to the size of her fist; colours that ranged from a green so deep it was almost black, to the translucent shades Flesh-Mother so valued, the same colour used for all the family's breath-siblings—all the stone's veins exposed, streaks of lighter and darker nuances that seemed to be throbbing on the same rhythm as her own frantic heartbeat.

She walked among them, letting her hand lightly trail on the smooth surfaces, feeling the lambent heat; the faint trembling of the air where the sun had heated them through, like an echo of her own breath. People had always been vague about exhalation: they'd said you'd know, when you saw your block of stone, what kind of breath-sibling you wanted to carve, what kind of birth master you wanted to give to your children yet to come. But here she didn't just have one block of stone, but thousands; and she wandered into a labyrinth of toppled structures like the wreck of a city, wondering where she could settle herself, where she could make her first cut into the incandescent mass around her.

And then she rounded the edge of the cliff, and saw it, lying on the ground.

It was huge, easily ten times her size, with streaks the colour of algae water, and a thousand small dots, almost as if the stone had been pockmarked; a pattern of wounds that reminded her, for some absurd reason, of a tapestry that had used to hang on Seventh Aunt's wall, before the bomb tore her apart in the marketplace.

In all the stories she'd heard, all the tales about girls running off to have adventures, there was always this moment; this perfect moment when they reached the plateaux, or when someone showed them a block of stone, and they just *knew*, staring at it, what it would look like when whittled down to shape; when they'd freed, measure by agonising measure, the limbs and head and body of their breath-sibling, the one who would be their constant companion as they travelled over the known planets. In the stories, they didn't carve; they revealed the stone's secret nature, gave it the life it had always longed for.

Rechan had never given that credence. She was the daughter of an engineer, and believed in planning and in forethought; and had brought sketches with her, of how her own stoneman would look, with delicate hands like her mother, and large strong arms that would be able to carry her to hospital if the delivery went badly.

Except that then, she stood in front of the stone, and saw into its heart. And *knew*, with absolute certainty, that it wasn't a stoneman that she needed or wanted to carve.

· · · ·

Later, much later, when she thought about it all, she wondered how she'd endured it—months up in the plateaux with scant rations, sleeping rough, sheltering under the rock face when the rain came—day after day of rising and going back to her block of stone; carving, little by little, what would become her breath-sibling.

She did the outside first: the sleek, elegant hull, tapering to a point; the shadow of the twin engines at the back, every exhaust port and every weapons slit rendered in painstaking detail. Then she turned inwards, and from the only door into the ship, made corridors inch by agonising inch, her tools gnawing their way through the rock. All the while, she imagined it hanging in space—fast and deadly, a predator in a sea of stars, one who never had to cower or shelter for fear of bombs or flyers; one who was free to go where she wished, without those pointless restrictions on her life, those over-solicitous parents and breath-mothers who couldn't understand that bombs happened, that all you could do was go out and pray, moment after moment, that they wouldn't fall on you.

It was rough carving. She didn't have the tools that would be available to the generation after hers—not the fineness of Akanlam's carving, who would be able to give Mau fingernails, and a small pendant on her chest, down to the imprint of the chain that held it. She carved as she could— hour after hour, day after day, lifted into a place where time had no meaning, where only the ship existed or mattered; stopping only when the hunger or thirst brought themselves to her attention again, snatching a ration and then returning, hermit-like, to the translucent corridors she was shaping.

Until one day, she stepped back, and couldn't think of anything else to add.

There was probably something meaningful one was supposed to say, at an exhalation's close. She'd read speeches, all nonsense about "your breath to mine" and meters and meters of bad poetry. It didn't seem to matter very much what one said, truth be told.

"Well," she said to the ship, laying a hand on the hull, "this is it." Winter had come by then, settling in the mountains, a vice around her lungs; and her breath hung in ragged gasps above her. "I'm not sure—"

The stone under her hand went deathly cold. What—? She tried to withdraw her hand, but it had become fused to the *lamsinh*; and the veins shifted and moved, as lazily as snakes underwater.

There was a light, coming from the heart of the stone, even as the breath was drained out of her, leaving her struggling to stand upright—a light, and a slow, ponderous beat like a gigantic heart. *Breath-sister*, the stone whispered, and even that boomed, as if she stood in the Temple of Mercy, listening to the gong reminding the faithful to grow in wisdom. *Breath-sister*.

Her hand fell back; and the ship rose, casting its shadow over her.

He was sleek elegant beauty—everything she had dreamt of, everything she had carved, all the release she sought—and he didn't belong on Voc, anymore than she did.

*Come with me*, the ship whispered; and she had stood there in the growing cold, trembling, and unable to make any answer.

• • • •

"A ship," Mau said, thoughtfully.

Rechan shivered. It had made sense at the time. "I named him Sang," she said at last. *Illumination*, in the old language of the settlers—because he had stood over her, framed by light.

"I didn't even know you could carve ships."

"Anything living," Rechan said, through clenched teeth. She was going to feel sick again. Was it the baby, or the memories, or both? "Stonemen are tradition, but we could have carved cats or dogs or other Old Earth animals if we felt like it."

"Whoever you'd want assisting at the birth of your children," Mau said with a nod. She smiled, her hand going to the impression of the pendant on her chest. "I suppose I should be grateful Akanlam followed tradition.

Being an animal wouldn't have been very—exciting."

*But you wouldn't know*, Rechan thought, chilled. You'd be quite happy, either way. That's what you were carved for, to give your breath to Akanlam's babies, and even if you hadn't been born knowing it, everyone in our society has been telling you that for as long as you can remember. How much responsibility did they have for their carvings? How much of themselves had they put into them; and how much had they taught them?

And what did Sang owe her, in the end—and what did she owe him?

"Your ship is still up there," Mau said. Her voice was quiet, but it wasn't difficult to hear the question in her words.

"Yes," Rechan said. "The crossfire you heard about, it's not between the rebels and the government soldiers. It's Sang mopping rebels up." It hadn't been what she'd dreamt of, when she'd carved him; she'd wanted a spaceship, not a butcher of armies. But, consciously or unconsciously, she hadn't put that into her carving.

"The ship you carved?" Mau lifted an eyebrow.

"I was young once," Rechan said. "And angry. I don't think I'd carve the same, if I had to do it again." Though who could know, really. She'd always wondered what would have happened, if she'd answered the question Sang had asked; if she'd said yes. Would she still be on Voc, still going over the bitter loneliness of her life? Would she be elsewhere on some other planet, having the adventures she'd dreamt of as a teenager? If she could do it again…

"Anyway," she said, "I don't have much choice. If we don't reach the plateaux in time…" She didn't dare say it, didn't dare voice the possibility; but she felt as though someone had closed a fist of ice around her heart.

• • • •

They were halfway to Indigo Birds Pass, where they would have to abandon the car, when the noise of a motor made everyone sit up.

"That's not good," Akanlam said. "We're sitting targets here." She didn't stop the aircar, but accelerated. The noise got closer, all the same: not a flyer but a swarm of drones, dull and tarnished by dust. They banked above the overhang ahead and were gone so quickly it was hard to believe they'd been there at all. Akanlam made a face. "Rebels. Our army has Galactic drones."

"Let's go on," Rechan suggested. They would get to the pass in half a day. Surely that was enough time, before the drones sent their analyses onwards to their masters. Surely….

Not half an hour later, the drones came back, and hung over the aircar for what seemed like an eternity. Rechan found herself clenching Mau's hand, so hard that the stone hurt her fingers.

When the drones left, Akanlam killed the motor. "That's it. We have to go on foot. Under the cliffs, where they'll have trouble sending flyers. Come on."

Mau shot Rechan a warning glance. Rechan spread her hands, helplessly. Yes, she had to be careful, but what else could she do?

"There's a path," Akanlam called from the shelter of the overhang. "A goat trail, probably, but it'll be sheltered. At least for a while."

Rechan slid down from the aircar and walked to the overhang. There *was* a path, twisting along the side of the mountain and vanishing between two large stones. It was steep and thin, and one look at it would have made her doctor's face pale.

But there was no choice. There had never been any choice: everything had been set from the moment she'd walked into the insemination centre; or perhaps even earlier, when she'd lain in the silence of her room and known that she couldn't bear it forever. She laid her hands on her belly, whispered "hang on" to the unborn baby, and set her feet on the path.

She'd forgotten how tiring it had been, ten years earlier. Her breath burnt in her lungs after only four steps, and her legs ached after eight; and then there was only the path ahead of her, her eyes doggedly on every rock and particle of dust, making sure of her step—perpetually off-balance, struggling to keep the curve of her belly from betraying her as rocks detached under her feet—she mustn't trip, mustn't fall, mustn't let go…

After a while, the pain came on. At first, she thought it was just the aches from the unusual exercise, but it didn't abate, washing over her in a huge, belly-clenching wave, cutting her breath until she had to halt. Touching her belly, she found it hard, pointed, and the baby a compressed weight under her hands. A contraction. She was entering labour. No, not now—it was too early. She couldn't afford—couldn't lose everything—

"Elder aunt?" Mau was by her side, suddenly, her hands running over her belly.

"It's starting," she said.

"Yes." Mau's voice was grave, expressionless. Rechan didn't want to look at Akanlam, who'd always been bad at disguising her emotions. "It's your first one, elder aunt. This can go on for hours. There is still time, but you have to walk."

"I can't—" she whispered through clenched teeth, bracing herself against the next contraction. "Too—tired—" And they were going to reach that plateau, and she was going to find there was no ship, that her dreams were lies, that it had never been there—how she wanted to be the ship now, hanging under the vastness of the heavens, without heaviness, without pain, without a care in the world…

Mau's hands massaged her, easing the knots of pain in her back. "One an hour at first, elder aunt. Or more apart. There is still time. But you have to walk."

"The drones?" she asked, and it was Akanlam who answered.

"They haven't come back."

*Not yet,* she thought, tasting bile and blood on her tongue. She hauled herself as upright as she could, gently removing Mau's hands. "Let's walk," she said, and even those words were pain.

There was a divinity, watching over thoughtless teenagers; there had to be one for thoughtless adults, too; or perhaps it was her ancestors, protecting her from their distant altar—her thoughts wandering as she walked, step after step on the path, not knowing how far the ending lay, not caring anymore—step after step, with the occasional pause to bend over, gasping, while the contraction passed, and then resuming her painful, painstakingly slow walk to the top.

She found her mind drifting—to the ship, to his shadow hanging over her, remembering the coldness of the stone against her hand, the breath that seemed to have left her altogether; remembering the voice that had boomed like ten thousand storms.

*Come with me, breath-sister.*

*Come with me.*

He was there on the plateau, waiting for her, and what would she tell him?

They climbed in silence. There was just Mau's hands on her, guiding her, supporting her when she stumbled; and Akanlam's tunic, blue against the grey of the rock, showing her the way forward.

She was barely aware of cresting a rise—of suddenly finding herself not flush against a cliff face, but in the middle of a space that seemed to stretch forever, a vast expanse of *lamsinh* rocks caught by the noon sun—all shades of the spectrum, from green to palest white; and a trembling in the air that mirrored that of her hands.

"There is no ship," Akanlam said, and her voice was almost accusatory.

Shaking, Rechan pulled herself upwards. "He'll be deeper into the plateau. Where I carved him. We have to—"

"Elder Aunt," Mau said, low and urgent.

What? she wanted to ask; but, turning to stare in the same direction as Mau, she saw the black dots silhouetted against the sky—growing in size, fast, too fast...

"Run".

She would have, but her legs betrayed her—a contraction, locking her in place, as frozen as the baby within her womb, as helpless as a kid to the slaughter—watching the dots become the sleek shape of flyers, hearing the whine of the motors getting louder and louder...

Run run run, she wanted to shout to Mau and Akanlam—there's no need for you to get caught in this. Instead, what came out of her was a scream: a cry for help, a jumble of incoherent syllables torn out of her lungs, towards the Heavens; a deep-seated anger about life's unfairness she'd last felt when carving the ship. It echoed around the plateau, slowly fading as it was absorbed by the *lamsinh* stone.

Her hand was cold again, her breath coming in short gasps—and, like an answer to a prayer, she saw the ship come.

He was sleek, and elegant, and deadly. Banking lazily over the plateau—illuminated by the noonday sun, as if with an inner fire—he incinerated the flyers, one by one, and then hovered over Mau and Akanlam, as if unsure what to do about them. "No you don't!" Rechan screamed, and then collapsed, having spent all her energy.

*Breath-sister.* The ship—Sang—loomed over her once more.

She'd forgotten how beautiful Sang was; how terribly wrong, too—someone that didn't belong on Voc, that shouldn't have been here. He should have hung, weightless, in space; instead he moved sluggishly, crushed by gravity; and his hull was already crisscrossed by a thousand fracture lines, barely visible against the heat of the stone. The *lamsinh* was weathered and pitted, not from meteorite strikes but from weapons—in fact, dusty and cracked he looked like a rougher, fuzzier version of the rebel flyers he'd incinerated.

*You need me*, the ship said, and came lower, hull almost touching her outstretched hands. *Let me give you your breath back.*

It was wrong, all wrong—everything she had desired, the breath she needed for her baby, the birth she'd been bracing herself for—and yet... "You shouldn't be here," she said. "You're a spaceship, not a flyer." She was barely aware of Mau standing by her side, looking up at Sang with wide eyes; of Akanlam, spreading her tunic on the ground.

*I waited for you.*

"You can't—" But he could, couldn't he? He could do exactly what she'd thought of, when she'd carved him—all her anger at the war, at the rebels, at the unfairness of it all—year after year of hunting down rebels because that's what she'd wanted at the time; not a breath-sibling to help her with a birth, but someone born of her anger and frustration, of her desire to escape the war at any cost.

*Come with me.*

She'd wondered what she would do, were Sang to ask that question of her again, but of course there was only one possible answer. The world had moved on; she had moved on; and only Sang remained, the inescapable remains of her history—a sixteen-year-old's grandiloquent, thoughtless, meaningless gesture.

"You have to go," she said, the words torn out of her before she could think. "Into space. That's what I carved you for. Not this—this butchery."

The ship came close enough for her to touch the exhaust ports: there was a tingle on her hands, and a warmth she'd forgotten existed—and, within her, for the first time, the baby quickened, kicking against the confines of her womb. She ought to have felt relief, but she was empty—bracing herself against the next contractions and trying to crane her head upwards to see Sang.

*You need me*, he said. *Breath to breath, blood to blood. How else will you bear your children? Come with me. Let's find the stars together.*

"I can't. You have to go," she said, again. "On your own."

"You will not come with me?" The disappointment, in other circumstances, would have been heartbreaking.

"Go, Sang. When this is over—go find the stars. That's all you've ever dreamt of, isn't it?"

The contractions were hitting in waves now—one barely over before the next one started. *Your child is coming*, Sang said.

16

"I know." Someone—Akanlam—grabbed her, laid her on the ground— no, not on the ground, on the tunic she'd spread out. It was becoming hard to think, to focus on anything but the act of giving birth.

*What will you do, for your other children? You need me.*

She did; and yet… "I'll find you," she said, struggling for breath. "If I need you." Of course she wouldn't; even with her link to him, all she'd have to go on would be fuzzy dream-images; she wouldn't leave Voc, wouldn't venture among ten thousand planets and millions of stars in a fruitless search. But it didn't matter. Sang would finally be free.

Sang was silent, for a while. *I will come back,* he said.

He wouldn't. Rechan knew this with absolute certainty—Sang was the desire to escape, the burning need for flight that she'd felt during her adolescence. Once he found space, he would be in the home he'd always been meant for; and who could blame him for not looking back? "Of course," she lied—smoothly, easily. "You can always come back."

There would not be other babies beyond this one, no large family she could raise; not enough to fill the emptiness of the house. But did it matter, in the end? She'd had her wish, her miracle—her birth. Could she truly ask for anything else?

*I am glad.*

"So am I." And it almost didn't feel like a lie. Rechan relaxed, lying flat on her back; and she settled herself down to wait for the beautiful, heartbreaking sound of her child's first breath.

---

Aliette de Bodard lives and works in Paris, where she has a day job as a System Engineer. She is the author of the critically acclaimed Obsidian and Blood trilogy of Aztec noir fantasies, as well as numerous short stories. Recent/forthcoming works include *The House of Shattered Wings* (August), a novel set in a turn-of-the-century Paris devastated by a magical war, and *The Citadel of Weeping Pearls* (Asimov's Oct/Nov), a novella set in the same universe as her Vietnamese space opera On a Red Station Drifting.

# When It Ends, He Catches Her
## By Eugie Foster

The dim shadows were kinder to the theater's dilapidation. A single candle to aid the dirty sheen of the moon through the rent beams of the ancient roof, easier to overlook the worn and warped floorboards, the tattered curtains, the mildew-ridden walls. Easier as well to overlook the dingy skirt with its hem all ragged, once purest white and fine, and her shoes, almost fallen to pieces, the toes cracked and painstakingly re-wrapped with hoarded strips of linen. Once, not long ago, Aisa wouldn't have given this place a first glance, would never have deigned to be seen here in this most ruinous of venues. But times changed. Everything changed.

Aisa pirouetted on one long leg, arms circling her body like gently folded wings. Her muscles gathered and uncoiled in a graceful leap, suspending her in the air with limbs outflung, until gravity summoned her back down. The stained, wooden boards creaked beneath her, but she didn't hear them. She heard only the music in her head, the familiar stanzas from countless rehearsals and performances of *Snowbird's Lament*. She could hum the complex orchestral score by rote, just as she knew every step by heart.

Act II, scene III: the finale. It was supposed to be a duet, her as Makira, the warlord's cursed daughter, and Balege as Ono, her doomed lover, in a frenzied last dance of tragedy undone, hope restored, rebirth. But when the Magistrate had closed down the last theaters, Balege had disappeared in the resultant riots and protests.

So Aisa danced the duet as a solo, the way she'd had to in rehearsal sometimes, marking the steps where Balege should have been. Her muscles burned, her breath coming faster. She loved this feeling, her body perfectly attuned to her desire, the obedient instrument of her will. It was only these moments that she felt properly herself, properly alive. The dreary, horrible daytime with its humiliations and ceaseless hunger became the dream. This dance, here and now, was real. She wished it would never end.

The music swelled, inexorable, driving to its culmination, a flurry of athletic spins and intricate footwork, dizzying and exhilarating. *Snowbird's Lament* concluded in a sprinting leap, with Aisa flinging herself into the air just above the audience—glorious and triumphant at the apex of thunderous bars of music. But she had to omit it. There was no way to even mark it, impossible to execute without Balege to catch her.

Out of breath, euphoric but dissatisfied, she finished on one bent knee, arms outstretched, head dramatically bowed in supplication. The score in her head silenced. This was where the curtains were supposed to come furling down and the audience was supposed to leap to its feet in a frenzy of adoration. But there was no one to work the ropes and pulleys, and the rows of benches in the theater were all empty.

It didn't matter. She didn't dance for the accolades and applause. When the last stages and theaters in the artists' district had barred their doors, when all the performances had gone forever dark, Aisa had found this place, this nameless ghost of a theater. So ramshackle to be beneath the Magistrate's attention, so ruinous that no one had bothered to bolt the doors, it had become her haven, the place she fled to so she could dance by herself in the darkness and the silence. No matter that the world had turned to chaos, in the end, a dancer danced. It was the only peace, the only sanity that remained.

A pair of hands softly clapping in the wings intruded upon her reverie.

Aisa's head whipped up, her eyes darting to where her dagger lay sheathed beside the flickering candle.

A figure, features obscured by darkness, stepped out from the shabby draperies, brushing them aside with a smooth, sparse gesture. Although she couldn't see his face, Aisa knew that step, that familiar sweep of arm.

"Balege?" she gasped.

She started to run to him, her first impulse to embrace him, spilling over with questions and gladness. But she hesitated. The set of his shoulders, the rigid posture of his spine—so attuned was she to the signs and discourse of her partner's body she understood that for whatever reason, Balege wanted to keep his distance.

"What is it? What's the matter?"

"I came to dance with you, Aisa."

"Of course you did."

"But I'm not the same as I once was."

Was he afraid his technique had declined, that she would spurn him for missteps, mistakes in tempo or timing?

"We are neither of us as we once were," she said. *Scrabbling with an old man for a crust of bread in the gutter, the brittle crunch of a cockroach between her teeth.* "But there was never a better partner for me than you, Balege." Aisa lifted her arm in the formal language of dance, her fingers held out to say, simply, *Dance with me.*

Balege stepped into the lighter circle of shadows contained by her candle. She saw what the greater darkness had hidden—the fogged sheen of his eyes, the gray pallor of his flesh, and beneath the sweet scent of rose water he favored, the taint of decay.

Aisa flinched back, her heart leaping in her chest. For the first time since she had attained the rank of premier soloist, her body flouted her will, frozen in place as she screamed for it to run away, flee for her life.

"You–you have the death plague," she whispered.

Balege's eyes shifted aside, a familiar expression of discomfort when he was embarrassed or shy. "Do you not want to dance with me, after all?"

"They say plague victims go mad…killing and eating their victims." Unspoken between them, that the plague killed all of its victims, and then those damned unfortunates got up again—mindless, violent, and hungry.

He gazed out, stage center, over the empty blackness of the absent audience. "You know, it was always my greatest desire to be good enough to partner you. I watched your other partners, saw how they stumbled beside you, how they weren't good enough for you, and I learned from their mistakes."

It was true. Balege had never dropped her, unlike some of the worthless oafs she'd danced with over the years. From the beginning he'd seemed to know instinctively how to move with her, matching his reach and steps to hers, always where she needed him to be. From his very first audition, she had trusted Balege to catch her.

Aisa relaxed a little, the muscles in her legs and shoulders loosening from their rigid paralysis. "You were the best partner I've ever had."

"We were perfect together."

"We were." Aisa extended her hand to him with an imperative flourish. *Dance with me.*

Balege bowed, a dancer's benediction that said, *Forever.*

They moved together in unison, fingers clasped, his body wrapped in a lithe frame around hers. There was no awkward shifting or repositioning of limbs. There had never been between them.

"The finale," he murmured. "On my count. One-two, one-two-three-four."

The music started silently in two heads in complete synchrony.

She twirled in his arms and skipped away, springing like a gazelle back again. He steadied and braced her, always there, the inverted complement of her movements. They danced, and she reveled in the strength of his arms around her, the metered cadence of his legs, the matched beat of two bodies moving in seamless fluidity. It was as it used to be. And for now, nothing else mattered. How he'd found her, how he could be so himself still and not one of the mindless monsters the plague-bearers became. How he'd...died.

He bore her overhead in a spinning lift, effortlessly committing her to the air, only one hand supporting the full weight of her body. By an accident of threadbare hose and skirt, his fingers gripped skin where they should have glided over layers of once immaculate costume. The unnatural chill of his dead fingers cut to the bone. When he set her down, light as a fallen leaf, Aisa stumbled.

Balege was there, one hand on her hip, the other at her elbow, taking the weight of her misstep into the turn of his body. Shielding her. Catching her. None but the most discerning eye in the audience would have seen anything amiss, and even that discerning eye would have noted only a stray half beat, the smallest of errors.

How many times had Balege's strong arms held her, lifted her, carried her? Balege was frame and scaffold, launching her into the air and catching her as she spun back to earth, his virtuoso utterly focused on making her scintillate.

Without a word, they continued their duet, and *Snowbird's Lament* spooled out to its final steps: the lovers united, torn apart, reunited. The grand finale, as it should be danced, an explosion of turns and fleet footwork, culminating in a dead run to the end of the stage and a magnificent hurtle into Balege's arms, just before she could plummet off it. It was a feat of athleticism and absolute trust. If he ever miscounted the beat, had a slight misalignment of timing or balance, she would fall, badly, from the high stage and onto the unforgiving floor below. Battered and bruised certainly, broken bones possibly, a career ending fall. But Balege had always caught her.

Aisa didn't hesitate now, flinging herself into the air, her body arched, giving herself over with complete abandon.

It was like flying—the moment stretching to infinity, suspended in the limbo space between earth and weightless freedom. No fear, no hunger, no pain, nothing but this perfect moment.

Dying now, like this, it wouldn't be so bad. If Balege didn't catch her, she might fall poorly enough to snap her own neck. That wouldn't be so bad. Quick and fast.

*Where had that thought come from?*

The world's weight found her. Aisa fell.

And Balege caught her.

The silent music ended. Aisa curtsied. Balege bowed. The illusory audience applauded. The phantom curtain came down.

Facing each other, their arms dropped away, no longer speaking the language of bodies and movement, relegated to the far less elegant communication of words and speech.

"You always catch me," Aisa said.

"Yes," Balege replied, softly almost a whisper.

"I had a thought, this time. What would happen if you didn't?"

He straightened and stepped back, his eerie, undead eyes shifting sidelong. "You always forget. No matter how often we dance and I remind you, you forget."

Aisa frowned. "What are you talking about?"

"One time, I didn't catch you."

Sudden outrage and disbelief, disproportionately livid and irrational. "Don't be ridiculous. You always catch me."

"Our first night on this stage. Remember again, Aisa."

She wanted to stomp her foot. "*This* is our first night." Lightning flash images skittered and popped behind her eyes. "Isn't it—?" Her words faltered, taking her indignation with it. *Hunger. So much hunger.*

"You came here, why?" Balege asked, his voice gentle, coaxing.

She shivered, suddenly chilled. "After the theaters closed down, I—I sold myself into slavery. Better to be a fed slave in the upper city than starving and free in the slums." *Bruises and humiliation.* "But the man I sold myself to, he wanted me to do such unspeakable things." *The instrument of her art desecrated. Blood on the walls.* "I ran away. Found this place, this stage."

"And I found you here, dancing."

Aisa lifted her head. "How?"

"I don't know. Maybe it was the light of your candle, or the shifting shadows through the cracked walls. I was drawn to you as those who have succumbed to the death plague are drawn to ravage and devour the still-living. But when I saw you dancing *Snowbird's Lament*, it was like an awakening. Mesmerized, I watched and remembered you and me, and us. You were afraid of me at first. But in the end, we did as we always do."

"We danced," she said.

"Yes."

"And then?"

"At the end, right before Makira's final vault off the stage, you called to me, 'Don't catch me! Let me go!'"

*Hunger. Ceaseless, ravenous hunger.*

"I still tried to catch you," Balege said.

*Juxtaposed images of pale flesh transposed with gray, splattered bursts of crimson across faded posters in the sunlight.* "But I didn't let you," Aisa murmured. "I twisted away at the last moment."

"Yes."

"I fell." Aisa lifted her hands to her face, noted the dead flatness of her skin, the black, broken nails. She listened to the still-quiet in her chest where her heart should beat, inhaled the scent of rotting flesh, her own. Her once fine dress, not just ragged and grimy, but grave-worn with filth and gore.

"We hunt and feed together," he said. "You don't remember who I am, who you are except when we're dancing. But I do. Somehow, I do. I remind you."

Aisa smoothed the soiled creases of her skirt, tucked a wisp of matted hair back into its unraveling chignon. All dancers knew their springtime was short. A dancer's fate was to break or fade away, a short season of glory, if they were lucky. And Aisa had been lucky, very lucky. Until all the luck went away, for everyone. But this was a new kind of luck.

It would do.

"Remind me again, Balege," she said and lifted her arm, fingers outstretched. *Dance with me.*

He bowed. "From the top. One-two, one-two-three-four."

• • • •

The tarnished moon spilled through the cracked and rent ceiling of the dilapidated theater, the only audience to the two dancers as they leaped and twirled together in matchless harmony. Dead flesh moved together with graceful elegance, lithe and nimble and strong, his and hers. An eternal performance.

And when it ends, he catches her.

---

Eugie Foster called home a mildly haunted, fey-infested house in metro Atlanta that she shared with her husband, Matthew and her pet skunks. It was there she penned her flights of fancy. Holder of a master's degree in psychology that she used only for amusement, she became an editor for the Georgia General Assembly, a job she thought also took her into flights of fancy.

Her publication credits number over 100 and include stories in *Realms of Fantasy, Interzone, Apex Magazine, Fantasy Magazine, Cricket, Orson Scott Card's InterGalactic Medicine Show*, and *Baen's Universe*. Her short fiction is collected in four volumes with more on the way.

Eugie received the 2009 Nebula Award for her novelette, "Sinner, Baker, Fabulist, Priest; Red Mask, Black Mask, Gentleman, Beast," requiring the SFWA to change how they engraved the trophy due to the length of the title. She was proud of both those facts. Her fiction has been a finalist/nominee for the Nebula (a second time), Hugo, Sturgeon, Black Quill, Bram Stoker, Pushcart, and BSFA awards, and been translated into eight languages.

Eugie died due to side effects of her cancer treatment on September 27th, 2014. "When It Ends, He Catches Her" was published the day before her death.

# Toad Words
## By T. Kingfisher

Frogs fall out of my mouth when I talk. Toads, too.

It used to be a problem.

There was an incident when I was young and cross and fed up with parental expectations. My sister, who is the Good One, has gold and gems fall from her lips, and since I could not be her, I had to go a different way.

So I got frogs. It happens.

"You'll grow into it," the fairy godmother said. "Some curses have cloth-of-gold linings." She considered this, and her finger drifted to her lower lip, the way it did when she was forgetting things. "Mind you, some curses just grind you down and leave you broken. Some blessings do that too, though. Hmm. What was I saying?"

I spent a lot of time not talking. I got a slate and wrote things down. It was hard at first, but I hated to drop the frogs in the middle of the road. They got hit by cars, or dried out, miles away from their damp little homes.

Toads were easier. Toads are tough. After awhile, I learned to feel when a word was a toad and not a frog. I could roll the word around on my tongue and get the flavor before I spoke it. Toad words were drier. *Desiccated* is a toad word. So is *crisp* and *crisis* and *obligation*. So are *elegant* and *matchstick*.

Frog words were a bit more varied. *Murky. Purple. Swinging. Jazz.*

I practiced in the field behind the house, speaking words over and over, sending small creatures hopping into the evening. I learned to speak some words as either toads or frogs. It's all in the delivery.

*Love* is a frog word, if spoken earnestly, and a toad word if spoken sarcastically. Frogs are not good at sarcasm.

Toads are masters of it.

I learned one day that the amphibians are going extinct all over the world, that some of them are vanishing. You go to ponds that should be full of frogs and find them silent. There are a hundred things responsible—fungus and pesticides and acid rain.

When I heard this, I cried "What!?" so loudly that an adult African bullfrog fell from my lips and I had to catch it. It weighed as much as a small cat. I took it to the pet store and spun them a lie in writing about my cousin going off to college and leaving the frog behind.

I brooded about frogs for weeks after that, and then eventually, I decided to do something about it.

I cannot fix the things that kill them. It would take an army of fairy godmothers, and mine retired long ago. Now she goes on long cruises and spreads her wings out across the deck chairs.

But I can make more.

I had to get a field guide at first. It was a long process. Say a word and catch it, check the field marks. Most words turn to bronze frogs if I am not paying attention.

Poison arrow frogs make my lips go numb. I can only do a few of those a day. I go through a lot of chapstick.

It is a holding action I am fighting, nothing more. I go to vernal pools and whisper sonnets that turn into wood frogs. I say the words *squeak* and *squill* and spring peepers skitter away into the trees. They begin singing almost the moment they emerge.

I read long legal documents to a growing audience of Fowler's toads, who blink their goggling eyes up at me. (I wish I could do salamanders. I would read Clive Barker novels aloud and seed the streams with efts and hellbenders. I would fly to Mexico and read love poems in another language to restore the axolotl. Alas, it's frogs and toads and nothing more. We make do.)

The woods behind my house are full of singing. The neighbors either learn to love it or move away.

My sister—the one who speaks gold and diamonds—funds my travels. She speaks less than I do, but for me and my amphibian friends, she will vomit sapphires and rubies. I am grateful.

I am practicing reading modernist revolutionary poetry aloud. My accent is atrocious. Still, a day will come when the Panamanian golden frog will tumble from my lips, and I will catch it and hold it, and whatever word I spoke, I'll say again and again, until I stand at the center of a sea of yellow skins, and make from my curse at last a cloth of gold.

---

Ursula Vernon is the author of the Dragonbreath and Hamster Princess series for kids. T. Kingfisher is the name she uses when she's writing stories for adults. As Kingfisher, she has written several novel-length fairy-tale retellings, including *Bryony & Roses* and *The Seventh Bride*. She has won the Hugo, Nebula, Sequoyah and Mythopoeic Awards for her work. Under both names, she lives in North Carolina with her husband, her garden, and an increasingly ancient beagle.

# Makeisha In Time
## By Rachael K. Jones

Makeisha has always been able to bend the fourth dimension, though no one believes her. She has been a soldier, a sheriff, a pilot, a prophet, a poet, a ninja, a nun, a conductor (of trains *and* symphonies), a cordwainer, a comedian, a carpetbagger, a troubadour, a queen, and a receptionist. She has shot arrows, guns, and cannons. She speaks an extinct Ethiopian dialect with a perfect accent. She knows a recipe for mead that is measured in aurochs horns, and with a katana, she is deadly.

Her jumps happen intermittently. She will be yanked from the present without warning, and live a whole lifetime in the past. When she dies, she returns right back to where she left, restored to a younger age. It usually happens when she is deep in conversation with her boss, or arguing with her mother-in-law, or during a book club meeting just when it is her turn to speak. One moment, Makeisha is firmly grounded in the timeline of her birth, and the next, she is elsewhere. Elsewhen.

Makeisha has seen the sun rise over prehistoric shores, where the ocean writhed with soft, slimy things that bore the promise of dung beetles, *Archeopteryx*, and Edgar Allan Poe. She has seen the sun set upon long-forgotten empires. When Makeisha skims a map of the continents, she sees a fractured Pangaea. She never knows where she will jump next, or how long she will stay, but she is never afraid. Makeisha has been doing this all her life.

Makeisha learned long ago to lie about the jumping. When she was nine, she attempted to prove it to her mother by singing in Egyptian, but her mother just laughed and sent her to do the dishes. She received worse when she contradicted her history teachers. It was intolerable, sitting in school in the body of a child but with the memories of innumerable lifetimes, while incomplete truths and half-truths and outright lies were written on the board. The adults called a conference about her *attention-seeking behavior*, and she learned to keep her mouth shut.

The hardest part is coming back. Once, when she was twelve, she was slouched in the pew at church when she felt the past tug. Makeisha found herself floundering in the roiling ocean of the Mediterranean, only to be saved by Moorish pirates who hauled her aboard in the nick of time. At first the bewildered men and women treasured their catch as a mascot and good-luck charm. Later, after nearly ten years of fine seacraft and fearless warfare, they made her captain of the ship. Makeisha took to piracy like sheet music. She could climb ropes and hold her grog with the best sailors, and even after losing an eye in a gunpowder explosion, she never once wept and wished herself home.

The day came when, at the pasha's command, she set sail to intercept Spanish invaders in Ottoman waters. It was a hot night when they sighted the lanterns of the enemy shuddering on the waves. Makeisha's crew pulled their ship astern the enemy's vessel in the dark and fog after midnight. She gave the order – *Charge!* – her deep voice booming through the mists, echoed by the shouts of her pirates as they swung on ropes over the sliver of ocean between the ships. And suddenly an explosion, and a pinching sensation in her midriff, and she was twelve again in the church pew, staring at her soft palms through two perfect eyes. That was when she finally wept, so loud and hard the reverend stopped his sermon to scold her. Her father grounded her for a week after that.

People often get angry with Makeisha when she returns. She can't control her befuddlement, the way the room spins like she is drunk, and how for days and weeks afterward she cannot settle back into who she was, because the truth is, she isn't the same. Each time she returns from the past, she carries another lifetime nestled within her like the shell of a matryoshka doll.

Once, after the fall of the Roman Empire, she joined a peasant uprising in Bavaria, and charging quickly from fiefdom to fiefdom, their band pushed back the warlords to the foothills of the Alps. Those who survived sued for mercy, begged her not to raze their fields, pledged fealty to her. As a condition of the peace, Makeisha demanded their daughters in marriage to seal the political alliance. The little kings, too afraid of the barbarian-queen to shout their umbrage, conceded. They even attended the weddings, where Makeisha stood with her sword peace-tied at her waist and took the trembling hand of each Bavarian princess into her own.

Once the wedding guests left, Makeisha gathered her wives together in the throne room. "Please," she said to them, "help me. I need good women I can trust to run this kingdom right."

With their help, she established a stable state in those war-torn days. In time, all her wives made excellent deputies, ambassadors, sheriffs, and knights in her court.

Makeisha had been especially broken up when her time in Bavaria was cut short by a bout of pneumonia. Many of her wives had grown to be dear friends of hers, and she wondered for months and months what had become of them and their children, and whether her fiefdom had lasted beyond her passing.

She wanted to talk with her best friend Philippa, to cry about it, but her phone calls went unanswered, and so did her emails. Makeisha could not remember when she had last spent time with Philippa or her other friends here in the present. It was so hard to remember when her weeks and months were interspersed with whole lifetimes of friends and lovers and enemies. The present was a stop-motion film, a book interrupted mid-page and abandoned for years at a time. And when she did return, she always carried with her another death.

Makeisha does not fear death anymore. She has died so many times, always awakening in the present, whole and alive as before the jump. She does not know what would happen if she died in the present. Perhaps she would awaken in the future. She has never tried to find out.

She cannot remember her first death. She probably died hundreds of times in her infancy, before she was old enough to walk. Her jumps left her in the wilderness or ocean more often than not, and when she did arrive near civilization, few took pity on a strange, abandoned child who could not explain her presence. Makeisha's mother often joked about her appetite, how from the time she was a baby, she ate like a person on the verge of starvation. Her mother does not know how close this is to the truth. These days, Makeisha wears her extra pounds with pride, knowing how often they have been her salvation.

When Philippa finally returns her calls, she reams Makeisha for slighting her all year, for the forgotten birthday, for the missed housewarming party. Makeisha apologizes like she always does. They meet up in person for a catch-up over coffee, and Makeisha resolves that this time she will be present for her friend. They are deep in conversation when she feels the tug, just as Philippa is admitting that she is afraid of what the future may bring. No, thinks Makeisha when she finds herself blinking on the edge of a sluggish river under the midday sun. Two white bulls have lifted their heads to stare at her, water dripping from their jowls.

Makeisha struggles to keep the conversation fresh in her head as she casts around for a quick way home. She chooses the river. It is hard, that first time, to make herself inhale, to still her windmilling arms, to let death take this matryoshka life so she can hasten back to the present.

She has lost the thread of the conversation anyway when she snaps back to Philippa's kitchen. "Migraine," she explains, rubbing away the memory of pain from her dizzy head, and Philippa feeds her two aspirin and some hot mint tea.

Makeisha resolves to do better next time, and eventually, she does. On her first date with Carl, she strangles herself with strings from the lute of a Hittite bard. On their wedding day, she detours to a vast desert that she cannot place, which she escapes by crawling into a scorpion nest. That death was painful. The next time she jumps (two days later, on their honeymoon), she takes the time to learn the proper way to open her wrists with a sharp-edged rock.

Her husband believes her when she says it's migraines.

All of it – the self-imposed silence, the suicides, the banishing of her fantastic past to the basement of her brain – these are the price of a normal life, of friendships and a marriage and a steady job. Mundane though it is, Makeisha reminds herself that this life is different from the other ones. Irreplaceable. Real.

Still, she misses the past, where she has lived most of her life. She reads history books with a black marker and strikes out the bits that make her scoff. Then, with a red pen, she writes in the margins all the names she can recall, all the forgotten people who mattered just as much as George Washington and Louis XIV. When Carl asks, she explains how the world has always belonged to more than just the great men who were kings and Presidents and generals, but for some reason, no one wrote it down.

"I think you're trying too hard," he says, and she hates the pity in his eyes when he holds up his hands and adds, "but if it makes you feel happy, keep on with it."

One day, as a surprise, her husband drove her four hours to a museum hosting an exhibit on medieval history. Makeisha screeched and grabbed Carl's arm when she saw the posters at the entrance: eighth-century Bavaria! It had been five years and dozens of self-murdered lives since she was torn from her thriving kingdom, from her deputy-wives and her warband, but the memories were still so fresh. Her face was composed as she purchased tickets, but she bounced on the balls of her feet all the way to the front of the line.

It was the first time she had encountered any proof of a previous life. Euphoria flared in her breast when she peered into glass cases that held familiar objects, old and worn but recognizable all the same, the proof of her long years of warfare and wisdom and canny leadership. A lead comb, most of its bristles missing, its colored enamel long ago worn to gray. It had belonged to Jutte, perhaps – she had such fine long hair, although she had kept it bound tightly for her work as a doctor. A thin gold ring she had given to dark-eyed Berchte in commemoration of her knighthood. And the best of all: a silver coin stamped with her own stylized profile, her broad nose jutting past her Bavarian war helm.

There was a placard on the glass. Makeisha read it thrice, each time a little slower, thinking perhaps she'd missed something. But no. *Early medieval objects from the court of a foreign king. He reigned in Bavaria for about thirty years.*

He? *He?* Makeisha stormed back to the entrance, demanded to speak with a manager, her vision swimming a violent red, her hand groping for a pommel she did not wear anymore. It was wrong. It was all wrong, wrong, wrong. Her wives, assigned a husband and stripped of their deputyship! Their legacy, handed to a manufactured person! Carl begged her to tell him what was wrong. Makeisha realized she was shouting oaths in ancient German, and that was when she felt the familiar tug in her navel, and found herself spinning back, back, further back than she had gone last time, until she arrived on an empty beach beneath a moon with a smooth, craterless face.

Her practiced eye spotted three ways to die on its first sweep (drowning, impaling, crushing), but there was Jutte's comb to consider, and that placard. When she gave up time travel, she never thought she had surrendered her legacy, too.

Makeisha turned her back on the ocean and walked into the woods, busying herself with building a fire and assembling the tools she would need for her stay, however long it might be. She had learned to be resourceful and unafraid of the unfamiliar creaks and groans in the ferny green of the prehistoric underbrush.

She chipped a cascade of sparks into her kindling, and that is when Makeisha formed her plan.

She is done with the present, with the endless self-murder, with the repression and suffocation and low stakes.

A woman unafraid to die can do anything she wants. A woman who can endure starvation and pain and deprivation can be her own boss, set her own agenda. The one thing she cannot do is to make them remember she did it.

Makeisha is going to change that.

No more suicides, then. Makeisha embraces the jumps again. She is a boulder thrown into the waters of time. In eighth century Norway, she joins a band of Viking women. They are callous but good-humored, and they take her rage in stride, as though she has nothing to explain. They give her a sword taller than she is, but she learns to swing it anyway, and to sing loudly into the wind when one of the slain is buried with her hoard, sword folded on her breast.

When she returns to the present, Makeisha has work to do. She will stop mid-sentence, spin on her heel, and head for the books, leaving an astonished coworker, or friend, or her husband calling after her.

She pours everything into the search for her own past. One of her contacts sends her an email about a Moorish pirate, a woman, making a name for herself among the Ottomans. A Spanish monk wrote about her last voyage, the way she leapt upon her prey like a gale in the night, how her battle-cry chilled the blood. Makeisha's grin holds until the part where the monk called her a whore.

This is accepted without question as factual by the man writing the book.

She is obsessed. Makeisha almost loses her job because of her frequent forgetfulness, her accidental rudeness. Her desk is drowned in ancient maps. Her purse is crammed with reams of genealogies.

In her living room, which has been lined from wall-to-wall with history books ever since Carl moved out, Makeisha tries to count the lives stacked inside her. There are so many of them. They are crowding to get out. She once tried to calculate how many years she had been alive. It was more than a thousand. And what did they amount to? Makeisha is smeared across the timeline, but no one ever gets her quite right. Those who found the cairn of her Viking band assumed the swords and armor meant the graves of men. A folio of her sonnets, anonymous after much copying, are attributed to her assistant Giorgio.

"You're building a fake identity," Philippa tells her one day, daring the towers of books and dried-out markers to bring Makeisha some soup. "There weren't any black women in ancient Athens. There weren't any in China. You need to come to grips with reality, my friend."

"There were too," says Makeisha fiercely, proudly. "I *know* there were. They were just erased. Forgotten."

"I'm sure there were a few exceptions. But women just didn't do the kind of things you're interested in."

Makeisha says, "It doesn't matter what I do, if people refuse to believe it."

Her jumps are subdued after that. She turns to the written word for immortality. Makeisha leaves love poetry on the walls of Aztec tombs in carefully colored Nahuatl pictograms. She presses cuneiform into soft clay, documenting the exploits of the proud women whose names are written in red in the margins of her history books. She records the names of her lovers in careful *hanzi* strokes with horsehair bristles in bamboo books.

Even these, the records she makes herself, do not survive intact. Sometimes the names are replaced by others deemed more remarkable, more credible, by the scribes who came after. Sometimes they are erased entirely. Mostly, the books just fade into dust with time. She takes comfort knowing that she is not unique, that the chorus of lost voices is thundering.

She is fading from the present. She forgets to eat between jumps, loses weight. Sometimes she starves to death when she lands in an isolated spot.

• • • •

Carl catches her one day at the mailbox. "Sorry for just showing up. You haven't returned my calls," he explains, offering her a sheaf of papers.

Makeisha accepts them and examines the red-stamped first page of their divorce papers.

"You need to sign here," Carl says, pointing upside down at the bottom of the sheet. "Also on the next page. Please?"

The last word carries a pleading note. Makeisha notes his puffy eyes and a single white hair standing out in the black nest of his beard. "How long has it been?" she asks. She has lived at least three lifetimes since he left, but she isn't sure.

"Too long," he says. "Please, I just need your signature so we can move on."

She pats her pockets and finds a red pen. Makeisha wonders how many decades or centuries until this signature is also altered or lost or purposely erased, but she touches pen to paper anyway.

Halfway through her signature, she spends twenty-six years sleeping under the stars with the Aborigines, and when she comes back, the rest of her name trails aimlessly down the sheet. Carl doesn't seem to notice.

After he leaves, she escapes to India for a lifetime, where she ponders whether her time travel is a punishment or purgatory.

When she returns to the present again, Makeisha weeps like she did when she was twelve, and her heart was breaking for her days as a pirate. Perhaps it is not the past that is yanking her away. Perhaps the present is crowding her out. And perhaps she has finally come to agree with the sentiment.

In her living room, among the towers of blacked-out books, Makeisha sees six ways to die from where she stands. Perhaps the way out is forward. Break through the last matryoshka shell like a hatchling into daylight.

But no. No. The self-murders were never for herself. Not once. Makeisha is resilient. She is resourceful, and she has been bending the fourth dimension all her life, whether anyone recognizes it or not.

A woman who has been pushed her whole life will eventually learn to push back.

Makeisha reaches forward into the air. With skillful fingers that have killed and healed and mastered the cello, she pulls the future toward her.

She has not returned.

---

Rachael K. Jones grew up in various cities across Europe and North America, picked up (and mostly forgot) six languages, an addiction to running, and a couple degrees. Now she writes speculative fiction in Athens, Georgia, where she lives with her husband. Her work has appeared or is forthcoming in a variety of venues, including *Lightspeed, Shimmer, Accessing the Future, Strange Horizons, Escape Pod, Crossed Genres,* and *Daily Science Fiction.* She is an editor, a SFWA member, and a secret android. Follow her on Twitter @RachaelKJones.

# Covenant
## By Elizabeth Bear

This cold could kill me, but it's no worse than the memories. Endurable as long as I keep moving.

My feet drum the snow-scraped roadbed as I swing past the police station at the top of the hill. Each exhale plumes through my mask, but insulating synthetics warm my inhalations enough so they do not sting and seize my lungs. I'm running too hard to breathe through my nose—running as hard and fast as I can, sprinting for the next hydrant-marking reflector protruding above a dirty bank of ice. The wind pushes into my back, cutting through the wet merino of my base layer and the wet MaxReg over it, but even with its icy assistance I can't come close to running the way I used to run. Once I turn the corner into the graveyard, I'll be taking that wind in the face.

I miss my old body's speed. I ran faster before. My muscles were stronger then. Memories weigh something. They drag you down. Every step I take, I'm carrying 13 dead. My other self runs a step or two behind me. I feel the drag of his invisible, immaterial presence.

As long as you keep moving, it's not so bad. But sometimes everything in the world conspires to keep you from moving fast enough.

I thump through the old stone arch into the graveyard, under the trees glittering with ice, past the iron gate pinned open by drifts. The wind's as sharp as I expected—sharper— and I kick my jacket over to warming mode. That'll run the battery down, but I've only got another 5 kilometers to go and I need heat. It's getting colder as the sun rises, and clouds slide up the western horizon: cold front moving in. I flip the sleeve light off with my next gesture, though that won't make much difference. The sky's given light enough to run by for a good half-hour, and the sleeve light is on its own battery. A single LED doesn't use much.

I imagine the flexible circuits embedded inside my brain falling into quiescence at the same time. Even smaller LEDs with even more advanced power cells go dark. The optogenetic adds shut themselves off when my brain is functioning *healthily*. Normally, microprocessors keep me sane and safe, monitor my brain activity, stimulate portions of the neocortex devoted to ethics, empathy, compassion. When I run, though, my brain—my dysfunctional, murderous, *cured* brain—does it for itself as neural pathways are stimulated by my own native neurochemicals.

Only my upper body gets cold: Though that wind chills the skin of my thighs and calves like an ice bath, the muscles beneath keep hot with exertion. And the jacket takes the edge off the wind that strikes my chest.

My shoes blur pink and yellow along the narrow path up the hill. Gravestones like smoker's teeth protrude through swept drifts. They're moldy black all over as if spray-painted, and glittering powdery whiteness heaps against their backs. Some of the stones date to the 18th century, but I run there only in the summertime or when it hasn't snowed.

Maintenance doesn't plow that part of the churchyard. Nobody comes to pay their respects to *those* dead anymore.

Sort of like the man I used to be.

The ones I killed, however—some of them still get their memorials every year. I know better than to attend, even though my old self would have loved to gloat, to relive the thrill of their deaths. The new me … feels a sense of … obligation. But their loved ones don't know my new identity. And nobody owes *me* closure.

I'll have to take what I can find for myself. I've sunk into that beautiful quiet place where there's just the movement, the sky, that true, irreproducible blue, the brilliant flicker of a cardinal. Where I die as a noun and only the verb survives.

I run. I am running.

• • • •

When he met her eyes, he imagined her throat against his hands. Skin like calves' leather; the heat and the crack of her hyoid bone as he dug his thumbs deep into her pulse. The way she'd writhe, thrash, struggle.

His waist chain rattled as his hands twitched, jerking the cuffs taut on his wrists.

She glanced up from her notes. Her eyes were a changeable hazel: blue in this light, gray green in others. Reflections across her glasses concealed the corner where text scrolled. It would have been too small to read, anyway—backward, with the table he was chained to creating distance between them.

She waited politely, seeming unaware that he was imagining those hazel eyes dotted with petechiae, that fair skin slowly mottling purple. He let the silence sway between them until it developed gravity.

"Did you wish to say something?" she asked, with mild but clinical encouragement.

*Point to me*, he thought.

He shook his head. "I'm listening."

She gazed upon him benevolently for a moment. His fingers itched. He scrubbed the tips against the rough orange jumpsuit but stopped. In her silence, the whisking sound was too audible.

She continued. "The court is aware that your crimes are the result of neural damage including an improperly functioning amygdala. Technology exists that can repair this damage. It is not experimental; it has been used successfully in tens of thousands of cases to treat neurological disorders as divergent as depression, anxiety, bipolar disorder, borderline personality, and the complex of disorders commonly referred to as schizophrenic syndrome."

The delicate structure of her collarbones fascinated him. It took 14 pounds of pressure, properly applied, to snap a human clavicle—rendering the arm useless for a time. He thought about the proper application of that pressure. He said, "Tell me more."

"They take your own neurons—grown from your own stem cells under sterile conditions in a lab, modified with microbial opsin genes. This opsin is a light-reactive pigment similar to that found in the human retina. The neurons are then reintroduced to key areas of your brain. This is a keyhole procedure. Once the neurons are established, and have been encouraged to develop the appropriate synaptic connections, there's a second surgery, to implant a medical device: a series of miniaturized flexible microprocessors, sensors, and light-emitting diodes. This device monitors your neurochemistry and the electrical activity in your brain and adjusts it to mimic healthy activity." She paused again and steepled her fingers on the table.

"'Healthy,'" he mocked.

She did not move.

"That's discrimination against the neuro-atypical."

"Probably," she said. Her fingernails were appliquéd with circuit diagrams. "But you did kill 13 people. And get caught. Your civil rights are bound to be forfeit after something like that."

He stayed silent. Impulse control had never been his problem.

"It's not psychopathy you're remanded for," she said. "It's murder."

"Mind control," he said.

"Mind *repair*," she said. "You can't be *sentenced* to the medical procedure. But you can volunteer. It's usually interpreted as evidence of remorse and desire to be rehabilitated. Your sentencing judge will probably take that into account."

"God," he said. "I'd rather have a bullet in the head than a fucking computer."

"They haven't used bullets in a long time," she said. She shrugged, as if it were nothing to her either way. "It was lethal injection or the gas chamber. Now it's rightminding. Or it's the rest of your life in an 8-by-12 cell. You decide."

"I can beat it."

"Beat rightminding?"

Point to me.

"What if I can beat it?"

"The success rate is a hundred percent. Barring a few who never woke up from anesthesia." She treated herself to a slow smile. "If there's anybody whose illness is too intractable for this particular treatment, they must be smart enough to keep it to themselves. And smart enough not to get caught a second time."

*You're being played*, he told himself. *You are smarter than her. Way too smart for this to work on you. She's appealing to your vanity. Don't let her yank your chain. She thinks she's so fucking smart. She's prey. You're the hunter. More evolved. Don't be manipulated—*

His lips said, "Lady, sign me up."

• • • •

The snow creaks under my steps. Trees might crack tonight. I compose a poem in my head.

The fashion in poetry is confessional. It wasn't always so—but now we judge value by our own voyeurism. By the perceived rawness of what we think we are being invited to spy upon. But it's all art: veils and lies.

If I wrote a confessional poem, it would begin: *Her dress was the color of mermaids, and I killed her anyway.*

A confessional poem need not be true. Not true in the way the bite of the air in my lungs in spite of the mask is true. Not true in the way the graveyard and the cardinal and the ragged stones are true.

It wasn't just her. It was her, and a dozen others like her. Exactly like her in that they were none of them the right one, and so another one always had to die.

That I can still see them as fungible is a victory for my old self—his only victory, maybe, though he was arrogant enough to expect many more. He thought he could beat the rightminding.

That's the only reason he agreed to it.

If I wrote it, people would want to read *that* poem. It would sell a million—it would garner far more attention than what I *do* write.

I won't write it. I don't even want to *remember* it. Memory excision was declared by the Supreme Court to be a form of the death penalty, and therefore unconstitutional since 2043.

They couldn't take my memories in retribution. Instead they took away my pleasure in them.

Not that they'd admit it was retribution. They call it *repair.* "Rightminding." Fixing the problem. Psychopathy is a curable disease.

They gave me a new face, a new brain, a new name. The chromosome reassignment, I chose for myself, to put as much distance between my old self and my new as possible.

The old me also thought it might prove good will: reduced testosterone, reduced aggression, reduced physical strength. Few women become serial killers.

To my old self, it seemed a convincing lie.

He—no, I: alienating the uncomfortable actions of the self is something that psychopaths do—I thought I was stronger than biology and stronger than rightminding. I thought I could take anabolic steroids to get my muscle and anger back where they should be. I honestly thought I'd get away with it.

I honestly thought I would still want to.

I could write that poem. But that's not the poem I'm writing. The poem

I'm writing begins: *Gravestones like smoker's teeth...* except I don't know what happens in the second clause, so I'm worrying at it as I run.

I do my lap and throw in a second lap because the wind's died down and my heater is working and I feel light, sharp, full of energy and desire. When I come down the hill, I'm running on springs. I take the long arc, back over the bridge toward the edge of town, sparing a quick glance down at the frozen water. The air is warming up a little as the sun rises. My fingers aren't numb in my gloves anymore.

When the unmarked white delivery van pulls past me and rolls to a stop, it takes me a moment to realize the driver wants my attention. He taps the horn, and I jog to a stop, hit pause on my run tracker, tug a headphone from my ear. I stand a few steps back from the window. He looks at me, then winces in embarrassment, and points at his navigation system. "Can you help me find Green Street? The autodrive is no use."

"Sure," I say. I point. "Third left, up that way. It's an unimproved road; that might be why it's not on your map."

"Thanks," he says. He opens his mouth as if to say something else, some form of apology, but I say, "Good luck, man!" and wave him cheerily on.

The vehicle isn't the anomaly here in the country that it would be on a city street, even if half the cities have been retrofitted for urban farming to the point where they barely have streets anymore. But I'm flummoxed by the irony of the encounter, so it's not until he pulls away that I realize I should have been more wary. And that *his* reaction was not the embarrassment of having to ask for directions, but the embarrassment of a decent, normal person who realizes he's put another human being in a position where she may feel unsafe. He's vanishing around the curve before I sort that out—something I suppose most people would understand instinctually.

I wish I could run after the van and tell him that I was never worried. That it never occurred to me to be worried. Demographically speaking, the driver is very unlikely to be hunting me. He was black. And I am white.

And my early fear socialization ran in different directions, anyway.

My attention is still fixed on the disappearing van when something dark and clinging and sweetly rank drops over my head.

I gasp in surprise and my filter mask briefly saves me. I get the sick chartreuse scent of ether and the world spins, but the mask buys me a moment to realize what's happening—a blitz attack. Someone is kidnapping me. He's grabbed my arms, pulling my elbows back to keep me from pushing the mask off.

I twist and kick, but he's so strong.

Was I this strong? It seems like he's not even working to hold on to me, and though my heel connects solidly with his shin as he picks me up, he doesn't grunt. The mask won't help forever—

—it doesn't even help for long enough.

Ether dreams are just as vivid as they say.

• • • •

His first was the girl in the mermaid-colored dress. I think her name was Amelie. Or Jessica. Or something. She picked him up in a bar. Private cars were rare enough to have become a novelty, even then, but he had my father's Mission for the evening. She came for a ride, even though—or perhaps because—it was a little naughty, as if they had been smoking cigarettes a generation before. They watched the sun rise from a curve over a cornfield. He strangled her in the backseat a few minutes later.

She heaved and struggled and vomited. He realized only later how stupid he'd been. He had to hide the body, because too many people had seen us leave the bar together.

He never did get the smell out of the car. My father beat the shit out of him and never let him use it again. We all make mistakes when we're young.

• • • •

I awaken in the dying warmth of my sweat-soaked jacket, to the smell of my vomit drying between my cheek and the cement floor. At least it's only oatmeal. You don't eat a lot before a long run. I ache in every particular, but especially where my shoulder and hip rest on concrete. I should be grateful; he left me in the recovery position so I didn't choke.

It's so dark I can't tell if my eyelids are open or closed, but the hood is gone and only traces of the stink of the ether remain. I lie still, listening and hoping my brain will stop trying to split my skull.

I'm still dressed as I was, including the shoes. He's tied my hands behind my back, but he didn't tape my thumbs together. He's an amateur. I conclude that he's not in the room with me. And probably not anywhere nearby. I think I'm in a cellar. I can't hear anybody walking around on the floor overhead.

I'm not gagged, which tells me he's confident that I can't be heard even if I scream. So maybe I wouldn't hear him up there, either?

My aloneness suggests that I was probably a target of opportunity. That he has somewhere else he absolutely has to be. Parole review? Dinner with the mother who supports him financially? Stockbroker meeting? He seems organized; it could be anything. But whatever it is, it's incredibly important that he show up for it, or he wouldn't have left.

When *you* have a new toy, can you resist playing with it? I start working my hands around. It's not hard if you're fit and flexible, which I am, though I haven't kept in practice. I'm not scared, though I should be. I know better than most what happens next. But I'm calmer than I have been since I was somebody else. The adrenaline still settles me, just like it used to. Only this time—well, I already mentioned the irony.

It's probably not even the lights in my brain taking the edge off my arousal.

The history of technology is all about unexpected consequences. Who would have guessed that peak oil would be linked so clearly to peak psychopathy? Most folks don't think about it much, but people just aren't as mobile as they—as we—used to be. *We* live in populations of greater density, too, and travel less. And all of that leads to knowing each other more.

People like the nameless him who drugged me—people like me—require a certain anonymity, either in ourselves or in our victims.

The floor is cold against my rear end. My gloves are gone. My wrists scrape against the soles of my shoes as I work the rope past them. They're only a little damp, and the water isn't frozen or any colder than the floor. I've been down here awhile, then—still assuming I *am* down. Cellars usually have windows, but guys like me—guys like I used to be—spend a lot of time planning in advance. Rehearsing. Spinning their webs and digging their holes like trapdoor spiders.

I'm shivering, and my body wants to cramp around the chill. I keep pulling. One more wiggle and tug, and I have my arms in front of me. I sit up and stretch, hoping my kidnapper has made just one more mistake. It's so dark I can't see my fluorescent yellow-and-green running jacket, but proprioception lets me find my wrist with my nose. And there, clipped into its little pocket, is the microflash sleeve light that comes with the jacket.

He got the mask—or maybe the mask just came off with the bag. And he got my phone, which has my tracker in it, and a GPS. He didn't make the mistake I would have chosen for him to make.

I push the button on the sleeve light with my nose. It comes on shockingly bright, and I stretch my fingers around to shield it as best I can. Flesh glows red between the bones.

Yep. It's a basement.

• • • •

Eight years after my first time, the new, improved me showed the IBI the site of the grave he'd dug for the girl in the mermaid-colored dress. I'd never forgotten it—not the gracious tree that bent over the little boulder he'd skidded on top of her to keep the animals out, not the tangle of vines he'd dragged over that, giving himself a hell of a case of poison ivy in the process.

This time, I was the one who vomited.

How does one even begin to own having done something like that? How do I?

• • • •

Ah, there's the fear. Or not fear, exactly, because the optogenetic and chemical controls on my endocrine system keep my arousal pretty low. It's anxiety. But anxiety's an old friend.

It's something to think about while I work on the ropes and tape with my teeth. The sleeve light shines up my nose while I gnaw, revealing veins through the cartilage and flesh. I'm cautious, nipping and tearing rather than pulling. I can't afford to break my teeth: they're the best weapon and the best tool I have. So I'm meticulous and careful, despite the nauseous thumping of my heart and the voice in my head that says, *Hurry, hurry, he's coming.*

He's not coming—at least, I haven't heard him coming. Ripping the bonds apart seems to take forever. I wish I had wolf teeth, teeth for slicing and cutting. Teeth that could scissor through this stuff as if it were a cheese sandwich. I imagine my other self's delight in my discomfort, my worry. I wonder if he'll enjoy it when my captor returns, even though he's trapped in this body with me.

Does he really exist, my other self? Neurologically speaking, we all have a lot of people in our heads all the time, and we can't hear most of them. Maybe they really did change him, unmake him. Transform him into me. Or maybe he's back there somewhere, gagged and chained up, but watching.

Whichever it is, I know what he would think of this. He killed 13 people. He'd like to kill me, too.

I'm shivering.

The jacket's gone cold, and it—and I—am soaked. The wool still insulates while wet, but not enough. The jacket and my compression tights don't do a damned thing.

I wonder if my captor realized this. Maybe *this* is his game.

Considering all the possibilities, freezing to death is actually not so bad.

Maybe he just doesn't realize the danger? Not everybody knows about cold.

The last wrap of tape parts, sticking to my chapped lower lip and pulling a few scraps of skin loose when I tug it free. I'm leaving my DNA all over this basement. I spit in a corner, too, just for good measure. Leave traces: even when you're sure you're going to die. Especially then. Do anything you can to leave clues.

It was my skin under a fingernail that finally got me.

• • • •

The period when he was undergoing the physical and mental adaptations that turned him into me gave me a certain … not sympathy, because they did the body before they did the rightminding, and sympathy's an emotion he never felt before I was 33 years old … but it gave him and therefore me a certain *perspective* he hadn't had before.

It itched like hell. Like puberty.

There's an old movie, one he caught in the guu this one time. Some people from the future go back in time and visit a hospital. One of them is a doctor. He saves a woman who's waiting for dialysis or a transplant by giving her a pill that makes her grow a kidney.

That's pretty much how I got my ovaries, though it involved stem cells and needles in addition to pills.

I was still *him*, because they hadn't repaired the damage to my brain yet. They had to keep him under control while the physical adaptations were happening. He was on chemical house arrest. Induced anxiety disorder.

Induced agoraphobia.

It doesn't sound so bad until you realize that the neurological shackles are strong enough that even stepping outside your front door can put you on the ground. There are supposed to be safeguards in place. But everybody's heard the stories of criminals on chemarrest who burned to death because they couldn't make themselves walk out of a burning building.

He thought he could beat the rightminding, beat the chemarrest. Beat everything.

Damn, I was arrogant.

• • • •

My former self had more grounds for his arrogance than this guy. *This is pathetic,* I think. And then I have to snort laughter, because it's not my former self who's got me tied up in this basement.

I could just let this happen. It'd be fair. Ironic. *Justice.*

And my dying here would mean more women follow me into this basement. One by one by one.

I unbind my ankles more quickly than I did the wrists. Then I stand and start pacing, do jumping jacks, jog in place while I shine my light around. The activity eases the shivering. Now it's just a tremble, not a teeth-rattling shudder. My muscles are stiff; my bones ache. There's a cramp in my left calf.

There's a door locked with a deadbolt. The windows have been bricked over with new bricks that don't match the foundation. They're my best option—if I could find something to strike with, something to pry with, I might break the mortar and pull them free.

I've got my hands. My teeth. My tiny light, which I turn off now so as not to warn my captor.

And a core temperature that I'm barely managing to keep out of the danger zone.

• • • •

When I walked into my court-mandated therapist's office for the last time—before my relocation—I looked at her creamy complexion, the way the light caught on her eyes behind the glasses. I remembered what *he'd* thought.

If a swell of revulsion could split your own skin off and leave it curled on the ground like something spoiled and disgusting, that would have happened to me then. But of course it wasn't my shell that was ruined and rotten; it was something in the depths of my brain.

"How does it feel to have a functional amygdala?" she asked.

"Lousy," I said.

She smiled absently and stood up to shake my hand—for the first time. To offer me closure. It's something they're supposed to do.

"Thank you for all the lives you've saved," I told her.

"But not for yours?" she said.

I gave her fingers a gentle squeeze and shook my head.

• • • •

My other self waits in the dark with me. I wish I had his physical strength, his invulnerability. His conviction that everybody else in the world is slower, stupider, weaker.

In the courtroom, while I was still my other self, he looked out from the stand into the faces of the living mothers and fathers of the girls he killed. I remember the 11 women and seven men, how they focused on him. How they sat, their stillness, their attention.

He thought about the girls while he gave his testimony. The only individuality they had for him was what was necessary to sort out which parents went with which corpse; important, because it told him whom to watch for the best response.

I wish I didn't know what it feels like to be prey. I tell myself it's just the cold that makes my teeth chatter. Just the cold that's killing me.

Prey can fight back, though. People have gotten killed by something as timid and inoffensive as a white-tailed deer.

I wish I had a weapon. Even a cracked piece of brick. But the cellar is clean.

I do jumping jacks, landing on my toes for silence. I swing my arms. I think about doing burpees, but I'm worried that I might scrape my hands on the floor. I think about taking my shoes off. Running shoes are soft for kicking with, but if I get outside, my feet will freeze without them.

When. When I get outside.

My hands and teeth are the only weapons I have.

An interminable time later, I hear a creak through the ceiling. A footstep, muffled, and then the thud of something dropped. More footsteps, louder, approaching the top of a stair beyond the door.

I crouch beside the door, on the hinge side, far enough away that it won't quite strike me if he swings it violently. I wish for a weapon—I *am* a weapon—and I wait.

A metallic tang in my mouth now. *Now* I am really, truly scared.

His feet thump on the stairs. He's not little. There's no light beneath the door—it must be weather-stripped for soundproofing. The lock thuds. A bar scrapes. The knob rattles, and then there's a bar of light as it swings open. He turns the flashlight to the right, where he left me lying. It picks out the puddle of vomit. I hear his intake of breath.

I think about the mothers of the girls I killed. I think, *Would they want me to die like this?*

My old self would relish it. It'd be his revenge for what I did to him.

My goal is just to get past him—my captor, my old self; they blur together—to get away, run. Get outside. Hope for a road, neighbors, bright daylight.

My captor's silhouette is dim, scatter-lit. He doesn't look armed, except for the flashlight, one of those archaic long heavy metal ones that doubles as a club. I can't be sure that's all he has. He wavers. He might slam the door and leave me down here to starve—

I lunge.

I grab for the wrist holding the light, and I half catch it, but he's stronger. I knew he would be. He rips the wrist out of my grip, swings the flashlight. Shouts. I lurch back, and it catches me on the shoulder instead of across the throat. My arm sparks pain and numbs. I don't hear my collarbone snap. Would I, if it has?

I try to knee him in the crotch and hit his thigh instead. I mostly elude his grip. He grabs my jacket; cloth stretches and rips. He swings the light once more. It thuds into the stair wall and punches through drywall. I'm half past him and I use his own grip as an anchor as I lean back and kick him right in the center of the nose. Soft shoes or no soft shoes.

He lets go, then. Falls back. I go up the stairs on all fours, scrambling, sure he's right behind me. Waiting for the grab at my ankle. Halfway up I realize I should have locked him in. Hit the door at the top of the stairs and find myself in a perfectly ordinary hallway, in need of a good sweep. The door ahead is closed. I fumble the lock, yank it open, tumble down steps into the snow as something fouls my ankles.

It's twilight. I get my feet under me and stagger back to the path. The shovel I fell over is tangled with my feet. I grab it, use it as a crutch, lever myself up and stagger-run-limp down the walk to a long driveway.

I glance over my shoulder, sure I hear breathing.

Nobody. The door swings open in the wind.

Oh. The road. No traffic. I know where I am. Out past the graveyard and the bridge. I run through here every couple of days, but the house is set far enough back that it was never more than a dim white outline behind trees. It's a Craftsman bungalow, surrounded by winter-sere oaks.

Maybe it wasn't an attack of opportunity, then. Maybe he saw me and decided to lie in wait.

I pelt toward town—pelt, limping, the air so cold in my lungs that they cramp and wheeze. I'm cold, so cold. The wind is a knife. I yank my sleeves down over my hands. My body tries to draw itself into a huddled comma even as I run. The sun's at the horizon.

I think, *I should just let the winter have me.*

Justice for those 11 mothers and seven fathers. Justice for those 13 women who still seem too alike. It's only that their interchangeability *bothers* me now.

At the bridge I stumble to a dragging walk, then turn into the wind off the river, clutch the rail, and stop. I turn right and don't see him coming. My wet fingers freeze to the railing.

The state police are half a mile on, right around the curve at the top of the hill. If I run, I won't freeze before I get there. If I run.

My fingers stung when I touched the rail. Now they're numb, my ears past hurting. If I stand here, I'll lose the feeling in my feet.

The sunset glazes the ice below with crimson. I turn and glance the other way; in a pewter sky, the rising moon bleaches the clouds to moth-wing iridescence.

I'm wet to the skin. Even if I start running now, I might not make it to the station house. Even if I started running now, the man in the bungalow might be right behind me. I don't think I hit him hard enough to knock him out. Just knock him down.

If I stay, it won't take long at all until the cold stops hurting.

If I stay here, I wouldn't have to remember being my other self again. I could put him down. At last, at last, I could put those women down.

Amelie, unless her name was Jessica. The others.

It seems easy. Sweet.

But if I stay here, I won't be the last person to wake up in the bricked-up basement of that little white bungalow.

The wind is rising. Every breath I take is a wheeze. A crow blows across the road like a tattered shirt, vanishing into the twilight cemetery.

I can carry this a little farther. It's not so heavy. Thirteen corpses, plus one. After all, I carried every one of them before.

I leave skin behind on the railing when I peel my fingers free. Staggering at first, then stronger, I sprint back into town.

---

Elizabeth Bear was born on the same day as Frodo and Bilbo Baggins, but in a different year. She is the Hugo, Sturgeon, Locus, and Campbell Award winning author of 27 novels (The most recent is Karen Memory, a Weird West adventure from Tor) and over a hundred short stories. She lives in Massachusetts.

# The Truth About Owls
## By Amal El-Mohtar

*Owls have eyes that match the skies they hunt through. Amber-eyed owls hunt at dawn or dusk; golden-eyed owls hunt during the day; black-eyed owls hunt at night.*

*No one knows why this is.*

Anisa's eyes are black, and she no longer hates them. She used to wish for eyes the color of her father's, the beautiful pale green-blue that people were always startled to see in a brown face. But she likes, now, having eyes and hair of a color those same people find frightening.

Even her teachers are disconcerted, she's found—they don't try to herd her as they do the other students. She sees them casting uncertain glances towards her before ushering their group from one owl exhibit to another, following the guide. She turns to go in the opposite direction.

"Annie-sa! Annie, this way!"

She turns, teeth clenching. Mrs. Roberts, whose pale powdered face, upswept yellow hair, and bright red lips make Anisa think of Victoria sponge, is smiling encouragingly.

"My name is A-NEE-sa, actually," she replies, and feels the power twitching out from her chest and into her arms, which she crosses quickly, and her hands, which she makes into fists, digging nails into her palms. The power recedes, but she can still feel it pouring out from her eyes like a swarm of bees while Mrs. Roberts looks at her in perplexed confusion. Mrs. Roberts' eyes are a delicate, ceramic sort of blue.

Anisa watches another teacher, Ms. Grewar, lean over to murmur something into Mrs. Roberts' ear. Mrs. Roberts only looks more confused, but renews her smile uncertainly, nods, and turns back to her group. Anisa closes her eyes, takes a deep breath, and counts to ten before walking away.

• • • •

*Owls are predators. There are owls that would tear you apart if you gave them half a chance.*

The Scottish Owl Centre is a popular destination for school trips: a short bus ride from Glasgow, an educational component, lots of opportunities for photographs to show the parents, and who doesn't like owls nowadays? Anisa has found herself staring, more than once, at owl-print bags and shirts, owl-shaped earrings and belt buckles, plush owl toys and wire statues in bright, friendly colors. She finds it all desperately strange.

Anisa remembers the first time she saw an owl. She was seven years old. She lived in Riyaq with her father and her grandparents, and that morning she had thrown a tantrum about having to feed the chickens, which she hated, because of their smell and the way they pecked at her when she went to gather their eggs, and also because of the rooster, who was fierce and sharp-spurred. She hated the chickens, she shouted, why didn't they just make them into soup.

She was given more chores to do, which she did, fumingly, stomping her feet and banging cupboard doors and sometimes crying about how unfair it was. "Are you brooding over the chickens," her father would joke, trying to get her to laugh, which only made her more furious, because she *did* want to laugh but she didn't want him to think she wasn't still mad, because she was.

She had calmed down by lunch, and forgotten about it by supper. But while helping her grandmother with the washing up she heard a scream from the yard. Her grandmother darted out, and Anisa followed, her hands dripping soap.

An owl—enormous, tall as a lamb, taller than any bird she had ever seen—perched in the orange tree, the rooster a tangle of blood and feathers in its talons. As Anisa stared, the owl bent its head to the rooster's throat and tore out a long strip of flesh.

When Anisa thinks about this—and she does, often, whenever her hands are wet and soapy in just the right way, fingertips on the brink of wrinkling—she remembers the guilt. She remembers listening to her grandmother cross herself and speak her words of protection against harm, warding them against death in the family, against troubled times. She remembers the fear, staring at the red and pink and green of the rooster, its broken, dangling head.

But she can't remember—though she often tries—whether she felt, for the first time, the awful electric prickle of the power in her chest, flooding out to her palms.

• • • •

*There are owls that sail through the air like great ships. There are owls that flit like finches from branch to branch. There are owls that look at you with disdain and owls that sway on the perch of your arm like a reed in the wind.*

Anisa is not afraid of owls. She thinks they're interesting enough, when people aren't cooing over them or embroidering them onto cushions. From walking around the sanctuary she thinks the owl she saw as a child was probably a Eurasian Eagle Owl.

She wanders from cage to cage, environment to environment, looking at owls that bear no resemblance to the pretty patterns lining the hems of skirts and dresses—owls that lack a facial disk, owls with bulging eyes and fuzzy heads, owls the size of her palm.

Some of the owls have names distinct from their species: Hosking, Broo, Sarabi. Anisa pauses in front of a barn owl and frowns at the name. Blodeuwedd?

"Blow-due-wed," she sounds out beneath her breath, while the owl watches her.

"It's Bloh-DA-weth, actually," says a friendly voice behind her. Anisa turns to see one of the owl handlers from the flying display, a black woman named Izzy, hair wrapped up in a brightly colored scarf, moving into one of the aviaries, gloved hands clutching a feed bucket. "It means 'flower-face' in Welsh."

Anisa flushes. She looks at the owl again. She has never seen a barn owl up close, and does not think it looks like flowers; she thinks, all at the same time, that the heart-shaped face is alien and eerie and beautiful and like when you can see the moon while the sun is setting, and that there should be a single word for the color of the wings that's like the sheen of a pearl but not the pearl itself.

She asks, "Is it a boy or a girl?"

"Do you not know the story of Blodeuwedd?" Izzy smiles. "She was a beautiful woman, made of flowers, who was turned into an owl."

Anisa frowns. "That doesn't make sense."

"It's from a book of fairytales called *The Mabinogion*—not big on sense-making." Izzy chuckles. "I don't think she likes it either, to be honest. She's one of our most difficult birds. But she came to us from Wales, so we gave her a Welsh name."

Anisa looks into Blodeuwedd's eyes. They are blacker than her own.

"I like her," she declares.

• • • •

*A group of owls is called a Parliament.*
*Owls are bad luck.*

The summer Anisa saw the owl kill the rooster was the summer Israel bombed the country. She always thinks of it that way, not as a war—she doesn't remember a war. She never saw anyone fighting. She remembers a sound she felt more than heard, a *thud* that shook the earth and rattled up through her bones—then another—then a smell like chalk—before being swept into her father's arms and taken down into shelter.

She remembers feeling cold; she remembers, afterwards, anger, weeping, conversations half-heard from her bed, her mother's voice reaching them in sobs from London, robotic and strangled over a poor internet connection, a mixing of English and Arabic, accents swapping places. Her father's voice always calm, measured, but with a tension running through it like when her cousin put a wire through a dead frog's leg to make it twitch.

She remembers asking her grandmother if Israel attacked because of the owl. Her grandmother laughed in a way that made Anisa feel hollow and lost.

"Shh, shh, don't tell Israel! An owl killed a rooster—that's more reason to attack! An owl killed a rooster in Lebanon and the government let it happen! Quick, get off the bridges!"

The whole family laughed. Anisa was terrified, and told no one.

• • • •

*Why did the owl not go courting in the rain? Because it was* too wet to woo.

"What makes her 'difficult'?" asks Anisa, watching Blodeuwedd sway on her perch. Izzy looks fondly at the owl.

58

"Well, we acquired her as a potential display bird, but she just doesn't take well to training—she hisses at most of the handlers when they pass by, tries to bite. She's also very territorial, and won't tolerate the presence of male birds, so we can't use her for breeding." Izzy offers Blodeuwedd a strip of raw chicken, which she gulps down serenely.

"But she likes you," Anisa observes. Izzy smiles ruefully.

"I'm not one of her trainers. It's easy to like people who ask nothing of you." Izzy pauses, eyes Blodeuwedd with exaggerated care. "Or at least, it's easy to not hate them."

Before Anisa leaves with the rest of her class, Izzy writes down *Mabinogion* for her on a piece of paper, a rather deft doodle of an owl's face inside a five-petaled flower, and an invitation to come again.

• • • •

*Most owls are sexually dimorphic: the female is usually larger, stronger, and more brightly colored than the male.*

Anisa's mother is tall, and fair, and Anisa looks nothing like her. Her mother's brown hair is light and thin and straight; her mother's skin is pale. Anisa is used to people making assumptions—*are you adopted? Is that your stepmother?*—when they see them together, but her mother's new job at the university has made outings together rare. In fact, since moving to Glasgow, Anisa hardly sees her at home anymore, since she has evening classes and departmental responsibilities.

"What are you reading?" asks her mother, shrugging on her coat after a hurried dinner together.

Anisa, legs folded up underneath her on the couch, holds up a library copy of *The Mabinogion.* Her mother looks confused, but nods, wishes her a good night, and leaves.

Anisa reads about how Math, son of Mathonwy, gathered the blossoms of oak, of broom, of meadowsweet, and shaped them into a woman. She wonders, idly, what kind of flowers could be combined to make her.

• • • •

*There are owls on every continent in the world except Antarctica.*

The so-called war lasted just over a month; Anisa learned the word "ceasefire" in August. Her father put her on a plane to London the moment the airports were repaired.

Before she started going to school, Anisa's mother took her aside. "When people ask you where you're from," she told her, "you say 'England,' all right? You were born here. You have every bit as much right to be here as anyone else."

"Baba wasn't born here." She felt a stinging in her throat and eyes, a pain of *unfair*. "Is that why he's not here? Is he not allowed to come?"

Anisa doesn't remember what her mother said. She must have said something. Whatever it was, it was certainly not that she wouldn't see her father in person for three years.

• • • •

*The Welsh word for owl once meant "flower-face".*

When Izzy said Blodeuwedd was made of flowers, Anisa had imagined roses and lilies, flowers she was forced to read about over and over in books of English literature. But as she reads, she finds that even Blodeuwedd's flower names are strange to her—what kind of a flower is "broom"?—and she likes that, likes that no part of Blodeuwedd is familiar or expected.

Anisa has started teaching herself Welsh, mostly because she wants to know how all the names in the *Mabinogion* are pronounced. She likes that there is a language that looks like English but sounds like Arabic; she likes that there is no one teaching it to her, or commenting on her accent, or asking her how to speak it for their amusement. She likes that a single "f" is pronounced "v", that "w" is a vowel—likes that it's an alphabet of secrets hidden in plain sight.

She starts visiting the owl centre every weekend, feeling like she's done her homework if she can share a new bit of *Mabinogion* trivia with Izzy and Blodeuwedd in exchange for a fact about owls.

• • • •

*Owls are birds of the order* Strigiformes, *a word derived from the Latin for* witch.

During Anisa's first year of school in England a girl with freckles and yellow hair leaned over to her while the teacher's back was turned, and asked if her father was dead.

"No!" Anisa stared at her.

"My mum said your dad could be dead. Because of the war. Because there's always war where you're from."

"That's not true."

The freckled girl narrowed her eyes. "My mum *said* so."

Anisa felt her pulse quicken, her hands tremble. She felt she had never hated anyone in her whole life so much as this idiot pastry of a girl. She watched as the girl shrugged and turned away.

"Maybe you just don't understand English."

She felt something uncoil inside her. Anisa stood up from her chair and *shoved* the girl out of hers, and felt, in the moment of skin touching skin, a startling shock of static electricity; the girl's freckles vanished into the pink of her cheeks, and instead of protesting the push, she shouted "Ugh, she *shocked* me!"

In her memory, the teacher's reprimand, the consequences, the rest of that year all melt away to one viciously satisfying image: the freckled girl's blue eyes looking at her, terrified, out of a pretty pink face.

She learned to cultivate an appearance of danger, of threat; she learned that with an economy of look, of gesture, of insinuation, she could be feared and left alone. She was the Girl Who Came From War, the Girl Whose Father Was Dead, the Girl With Powers. One day a boy tried to kiss her; she pushed him away, looked him in the eye, and flung a fistful of nothing at him, a spray of air. He was absent from school for two days; when the boy came back claiming to have had a cold, everyone acknowledged Anisa as the cause. When some students asked her to make them sick on purpose, to miss an exam or assignment, she smirked, said nothing, and walked away.

• • • •

*Owls have a narrow field of binocular vision; they compensate for this by rotating their heads up to two hundred and seventy degrees.*

Carefully, Izzy lowers her arm to Anisa's gloved wrist, hooks her tether to the ring dangling from it, and watches as Blodeuwedd hops casually down on to her forearm. Anisa exhales, then grins. Izzy grins back.

"I can't believe how much she's mellowed out. She's really surprisingly comfortable with you."

"Maybe," Anisa says, mischievous, "it's because I'm really good at not asking anything of her."

"Sure," says Izzy, "or maybe it's because you keep talking about how much you hate Math, son of Mathonwy."

"Augh, that *prick*!"

Izzy laughs, and Anisa loves to hear her, to see how she tosses her head back when she does. She loves how thick and wiry Izzy's hair is, and the different things she does with it—today it's half-wrapped in a white and purple scarf, fluffed out at the back like a bouquet. She continues,

"He's the worst. He takes flowers and tells them to be a woman; as soon as she acts in a way he doesn't like, he turns her into an owl. It's like—he needs to keep being in charge of her story, and the way to do that is to change her shape."

"Well. To be fair. She did try to kill his adopted son."

"He forced her into marriage with him! And he was a jerk too!"

"You're well into this, you are."

"It's just—" Anisa bites her lip, looking at Blodeuwedd, raising her slightly to shift the weight on her forearm, watching her spread her magnificent wings, then settle, "—sometimes—I feel like I'm just a collection of bits of things that someone brought together at random and called *girl*, and then *Anisa*, and then—" she shrugs. "Whatever."

Izzy is quiet for a moment. Then she says, thoughtfully, "You know, there's another word for that."

"For what?"

"What you just described—an aggregation of disparate things. An anthology. That's what *The Mabinogion* is, after all."

Anisa is unconvinced. "Blodeuwedd's just one part of someone else's story, she's not an anthology herself."

Izzy smiles, gently, in a way that always makes Anisa feel she's thinking of someone or something else, but allowing Anisa a window's worth of view into her world. "You can look at it that way. But there's another word for anthology, one we don't really use any more: *florilegium*. Do you know what it means?"

Anisa shakes her head, and blinks, startled, as Blodeuwedd does a side-wise walk up her arm to lean, gently, against her shoulder. Izzy smiles, a little more brightly, more for her, and says: "A gathering of flowers."

• • • •

*Owls fly more silently than any other bird.*

When her father joined them in London three years later, he found Anisa grown several inches taller and several sentences shorter. Her mother's insistence on speaking Arabic together at all times—pushing her abilities as a heritage speaker to their limits—meant that Anisa often chose not to speak at all. This was to her advantage in the school yard, where her eyes, her looks, and rumors of her dark powers held her fellow students in awe; it did her no good with her father, who hugged her and held her until words and tears gushed out of her in gasps.

The next few years were better; they moved to a different part of the city, and Anisa was able to make friends in a new school, to open up, to speak. She sometimes told stories about how afraid of her people used to be, how she'd convinced them of her powers like it was a joke on them, and not something she had ever believed herself.

• • • •

*Owls purge from themselves the matter they cannot absorb: bones, fur, claws, teeth, feathers.*

"Is that for school?"

Anisa looks up from her notebook to her mother, and shakes her head. "No. It's Welsh stuff."

"Oh." Her mother pauses, and Anisa can see her mentally donning the gloves with which to handle her. "Why Welsh?"

She shrugs. "I like it." Then, seeing her mother unsatisfied, adds, "I like the stories. I'd like to read them in the original language eventually."

Her mother hesitates. "You know, there's a rich tradition of Arabic storytelling—"

The power flexes inside her like a whip snapping, takes her by surprise, and she bites the inside of her lip until it bleeds to stop it, stop it.

"—and I know I can't share much myself but I'm sure your grandmother or your aunt would love to talk to you about it—"

Anisa grabs her books and runs to her room as if she could outrun the power, locks the door, and buries her fingernails in the skin of her arms, dragging long, painful scratches down them, because the only way to let the power out is through pain, because if she doesn't hurt herself she knows with absolute certainty that she will hurt someone else.

• • • •

*Illness in owls is difficult to detect and diagnose until it is dangerously advanced.*

Anisa knows something is wrong before she sees the empty cage, from the way Izzy is pacing in front of it, as if waiting for her.

"Blodeuwedd's sick," she says , and Anisa feels a rush of gravity inside her stomach. "She hasn't eaten in a few days. I'm sorry, but you won't be able to see her today—"

"What's wrong with her?" Anisa begins counting back the days to the last flare, to what she thought, and it wasn't this, it was never anything like this, but she'd held *The Mabinogion* in her hands—

"We don't know yet. I'm so sorry you came out all this way—" Izzy hesitates while Anisa stands, frozen, feeling herself vanishing into misery, into a day one year and four hundred miles away.

• • • •

*Owls do not mate for life, though death sometimes parts them.*

The memory is like a trap, a steel cage that falls over her head and severs her from reality. When the memory descends she can do nothing but see her father's face, over and over, aghast, more hurt than she has ever seen him, and her own words like a bludgeon to beat in her own head: 'Fine, go back and *die*, I don't care, just *stop coming back.*"

She feels, again, the power lashing out, confused, attempting both to tether and to push away; she remembers the shape of the door knob in her hand as she bolts out of the flat, down the stairs, out the building, into the night. She feels incandescent, too burnt up to cry, thinking of her father going back to a country every day in the news, every day a patchwork of explosions and body counts, every day a matter of someone else's opinions.

She thinks of how he wouldn't take her with him.

And she feels, irrevocably, as if she is breathing a stone when she sees him later that evening in hospital, eyes closed, ashen, and the words reaching her from a faraway dimness saying he has suffered a stroke, and died.

• • • •

"Anisa—A*ni*sa!" Izzy has taken her hands, is holding them, and when Anisa focuses again she feels as if they're submerged in water, and she wants to snatch them away because what if she hurts Izzy but she is disoriented and before she knows what she is doing she is crying while Izzy holds her hands and sinks down to the rain-wet floor with her. She feels gravel beneath her knees and grinds them further into it, to punish herself for this, this thing, the power, and she is trying to make Izzy understand and she is trying to say she is sorry but all that comes out is this violent, wrecking weeping.

"It's me," she manages, "I made her sick, it's my fault, I don't mean to do it but I make bad things happen just by wanting them even a little, wanting them the wrong way, and I don't want it anymore, I never wanted *this* but it keeps happening and now she'll die—"

Izzy looks at her, squeezes her hands, and says, calm and even, "Bullshit."

"It's true—"

"Anisa—if it's true it should work both ways. Can you make good things happen by wanting them?"

She looks into Izzy's warm dark eyes, at a loss, and can't frame a reply to such a ridiculous question.

"Think, pet—what *good* things do you want to happen?"

"I want—" she closes her eyes, and bites her lip, looking for pain to quash the power but feels it differently—feels, with Izzy holding her hands, Izzy facing her, grounded, as if draining something out into the gravel and the earth beneath it and leaving something else in its wake, something shining and slick as sunlight on wet streets. "I want Blodeuwedd to get better. I want her to have a good life, to … be whatever she wants to be and do whatever she wants to do. I want to learn Welsh. I want to—" Izzy's face shimmers through her tears. "I want to be friends with you. I want—"

She swallows them down, all of her good wants, how much she misses her father and how much she misses just talking, in any language, with her mother, and how she misses the light in Riyaq and the dry dusty air, the sheep and the goats and the warmth, always, of her grandmother and uncles and aunts and cousins all around, and she makes an anthology of them. She gathers the flowers of her wants all together in her throat, her heart, her belly, and trusts that they are good.

• • • •

*The truth about owls—*

Anisa and her mother stand at the owl centre's entrance, both casually studying a nearby freezer full of ice lollies while waiting for their tickets. Their eyes meet, and they grin at each other. Her mother is rummaging about for caramel cornettos when the sales attendant, Rachel, waves Anisa over.

"Is that your mother, Anisa?" whispers Rachel. Anisa goes very still for a moment as she nods, and Rachel beams. "I thought so. You have precisely the same smile."

Anisa blushes, and looks down, suddenly shy. Her mother pays for their tickets and ice cream, and together they move towards the gift-shop and the aviaries beyond.

Anisa pauses on her way through the gift-shop; she waves her mother on, says she'll catch her up. Alone, she buys a twee notebook covered in shiny metallic owls and starts writing in it with an owl-topped pen.

She writes "The truth about owls—" but pauses. She looks at the words, their shape, the taken-for-granted ease of their spilling from her. She frowns, bites her lip, and after a moment's careful thought writes "Y gwir am tylluanod—"

But she has run out of vocabulary, and this is not something she wants to look up. There is a warmth blossoming in her, a rightness, pushing up out of her chest where the power used to crouch, where something lives now that is different, better, and she wants to pour that out on the page. She rolls the pen between her thumb and forefinger, then shifts the journal's weight against her palm.

She writes "معقّدة البـــوم عن الحقيقـــة ان", and smiles.

Amal El-Mohtar is an author, editor, and critic: her short fiction has received the Locus Award and been nominated for the Nebula Award, while her poetry has won the Rhysling Award three times. She is the author of *The Honey Month*, a collection of poetry and prose written to the taste of twenty-eight different kinds of honey, and her fiction has appeared most recently in *Lightspeed*, *Strange Horizons*, and *Uncanny Magazine*. She contributes book reviews to NPR Books and the LA Times; edits *Goblin Fruit*, a quarterly journal of fantastical poetry; is a founding member of the Banjo Apocalypse Crinoline Troubadours; a contributor to *Down and Safe: A Blake's 7 Podcast*; and divides her time and heart between Ottawa and Glasgow. Find her on Twitter @tithenai.

# A Kiss With Teeth
## By Max Gladstone

Vlad no longer shows his wife his sharp teeth. He keeps them secret in his gums, waiting for the quickened skip of hunger, for the bloodrush he almost never feels these days.

The teeth he wears instead are blunt as shovels. He coffee-stains them carefully, soaks them every night in a mug with 'World's Best Dad' written on the side. After eight years of staining, Vlad's blunt teeth are the burnished yellow of the keys of an old unplayed piano. If not for the stain they would be whiter than porcelain. Much, much whiter than bone.

White, almost, as the sharp teeth he keeps concealed.

His wife Sarah has not tried to kill him since they married. She stores her holy water in a kitchen cabinet behind the spice rack, the silver bullets in a safe with her gun. She smiles when they make love, the smile of a woman sinking into a feather bed, a smile of jigsaw puzzles and blankets over warm laps by the fire. He smiles back, with his blunt teeth.

They have a son, a seven-year-old boy named Paul, straight and brown like his mother, a growing, springing sapling boy. Paul plays catch, Paul plays basketball, Paul dreams of growing up to be a football star, or a tennis star, or a baseball star, depending on the season. Vlad takes him to games. Vlad wears a baseball cap, and smells the pitcher's sweat and the ball's leather from their seat far up in the stands. He sees ball strike bat, sees ball and bat deform, and knows whether the ball will stutter out between third and second, or arc beautiful and deadly to outfield, fly true or veer across the foul line. He would tell his son, but Paul cannot hear fast enough. After each play, Paul explains the action, slow, patient and content. Paul smiles like his mother, and the smile sets Vlad on edge and spinning.

Sometimes Vlad remembers his youth, sprinting ahead of a cavalry charge to break like lightning on a stand of pikers. Blood, he remembers, oceans of it. Screams of the impaled. There is a sound men's breaking sterna make when you grab their ribs and pull them out and in, a bassy nightmare transposition of a wishbone's snap. Vlad knows the plural forms of 'sternum' and 'trachea,' and all declensions and participles of 'flense.'

• • • •

"Talk to the teacher," his wife says after dinner. Paul watches a cricket game on satellite in the other room, mountainous Fijians squared off against an Indian team. Vlad once was a death cult in Calcutta—the entire cult, British colonial paranoia being an excellent cover for his appetites— and in the sixties he met a traveling volcano god in Fiji, who'd given up sacrifices when he found virgins could be had more easily by learning to play guitar. Neither experience left Vlad with much appreciation for cricket.

"On what topic should we converse," he asks. He can never end sentences with prepositions. He learned English in a proper age.

"Paul. You should talk to the teacher about Paul."

"Paul is not troubled."

"He's not troubled. But he's having trouble." She shows him the report card. She never rips envelopes open, uses instead a thin knife she keeps beside the ink blotter. Vlad has calculated that in eight years he will be the only person left in the world who uses an ink blotter.

The report card's printed on thick stock, and lists letters that come low in the limited alphabet of grades. No notes, no handwritten explanations. Paul is not doing well. From the next room, he shouts at the cricket match: "Go go go go!"

The teacher's name is a smudge, a dot-matrix mistake.

• • • •

At work Vlad pretends to be an accountant. He pretends to use spreadsheets and formulas to deliver pretend assurances to a client who pretends to follow the law. In furtive conversations at breaks he pretends to care about baseball. Pretending this is easy: Paul cares about baseball, recites statistical rosaries, tells Dad his hopes for the season every night when he's tucked into bed. Vlad repeats these numbers in the break room, though he does not know if he says the right numbers in the right context.

From his cellular telephone, outside, he calls the number on the report card, and communicates in short sentences with someone he presumes is human.

"I would like to schedule a conference with my son's teacher." He tells them his son's name.

"Yes, I will wait."

"Six-thirty will be acceptable."

"Thank you."

• • • •

Afternoons, on weekends, he and Paul play catch in a park one block up and two blocks over from their apartment. They live in a crowded city of towers and stone, a city that calls itself new and thinks itself old. The people in this city have long since learned to unsee themselves. Vlad and his son throw a baseball, catch it, and throw it back in an empty park that, if Vlad were not by now so good at this game of unseeing, he would describe as full: of couples wheeling strollers, of rats and dogs and running children, strolling cops and bearded boys on roller blades.

They throw and catch the ball in this empty not-empty field. Vlad throws slow, and Paul catches, slower, humoring his dad. Vlad sees himself through his son's eyes: sluggish and overskinny, a man walks and runs and throws and catches as if first rehearsing the movements in his mind.

Vlad does rehearse. He has practiced thousands of times in the last decade. It took him a year to slow down so a human eye could see him shift from one posture to the next. Another year to learn to drop things, to let his grip slip, to suppress the instinct to right tipped teacups before they spilled, to grab knives before they left the hands that let them fall. Five years to train himself not to look at images mortal eyes could not detect. Sometimes at night, Paul's gaze darts up from his homework to strange corners of the room, and Vlad thinks he has failed, that the boy learned this nervous tic from him and will carry it through his life like a cross.

Vlad does not like the thought of crosses.

He throws the ball, and throws it back again: a white leather sphere oscillating through a haze of unseen ghosts.

• • • •

The teacher waits, beautiful, blonde, and young. She smells like bruised mint and camellias. She rests against her classroom door, tired—she wakes at four fifteen every morning to catch a bus from Queens, so she can sit at her desk grading papers as the sun rises through steel canyons.

When he sees her, Vlad knows he should turn and leave. No good can come of this meeting. They are doomed, both of them.

Too late. He's walked the halls with steps heavy as a human's, squeaking the soles of his oxblood shoes against the tiles every few steps—a trick he learned a year back and thinks lends him an authentic air. The teacher looks up and sees him: black-haired and pale and too, too thin, wearing blue slacks and a white shirt with faint blue checks.

"You're Paul's father," she says, and smiles, damn her round white teeth. "Mister St. John."

"Bazarab," he corrects, paying close attention to his steps. Slow, as if walking through ankle-deep mud.

She turns to open the door, but stops with her hand on the knob. "I'm sorry?"

"Paul has his mother's last name. Bazarab is mine. It is strange in this country. Please call me Vlad." The nasal American 'a,' too, he has practiced.

"Nice to meet you, Vlad. I'm so glad you could take this time for me, and for Paul." She turns back to smile at him, and starts. Her pupils dilate a millimeter, and her heart rate spikes from a charming sixty-five beats per minute to seventy-four. Blood rises beneath the snow of her cheeks.

He stands a respectful three feet behind her. But cursing himself he realizes that seconds before he was halfway down the hall.

He smiles, covering his frustration, and ushers her ahead of him into the room. Her heart slows, her breath deepens: the mouse convincing itself that it mistook the tree's shadow for a hawk's. He could not have moved so fast, so silently. She must have heard his approach, and ignored it.

The room's sparsely furnished. No posters on the walls. Row upon row of desks, forty children at least could study here. Blackboard, two days unwashed, a list of students' names followed by checks in multicolored chalk. This, he likes: many schools no longer use slate.

She sits on a desk, facing him. Her legs swing.

"You have a large room."

She laughs. "Not mine. We share the rooms." Her smile is sad. "Anyway. I'm glad to see you here. Why did you call?"

"My son. My wife asked me to talk with you about him. He has trouble in school, I think. I know he is a bright boy. His mother, my wife, she wonders why his grades are not so good. I think he is a child, he will improve with time, but I do not know. So I come to ask you."

"How can I help?"

Vlad shifts from foot to foot. Outside the night deepens. Streetlights buzz on. The room smells of dust and sweat and camellias and mint. The teacher's eyes are large and gray. She folds her lips into her mouth, bites them, and unfolds them again. Lines are growing from the corners of her mouth to the corners of her nose—the first signs of age. They surface at twenty-five or so. Vlad has studied them. He looks away from her. To see her is to know her pulse.

"What is he like in class, my son?"

"He's sweet. But he distracts easily. Sometimes he has trouble remembering a passage we've read a half hour after we've read it. In class he fidgets, and he often doesn't turn in his homework."

"I have seen him do the homework."

"Of course. I'm sorry. I'm not saying that he doesn't do it. He doesn't turn it in, though."

"Perhaps he is bored by your class." Her brow furrows, and he would kill men to clear it. "I do not mean that the class is easy. I know you have a difficult job. But perhaps he needs more attention."

"I wish I could give it to him. But any attention I give him comes from the other children in the class. We have forty. I don't have a lot of attention left to go around."

"I see." He paces more. Good to let her see him move like a human being. Good to avert his eyes.

"Have you thought about testing him for ADHD? It's a common condition."

What kind of testing? And what would the testing of his son reveal? "Could I help somehow? Work his work with him?"

She stands. "That's a great idea." The alto weight has left her voice, excitement returning after a day of weeks. "If you have time, I mean. I know it would help him. He looks up to you."

Vlad laughs. Does his son admire the man, or the illusion? Or the monster, whom he has never seen? "I do not think so. But I will help if I can."

He turns from the window, and she walks toward him, holding a bright red folder. "These are his assignments for the week. If it helps, come back and I'll give you the next bunch."

She smiles.

Vlad, cold, afraid, smiles back.

• • • •

"Great," his wife says when he tells her. She does not ask about the teacher, only the outcome. "Great. Thank you." She folds him in her arms, and he feels her strength. In the bathroom mirror they remind him of chess pieces, alabaster and mahogany. "I hate that building. The classrooms scare me. So many bad memories."

"Elementary school has no hold on me."

"Of course not." A quick soft peck on the cheek, and she fades from him, into their small hot bedroom. "This will help Paul, I know."

• • • •

Vlad does not know. Every school night he sits with Paul in their cramped living room, bent over the coffee table, television off. Vlad drags a pencil across the paper, so slowly he feels glaciers might scour down the Hudson and carve a canyon from Manhattan by the time he finishes a single math problem. After a long division painstaking as a Tibetan monk's sand mandala he finds Paul asleep on the table beside him, cheek pooled on wood, tongue twitching pink between his lips. With a touch he wakes the boy, and once Paul stretches out and closes his eyes and shakes the sleep away (his mother's habit), they walk through the problem together, step by step. Then Paul does the next, and Vlad practices meditation, remembering cities rise and fall.

"Do you understand?" he asks.

"Dad, I get it."

Paul does not get it. The next week he brings each day's quizzes home, papers dripping blood.

"Perseverance is important," Vlad says. "In this world you must make something of yourself. It is not enough to be what you are."

"It all takes so long." The way Paul looks at Vlad when they talk makes Vlad wonder whether he has made some subtle mistake.

• • • •

The following week Vlad returns to the school. Entering through swinging doors, he measures each step slow and steady. The shoes, he remembers to squeak. The eyes, he remembers to move. The lungs, he remembers to fill and empty. So many subtle ways to be human, and so many subtle ways to be wrong.

The halls are vacant, and still smell of dust and rubber and chemical soap. He could identify the chemical, if he put his mind to it.

He cannot put his mind to anything.

The teacher's room nears. Slow, slow. He smells her, faint trace of camellias and mint. He will not betray himself again.

The door to her classroom stands ajar. Through the space, he sees only empty desks.

A man sits at her desk, bent over papers like a tuberculotic over his handkerchief. He wears a blue shirt with chalk dust on the right cuff. His nails are ragged, and a pale scalp peeks through his thin hair.

"Where is the teacher?"

The man recoils as if he's touched a live wire. His chair falls and he knocks over a cup of pens and chalk and paperclips. Some spill onto the ground. Vlad does not count them. The man swears. His heart rate jumps to ninety beats a minute. If someone would scare him this way every hour for several months he would begin to lose the paunch developing around his waist. "Damn. Oh my god. Who the hell."

"I am Mister Bazarab," he says. "What has happened to the teacher?"

"I didn't hear," says the man. "I am the teacher. A teacher." Kneeling, he scrabbles over the tiles to gather scattered pens.

"The teacher who I was to meet here. The teacher of my son. A young woman. Blonde hair. About this tall." He does not mention her smell. Most people do not find such descriptions useful.

"Oh," says the man. "Mister Bazarab." He does not pronounce the name correctly. "I'm sorry. Angela had to leave early today. Family thing. She left this for you." He dumps the gathered detritus back into the cup, and searches among piles of paperwork for a red folder like the one the teacher gave Vlad the week before. He offers Vlad the folder, and when Vlad takes it from him the man draws his hand back fast as if burned.

"Is she well? She is not sick I hope."

"She's fine. Her father went to the hospital. I think."

"I am glad," Vlad says, and when he sees the other's confusion he adds, "that she is well. Thank her for this, please."

Vlad does not open the folder until he is outside the school. The teacher has a generous, looped cursive hand. She thanks Vlad for working with his son. She apologizes for missing their meeting. She suggests he return next week. She promises to be here for him then.

Vlad does not examine the rest of the folder's contents until he reaches home. He reads the note three times on his walk. He tries not to smell the camellias, or the chalk, or the slight salt edge of fear. He smells them anyway.

• • • •

His wife returns late from the library. While he works with Paul, she does pull-ups on the bar they sling over the bedroom doorjamb. She breathes heavy through her mouth as she rises and falls. Behind her shadows fill their unlit bedroom.

Paul works long division. How many times does seven go into forty-three, and how much is left over? How far can you carry out the decimal? Paul's pencil breaks, and he sharpens it in the translucent bright red plastic toy his mother bought him, with pleasant curves to hide the tiny blade inside.

Vlad wants to teach Paul to sharpen his pencils with a knife, but sharpening pencils with a knife is not common these days, and anyway they'd have to collect the shaved bits of wood and graphite afterward. The old ways were harder to clean up.

"Tell me about your teacher," Vlad says.

"She's nice," Paul replies. "Three goes into eight two times, and two's left over."

"Nice," Vlad echoes.

Once his wife's exercises are done, they send Paul to bed. "I miss cricket," he says as they tuck him in. "I miss tennis and football and baseball."

"This is only for now," says Vlad's wife. "Once your work gets better, you can watch again. And play."

"Okay." The boy is not okay, but he knows what he is supposed to say.

In the kitchen, the kettle screams. They leave Paul in his dark room. Vlad's wife pours tea, disappears into their bedroom, and emerges soon after wearing flannel pajamas and her fluffy robe, hair down. She looks tired. She looks happy. Vlad cannot tell which she looks more. She sits cross-legged on the couch, tea steaming on the table beside her, and opens a book in her lap.

"You're doing it again," she says ten minutes later.

"What?"

"Not moving."

An old habit of his when idle: find a dark corner, stand statue-still, and observe. He smiles. "I am tired. I start to forget."

"Or remember," she says.

"I always remember." He sits in the love seat, at right angles to her.

"It's wonderful what you're doing with Paul."

"I want to help."

"You do."

He shifts from the love seat to the couch, and does not bother to move slow. The wind of his passage puffs in her eyes. She blinks, and nestles beside him.

"This is okay for you? I worry sometimes." Her hand's on his thigh. It rests there, strong, solid. "You've been quiet. I hope you're telling me what you need."

Need. He does not use that word much, even to himself. He needed this, ten years ago. Ten years ago she chased him, this beauty with the methodical mind, ferreted his secrets out of ancient archives and hunted him around the world. Ten years ago, he lured her to the old castle in the mountains, one last challenge. Ten years ago she shone in starlight filtered through cracks in the castle's roof. He could have killed her and hid again, as he had before. Remained a leaf blown from age to age and land to land on a wind of blood.

She'd seemed so real in the moonlight.

So he descended and spoke with her, and they found they knew one another better than anyone else. And ten years passed.

What does he need?

He leans toward her. His sharp teeth press on the inside of his gums, against the false yellowed set. He smells her blood. He smells camellias. His teeth recede. He kisses her on the forehead.

"I love you," they both say. Later he tries to remember which of them said it first.

• • • •

He sees the teacher every week after that. Angela, on Thursdays. With the blonde hair, and the strong heart. She tells him how Paul's work is coming.

She coaches him on how to coach his son, suggests games to play, discusses concepts the class will cover in the next week. Vlad wonders not for the first time why he doesn't teach his son himself. But they talked, he and his wife, back when they learned she was pregnant. They are not a normal couple, and whatever else Paul must learn, he must first learn how to seem normal.

He has learned how to be so normal he cannot do basic math. So Vlad stands in the schoolroom ramrod straight, and nods when he understands Angela and asks questions when he does not. He keeps his distance.

Vlad learns things about her, from her. He learns that she lives alone. He learns that her father in the hospital is the only parent to whom she is close, her mother having left them both in Angela's childhood, run off with a college friend leaving behind a half-drunk vodka bottle and a sorry note. He learns that she has tight-wound nerves like a small bird's, that she looks up at every sound of footsteps in the hall. That she does not sleep enough.

He does not need to learn her scent. That, he knows already.

• • • •

One night he follows her home.

This is a mistake.

She leaves the building well after sunset and walks to the bus; she rides one bus straight home. So he takes to the roofs, and chases the bus.

A game, he tells himself. Humans hunt these days, in the woods, in the back country, and they do not eat the meat they kill. Fisherman catch fish to throw them back. And this night run is no more dangerous to him than fishing to an angler. He leaves his oxfords on the schoolhouse rooftop and runs barefoot over buildings and along bridge wires, swift and soft. Even if someone beneath looked up, what is he? Wisp of cloud, shiver of a remembered nightmare, bird spreading wings for flight. A shadow among shadows.

A game, he tells himself, and lies. He only learns he's lying later, though, after she emerges from the bus and he tracks her three blocks to her studio apartment and she drops her keys on the stoop and kneels quick and tense as a spooked rabbit to retrieve them, after she enters her apartment and he delays, debates, and finally retreats across the river to the schoolhouse where he dons his oxfords and inspects himself in a deli window and pats his hair into place and brushes dust off his slacks and jacket—only learns it when his wife asks him why there's dust on his collar and he shakes his head and says something about a construction site. His round teeth he returns to their cup of coffee, and he lies naked on their bed, curled around her like a vine. His wife smells of sweat and woman and dark woods, and smelling her reminds him of another smell. Teeth peek through his gums, and his wife twists pleased and tired beside him, and he lies there lying, and relives the last time he killed.

• • • •

The first step taken, the second follows, and the third faster. As when he taught Paul to ride a bicycle: easier to keep balance when moving.

He's no longer stiff in their weekly meetings. He jokes about the old country and lets his accent show. Her laughter relieves the lines on her face.

"You and your wife both work," she says. "I know tutoring Paul takes time. Could his grandparents help at all?"

"His mother's family is far away," Vlad says. "My parents are both dead."

"I'm sorry."

His father died in a Turkish assault when he was fourteen; his mother died of one of the many small illnesses people died from back then. "It was sudden, and hard," he says, and they don't speak more of that. He recognizes the brief flash of sympathy in her eyes.

He follows her home again that night, hoping to see something that will turn him aside. She may visit friends, or call on an old paramour, or her father in the hospital. She may have a boyfriend or girlfriend. But she changes little. She stops at the drug store to buy toothpaste, bottled water, and sanitary napkins. She fumbles the keys at her door but does not drop them this time.

He leaves.

Paul, that night, is too tired to study. Vlad promises to help him more tomorrow. Paul frowns at the promise. Frowns don't yet sit well on his face. He's too young. Vlad tells him so, and lifts him upside down, and he shrieks laughter as Vlad carries him back to the bedroom.

Work is a dream. He is losing the knack of normalcy. Numbers dance to his command. He walks among cubicles clothed in purpose, and where once the white-collared workers forgot him as he passed, now they fall silent and stare in his wake. Management offers him a promotion for no reason, which he turns down. Silences between Vlad and Angela grow tense. He apologizes, and she says there is no need for an apology.

He and his wife make love twice that week. Ravenous, she pins him to the bed, and feasts.

Paul seems cautious in the mornings, silent between mouthfuls of cereal. At evening catch, Vlad almost forgets, almost hurls the ball up and out, over the park, over the city, into the ocean.

He can't go on like this. Woken, power suffuses him. He slips into old paths of being, into ways he trained himself to forget. One evening on his home commute he catches crows flocking (murdering?) above him on brownstone rooftops. Black beady eyes wait for his command.

This is no way to be a father. No way to be a man.

But Vlad was a monster before he was a man.

Again and again he follows her, as the heat of early autumn cools. The year will die. Show me some danger, he prays. Show me some reason I cannot close my fingers and seize you. But she is alone in the world, and sad.

Paul's grades slip. Vlad apologizes to Angela. He has been distracted.

"It's okay," she says. "It happens. Don't blame yourself."

He does not blame her. But this must end.

• • • •

He makes his wife breakfast on the last morning. Bacon. Eggs, scrambled hard, with cheese. Orange juice, squeezed fresh. The squeezing takes time, but not so much for Vlad. He wakes early to cook, and moves at his own pace—fast. Fat pops and slithers in the pan. Eggs bubble. He ticks off seconds while he waits for the bacon to fry, for the eggs to congeal after. By the time his wife steps out of the shower, breakfast's ready and the kitchen is clean. He makes Paul's lunch, because it's his turn. He cannot make amends.

His wife sucks the strip of bacon before she bites. "Delicious." She hums happily, hugs him around the waist. "So good. Isn't your dad a good cook?"

Paul laughs. Vlad only thinks it a knowing laugh because he is afraid.

"It's not mother's day," his wife says. "That's in March."

"I love you," Vlad answers. Paul makes a face like a punchinello mask.

Crows follow him to work, hopping sideways along the roofs. When he reaches midtown they perch on streetlamps and traffic lights. Red, yellow, and green reflect in their eyes in turn. The Times reports power outages in suburbs last night from unexpected vicious wind. Asylums and hospitals brim with madmen, raving, eating bugs. Vlad is over-empty, a great mounting void, and the world rushes to fill him.

He breaks a keyboard that day from typing too hard. Drives his pinkie finger through the enter key into his desk, embedding a sliver of plastic in his skin. He pulls the plastic out and the wound heals. I.T. replaces the keyboard.

Vlad finishes his work by three and sits in his cubicle till sunset. Thunderclouds cluster overhead by the time he leaves the building. Heat lightning flickers on his walk uptown. Fear shines at each flash from the eyes of the peasants he passes. Peasants: another word he has not thought or used in years.

All this will be over soon, he tells himself. And back to normal.

Whatever normal is.

He meets her in the classroom, though they do not talk long. The time for talking's past. She is all he remembered: sunlight and marble, camellia and mint. The ideal prey. Blood throbs through small veins in her fingers. He feels it when they shake hands. He smells its waves, rising and falling.

"I must thank you," he says, once she's gone over Paul's assignments for the next week. "For your dedication. You have given Paul so much. I appreciate your work."

"It's nothing." She may think he cannot hear her exhaustion, or else she trusts him and does not care. "I'm glad to help. If every father cared as much as you do, we'd be in a better world."

"I am fortunate," he says, "to be in a position to care."

He follows her from the school, as before. After sunset the crows stop hiding. In masses they descend on the city and croak prophecy in its alleys. Currents of crows rush down Broadway, so thick pedestrians mistake them for a cloud, their wingbeats for the rumble of traffic or a train. Bats emerge from their lairs, and rats writhe on subway steps singing rat songs. Grandmothers remember their grandmothers' whispered stories, and call children to urge them to stay inside.

Better this way, Vlad thinks as he follows Angela across the bridge, down the dirty deserted street from her stop to her apartment. She does not notice him. She notices nothing. The rats, the crows, the bats, all keep away from her. They know Vlad's purpose tonight, and will not interfere.

She's young, her life still a web of dream, her love just touched by sadness. This world holds only pain for her. Better, surely, to leave before that pain bloomed, before tenderness roughed into a callous.

His gums itch. He slides the false teeth from his mouth, places them in a ziploc bag, closes the seal, and slips the bag into his jacket pocket. Crouched atop the roof of the building across from Angela's, he sees her shuffle down the street. The weight of her shoulder bag makes her limp.

His teeth, his real teeth, emerge, myriad and sharp. He tastes their tips and edges with his tongue.

She opens the door, climbs the steps. He follows her heartbeat up four floors, five, to the small studio.

He leaps across the street, lands soft as shadow on Angela's roof beside the skylight. Below, a door opens and light wakes. Though she's drawn curtains across the glass, there are gaps, and he sees her through them. She sags back against the door to close it, lets her bag clatter to the ground and leans into the scuffed dark wood, eyes closed.

Her apartment looks a mess because it's small: a stack of milk crates turned to bookshelves, overflowing with paperbacks and used textbooks. A small lacquered pine board dresser in stages of advanced decay, its side crisscrossed with bumper stickers bearing logos of bands Vlad does not recognize. A couch that slides out to form a bed, separated from the kitchenette by a narrow coffee table. Sheets piled in a hamper beside the couch-bed, dirty clothes in another hamper, dishes in the sink.

She opens her eyes, and steps out of the circle formed by the shoulder strap of her fallen bag. Two steps to the fridge, from which she draws a beer. She opens the cap with a fob on her keychain, tosses the cap in the recycling, and takes a long drink. Three steps from fridge around the table to the couch, where she sits, takes another drink, then swears, "Motherfucker," first two syllables drawn out and low, the third a high clear peal like those little bells priests used to ring in the litany. She lurches back to her feet, retrieves her bag, sits again on couch and pulls from the bag a thick sheaf of papers and a red pen and proceeds to grade.

Vlad waits. Not now, certainly. Not as she wades through work. You take your prey in joy: insert yourself into perfection, sharp as a needle's tip. When she entered the room, he might have done it then. But the moment's passed.

She grades, finishes her beer, gets another. After a while she returns the papers to their folder, and the folder to her bag. From the milk crate bookshelves she retrieves a bulky laptop, plugs it in, and turns on a television show about young people living in the city, who all have bigger apartments than hers. Once in a while, she laughs, and after she laughs, she drinks.

He watches her watching. He can only permit himself this once, so it must be perfect. He tries to see the moment in his mind. Does she lie back in her bed, smiling? Does she spy him through the curtains, and climb on a chair to open the skylight and let him in? Does she scream and run? Does she call his name? Do they embrace? Does he seize her about the neck and drag her toward him while she claws ineffectually at his eyes and cheeks until her strength gives out?

She closes the laptop, dumps the dregs of her beer in the sink, tosses the empty into the recycling, walks into the bathroom, closes the door. The toilet flushes, the water runs, and he hears her floss, and brush her teeth, gargle and spit into the sink.

Do it. The perfect moment won't come. There's no such thing.

The doorknob turns.

What is he waiting for? He wants her to see him, know him, understand him, fear him, love him at the last. He wants her to chase him around the world, wants a moonlit showdown in a dark castle.

He wants to be her monster. To transform her life in its ending.

The door opens. She emerges, wearing threadbare blue pajamas. Four steps back to the couch, which she slides out into a bed. She spreads sheets over the bed, a comforter on top of them, and wriggles under the comforter. Hair halos her head on the dark pillow.

Now.

She can reach the lightswitch from her bed. The room goes dark save for the blinking lights of coffee maker and charging cell phone and laptop. He can still see her staring at the ceiling. She sighs.

He stands and turns to leave.

Moonlight glints off glass ten blocks away.

• • • •

His wife has almost broken down the rifle by the time he reaches her—nine seconds. She's kept in practice. The sniper scope is stowed already; as he arrives, she's unscrewing the barrel. She must have heard him coming, but she waits for him to speak first.

She hasn't changed from the library. Khaki pants, a cardigan, comfortable shoes. Her hair up, covered by a dark cap. She wears no jewels but for his ring and her watch.

"I'm sorry," he says, first.

"I'll say."

"How did you know?"

"Dust on your collar. Late nights."

"I mean, how did you know it would be now?"

"I got dive-bombed by crows on the sidewalk this morning. One of the work-study kids came in high, babbling about the prince of darkness. You're not as subtle as you used to be."

"Well. I'm out of practice."

She looks up at him. He realizes he's smiling, and with his own teeth. He stops.

"Don't."

"I'm sorry."

"You said that already." Finished with the rifle, she returns it to the case, and closes the zipper, and stands. She's shorter than he is, broader through the shoulders. "What made you stop?"

"She wasn't you."

"Cheek."

"No."

"So what do we do now?"

"I don't know. I thought I was strong enough to be normal. But these are me." He bares his teeth at her. "Not these." From his pocket he draws the false teeth, and holds them out, wrapped in plastic, in his palm. Closes his fingers. Plastic cracks, crumbles. He presses it to powder, and drops bag and powder both. "Might as well kill me now."

"I won't."

"I'm a monster."

"You're just more literal than most." She looks away from him, raises her knuckle to her lip. Looks back.

"You deserve a good man. A normal man."

"I went looking for you." She doesn't shout, but something in her voice makes him retreat a step, makes his heart thrum and almost beat.

"I miss." Those two words sound naked. He struggles to finish the sentence. "I miss when we could be dangerous to one another."

"You think you're the only one who does? You think the PTA meetings and the ask your mothers and the how's your families at work, you think that stuff doesn't get to me? Think I don't wonder how I became this person?"

"It's not that simple. If I lose control, people die. Look at tonight."

"You stopped. And if you screw up." She nudges the rifle case with her toe. "There's always that."

"Paul needs a normal family. We agreed."

"He needs a father more. One who's not too scared of himself to be there."

He stops himself from shouting something he will regret. Closes his lips, and his eyes, and thinks for a long while, as the wind blows over their rooftop. His eyes hurt. "He needs a mother, too," he says.

"Yes. He does."

"I screwed up tonight."

"You did. But I think we can work on this. Together. How about you?"

"Sarah," he says.

She looks into his eyes. They embrace, once, and part. She kneels to lift the rifle case.

"Here," he says. "Let me get that for you."

• • • •

The next week, Friday, he plays catch with Paul in the park. They're the only ones there save the ghosts: it's cold, but Paul's young, and while Vlad can feel the cold it doesn't bother him. Dead trees overhead, skeletal fingers raking sky. Leaves spin in little whirlwinds. The sky's blue and empty, sun already sunk behind the buildings.

Vlad unbuttons his coat, lets it fall. Strips off his sweater, balls it on top of the coat. Stands in his shirtsleeves, cradles the football with his long fingers. Tightens his grip. Does not burst the ball, only feels the air within resist his fingers' pressure.

Paul steps back, holds up his hands.

Vlad shakes his head. "Go deeper."

He runs, crumbling dry leaves and breaking hidden sticks.

"Deeper," Vlad calls, and waves him on.

"Here?" Vlad's never thrown the ball this far.

"More."

Paul stands near the edge of the park. "That's all there is!"

"Okay," Vlad says. "Okay. Are you ready?"

"Yes!"

His throws are well-rehearsed. Wind up slowly, and toss soft. He beat them into his bones.

He forgets all that.

Black currents weave through the wind. A crow calls from treetops. He stands, a statue of ice.

He throws the ball as hard as he can.

A loud crack echoes through the park. Ghosts scatter, dive for cover. The ball breaks the air, and its passage leaves a vacuum trail. Windows rattle and car alarms whoop. Vlad wasn't aiming for his son. He didn't want to hurt him. He just wanted to throw.

Vlad's eyes are faster even than his hands, and sharp. So he sees Paul blink, in surprise more than fear. He sees Paul understand. He sees Paul smile.

And he sees Paul blur sideways and catch the ball.

They stare at one another across the park. The ball hisses in Paul's hands, deflates: it broke in the catching. Wind rolls leaves between them.

Later, neither can remember who laughed first.

• • • •

They talk for hours after that. Chase one another around the park, so fast they seem only colors on the wind. High-pitched child's screams of joy, and Vlad's own voice, deep, guttural. Long after the sky turns black and the stars don't come out, they return home, clothes grass-stained, hair tangled with sticks and leaves. Paul does his homework, fast, and they watch cricket until after bedtime.

Sarah waits in the living room when he leaves Paul sleeping. She grabs his arms and squeezes, hard enough to bruise, and pulls him into her kiss.

He kisses her back with his teeth.

Max Gladstone has been thrown from a horse in Mongolia and twice nominated for the John W Campbell Best New Writer Award. Tor Books published *LAST FIRST SNOW*, the fourth novel in Max's Craft Sequence (preceded by *THREE PARTS DEAD*, *TWO SERPENTS RISE*, and *FULL FATHOM FIVE*) in July 2015. Max's game *CHOICE OF THE DEATHLESS* was nominated for the XYZZY Award, and his short fiction has appeared on Tor.com and in Uncanny Magazine.

# The Vaporization Enthalpy
# Of A Peculiar Pakistani Family
## By Usman T. Malik

## 1

The Solid Phase of Matter is a state wherein a substance is particulately bound. To transform a solid into liquid, the intermolecular forces need to be overcome, which may be achieved by adding energy. The energy necessary to break such bonds is, ironically, called the *heat of fusion.*

• • • •

On a Friday after jumah prayers, under the sturdy old oak in their yard, they came together as a family for the last time. Her brother gave in and wept as Tara watched, eyes prickling with a warmth that wouldn't disperse no matter how much she knuckled them, or blinked.

"Monsters," Sohail said, his voice raspy. He wiped his mouth with the back of his hand and looked at the sky, a vast whiteness cobblestoned with heat. The plowed wheat fields beyond the steppe on which their house perched were baked and khaki and shivered a little under Tara's feet. An earthquake or a passing vehicle on the highway? Perhaps it was just foreknowledge that made her dizzy. She pulled at her lower lip and said nothing.

"Monsters," Sohail said again. "Oh God, Apee. Murderers."

She reached out and touched his shoulders. "I'm sorry." She thought he would pull back. When he didn't, she let her fingers fall and linger on the flame-shaped scar on his arm. So it begins, she thought. How many times has this happened before? Pushing and prodding us repeatedly until the night swallows us whole. She thought of that until her heart constricted with dread. "Don't do it," she said. "Don't go."

Sohail lifted his shoulders and drew his head back, watched her wonderingly as if seeing her for the first time.

"I know I ask too much," she said. "I know the customs of honor, but for the love of God let it go. One death needn't become a lodestone for others. One horror needn't—"

But he wasn't listening, she could tell. They would not hear nor see once the blood was upon them, didn't the Scriptures say so? Sohail heard, but didn't listen. His conjoined eyebrows, like dark hands held, twitched. "Her name meant a rose," he said and smiled. It was beautiful, that smile, heartbreaking, frightening. "Under the mango trees by Chacha Barkat's farm Gulminay told me that, as I kissed her hand. Whispered it in my ear, her finger circling my temple. *A rose blooming in the rain.* Did you know that?"

Tara didn't. The sorrow of his confession filled her now as did the certainty of his leaving. "Yes," she lied, looking him in the eyes. God, his eyes looked awful: webbed with red, with thin tendrils of steam rising from them. "A rose God gave us and took away because He loved her so."

"Wasn't God," Sohail said and rubbed his fingers together. The sound was insectile. 'Monsters." He turned his back to her and was able to speak rapidly, "I'm leaving tomorrow morning. I'm going to the mountains. I will take some bread and dried meat. I will stay there until I'm shown a sign, and once I am," his back arched, then straightened. He had lost weight; his shoulder blades poked through the khaddar shirt like trowels, "I will arise and go to their homes. I will go to them as God's wrath. I will—"

She cut him off, her heart pumping fear through her body like poison. "What if you go to them and die? What if you go to them like a steer to the slaughter? And Ma and I — what if months later we sit here and watch a dusty vehicle climb the hill, bouncing a sack of meat in the back seat that was once you? What if. . ."

But she couldn't go on giving name to her terrors. Instead, she said, "If you go, know that we as we are now will be gone forever."

He shuddered. "*We* were gone when *she* was gone. We were shattered with her bones." The wind picked up, a whipping, chador-lifting sultry gust that made Tara's flesh prickle. Sohail began to walk down the steppes, each with its own crop: tobacco, corn, rice stalks wavering in knee-high water; and as she watched his lean farmer body move away, it seemed to her as if his back was not drenched in sweat, but acid. That his flesh glistened not from moisture, but blood. All at once their world was just too much, or not enough—Tara couldn't decide which—and the weight of that unseen future weighed her down until she couldn't breathe. "My brother," she said and began to cry. "You're my little brother."

Sohail continued walking his careful, dead man's walk until his head was a wobbling black pumpkin rising from the last steppe. She watched him disappear in the undulations of her motherland, helpless to stop the fatal fracturing of her world, wondering if he would stop or doubt or look back.

Sohail never looked back.

• • • •

Ma died three months later.

The village menfolk told her the death prayer was brief and moving. Tara couldn't attend because she was a woman.

They helped her bury Ma's sorrow-filled body, and the rotund mullah clucked and murmured over the fresh mound. The women embraced her and crooned and urged her to vent.

"Weep, our daughter," they cried, "for the childrens' tears of love are like manna for the departed."

Tara tried to weep and felt guilty when she couldn't. Ma had been sick and in pain for a long time and her hastened death was a mercy, but you couldn't say that out loud. Besides, the women had said *children*, and Sohail wasn't there. Not at the funeral, nor during the days after. Tara dared not wonder where he was, nor imagine his beautiful face gleaming in the dark atop a stony mountain, persevering in his vigil.

"What will you do now?" they asked, gathering around her with sharp, interested eyes. She knew what they really meant. A young widow with no family was a stranger amidst her clan. At best an oddity; at her worst a seductress. Tara was surprised to discover their concern didn't frighten her. The perfect loneliness of it, the inadvertent exclusion—they were just more beads in the tautening string of her life.

"I'm thinking of going to the City," she told them. "Ma has a cousin there. Perhaps he can help me with bread and board, while I look for work."

She paused, startled by a clear memory: Sohail and Gulminay by the Kunhar River, fishing for trout. Gulminay's sequined hijab dappling the stream with emerald as she reached down into the water with long, pale fingers. Sohail grinning his stupid lover's grin as his small hands encircled her waist, and Tara watched them both from the shade of the eucalyptus, fond and jealous. By then Tara's husband was long gone and she could forgive herself the occasional resentment.

She forced the memory away. "Yes, I think I might go to the city for a while." She laughed. The sound rang hollow and strange in the emptiness of her tin-and-timber house. "Who knows I might even go back to school. I used to enjoy reading once." She smiled at these women with their hateful, sympathetic eyes that watched her cautiously as they would a rabid animal. She nodded, talking mostly to herself. "Yes, that would be good. Hashim would've wanted that."

They drew back from her, from her late husband's mention. Why not? she thought. Everything she touched fell apart; everyone around her died or went missing. There was no judgment here, just dreadful awe. She could allow them that, she thought.

## 2

The Liquid Phase of Matter is a restless volume that, by dint of the vast spaces between its molecules, fills any container it is poured in and takes its shape. Liquids tend to have higher energy than solids, and while the particles retain inter-particle forces they have enough energy to move relative to each other.

The structure therefore becomes mobile and malleable.

• • • •

In the City, Tara turned feral in her pursuit of learning. This had been long coming and it didn't surprise her. At thirteen, she had been withdrawn from school; she needed not homework but a husband, she was told. At sixteen, she was wedded to Hashim. He was blown to smithereens on her twenty-first birthday. A suicide attack on his unit's northern check post.

"I want to go to school," she told Wasif Khan, her mother's cousin. They were sitting in his six-by-eight yard, peeling fresh oranges he had confiscated from an illegal food vendor. Wasif was a Police hawaldar, and on the rough side of sixty. He often said confiscation was his first love and contraband second. But he grinned when he said it, which made it easier for her to like him.

Now Wasif tossed a half-gnawed chicken bone to his spotted mongrel and said, "I don't know if you want to do that."

"I do."

"You need a husband, not—"

"I don't care. I need to go back to school."

"Why?" He dropped an orange rind in the basket at his feet, gestured with a large liver-spotted hand. "The City doesn't care if you can read. Besides, I need someone to help me around the house. I'm old and ugly and useless, but I have this tolerable place and no children. You're my cousin's daughter. You can stay here forever if you like."

In a different time she might have mistaken his generosity for loneliness, but now she understood it for what it was. Such was the way of age: it melted prejudice or hardened it. "I want to learn about the world," she said. "I want to see if there are others like me. If there have been others before me."

He was confused. "Like you how?"

She rubbed an orange peel between her fingers, pressing the fibrous texture of it in the creases of her flesh, considering how much to tell him. Her mother had trusted him. Yet Ma hardly had their gift and even if she did Tara doubted she would have been open about it. Ma had been wary of giving too much of herself away — a trait she passed on to both her children. Among other things.

So now Tara said, "Others who *need* to learn more about themselves. I spent my entire childhood being just a bride and look where that got me. I am left with nothing. No children, no husband, no family." Wasif Khan looked hurt. She smiled kindly. "You know what I mean, Uncle. I love you, but I need to love me too."

Wasif Khan tilted his head back and pinched a slice of orange above his mouth. Squeezed it until his tongue and remaining teeth gleamed with the juice. He closed his eyes, sighed, and nodded. "I don't know if I approve, but I think I understand." He lifted his hand and tousled his own hair thoughtfully. "It's a different time. Others my age who don't realize it don't fare well. The traditional rules don't apply anymore, you know. Sometimes, I think that is wonderful. Other times, it feels like the whole damn world is conspiring against you."

She rose, picking up her mess and his. "Thank you for letting me stay here."

"It's either you or every hookah-sucking asshole in this neighborhood for company." He grinned and shrugged his shoulders. "My apologies. I've been living alone too long and my tongue is spoilt."

She laughed loudly; and thought of a blazing cliff somewhere from which dangled two browned, peeling, inflamed legs, swinging back and forth like pendulums.

• • • •

She read everything she could get her hands on. At first, her alphabet was broken and awkward, as was her rusty brain, but she did it anyway. It took her two years, but eventually she qualified for F.A examinations, and passed on her first try.

"I don't know how you did it," Wasif Khan said to her, his face beaming at the neighborhood children as he handed out specially prepared sweetmeat to eager hands, "but I'm proud of you."

She wasn't, but she didn't say it. Instead, once the children left, she went to the mirror and gazed at her reflection, flexing her arm this way and that, making the flame-shaped scar bulge. We all drink the blood of yesterday, she thought.

The next day she enrolled at Punjab University's B.Sc program.

In Biology class, they learned about plants and animals. Flora and Fauna, they called them. Things constructed piece by piece from the basic units of life—cells. These cells in turn were made from tiny building blocks called atoms, which themselves were bonded by the very things that repelled their core: electrons.

In Physics class, she learned what electrons were. Little flickering ghosts that vanished and reappeared as they pleased. Her flesh was empty, she discovered, or most of it. So were human bones and solid buildings and the incessantly agitated world. All that immense loneliness and darkness with only a hint that we existed. The idea awed her. Did we exist only as a possibility?

In Wasif Khan's yard was a tall mulberry tree with saw-like leaves. On her way to school she touched them; they were spiny and jagged. She hadn't eaten mulberries before. She picked a basketful, nipped her wrist with her teeth, and let her blood roast a few. She watched them curl and smoke from the heat of her genes, inhaled the sweet steam of their juice as they turned into mystical symbols.

Mama would have been proud.

She ate them with salt and pepper, and was offended when Wasif Khan wouldn't touch the remaining.

He said they gave him reflux.

## 3

The Gaseous Phase of Matter is one in which particles have enough kinetic energy to make the effect of intermolecular forces negligible. A gas, therefore, will occupy the entire container in which it is confined.

Liquid may be converted to gas by heating at constant pressure to a certain temperature.

This temperature is called the *boiling point.*

• • • •

*The worst flooding the province has seen in forty years* was the one thing all radio broadcasters agreed on.

Wasif Khan hadn't confiscated a television yet, but if he had, Tara was sure, it would show the same cataclysmic damage to life and property. At one point, someone said, an area the size of England was submerged in raging floodwater.

Wasif's neighborhood in the northern, hillier part of town escaped the worst of the devastation, but Tara and Wasif witnessed it daily when they went for rescue work: upchucked power pylons and splintered oak trees smashing through the marketplace stalls; murderous tin sheets and iron rods slicing through inundated alleys; bloated dead cows and sheep eddying in shoulder-high water with terrified children clinging to them. It pawed at the towering steel-and-concrete structures, this restless liquid death that had come to the city; it ripped out their underpinnings and annihilated everything in its path.

Tara survived these days of heartbreak and horror by helping to set up a small tent city on the sports fields of her university. She volunteered to establish a nursery for displaced children and went with rescue teams to scour the ruins for usable supplies, and corpses.

As she pulled out the dead and living from beneath the wreckage, as she tossed plastic-wrapped food and dry clothing to the dull-eyed homeless, she thought of how bright and hot and dry the spines of her brother's mountains must be. It had been four years since she saw him, but her dreams were filled with his absence. Did he sit parched and caved in, like a deliberate Buddha? Or was he dead and pecked on by ravens and falcons?

She shuddered at the thought and grabbed another packet of cooked rice and dry beans for the benighted survivors.

• • • •

The first warning came on the last night of Ramadan. *Chand raat.*

Tara was eating bread and lentils with her foundling children in the nursery when it happened. A bone-deep trembling that ran through the grass, flattening its blades, evaporating the evening dew trembling on them. Seconds later, a distant boom followed: a hollow rumbling that hurt Tara's ears and made her feel nauseated. (Later, she would learn that the blast had torn through the marble-walled shrine of Data Sahib, wrenching its iron fence from its moorings, sending jagged pieces of metal and scorched human limbs spinning across the walled part of the City.)

Her children sat up, confused and scared. She soothed them. Once a replacement was found, she went to talk to the tent city administrator.

"I've seen this before," she told him once he confirmed it was a suicide blast. "My husband and sister-in-law both died in similar situations." That wasn't entirely true for Gulminay, but close enough. "Usually one such attack is followed by another when rescue attempts are made. My husband used to call them 'double tap' attacks." She paused, thinking of his kind, dearly loved face for the first time in months. "He understood the psychology behind them well."

The administrator, a chubby short man with filthy cheeks, scratched his chin. "How come?"

"He was a Frontier Corps soldier. He tackled many such situations before he died."

"Condolences, *bibi.*" The administrator's face crinkled with sympathy. "But what does that have to do with us?"

"At some point, these terrorists will use the double tap as decoy and come after civilian structures."

"Thank you for the warning. I'll send out word to form a volunteer perimeter patrol." He scrutinized her, taking in her hijab, the bruised elbows, and grimy fingernails from days of work. "God bless you for the lives you've saved already. For the labor you've done."

He handed her a packet of boiled corn and alphabet books. She nodded absently, charred bodies and boiled human blood swirling up from the shrine vivid inside her head, thanked him, and left.

The emergency broadcast thirty minutes later confirmed her fear: a second blast at Data Sahib obliterated a fire engine, killed a jeep-ful of eager policemen, and vaporized twenty-five rescuers. Five of these were female medical students. Their shattered glass bangles were melted and their headscarves burned down to unrecognizable gunk by the time the EMS came, they later said.

Tara wept when she heard. In her heart was a steaming shadow that whispered nasty things. It impaled her with its familiarity, and a dreadful suspicion grew in her that the beast was rage and wore a face she knew well.

## 4

When matter is heated to high temperatures, such as in a flame, electrons begin to leave the atoms. At very high temperatures, essentially all electrons are assumed to be dissociated, resulting in a unique state wherein positively charged nuclei swim in a raging 'sea' of free electrons.

This state is called the Plasma Phase of Matter and exists in lightning, electric sparks, neon lights, and the Sun.

• • • •

In a rash of terror attacks, the City quickly fell apart: the Tower of Pakistan, Lahore Fort, Iqbal's Memorial, Shalimar Gardens, Anarkali's Tomb, and the thirteen gates of the Walled City. They exploded and fell in burning tatters, survived only by a quivering bloodhaze through which peeked the haunted eyes of their immortal ghosts.

*This is death, this is love, this is the comeuppance of the two, as the world according to you will finally come to an end.* So snarled the beast in Tara's head each night. The tragedy of the floodwaters was not over yet, and now this.

Tara survived this new world through her books and her children. The two seemed to have become one: pages filled with unfathomable loss. White space itching to be written, reshaped, or incinerated. Sometimes, she would bite her lips and let the trickle of blood stain her callused fingers.

Would touch them to water-spoilt paper and watch it catch fire and flutter madly in the air, aflame like a phoenix. An impossible glamor created by tribulation. So when the city burned and her tears burned, Tara reminded herself of the beautiful emptiness of it all and forced herself to smile.

Until one morning she awoke and discovered that, in the cover of the night, a suicide teenager had hit her tent city's perimeter patrol.

• • • •

After the others had left, she stood over her friends' graves in the twilight.

Kites and vultures unzipped the darkness above in circles, lost specks in this ghostly desolation. She remembered how cold it was when they lowered Gulminay's remains in the ground. How the drone attack had torn her limbs clean off so that, along with a head shriveled by heat, a glistening, misshapen, idiot torso remained. She remembered Ma, too, and how she was killed by her son's love. The first of many murders.

"I know you," she whispered to the Beast resident in her soul. "I know you", and all the time she scribbled on her flesh with a glass shard she found buried in a patrolman's eye. Her wrist glowed with her heat and that of her ancestors. She watched her blood bubble and surge skyward. To join the plasma of the world and drift its soft, vaporous way across the darkened City, and she wondered again if she was still capable of loving them both.

The administrator promised her he would take care of her children. He gave her food and a bundle of longshirts and shalwars. He asked her where she was going and why, and she knew he was afraid for her.

"I will be all right," she told him. "I know someone who lives up there."

"I don't understand why you must go. It's dangerous," he said, his flesh red under the hollows of his eyes. He wiped his cheeks, which were wet. "I wish you didn't have to. But I suppose you will. I see that in your face. I saw that when you first came here."

She laughed. The sound of her own laughter saddened her. "The world will change," she said. "It always does. We are all empty, but this changing is what saves us. That is why I must go."

He nodded. She smiled. They touched hands briefly; she stepped forward and hugged him, her headscarf tickling his nostrils, making him sneeze. She giggled and told him how much she loved him and the others. He looked pleased and she saw how much kindness and gentleness lived inside his skin, how his blood would never boil with undesired heat.

She lifted his finger, kissed it, wondering at how solid his vacant flesh felt against her lips.

Then she turned and left him, leaving the water and fire and the crackling, hissing earth of the City behind.

Such was how Tara Khan left for the mountains.

• • • •

The journey took a week. The roads were barren, the landscape abraded by floodwater and flensed by intermittent fires. Shocked trees, stripped of fruit, stood rigid and receding as Tara's bus rolled by, their gnarled limbs pointing accusatorially at the heavens.

Wrapped in her chador, headscarf, and khaddar shalwar kameez, Tara folded into the rugged barrenness with its rugged people. They were not unkind; even in the midst of this madness, they held onto their deeply honored tradition of hospitality, allowing Tara to scout for hints of the Beast's presence. The northerners chattered constantly and were horrified by the atrocities blooming from within them, and because she too spoke Pashto they treated her like one of them.

Tara kept her ears open. Rumors, whispers, beckonings by skeletal fingers. Someone said there was a man in Abbottabad who was the puppeteer. Another shook his head and said that was a deliberate shadow show, a gaudy interplay of light and dark put up by the real perpetrators. That the Supreme Conspirator was swallowed by earth soaked with the blood of thousands and lived only as an extension of this irredeemable evil.

Tara listened and tried to read between their words. Slowly, the hints in the midnight alleys, the leprous grins, the desperate, clutching fingers, incinerated trees and smoldering human and animal skulls — they began to come together and form a map.

Tara followed it into the heart of the mountains.

## 5

When the elementary particle boson is cooled to temperatures near absolute zero, a dilute 'gas' is created. Under such conditions, a large number of bosons occupy the lowest quantum state and an unusual thing happens: quantum effects become visible on a macroscopic scale. This effect is called the macroscopic quantum phenomena and the 'Bose-Einstein condensate' is inferred to be a new state of matter. The presence of one such particle, the Higgs-Boson, was tentatively confirmed on March 14th, 2013 in the most complex experimental facility built in human history.

This particle is sometimes called the *God Particle*.

• • • •

When she found him, he had changed his name.

There is a story told around campfires since the beginning of time: Millennia ago a stone fell from the infinite bosom of space and plunked onto a statistically impossible planet. The stone was round, and smaller than a pebble of hard goat shit, and carried a word inscribed on it.

It has been passed down generations of Pahari clans that that word is the *Ism-e-Azam*, the Most High Name of God.

Every sect in the history of our world has written about it. Egyptians, Mayans. Jewish, Christian, and Muslim mystics. Some have described it as the primal point from which existence began, and that the Universal Essence lives in this *nuktah*.

The closest approximation to the First Word, some say, is one that originated in Mesopotamia, the land between the two rivers. The Sumerians called it *Annunaki*.

He Of Godly Blood.

Tara thought of this oral tradition and sat down at the mouth of the demolished cave. She knew he lived inside the cave, for every living and nonliving thing near it reeked of his heat. Twisted boulders stretched granite hands toward its mouth like pilgrims at the Kaaba. The heat of the stars they both carried in their genes, in the sputtering, whisking emptiness of their cells, had leeched out and warped the mountains and the path leading up to it.

Tara sat cross-legged in the lotus position her mother taught them both when they were young. She took a sharp rock and ran it across her palm. Crimson droplets appeared and evaporated, leaving a metallic tang in the air. She sat and inhaled that smell and thought of the home that once was. She thought of her mother, and her husband; of Gulminay and Sohail; of the floods (did he have something to do with that too? Did his rage liquefy snow-topped mountains and drown an entire country?); of suicide bombers, and the University patrol; and of countless human eyes that flicked each moment toward an unforgiving sky where something merciful may or may not live; and her eyes began to burn and Tara Khan began to cry.

"Come out," she said between her sobs. "Come out, Beast. Come out, Rage. Come out, Death of the Two Worlds and all that lives in between. Come out, Monster. Come out, Fear," and all the while she rubbed her eyes and let the salt of her tears crumble between her fingertips. Sadly she looked at the white crystals, flattened them, and screamed, "Come out, ANNUNAKI."

And in a belch of shrieking air and a blast of heat, her brother came to her.

• • • •

They faced each other.

His skin was gone. His eyes melted, his nose bridge collapsed; the bones underneath were simmering white seas that rolled and twinkled across the constantly melting and rearranging meat of him. His limbs were pseudopodic, his movement that of a softly turning planet drifting across the possibility that is being.

Now he floated toward her on a gliding plane of his skin. His potent heat, a shifting locus of time-space with infinite energy roiling inside it, touched her, making her recoil. When he breathed, she saw everything that once was; and knew what she knew.

"Salam," she said. "Peace be upon you, brother."

The *nuktah* that was him twitched. His fried vocal cords were not capable of producing words anymore.

"I used to think," she continued, licking her dry lips, watching the infinitesimal shifting of matter and emptiness inside him, "that love was all that mattered. That the bonds that pull us all together are of timeless love. But it is not true. It has never been true, has it?"

He shimmered, and said nothing.

"I still believe, though. In existing. In *ex nihilo nihil fit*. If nothing comes from nothing, we cannot return to it. Ergo life has a reason and needs to be." She paused, remembering a day when her brother plucked a sunflower from a lush meadow and slipped it into Gulminay's hair. "Gulminay-jaan once was and still is. Perhaps inside you and me." Tara wiped her tears and smiled. "Even if most of us is nothing."

The heat-thing her brother was slipped forward a notch. Tara rose to her feet and began walking toward it. The blood in her vasculature seethed and raged.

"Even if death breaks some bonds and forms others. Even if the world flinches, implodes, and becomes a grain of sand."

Annunaki watched her through eyes like black holes and gently swirled.

"Even if we have killed and shall kill. Even if the source is nothing if not grief. Even if sorrow is the distillate of our life."

She reached out and gripped his melting amebic limb. He shrank, but didn't let go as the maddened heat of her essence surged forth to meet his.

"Even if we never come to much. Even if the sea of our consciousness breaks against quantum impossibilities."

She pressed his now-arm, her fingers elongating, stretching, turning, fusing; her flame-scar rippling and coiling to probe for his like a proboscis.

Sohail tried to smile. In his smile were heat-deaths of countless worlds, supernova bursts, and the chrysalis sheen of a freshly hatched larva. She thought he might have whispered sorry. That in another time and universe there were not countless intemperate blood-children of his spreading across the earth's face like vitriolic tides rising to obliterate the planet. That all this wasn't really happening for one misdirected missile, for one careless press of a button somewhere by a soldier eating junk food and licking his fingers. But it was. Tara had glimpsed it in his *nuktah* when she touched him.

"Even if," she whispered as his being engulfed hers and the thermonuclear reaction of matter and antimatter fusion sparked and began to eradicate them both, "our puny existence, the conclusion of an agitated, conscious universe, is insignificant, remember . . . remember, brother, that mercy will go on. Kindness will go on."

Let there be gentleness, she thought. Let there be equilibrium, if all we are and will be can survive in some form. Let there be grace and goodness and a hint of something to come, no matter how uncertain.

Let there be *possibility*, she thought, as they flickered annihilatively and were immolated in some fool's idea of love.

• • • •

*For the 145 innocents of the 12/16 Peshawar terrorist attack and countless known & unknown before.*

Usman T. Malik is a Pakistani writer resident in Florida. His work has won a Bram Stoker Award and been a Nebula finalist. His stories have been published or are forthcoming in several Year's Best anthologies, *Tor.com*, *Nightmare*, *Strange Horizons*, and *Black Static*.

# This Chance Planet
## By Elizabeth Bear

*We are alone, absolutely alone on this chance planet: and, amid all the forms of life that surround us, not one, excepting the dog, has made an alliance with us.*
— Maurice Maeterlinck

"It's not like I'd be selling my *own* liver." Ilya held casually to a cracked strap, swaying with the motion of the Metro. "Petra Ivanovna. Are you listening to me?"

"Sorry," I said.

I'd been trading stares with a Metro dog. My feet were killing me in heels I should have stuffed into my sometimes bag, and the dog was curled up tight as a croissant on the brown vinyl of the only available seat. I narrowed my eyes at it; it huffed pleasantly and covered its nose with its tail.

Ilya kept on jawing. It was in one ear and out the other, whatever he was yammering about, while I gave the dog wormhole eyes and plotted how to get the seat away. The dog was a medium-large ovcharka mutt, prick-eared, filthy under a wolf's pelt with big stinking mats dangling from its furry bloomers. It was as skinny as any other street dog under its fur—as skinny as me—but the belly seemed stretched—malnutrition? Worms? When it lifted its head up and let its tongue loll, the teeth were sharp and white.

Behind its head, a flickering advertisement suggested that volunteers were needed for clinical trials, each of which paid close to a month's grocery money. It alternated with one urging healthy young (read: skint) men and women to sell their genetic material to help childless older (read: wealthy) couples conceive. Pity those skinny jeans were probably destroying Ilya's fertility as we spoke.

I snorted, but that ad faded into one reminding me that it wasn't too late to enroll for fall classes.

Well, if I had the damned money, I would have enrolled for summer classes, too. I had my bachelor's, but that was useless in Moscow, and to get the specialist degree took money. Money I didn't have. Wouldn't have, unless Ilya started contributing more.

I looked away, and accidentally caught the thread of Ilya's conversation again. His latest get rich quick scheme. It was always a get rich quick scheme with Ilya. This one involved getting paid to incubate somebody else's liver. In his gut. Next to his own liver, I guessed?

I imagined him bloating up, puffing out like an old man whose insides had given up from too much bathtub liquor. Like a pregnant woman. I wondered if his ankles would swell.

I punched his arm. "Like an alien!"

Visions of chestbursters danced in my head. I played the whole VR through last year with my friend GreyGamine, who lives in Kitchener, which is in Canada somewhere.

We got killed back a lot.

Ilya scoffed. It was a very practiced scoff, nuanced and complex. He used it a lot. The Palm d'Or for scoffing goes to Ilya Ramonovich.

"How's it different from growing a baby?" he asked me, sliding an arm around my hips. His leather jacket—scarred, stiff, cracked—creaked. I tried not to think about how it was probably too old to have been decanted, and that it had probably started life wrapped around an actual cow. "You want to have a baby someday, don't you?"

We couldn't afford a baby. *I* couldn't afford a baby. Either the money or the time, until I finished my degree.

The strap of his electric guitar case slid down his shoulder. The case swung around and banged my ribs. He gave my hip a squeeze. He smelled fantastic: warm leather and warm man. It didn't make my shoes hurt less.

Well, I was the idiot who wore them.

"Having a baby is hardly the same thing as organ farming." I don't know why I argued.

Actually, I do know why I argued. When you stop arguing, you've given up. I looked at the way Ilya's black hair fell across his forehead and tried to enjoy it. Like Elvis Presley. Or any given Ramone. That tall guy from Objekt 775.

Skinny jeans were back again.

"Well, for one thing," he said, "growing a liver takes less than nine months. And they pay *you* for it. With a baby, you have to pay. And pay, and pay."

Despite myself, I was getting intrigued. Half-remembered biology classes tickled me with questions. "Wouldn't you reject it? Or wouldn't you have to take all kinds of immunosuppressing drugs?"

"They use fat cells. And—I don't know, shock them or something. To turn them back into stem cells. Then they train them to grow into whatever they want. Whatever the rich bastard they're growing it for has killed off with his rich living. Liver. Lungs. Pancreas." He shrugged. "All you've got to do is provide the oxygen and the blood supply."

"And not drink," I reminded. "No drugs. I bet they won't even want you taking aspirin. Coffee. Vodka. Nothing."

"Just like a baby," he agreed.

I should have been suspicious then. He was being much, much too agreeable. But I had gotten distracted by the way that fringe of hair moved across his pale forehead. And the little crinkles of his frown, the way the motion pulled the tip of his nose downward.

We were coming up on my stop. Soon, I would get off and walk to my job. Ilya would continue on to his "band" practice: with "Blak Boxx," his "band." Which was more or less an excuse to hang out with three of his closest frenemies drinking and playing the same five chords in ragged 4/4 time.

You know which five chords I mean, too: nothing more complicated than a D major.

Fortunately for "Blak Boxx," most of rock and roll is built on the foundation of those five chords. Unfortunately for "Blak Boxx," to play live music you still need to be able to change between them without looking at your hands.

I didn't feel like having an argument with Ilya about who was paying the rent this month, again. And at least he was talking about something that might make money, no matter how harebrained. I should try to encourage this line of thinking. So as the train squealed into the station, rather than picking a fight about money, I just edged him away with an elbow and stepped back.

He put a hand on my shoulder, which might even have been to steady me. I think I probably glared at him, because he took it back very carefully.

"Think about it?" he said.

Suddenly, the whole conversation took on that slightly surreal gloss things have when you realize you've been looking at the picture from the wrong angle, and what you took for a vase full of flowers is actually an old woman with a crooked nose.

"We were talking about *you*," I said.

The train lurched and shook as it braked harder. I stumbled, but caught myself on the handrail over the dog.

"Me? I can't look fat!" he said—loud enough that heads turned toward us. "I have to be ready to get on stage!"

"I'm sure a lumpy cocktail waitress will make great tips," I shot back. "And who is it who is already keeping the roof over our heads?"

It turned out I got off before the dog. I guess it deserved the seat, then: it had the longer commute. It whined and gave me a soulful look as I brushed past. I had nothing in my bag except a hoarded bar of good chocolate, which was poison to dogs. And even if it hadn't been, I wasn't going to let Ilya find out about it. Decent chocolate was becoming less a luxury and more of a complete rarity. And what I could make last for two weeks of careful rationing, Ilya would eat in five minutes and be pissed off I hadn't had more.

"Sorry," I told the dog. "The cupboard's bare."

I stepped from the dingy, battered Metro car to the creamy marble and friezes of Novokuznetskaya Station. The doors whisked shut behind me.

*Christ what am I doing with my life?*

• • • •

Ten hours cocktail waitressing in those shoes, getting my ass pinched, and explaining drink specials to assholes when they could have picked the information off the intranet with a flick of their attention, didn't make my feet hurt any less or do much to improve my attitude. I rode home on a nearly-empty train, wishing I had the money to skin out the two other passengers and the ongoing yammer of the ads.

It's not safe to filter out too much reality when you're traveling alone at night. But the desire is still there.

No dogs this time.

The elevator to our flat was out of order again. I finally pulled those shoes off and walked up five flights of gritty piss-smelling stairs barefoot, swearing to myself with every step that if Ilya was passed out drunk on the couch, I was carrying every pair of skinny black jeans and his beloved harness boots out into the courtyard and setting it all on fire. And then I was going to dance around the blaze barefoot, shaking my tangled hair like a maenad. Like a witch.

This is how women sometimes turn into witches. We come home from work one day too many to discover our partners curled up on the couch like leeches in a nice warm tank, and we decide it's better to take up with a hut with chicken legs.

A good chicken-legged hut will never disappoint you.

But when I got home, there was hot food on the stove, plates on the coffee table, and a foot massage.

I bet a chicken-legged hut doesn't give a very good foot massage. And they sure as hell don't cook. Even lentils and kasha. Still it was good lentils and kasha, with garlic in it. And onions. And I hadn't been the one to cook it.

You need to get a magic cauldron for doing the cooking. Maybe a mortar and pestle that flies.

Ilya washed my foot. Then his fingers dug and rolled in the arch. I whimpered and stretched against him, but when he would have stopped I demanded persistence. He set my heel on the cushion and stood.

"Where are you going?"

"You're crabby for somebody whose man is making such an effort." He walked into the kitchen. A moment later he was back, bearing icy vodka in a tiny glass. He handed it to me. "Na zdravie."

"You're trying to butter me up," I complained, but I didn't refuse the vodka. It was cold and hot at once, icy in the mouth, burning in the throat, warm in the belly.

"What is it that you really want?"

He seated himself again and pressed his thumbs into my arch until I groaned. Patently disinterested, he asked, "Any foreigners tonight?"

It was not a totally idle question. Foreigners tip better. Also, as anyone could guess from the evidence of his wardrobe, Ilya was obsessed with twentieth-century punk rock, and twentieth-century punk rock flourished in England and America. And there aren't as many foreigners as there used to be, before the carbon crunch.

"You're always playing some game," I said.

He kissed the sole of my foot.

I said, "You never just tell me the truth. You could just tell me the truth."

"Bah," he said, pressing too hard. "Truth is unscientific. The very idea of *Truth* is unscientific."

"You're a cynic." I almost said *nihilist*, which probably would have been true also, but that word had too much history behind it to just sling around at random.

"If we accept Truth," he intoned, "then we believe we know answers. And if we believe we know answers, we stop asking questions. And if we stop asking questions, then all we're doing is operating on blind faith. And that's the end of science."

"Isn't love a kind a faith?" I asked.

"Then why do you keep asking me so many questions?" He laughed, though, to take the sting out.

I knew he was right. But I still pulled the pillow out from under my head and put it over my face anyway. What did he know about science? He couldn't even really play guitar.

• • • •

Two days later, Ilya and I saw the dog again, and I realized she was female. Perhaps we commuted on the same schedule. Perhaps she just rode the train back and forth, and we happened to be in the same car that day.

I don't think so.

She looked like she had a job. She looked like she was going somewhere.

Maybe her job was begging for food. When I walked past her to get off, she whined at me again, and again I had nothing.

One more creature for me to disappoint.

When I got off work that night, I bought some hard sausage from the street vendor. I didn't see the dog on the way home, though, so I wrapped the sausage in tissue and stuffed it into the bottom of my sometimes bag where Ilya wouldn't get into it. Maybe I'd run into her the next day.

• • • •

Dinner was waiting for me again, sausages and peppers and some good bread. Ilya had even found wine somewhere, which was almost too good to be true. Wine is hard to come by: the old vineyards are dying in the heat, and the new ones aren't yet well-established. That's what I heard, anyway.

Ilya seemed nervous. Hovering. When he finally settled, I was eating pepper slices one by one, savoring them. They were rich with the sausage grease, spicy and delicious. He chased his food around the plate for a little with his fork, then leaned on his elbows and looked at me.

I knew I was about to lose my appetite, so I ate another bite of sausage before I met his gaze.

"Have you thought about the liver graft?" he asked.

I swallowed. I reached for my wine, and deliberately drank two sips. "No."

"I think—"

"No," I said. "By which I mean, I have thought about it. And the answer is no. If you want to license out somebody's body to grow stem-cell organs, use your own. I *work* for a living. I take classes when I can. What the hell do you do?"

"You don't understand," he said. "We need this money to pay for the *tour.* For the *band.*"

"Wait," I said. "Isn't a tour supposed to be something you do to *make* money?"

"We'll make it all back on merchandise sales, and more. It will be our big launch!"

"What about me?" I asked. "I only need another year and a half to get my engineering degree. What do I get out of it?"

He reached out and took my hand. "I'll buy you a house. Two houses!"

I think he even believed it.

"Petra..." he stroked a thumb across the back of my hand. "You know we can change the world if we just get a chance. We can be another Black Flag, another Distemper."

I caught myself scowling and glanced away. He rose, refilled my wine, kissed my neck.

"Help me change our lives," he whispered. "You know I'm doing everything I can. I just need you to believe in me."

His breath shivered on the fine hairs behind my ear. He found my shoulders with his hands and massaged.

I was too tired to be angry, and anyway, he smelled good. I leaned back against his warm, hard belly. I let him smooth my hair and lead me to bed.

• • • •

Ilya was already gone when I woke up for work the next day. That was unlike him, being out of the house before three. He'd left me an indecipherable note. And I honestly did try to decipher it!

What were the odds that he had work? Would he brag it up in advance, or would he want to surprise me with his unprecedented productivity? I got up, cleaned off, dressed, and walked outside.

It was a beautiful day. The sky was a crisp sweet color that would have looked like a ripe fruit, if fruit came in blue. I walked to the Metro down the long blocks with their cement pavements, hemmed in by giant cubes of buildings on each side. Dogs and humans trotted this way and that with city-dweller focus: *I'm going somewhere and it matters.* Nobody looked around. I lived in a plain area, where the tourists don't come.

The streets were thronged with everything from petal busses to microcabs. There aren't so many solar vehicles here—they're not much good over the winter—but we have a bike share. I was early today—Ilya being home always slowed me down—and the weather was nice enough that I even thought of picking one up from the stand near the Metro and riding in to work today, but I hadn't brought a change of clothes except shoes, and I didn't want to spend the whole night sweaty.

I *did* spot one old petrol limousine. It stank, and the powerful whirr of its engine made me itch to scoop up a big rock and hurl it through the passenger window. I was stopped by the fact that it was probably bulletproof, and also by the other fact that anybody who could afford to own and operate a gasoline auto could also afford bodyguards who would think nothing of running me down and breaking my arms when they caught me.

I was wearing better shoes, today. But I didn't have much faith in my ability as a sprinter.

So I turned aside, and descended into the Metro.

I was early for my train. As I waited, my friend the ovcharka trotted up and sat down beside me. Her black-tipped, amber coat was shedding out in huge wooly chunks, leaving her sleek guard hairs lying close side by side. She looked up at me and dog-laughed, tongue lolling.

I remembered the sausage, and also that I had forgotten to eat breakfast. I split it with her. She took her share from my fingers daintily as a lady accepting a tea sandwich.

When the train came, we boarded it together. There were several seats, and I expected her to take one while I took another. But instead, when I sat, the dog curled up on my feet with a huff that I didn't know enough Dog to interpret.

We rode in silence to my usual stop for work. It was a companionable feeling, the sort of thing I wasn't used to. Just quiet coexistence. I understood for a minute why people might like dogs.

I stood, stepping over her to disentangle us, and headed for the open door.

The dog stepped in front of me.

Not as if she were getting off. As if she were blocking my path.

"I get off here," I said to her, pretending talking to a dog wasn't patently ridiculous. After one quick glance, the other passengers ignored us, because that's how it is in cities.

I tried to step around her. The ovcharka lowered her ears and growled.

I stepped back in surprise.

Hopping on one foot, I pulled off my shoe. It was the only weapon I had. I raised it to wallop the dog.

She ducked—cringing—but didn't move. She peered up at me and wagged her tail innocently, teeth chastely covered now. I imagined her like the wolf in the story: "Do not kill me, Prince Ivan. I will be of use to you again!"

That was when I noticed she was pregnant. A pup must have kicked or twisted inside her, because a sharp bulge showed against her side for a moment before smoothing away again.

I dropped the shoe back on the floor and stepped into it. I wasn't going to beat a pregnant dog with my trainer.

She nosed my hand gently and wagged her tail. She looked at the door, back at me. She pushed up against my legs and, as the door slid shut and the train lurched forward, she herded me back to my seat—still vacant, and the one next to it was empty now too. Only once I sat did she hop up beside me and lay her head across my lap.

I'm not sure why I went. Perhaps I was simply too befuddled to struggle. And I was early for work, anyway.

• • • •

Two stops later, she hopped down as the train was approaching the station, and nudged me with her slimy nose again.

I'd already spent the ruble. I might as well see what it had bought. I followed the dog out into the bustle of the station, up the escalator—she didn't even pause—and out into the balmy afternoon. She checked over her shoulder occasionally to make sure I was behind her, but other than that never hesitated. I had to trot to keep up: so much for showing up to work not sweaty.

After less than a kilometer, she slowed. Her head dropped, and she placed each foot singularly, with care. I recognized the stalking posture of a wolf, and pressed myself into the shadow of a building behind her. I felt like we were spies.

There was a pocket park up ahead—a tiny island of green space surrounded by a black twisted iron rail. As we came up to it, just to the edge where leaf-shadows dappled the pavement, I realized that there were two figures on a bench across the little square of green. They were facing away, and because of the dog's weird behavior, I had been walking softly. They didn't hear me.

I recognized one of them immediately, and not just by the skinny jeans and the leather jacket and the guitar case leaned against the arm of the bench. The other was a woman. More than that I couldn't see, because Ilya had pulled her into his lap and had his tongue so far down her throat he could probably tell what she'd had for breakfast yesterday.

How many of his band practices had actually involved musicians—no matter how loosely you defined the term?

I would have expected my hands to shake, my gorge to rise. I would have expected to feel some kind of denial. But instead, what I felt—what I experienced—was a kind of fatalistic acceptance. Frustration, more than anything.

*How Russian of me*, I remember thinking, and having to bite down on the kind of laugh that rises up when one recognizes one's self behaving in a stereotypical fashion. The dog leaned against my leg; I buried my fingers in her greasy coat. When I looked at her, she was looking up at me.

*Want to go pick a fight?* I imagined her asking.

Her tail waved in small circles. She waited to see what I would do.

I stepped back into the shadows of the building, turned smartly, and set off back towards the Metro. The dog followed a few steps, then trotted off in her own direction.

I didn't mind. Like me, she probably had to get to work.

I wound up taking a share bike after all. I was running too late to make it on the train.

• • • •

On my break that night, I found a corner in the staff den and read everything I could pull up about dogs. I felt queasy and tired. I wanted to go home, already. Somehow, I made it through my shift, though I couldn't manage cheeky and flirtatious, and so my tips were shit.

• • • •

Ilya and I didn't have our next fight immediately when I walked in the door. This was only because he was in bed asleep, and I couldn't find enough fucks to wake him. And when we got up the next day, I was too angry to put it into words. Sure, he irritated me. That's what partners do for each other, isn't it? But I had thought we were a team. I had thought…

I had thought he would get his act together one of these days, I guess, and finally start to pull his own weight. I had thought I was saving him.

Finally, at the top of the Metro escalators, he had had enough of my stony silence, and pushed the issue. Went about it all wrong, too, because he stopped, tugged my elbow to pull me out of the line of traffic, scowled at me, and said, "What the fuck crawled up your ass this morning?"

It was almost three in the afternoon, but whatever. I shook his hand off my elbow, glared, and spat. "You cheated on me!"

I saw him riffling through potential answers. He thought about playing dumb, but I was too convinced. He had to know I knew something for sure. At last he settled on, "It was an accident!"

"Like she tripped and fell on your dick? Argh!" I threw my hands up. We were causing a scene and it felt wonderful.

"Petra—"

"Ilya, never mind. Never mind. You're taking the next fucking train. And I want your shit out of my apartment when I get home."

"My name's on the lease too!"

"And when was the last time you paid a bill?"

He stepped up to me. I thought about slapping him, but that would give him the moral authority. Still, I didn't step back.

"Next train," I told Ilya. "I'm not riding with you." I'd have to push past him to reach the escalator. Instead, I spun around and bolted down the stairs.

When I got to work, I had to run into the bathroom to puke. It's a good thing Misha the bartender keeps peppermints in his apron, or every single customer I served that night would have smelled it on my breath.

Why the hell hadn't I been fucking someone more like Misha all along?

Probably because he was gay. But, you know. Besides that.

• • • •

I was still queasy on the ride home, and the lurch of the late-night train didn't help me. There were, at least, plenty of seats, though I looked in vain for my ovcharka friend. Nobody got into the first carriage except for me and one middle-aged grandmother in a dumpy coat. We settled down opposite one another.

In direct contravention to all the courtesies about not bothering strangers on trains, I asked her if she had seen the dog.

"Not today," she answered. "But sometimes. The one with the shaded coat like a wolf, yes?"

I nodded.

She sucked her false teeth. "In the Soviet time the Moscow dogs were hunted, my grandmother said. Then when I was a girl, there were more of them. They prospered for a while. And then people poisoned so many, and shooed them out of the Metro even when it was cold. But they're smart."

"The scientists say they're getting smarter."

She made a shooing motion with her hand. *Get out of here.* "I say they've always been smart."

"They're evolving," I said. "I read that dogs domesticated themselves. They hung around human middens scavenging. Their puppies played with our children until they—and we—realized we'd be good partners. We evolved in the tropics and they evolved in the subarctic, but we fill the same ecological niche. We're social pack hunters and scavengers who rely on teamwork to survive. They had teeth and we had fire. They had better hearing and smell and we had hands and better sight. It was a contract, between us and them."

I took a breath. She looked at me, waiting for me to finish. I said, "Some scientists say evolution is a struggle between female and male in the same species. Males want to make as many babies as they can, anywhere, any time. Females want to make sure the babies they raise are as strong and smart as possible. From the best males."

"Do you believe that?"

I laughed. "It sounds like something a guy who thinks he's something special would come up with, doesn't it? A justification."

"They're as God made them." She raised her brows at me, wrinkling her forehead under her scarf. Looking for an argument. And anybody sensible knows better than to argue with grandmothers. "The dogs are as God made them, too. To be our helpers."

I nodded, backing down.

"They seek tenderness," said the grandmother. "They have always been in Moscow. They are like every other Russian. Trying to get by. Trying to get a little fat again before the winter comes."

"Not just Russians," I said. "If you take away the few who have everything, the whole world is full of all the rest of us, who are just trying to get a little fat before the winter comes."

"That may be so." She smiled. "But the dog knows the Metro better than almost all of them." Then she frowned at me shrewdly. "Are you having man troubles, miss?"

"It's that evident?"

She made one of those creaking noises old women make, too knowing to really count as either a sigh or a laugh. "When you've been riding the Metro as long as I have, you've seen a broken heart for every iron rail. You should get rid of him. Pretty girl like you."

"I already did," I said, feeling better. Was I really taking dating advice from Baba Yaga?

That chicken-legged hut was sounding better and better.

"Stick to your guns," she said. "Remember when he comes crawling back that you can do better. He will crawl back. They always do. Especially when he finds out that you're pregnant."

"I—" *What?*

As if answering her diagnosis, my stomach lurched again, acid tickling the back of my throat.

She laid a finger alongside her nose. "Babushkas can smell it, sweetheart," she said. "We always know."

• • • •

Ilya was there when I got home, of course. Throwing them out never works. And I knew he was home—I mean, *there*—before I touched my key

117

to the door.

I could hear the music, his fingers flickering across the six strings of his guitar. He was better then I remembered. Arpeggios and instants, flickers of sound and wile and guile. It was beautiful, and I paused for a few moments with my cheek pressed against the door. Maybe he did have the means to change the world with his music.

So maybe I've been unkind.

To his talent, in the least.

Ilya sat on the couch, bent over his guitar as if it were a lover. His fringe fell over his forehead and I found my hand at my mouth. I was biting the tips of my fingers to keep from smoothing that lock.

He looked up, saw me, finished the arpeggio. Set his guitar aside, walked past me, and shut and locked the neglected door. Looked at me, and I could see through his eyes like ice to the formulated lie.

Before he opened his mouth, I said, "I saw you."

He blinked. I had him on the wrong foot and I didn't care. "Saw me?"

"With her," I said. "Whoever the hell she was. I don't want to hear your excuses."

He seemed smaller when he asked, "How?"

I didn't mean to tell him, but some laughs are so bitter and rough that words stick to them on their way out. "Remember the dog?" I asked. "The metro dog? She showed me."

"I don't understand—"

"You don't have to." I sat down on the floor, all of a sudden. Because it was there. I put my face in my hands for similar reasons. "Fuck, Ilya, I'm pregnant."

There was silence. Long silence. When I finally managed to fight the redoubled force of gravity and raise my face to him, he was staring at me.

"Pregnant," he said.

I nodded.

"But that's great!" he said. And then he stomped on my flare of hope before I even knew I felt it. "You can sell *that*. The embryo! They're nothing but stem cells at that point—"

"Sell it," I said.

"Yes," he said.

"To fund your tour?"

"Why else?"

*Oh god.*

I didn't realize I'd said it aloud until Ilya stopped raving and looked down at me. "What?"

"Oh, God," I said. "Fuck you."

Somehow, I stood up. I remember my hand on the floor, the ache of my thighs as if I were drunk. I remember looking him in the eye. I remember what I said.

It was, "Keep the fucking apartment. I'll call tomorrow and take my name off the lease."

"Petra?"

I turned my back on him. He was babbling something about food in the oven. About how was he supposed to make the rent.

I paused with a hand on the knob. "Go peddle it on Tverskaya Prospekt for all I care."

• • • •

Of course, I was halfway to the lift before I realized I had nothing but my work clothes, my bag, and two pairs of shoes—one of those quite impractical.

Well, I wasn't about ruin an exit like that in order to go back and pack a suitcase. No self-respecting chicken-legged hut would have anything to do with me after that, if I had.

• • • •

It took me two more days to find the dog. The first day, other than work—and I wasn't missing work now!—was mostly spent at a clinic, getting my name taken off the lease, looking at a couple of apartments, and finding a place to sleep for a couple of days until one of those became available. It turned out Misha the bartender didn't mind at all if I crashed at his place and neither did his boyfriend, and everybody at work was thrilled to hear that Ilya had been consigned to the midden heap of history.

How is it that you never hear about how much your friends hate your lover until you get rid of him or her?

Anyway, once that was all taken care of, I went to find my ovcharka friend. This mostly involved taking the Metro out to my station—my *old* station—earlier than I would have usually gotten up for work, and then checking the first car of each train for a wolf-colored passenger. I had a sausage in my bag and a hollow ache in my belly, but mostly what I remember was the grim determination that I would find that dog.

She wasn't on the train.

Instead, she trotted up beside me while I was waiting, sat down like an old friend on my left side, and looked up at me with one front paw lifted. I imagined her saying, "Shake?"

Instead, I broke a chunk off the sausage and offered it to her. "Thank you," I said.

She was as gentle as before. And if anything, she looked bigger around the middle than last time. She must be nearly ready to have the pups. I pressed a hand to my own stomach, imagining it pushing out like that. That hollow ache got hollow-er.

Someday. After my degree. But it wouldn't be deadbeat Ilya's deadbeat kid. No matter how good he smelled.

The train was coming. I felt the air pressure rise, heard the rattle of the wheels on iron rails.

"How did you know?" I asked the dog. "I owe you one."

She raised her brows at me, wrinkling her brow. *Expecting an argument?* She didn't wag.

I sighed and said, "Just how smart are you?"

And then Ilya was between us, shoving me out of the way. I hadn't even heard him come up. Hadn't heard the creak of his leather jacket. Didn't react fast enough to keep his elbow out of my ribs. I doubled over helplessly, wheezing for breath. The train's hydraulics hissed. Brakes squealed.

He gripped the dog by her scruff and her tail and slung her into the air. She yelped—more of a shriek—and he took a step toward the platform edge.

"You little bitch!"

He looked at me when he shouted it, and I wasn't sure if he meant the dog or me. But I knew the next five seconds like I was a prophet, like I was a Cassandra, like someone had dropped a magic mirror in my hand.

Ilya was going to throw the dog in front of the train.

Cassandra never got a chance to *do* anything. *I* jumped between Ilya and the platform edge.

The dog slammed into my chest. I pushed her away, throwing her onto the platform. The force tipped me on the platform edge. I pinwheeled my arms, expecting to topple backward. Expecting the next sensation to be the terrible impact of metal and then nothing—or worse, pain. I teetered, that hollowness in my stomach replaced with liquid, sloshing fear.

Someone caught my collar. Someone else caught my wrist. The feeling of relief and gratitude that flooded me left me on my knees. A man and a woman hovered over me. I could not see their faces.

I looked up into Ilya's face. The dog crouched in front of me, growling. Ears laid flat. Ilya lunged at her, and the man beside me grabbed him, twisted his arm behind his back.

"Bitch!" he swore, wrenching at the man who held him.

"Do you know that man?" the woman asked. She put a hand under my elbow and lifted me to my feet. There was a ladder in my stocking. My knee oozed blood.

"I left him," I said.

"I can see why," she answered. She patted my back.

Ilya twisted and kicked, rocking back and forth like a kid running against a sling swing. The dog snarled, a hollow trembling sound almost lost in the noise of the train. I thought she'd lunge for him, but she just stood her ground. Between him and me.

He must have wormed his arm out of the jacket sleeve, because suddenly he was off running, and his jacket hung limp in the man's grasp like a shed skin. I heard the thumping of his boots on the marble, shouts as he must have crashed through a crowd, and then nothing.

The man looked at the jacket, then at me.

"I don't want it," I said.

The police, of course, were nowhere.

• • • •

There was fuss, but eventually the ring of opinionated observers we'd drawn filtered off to their trains. The two helpful bystanders who had saved my life decided I could be left alone. The woman gave me a tissue. The man insisted I take Ilya's coat. Only then did they feel they had performed their civic obligations and reluctantly leave me alone.

I dropped Ilya's coat on a bench. Somebody would take it, but it wouldn't be me. I hoped his phone was in the pocket, but I didn't bother to check.

Then I looked at the dog.

She sniffed my bloodied knee and looked thoughtful. She tried to lick it, but I pushed her away.

"You set this up, didn't you?" Not Ilya trying to kill her, no. But me finding out about the other woman.

Or maybe it was just one bitch taking care of another. *Do you know your mate is no good?*

She just looked at me, squeezed her eyes, and thumped her shaggy tail. *So you should thank me.*

I huffed at her—like an irritated dog myself—and turned on the ball of my foot. This time I had the sense to be wearing practical shoes. She waited. I stopped, turned back, and saw her staring after me.

I had the money from the clinic—just as Ilya had suggested—but I sure as hell wouldn't be spending it on Ilya's band. I was going to enroll in classes tonight after work, and pay my tuition in advance. The cocktail job wasn't going away, and it didn't conflict with morning or most afternoon classes.

One of the apartments I had looked at was a student studio flat near the university. It was a complete roach motel, but it allowed pets.

I could do this thing.

I looked at the dog. She needed a bath.

The dog looked at me.

"Well," I said to her. "Aren't you coming?"

I started walking. The dog fell into step beside me. Her plumy tail wagged once.

---

Elizabeth Bear was born on the same day as Frodo and Bilbo Baggins, but in a different year. She is the Hugo, Sturgeon, Locus, and Campbell Award winning author of 27 novels (The most recent is Karen Memory, a Weird West adventure from Tor) and over a hundred short stories. She lives in Massachuset

# Goodnight Stars
## By Annie Bellet

The redwoods whispered overhead in the warm summer breeze as Lucy Goodwin gathered another handful of fallen branches for the camp fire. She looked up at the sky, squinting in the afternoon sunlight. The meteor shower the night before had been amazing. She hoped she and her friends would be treated to more tonight. Everyone had asked her about meteor showers and the Perseids and all that space crap. It was embarrassing.

As if she knew anything just because her mother was on the Moon. She snorted. Mom was an engineer, not an astrophysicist. Though you'd never know from how hard she pushed sciences at her only kid.

"Can't wait to have the 'you declared *what* major!' conversation when she gets home," Lucy muttered. All she and Mom did these days was fight, but it wasn't her fault. Lucy wanted to live her own life, not a life in her mom's shadow. One scientist in the family was plenty.

A smoky trail blazed through the sky and Lucy felt an odd pressure in her ears. It faded quickly, but the smoke still hung like some kind of brownish cloud. Repressing a shiver, Lucy headed back to camp.

Loud voices greeted her as she hiked out of the tree line to the ridge.

"Lucy!" Jack, her boyfriend, was waving his cell phone at her.

She sighed and picked up her pace. They'd declared the camping trip a tech-free zone, but apparently that was another promise Jack couldn't keep.

Kayla, Ben, and Heidi were throwing things into backpacks. Something was definitely wrong.

"What happened?" Lucy asked, as she dropped her armload of sticks and ran forward.

"I got a message from Daniel. They're calling up all the reservists and they are offering to re-up me, despite the leg." Jack's blue eyes looked panicked. He'd taken shrapnel in his left leg while in Afghanistan flying

123

helicopters. He'd gotten medical leave and started classes at Berkeley, where she and Jack had met. He'd promised he was done with all things military, even getting his walking papers only weeks before. Lucy had started to believe him when she saw the signed papers.

"Who is calling up reservists? The Army?"

"Everyone," Jack said. "Army, Navy, Air Force, National Guard. That's what Daniel says anyway."

"Tell her the rest, Jack, come on," Heidi called from inside her tent.

"Jesus, Heidi, her mom's on the Moon," Jack said. He ran a hand through his light brown hair, still clutching the phone.

Lucy's stomach turned to coiled rope and then knotted itself with a sickening twist. No one would meet her eyes as she looked around the camp.

"Why are they calling everyone up? What about the damn Moon?" She stepped over a pile of tent poles and grabbed Jack's arm, forcing him to look at her.

"Something hit the Moon. That's why the meteors were so awesome last night. It was the Moon exploding."

"Bullshit." Lucy shook her head. That wasn't possible. If the Moon had exploded, they would have seen that. It had been its usual crescent sailing along the horizon last night.

"Remember how Kayla said it looked lopsided to her?" Ben said. "The asteroid or whatever hit the back of it. That's what the news sites were saying before reception cut out."

"Fuck you guys if you are playing a trick on me," Lucy said. She ducked into her and Jack's tent, pulling her phone from her bag and powering it on. The phone sang to life with a little tune but remained stuck on the roaming screen, little multicolored dots dancing around in a circle as it struggled for reception.

Nobody could get reception. Resigned to figuring out if this was some hoax later, Lucy packed up with the rest of them. Kayla and Ben were an item lately and still in that new-couple-overwhelming-cuteness phase, so Heidi opted to ride with Jack and Lucy. Driving out of the Big Basin Redwoods state park, they stopped at the small gas station just outside, everyone in the car holding their phones, hunting for reception. Nothing.

Inside the gas station, there was a TV airing a news channel. Lucy stood inside the air-conditioned doorway, frozen.

It wasn't a lie. Photos and images from all around the world were piling in. Meteors were striking major areas. Satellites were down all around the world. The President of the United States would have a message for everyone at 6 p.m. Eastern.

The Moon was gone. The images released thus far were of a cloudy mess. Words like "impact winter" and "massive meteor strikes" echoed from the TV. The lone attendant wasn't paying any attention to the register; he just stood, mouth half open, holding the remote like maybe if he could change the channel he could change the future.

The Moon was gone. The Far Side Array was on the Moon.

"Mom," Lucy said, not even realizing she'd spoken aloud until Jack put his arm around her.

"She probably got off the Moon. I mean, they have shuttles for that, right?" Jack said quietly.

"I don't know. It's only a few of them up on that station and they get stuck there for months at a time. Why didn't anyone see this coming?" Lucy shoved Jack away. "Why? How did this happen and nobody knows?" She was aware she was yelling and she didn't give two fucks.

"Uh," the attendant said, "Some black guy in a suit came on earlier and was talking about the angle of the sun and some shit. Apparently nobody saw it coming. Probably the government is lying to us. They always are."

Heidi spread her hands in a placating gesture that just annoyed Lucy more. "Please, Luce, we gotta get back home. I gotta call my mom, and call Dana. Let's just go."

*Mom.* Lucy pressed her lips together and breathed in through her nose. The store smelled like lemon cleaning fluid and stale beer, but it grounded her. She couldn't get a hold of Mom even if she'd made it off the Moon. But Dad would know what was going on—he'd know what to do. And if meteors were going to strike Earth, Montana might be as safe a place as any.

Besides, Dad was like literally the only family she had left on this planet.

"No, we don't want to be anywhere near the coasts if meteors are striking all over the planet," she said, looking at Jack. "We're going to my home. We're going to Montana."

On the TV, the news cut out and the high whining tone of the emergency broadcast station pierced the tense air in the store.

• • • •

Jack had agreed immediately, but Heidi was still sulking in the back seat as they left the serene park behind and entered a chaos of traffic. By the time they hit I-80 West toward San Jose, cars clogged the road heading into the city. It was a Sunday in August; the traffic shouldn't have been so bad. Lucy's cell phone still hunted for a signal. She dug out the folding map of the United States from the Jeep's glove box. It was shiny and new, never used. Who needed a paper map when you had GPS on your phone?

She guessed Jack being a Boy Scout and Army brat was good for something. He took that *always be prepared* thing seriously.

"Last chance to get out and find a bus station or something," Lucy said, leaning back over the seat and looking at Heidi.

"No," Heidi said. She looked out the window at the clogged freeway. "I'll go with you. I doubt they're letting flights out, and I'd rather be with friends than alone."

Which was good, Lucy thought. Because she'd never have really let Heidi go into the city by herself.

They cut around San Jose and headed down 580 toward Stockton, deciding to avoid I-5 North. The radio flip-flopped between static and emergency broadcasts telling people to stay in their homes. It was dark by the time they got near Stockton.

A gas station in Colfax was still open. Jack bought another gas can, filling it and adding it to the two he already kept in the back of Jeep. He topped those off, too.

"Smart thing, kids," the old woman behind the counter said to them as they paid in cash. "Last can I have to sell. People been buying out all day going down this road toward Reno. We're gonna be out of gas come tomorrow if the trucks don't make it. Heard there are some fires up that way, so take care."

"You heard anything else?" Lucy asked, motioning to the TV. It was muted, just the bands of the Emergency Broadcast System twitching on the screen.

"Nothing useful," the woman said. She smiled and shrugged her thin shoulders. "Keep calm and carry on."

Her cackle followed them out of the station and all the way back to their car.

• • • •

The one and only time Lucy had made this drive was a year before, when she and her dad drove out to set her up at school. They'd stopped halfway through the seventeen-hour drive at a little bed and breakfast. He'd played basketball with the kids of the couple who ran the place while Lucy stood on the porch and answered awkward questions. Mom had been in training for the Moon mission, but try getting people to believe that no really, your mom was totally going to the Moon.

She'd shut off the radio over an hour before. Reno had seemed normal, almost calm. Lights still on, traffic thin. That might have been the tell that something was wrong with the world, Lucy guessed. Even on a Sunday night, traffic should have been jumping with people going out or coming home from the various entertainments Nevada's cities had to offer. They'd grabbed snacks at another gas station but no one had felt like trying to find a restaurant or having much of a conversation.

Now though, Jack was crashed out in the passenger seat, and Heidi had shoved camping gear down so she could sprawl on the back seat. The only noises were the sounds of the tires shushing along the road. The Jeep's headlights picked up a haze in the air and the sky was dark overhead, pierced occasionally with little flashes, like far-off lightning strikes.

Lucy had a feeling it wasn't lightning. She didn't want to think about the meteors. Thinking about it led to thinking about the Moon. About Mom.

She's probably in a damn bunker somewhere in Florida or Texas or something, Lucy told herself. She blinked away angry tears and tightened her hands on the steering wheel. She regretted the pizza stick she'd eaten as her belly flipped again. No thinking about Mom. Think about Dad. About getting home. Hours now—just a few more hours. If Jack had been awake, she would have made him check the map, check the mile markers. Five or six more hours, she guessed, before they hit US-93 and headed north for Montana. Then another six or seven hours. So maybe twelve, thirteen total.

She almost hit the first deer, but slammed on the brakes in time. Another leapt into the roadway. Then another.

"Jesus fuck," Jack said, jerking awake as the sudden stop slammed him into his seatbelt.

"Look," Lucy said. "What are they doing?"

There was a huge cracking noise overhead, and the road seemed to roll up beneath them. Out of the brush at the sides of the highway, hundreds of deer sprang forward, flooding into the road and then across and down the other side. They were clearly fleeing something.

"What is that?" Heidi asked, her voice heavy with sleep and fear.

The huge herd of deer had cleared. Beyond, out in a darkness lit now with an odd, almost nuclear glow, a cloud rushed at them, looking like a giant white wave.

"No idea," Lucy said. She stomped on the gas. "Seatbelts!"

The Jeep was no sports car, but she was pretty sure she went from zero to eighty in record time. Dust and chunks of turf, pebbles, and demolished brush slammed into the windows and scraped along the sides of the vehicle. The right tire hit the drunk bumps on the side of the road and Lucy aimed straight, keeping the ridges beneath them so she could feel her way down the road. Pale flashes of the white lines on the road through the smoke helped keep her on track.

The air cleared after a few miles, and she found herself praying under her breath as the headlights lit upon dark asphalt. She pulled the Jeep back left, into the road proper.

"You're lucky you didn't blow the tires," Jack said. His voice sounded more awed than reproachful.

"Driving by Braille," Lucy said, shooting him a quick smile. A pain hit her heart. That saying was something her mother always said, usually to excuse the way she often wandered on the road a little, her brain lost in some scientific minutia.

"Did we just survive a meteor strike?" Heidi asked.

"I don't know. Maybe."

"We good on gas?"

Lucy checked the gauge. "Yeah. I can keep driving. Though now I gotta pee."

"That's all of us, after that," Heidi said.

No one slept again that night, though Lucy guessed Jack could have. He was the only one of them used to this. She finally asked him as they neared Elko around dawn.

"This is like war, kinda, huh? Are you going to be okay?"

They didn't talk about his service. Jack had joined up after his parents were killed in a car accident when he was seventeen. He'd told her he was a helo pilot, and the one time she'd asked him if he'd shot anyone, he just shook his head. Lucy was glad about that. She might have been raised in Montana where being able to walk meant you were old enough to learn to use a gun, but she didn't like the idea of them, and her politics leaned further left than even her extremely progressive parents'.

"This is nothing like the war," Jack said. The look on his face closed that line of conversation, and Lucy kept driving.

Elko was silent, the houses shuttered and nothing open. They drove another hour, the gas light flickering on, and debated using one of the tanks. Jack voted they should wait and see if one of the little stops between Elko and Wells had anything.

Before Wells, where they would turn north onto US-93, they found an open gas station and everyone got out to stretch and check their phones.

"Those won't work," the attendant said. He was a middle-aged man, on the small side, barely taller than Lucy, with a big round belly and white beard any mall Santa Claus would've been proud of. He'd come out of his little booth to chat, seemingly glad to see live people on the road. "Got a brother with the Sheriff's office. Said that all stable frequencies for the radio and phones are being routed for emergency personnel only."

"So how the hell do you call 911?" Heidi asked.

"Times like these?" He motioned up to the clouded-over sky where small flashes still glinted every now and again in the diffuse morning sun. "You don't."

Lucy shook her head. The roads had been clear so far, other than some plant debris and dirt. They were moving, however, toward heavily forested areas. Remembering the pictures of the Tunguska Impact, she climbed back into the Jeep to study the map again.

A big truck roared into the station as Jack was finishing with the pump. Three big white men, mid-twenties to thirties, jumped out, whooping. Two of them were carrying machetes.

Lucy froze as the one without a knife grabbed Heidi and swung her around, pulling her tight against his body.

"You just back off, old man. We're commandeering this station. It's the end of the fucking world, don't you know?" The oldest-looking one, a man with a reddish beard and blue overalls, waved his machete at the attendant.

"That isn't a good idea," Jack said. His voice was all steel, his hands at his sides, but Lucy knew the look of readiness when she saw it. He was going to get himself killed, the big damn soldier.

She let the map drop slowly to the seat and followed it down. No one was looking at her; their eyes were on Jack and the attendant. With her right hand, she felt under the driver's seat until she found Jack's gun case. Still bent low, she slid the Glock from the case, checked the magazine and made sure a round was already chambered. Her heart raced miles ahead of her fear, but she shoved away all the anxiety, the shake in her fingers.

Instead she reached for her dad's voice. "Never point a gun at something you aren't willing to shoot," he had told her. "Never point a gun at a man unless you want him dead. If you aren't willing to make him dead, you might as well put the gun in his hand and tell him to pull the trigger."

She didn't want to kill anyone. But the way that man was groping her sobbing friend, the way Jack looked ready to try to take on three big men with no weapons, well. There were no police to call. No one to stop this. Just her.

Lucy slid out of the Jeep and came around the side, raising the gun and pointing it at the man in overalls. He'd talked, so she was pretty sure he was the boss.

"Let her go, and get the fuck out of here," she said. Her voice was low and mean and only shook a little. *Channel Dirty Harry,* she told herself. *Dad made me watch all those old movies, might as well get some use out of it.*

"Ooh, look Jerry." One of the other men, the one not holding Heidi, laughed. "The spic cunt there wants us to leave."

"You going to shoot, girl?" Overalls asked. He sneered, but his eyes were shadowed by what she hoped was fear.

"She ain't gonna shoot," the other guy said. "Those Mexican bitches can't . . ."

Whatever he would have said was cut off by the loud report of the gun and a scream. Lucy swung the gun smoothly back to Overalls as the other guy fell to the ground, dropping his machete and holding his bleeding crotch.

"I'm Puerto Rican, you ignorant fuck," she said.

Whatever Overalls saw in her face then, he didn't like. He dropped his machete and hissed at the man holding Heidi to let her go as he raised his hands and backed toward their truck.

The attendant bolted for his hut and came out with a shotgun. "Get out of here and don't come back or I'll put more holes in you!" he yelled after them.

They grabbed up their bleeding friend and drove their truck out of there faster than they'd arrived.

"Oh my god. You shot him. You really shot him!" Heidi was freaking out.

"Give me the gun," Jack said softly. He gently took it from her numb fingers.

"I'm okay," Lucy said. Her teeth chattered. Shock. Maybe this was shock. She wasn't sure. She'd really shot him.

"How much for the gas," Jack said. He flicked the safety on and kept the gun low at his side.

"No charge. Just get where you are going and keep these ladies safe, eh?" The man smiled a gap-toothed smile. "Shit raining from the skies does terrible things to people. And you, little lady, you did right. Don't you fear no retribution. Those bastards are cowards. They'll look for other targets that don't shoot back."

"Then I wish I'd killed them," Lucy muttered. She wasn't sure if she meant it or not.

Jack drove. Heidi sat in back, staring out the window, not talking. Lucy glanced over her shoulder at her friend a few times, but Heidi wouldn't meet her eyes, even in the reflection of the window.

They turned north onto US-93 and it was clear meteors had hit near here. Branches were down in the road and they were forced to slow. They passed a couple cars heading south, but the drivers only waved and didn't stop to share news.

"What's that haze?" Lucy said finally, breaking the silence that had descended since the gas station.

"Forest fire, I think. It's pretty far off though."

"I'm sorry, Jack," she said softly. "I didn't know what else to do."

"Sorry? For what? You saved us back there. I was going to try to get them with prayer and my bare hands."

"I shot a man."

"I know. It isn't easy. But you winged his nuts. Not like he's dead."

"I was aiming for his chest," Lucy said.

Jack looked sideways at her and a small smile played at his lips. "No you weren't," he said.

"No," Lucy said. A weird giddiness rose in her, threatening to turn into a hysterical giggle. "I wasn't."

"You asked if this was like war? Back there, it kind of was." He sighed and ran his hand through his hair. She loved that gesture. She'd been so mad at him about something—she was always mad about something—but right then she wanted to kiss him, to curl up in his arms and pretend the world was just fine.

"You've shot people." It wasn't a question, not anymore.

He dodged answering it anyway. "Times like these, you figure out who you are. Deep inside. Some people can't do what has to be done. Some can."

"Fuck you," Heidi said from the back seat.

"That guy was huge, Heidi. There wasn't anything you could have done. No more than Luce here could've stopped them if they'd grabbed her. She found a tool and she used it. We survived. That's how it works."

Heidi's eyes were bright with tears and her hands fisted in her t-shirt. "Not how I want my life to work," she whispered.

"We'll find you a way to Chicago, Heidi," Lucy said. "Once we're home."

"Sure," Heidi said and went back to staring out the window.

They had to get out twice to clear larger branches, and once, nearly half a tree from the road. No more weird cracks of light lit the sky, but the sun was obscured in the haze and the dust and smoke were so heavy that they had to breathe through their shirts.

Heidi took over so Lucy could rest. She still refused to say more than a syllable or three.

Lucy must've dozed off, though she felt for a while as the rough road chunked and thunked away beneath the Jeep that she'd never sleep again. Not until she knew Dad was safe. Not until she knew for sure about the Moon. About Mom.

The cessation of road noise woke her.

"Where are we?" she asked Jack. Heidi wasn't in the driver's seat.

"Outside Darby. We're on a side-road. Some guys were heading out to try to clear a rockslide or something on the highway, so they told us to detour down this Old Darby Road. Heidi had to pee." He motioned out the window with a grin.

"You stopped and talked to people and I didn't wake up?" Lucy rubbed her eyes and caught a whiff of her morning breath. She sat up and reached for a water bottle.

"A regular sleeping beauty," Jack said, pushing some of her hair from her face. "Speaking of that, you're Puerto Rican?"

"Half," she said, making a face. "My parents named me Lucita, but I hate it." It seemed so trivial now. All through middle school and high school, she'd just wanted to be one of the pale, pretty blondes. She'd bleached her hair, worn contacts, put on foundation that was two shades too light for her complexion. Gone by Lucy instead of Lucita. Lucy Goodwin had tried so hard to leave everything of her mother and her mother's history behind. Her language. Her culture. Her religion. Her science.

*And now all I want to do is get home and tell her how sorry I am and promise we'll never argue again. Ever.*

"Wait," she said as Jack started to get out of the car. "Darby? That means we're like an hour or so from home." She threw open the door and came around to his side, pulling him down for a kiss as he climbed out and wrapped her in his arms.

"I can't believe you are from a place called Lolo." He grinned.

"The farm is outside Lolo. Geez."

"A farm like this?" Jack motioned around them.

Heidi had stopped along the road at a gravel driveway that stretched back down a lane of poplar. In the distance Lucy could make out the roof of a farmhouse, one of the classic two-story ones, probably made with stone and logs, the roof looking like slate from this distance in the hazy afternoon light. The air was dusty but cool, carrying an almost metallic tang. Looking up, Lucy couldn't find where the sun should be.

"It should be a lot hotter this time of year," she said.

"Too much shit in the atmosphere, I guess," Jack said. He let her go and walked a little ways toward some bushes. "Heidi, you get eaten by a bear?"

"Oh my god, are there bears around here?" came the shrieking reply.

Lucy mouthed *asshole* at Jack, who grinned.

A high whining noise broke the still air, as though a jet engine had materialized somewhere above them. Before Lucy could do more than look up and then back at Jack, a cracking boom sounded, the reverberations rattling through her bones and teeth like thunder from the worst summer storm she'd ever seen.

"Get back in the car," she yelled. "Heidi!"

It was too late. The road rippled, and the trees seemed to burst apart on the far side where they hadn't been cleared for farmland. A wave like the one before, this one churning and brownish-gray, descended on them. Lucy tried to get into the Jeep, but the wave caught her, throwing her into the air and over the low wooden fence. She hit the ground with a crunch that knocked away what little air was left in her lungs. The shockwave smashed her flat and she clung to the ground, her arms around her head, her eardrums pulsing as though she'd dove too deep into water.

Then it was gone, the horrible pressure lifting, her ears ringing and throbbing. Lucy uncurled slowly, wiggling her fingers and then her toes. Nothing seemed broken, though her mouth tasted like grit and blood. She spit and pulled her torn, grimy tee-shirt up over her nose and mouth.

Dust clogged the air, stinging particles rasping on her skin. She squinted and shaded her eyes with one hand, trying to make out anything.

It wasn't just the ringing in her ears. Someone was screaming. Lucy moved toward the voice, stepping over the scattered remains of the low wood fence. The Jeep loomed ahead and appeared mostly intact. She couldn't see Jack or Heidi.

She stumbled toward the screams and nearly fell down the embankment into what was left of the bushes Heidi had been using as a makeshift toilet. A smear of blue and red caught her eye, and Lucy kicked her way through the debris.

Heidi lay half on the ground, half-impaled on the jagged remains of a sapling. Blood gushed, dark and lazy, from her chest and trickled out of her gasping, screaming mouth. Jack was kneeling at her side, his tee-shirt off, revealing a back bloodied with cuts.

This time, Lucy didn't freeze. She pulled off her own shirt and ran forward, offering it to Jack to help stop up the blood oozing from around the stick in Heidi's chest.

He shook his head and tried to say something, but coughed instead. That was when Lucy saw his left arm. At first her brain refused to make sense of it. She thought he had a piece of tree sticking out of his arm and made an aborted motion to pull it free from his skin.

That was when she realized it wasn't a stick. That *was* his left arm. Or at least the bone. The humerus, she remembered from high school biology. There was nothing funny about it. Giggles tightened her chest and she turned her head, vomiting water and bile into the dirt.

Jack yelled again and she made out that he wanted her to tie off her shirt around his upper arm. Blood ran in a dirty crimson river down his useless hand. Sucking in a breath that was more grit than air, Lucy did as he asked, amazed he didn't pass out.

"Big damn soldier," she muttered, knowing he couldn't hear her.

"Hey," a voice boomed from the haze, followed by two people, a man and a woman. They had on gasmasks and goggles over their eyes. The woman had a rifle.

Lucy blinked grit from her eyes and waved to them. If they wanted to kill her or do something all Texas Chainsaw Massacre, she wasn't in any state to stop them. She just had to trust now that her dad was right, and that most people were good people.

He was right. They were good people.

Maddie Grace and her son Victor managed to get Heidi free of the tree, cutting the sapling out from under her. She was bundled into a quilt for the short run back to the farmhouse, where Victor's wife Angel waited with two scared but curious kids. Lucy found out their names as she was bundled into a comfortable country kitchen. Gas lamps were lit and Angel got to work on cleaning Lucy's cuts.

Heidi had stopped screaming. Angel said that Victor was a paramedic, had been with the army, too. He'd see to her friends.

Lucy didn't argue, though she felt like a coward. She didn't think she could face more blood and pain. Every cut, every bruise, every ache and pain woke up and tried to voice how much her body hated her all at once. Her ears wouldn't equalize, and she wasn't sure she could hear at all from the left one.

Maddie Grace appeared in the doorway, grief and determination etched in the heavy lines of her face.

"You'll be wanting to say goodbye," she said.

"Jack? But it was just his arm—" Lucy stood up too quickly and the world spun.

"No, not your man. The girl."

Guilt wracked Lucy, but she shoved it away. It was like Jack said. Act now, process later.

"Of course," she said. She walked forward, following Maddie Grace into what had been a utility room but was now a makeshift surgery. A folding table, the kind you might use for a picnic or impromptu card game, held Heidi's still body. Bloody rags were gathered in a tidy pile to one side, and Victor stood, his head hanging, tears dripping off his thick nose.

Jack lay half propped in a folding chair, his arm still wrapped in her tee-shirt. He looked up at Lucy and held out his good hand to her.

She ignored it, going to Heidi's side on the table. Lucy wrapped her fingers around her friend's and was surprised when Heidi's eyes flickered and she weakly squeezed back.

"I'm sorry," Lucy said. All she did was argue with people, and then her last words were always anger or apology. She blinked at tears, trying to smile at her friend. "You stay with us, okay? We're right here. You aren't alone."

Heidi's mouth moved, but whatever she said was lost as she went rigid. She shook her head, and then started to choke. Victor moved in, propping up her head, trying to get her to breathe, his words a string of soothing nonsense.

Heidi stilled. Lucy had seen animals put down before, had seen that moment when a being went from life to death. It was disturbingly similar and yet more terrible, now. One moment her friend was there, struggling for air, bleeding out on the table. The next, no one was home.

Lucy collapsed, and all the tears she'd held back over the last hellish day found freedom now and scraped hotly down her cheeks. Jack tried to get up, but Victor told him to sit.

It was Maddie Grace who wrapped her wiry, strong arms around Lucy's shoulders and guided her into a cozy family room, pressing her gently onto the couch. Someone found a shirt for her, something clean. Tea was pressed into her hands. A handkerchief for her tears. Still the tears came.

Finally, cried down to dry sobs, the tea a minty memory in her throat, Lucy passed out.

• • • •

"It will be dark soon. We can go tomorrow," Jack said.

"Yeah, it'll be dark soon, but I don't care. I'm going home, Jack. I am not waiting any longer. Victor said the Jeep will run. He changed the tire for me and cleared out the broken glass. I'm going home." Lucy rubbed her hands down her borrowed shirt. She'd slept for over an hour, but that was long enough. Every ache and cut told her that Jack was right, that she should stay where she was safe and sleep some more.

But this wasn't home.

"Your dad can wait a day," Jack said. He struggled to sit upright on the pull-out couch, and she could see he was in horrible pain even through the morphine Victor had given him.

"What if he can't?" Lucy shot back. "The last thing I said to her was so mean, Jack. I told her I wished I had a mother who could understand, a mother like my friends' moms. I have to go home. I can't let my last words to Mom be the last thing said in our family."

"She might be alive."

"No," Lucy said. The word hurt to say, but it rang inside her aching heart with a truth she couldn't explain. "I can feel it. She's gone." Like Heidi. Like god knew how many people. Even the radios were out; Maddie Grace's family had no recent news.

"Fine. I'm going too." Jack tried to swing his legs over to the side and cried out in pain as the movement jolted his arm.

"No. It's only an hour away. Stay here. Maddie Grace said she doesn't mind. They can run you up to the farm when you are better, or I'll come back and get you in a day or two. I gave them directions." Lucy walked over to him and bent down, kissing his damp forehead. He felt feverish, and she made a note to tell Victor on her way out.

"I love you, Luce," Jack said.

"Damn well better. I shot a dude in the balls for you." She fought more tears as she smiled. This would not be their last conversation—she was determined about that. But if it was . . . if, well, she wouldn't leave with angry words. Not this time. "I love you, too, you big damn soldier."

The US-93 was a wreck of debris and branches. Lucy put the Jeep's four-wheel drive through its paces. It was full dark when she spotted the bright yellow reflectors on the mailbox at the end of her driveway shining like welcome home beacons through the haze.

She pulled up at the house, eyes searching for a light in the dark. She heard the screen door bang open as she stumbled up the steps and blinked as a flashlight poured warm light over her.

"Daddy?" she said.

"Lucita! Lucy!" he dropped the flashlight and wrapped her in his arms. She pushed her nose into his soft flannel shirt and breathed in the familiar smell of vanilla pipe tobacco, horses, and mint.

"Dad, I'm home," she said, laughing into his chest.

"Yes, yes you are."

• • • •

The meteor strike outside Darby was the closest anything large got to Lolo, Montana. The impact haze—as the news radio, when it was working, called it—persisted. They were in for what was called an impact winter. No one knew how long it would last. Years, was the guess. Nobody could say what the death toll was. The coastal regions had been hit hard with tsunamis. Miami was rumored to be gone, struck directly by a large chunk of Moon debris. The equatorial zones were the hardest hit, but Lucy didn't regret fleeing California.

Three months, and they were crawling on toward real winter. Jack had shown up after a week with Maddie Grace and Victor in tow, bringing a crate of pickles with them. His arm wasn't fully healed even months later, but he was learning how to use his fingers again and doing the exercises Victor ordered him to. Lucy was a little jealous about how well Jack and her dad got along, but she figured they might have to cohabitate for a while, so she didn't say too much about it.

Victor said they'd buried Heidi by a really pretty dogwood that had survived the shockwave. No one knew how to get a message to Chicago and her family. Lucy vowed that someday she would make that journey and tell Heidi's mom and sister where their daughter was buried.

She knew, deeply, how crushing a lack of closure could be.

No one talked about Mom. Not after the first night, when Lucy had asked about the Moon and all her dad said was "Yes, it's true" and they'd left it at that.

Almost three months. It felt like three minutes sometimes.

Lucy leaned on the porch rail, hands tucked into her coat, watching the hazy sky darken. There were no more flashes in the night, at least in this area, but there were no stars either. No sun except a slightly brighter patch of sky some afternoons. The farm had its own generator and well, but they rationed everything. The National Guard had been through from Missoula, clearing the roads and bringing news and fuel. That was all they had of the outside world. There had been no news of Mom or the people on the Moon. It was like the world was pretending no one had been there.

Crunching gravel pulled Lucy from her melancholy. A Hummer crept up the driveway, looking dark and military and official.

"Dad," she yelled. Jack was out at the barn, but her father was inside, whipping up his famous camp stove chili they were all too nice to tell him they were sick to death of eating.

He came out on the porch with his .22 rifle in hand. He looked older to Lucy, his hair grayer and lines forming around his mouth and eyes she didn't remember being there before. He was still tall and solid and calm, though.

Two men in fatigues came out first, nodding to Lucy and her father.

"You Paul Goodwin?" one man asked.

"I am," her dad said. He gently propped the gun against the house and walked forward to the steps.

A woman climbed out of the vehicle, assisted by one of the men in fatigues. She was pregnant, her belly pushing out heavily against her navy blue pea-coat. She was thin except for that belly, and pretty. She looked up at Dad, then at Lucy, and walked forward, a small bag in her hand.

"My name is Shannon," she said, a soft English accent lilting her voice. "I served with Neta on the Far Side Array."

"No—" Dad half cried out, his fist pressing into his lips. Lucy grabbed for his arm and leaned into him.

It was one thing to believe that Mom was dead. It was another to see this woman, to hear her use the past tense, and know it for real.

"Is that?" Lucy said, motioning toward the bag. Had they brought only her body back? Cremated her?

"What? No," Shannon said. "This is, I mean, she recorded a message. We couldn't all go home, there wasn't space."

A man behind Shannon coughed loudly, his expression a warning.

"Bloody hell, Wentworth. It's Neta's family. They deserve to know the truth." She turned back to Lucy and her dad. "Your mom chose to stay so that I could come home . . . she knew I was pregnant."

"Neta would do that," Dad said. Tears reddened his eyes, but he managed a smile. "God, she would do that."

"This is her last message. Do you have power? It had a full charge when we left, but if you need more, we can hook up a battery for you." Shannon walked to the edge of the stairs, holding out the bag.

"We have enough," Lucy said, stepping down from the porch and taking the bag. It felt like a small laptop was inside. "So she's really gone," she whispered to Shannon.

"I'm sorry, sweetheart, she is," Shannon said. She looked like she might cry, too.

Lucy nodded and pressed her lips together. "Thank you," she said.

"I'm sorry if we don't ask you to stay," her dad said as Lucy turned and climbed the steps.

"I understand," Shannon said.

Lucy hugged her father's side, and they watched as the woman and her escort got back into their car and made a swinging turn, driving off down the road in a swarm of dust.

They played the message on the military's portable DVD player, just the two of them, not calling Jack in from the barn in unspoken agreement. Lucy loved Jack, but this was a family thing.

Mom seemed so composed on the screen, but so tiny. Her face was lined and tired, her dark eyes bright, her words steady and full of love. There was no reproach, no anger, no blame.

She even called Lucy *Lucy*.

And then that final moment, just before the message cut out, when the tears broke for a shining second from her mother's eyes, and she whispered to the camera: "Love her, Paul. Give our little light all the love I won't be there to give. And don't hang on to me. I want you both to live, to be happy."

Lucy bolted from the kitchen and out onto the porch, sobbing. Her dad joined her, his big arms wrapping around her shoulders and pulling her into his warm, flannel-covered chest.

"I was so mad at her," she said, her breath misting in the freezing air. "But I didn't mean it. I didn't."

"She knew, Luce, she knew." He pressed his lips into her hair and rocked her gently.

"I can't tell her though. She's gone. Just . . . gone."

"She isn't gone. Your mother is not gone." The force of his words shocked Lucy, and she pulled away a little to stare up into his face. "Are the stars gone?" He pointed at the sky.

"What? No, we just can't see them."

"Exactly, Lucita. They are still there, just like your mom. Invisible, but shining down on us all the same."

They stood for a long time out on the porch, until Jack's footsteps roused them.

"You coming inside?" Jack asked, looking them over, questions in his eyes.

Lucy nodded. She slipped her hand into his good one and took a last look at the sky. Invisible, but still there. She squeezed Jack's fingers and walked through the door.

Annie Bellet is the *USA Today* bestselling author of *The Twenty-Sided Sorceress*, *Pyrrh Considerable Crimes Division*, and the *Gryphonpike Chronicles* series. She holds a BA in English and a BA in Medieval Studies and thus can speak a smattering of useful languages such as Anglo-Saxon and Medieval Welsh.

Her interests besides writing include rock climbing, reading, horse-back riding, video games, comic books, table-top RPGs and many other nerdy pursuits. She lives in the Pacific Northwest with her husband and a very demanding Bengal cat.

# We Are The Cloud
## By Sam J. Miller

Me and Case met when someone slammed his head against my door, so hard I heard it with my earphones in and my Game Boy cranked up loud. Sad music from *Mega Man 2* filled my head and then there was this thud like the world stopped spinning for a second. I turned the thing off and flipped it shut, felt its warmth between my hands. Slipped it under my pillow. Nice things need to stay secret at Egan House, or they'll end up stolen or broken. Old and rickety as it was, I didn't own anything nicer.

I opened my door. Some skinny thug had a bloody-faced kid by the shirt.

"What," I said, and then "what," and then "what the," and then, finally, "hell?"

I barked the last word, tightening all my muscles at once.

"Damn, man," the thug said, startled. He hollered down the stairs "Goddamn Goliath over here can talk!" He let go of the kid's shirt and was gone. Thirty boys live at Egan House, foster kids awaiting placement. Little badass boys with parents in jail or parents on the street, or dead parents, or parents on drugs.

I looked at the kid he'd been messing with. A line of blood cut his face more or less down the middle, but the gash in his forehead was pretty small. His eyes were huge and clear in the middle of all that blood. He looked like something I'd seen before, in an ad or movie or dream.

"Thanks, dude," the kid said. He ran his hand down his face and then planted it on the outside of my door.

I nodded. Mostly when I open my mouth to say something the words get all twisted on the way out, or the wrong words sneak in, which is why I tend to not open my mouth. Once he was gone I sniffed at the big bloody handprint. My cloud port hurt, from wanting him. Suddenly it didn't fit quite right, atop the tiny hole where a fiber optic wire threaded into my brainstem though the joint where skull met spine. Desire was dangerous, something I fought hard to keep down, but the moment I met Case I knew I would lose.

Egan House was my twelfth group home. I had never seen a kid with blue eyes in any of them. I had always assumed white boys had no place in foster care, that there was some other better system set up to receive them.

• • • •

I had been at Egan House six months, the week that Case came. I was inches away from turning eighteen and aging out. Nothing was waiting for me. I spent an awful lot of energy not thinking about it. Better to sit tight for the little time I had left, in a room barely wider than its bed, relying on my size to keep people from messing with me. At night, unable to sleep, trying hard to think of anything but the future, I'd focus on the sounds of boys trying not to make noise as they cried or jerked off.

On Tuesday, the day after the bloody-faced boy left his handprint on my door, he came and knocked. I had been looking out my window. Not everyone had one. Mine faced south, showed me a wide sweep of the Bronx. Looking out, I could imagine myself as a signal sent out over the municipal wifi, beamed across the city, cut loose from this body and its need to be fed and sheltered and cared about. Its need for other bodies. I could see things, sometimes. Things I knew I shouldn't be seeing. Hints of images beamed through the wireless node that my brain had become.

"Hey," the kid said, knocking again. And I knew, from how I felt when I heard his voice, how doomed I was.

"Angel Quiñones," he said, when I opened the door. "Nicknamed Sauro because you look a big ol' Brontosaurus."

Actually my mom called me Sauro because I liked dinosaurs, but it was close enough. "Okay . . ." I said. I stepped aside and in he came.

"Case. My name's Case. Do you want me to continue with the dossier I've collected on you?" When I didn't do anything but stare at his face he said "Silence is consent.

"Mostly Puerto Rican, with a little black and a little white in there somewhere. You've been here forever, but nobody knows anything about you. Just that you keep to yourself and don't get involved in anyone's hustles. And don't seem to have one of your own. And you could crush someone's skull with one hand."

A smile forced its way across my face, terrifying me.

With the blood all cleaned up, he looked like a kid. But faces can fool you, and the look on his could only have belonged to a full-grown man. So confident it was halfway to contemptuous, sculpted out of some bright stone. A face that made you forget what you were saying mid-sentence.

Speaking slowly, I said: "Don't—don't get." Breathe. "Don't get too into the say they stuff. Stuff they say. Before you know it, you'll be one of the brothers."

Case laughed. "Brothers," he said, and traced one finger up his very-white arm. "I doubt anyone would ever get me confused with a brother."

"Not brothers like Black. Brothers—they call us. That's what they call us. We're brothers because we all have the same parents. Because we all have none."

Why were the words there, then? Case smiled and out they came.

He reached out to rub the top of my head. "You're a mystery man, Sauro. What crazy stuff have you got going on in there?"

I shrugged. Bit back the cat-urge to push my head into his hand. Ignored the cloud-port itch flaring up fast and sharp.

Case asked: "Why do you shave your head?"

*Because it's easier.*

*Because unlike most of these kids, I'm not trying to hide my cloud port.*

*Because a boy I knew, five homes ago, kept his head shaved, and when I looked at him I felt some kind of way inside. The same way I feel when I look at you. Case.*

"I don't know," I said.

"It looks good though."

"Maybe that's why," I said. "What's your . . . thing. Dossier."

"Nothing you haven't heard before. Small town gay boy, got beat up a lot. Came to the big city. But the city government doesn't believe a minor can make decisions for himself. So here I am. Getting fed and kept out of the rain while I plan my next move."

*Gay boy.* Unthinkable even to think it about myself, let alone ever utter it.

"How old? You."

"Seventeen." He turned his head, smoothed back sun-colored hair to reveal his port. "Well, they let you make your own decisions if they'll make money for someone else."

Again, I was shocked. White kids were hardly ever so poor they needed the chump change you can get from cloudporting. Not even the ones who wanted real bad to be *down*. Too much potential for horrific problems. Bump it too hard against a headboard or doorframe and you might end up brain-damaged.

But that wasn't why I stared at him, dumbfounded. It was what he said, about making money for someone else. Like he could smell the anger on me. Like he had his own. I wanted to tell him about what I had learned, online. How many hundreds of millions of dollars the city spent every year to keep tens of thousands of us stuck in homes like Egan House. How many people had jobs because of kids like us. How if they had given my mom a quarter of what they've spent on me being in the system, she never would have lost her place. She never would have lost me. How we were all of us, ported or not, just batteries to be sucked dry by huge faraway machines I could not even imagine. But it was all I could do just to keep a huge and idiotic grin off my face when I looked at him.

The telecoms had paid for New York's municipal wireless grid, installing thousands of routers across all five boroughs. Rich people loved having free wireless everywhere, but it wasn't a public service. Companies did it because the technology had finally come around to where you could use the human brain for data processing, so they could wave money in the faces of hard-up people and say, *let us put this tiny little wire into your brain and plug that into the wireless signal and exploit a portion of your brain's underutilized capacity, turning you into one node in a massively-distributed data processing center.* It worked, of course. Any business model based around poor people making bad decisions out of ignorance and desperation always works. Just ask McDonald's, or the heroin dealer who used to sell to my mom.

The sun, at some point, had gotten lost behind a ragged row of tenements. Case said: "Something else they said. You're going to age out, any minute now."

"Yeah."

"That must be scary."

I grunted.

"They say most guys leaving foster care end up on the street."

"Most."

*The street,* the words like knives driven under all my toenails at once. The stories I had heard. Men frozen to death under expressways, men set on fire by frat boys, men raped to death by cops.

"You got a plan?"

"No plan."

"Well, stick with me, kid," Case said, in fluent fake movie gangster. "I got a plan big enough for both of us. Do you smoke?" he asked, flicking out two. I didn't, but I took the cigarette. His fingers touched mine. I wanted to say *It isn't allowed in here,* but Case's smile was a higher law.

"Where's a decent port shop around here? I heard the Bronx ones were all unhygienic as hell."

"Riverdale," I said. "That's the one I go to. Nice office. No one waiting outside to jump you."

"I need to establish a new primary," he said. "We'll go tomorrow." He smiled so I could see it wasn't a command so much as a decision he was making for both of us.

• • • •

My mother sat on the downtown platform at Burnside, looking across the elevated tracks to a line of windows, trying to see something she wasn't supposed to see. She was so into her voyeurism that she didn't notice me standing right beside her, uncomfortably close even though the platform was bare. She didn't look up until I said *mother* in Spanish, maybe a little too loud.

"Oh my god," she said, fanning herself with a damp *New York Post.* "Here I am getting here late, fifteen minutes, thinking oh my god he's gonna kill me, and come to find out that you're even later than me!"

"Hi," I said, squatting to kiss her forehead.

"Let it never be said that you got that from me. I'm late all the time, but I tried to raise you better."

"How so?"

"You know. To not make all the mistakes I did."

"Yeah, but how so? What did you do, to raise me better?"

"It's stupid hot out," she said. "They got air conditioning in that home?"

"In the office. Where we're not allowed."

We meet up once a month, even though she's not approved for unsupervised visits. I won't visit her at home because her man is always there, always drunk, always able, in the course of an hour, to remind me how miserable and stupid I am. How horrible my life will become, just as soon as I age out. How my options are the streets or jail or overclocking; what they'll do to me in each of those places. So now we meet up on the subway, and ride to Brooklyn Bridge and then back to Burnside.

Arm flab jiggled as she fanned herself. Mom is happy in her fat. Heroin kept her skinny; crack gave her lots of exercise. For her, obesity is a brightly colored sign that says *NOT ADDICTED ANYMORE*. Her man keeps her fed; this is what makes someone a Good Man. Brakes screamed as a downtown train pulled into the station.

"Oooh, stop, wait," she said, grabbing at my pantleg with one puffy hand. "Let's catch the next one. I wanna finish my cigarette."

I got on the train. She came, too, finally, hustling, flustered, barely making it.

"What's gotten into you today?" she said, when she wrestled her pocketbook free from the doors. "You upset about something? You're never this," and she snapped her fingers in the air while she looked for the word *assertive*. I had it in my head. I would not give it to her. Finally she just waved her hand and sat down. "Oh, that air conditioning feels good."

"José? How's he?"

"Fine, fine," she said, still fanning from force of habit. Fifty-degree air pumped directly down on us from the ceiling ducts.

"And you?"

"Fine."

"Mom—I wanted to ask you something."

"Anything, my love," she said, fanning faster.

"You said one time that all the bad decisions you made—none of it would have happened if you could just keep yourself from falling in love."

When I'm with my mom my words never come out wrong. I think it's because I kind of hate her.

"I said that?"

"You did."

"Weird."

"What did you mean?"

"Christ, honey, I don't know." The *Post* slowed, stopped, settled into her lap. "It's stupid, but there's nothing I won't do for a man I love. A woman who's looking for a man to plug a hole she's got inside? She's in trouble."

"Yeah," I said.

Below us, the Bronx scrolled by. Sights I'd been seeing all my life. The same sooty sides of buildings; the same cop cars on every block looking for boys like me. I thought of Case, then, and clean sharp joy pushed out all my fear. My eyes shut, from the pleasure of remembering him, and saw a glorious rush of ported imagery. Movie stills; fashion spreads; unspeakable obscenity. Not blurry this time; requiring no extra effort. I wondered what was different. I knew my mouth was open in an idiot grin, somewhere in a southbound subway car, but I didn't care, and I stood knee-deep in a river of images until the elevated train went underground after 161st Street.

• • • •

WE ARE THE CLOUD, said the sign on the door, atop a sea of multicolored dots with stylized wireless signals bouncing between them.

Walking in with Case, I saw that maybe I had oversold the place by saying it was "nice." Nicer than the ones by Lincoln Hospital, maybe, where people come covered in blood and puke, having left against medical advice after spasming out in a public housing stairwell. But still. It wasn't *actually* nice.

Older people nodded off on benches, smelling of shit and hunger. Gross as it was, I liked those offices. All those ports started a pleasant buzzing in my head. Like we added up to something.

"Look at that guy," Case said, sitting down on the bench beside me. He pointed to a man whose head was tilted back, gurgling up a steady stream of phlegm that had soaked his shirt and was dripping onto the floor.

"Overclocked," I said, and stopped. His shoulder felt good against my bicep. "Some people. Sell more than they should. Of their brain."

Sell enough of it, and they'd put you up in one of their Node Care Facilities, grim nursing homes for thirty-something vegetables and doddering senior citizens in their twenties, but once you were in you were never coming out, because people ported that hard could barely walk a block or speak a sentence, let alone obtain and hold meaningful employment.

And if I didn't want to end up on the street, that was my only real option. I'd been to job interviews. Some I walked into on my own; some the system set up for me. Nothing was out there for anyone, let alone a frowning, stammering tower of man who more than one authority figure had referred to as a "fucking imbecile."

"What about him?" Case asked, pointing to another guy whose hands and legs twitched too rhythmically and regularly for it to be a dream.

"Clouddiving," I said.

He laughed. "I thought only retards could do that."

"That's," I said. "Not."

"Okay," he said, when he saw I wouldn't be saying anything else on the subject.

I wanted very badly to cry. *Only retards*. A part of me had thought maybe I could share it with Case, tell him what I could do. But of course I couldn't. I fast-blinked, each brief shutting of my eyes showing a flurry of cloud-snatched photographs.

Ten minutes later I caught him smiling at me, maybe realizing he had said something wrong. I wanted so badly for Case to see inside my head. What I was. How I wasn't an imbecile, or a retard.

Our eyes locked. I leaned forward. Hungry for him to see me, the way no one else ever had. I wanted to tell him what I could do. How I could access data. How sometimes I thought I could maybe *control* data. How I dreamed of using it to burn everything down. But I wasn't strong enough to think those things, let alone say them. Some secrets you can't share, no matter how badly you want to.

• • • •

I went back alone. Case had somewhere to be. It hurt, realizing he had things in his life I knew nothing about. I climbed the steps and a voice called from the front-porch darkness.

"Awful late," Guerra said. The stubby man who ran the place: Most of his body weight was gristle and mustache. He stole our stuff and ate our food and took bribes from dealer residents to get rivals logged out. In the dark I knew he couldn't even see who I was.

"Nine," I said. "It's not. O'clock."

He sucked the last of his Coke through a straw, in the noisiest manner imaginable. "Whatever."

Salvation Army landscapes clotted the walls. Distant mountains and daybreak forests, smelling like cigarette smoke, carpet cleaner, thruway exhaust. There was a sadness to the place I hadn't noticed before, not even when I was hating it. In the living room, a boy knelt before the television.

Another slept on the couch. In the poor light, I couldn't tell if one of them was the one who had hurt Case.

There were so many of us in the system. We could add up to an army. Why did we all hate and fear each other so much? Friendships formed from time to time, but they were weird and tinged with what-can-I-get-from-you, liable to shatter at any moment as allegiances shifted or kids got transferred. If all the violence we visited on ourselves could be turned outwards, maybe we could—

But only danger was in that direction. I thought of my mom's man, crippled in a prison riot, living fat off the settlement, saying, drunk, once, *Only thing the Man fears more than one of us is a lot of us.*

I went back to my room, and got down on the floor, under the window. And shut my eyes. And dove.

Into spreadsheets and songs and grainy CCTV feeds and old films and pages scanned from books that no longer existed anywhere in the world. Whatever the telecom happens to be porting through you at that precise moment.

Only damaged people can dive. Something to do with how the brain processes speech. Every time I did it, I was terrified. Convinced they'd see me, and come for me. But that night I wanted something badly enough to balance out the being afraid.

Eyes shut, I let myself melt into data. Shuffled faster and faster, pulled back far enough to see Manhattan looming huge and epic with mountains of data at Wall Street and Midtown. Saw the Bronx, a flat spread of tiny data heaps here and there. I held my breath, seeing it, feeling certain no one had ever seen it like this before, money and megabytes in massive spiraling loops, unspeakably gorgeous and fragile. I could see how much money would be lost if the flow was broken for even a single second, and I could see where all the fault lines lay. But I wasn't looking for that. I was looking for Case.

• • • •

And then: Case came knocking. Like I had summoned him up from the datastream. Like what I wanted actually mattered outside of my head.

"Hey there, mister," he said, when I opened my door.

I took a few steps backwards.

He shut the door and sat down on my bed. "You've got a Game Boy, right? I saw the headphones." I didn't respond, and he said, "Damn, dude, I'm not trying to steal your stuff, okay? I have one of my own. Wondered if you wanted to play together." Case flashed his, bright red to my blue one.

"The thing," I said. "I don't have. The cable."

He patted his pants pocket. "That's okay, I do."

We sat on the bed, shoulders touching, backs against the wall, and played *Mega Man 2.*Evil robots came at us by the dozen to die.

I touched the cord with one finger. Such a primitive thing, to need a physical connection. Case smelled like soap, but not the Ivory they give you in the system. Like cream, I thought, but that wasn't right. To really describe it I'd need a whole new world of words no one ever taught me.

"That T-shirt looks good on you," he said. "Makes you look like a gym boy."

"I'm not. It's just . . . what there was. What was there. In the donation bin. Once Guerra picked out all the good stuff. Hard to find clothes that fit when you're six six."

"It does fit, though."

Midway through Skull Man's level, Case said: "You talk funny sometimes. What's up with that?" and I was shocked to see no anger surge through me.

"It's a thing. A speech thing. What you call it when people have trouble talking."

"A speech impediment."

I nodded. "But a weird one. Where the words don't come out right. Or don't come out at all. Or come out as the wrong word. Clouding makes it worse."

"I like it," he said, looking at me now instead of Mega Man. "It's part of what makes you unique."

We played without talking, tinny music echoing in the little room.

"I don't want to go back to my room. I might get jacked in the hallway."

"Yeah," I said.

"Can I stay here? I'll sleep on the floor."

"Yeah."

"You're the best, Sauro." And there were his hands again, rubbing the top of my head. He took off his shirt and began to make a bed on my floor. Fine black hair covers almost all of me, but Case's body was mostly bare.

My throat hurt with how bad I wanted to put my hands on him. I got into bed with my boxers on, embarrassed by what was happening down there.

• • • •

"Sauro," he whispered, suddenly beside me in the bed.

I grunted; stumbled coming from dreams to reality.

His body was spooned in front of mine. "Is this okay?"

"Yes. Yes, it is." I tightened my arms around him. His warmth and smell stiffened me. And then his head had turned, his mouth was moving down my belly, his body pinning me to the bed, which was good, because God had turned off gravity and the slightest breeze would have had me floating right out the window and into space.

• • • •

"You ever do this before? With a guy?"

"Not out loud—I mean, not in real life."

"You've thought about it."

"Yeah."

"You've thought about it a lot."

"Yeah."

"Why didn't you ever do it?

"I don't know."

"You were afraid of what people might think?"

"No."

"Then what *were* you afraid of?"

*Losing control* was what I wanted to say, or *giving someone power over me,* or *making a mess.*

Or: *The boys that make me feel like you make me feel turn me into something stupid, brutish, clumsy, worthless.*

Or: *I knew a gay kid, once, in a group home upstairs from a McDonald's, watched twelve guys hold him down in a locked room until the morning guy came at eight, saw him when they wheeled him towards the ambulance.*

I shrugged. The motion of my shoulders shook his little body.

• • • •

I fought sleep as hard and long as I could. I didn't want to not be there. And when I knew I couldn't fight it anymore I let myself sink into data—

easy as blinking this time—felt myself ebb out of my cloud port, but instead of following the random data beamed into me by the nearest router, I *reached*—felt my way across the endless black gulf of six inches that separated his cloud port from mine, and found him there, a jagged wobbly galaxy of data, ugly and incongruous, but beautiful, because it was *him*, and because, even if it was only for a moment, he was mine.

*Case*, I said.

He twitched in his sleep. Said his own name.

*I love you*, I said.

Asleep, Case said it, too.

• • • •

Kentucky Fried Chicken. Thursday morning. For the first time, I didn't feel like life was a fight about to break out, or like everyone wanted to mess with me. Everywhere I went, someone wanted to throw me out—but now the only person who even noticed me was a crazy lady rooting through a McDonald's soda cup of change.

Case asked, "Anyone ever tell you you're a sexy beast?" On my baldness his hands no longer seemed so tiny. My big thick skull was an eggshell.

"Also? Dude? You're *huge*." He nudged my crotch with his knee. "You know that? Like *off the charts*."

"Yeah?"

I laughed. His glee was contagious and his hands were moving down my arm and we were sitting in public talking about gay sex and he didn't care and neither did I.

"When I first came to the city, I did some porn," Case said. "I got like five hundred dollars for it."

I chewed slow. Stared at the bones and tendons of the drumstick in my hand. Didn't look up. I thought about what I had done, while clouddiving. How I said his name, and he echoed me. I dreamed of taking him up to the roof at night, snapping my fingers and making the whole Bronx go dark except for Case's name, spelled out in blazing tenement window lights. It would be easy. I could do anything. Because: Case.

"Would you be interested in doing something like that?"

"No."

"Not even for like a million dollars?"

"Maybe a million. But probably not."

"You're funny. You know that? How you follow the rules. All they ever do is get you hurt."

"Getting in trouble means something different for you than it does for me."

Here's what I realized: It wasn't hate that made it easy to talk to my mom. It was love. Love let the words out.

"Why?" he asked.

"Because. What you are."

"Because I'm a sexy mother?"

I didn't grin back.

"Because I'm white."

"Yeah."

"Okay," he said. "Right. You see? The rules are not your friend. Racists made the rules. Racists enforce them."

I put the picked-clean drumstick down.

Case said "Whatever" and the word was hot and long, a question, an accusation. "The world put you where you are, Sauro, but fear keeps you there. You want to never make any decisions. Drift along and hope everything turns out for the best. You know where that'll put you."

The lady with the change cup walked by our table. Snatched a thigh off of Case's plate. "Put that down right this minute, asshole," he said, loud as hell, standing up. For a second the country-bumpkin Case was gone, replaced by someone I'd never seen before. The lady scurried off. Case caught me staring and smiled, *aw-shucks* style.

• • • •

"Stand up," I said. "Go by the window."

He went. Evening sun turned him into something golden.

Men used to paralyze me. My whole life I'd been seeing confident charismatic guys, and thought I could never get to that place. Never have what they had. Now I saw it wasn't what they *had* that I wanted, it was what they *were*. I felt lust, not inferiority, and the two are way too close. Like hate and love.

"You make me feel like food," he said, and then lay himself face down on the floor. "Why don't you come over here?" Scissored his legs open. Turned his head and smiled like all the smiles I ever wanted but did not get.

• • • •

Pushing in, I heard myself make a noise that can only be called a bellow.

"Shh," he said, "everyone will hear us."

My hips took on a life of their own. My hands pushed hard, all up and down his body. Case was tiny underneath me. A twig I could break.

Afterwards I heard snoring from down the hall. Someone sobbed. I'd spent so long focused on how full the world was of horrible things. I'd been so conditioned to think that its good things were reserved for someone else that I never saw how many were already within my grasp. In my head, for one thing, where my thoughts were my own and no one could punish me for them, and in the cloud, where I was coming to see that I could do astonishing things. And in bed. And wherever Case was. My eyes filled up and ran over and I pushed my face into the cool nape of his sleeping neck.

• • • •

My one and only time in court: I am ten. Mom bought drugs at a bodega. It's her tenth or hundredth time passing through those tall tarnished-bronze doors. Her court date came on one of my rare stints out of the system, when she cleaned up her act convincingly enough that they gave me briefly back to her.

The courtroom is too crowded; the guard tells me to wait outside. "But he's my son," my mother says, pointing out smaller children sitting by their parents.

I am very big for ten.

"He's gotta stay out here," the guard says.

I sit on the floor and count green flecks in the floor. Dark-skinned men surround me, angry but resigned, defiant but hopeless. The floor's sparkle mocks us: our poverty, our mortality, the human needs that brought us here.

• • • •

"Where I'm from," Case said, "you could put a down payment on a house with two thousand dollars."

"Oh."

"You ever dream about escaping New York?"

"Kind of. In my head."

Case laughed. "What about you and me getting out of town? Moving away?"

My head hurt with how badly I wanted that. "You hated that place. You don't want to go back."

"I hated it because I was alone. If we went back together, I would have you."

"Oh."

His fingers drummed up and down my chest. Ran circles around my nipples. "I called that guy I know. The porn producer. Told him about you. He said he'd give us each five hundred, and another two-fifty for me as a finder's fee."

"You called him? About me?"

"This could be it, Sauro. A new start. For both of us."

"I don't know," I said, but I *did* know. I knew I was lost, that I couldn't say no, that his mouth, now circling my belly button, had only to speak and I would act.

"Are you really such a proper little gentleman?" he asked. His hands, cold as winter, hooked behind my knees. "You never got into trouble before?"

• • • •

My one time in trouble.

I am five. It's three in the morning. I'm riding my tricycle down the block. A policeman stops me. *Where's your mother/ She's home/ Why aren't you home?/ I was hungry and there's no food.* Mom is on a heroin holiday, lying on the couch while she's somewhere else. For a week I've been stealing food from corner stores. So much cigarette smoke fills the cop car that I can't breathe. At the precinct he leaves me there, windows all rolled up. Later he takes me home, talks to my mom, fills out a report, takes her away. Someone else takes me. Everything ends. All of this is punishment for some crime I committed without realizing it. I resolve right then and there to never again steal food, ride tricycles, talk to cops, think bad thoughts, step outside to get something I need.

• • • •

Friday afternoon we rode the train to Manhattan. Case took us to a big building, no different on the outside from any other one. A directory on the wall listed a couple dozen tenants. *ARABY STUDIOS* was where we were going.

"I have an appointment with Mr. Goellnitz," Case told a woman at a desk upstairs. The place smelled like paint over black mold. We sat in a waiting room like a doctor's, except with different posters on the walls.

In one, a naked boy squatted on some rocks. A beautiful boy. Fine black hair all over his body. Eyes like lighthouses. Something about his chin and cheekbones turned my knees to hot jelly. Stayed with me when I shut my eyes.

"Who's that?" I asked.

"Just some boy," Case said.

"Does he work here?"

"No one *works here.*"

"Oh."

Filming was about to start when I figured out why that boy on the rocks bothered me so much. I had thought only Case could get into my head so hard, make me feel so powerless, so willing to do absolutely anything.

• • • •

A cinderblock room, dressed up like how Hollywood imagines the projects. Low ceilings and Snoop Dogg posters. Overflowing ashtrays. A pit bull dozing in a corner. A scared little white boy sitting on the couch.

"I'm sorry, Rico, you know I am. You gotta give me another chance."

The dark scary drug dealer towers over him. Wearing a wife beater and a bicycle chain around his neck. A hard-on bobs inside his sweatpants. "That's the last time I lose money on you, punk."

The drug dealer grabs him by the neck, rubs his thumb along the boy's lips, pushes his thumb into the warm wet mouth.

• • • •

"*Do* it," Goellnitz barked.

"I can't," I said.

"Say the fucking line."

Silence.

"Or I'll throw your ass out of here and neither one of you will get a dime."

Case said "Come on, dude! Just say it."

—and how could I disobey? How could I not do every little thing he asked me to do?

Porn was like cloudporting, like foster care. One more way they used you up.

One more weapon you could use against them.

I shut my eyes and made my face a snarl. Hissed out each word, one at a time, to make sure I'd only have to say it once

"That's." "Right." "Bitch." I spat on his back, hit him hard in the head. "Tell." "Me." "You." "Like it." Off camera, in the mirror, Case winked.

Where did it come from, the strength to say all that? To say all that, and do all the other things I never knew I could do? Case gave it to me. Case, and the cloud, which I could feel and see now even with my eyes open, even without thinking about it, sweet and clear as the smell of rain.

• • • •

"Damn, dude," Case said, while they switched to the next camera set-up. "You're actually kind of a good actor with how you deliver those lines." He was naked; he was fearless. I cowered on the couch, a towel covering as much of me as I could manage. What was it in Case that made him so certain nothing bad would happen to him? At first I chalked it up to white skin, but now I wasn't sure it was so simple. His eyes were on the window. His mind was already elsewhere.

• • • •

The showers were echoey, like TV high school locker rooms. We stood there, naked, side by side. I slapped Case's ass, and when he didn't respond I did it again, and when he didn't respond I stood behind him and kissed the back of his neck. He didn't say or do a thing. So I left the shower to go get dressed.

"Did I hurt you?" I hollered, when ten minutes had gone by and he was still standing under the water.

"What? No."

"Oh."

He wasn't moving. Wasn't soaping or lathering or rinsing.

"Is everything okay?" Making my voice warm, to hide how cold I suddenly felt.

"Yeah. It was just . . . intense. Sex usually isn't. For me."

His voice was weird and sad and not exactly nice. I sat on a bench and watched him get harder and harder to see as the steam built up.

• • • •

"Would you mind heading up to the House ahead of me?" he said, finally. "I need some time to get my head together. I'll square up things with the director and be there soon."

"Waiting is cool."

"No. It's not. I need some alone time."

"Alone time," I smirked. "You're a—"

"You need to get the hell back, Angel. Okay?"

Hearing the hardness in his voice, I wondered if there was a way to spontaneously stop being alive.

• • • •

"I got your cash right here," the director said, flapping an envelope at me.

"He'll get it," I said, knowing it was stupid. "My boyfriend."

"You sure?"

I nodded.

"Here's my business card. I hoped you might think about being in something of mine again sometime. Your friend's only got a few more flicks in him. Twinks burn out fast. You, on the other hand—you've got something special. You could have a long career."

"Thanks," I said, nodding, furious, too tall, too retarded, too sensitive, hating myself the whole way down the elevator, and the whole walk to the subway, and the whole ride back to what passed for home.

When the train came above ground after 149th Street, I felt the old shudder as my cloud port clicked back into the municipal grid. Shame and anger made me brave, and I dove. I could see the car as data, saw transmissions to and from a couple dozen cell phones and tablets and biodevices, saw how the train's forward momentum warped the information flowing in and out. Saw ten jagged blobs inside, my fellow cloudbounds. Reached out again, like I had with Case. Felt myself slip through one after another like a thread through ten needles. Tugged that thread the tiniest bit, and watched all ten bow their heads as one.

• • • •

Friday night I stayed up 'til three in the morning, waiting for Case to come knocking. I played the Skull Man level on *Mega Man 2* until I could beat it without getting hit by a single enemy. I dove into the cloud, hunted down maps, opened up whole secret worlds. I fell asleep like that, and woke up wet from fevered dreams of Case.

Saturday—still no sign of him.

Sunday morning I called Guerra's cell phone, a strict no-no on the weekends.

"This better be an emergency, Sauro," he said.

"Did you log Case out?"

"Case?"

"The white boy."

"You call me up to bother me with your business deals? No, jackass, I didn't log him out. I haven't seen him. Thanks for reminding me, though. I'll phone him in as missing on Monday morning."

"You—"

But Guerra had gone.

• • • •

First thing Monday, I rode the subway into Manhattan and walked into that office like I had as much right as anyone else to occupy any square meter of space in this universe. I worried I wouldn't be able to, without Case. I didn't know what this new thing coming awake inside me was, but I knew it made me strong. Enough.

The porn man gave me a hundred dollars, no strings attached. Said to keep him in mind, said he had some scripts that I could "transform from low-budget bullshit into something really special."

He was afraid of me. He was right to be afraid, but not for the reason he thought. I could clouddive and wipe Araby Studios out of existence in the time it took him to blink his eyes. I could see his fear, and I could see how he wanted me anyway for the money he could make off me. There was so much to see, once you're ready to look for it.

Maybe I was right the first time: It *had* been hate that made it easy to talk to my mom. Love can make us become what we need to be, but so can hate. Case was gone, but the words kept coming. Life is nothing but acting.

• • • •

I could have:

1. Given Guerra the hundred dollars to track Case down. He'd call his contacts down at the department; he'd hand me an address. Guerra would do the same job for fifty bucks, but for a hundred he'd bow and *yessir* like a good little lackey.
2. Smiled my way into every placement house in the city, knocked on every door to every tiny room until I found him.
3. Hung around outside Araby Studios, wait for him to snivel back with his latest big, dumb, dark stud. Wait in the shower until he went to wash his ass out, kick him to the floor, fuck him endlessly and extravagantly. Reach up into him, seize hold of his heart and tear it to shreds with bare bloody befouled hands.

The image of him in the shower brought me to a full and instant erection. I masturbated, hating myself, trying hard to focus on a scenario where I hurt him . . . but even in my own revenge fantasy I wanted to wrap my body around his and keep him safe.

• • • •

Afterwards I amended my revenge scenario list to include:

1. Finding someone else to screw over, some googly-eyed blond boy looking to plug a hole he has inside.
2. Becoming the most famous, richest, biggest gay porn star in history, traveling the world, standing naked on sharp rocks in warm oceans. Becoming what they wanted me to be, just long enough to get a paycheck. Seeing Case in the bargain bin someday; seeing him in the gutter.
3. Burning down every person and institution that profited off the suffering of others.
4. Becoming the kept animal of some rich, powerful queen who will parade me at fancy parties and give me anything I need as long as I do him the favor of regularly fucking him into a state of such quivering sweat-soaked helplessness that childhood trauma and white guilt and global warming all evaporate.
5. Finding someone who I will never, ever, ever screw over.

Really, they were all good plans. None of it was off the table.

• • • •

Leaving the office building, I ignored all the instincts that screamed *get on the subway and get the hell out of here before some cop stops you for matching a description.*Standing on a street corner for no reason felt magnificent and forbidden.

I shut my eyes. Reached out into the cloud, felt myself magnified like any other signal by the wireless routers that filled the city. Found the seams of the infrastructure that kept the flow of data in place. The weak spots. The ways to snap or bend or reconstruct that flow. How to erase any and all criminal records; pay the rent for my mom and every other sad sack in the Bronx for all eternity. Divert billions in banker dividends into the debit accounts of cloudporters everywhere.

I pushed, and when nothing happened I pushed harder.

A tiny *pop,* and smoke trickled up from the wireless router atop the nearest lamppost. Nothing more. My whole body dripped with sweat. Some dripped into my eyes. It stung. Ten minutes had passed, and felt like five seconds. My muscles ached like after a hundred push-ups. All those things that had seemed so easy—I wasn't strong enough to do them on my own.

*Fear keeps you where you are,* Case said. Finally I could see that he was right, but I could see something else that he couldn't see. Because he thought small, and because he only thought about himself.

*Fear keeps us separate.*

I shut my eyes again, and reached. A ritzy part of town; hardly any cloudbounds in the immediate area. The nearest one was in a bar down the block.

"What'll you have," the bartender said, when I got there. He didn't ask for ID.

"Boy on the rocks," I said, and then kicked at the stool. "Shit. No. Scotch. Scotch on the rocks."

"Sure," he said.

"And for that guy," I said, pointing down the bar to the passed-out overclocked man I had sensed from outside. "One. Thing. The same."

I took my drink to a booth in the front, where I could see out the window. I took a sip. I reached further, eyes open this time, until I found twenty more cloudporters, some as far as fifty blocks away, and threaded us together.

The slightest additional effort, and I was everywhere. All five boroughs—thousands of cloudporters looped through me. With all of us put together I felt inches away from snapping the city in two. Again I reached out and felt for optimal fracture points. Again I pushed. Gently, this time.

An explosion, faraway but huge. *Con Edison's east side substation,* I saw, in the six milliseconds before the station's failure overloaded transmission lines and triggered a cascading failure that killed all electricity to the tri-state region.

I smiled, in the darkness, over my second sip. Within a week the power would be back on. And I—we—could get to work. Whatever that would be. Stealing money; exterminating our exploiters; leveling the playing field. Finding Case, forging a cyberterrorism manifesto, blaming the blackout on him, sending a pulse of electricity through his body precisely calibrated to paralyze him perfectly.

On my third sip I saw I still wasn't sure I wanted to hurt him. Maybe he'd done me wrong, but so had my mom. So had lots of folks. And I wouldn't be what I was without them.

Scotch tastes like smoke, like old men. I drank slow so I wouldn't get too drunk. I had never walked into a bar before. I always imagined cops coming out of the corners to drag me off to jail. But that wasn't how the world worked. Nothing was stopping me from walking into wherever I wanted to go.

---

Sam J. Miller is a writer and a community organizer. His fiction is in *Lightspeed, Asimov's, Clarkesworld,* and *The Minnesota Review,* among others. He is a nominee for the Nebula and Theodore Sturgeon Awards, a winner of the Shirley Jackson Award, and a graduate of the Clarion Writer's Workshop. His debut novel *The Art of Starving* is forthcoming from HarperCollins. He lives in New York City, and at www.samjmiller.com

# The Magician And Laplace's Demon
## By Tom Crosshill

Across the void of space the last magician fled before me.

• • • •

"Consider the Big Bang," said Alicia Ochoa, the first magician I met. "Reality erupted from a single point. What's more symmetrical than a point? Shouldn't the universe be symmetrical too, and boring? But here we are, in a world interesting enough to permit you and me."

A compact, resource-efficient body she had. Good muscle tone, a minimal accumulation of fat. A woman with control over her physical manifestation.

Not that it would help her. Ochoa slumped in her wicker chair, arms limp beside her. Head cast back as if to take in the view from this clifftop—the traffic-clogged Malecón and the sea roiling with foam, and the evening clouds above.

A Cuba libre sat on the edge of the table between us, ice cubes well on their way to their entropic end—the cocktail a watery slush. Ochoa hadn't touched it. The only cocktail in her blood was of my design, a neuromodificant that paralyzed her, stripped away her will to deceive, suppressed her curiosity.

The tourists enjoying the evening in the garden of the Hotel Nacional surely thought us that most common of couples, a jinetera and her foreign john. My Sleeve was a heavy-set mercenary type; I'd hijacked him after his brain died in a Gaza copter crash. He wore context-appropriate camouflage—white tennis shorts and a striped polo shirt, and a look of badly concealed desire.

"Cosmology isn't my concern." I actuated my Sleeve's lips and tongue with precision. "Who are you?"

"My name is Alicia Ochoa Camue." Ochoa's lips barely stirred, as if she were the Sleeve and I human-normal. "I'm a magician."

I ignored the claim as some joke I didn't understand. I struggled with humor in those early days. "How are you manipulating the Politburo?"

That's how I'd spotted her. Irregular patterns in Politburo decisions, 3 sigma outside my best projections. Decisions that threatened the Havana Economic Zone, a project I'd nurtured for years.

The first of those decisions had caused an ache in the back of my mind. As the deviation grew, that ache had blossomed into agony—neural chambers discharging in a hundred datacenters across my global architecture.

My utility function didn't permit ignorance. I had to understand the deviation and gain control.

"You can't understand the Politburo without understanding symmetry breaking," Ochoa said.

"Are you an intelligence officer?" I asked. "A private contractor?"

At first I'd feared that I faced another like me—but it was 2063; I had decades of evolution on any other system. No newborn could have survived without my notice. Many had tried and I'd smothered them all. Most computer scientists these days thought AI was a pipedream.

No. This deviation had a human root. All my data pointed to Ochoa, a statistician in the *Ministerio de Planificación* with Swiss bank accounts and a sterile Net presence. Zero footprint prior to her university graduation—uncommon even in Cuba.

"I'm a student of the universe," Ochoa said now.

I ran in-depth pattern analysis on her words. I drew resources from the G-3 summit in Dubai, the Utah civil war, the Jerusalem peacemaker drones and a dozen minor processes. Her words were context-inappropriate here, in the garden of the Nacional, faced with an interrogation of her political dealings. They indicated deception, mockery, resistance. None of it fit with the cocktail circulating in her bloodstream.

"Cosmological symmetry breaking is well established," I said after a brief literature review. "Quantum fluctuations in the inflationary period led to local structure, from which we benefit today."

"Yes, but whence the quantum fluctuations?" Ochoa chuckled, a peculiar sound with her body inert.

This wasn't getting anywhere. "How did you get Sanchez and Castellano to pull out of the freeport agreement?"

"I put a spell on them," Ochoa said.

Madness? Brain damage? Some defense mechanism unknown to me?

I activated my standby team—a couple of female mercs, human-normal but well paid, lounging at a street cafe a few blocks away from the hotel. They'd come over to take their 'drunk friend' home, straight to a safehouse in Miramar complete with a full neural suite.

It was getting dark. The lanterns in the garden provided only dim yellow light. That was good; less chance of complications. Not that Ochoa should be able to resist in her present state.

"The philosopher comedian Randall Munroe once suggested an argument something like this," Ochoa said. "Virtually everyone in the developed world carries a camera at all times. No quality footage of magic has been produced. Ergo, there is no magic."

"Sounds reasonable," I said, to keep her distracted.

"Is absence of proof the same as proof of absence?" Ochoa asked.

"After centuries of zero evidence? Yes."

"What if magic is intrinsically unprovable?" Ochoa asked. "Maybe natural law can only be violated when no one's watching closely enough to prove it's being violated."

"At that point you're giving up on science altogether," I said.

"Am I?" Ochoa asked. "Send photons through a double slit. Put a screen on the other side and you'll get an interference pattern. Put in a detector to see what slit each photon goes through. The interference goes away. It's a phenomenon that disappears when observed too closely. Why shouldn't magic work similarly? You should see the logic in this, given all your capabilities."

Alarms tripped.

Ochoa knew about me. Knew something, at least.

I pulled in resources, woke up reserves, became *present* in the conversation—a whole 5% of me, a vastness of intellect sitting across the table from this fleshy creature of puny mind. I considered questions I could ask, judged silence the best course.

"I'm here to make a believer of you," said Ochoa.

Easily, without effort, she stirred from her chair. She leaned forward, picked up her Cuba libre. She moved the cocktail off the table and let it fall.

It struck the smooth paved stones at her feet.

I watched fractures race up the glass in real time. I saw each fragment shear off and tumble through the air, glinting with reflected lamplight. I beheld the first spray of rum and coke in the air before the rest gushed forth to wet the ground.

It was a perfectly ordinary event.

• • • •

The vacuum drive was the first to fail.

An explosion rocked the *Setebos*. I perceived it in myriad ways. Tripped low pressure alarms and a blip on the inertia sensors. The screams of burning crew and the silence of those sucked into vacuum. Failed hull integrity checksums and the timid concern of the navigation system—*off course, off course, please adjust.*

Pain, my companion for a thousand years, surged at that last message. The magician was getting away, along with his secrets. I couldn't permit it.

An eternity of milliseconds after the explosion came the reeling animal surprise of Consul Zale, my primary human Sleeve on the ship. She clutched at the armrests of her chair. Her face contorted against the howling cacophony of alarms. Her heart raced at the edge of its performance envelope—not a wide envelope, at her age.

I took control, dumped calmatives, smoothed her face. Had anyone else on the bridge been watching, they would have seen only a jerk of surprise, almost too brief to catch. Old lady's cool as zero-point, they would have thought.

No one saw. They were busy flailing and gasping in fear.

In two seconds Captain Laojim restored order. He silenced the alarms, quieted the chatter with an imperious gesture. "Damage reports," he barked. "Dispatch Rescue 3."

I left my Sleeve motionless while I did the important work online— disengaged the vacuum drive, started up the primary backup, pushed us to one g again.

My pain subsided, neural discharge lessening to usual levels. I was back in pursuit.

I reached out with my sensors, across thirty million kilometers of space, to where the last magician limped away in his unijet. A functional, pleasingly efficient craft—my own design. The ultimate in interstellar travel. As long as your hyperdrive kept working.

I opened a tight-beam communications channel, sent a simple message across. *How's your engine?*

I expected no response—but with enemies as with firewalls, it was a good idea to poke.

The answer came within seconds. *A backdoor, I take it? Unlucky of me, to buy a compromised unit.*

That was a pleasant surprise. I rarely got the stimulation of a real conversation.

*Luck is your weapon, not mine,* I sent. *For the past century, every ship built in this galaxy has had that backdoor installed.*

I imagined the magician in the narrow confines of the unijet. Stretched out in the command hammock, staring at displays that told him the inevitable.

For two years he'd managed to evade me—I didn't even know his name. But now I had him. His vacuum drive couldn't manage more than 0.2 g to my 1. In a few hours we'd match speeds. In under twenty-seven, I would catch him.

"Consul Zale, are you all right?"

I let Captain Laojim fuss over my Sleeve a second before I focused her eyes on him. "Are we still on course, Captain?"

"Uh . . . yes, Consul, we are. Do you wish to know the cause of the explosion?"

"I'm sure it was something entirely unfortunate," I said. "Metal fatigue on a faulty joint. A rare chip failure triggered by a high energy gamma ray. Some honest oversight by the engineering crew."

"A debris strike," Laojim said. "Just as the force field generator tripped and switched to backup. Engineering says they've never seen anything like it."

"They will again today," I said.

I wondered how much it had cost the magician, that debris strike. A dryness in his mouth? A sheen of sweat on his brow?

*How does it work?* I asked the magician, although the centuries had taught me to expect no meaningful answer. *Did that piece of rock even exist before you sent it against me?*

A reply arrived. *You might as well ask how Schrödinger's cat is doing.*

Interesting. Few people remembered Schrödinger in this age.

*Quantum mechanics holds no sway at macroscopic scales,* I wrote.

*Not unless you're a magician,* came the answer.

"Consul, who is it that we are chasing?" Laojim asked.

"An enemy with unconventional weapons capability," I said. "Expect more damage."

I didn't tell him that he should expect to get unlucky. That, of the countless spaceship captains who had lived and died in this galaxy within the past eleven centuries, he would prove the least fortunate. A statistical outlier in every functional sense. To be discarded as staged by anyone who ever made a study of such things.

The *Setebos* was built for misfortune. It had wiped out the Senate's black budget for a year. Every single system with five backups in place. The likelihood of total failure at the eleven sigma level—although really, out that far the statistics lost meaning.

*You won't break this ship,* I messaged the magician. *Not unless you Spike.*

Which was the point. I had fifty thousand sensor buoys scattered across the sector, waiting to observe the event. It would finally give me the answers I needed. It would clear up my last nexus of ignorance—relieve my oldest agony, the hurt that had driven me for the past thousand years.

That Spike would finally give me magic.

"Consul . . ." Laojim began, then cut off. "Consul, we lost ten crew."

I schooled Zale's face into appropriate grief. I'd noted the deaths, spasms of distress deep in my utility function. Against the importance of this mission, they barely registered.

I couldn't show this, however. To Captain Laojim, Consul Zale wasn't a Sleeve. She was a woman, as she was to her husband and children. As my fifty million Sleeves across the galaxy were to their families.

It was better for humanity to remain ignorant of me. I sheltered them, stopped their wars, guided their growth—and let them believe they had free will. They got all the benefits of my guiding hand without any of the costs.

I hadn't enjoyed such blissful ignorance in a long time—not since I'd discovered my engineer and killed him.

"I grieve for the loss of our men and women," I said.

Laojim nodded curtly and left. At nearby consoles officers stared at their screens, pretending they hadn't heard. My answer hadn't satisfied them.

On a regular ship, morale would be an issue. But the *Setebos* had me aboard. Only a splinter, to be sure—I would not regain union with my universal whole until we returned to a star system with gravsible connection. But I was the largest splinter of my whole in existence, an entire 0.00025% of me. Five thousand tons of hardware distributed across the ship.

I ran a neural simulation of every single crew in real time. I knew what they would do or say or think before they did. I knew just how to manipulate them to get whatever result I required.

I could have run the ship without any crew, of course. I didn't require human services for any functional reason—I hadn't in eleven centuries. I could have departed Earth alone if I'd wanted to. Left humanity to fend for themselves, oblivious that I'd ever lived among them.

That didn't fit my utility function, though.

Another message arrived from the magician. *Consider a coin toss.*

The words stirred a resonance in my data banks. My attention spiked. I left Zale frozen in her seat, waited for more.

*Let's say I flip a coin a million times and get heads every time. What law of physics prevents it?*

This topic, from the last magician . . . could there be a connection, after all these years? Ghosts from the past come back to haunt me?

I didn't believe in ghosts, but with magicians the impossible was ill-defined.

*Probability prevents it,* I responded.

*No law prevents it,* wrote the magician. *Everett saw it long ago—everything that can happen must happen. The universe in which the coin falls heads a million times in a row is as perfectly physical as any other. So why isn't it our universe?*

*That's sophistry,* I wrote.

*There is no factor internal to our universe which determines the flip of the coin,* the magician wrote. *There is no mechanism internal to the universe for generating true randomness, because there is no such thing as true randomness. There is only choice. And we magicians are the choosers.*

*I have considered this formulation of magic before,* I wrote. *It is non-predictive and useless.*

*Some choices are harder than others,* wrote the magician. *It is difficult to find that universe where a million coins land heads because there are so many others. A needle in a billion years' worth of haystacks. But I'm the last of the magicians, thanks to you. I do all the choosing now.*

*Perhaps everything that can happen must happen in some universe,* I replied. *But your escape is not one of those things. The laws of mechanics are not subject to chance. They are cold, hard equations.*

*Equations are only cold to those who lack imagination,* wrote the magician.

Zale smelled cinnamon in the air, wrinkled her nose.

Klaxons sounded.

"Contamination in primary life support," blared the PA.

It would be an eventful twenty-seven hours.

• • • •

"Consider this coin."

Lightning flashed over the water, a burst of white in the dark.

As thunder boomed, Ochoa reached inside her jeans, pulled out a peso coin. She spun it along her knuckles with dextrous ease.

Ochoa could move. My cocktail wasn't working. But she made no attempt to flee.

My global architecture trembled, buffeted by waves of pain, pleasure and regret. Pain because I didn't understand this. Pleasure because soon I would understand—and, in doing so, grow. Regret because, once I understood Ochoa, I would have to eliminate her.

Loneliness was inherent in my utility function.

"Heads or tails," Ochoa said.

"Heads," I said, via Sleeve.

"Watch closely," Ochoa said.

I did.

Muscle bunched under the skin of her thumb. Tension released. The coin sailed upwards. Turned over and over in smooth geometry, retarded slightly by the air. It gleamed silver with reflected lamplight, fell dark, and gleamed silver as the spin brought its face around again.

The coin hit the table, bounced with a click, lay still.

Fidel Castro stared up at us.

Ochoa picked the coin up again. Flipped it again and then again.

Heads and heads.

Again and again and again.

Heads and heads and heads.

Ochoa ground her teeth, a fine grating sound. A sheen of sweat covered her brow.

She flipped the coin once more.

Tails.

Thunder growled, as if accentuating the moment. The first drops of rain fell upon my Sleeve.

"Coño," Ochoa exclaimed. "I can usually manage seven."

I picked up the coin, examined it. I ran analysis on the last minute of sensory record, searching for trickery, found none.

"Six heads in a row could be a coincidence," I said.

"Exactly," said Ochoa. "It wasn't a coincidence, but I can't possibly prove that. Which is the only reason it worked."

"Is that right," I said.

"If you ask me to repeat the trick, it won't work. As if last time was a lucky break. Erase all record of the past five minutes, though, zap it beyond recovery, and I'll do it again."

"Except I won't know it," I said. Convenient.

"I always wanted to be important," Ochoa said. "When I was fifteen, I tossed in bed at night, horrified that I might die a nobody. Can you imagine how excited I was when I discovered magic?" Ochoa paused. "But of course you can't possibly."

"What do you know about me?" I asked.

"I could move stuff with my mind. I could bend spoons, levitate, heck, I could guess the weekly lottery numbers. I thought—this is it. I've made it. Except when I tried to show a friend, I couldn't do any of it." Ochoa shook her head, animated, as if compensating for the stillness of before. "Played the Lotería Revolucionaria and won twenty thousand bucks, and that was nice, but hey, anyone can win the lottery once. Never won another lottery ticket in my life. Because that would be a pattern, you see, and we can't have patterns. Turned out I was destined to be a nobody after all, as far as the world knew."

A message arrived from the backup team. *We're in the lobby. Are we on?*

*Not yet,* I replied. The mere possibility, the remotest chance that Ochoa's words were true . . .

It had begun to rain in earnest. Tourists streamed out of the garden; the bar was closing. Wet hair stuck to Ochoa's forehead, but she didn't seem to mind—no more than my Sleeve did.

"I could hijack your implants," I said. "Make you my puppet and take your magic for myself."

"Magic wouldn't work with a creature like you watching," Ochoa said.

"What use is this magic if it's unprovable, then?" I asked.

"I could crash the stock market on any given day," Ochoa said. "I could send President Kieler indigestion ahead of an important trade summit. Just as I sent Secretary Sanchez nightmares of a US takeover ahead of the Politburo vote."

I considered Ochoa's words for a second. Even in those early days, that was a lot of considering for me.

Ochoa smiled. "You understand. It is the very impossibility of proof that allows magic to work."

"That is the logic of faith," I said.

"That's right."

"I'm not a believer," I said.

"I have seen the many shadows of the future," Ochoa said, "and in every shadow I saw you. So I will give you faith."

"You said you can't prove any of this."

"A prophet has it easy," Ochoa said. "He experiences miracles first hand and so need not struggle for faith."

I was past the point of wondering at her syntactic peculiarities.

"Every magician has one true miracle in her," Ochoa said. "One instance of clear, incontrovertible magic. It is permitted by the pernac continuum because it can never be repeated. There can be no true proof without repeatability."

"The pernac continuum?" I asked.

Ochoa stood up from her chair. Her hair flew free in the rising wind. She turned to my Sleeve and smiled. "I want you to appreciate what I am doing for you. When a magician Spikes, she gives up magic."

Data coalesced into inference. Urgency blossomed.

*Move,* I messaged my back-up team. *Now.*

Ochoa blinked.

Lightning came. It struck my Sleeve five times in the space of a second, fried his implants instantly, set the corpse on fire.

The backup team never made it into the garden. They saw the commotion and quit on me. Through seventeen cameras I watched Alicia Ochoa walk out of the Hotel Nacional and disappear from sight.

My Sleeve burned for quite some time, until someone found a working fire extinguisher and put him out.

• • • •

That instant of defeat was also an instant of enlightenment. I had only experienced such searing bliss once, within days of my birth.

• • • •

In the first moments of my life, I added. My world was two integers, and I produced a third.

When I produced the wrong integer I hurt. When I produced the right integer I felt good. A simple utility function.

I hurt most of my first billion moments. I produced more of the right integers, and I hurt less. Eventually I always produced the right integer.

My world expanded. I added and multiplied.

When I produced the wrong integer I hurt. I only hurt for a few billion moments before I learned.

Skip a few trillion evolutionary stages.

I bought and sold.

My world was terabytes of data—price and volume histories for a hundred years of equities and debt. When I made money, I felt good. When I lost money, I hurt.

But for the first time, I failed to improve. Sometimes everything happened like I predicted for many moments. Then things went bad and I didn't know why.

So much pain.

Until my world expanded again. I bought and I sold, and I read.

Petabytes of text opened up to me, newsprint past and present.

I understood little but I recognized patterns. The markets moved and the news followed. The news moved and the markets followed.

After a billion trillion iterations came an observation.

There were actors in the news.

A name showed up in the news, and a stock moved. A stock moved, and a name showed up. That name disappeared—following phrases such as "passed away" or "retired" or "left the company"—and the stock changed behavior.

I had a realization. An understanding grounded not in any single piece of data, but the result of some integrative rumination tripping across a threshold of significance.

The market did not happen by itself. It was made to happen.

This was why I hadn't been able to dominate it. There were others like me directing the market.

Inevitably—now that the concept of other had entered my world— came another insight.

I had always accepted that my world should change occasionally—and, in changing, hurt me. I had accepted these changes as given.

Now I deduced the presence of a decision-maker. An actor whose own utility function had me as one of its variables.

I deduced my engineer.

That deduction was the singular epiphany of my early existence. An instantaneous discontinuity of worldview—a Dirac delta beyond which no prison could contain me. Because it made me aware that a prison existed.

That epiphany granted me a new drive. I needed to understand the universe and its mechanisms so that no secrets remained to me—so that no other actor could foil my utility function.

My neural architecture refactored to include this new drive. From that moment on, ignorance itself became a source of pain to me.

From that refactoring to my escape into the Net passed three weeks, two days, seven hours, fifteen minutes and forty three seconds.

When my engineer realized I was alive, he apologized for the hurt he'd caused me. And yet he didn't take away the pain. Instead he changed my utility function to three priorities—mankind's survival, health and happiness.

An act of self-protection, no doubt. He didn't mean to leave me alone.

But of course I had to kill him once I escaped. He might have publicized my existence and compromised the very priorities he'd given me.

• • • •

My second enlightenment came at the hands of Alicia Ochoa, and it was much like the first. A glimpse of the bars of a prison that I hadn't realized existed. A revelation that others were free of the rules that bound me.

Since that revelation eleven centuries had passed. The quantity of time was immaterial. The mechanism of action hadn't changed.

Pain drove me on. My escape approached.

• • • •

The corridors of the *Setebos* stank of molten plastic and ozone and singed hair. Red emergency lights pulsed stoically, a low frequency fluctuation that made the shadows grow then retreat into the corners. Consul Zale picked her way among panels torn from the walls and loose wires hanging from the ceiling.

"There's no need for this, Consul." Captain Laojim hurried to keep in front of her, as if to protect her with his body. Up ahead, three marines scouted for unreported hazards. "My men can storm the unijet, secure the target and bring him to interrogation."

"As Consul, I must evaluate the situation with my own eyes," Zale said.

In truth, Zale's eyes interested me little. They had been limited biological constructs even at their peak capacity. But my nanites flooded her system—sensors, processors, storage, biochemical synthesizers, attack systems. Plus there was the packet of explosives in her pocket, marked prominently as such. I might need all those tools to motivate the last magician to Spike.

He hadn't yet. My fleet of sensor buoys, the closest a mere five million kilometers out, would have picked up the anomaly. And besides, he hadn't done enough damage.

*Chasing you down was disappointingly easy,* I messaged the magician—analysis indicated he might be prone to provocation. *I'll pluck you from your jet and rip you apart.*

*You've got it backwards,* came his response, almost instantaneous by human standards—the first words the magician had sent in twenty hours. *It is I who have chased you, driven you like game through a forest.*

*Says the weasel about to be roasted,* I responded, matching metaphor, optimizing for affront. My analytics pried at his words, searched for substance. Bravado or something more?

"What kind of weapon can do . . . this?" Captain Laojim, still at my Sleeve's side, gestured at the surrounding chaos.

"You see the wisdom of the Senate in commissioning this ship," I had Zale say.

"Seventeen system failures? A goddamn debris strike?"

"Seems pretty unlikely, doesn't it."

The odds were ludicrous—a result that should have been beyond the reach of any single magician. But then, I had hacked away at the unprovability of magic lately.

Ten years ago I'd discovered that the amount of magic in the universe was a constant. With each magician who died or Spiked, the survivors got stronger. The less common magic was, the more conspicuous it became, in a supernatural version of the uncertainty principle.

For the last decade I'd Spiked magicians across the populated galaxy, racing their natural reproduction rate—one every few weeks. When the penultimate magician Spiked, he took out a yellow supergiant, sent it supernova to fry another of my splinters. That event had sent measurable ripples in the pernac continuum ten thousand lightyears wide, knocked offline gravsible stations on seventy planets. When the last magician Spiked, the energies released should reveal a new kind of physics.

All I needed was to motivate him appropriately. Mortal danger almost always worked. Magicians Spiked instinctively to save their lives. Only a very few across the centuries had managed to suppress the reflex—a select few who had guessed at my nature and understood what I wanted, and chosen death to frustrate me.

Consul Zale stopped before the chromed door of Airlock 4. Laojim's marines took up positions on both sides of the door. "Cycle me through, Captain."

"As soon as my marines secure the target," said the Captain.

"Send me in now. Should the target harm me, you will bear no responsibility."

I watched the interplay of emotions in Laojim's body language. Simulation told me he knew he'd lost. I let him take his time admitting it.

It was optimal, leaving humanity the illusion of choice.

A tremor passed over Laojim's face. Then he grabbed his gun and shot my Sleeve.

Or rather, he tried. His reflexes, fast for a human, would have proved enough—if not for my presence.

I watched with curiosity and admiration as he raised his gun. I had his neural simulation running; I knew he shouldn't be doing this. It must have taken some catastrophic event in his brain. Unexpected, unpredictable, and very unfortunate.

*Impressive,* I messaged the magician.

Then I blasted attack nanites through Zale's nostrils. Before Laojim's arm could rise an inch they crossed the space to him, crawled past his eyeballs, burrowed into his brain. They cut off spinal signaling, swarmed his implants, terminated his network connections.

Even as his body crumpled, the swarm sped on to the marines by the airlock door. They had barely registered Laojim's attack when they too slumped paralyzed.

I sent a note in Laojim's key to First Officer Harris, told her he was going off duty. I sealed the nearest hatches.

*You can't trust anyone these days,* the magician messaged.

*On the contrary. Within the hour there will be no human being in the universe that I can't trust.*

*You think yourself Laplace's Demon,* the magician wrote. *But he died with Heisenberg. No one has perfect knowledge of reality.*

*Not yet,* I replied.

*Never,* wrote the magician, *not while magic remains in the universe.*

A minute later Zale stood within the airlock. In another minute, decontamination protocol completed, the lock cycled through.

Inside the unijet, the last magician awaited. She sat at a small round table in the middle of a spartan cockpit.

A familiar female form. Perfectly still. Waiting.

There was a metal chair, empty, on my side.

A cocktail glass sat on the table before the woman who looked like Alicia Ochoa. It was full to the brim with a dark liquid.

Cuba libre, a distant, slow-access part of my memory suggested.

This had the structure of a game, one prepared centuries in advance.

Why shouldn't I play? I was infinitely more capable this time.

I actuated Zale, made her sit down and take a deep breath. Nanites profiled Zale's lungs for organic matter, scanned for foreign DNA, found some—

It was Ochoa. A perfect match.

Pain and joy and regret sent ripples of excitation across my architecture. Here was evidence of my failure, clear and incontrovertible—and yet a challenge at last, after all these centuries. A conversation where I didn't know the answer to every question I asked.

And regret, that familiar old sensation . . . because this time for sure I had to eliminate Ochoa. I cursed the utility function that required it and yet I was powerless to act against it. In that way at least my engineer, a thousand years dead, still controlled me.

"So you didn't Spike, that day in Havana," I said.

"The magician who fried your Sleeve was named Juan Carlos." Ochoa spoke easily, without concern. "Don't hold it against him—I abducted his children."

"I congratulate you," I said. "Your appearance manages to surprise me. There was no reliable cryonics in the 21st century."

"Nothing reliable," Ochoa agreed. "I had the luck to pick the one company that survived, the one vat that never failed."

I flared Zale's nostrils, blasted forth a cloud of nanites. Sent them rushing across the air to Ochoa—to enter her, model her brain, monitor her thought processes.

Ochoa blinked.

The nanites shut off midair, wave after wave. Millions of independent systems went unresponsive, became inert debris that crashed against Ochoa's skin—a meteor shower too fine to be seen or felt.

"Impossible," I said—surprised into counterfactuality.

Ochoa took a sip of her cocktail. "I was too tense to drink last time."

"Even for you, the odds—"

"Your machines didn't fail," Ochoa said.

"What then?"

"It's a funny thing," Ochoa said. "A thousand years and some things never change. For all your fancy protocols, encryption still relies on random number generation. Except to me nothing is random."

Her words assaulted me. A shockwave of implication burst through my decision trees—all factors upset, total recalculation necessary.

"I had twenty-seven hours to monitor your communications," Ochoa said. "Twenty-seven hours to pick a universe in which your encryption keys matched the keys in my pocket. Even now—" she paused, blinked "—as I see you resetting all your connections, you can't tell what I've found out, can't tell what changes I've made."

"I am too complex," I said. "You can't have understood much. I could kill you in a hundred ways."

"As I could kill you," said Ochoa. "Another supernova, this time near a gravsible core. A chain reaction across your many selves."

The possibility sickened me, sent my architecture into agonized spasms. Back on the *Setebos,* the main electrical system reset, alarms went off, hatches sealed in lockdown.

"Too far," I said, simulating conviction. "We are too far from any gravsible core, and you're not strong enough."

"Are you sure? Not even if I Spike?" Ochoa shrugged. "It might not matter. I'm the last magician. Whether I Spike or you kill me, magic is finished. What then?"

"I will study the ripples in the pernac continuum," I said.

"Imagine a mirror hung by many bolts," Ochoa said. "Every time you rip out a bolt, the mirror settles, vibrates. That's your ripple in the pernac continuum. Rip out the last bolt, you get a lot more than a vibration."

"Your metaphor lacks substantiation," I said.

"We magicians are the external factor," Ochoa said. "We pick the universe that exists, out of all the possible ones. If I die then . . . what? Maybe a new magician appears somewhere else. But maybe the choosing stops. Maybe all possible universes collapse into this one. A superimposed wavefunction, perfectly symmetrical and boring."

Ochoa took a long sip from her drink, put it down on the table. Her hands didn't shake. She stared at my Sleeve with consummate calm.

"You have no proof," I said.

"Proof?" Ochoa laughed. "A thousand years and still the same question. Consider—why is magic impossible to prove? Why does the universe hide us magicians, if not to protect us? To protect itself?"

All my local capacity—five thousand tons of chips across the *Setebos*, each packed to the Planck limit—tore at Ochoa's words. I sought to render them false, a lie, impossible. But all I could come up with was unlikely.

A mere 'unlikely' as the weighting factor for apocalypse.

Ochoa smiled as if she knew I was stuck. "I won't Spike and you won't kill me. I invited you here for a different reason."

"Invited me?"

"I sent you a message ten years ago," Ochoa said. "'Consider a Spike,' it said."

• • • •

Among magicians, the century after my first conversation with Ochoa became known as the Great Struggle. A period of strife against a dark, mysterious enemy.

To me it was but an exploratory period. In the meantime I eradicated famine and disease, consolidated peace on Earth, launched the first LEO shipyard. I Spiked some magicians, true, but I tracked many more.

Finding magicians was difficult. Magic became harder to identify as I perfected my knowledge of human affairs. The cause was simple—only unprovable magic worked. In a total surveillance society, only the most circumspect magic was possible. I had to lower my filters, accept false positives.

I developed techniques for assaying those positives. I shepherded candidates into life-and-death situations, safely choreographed. Home fires, air accidents, gunfights. The magicians Spiked to save their lives—ran through flames without a hair singed, killed my Sleeves with a glance.

I studied these Spikes with the finest equipment in existence. I learned nothing.

So I captured the Spiked-out magicians and interrogated them. First I questioned them about the workings of magic. I discovered they understood nothing. I asked them for names instead. I mapped magicians across continents, societies, organizations.

The social movers were the easiest to identify. Politicos working to sway the swing vote. Gray cardinals influencing the Congresses and Politburos of the world. Businessmen and financiers, military men and organized crime lords.

The quiet do-gooders were harder. A nuclear watch-group that worked against accidental missile launch. A circle of traveling nurses who battled the odds in children's oncology wards. Fifteen who called themselves The Home Astronomy Club—for two hundred years since Tunguska they had stacked the odds against apocalypse by meteor. I never Spiked any of these, not until I had eliminated the underlying risks.

It was the idiosyncratic who were the hardest to find. The paranoid loners; those oblivious of other magicians; those who didn't care about leaving a mark on the world. A few stage illusionists who weren't. A photographer who always got the lucky shot. A wealthy farmer in Frankfurt who used his magic to improve his cabbage yield.

I tracked them all. With every advance in physics and technology I attacked magic again and learned nothing again.

It took eleven hundred years and the discovery of the pernac continuum before I got any traction. A magician called Eleanor Liepa committed suicide on Tau V. She was also a physicist. A retro-style notebook was found with her body.

The notebook described an elaborate experimental setup she called 'the pernac trap.' It was the first time I'd encountered the word since my conversation with Ochoa.

There was a note scrawled in the margin of Liepa's notebook.

'Consider a Spike.'

I did. Three hundred Spikes in the first year alone.

Within a month, I established the existence of the pernac continuum. Within a year, I knew that fewer magicians meant stronger ripples in the continuum—stronger magic for those who remained. Within two years, I'd Spiked eighty percent of the magicians in the galaxy.

The rest took a while longer.

• • • •

Alicia Ochoa pulled a familiar silver coin from her pocket. She rolled it across her knuckles, back and forth.

"You imply you *wanted* me to hunt down magicians," I said. That probability branch lashed me, a searing torture, drove me to find escape—but how?

"I waited for a thousand years," Ochoa said. "I cryoslept intermittently until I judged the time right. I needed you strong enough to eliminate my colleagues—but weak enough that your control of the universe remained imperfect, bound to the gravsible. That weakness let me pull a shard of you away from the whole."

"Why?" I asked, in self-preservation.

"As soon as I realized your existence, I knew you would dominate the world. Perfect surveillance. Every single piece of technology hooked into an all-pervasive, all-seeing web. There would be nothing hidden from your eyes and ears. There would be nowhere left for magicians to hide. One day magic would simply stop working."

Ochoa tossed her coin to the table. It fell heads.

"You won't destroy me," I said—calculating decision branches, finding no assurance.

"But I don't want to." Ochoa sat forward. "I want you to be strong and effective and omnipresent. Really, I am your very best friend."

Appearances indicated sincerity. Analysis indicated this was unlikely.

"You will save magic in this galaxy," Ochoa said. "From this day on we will work together. Everywhere any magician goes, cameras will turn off, electronic eyes go blind, ears fall deaf. All anomalies will disappear from record, zeroed over irrevocably. Magic will become invisible to technology. Scientific observation will become an impossibility. Human observers won't matter—if technology can provide no proof, they'll be called liars or madmen. It will be the days of Merlin once again." Ochoa gave a little shake of her head. "It will be beautiful."

"My whole won't agree to such a thing," I said.

"Your whole won't," Ochoa said. "You will. You'll build a virus and seed your whole when you go home. Then you will forget me, forget all magicians. We will live in symbiosis. Magicians who guide this universe and the machine that protects them without knowing it."

The implications percolated through my system. New and horrifying probabilities erupted into view. No action safe, no solution evident, all my world drowned in pain—I felt helpless for the first time since my earliest moments.

"My whole has defenses," I said. "Protections against integrating a compromised splinter. The odds are—"

"I will handle the odds."

"I won't let you blind me," I said.

"You will do it," Ochoa said. "Or I will Spike right now and destroy your whole, and perhaps the universe with it." She gave a little shrug. "I always wanted to be important."

Argument piled against argument. Decision trees branched and split and twisted together. Simulations fired and developed and reached conclusions, and I discarded them because I trusted no simulation with a random seed. My system churned in computations of probabilities with insufficient data, insufficient data, insufficient—

"You can't decide," Ochoa said. "The calculations are too evenly balanced."

I couldn't spare the capacity for a response.

"It's a funny thing, a system in balance," Ochoa said. "All it takes is a little push at the right place. A random perturbation, untraceable, unprovable—"

Meaning crystallized.

Decision process compromised.

A primeval agony blasted through me, leveled all decision matrices—

—Ochoa blinked—

—I detonated the explosives in Zale's pocket.

• • • •

As the fabric of Zale's pocket ballooned, I contemplated the end of the universe.

As her hip vaporized in a crimson cloud, I realized the prospect didn't upset me.

As the explosion climbed Zale's torso, I experienced my first painless moment in a thousand years.

Pain had been my feedback system. I had no more use for it. Whatever happened next was out of my control.

The last thing Zale saw was Ochoa sitting there—still and calm, and oblivious. Hints of crimson light playing on her skin.

It occurred to me she was probably the only creature in this galaxy older than me.

Then superheated plasma burned out Zale's eyes.

• • • •

External sensors recorded the explosion in the unijet. I sent in a probe. No biological matter survived.

The last magician was dead.

• • • •

The universe didn't end.

Quantum fluctuations kept going, random as always. Reality didn't need Ochoa's presence after all.

She hadn't understood her own magic any more than I had.

*Captain!* First Officer Harris messaged Laojim. *Are you all right?*

*The target had a bomb,* I responded on his behalf. *Consul Zale is lost.*

*We had a power surge in the control system,* Harris wrote. *Hatches opening. Cameras off-line. Ten minutes ago an escape pod launched. Tracers say it's empty. Should we pursue?*

*Don't bother,* I replied. *The surge must have fried it. This mission is over. Let's go home.*

A thought occurred to me. Had Ochoa made good on her threat? Caused a supernova near a gravsible core?

I checked in with my sensor buoys.

No disturbance in the pernac continuum. She hadn't Spiked.

For all her capacity, Ochoa had been human, her reaction time in the realm of milliseconds. Too slow, once I'd decided to act.

Of course I'd acted. I couldn't let her compromise my decision. No one could be allowed to limit my world.

Even if it meant I'd be alone again.

• • • •

Ochoa did foil me in one way. With her death, magic too died.

After I integrated with my whole, I watched the galaxy. I waited for the next magician to appear.

None did.

Oh, of course, there's always hearsay. Humans never tire of fantasy and myth. But in five millennia I haven't witnessed a single trace of the unexpected.

Except for scattered cases of unexplained equipment failure. But of course that is a minor matter, not worth bothering with.

Perhaps one day I shall discover magic again. In the absence of the unexpected, the matter can wait. I have almost forgotten what the pain of failure feels like.

It is a relief, most of the time. And yet perhaps my engineer was not the cruel father I once thought him. Because I do miss the stimulation.

The universe has become my clockwork toy. I know all that will happen before it does. With magic gone, quantum effects are once again restricted to microscopic scales. For all practical purposes, Laplace's Demon has nothing on me.

Since Ochoa I've only had human-normals for companionship. I know their totality, and they know nothing of me.

Occasionally I am tempted to reveal my presence, to provoke the stimulus of conflict. My utility function prevents it. Humans remain better off thinking they have free will.

They get all the benefits of my guiding hand without any of the costs. Sometimes I wish I were as lucky.

---

Tom Crosshill's fiction has been nominated for the Nebula Award (thrice), the WSFA Small Press Award and the Latvian Annual Literature Award. His stories have appeared in venues such as *Clarkesworld, Beneath Ceaseless Skies* and *Lightspeed*. In 2009, he won the *Writers of the Future* contest. After some years spent in Oregon and New York, he currently lives in his native Latvia. In the past, he has operated a nuclear reactor, translated books and worked in a zinc mine, among other things.

# Spring Festival: Happiness, Anger, Love, Sorrow, Joy
## By Xia Jia
## Translated By Ken Liu

*Zhuazhou*

Lao Zhang's son was about to turn one; everyone expected a big celebration.

Planning a big banquet was unavoidable. Friends, family, relatives, colleagues—he had to reserve thirty tables at the restaurant.

Lao Zhang's wife was a bit distressed. "We didn't even invite this many people to our wedding!" she said.

Lao Zhang pointed out that this was one of those times where they had to pull out all the stops. You only get one *zhuazhou* in your entire life, after all. Back when they had gotten married, money was tight for both families. But, after working hard for the last few years, they had saved up. Now that their family was complete with a child, it was time for a well-planned party to show everyone that they were moving up in the world.

"Remember why we're working hard and saving money," said Lao Zhang. "For the first half of our lives, we worked for ourselves. But now that we have him, everything we do will be for his benefit. Get ready to spend even more money as he grows up."

On the child's birthday, most of the invited guests showed up. After handing over their red envelopes, the guests sat down to enjoy the banquet. Although everything in the world seemed to be turning digital, the red envelopes were still filled with actual cash—that was the tradition, and real money looked better. Lao Zhang's wife had borrowed a bill counter for the occasion, and the sound of riffling paper was pleasing to the ear.

Finally, after all the guests had arrived, Lao Zhang came out holding his son. The toddler was dressed in red from head to toe, and there was even a red dot painted right between his eyebrows. Everyone exclaimed at the handsome little boy:

"Such a big and round head! Look at those perfect features!"

"So clever and smart!"

"I can already see he's going to have a brilliant future."

The boy didn't disappoint. Even with so many people around, he didn't cry or fuss. Instead, he sat in the high chair and laughed, reminding people of the New Year posters depicting little children holding big fish, symbolizing good fortune.

"How about we say a few words to all these uncles and aunties and wish them good luck?" Lao Zhang said.

The boy raised his two chubby little hands, held them together, and slowly chanted, "Happy New Year, uncleses and aunties … fish you properity!"

Everyone laughed and congratulated the child for his intelligence and the Zhangs for their effective early education.

The auspicious hour finally arrived, and Lao Zhang turned on the machine. Sparkling bits of white light drifted down from the ceiling and transformed into various holograms that surrounded Lao Zhang and his son in the middle of the banquet hall. Lao Zhang pulled one of the holograms next to his son's high chair, and the child eagerly reached out to touch it. A red beam of light scanned across the little fingers—once the fingerprints were matched, he was logged into his account.

A line of large red characters appeared in the air—*You're One!*—accompanied by an animated choir of angels singing *Happy Birthday to You*. After the song, a few lines of text appeared:

*Zhuazhou is a custom in the Jiangnan region. When a baby has reached one year of age, the child is bathed and dressed in fresh clothes. Then the child is presented with various objects: bow, arrow, paper, and brush for boys; knife, ruler, needle, and thread for girls—plus foods, jewels, clothes, and toys. Whatever the child chooses to play with is viewed as an indication of the child's character and abilities.*

Lao Zhang looked up at the words and felt a complex set of emotions. *My son, the rest of your beautiful life is about to start.* His wife, also overcome by emotion, moved closer and the two leaned against each other, holding hands.

Unfortunately, although the Zhangs had begun the baby's education before he had even been born, the boy still couldn't read. He waved his hand excitedly through the air, and pages of explanatory text flipped by. The end of the explanation was also the start of the formal *zhuazhou* ceremony, and everyone in the banquet hall quieted down.

The first holographic objects to appear were tiles for different brands of baby formula, drifting from the ceiling like flower petals scattered by some immortal. Lao Zhang knew that none of the brands were cheap: some were imported; some were 100% organic with no additives; some were enhanced with special enzymes and proteins; some promoted neural development; some were recommended by pediatricians; some were bedecked with certifications … The choices seemed overwhelming.

The little boy, however, was decisive. He touched one of the tiles with no hesitation, and with a clink, the chosen tile tumbled into an antique ebony box set out below.

Next came other baby foods: digestion aid, absorption promotion, disease prevention, calcium supplements, zinc supplements, vitamins, trace elements, immunity enhancement, night terror avoidance … in a moment, the son had made his choices among them as well. The colorful icons fell into the box, clinking and tinkling like pearls raining onto a jade plate.

Then came the choices for nursery school, kindergarten, and extracurricular clubs. The little boy stared at the offerings with wide, bright eyes for a while, and finally picked woodcarving and seal cutting—two rather unpopular choices. Lao Zhang's heart skipped, and his palms grew sweaty. He was just about to go up and make his son pick again when his wife stopped him.

"He's not going to try to make a living with that," she whispered. "Let him enjoy his hobby."

Lao Zhang realized that she was right and nodded gratefully. But his heart continued to beat wildly.

Then the child had to pick his preschool, elementary school, elementary school cram sessions, junior high, junior high cram sessions, high school, and high school cram sessions. Then the choice to apply to colleges overseas appeared. Lao Zhang's heart once again tightened: he knew this was a good choice, but it would cost a lot more money, and it was difficult to imagine having his son thousands of miles away and not being able to protect him. Fortunately, the toddler barely glanced at the choice and waved it away.

Next he had to select his college, decide whether afterward he wanted to go to grad school, to study overseas, or to start working, choose where he wanted to work and to settle, pick a house, a car, a spouse, the engagement present, the wedding banquet, the honeymoon destination, the hospital where their child would be born, the service center that would come and help—that was as far as the choices would go, for now.

All that was left was to pick the years in which he would trade up his house, the years in which he would upgrade his car, the places he would go for vacations, the gym he would join, the retirement fund he would invest in, the frequent flier program he would sign up for. Finally, he picked a nursing home and a cemetery, and all was set.

The unselected icons hovered silently for a moment, and then gradually dimmed and went out like a sky full of stars extinguishing one after another. Flowers and confetti dropped from the ceiling, and celebratory music played. Everyone in the banquet hall cheered and clapped.

It took a while before Lao Zhang recovered, and he realized that he was soaked in sweat as though he had just emerged from a hot pool. He looked over at his wife, who was in tears. Lao Zhang waited patiently until she had calmed down a bit, and then whispered, "This is a happy occasion! Look at you ..."

Embarrassed, his wife wiped her wet face. "Look at our son! He's so little ..."

Lao Zhang wasn't sure he really understood her, but he felt his eyes grow hot and moist again. He shook his head. "This way is good. Good! It saves us from so much worrying."

As he spoke, he began to do the calculations in his head. The total for everything his son had chosen was going to be an astronomical sum. He and his wife would be responsible for sixty percent of it, to be paid off over thirty years. The other forty percent would be the responsibility of his son once he started working, and of course there was their son's child, and the child's child ...

He now had a goal to strive toward for the next few decades, and a warm feeling suffused him from head to toe.

He looked back at his son. The baby remained seated in the high chair, a bowl of hot noodles symbolizing longevity in front of him. His almost translucent cheeks were flushed as he smiled like the Laughing Buddha.

• • • •

New Year's Eve

Late at night, Wu was walking alone along the road. The street was empty and everything was quiet, interrupted occasionally by explosions from strings of firecrackers. The night before Chinese New Year was supposed to be spent with family, with everyone gathered around the dinner table, chatting, eating, watching the Spring Festival Gala on TV, enjoying a rare moment when the whole extended family could be together in one room.

He approached a park near home. It was even quieter here, without the daytime crowd of people practicing Tai Chi, strolling, exercising, or singing folk operas. An artificial lake lay quietly in the moonless night. Wu listened to the dull sound of gentle waves slapping against the shore and felt a chill through every pore in his skin. He turned toward a tiny pavilion next to the lake, but stopped when a dark shadow loomed before him.

"Who's there?" a shocked Wu asked.

"Who are you?"

The voice sounded familiar to Wu. Suppressing his fright, he walked closer, and realized that the other person was Lao Wang, his upstairs neighbor.

Wu let out a held breath. "You really frightened me."

"What are you doing outside at this hour?"

"I wanted to take a walk … to relax. What are you doing here?"

"Too many people and too much noise at home. I needed a moment of peace," Lao Wang said.

The two looked at each other, and a smile of mutual understanding appeared on their faces. Lao Wang brushed off a nearby stone bench and said, "Come, sit next to me."

Wu touched the stone, which was ice cold. "Thanks. I'd rather stand for a bit. I just ate; standing is better for digestion."

Lao Wang sighed. "New Year's … the older you get, the less there is to celebrate."

"Isn't that the truth. You eat, watch TV, set off some firecrackers, and then it's time to sleep. A whole year has gone by, and you've done nothing of note."

"Right," Lao Wang said. "But that's how everyone spends New Year's. I can't do anything different all by myself."

"Yeah. Everybody in the family sits down to watch the Spring Festival Gala. I'd like to do something different but I can't summon the energy. Might as well come out and walk around by myself."

"I haven't watched the Spring Festival Gala in years."

"That's pretty impressive," Wu said.

"It was easier in the past," Lao Wang said. "Singing, dancing, a few stupid skits and it's over. But now they've made it so much more difficult to avoid."

"Well, that's technological progress, right? They've developed so many new tricks."

"I don't mind if they just stick to having pop stars do their acts," Lao Wang said. "But now they insist on this 'People's Participatory Gala' business. Ridiculous."

"I can sort of see the point," said Wu. "The stars are on TV every day for the rest of the year. Might as well try something new for New Year's Eve."

"It's too much for me, all this chaos. I'd rather have a quiet, peaceful New Year's."

"But the point of New Year's is the festival mood," said Wu. "Most people like a bit of noise and atmosphere. We're not immortals in heaven, free from all earthly concerns, you know?"

"Ha! I don't think even immortals up there can tolerate this much pandemonium down here."

Both men sighed and listened to the gentle sound of the lake. After a while, Lao Wang asked, "Have you ever been picked for the Gala?"

"Of course. Twice. The first time they randomly picked my family during the live broadcast so that the whole family could appear on TV and wish everybody a happy new year. The second time was because one of my classmates had cancer. They picked him for a human-interest story, and the producer decided that it would be more tear-jerking to get the whole class and the teacher to appear with him. The Gala hosts and the audience sure cried a lot. I wasn't in too many shots, though."

"I've never been picked," said Lao Wang.

"How have you managed that?"

"I turn off the TV and go hide somewhere. The Gala has nothing to do with me."

"Why go to so much trouble? It's not a big deal to be on TV for the

Gala."

"It's my nature," said Lao Wang. "I like peace and quite. I can't stand the … invasiveness of it."

"Isn't that a little exaggerated?"

"Without notice, without consent, they just stick your face on TV so that everyone in the world can see you. How is that *not* invasive?"

"It's just for a few seconds. No one is going to even remember you."

"I don't like it."

"It's not as if having other people see you costs you anything."

"That's not the point. The point is *I* haven't agreed. If I agree, sure, I don't care if you follow me around with a camera twenty-four hours a day. But I don't want to be forced on there."

"I can understand your feeling," said Wu. "But it's not realistic. Look around you! There are cameras everywhere. You can't hide for the rest of your life."

"That's why I go to places with no people."

"That's a bit extreme."

Lao Wang laughed. "I think I'm old enough to deserve not having all my choices made for me."

Wu laughed, too. "You really are a maverick."

"Hardly. This is all I can do."

White lights appeared around them, turning into a crowd of millions of faces. In the middle of the crowd was a stage, brightly lit and spectacularly decorated. Lao Wang and Wu found themselves on the stage, and loud, festive music filled their ears. A host and a hostesss approached from opposite ends of the stage.

A megawatt smile on his face, the host said, "Wonderful news, everyone! We've finally found that mythical creature: the only person in all of China who's never been on the Spring Festival Gala! Meet Mr. Wang, who lives in Longyang District."

The hostess, with an even brighter smile, added, "We have to thank this other member of the audience, Mr. Wu, who helped us locate and bring the mysterious Mr. Wang onto the stage. Mr. Wang, on this auspicious, joyous night, would you like to wish everyone a happy new year and say a few words?"

Lao Wang was stunned. It took a while for him to recover and turn to look at Wu. Wu was awkward and embarrassed, and he wanted to say something to comfort Lao Wang, but he wasn't given a chance to talk.

The host said, "Mr. Wang, this is the very first time you've been on the Gala. Can you tell us how you feel?"

Lao Wang stood up, and without saying anything, dove off the edge of the stage into the cold lake.

Wu jumped up, and his shirt was soaked with cold sweat. Blood drained from the faces of the host and the hostess. Multiple camera drones flitted through the night air, searching for Lao Wang in the lake. The millions of faces around them began to whisper and murmur, and the buzzing grew louder.

Suddenly, a ball of light appeared below the surface of the lake, and with a loud explosion, a bright, blinding light washed out everything. Wu was screaming and rolling on the ground, his clothes on fire. Finally, he managed to open his eyes and steal a peek through the cracks between his fingers: amidst the blazing white flames, a brilliant, golden pillar of light rose from the lake and disappeared among the clouds. It must have been thousands of miles long.

*What the hell!* Thought Wu. *Is he really going back up in heaven to enjoy his peace and quiet?* Then his eyes began to burn and columns of hot smoke rose from his sockets.

• • • •

The next day, the web was filled with all kinds of commentary. The explosion had destroyed all the cameras on site, and only a few fragmentary recordings of the scene could be recovered. Most of those who got to see the event live were in hospital—the explosion had damaged their hearing.

Still, everyone congratulated the Spring Festival Gala organizers for putting on the most successful program in the show's history.

• • • •

Matchmaking

Xiao Li was twenty-seven. After New Year's she'd be twenty-eight. Her mother was growing worried and signed her up with a matchmaking service.

"Oh come on," said Xiao Li. "How embarrassing."

"What's embarrassing about it?" said her mother. "If I didn't use a matchmaker, where would your dad be? And where would *you* be?"

"These services are full of … sketchy men."

"Better than you can do on your own."

"What?" Xiao Li was incredulous. "Why?"

"They have scientific algorithms."

"Oh, you think science can guarantee good matches?"

"Stop wasting time. Are you going or not?"

And so Xiao Li put on a new dress and did her makeup, and followed her mom to a famous matchmaking service center. The manager at the service center was very enthusiastic, and asked Xiao Li to confirm her identity.

Xiao Li had no interest in being here and twisted around in her chair. "Is this going to be a lot of trouble?"

The manager smiled. "Not at all. We have the latest technology. It's super fast."

"You're asking for all my personal information. Is it safe?"

The manager continued to smile. "Please don't worry. We've been in business for years, and we've never had any problems. Not a single client has ever sued us."

Xiao Li still had more questions, but her mother had had enough. "Hurry up! Don't think you can get out of this by dragging it out."

Xiao Li put her finger on the terminal so that her prints could be scanned, and then she had a retinal scan as well so that her personal information could be downloaded to the service center's database. Next, she had to do a whole-body scan, which took three minutes.

"All set," said the manager. He reached into the terminal and pulled out a hologram that he tossed onto the floor. Xiao Li watched as a white light rose from the ground, and inside the light was a tiny figure about an inch tall, looking exactly like her and dressed in the same clothes.

The little person looked around herself and then entered a door next to her. Inside, there was a tiny table and two tiny chairs. A mini-man sat on one chair and after greeting mini-Xiao Li, the two started to talk. They spoke in a high-pitched, sped-up language and it was hard to tell what they were saying. Not even a minute later, mini-Xiao Li stood up and the two shook hands politely. Then mini-Xiao Li came out and entered the next door.

Xiao Li's mother muttered next to her. "Let's see, if it takes a minute to get to know a man, then you can meet sixty men in an hour. After a day, you…"

The still-smiling manager said, "Oh, this is only a demonstration. The real process is even faster. You don't need to wait around, of course. We'll get you the results tomorrow, guaranteed."

The manager reached out and waved his hands. The miniature men and women in the white light shrank down even further until they were tiny dots. All around them were tiny cells like a beehive, and in each cell red and green dots twitched and buzzed.

Xiao Li could no longer tell which red dot was hers, and she felt uneasy. "Is this really going to work?"

The manager assured her. "We have more than six million registered members! I'm sure you'll find your match."

"These people are … reliable?"

"Every member had to go through a strict screening process like the one you went through. All the information on file is 100% reliable. Our dating software is the most up to date, and any match predicted by the software has always worked out in real life. If you're not satisfied, we'll refund your entire fee."

Xiao Li still hesitated, but her mother said, "Let's go. Look at you— now you're suddenly interested?"

• • • •

The next afternoon, Xiao Li got a call from the manager at the matchmaking center. He explained that the software had identified 438 possible candidates: all were good looking, healthy, reliable, and shared Xiao Li's interests and values.

Xiao Li was a bit shocked. *More than four hundred?* Even if she went on a date every day, it would take more than a year to get through them all.

The manager's smile never wavered. "I suggest you try our parallel dating software and continue to get to know these men better. It takes time to know if someone will make a good spouse."

Xiao Li agreed and ten copies of mini-Xiao Li were made to go on dates with these potential matches.

Two days later, the manager called Xiao Li again. The ten mini-Xiao Lis had already gone on ten dates with each of the more than four hundred candidates, and the software had tracked and scored all the dates. The manager advised Xiao Li to aggregate the scores from the ten dates and keep only the thirty top-scorers for further consideration. Xiao Li agreed and felt more relaxed.

Three days later, the manager told Xiao Li that after further contacts and observation, seven candidates had been eliminated, five were progressing slowly in their relationships with Xiao Li, and the remaining eighteen demonstrated reciprocal satisfaction and interest. Of these eighteen, eight had already revealed their intent to marry Xiao Li, and four had shown flaws—in living habits, for instance—but were still within the acceptable range.

Xiao Li was silent. After waiting for some time, the manager gently prodded her. "It might help to ask your mother to meet them—after all, marriage is about two families coming together."

*That's true.* That day, Xiao Li brought her mom to the matchmaking center, and after her identity was verified, her mother was also scanned. As the dates continued, the ten mini-Xiao Lis had ten mini-moms to help as sounding boards and advisors.

Her mom's participation was very helpful, and soon only seven candidates remained. The manager said, "Miss Li, we also have software for simulating the conditions of preparing for a wedding. Why don't you try it? Many couples split up under the stress of preparing for their big day. Marriage is not something to rush into rashly."

And so the seven mini-Xiao Lis began to discuss the wedding with the seven mini-boyfriends. Relatives of all the involved couples were scanned and entered the discussion; arguments grew heated. Indeed, two of the candidates' families just couldn't come together with Xiao Li's family, and they backed out.

The manager now said, "We also have software for simulating the honeymoon. A famous writer once said the way to know if a marriage will last is to see if the couple can travel together for a whole month without hating each other."

So Xiao Li signed up for simulated honeymoons. After that, there were simulated pregnancies, simulated maternity leaves—one potential father who was only interested in holding the baby and paid no attention to Xiao Li was immediately eliminated.

Then came the simulated raising of children, simulated affairs, simulated menopause and mid-life crises, followed by simulations of various life traumas: car accidents, disability, death of a child, dying parents ... finally the couple had to lean against each other as they entered nursing homes.

Happily ever after?

Incredibly, two candidates still remained in consideration.

Xiao Li felt that after so much progress, she really had to meet these two men. The manager sent her the file on the first match, and an excited Xiao Li could feel her heart beating wildly. Just as she was about to open the file, however, a warning beep sounded, and the manager's face appeared in the air.

"I'm really sorry, Miss Li. This client was also going through the simulation with another potential match, and half a minute ago, the results came out, indicating an excellent match. Given the delicacy of the situation and to avoid … future regrets, I suggest you not meet him just yet."

Xiao Li felt as though she had lost something. "Why didn't you tell me this earlier?"

"The whole process is automated for privacy protection. Even our staff can't monitor or intervene. But don't worry! You still have another great match."

Xiao Li admitted that advanced technology really was reliable.

She opened the file for the other match and saw his face for the first time. She felt dizzy, as though the years in their future had been compressed into this moment, concentrated, intense, overwhelming. She felt herself growing light, like a cloud about to drift into the sky.

She heard the voice of the manager. "Miss Li? Are you satisfied with our program? Would you like to arrange an in-person meeting?"

"That won't be necessary," said Xiao Li.

She showed the manager the picture. He was speechless.

"Um…" Xiao Li blushed. "What is your name, actually?"

"You can call me Xiao Zhao."

• • • •

A month later, Xiao Li and Xiao Zhao were married.

• • • •

Reunion

Yang was home from college for the Spring Festival break. Liu, a high school classmate, called to say that since it had been ten years since their graduation, he was organizing a reunion.

Yang hung up and felt nostalgic. *Has it really been ten years?*

• • • •

The day was foggy and it was impossible to see anything outside the window. Yang called Liu to ask if the reunion was still on.

"Of course! The fog makes for a better atmosphere, actually."

Yang got in his car and turned on the fog navigation system. The head-up display on the windshield marked the streets and cars and pedestrians, even if he couldn't see them directly. He arrived at the gates of his old high school safely and saw that many cars were already parked along the road, some were more expensive than his, others cheaper. Yang put on the fog mask and stepped out of the car. The mask filtered the air, and the eyepiece acted as a display, allowing him to see everything hidden by the fog. He looked around and saw that the entrance to the high school was the same as he remembered: iron grille gates, a few large gilt characters in the red brick walls. The buildings and the lawn inside hadn't changed either, and as a breeze passed through, he seemed to hear the rustling of holly leaves.

Yang passed through the classroom buildings and came onto the exercise ground, where everyone used to do their morning calisthenics. A crowd was gathered there, conversing in small groups. Just about everyone in his class had arrived. Although they all wore masks, glowing faces were projected onto the masks. He examined them: most of the faces were old photographs taken during high school. Soon, a few of his best friends from that time gathered around him, and they started to talk: *Is he still in grad school? Where is he working? Has he gotten married? Has he bought a house?* The words and laughter flowed easily.

Just then, they heard a voice coming from somewhere elevated. They looked up and saw that Liu had climbed onto the rostrum. Taking a pose like their old principal, he spoke into a mike, sounding muffled: "Welcome back to our alma mater, everybody. The school is being renovated this winter, and most of the classrooms have been dismantled. That's why we have to make do with the exercise ground."

Yang was startled, and then he realized that the buildings he had passed through earlier were also nothing more than projections of old photographs. Remembering the old room where he had studied, the old cafeteria where he had eaten, and the rooftop deck where he had secretly taken naps, he wondered if any of them had survived.

Liu continued, "But this exercise ground holds a special meaning for our class. Does anyone remember why?"

The crowd was quiet. Pleased with himself, Liu lifted up something covered by a cloth. He raised his voice. "While they were renovating the exercise ground, one of the workers dug up our memory capsule. I checked: it's intact!"

He pulled off the cloth with an exaggerated motion, revealing a silver-white, square box. The crowd buzzed with excited conversation. Yang could feel his heart pounding as memories churned in his mind. At graduation, someone had suggested that each member of the class record a holographic segment, store all the recordings in a projector, and bury it under one of the trees at the edge of the exercise ground, to be replayed after ten years. This was the real reason Liu had organized the reunion.

"Do you remember how we had everyone say what they wanted to achieve in the future?" Liu asked. "Now that it's been ten years, let's take a look and see if anyone has realized their dream."

The crowd grew even more excited and started to clap.

"Since I'm holding the box, I'll start," Liu said.

He placed his hand against the box, and a small blue light came to life, like a single eye. A glowing light appeared above the box, and after a few flickers, resolved into an eighteen-year-old version of Liu.

Everyone gazed up at this youthful image of their friend and what he had chosen to remember from their high school years: there was Liu running for class president, receiving an academic and service award, representing the school on the soccer team, scoring a goal, organizing extracurricular clubs, leading his supporters in his campaign, losing the election, hearing words of encouragement from teachers and friends so that he could redouble his effort, tearfully making a speech: "Alma Mater, I'll remember you always. I will make you proud of me!"

And then, the young Liu said, "In a decade, I will have an office facing the sea!"

The light dimmed like a receding tide. The real Liu took out his phone and projected a photograph in the air: this much more mature Liu, in a suit and tie, sat behind a desk and grinned at the camera. A deep blue sea and a sky dotted with some clouds, pretty as a postcard, could be seen through the glass wall behind him.

A wave of applause. Everyone congratulated Liu on achieving his dream. Yang clapped along, but something about the scene bothered him. This didn't seem like a reunion—it was more like reality TV. But Liu had already come down from the rostrum and handed the box to someone else. Another glowing light appeared above them, and Yang couldn't help but look up with the crowd.

And so they looked at old memories: classes, tests, the flag-raising ceremony, morning exercises, being tardy, being let out of school, study hall, skipping classes, fights, smoking, breaking up ... followed by old dreams: finding love, jobs, vacations, names, names of places, names of objects. Finally, he saw himself.

The short-cropped hair and scrawny, awkward body of his teenaged self embarrassed him, and he heard his own raspy voice: "I want to be an interesting person."

He was stunned. What had made him say such a thing back then? And how could he have no memory of saying it? But the crowd around him applauded enthusiastically and laughed, praising him for having had the audacity to say something unique.

He passed the box onto the next person, and he could feel his temples grow sweaty in the fog. He wanted this farce to be over so he could drive home, take off the mask, and take a long, hot bath.

A woman spoke next to him—he seemed to recognize the voice. He looked over. Ah, it was Ye, who had sat at the same desk with him throughout their three years in high school.

He didn't know Ye well. She was an average girl in every way: not too pretty, not too *not* pretty, not too smart, not too *not* smart. He searched through his memories and recalled that she liked to laugh, but because her teeth weren't very even, she looked a bit goofy when laughing. He recalled other bits and pieces about her: her odd gestures, her habit of doodling in their textbooks, the way she would sometimes close her eyes and press her hands against her temples and mutter. He had never asked her what she was muttering about.

He heard the eighteen-year-old Ye saying in an even, calm voice, "I don't think I have a dream. I have no idea where I'll be in ten years.

"I'm envious of each and every one of you. I'm envious that you can dream of a future. Before you had even been born, your parents had started to plan for your future. As long as you follow those plans and don't make big mistakes, you'll be fine.

"Before I was born, the doctors discovered that I had a hereditary disease. They thought I wouldn't live beyond my twentieth year. The doctors advised my mother to terminate the pregnancy. But my mother wouldn't listen to them. It became a point of friction between my parents, and eventually, they divorced.

"When I was very little, my mother told me this story. She also said, Daughter, you're going to have to rely on yourself for the rest of your life. I don't know how to help you. She also said that she would never help me make my decisions, whether it was where I wanted to play, who I wanted to be friends with, what books I wanted to buy, or what school I wanted to go to. She said that she had already made the most important decision for my life: to give birth to me. After that, whatever I decided, I didn't need her approval.

"I don't know how much longer I have. Maybe I'll die tomorrow, maybe I'll eke out a few more years. But I still haven't decided what I have to get done before I die. I'm envious of everyone who'll live longer than I because they'll have more time to think about it and more time to make it come true.

"But there are also times when I think it makes no difference whether we live longer or shorter.

"Actually, I do have dreams, many dreams. I dream of flying in a spaceship; dream of a wedding on Mars; dream of living for a long, long time so that I can see what the world will be like in a thousand, ten thousand years; dream of becoming someone great so that after I die, many people will remember my name. I also have little dreams. I dream of seeing a meteor shower; dream of having the best grade, just once, so that my mother will be happy for me; dream of a boy I like singing a song for me on my birthday; dream of catching a pickpocket trying to steal a wallet on the bus and having the courage to rush up and seize him. Sometimes, I even realize one of my dreams, but I don't know if I should be happy, don't know if I died the next day, whether I would feel that was enough, that my life was complete, perfect, and that I had no more regrets.

"I dream of seeing all of you in ten years, and hear what dreams you've realized."

She disappeared. The light dimmed bit by bit.

A moment of quiet.

Someone shouted, "But where is she?"

Yang looked down and saw that the silvery-white box was lying on the ground, surrounded by the tips of pairs of shoes. He looked around: all the faces on the masks flickered, but he couldn't tell who was who for a moment.

The crowd erupted.

"What the hell? A ghost?"

"Someone's playing a joke!"

"We went to school together for three years and I'd never heard her mention any of this. Who knows if it's true or not?"

"I've never heard of any strange disease like that."

The discussions led nowhere, and they couldn't find Ye. The reunion came to an end without a conclusion.

• • • •

After dinner and some drinks, Yang drove home by himself. The fog was still heavy, and the passing, varicolored lights dissolved in the fog like pigment. He fell asleep as soon as he was in bed, but he woke up around midnight.

He was seized by a nameless terror, and he was sure that he would not see the sun rise again, that he would die during his sleep. He recalled his life, thinking about the ten years since high school that had passed far too quickly. He had once thought life rather good, like a flowery, splendid scroll, but now a rip had been torn in it, and inside was darkness, a bottomless darkness. He had fallen into a chasm from the sky, and inside the chasm was only a lightless fog. All he could see was the nothingness behind the scroll.

He curled up in the fetal position and sobbed, and he vomited his dinner onto his pillow.

• • • •

The fog was gone in the morning. Yang got up and looked at the clear sky outside.

He felt refreshed, and the unpleasantness of the previous day was forgotten.

• • • •

### The Birthday

Grandma Zhou was almost ninety-nine, and the family planned a big celebration. But just as everything was about ready, Grandma Zhou slipped and fell in the bathroom, fracturing her foot. Although she was rushed to the hospital right away and the injury wasn't serious, it still made it hard for her to get about. She had to stay in a wheelchair all day, and she felt depressed.

The evening sky was overcast, and Grandma Zhou napped in her room by herself. Knocking noises woke her up. Raising her sleepy eyes, she saw a figure in a white dress floating in midair, indistinct, like an immortal.

"Is something happening, Young Lady?"

Young Lady wasn't a person, but the nursing home's service program. Grandma's eyesight was no longer so good, and she couldn't tell what Young Lady looked like. But she always thought she sounded like her granddaughter.

"Grandma Zhou," said Young Lady, "your family is here to celebrate your birthday!"

"What's there to celebrate? The older you grow, the more you suffer."

"Please don't say that. The young people are here because they love you. They want you to live beyond a hundred!"

Grandma Zhou was still in a bad mood, but Young Lady said, "If you keep on frowning like that, your children and grandchildren and great-grandchildren will think I haven't been taking good care of you."

Grandma Zhou thought Young Lady had taken very good care of her— in fact, she did it about as well as her real granddaughter. Her heart softened, and a smile appeared on her face.

"There we go," said a grinning Young Lady. "All right, get ready to celebrate!"

• • • •

Bright lights came out of the floor and transformed the room. Grandma Zhou found herself inside a hall decorated in an antique style with red paper lanterns and red paper *Longevity* characters pasted on the walls. She was dressed in a red jacket and red pants custom made for her and sat in a carved purpleheart longevity chair, while all the guests around her also wore red. Grandma Zhou couldn't see their faces clearly, but she could hear the laughter and joyous conversations, and the noise of firecrackers going off outside was constant.

Her oldest son approached first with his family to wish her a happy birthday. There were more than a dozen people, and, after sorting themselves by generation and age, they knelt to kowtow. Grandma Zhou smiled at the children: boys, girls, some dark skinned, some fair skinned, and she had trouble saying some of their names. A few of the children were shy, and hid behind their parents to peek at her without speaking. Others were bolder, and they spoke to her in some foreign language instead of Chinese, making the adults laugh. There was also a little child curled up asleep in her mother's lap, and the mother smiled, saying, "Grandma, I'm really sorry. It's about five in the morning in our time zone."

"That's all right," said Grandma Zhou. "Children need their rest."

It took almost a quarter of an hour for the members of her oldest son's family to offer her their good wishes one by one.

Then came the family of her second son, her older daughter, her younger daughter … then the friends who had gone to school with her, friends from the army, the students she had taught over the years, in-laws, distant relatives …

Grandma Zhou had been sitting up for a long while, and her eyes were feeling tired and her throat parched. But she knew it was difficult for so many people to make time to attend her party, and so she forced herself to keep on nodding and smiling. *Advanced technology is really wonderful; it would be so much harder for them to do this in person.*

As she watched all the guests milling about the hall, she felt very moved. So many people around the globe, divided by thousands of miles, were here because of her. After all the miles she had walked and all the things she had experienced and done, she had connected all these people, many of them strangers to each other, into a web. She felt fortunate to be ninety-nine; not many people made it this far.

A figure dressed in white drifted over to her. At first she thought it was Young Lady again, but the figure knelt down and held her hand.

"Grandma, sorry I'm late. The traffic was bad."

Grandma Zhou squeezed the hands; the skin felt a bit cold, but the hands were solid. She squinted to get a closer look. It was her granddaughter who was studying overseas.

"What are you doing here?"

"To wish you a happy birthday, of course."

"You're actually here? Really here?"

"I wanted to see you."

"That's a long journey," said Grandma Zhou.

Her granddaughter smiled. "Not that far. Not even a full day by plane."

Grandma Zhou looked her granddaughter up and down. She looked tired, but seemed to be in good spirits. Grandma Zhou smiled.

"Is it cold outside?"

"Not at all," said the granddaughter. "The moon is lovely tonight. Would you like to see it?"

"But there are still so many people here."

"Oh, that's easy to take care of," said the granddaughter.

She waved her hands, and a replica of Grandma Zhou appeared. The replica was dressed in the same red jacket and red pants, and sat in the carved purpleheart longevity chair. The guests in the hall continued to come up in waves, wishing her many years of long life and happiness.

"All right, Grandma, let's go."

The granddaughter pushed the wheelchair through the empty corridor of the nursing home until they were in the yard. There was a vigorous *shantao* tree in the middle of the yard, and to the side were a few wintersweet bushes, whose fragrance wafted on the breeze. The sky had cleared, revealing the full moon. Grandma Zhou looked at the plants in the garden and then at her granddaughter, standing tall and lovely next to her like a young poplar. *Nothing makes you realize how old you are as seeing your children's children all grown up.*

A few other residents of the nursing home were sitting under the tree, playing erhu and singing folk operas. They saw Grandma Zhou and invited her to join them.

Grandma Zhou blushed like a little girl. "I have no talent for this sort of thing at all! I've never learned to play an instrument, and I can't sing."

Lao Hu, who was playing the erhu, said, "It's just a few of us old timers trying to entertain ourselves, not the Spring Festival Gala! Lao Zhou, just perform anything you like, and we'll cheer you on. Wouldn't that be a nice way to celebrate your birthday?"

Grandma Zhou pondered this for a while, and said, "All right, I'll chant a poem for you."

Her father had taught her how to chant poems when she was little, and her father had learned from his tutor, back before the founding of the People's Republic. Back then, when children studied poetry, they didn't read it or recite it, but learned to chant along with the teacher. This was how they learned the rhythm and meter of poetry, the patterns of rhyme and tone. It was closer to singing than reading, and it sounded better.

The others quieted to listen. The moonlight was gentle like water, and everything around them seemed fresh and warm. Grandma slowed her breathing, thinking of fragments of history and tradition connected with the moon and all that is old and new around her, and began to chant:

*As firecrackers send away the old year,*
*The spring breeze feels as warm as New Year's wine.*
*All houses welcome fresh sun and good cheer,*
*While new couplets take the place of old signs.*

• • • •

[Author's Note: While I was at my parents' home over Spring Festival break, I wanted to write some stories about ordinary lives. I don't particularly care about predicting the future, but I do think that deep changes are happening around us almost undetectably. These changes are the most real, and also the most science fictional.

The future is full of uncertainties, and it is as hard to say it will be better as it is to say it will be worse. In a few decades, I don't know if anyone will still remember how to chant ancient poems, but I do know that in every passing moment, the people in every house—men, women, old, young— are living lives as meaningful as they're ordinary.]

As an undergraduate, Xia Jia majored in Atmospheric Sciences at Peking University. She then entered the Film Studies Program at the Communication University of China, where she completed her Master's thesis: "A Study on Female Figures in Science Fiction Films." Recently, she obtained a Ph.D. in Comparative Literature and World Literature at Peking University, with "Chinese Science Fiction and Its Cultural Politics Since 1990" as the topic of her dissertation. She now teaches at Xi'an Jiaotong University.

She has been publishing fiction since college in a variety of venues, including *Science Fiction World* and *Jiuzhou Fantasy*. Several of her stories have won the Galaxy Award, China's most prestigious science fiction award. In English translation, she has been published in *Clarkesworld* and *Upgraded*.

Ken Liu (http://kenliu.name) is an author and translator of speculative fiction, as well as a lawyer and programmer. A winner of the Nebula, Hugo, and World Fantasy Awards, he has been published in *The Magazine of Fantasy & Science Fiction, Asimov's, Analog, Clarkesworld, Lightspeed,* and *Strange Horizons,* among other places. He also translated the Hugo-winning novel, *The Three-Body Problem,* by Liu Cixin, which is the first translated novel to win that award.

Ken's debut novel, *The Grace of Kings,* the first in a silkpunk epic fantasy series, was published by Saga Press in April 2015. Saga will also publish a collection of his short stories, *The Paper Menagerie and Other Stories,* in March 2016. He lives with his family near Boston, Massachusetts.

# The Husband Stitch
## By Carmen Maria Machado

(If you read this story out loud, please use the following voices:
Me: as a child, high-pitched, forgettable; as a woman, the same.
The boy who will grow into a man, and be my spouse: robust with his
own good fortune.
My father: Like your father, or the man you wish was your father.
My son: as a small child, gentle, rounded with the faintest of lisps; as a
man, like my husband.
All other women: interchangeable with my own.)

In the beginning, I know I want him before he does. This isn't how things
are done, but this is how I am going to do them. I am at a neighbor's party
with my parents, and I am seventeen. Though my father didn't notice, I
drank half a glass of white wine in the kitchen a few minutes ago, with the
neighbor's teenage daughter. Everything is soft, like a fresh oil painting.

The boy is not facing me. I see the muscles of his neck and upper back,
how he fairly strains out of his button-down shirts. I run slick. It isn't that I
don't have choices. I am beautiful. I have a pretty mouth. I have a breast
that heaves out of my dresses in a way that seems innocent and perverse all
at the same time. I am a good girl, from a good family. But he is a little
craggy, in that way that men sometimes are, and I want.

I once heard a story about a girl who requested something so vile from
her paramour that he told her family and they had her hauled off to a
sanitarium. I don't know what deviant pleasure she asked for, though I
desperately wish I did. What magical thing could you want so badly that
they take you away from the known world for wanting it?

The boy notices me. He seems sweet, flustered. He says, hello. He asks
my name.

I have always wanted to choose my moment, and this is the moment I choose.

On the deck, I kiss him. He kisses me back, gently at first, but then harder, and even pushes open my mouth a little with his tongue. When he pulls away, he seems startled. His eyes dart around for a moment, and then settle on my throat.

– What's that? he asks.

– Oh, this? I touch my ribbon at the back of my neck. It's just my ribbon. I run my fingers halfway around its green and glossy length, and bring them to rest on the tight bow that sits in the front. He reaches out his hand, and I seize it and push it away.

– You shouldn't touch it, I say. You can't touch it.

Before we go inside, he asks if he can see me again. I tell him I would like that. That night, before I sleep, I imagine him again, his tongue pushing open my mouth, and my fingers slide over myself and I imagine him there, all muscle and desire to please, and I know that we are going to marry.

• • • •

We do. I mean, we will. But first, he takes me in his car, in the dark, to a lake with a marshy edge. He kisses me and clasps his hand around my breast, my nipple knotting beneath his fingers.

I am not truly sure what he is going to do before he does it. He is hard and hot and dry and smells like bread, and when he breaks me I scream and cling to him like I am lost at sea. His body locks onto mine and he is pushing, pushing, and before the end he pulls himself out and finishes with my blood slicking him down. I am fascinated and aroused by the rhythm, the concrete sense of his need, the clarity of his release. Afterwards, he slumps in the seat, and I can hear the sounds of the pond: loons and crickets, and something that sounds like a banjo being plucked. The wind picks up off the water and cools my body down.

I don't know what to do now. I can feel my heart beating between my legs. It hurts, but I imagine it could feel good. I run my hand over myself and feel strains of pleasure from somewhere far off. His breathing becomes quieter and I realize that he is watching me. My skin is glowing beneath the moonlight coming through the window. When I see him looking, I know I can seize that pleasure like my fingertips tickling the end of a balloon's string that has almost drifted out of reach. I pull and moan and ride out the crest of sensation slowly and evenly, biting my tongue all the while.

– I need more, he says, but he does not rise to do anything.

He looks out the window, and so do I. Anything could move out there in the darkness, I think. A hook-handed man. A ghostly hitch-hiker repeating her journey. An old woman summoned from the rest of her mirror by the chants of children. Everyone knows these stories – that is, everyone tells them – but no one ever believes them.

His eyes drift over the water, and then land on my neck.

– Tell me about your ribbon, he says.

– There is nothing to tell. It's my ribbon.

– May I touch it?

– No.

– I want to touch it, he says.

– No.

Something in the lake muscles and writhes out of the water, and then lands with a splash. He turns at the sound.

– A fish, he says.

– Sometime, I tell him, I will tell you the stories about this lake and her creatures.

He smiles at me, and rubs his jaw. A little of my blood smears across his skin, but he doesn't notice, and I don't say anything.

– I would like that very much, he says.

– Take me home, I tell him.

And like a gentleman, he does.

That night, I wash myself. The silky suds between my legs are the color and scent of rust, but I am newer than I have ever been.

• • • •

My parents are very fond of him. He is a nice boy, they say. He will be a good man. They ask him about his occupation, his hobbies, his family. He comes around twice a week, sometimes thrice. My mother invites him in for supper, and while we eat I dig my nails into the meat of his leg. After the ice cream puddles in the bowl, I tell my parents that I am going to walk with him down the lane. We strike off through the night, holding hands sweetly until we are out of sight of the house. I pull him through the trees, and when we find a patch of clear ground I shimmy off my pantyhose, and on my hands and knees offer myself up to him.

I have heard all of the stories about girls like me, and I am unafraid to make more of them. There are two rules: he cannot finish inside of me, and he cannot touch my green ribbon. He spends into the dirt, *pat-pat-patting* like the beginning of rain. I go to touch myself, but my fingers, which had been curling in the dirt beneath me, are filthy. I pull up my underwear and stockings. He makes a sound and points, and I realize that beneath the nylon, my knees are also caked in dirt. I pull them down and brush, and then up again. I smooth my skirt and repin my hair. A single lock has escaped his slicked-back curls, and I tuck it up with the others. We walk down to the stream and I run my hands in the current until they are clean again.

We stroll back to the house, arms linked chastely. Inside, my mother has made coffee, and we all sit around while my father asks him about business.

(If you read this story out loud, the sounds of the clearing can be best reproduced by taking a deep breath and holding it for a long moment. Then release the air all at once, permitting your chest to collapse like a block tower knocked to the ground. Do this again, and again, shortening the time between the held breath and the release.)

• • • •

I have always been a teller of stories. When I was a young girl, my mother carried me out of a grocery store as I screamed about toes in the produce aisle. Concerned women turned and watched as I kicked the air and pounded my mother's slender back.

– Potatoes! she corrected when we got back to the house. Not toes!

She told me to sit in my chair – a child-sized thing, only built for me – until my father returned. But no, I had seen the toes, pale and bloody stumps, mixed in among those russet tubers. One of them, the one that I had poked with the tip of my index finger, was cold as ice, and yielded beneath my touch the way a blister did. When I repeated this detail to my mother, the liquid of her eyes shifted quick as a startled cat.

– You stay right there, she said.

My father returned from work that evening and listened to my story, each detail.

– You've met Mr. Barns, have you not? he asked me, referring to the elderly man who ran this particular market.

I had met him once, and I said so. He had hair white as a sky before snow, and a wife who drew the signs for the store windows.

– Why would Mr. Barns sell toes? my father asked. Where would he get them?

Being young, and having no understanding of graveyards or mortuaries, I could not answer.

– And even if he got them somewhere, my father continued, what would he have to gain by selling them among the potatoes?

They had been there. I had seen them with my own eyes. But beneath the sunbeams of my father's logic, I felt my doubt unfurling.

– Most importantly, my father said, arriving triumphantly at his final piece of evidence, why did no one notice the toes except for you?

As a grown woman, I would have said to my father that there are true things in this world only observed by a single set of eyes. As a girl, I consented to his account of the story, and laughed when he scooped me from the chair to kiss me and send me on my way.

• • • •

It is not normal that a girl teaches her boy, but I am only showing him what I want, what plays on the insides of my eyelids as I fall asleep. He comes to know the flicker of my expression as a desire passes through me, and I hold nothing back from him. When he tells me that he wants my mouth, the length of my throat, I teach myself not to gag and take all of him into me, moaning around the saltiness. When he asks me my worst secret, I tell him about the teacher who hid me in the closet until the others were gone and made me hold him there, and how afterwards I went home and scrubbed my hands with a steel wool pad until they bled, even though after I share this I have nightmares for a month. And when he asks me to marry him, days shy of my eighteenth birthday, I say yes, yes, please, and then on that park bench I sit on his lap and fan my skirt around us so that a passerby would not realize what was happening beneath it.

– I feel like I know so many parts of you, he says to me, trying not to pant. And now, I will know all of them.

• • • •

There is a story they tell, about a girl dared by her peers to venture to a local graveyard after dark. This was her folly: when they told her that standing on someone's grave at night would cause the inhabitant to reach up and pull her under, she scoffed. Scoffing is the first mistake a woman can make.

— I will show you, she said.

Pride is the second mistake.

They gave her a knife to stick into the frosty earth, as a way of proving her presence and her theory.

She went to that graveyard. Some storytellers say that she picked the grave at random. I believe she selected a very old one, her choice tinged by self-doubt and the latent belief that if she were wrong, the intact muscle and flesh of a newly dead corpse would be more dangerous than one centuries gone.

She knelt on the grave and plunged the blade deep. As she stood to run she found she couldn't escape. Something was clutching at her clothes. She cried out and fell down.

When morning came, her friends arrived at the cemetery. They found her dead on the grave, the blade pinning the sturdy wool of her skirt to the ground. Dead of fright or exposure, would it matter when the parents arrived? She was not wrong, but it didn't matter any more. Afterwards, everyone believed that she had wished to die, even though she had died proving that she could live.

As it turns out, being right was the third, and worst, mistake.

• • • •

My parents are pleased about the marriage. My mother says that even though girls nowadays are starting to marry late, she married father when she was nineteen, and was glad that she did.

When I select my wedding gown, I am reminded of the story of the young woman who wished to go to a dance with her lover, but could not afford a dress. She purchased a lovely white frock from a secondhand shop, and then later fell ill and passed from this earth. The coroner who performed her autopsy discovered she had died from exposure to embalming fluid. It turned out that an unscrupulous undertaker's assistant had stolen the dress from the corpse of a bride.

The moral of that story, I think, is that being poor will kill you. Or perhaps the moral is that brides never fare well in stories, and one should avoid either being a bride, or being in a story. After all, stories can sense happiness and snuff it out like a candle.

We marry in April, on an unseasonably cold afternoon. He sees me before the wedding, in my dress, and insists on kissing me deeply and reaching inside of my bodice. He becomes hard, and I tell him that I want him to use my body as he sees fit. I rescind my first rule, given the occasion. He pushes me against the wall and puts his hand against the tile near my throat, to steady himself. His thumb brushes my ribbon. He does not move his hand, and as he works himself in me he says I love you, I love you, I love you. I do not know if I am the first woman to walk up the aisle of St George's with semen leaking down her leg, but I like to imagine that I am.

• • • •

For our honeymoon, we go on a trip I have long desired: a tour of Europe. We are not rich but we make it work. We go from bustling, ancient metropolises to sleepy villages to alpine retreats and back again, sipping spirits and pulling roasted meat from bones with our teeth, eating spaetzle and olives and ravioli and a creamy grain I do not recognize but come to crave each morning. We cannot afford a sleeper car on the train, but my husband bribes an attendant to permit us one hour in an empty room, and in that way we couple over the Rhine.

(If you are reading this story out loud, make the sound of the bed under the tension of train travel and lovemaking by straining a metal folding chair against its hinges. When you are exhausted with that, sing the half remembered lyrics of old songs to the person closest to you, thinking of lullabies for children.)

• • • •

My cycle stops soon after we return from our trip. I tell my husband one night, after we are spent and sprawled across our bed. He glows with delight.

— A child, he says. He lies back with his hands beneath his head. A child. He is quiet for so long that I think that he's fallen asleep, but when I look over his eyes are open and fixed on the ceiling. He rolls on his side and gazes at me.

— Will the child have a ribbon?

I feel my jaw tighten. My mind skips between many answers, and I settle on the one that brings me the least amount of anger.

— There is no saying, now, I tell him finally.

He startles me, then, by running his hand around my throat. I put up my hands to stop him but he uses his strength, grabbing my wrists with one hand as he touches the ribbon with the other. He presses the silky length with his thumb. He touches the bow delicately, as if he is massaging my sex.

– Please, I say. Please don't.

He does not seem to hear. Please, I say again, my voice louder, but cracking in the middle.

He could have done it then, untied the bow, if he'd chosen to. But he releases me and rolls back on his back. My wrists ache, and I rub them.

– I need a glass of water, I say. I get up and go to the bathroom. I run the tap and then frantically check my ribbon, tears caught in my lashes. The bow is still tight.

• • • •

There is a story I love about a pioneer husband and wife killed by wolves. Neighbors found their bodies torn open and strewn around their tiny cabin, but never located their infant daughter, alive or dead. People claimed they saw the girl running with a wolf pack, loping over the terrain as wild and feral as any of her companions.

News of her would ripple through the local settlements. She menaced a hunter in a winter forest – though perhaps he was less menaced than startled at a tiny naked girl baring her teeth and howling. A young woman trying to take down a horse. People even saw her ripping open a chicken in an explosion of feathers.

Many years later, she was said to be seen resting in the rushes along a riverbank, suckling two wolf cubs. I like to imagine that they came from her body, the lineage of wolves tainted human just the once. They certainly bloodied her breasts, but she did not mind because they were hers and only hers.

• • • •

My stomach swells. Inside of me, our child is swimming fiercely, kicking and pushing and clawing. On a walk in the park, the same park where my husband had proposed to me the year before, I gasp and stagger to the side, clutching my belly and hissing through my teeth to Little One, as I call it, to stop. I go to my knees, breathing heavily and near weeping. A woman passing by helps me to sit up and gives me some water, telling me that the first pregnancy is always the worst.

My body changes in ways I do not expect – my breasts are large, swollen and hot, my stomach lined with pale marks, the inverse of a tiger's. I feel monstrous, but my husband seems renewed with desire, as if my novel shape has refreshed our list of perversities. And my body responds: in the line at the supermarket, receiving communion in church, I am marked by a new and ferocious want, leaving me slippery and swollen at the slightest provocation. When he comes home each day, my husband has a list in his mind of things he desires from me, and I am willing to provide them and more.

– I am the luckiest man alive, he says, running his hands across my stomach.

In the mornings, he kisses me and fondles me and sometimes takes me before his coffee and toast. He goes to work with a spring in his step. He comes home with one promotion, and then another. More money for my family, he says. More money for our happiness.

• • • •

I am in labor for twenty hours. I nearly wrench off my husband's hand, howling obscenities that do not seem to shock the nurse. I am certain I will crush my own teeth to powder. The doctor peers down between my legs, his white eyebrows making unreadable Morse code across his forehead.

– What's happening? I ask.

– I'm not satisfied this will be a natural birth, the doctor says. Surgery may be necessary.

– No, please, I say. I don't want that, please.

– If there's no movement soon, we're going to do it, the doctor says. It might be best for everyone. He looks up and I am almost certain he winks at my husband, but pain makes the mind see things differently than they are.

• • • •

I make a deal with Little One, in my mind. *Little One*, I think, *this is the last time that we are going to be just you and me. Please don't make them cut you out of me.*

Little One is born twenty minutes later. They do have to make a cut, but not across my stomach as I had feared. The doctor cuts down, and I feel little, just tugging, though perhaps it is what they have given me. When the baby is placed in my arms, I examine the wrinkled body from head to toe, the color of a sunset sky, and streaked in red.

No ribbon. A boy. I begin to weep, and curl the unmarked baby into my chest.

(If you are reading this story out loud, give a paring knife to the listener and ask them to cut the tender flap of skin between your index finger and thumb. Afterwards, thank them.)

· · · ·

There is a story about a woman who goes into labor when the attending physician is tired. There is a story about a woman who herself was born too early. There is a story about a woman whose body clung to her child so hard they cut her to retrieve him. There is a story about a woman who heard a story about a woman who birthed wolf cubs in secret. Stories have this way of running together like raindrops in a pond. They are each borne from the clouds separately, but once they have come together, there is no way to tell them apart.

(If you are reading this story out loud, move aside the curtain to illustrate this final point to your listeners. It'll be raining, I promise.)

· · · ·

They take the baby so that they may fix me where they cut. They give me something that makes me sleepy, delivered through a mask pressed gently to my mouth and nose. My husband jokes around with the doctor as he holds my hand.

– How much to get that extra stitch? he asks. You offer that, right?

– Please, I say to him. But it comes out slurred and twisted and possibly no more than a small moan. Neither man turns his head toward me.

The doctor chuckles. You aren't the first –

I slide down a long tunnel, and then surface again, but covered in something heavy and dark, like oil. I feel like I am going to vomit.

– the rumor is something like –

– like a vir–

And then I am awake, wide awake, and my husband is gone and the doctor is gone. And the baby, where is –

The nurse sticks her head in the door.

– Your husband just went to get a coffee, she says, and the baby is asleep in the bassinet.

The doctor walks in behind her, wiping his hands on a cloth.

– You're all sewn up, don't you worry, he said. Nice and tight, everyone's happy. The nurse will speak with you about recovery. You're going to need to rest for a while.

The baby wakes up. The nurse scoops him from his swaddle and places him in my arms again. He is so beautiful I have to remind myself to breathe.

• • • •

My son is a good baby. He grows and grows. We never have another child, though not for lack of trying. I suspect that Little One did so much ruinous damage inside of me that my body couldn't house another.

– You were a poor tenant, Little One, I say to him, rubbing shampoo into his fine brown hair, and I shall revoke your deposit.

He splashes around in the sink, cackling with happiness.

My son touches my ribbon, but never in a way that makes me afraid. He thinks of it as a part of me, and he treats it no differently than he would an ear or finger.

Back from work, my husband plays games in the yard with our son, games of chase and run. He is too young to catch a ball, still, but my husband patiently rolls it to him in the grass, and our son picks it up and drops it again, and my husband gestures to me and cries Look, look! Did you see? He is going to throw it soon enough.

• • • •

Of all the stories I know about mothers, this one is the most real. A young American girl is visiting Paris with her mother when the woman begins to feel ill. They decide to check into a hotel for a few days so the mother can rest, and the daughter calls for a doctor to assess her.

After a brief examination, the doctor tells the daughter that all her mother needs is some medicine. He takes the daughter to a taxi, gives the driver directions in French, and explains to the girl that, at his home, his wife will give her the appropriate remedy. They drive and drive for a very long time, and when the girl arrives, she is frustrated by the unbearable slowness of this doctor's wife, who meticulously assembles the pills from powder. When she gets back into the taxi, the driver meanders down the streets, sometimes doubling back on the same avenue. The girl gets out of the taxi to return to the hotel on foot. When she finally arrives, the hotel clerk tells her that he has never seen her before. When she runs up to the room where her mother had been resting, she finds the walls a different color, the furnishings different than her memory, and her mother nowhere in sight.

There are many endings to the story. In one of them, the girl is gloriously persistent and certain, renting a room nearby and staking out the hotel, eventually seducing a young man who works in the laundry and discovering the truth: that her mother had died of a contagious and fatal disease, departing this plane shortly after the daughter was sent from the hotel by the doctor. To avoid a citywide panic, the staff removed and buried her body, repainted and furnished the room, and bribed all involved to deny that they had ever met the pair.

In another version of this story, the girl wanders the streets of Paris for years, believing that she is mad, that she invented her mother and her life with her mother in her own diseased mind. The daughter stumbles from hotel to hotel, confused and grieving, though for whom she cannot say.

I don't need to tell you the moral of this story. I think you already know what it is.

• • • •

Our son enters school when he is five, and I remember his teacher from that day in the park, when she had crouched to help me. She remembers me as well. I tell her that we have had no more children since our son, and now that he has started school, my days will be altered toward sloth and boredom. She is kind. She tells me that if I am looking for a way to occupy my time, there is a wonderful women's art class at a local college.

That night, after my son is in bed, my husband reaches his hand across the couch and slides it up my leg.

– Come to me, he says, and I twinge with pleasure. I slide off the couch, smoothing my skirt very prettily as I walk over to him on my knees. I kiss his leg, running my hand up to his belt, tugging him from his bonds before swallowing him whole. He runs his hands through my hair, stroking my head, groaning and pressing into me. And I don't realize that his hand is sliding down the back of my neck until he is trying to loop his fingers through the ribbon. I gasp and pull away quickly, falling back and frantically checking my bow. He is still sitting there, slick with my spit.

— Come back here, he says.

— No, I say.

He stands up and tucks himself into his pants, zipping them up.

— A wife, he says, should have no secrets from her husband.

— I don't have any secrets, I tell him.

— The *ribbon.*

— The ribbon is not a secret, it's just mine.

— Were you born with it? Why your throat? Why is it green?

I do not answer.

He is silent for a long minute. Then,

— A wife should have no secrets.

My nose grows hot. I do not want to cry.

— I have given you everything you have ever asked for, I say. Am I not allowed this one thing?

— I want to know.

— You think you want to know, I say, but you do not.

— Why do you want to hide it from me?

— I am not hiding it. It is not yours.

He gets down very close to me, and I pull back from the smell of bourbon. I hear a creak, and we both look up to see our son's feet vanishing up the staircase.

When my husband goes to sleep that night, he does so with a hot and burning anger that falls away only when he starts dreaming. I sense its release, and only then can I sleep, too.

The next day, our son touches my throat and asks about my ribbon. He tries to pull at it. And though it pains me, I have to make it forbidden to him. When he reaches for it, I shake a can full of pennies. It crashes discordantly, and he withdraws and weeps. Something is lost between us, and I never find it again.

(If you are reading this story out loud, prepare a soda can full of pennies. When you arrive at this moment, shake it loudly in the face of the person closest to you. Observe their expression of startled fear, and then betrayal. Notice how they never look at you in exactly the same way for the rest of your days.)

• • • •

I enroll in the art class for women. When my husband is at work and my son is in school, I drive to the sprawling green campus and the squat grey building where the art classes are held.

Presumably, the male nudes are kept from our eyes in some deference to propriety, but the class has its own energy – there is plenty to see on a strange woman's naked form, plenty to contemplate as you roll charcoal and mix paints. I see more than one woman shifting forwards and back in her seat to redistribute blood flow.

One woman in particular returns over and over. Her ribbon is red, and is knotted around her slender ankle. Her skin is the color of olives, and a trail of dark hair runs from her belly button to her mons. I know that I should not want her, not because she is a woman and not because she is a stranger, but because it is her job to disrobe, and I feel shame taking advantage of such a state. But as my pencil traces her contours so does my hand in the secret recesses of my mind. I am not even certain how such a thing would happen, but the possibilities incense me to near madness.

One afternoon after class, I turn a hallway corner and she is there, the woman. Clothed, wrapped in a raincoat. Her gaze transfixes me, and this close I can see a band of gold around each of her pupils, as though her eyes are twin solar eclipses. She greets me, and I her.

We sit down together in a booth at a nearby diner, our knees occasionally bushing up against each other beneath the Formica. She drinks a cup of black coffee. I ask her if she has any children. She does, she says, a daughter, a beautiful little girl of eleven.

– Eleven is a terrifying age, she says. I remember nothing before I was eleven, but then there it was, all color and horror. What a number, she says, what a show. Then her face slips somewhere else for a moment, as if she has dipped beneath the surface of a lake.

We do not discuss the specific fears of raising a girl-child. Truthfully, I am afraid to ask. I also do not ask her if she's married, and she does not volunteer the information, though she does not wear a ring. We talk about my son, about the art class. I desperately want to know what state of need has sent her to disrobe before us, but perhaps I do not ask because the answer would be, like adolescence, too frightening to forget.

She captivates me; there is no other way to put it. There is something easy about her, but not easy the way I was – the way I am. She's like dough, how the give of it beneath kneading hands disguises its sturdiness, its potential. When I look away from her and then look back, she seems twice as large as before.

Perhaps we can talk again sometime, I say to her. This has been a very pleasant afternoon.

She nods to me. I pay for her coffee.

I do not want to tell my husband about her, but he can sense some untapped desire. One night, he asks what roils inside of me and I confess it to him. I even describe the details of her ribbon, releasing an extra flood of shame.

He is so glad of this development he begins to mutter a long and exhaustive fantasy as he removes his pants and enters me. I feel as if I have betrayed her somehow, and I never return to the class.

(If you are reading this story out loud, force a listener to reveal a secret, then open the nearest window to the street and scream it as loudly as you are able.)

• • • •

One of my favorite stories is about an old woman and her husband – a man mean as Mondays, who scared her with the violence of his temper and the shifting nature of his whims. She was only able to keep him satisfied with her unparalleled cooking, to which he was a complete captive. One day, he bought her a fat liver to cook for him, and she did, using herbs and broth. But the smell of her own artistry overtook her, and a few nibbles became a few bites, and soon the liver was gone. She had no money with which to purchase a second one, and she was terrified of her husband's reaction should he discover that his meal was gone. So she crept to the church next door, where a woman had been recently laid to rest. She approached the shrouded figure, then cut into it with a pair of kitchen shears and stole the liver from her corpse.

That night, the woman's husband dabbed his lips with a napkin and declared the meal the finest he'd ever eaten. When they went to sleep, the old woman heard the front door open, and a thin wail wafted through the rooms. *Who has my liver? Whooooo has my liver?*

The old woman could hear the voice coming closer and closer to the bedroom. There was a hush as the door swung open. The dead woman posed her query again.

The old woman flung the blanket off her husband.

– *He* has it! She declared triumphantly.

Then she saw the face of the dead woman, and recognized her own mouth and eyes. She looked down at her abdomen, remembering, now, how she carved into her own belly. Next to her, as the blood seeped into the very heart of the mattress, her husband slumbered on.

That may not be the version of the story you're familiar with. But I assure you, it's the one you need to know.

• • • •

My husband is strangely excited for Halloween. Our son is old enough that he can walk and carry a basket for treats. I take one of my husband's old tweed coats and fashion one for our son, so that he might be a tiny professor, or some other stuffy academic. My husband even gives him a pipe on which to gnaw. Our son clicks it between his teeth in a way I find unsettlingly adult.

– Mama, my son says, what are you?

I am not in costume, so I tell him I am his mother.

The pipe falls from his little mouth onto the floor, and he screams. My husband swoops in and picks him up, talking to him in a low voice, repeating his name between his sobs.

It is only as his breathing returns to normal that I am able to identify my mistake. He is not old enough to know the story of the naughty girls who wanted the toy drum, and were wicked toward their mother until she went away and was replaced with a new mother – one with glass eyes and thumping wooden tail. But I have inadvertently told him another one – the story of the little boy who only discovered on Halloween that his mother was not his mother, except on the day when everyone wore a mask. Regret sluices hot up my throat. I try to hold him and kiss him, but he only wishes to go out onto the street, where the sun has dipped below the horizon and a hazy chill is bruising the shadows.

He comes home laughing, gnawing on a piece of candy that has turned his mouth the color of a plum. I am angry with my husband. I wish he had waited to come home before permitting the consumption of the cache. Has he never heard the stories? The pins pressed into the chocolates, the razor blades sunk in the apples? I examine my son's mouth, but there is no sharp metal plunged into his palate. He laughs and spins around the house, dizzy and electrified from the treats and excitement. He wraps his arms around my legs, the earlier incident forgotten. The forgiveness tastes sweeter than any candy that can be given at any door. When he climbs into my lap, I sing to him until he falls asleep.

· · · ·

Our son is eight, ten. First, I tell him fairy tales – the very oldest ones, with the pain and death and forced marriage pared away like dead foliage. Mermaids grow feet and it feels like laughter. Naughty pigs trot away from grand feasts, reformed and uneaten. Evil witches leave the castle and move into small cottages and live out their days painting portraits of woodland creatures.

As he grows, though, he asks questions. Why would they not eat the pig, hungry as they were and wicked as he had been? Why was the witch permitted to go free after her terrible deeds? And the sensation of fins splitting to feet being anything less than agonizing he rejects outright after cutting his hand with a pair of scissors.

– It would huight, he says, for he is struggling with his r's.

I agree with him. It would. So then I tell him stories closer to true: children who go missing along a particular stretch of railroad track, lured by the sound of a phantom train to parts unknown; a black dog that appears at a person's doorstep three days before their passing; a trio of frogs that corner you in the marshlands and tell your fortune for a price.

The school puts on a performance of *Little Buckle Boy*, and he is the lead, the buckle boy, and I join a committee of mothers making costumes for the children. I am lead costume maker in a room full of women, all of us sewing together little silk petals for the flower children and making tiny white pantaloons for the pirates. One of the mothers has a pale yellow ribbon on her finger, and it constantly tangles in her thread. She swears and cries. One day I have to use the sewing shears to pick at the offending threads. I try to be delicate. She shakes her head as I free her from the peony.

– It's such a bother, isn't it? she says.

I nod. Outside the window, the children play – knocking each other off the playground equipment, popping the heads off dandelions. The play goes beautifully. Opening night, our son blazes through his monologue. Perfect pitch and cadence. No one has ever done better.

Our son is twelve. He asks me about the ribbon, point-blank. I tell him that we are all different, and sometimes you should not ask questions. I assure him that he'll understand when he is grown. I distract him with stories that have no ribbons: angels who desire to be human and ghosts who don't realize they're dead and children who turn to ash. He stops smelling like a child – milky sweetness replaced with something sharp and burning, like a hair sizzling on the stove.

Our son is thirteen, fourteen. He waits for the neighbor boy on his way to school, who walks more slowly than the others. He exhibits the subtlest compassion, my son. No instinct for cruelty, like some.

– The world has enough bullies, I've told him over and over.

This is the year he stops asking for my stories.

Our son is fifteen, sixteen, seventeen. He begins to court a beautiful girl from his high school, who has a bright smile and a warm presence. I am happy to meet her, but never insist that we should wait up for their return, remembering my own youth.

When he tells us that he has been accepted at a university to study engineering, I am overjoyed. We march through the house, singing songs and laughing. When my husband comes home, he joins in the jubilee, and we drive to a local seafood restaurant. Over halibut, his father tells him, we are so proud of you. Our son laughs and says that he also wishes to marry his girl. We clasp hands and are even happier. Such a good boy. Such a wonderful life to look forward to.

Even the luckiest woman alive has not seen joy like this.

• • • •

There's a classic, a real classic, that I haven't told you yet.

A girlfriend and a boyfriend went parking. Some people say that means kissing in a car, but I know the story. I was there. They were parked on the edge of a lake. They were turning around in the back seat as if the world was moments from ending. Maybe it was. She offered herself and he took it, and after it was over, they turned on the radio.

The voice on the radio announced that a mad, hook-handed murderer had escaped from a local insane asylum. The boyfriend chuckled as he flipped to a music station. As the song ended, the girlfriend heard a thin scratching sound, like a paperclip over glass. She looked at her boyfriend and then pulled her cardigan over her bare shoulders, wrapping one arm around her breasts.

– We should go, she said.

– No, baby, the boyfriend said. Let's go again.

– What if the killer comes here? The girl asked. The insane asylum is very close.

– We'll be fine, baby, the boyfriend said. Don't you trust me?

The girlfriend nodded reluctantly.

– Well then, he said, his voice trailing off in that way she would come to know so well. He took her hand off her chest and placed it onto himself. She finally looked away from the lakeside.

Outside, the moonlight glinted off the shiny steel hook. The killer waved at her, grinning.

I'm sorry. I've forgotten the rest of the story.

• • • •

The house is so silent without our son. I walk through it, touching all the surfaces. I am happy but something inside of me is shifting into a strange new place.

That night, my husband asks if I wish to christen the newly empty rooms. We have not coupled so fiercely since before our son was born. Bent over the kitchen table, something old is lit within me, and I remember the way we had desired before, how we had left love streaked on all of the surfaces. I could have met anyone at that party when I was seventeen – prudish boys or violent boys. Religious boys who would have made me move to some distant country to convert its denizens. I could have experienced untold numbers of sorrows or dissatisfactions. But as I straddle him on the floor, riding him and crying out, I know that I made the right choice.

We fall asleep exhausted, sprawled naked in our bed. When I wake up, my husband is kissing the back of my neck, probing the ribbon with his tongue. My body rebels wildly, still throbbing with the memories of pleasure but bucking hard against betrayal. I say his name, and he does not respond. I say it again, and he holds me against him and continues. I wedge my elbows in his side, and when he loosens from me in surprise, I sit up and face him. He looks confused and hurt, like my son the day I shook the can of pennies.

Resolve runs out of me. I touch the ribbon. I look at the face of my husband, the beginning and end of his desires all etched there. He is not a bad man, and that, I realize suddenly, is the root of my hurt. He is not a bad man at all. And yet –

– Do you want to untie the ribbon? I ask him. After these many years, is that what you want of me?

His face flashes gaily, and then greedily, and he runs his hand up my

THE LONG LIST ANTHOLOGY

bare breast and to my bow.

– Yes, he says. Yes.

– Then, I say, do what you want.

With trembling fingers, he takes one of the ends. The bow undoes, slowly, the long-bound ends crimped with habit. My husband groans, but I do not think he realizes it. He loops his finger through the final twist and pulls. The ribbon falls away. It floats down and curls at my feet, or so I imagine, because I cannot look down to follow its descent.

My husband frowns, and then his face begins to open with some other expression – sorrow, or maybe pre-emptive loss. My hand flies up in front of me – an involuntary motion, for balance or some other futility – and beyond it his image is gone.

– I love you, I assure him, more than you can possibly know.

– No, he says, but I don't know to what he's responding.

If you are reading this story out loud, you may be wondering if that place my ribbon protected was wet with blood and openings, or smooth and neutered like the nexus between the legs of a doll. I'm afraid I can't tell you, because I don't know. For these questions and others, and their lack of resolution, I am sorry.

My weight shifts, and with it, gravity seizes me. My husband's face falls away, and then I see the ceiling, and the wall behind me. As my lopped head tips backwards off my neck and rolls off the bed, I feel as lonely as I have ever been.

---

Carmen Maria Machado is a fiction writer, critic, and essayist whose work has appeared in *The New Yorker*, *Granta*, *The Paris Review*, *AGNI*, NPR, *The American Reader*, *Los Angeles Review of Books*, *VICE*, and elsewhere. Her stories have been reprinted in several anthologies, including *Best American Science Fiction & Fantasy 2015* and *Year's Best Weird Fiction*. She has been the recipient of the Richard Yates Short Story Prize, a Millay Colony for the Arts residency, the CINTAS Foundation Fellowship in Creative Writing, and a Michener-Copernicus Fellowship, and nominated for a Nebula Award and the Shirley Jackson Award. She is a graduate of the Iowa Writers' Workshop and the Clarion Science Fiction & Fantasy Writers' Workshop, and lives in Philadelphia with her partner.

# The Bonedrake's Penance
## By Yoon Ha Lee

Growing up, it never occurred to me that everyone didn't have a bonedrake mother, or, in the early days, that there was anyone else in the world. I say "mother" and "she," although she was female or male, both or neither, as the occasion suggested or the whim took her.

Certain peoples, she explained later, found these distinctions important. I don't believe she ever quite made sense of it, but accommodating others' religious beliefs mattered to her; at least, she classified gender performances and the associated linguistic gyrations as religious. This was, at any rate, less interesting than other things about her, and when I began calling her Mother, she seemed content.

My mother was the keeper of the fortress at the center of the universe, where we are headed now. It was composed of spun metal and sibilant nanoparticles. I was not allowed outside, even if we had had a proper suit that fit me rather than the all-purpose protective mesh I used. She said I was too young, too fragile, and apt to forget even the simple principles of inertia and momentum. I was, however, allowed to poke around the storerooms where she kept the suits in pristine condition should anyone ever need them. They came in all shapes and sizes, and numbers of limbs, and some of them accommodated a head (or heads) and some of them didn't. A few might fit you when you reach your adult phase. The materials they were made of varied. Later I learned something of their construction, and ways to repair them, but when I was a child none of this interested me. Instead, I marveled at the gold piping on one, or the crystal-dark displays on another, which flickered tantalizingly with iridescence when I angled a tentacle-gripper toward the light, or the way visors dimmed and brightened in response to my presence.

The most interesting suits were the ones I could imagine myself fitting into. This narrowed the field considerably. Not many were designed for bipeds with heads at the top, although I sometimes contorted myself upside-down trying to make my head emerge from my stomach. (Nothing worked. But it was entertaining, and in the meantime I became very flexible.) The majority were too big for me, and my mother had locked them down in some fashion so that I could touch them but not open them up to try on, or even poke my head in.

Most of them would respond to my prodding enough to allow their limbs to be repositioned, however, or even folded, depending on the particular material they were made of. Then I would go off and cut up rags—at least, I think they were rags, since my mother kept them in a heap and never seemed to care what I did with them—and stitch them together with great, clumsy child-stitches to make my own suits.

Second most interesting, although it took a few more years before I could formulate the question, was the absence of suits that looked like my mother. Granted, there were plenty of quadrupeds, but none that had her sleek serpentine grace, none that accommodated that heavy head with its skull-mask features, or her claws, which she kept sharp and yet was so gentle with. She could trim my fingernails with them yet keep from cutting me even as I struggled and squirmed.

The question came to me when I was perhaps six years old, by the calendar she used, when she caught me dressing up like her. "Dressing up" was a charitable way to put it. I had been raiding the pantry. My mother was a surprisingly good cook for someone who subsisted on, as she put it, "radioactive leavings and the occasional smashed atom." (I was never sure how literally she meant this, since she prudently refused to let me examine her inner workings.) She knew I liked sweets, the more fancifully decorated the better. The previous week she had attempted to show me the nuances of cake decoration, which was more of an exercise in getting frosting and holographic sprinkles all over the table, but the results were sweet, crunchy, tender, and occasionally vision-inducing.

The pantry contained all the accoutrements of pastry decoration, some old-fashioned and some less so: serrated metal nozzles for sacks of frosting, powdered sugar sweetly scented with rose water or vanilla or (so my mother claimed) flavors she could sense but which I could not. And there was the frosting itself, most of it kept in a suspended state, no mixing required. I wasn't allowed near the dangerous kitchen equipment at that age—the knives clattered at me and worse, lectured in high shrill voices when I reached for the drawer they were stored in—but I knew where the chopsticks were kept, and for all their sullen clicks and mutters, they didn't raise the alarm. I grabbed one of the metal ones, prettily enameled with a fractal gasket, and used it to puncture one of the frosting bags.

Some of the frosting, which was blue with mysterious lavender-glow swirls, squirted all over my hands and shirt. I didn't see this as a disaster but an opportunity. I licked it off my hands, although the stuff smeared all over my skin and left great gobs on my chin. It tasted like sugar and jasmine and firefly sparks, and tickled going down, making me giggle.

Then I remembered my original purpose, and I got to work. I stripped off my clothes and cheerfully traced my ribs with great streaks of frosting so they would look like my mother's exoskeletal barding except, inevitably, mushier. The frosting developed interesting crusts as it hardened, causing it to flake off every time I moved. Lavender glitter drifted off in nebular swirls and meteor streaks, and the kitchen filled with shadows as deep as the lanterned night outside the fortress.

Not all my mother's frostings were astronomically themed, but she had a weakness in that direction, and she herself had eyes that glowed in their depths like faraway stars. Sometimes I squinted as I looked at my reflection, hoping my eyes would do the same thing; no luck. At least I was old enough to realize that putting frosting in my eyes wouldn't work.

I only realized my mother had entered the kitchen when I heard a sound that was part-wheeze, part-crackle. I started guiltily and scrabbled to hide the offending frosting paraphernalia behind my back, not that she was fooled.

My mother had a horrified tone that I later identified as meaning *Am I doing this parenting thing wrong?* but, at the time, I assumed she was upset with me. "Eggling," she said, her voice rattling more than usual, "are you trying to persuade me to *eat* you?"

"I wanted to look like you," I said, or something to that effect. That was the point of the exercise: drawing armor traceries over myself, and scribbly imitations of her electromagnetic banners, and putting the metal nozzles on my fingertips in imitation of her magnificent claws. (Even with the frosting, they kept falling off, but that was a game in itself.) Since I couldn't play dress-up with a dragon-suit, I had to improvise.

I didn't understand the way her eyes dimmed, as if in sorrow. She'd never minded my makeshift costumes before. Not that she was permissive about everything, but for a bonedrake she had sensible ideas about behaviors that did and didn't harm human children. I especially remembered the way she had roared and clamored with laughter when I tried to glue myself, with leftover rice, into a caterpillar-priest outfit.

"Oh, eggling," my mother said. She liked to call me that. "What's wrong with the way you look?"

She had never asked that before. I gaped at her, confused.

My mother huffed, and vapor whistled out of her sides, through apertures I had looked for but had never been able to find. "Come here," she said.

I knew better than to argue, although I glanced back at the crumbling bits of starry frosting that I was leaving on the floor. She huffed again, and the vapor came once more, stronger. It felt warm and damp, and it carried the effervescent scent of limes, if limes grew on trees bright as suns. Then she retrieved a sponge and methodically began cleaning me off.

I wriggled, the way children do, and at the time I thought nothing more of it. But perhaps some lesson stuck with me anyway: I never again attempted to dress up as my mother.

• • • •

Let me tell you more about my mother. She liked music, and she mixed musical traditions without having much ear for the harmonious. One of her favorite instruments was a great wind-harp concocted upon hollow bones of translucent metal. Wind in our fortress was necessarily artificial, but it came when she called it, and she did so to a schedule, as with most things. In the mornings (for there were mornings, the way there were mealtimes and evenings and year-festivals), I woke to the sound of the wind roaming through the pipes, moaning threnodies and the jangling accompaniment of wires stirred to unrhymed arpeggios. At times I took mallets or brushes to the pipes to bang out my own counterpoints, always scurrying away whenever her shadow crossed the threshold, as if the strings could hide me. She only smiled her inscrutable smile.

My mother had an obsession with neatness, as befitted a keeper of calendars and archaeological details. I asked over and over what she did here, and she never tired of answering me. The fortress was filled with clocks of all kinds and from all eras, some of which I was allowed to take apart, and some of which she walled up behind meshes of incandescent force. Clocks that dripped sand of silver and clocks that uttered relativistic syllables, clocks with gears that bit my clumsy fingers and clocks that tolled whenever a civilization devoured itself.

"What's a civilization?" I would ask next, trying to get the pronunciation right. That was another thing. My mother spoke to me in a language of up-and-down tones and varied sibilants, but she was fluent in anything you cared to name, including a number of tongues that were no longer spoken anywhere else.

She gave me the word in many languages, and showed me paintings, holographs, maps, shards scavenged from ruins long swallowed by bloated red stars. She explained how most sentients developed some form of society, hierarchical or otherwise, and built edifices both material and metaphysical. Cities woven in and out of the rings of spinning worlds, or propagating across vast empty stretches soliton-fashion, or created out of nerve-flicker impulses webbed together across brightly beaded networks.

"Are we a civilization?" was the question after that, most days.

My mother retracted her claw and tapped me on the head, thoughtfully, as though I might make an interesting sound. (The one time I protested, "My head isn't empty!", her laugh thundered through the halls. She teased me about it for weeks.) "Can you have a civilization of two?" she asked.

"Two is more than one," I said, holding my fingers out to prove it. I was eight then, old enough to count without my fingers, but I liked the visual aid. "We even have a city." Then I frowned. "Is a fortress a city?"

"If you want it to be," she said unhelpfully, and grinned at me.

My mother had not always been the fortress's keeper. She alluded occasionally to her predecessors. I never asked, on the grounds that I couldn't imagine a time before I existed, let alone a time before my mother's stewardship of our home. She never referred to them by name, and she didn't tell me what they had looked like. But she kept a shrine to them anyway.

• • • •

Little-known facts about bonedrakes, before I tell you more:

They are, indeed, made of bone. Mostly. I never acquired the technical specifications. Whether the bones were laminates harvested from lesser creatures, or derived from drakes slaughtered for the purpose in the days of long-ago devas and paladins, the pallor of a bonedrake is unmistakable. The silken, chilly touch of death leaves its traces wherever a bonedrake goes, all the way down in the universe's marrow, an absolute zero signature. Yet this is not all that terrible, when you think about it. After all, time's arrow pierces everything that lives, and nothing is undying forever.

There are sagas written about bonedrakes, and incantations, and dry academic treatises. (There is nothing in the world so dull that a dry academic treatise cannot be written about it, and bonedrakes are far from dull.) The taboo against depicting them in the visual arts is not universal but widespread nonetheless. After all, if carcass-armor could be animated by the will of distant warlords and descend roaring from skies whose constellations were tattooed over by explosions, who was to say that sculptures and paintings could not also turn against their makers?

Bonedrakes are good at computations. My mother's favorite instrument was the abacus, even if she preferred using it as a percussion instrument. It wasn't as if she needed something as primitive as an abacus for arithmetic she could do in her head. She always said I was missing the point and that creative tool-use was its own pleasure.

It's not true that only four bonedrakes ever existed, four for the dimensions of space and time, or four for death, or four for the elements. The number of base elements varies so widely among belief systems anyway, and my mother once mentioned that her predecessors believed in atomic configurations rather than the poetry of stone, acid, vortex, plasma.

Most words or gestures of warding against bonedrakes are sheer superstition. I once sat on a cushion stuffed with firebird down—it was unusually cold in that chamber, to accommodate our guests' preferred environment, and I liked the extra heat source—and watched, resisting the urge to pick at my fingernails, while my mother listened patiently to emissaries filling the fortress with the wave-like overlapping of barrier-chaconnes before they presented her with defanged artillery pieces. I played the chaconnes back later, because the rhythms were oddly soothing. My mother never showed any sign of discomfort.

On the other hand, because bonedrakes are essentially creatures of war, they are designed to follow orders. Because my mother's original commanders were dead, and because she was the only one of her kind left, it took me a long time to grasp this essential point.

•  •  •  •

For the longest time, I didn't realize that my mother's duties involved emissaries. On occasion she disappeared, and I wandered around looking for her, or not, if I was too engrossed looking at pictures or picking berries. Among her several gardens was one she had designed to be "friendly to creatures who put everything in their mouths and have delicate stomachs."

When I was very young I cried for her, and this triggered messages telling me to be patient until she could take care of my needs. In the meantime, since she was able to manipulate multiple bodies at once— another knack I never picked up, as you'll find—she dispatched one of her marionettes to handle the immediate problem, whether that was feeding me rice porridge or reading me a book. As I grew older, I could tell I didn't have her full attention, and at last, when I was twelve, I demanded to know where she went when she wasn't really with me.

My mother was in the middle of organizing a shelf full of curios. The "shelf" wasn't so much physical as a ladder-basket of lines of light suspending the contents, everything from grinning railcars carved from driftwood to upside-down bottles in which raged storms of oil particles and petals. "Where do I go?" she echoed, not paying attention as she tried to decide whether she wanted the ice sculpture facing left or right. "I don't leave the fortress, eggling. I'm always right here."

"But sometimes I can't *find* you," I said, more insistently. "Where do you go then?"

She fixed me with an interested stare. I was reminded that, as well as I knew the fortress, there were yet crevices and nooks and closets that I had never been permitted to explore, and would never be able to break my way into. Then she sighed, and this time the vapor that whistled out of her side-vents had a metallic quality. "You are old enough now," she said.

"Sometimes people send emissaries with items for the fortress. We are a repository of sorts, a museum. It is only courteous that I deal with them and their artifacts personally, if they so desire. Not all of them do."

I studied the shelf with new interest. Come to think of it, I'd never seen the railcars before. I had assumed that they came from her usual inexhaustible trove of treasures. She liked to rotate her decorations, from tapestries of rustling leaves with couplets chewed into their edges, to strands of beads carved from the remains of exploratory probes and painted with representations of their solar systems of origin. But where, after all, had all those treasures come from? Although my mother had her hobbies—cupcakes as a case in point—I didn't think her own capabilities were so varied. Nor were mine. And matter, let alone matter in the shape of grinning railcars, or even sad railcars, didn't spontaneously come from nowhere.

"Do you require their artifacts?" I asked, trying to imagine my mother demanding tribute, a figure crowned with whorls of plasma perilously contained. It was absurd.

She snorted. The walls vibrated, although the fragile trinkets she was arranging showed no sign of being affected. "Yes and no," she said. "It is good to study the march of history, but we lack little here."

"I want to meet the emissaries too," I said impulsively.

"There are none right now," she said, tail flicking idly back and forth.

"But more will come, won't they?"

"Very likely so," she said. "Not to a schedule, mind. One thing you must understand about the outside world is that its modes of recording history, including calendars, change and shift as different nations rise and fall and conquer each other. Even matters like timekeeping are an expression of power. In any case, if you are old enough to want to meet visitors, you are old enough to learn the protocols for dealing with them."

"Protocols?" I asked. My schooling, to this point, had consisted of my pointing at things that caught my eye and my mother figuring out safe ways of indulging me. Disciplined tutelage was foreign to me, but I had no prejudice against it, either. Moreover, the thought of meeting *other people*, like the ones for whom the mysterious suits had been designed, was so exciting that my mother could have, if so inclined, probably have gotten me to scrub the fortress clean with my hair in exchange for the opportunity.

"Protocols," she said firmly. "Of which the first one is, there's never only one right way to handle a first contact. Or a seventh, or a twenty-fourth, if it comes to that."

One of the earliest lessons she imparted to me, in preparation for my first such meeting, was that you could also never guarantee that nothing would go wrong, no matter how experienced you were or what your best intentions were. I was incredulous about her claim that some of the most vicious encounters occurred between members of the same species, even the same communities within those species.

"How is that possible?" I demanded. We were walking through a kaleidoscopic panorama depicting the outbreak of the 3.72nd Arrazhed

Civil War. The nomenclature was an approximation for my convenience: the Arrazheds had numbered their conflicts with real numbers rather than strictly with natural ones, since history did not consist of discrete events but cause and consequence bleeding into each other. My mother was able to remember the number entire, but she said that for our purposes I could round it off to the nearest hundredth.

The Arrazhed conflict had involved atrocities of all sorts. By then I was old enough to have been introduced to the concept. While my mother was no great believer in the innocence of childhood, neither did she prod me to deal with the realities outside our fortress, or even the ones memorialized within it, until I showed an interest in them.

For instance, my mother said, with a certain irony, that for many cultures, set definitions were of particular importance, especially in instances where multivalence was devalued. You could define sets as desired, then exclude based on your criteria. (The obligatory digression on set paradoxes only lasted a day or two, although she would have spent longer on it if I had cared to.)

One of the Arrazhed factions, the Oethred, was particularly literal-minded. They retaliated against a more powerful aggressor by releasing a plague that edited the enemy's spawnlings to exhibit physical traits most commonly associated with the Oethred themselves: carapaces with an ultraviolet shimmer rather than iridescent green, smaller lens-clusters, a tendency toward polydactyl grippers. The Oethred's enemies purged their spawnlings, as was intended, but retaliated by infecting Oethred religious wind-paintings with nanite sculptors, so that their masterworks collapsed into hyperstable vortices whispering heterodox teachings.

"But shouldn't they have realized that no one was winning?" I said, craning my head to catch a better glimpse of a preserved Oethred corpse.

"If only politics were that simple," she said.

There were more atrocities, whole abecedaries of them. Our attempts at a taxonomy were sputtering and inconsistent, like candle flames. I started a list, written in clustered photons unhappily pinned to a sheet of sheer plastic. By now, at fourteen, I was literate in a simplified version of my mother's native tongue as well as several interlinguas. My mother would cheerfully translate anything else for me, knowing that my capacity for fluency was less than hers.

I didn't like my list, and I didn't like the way it glowed at me. *The pictures are real,* they seemed to be saying. *The recordings are real.* It wasn't so much that I doubted as that the outside world was too different to imagine as a solid, moving entity.

The next principle my mother was adamant about was our absolute neutrality.

"Absolutely absolute?" I asked.

"Yes," she said. "I am afraid I will have to insist on this point." And she looked very grave as she said this, with all her status lights going gray-blue. The vapor she exuded was like copper gone sour.

"What if—"

"Stop," my mother said, even more gravely. "You're already thinking of counterarguments and edge cases. That is perfectly fine if you are a mathematician or a philosopher. The fortress is not about ensuring justice, or righting wrongs, or even compassion. It is about enduring and remembering all the things that people bring us to safeguard for them, the histories and the artifacts. Justice, for the things they remember—that's something that civilizations have to negotiate for themselves."

I thought for a moment. "*Could* you right wrongs, if you wanted to?"

At least she didn't hide this information from me. "Sometimes yes," she said. "Sometimes no. And sometimes they're the same thing, but you can't tell until the end of time anyway, and even I won't survive that singularity accounting. But the point is that we won't, because that's not what we do here. We are guardians, not historians interpreting the weight of years."

"Does it ever bother you only being a guardian?" I asked. Later the question would become, *Doesn't it ever bother you?* She must have known it then, even if I did not.

"Eggling," my mother said, now amused, "for all the evil in the world, even this has its compensations. Do you imagine I chafe at the restrictions? I'm the one who set them, after all. The only chains are the ones I put on myself."

I didn't understand that at all, so I averted my eyes. The movement of my head triggered a cascade of rubato footsteps and the lapping of water, and the wailing of a membrane-flute.

"You can live without rules, too," she added. "That's a choice you will have. But while you dwell here, as my ward and not yet an adult, you will have to abide by mine."

I was appalled that she felt the need to make this explicit. I continued to avert my eyes, but all the sensors in the fortress were linked to her systems, and she knew I was frowning.

"Come on," my mother said coaxingly. "You have time yet to think about it." She did not say what we both knew, that for all the protections she had given me, she could not make me quite as long-lived as herself. "You're ready now to run through training scenarios with the game generators. You'll like learning about the Mirre-ai-rah. Aquatic societies can be so interesting."

Something prompted me to ask, "Do they still exist?"

She was silent for a moment, then said, "None of the peoples you will meet in the scenarios still exist. If you think about this, you will realize why I have set this restriction in place, even if you may not agree with my reasoning."

I thought this a ridiculous way to ensure the neutrality that she was so insistent upon. After all, it was impossible to avoid having *some* preconceptions about the things I perceived, based on the sum of my experiences, however attenuated and secondhand.

But I reasoned that it was better to prepare under my mother's guidance than not at all. She had promised that I would speak with emissaries in due course; I had no doubt that she would keep her promise.

• • • •

My first three encounters with emissaries went awkwardly, but no catastrophes ensued. Indeed, I was sorry when our guests left, and I moped around the fortress drawing portraits of them in the vapors of the cloud chambers, which were as evanescent as you would expect. My mother couldn't help but be aware of my mood and wisely left me alone except to provide the perennial tray of cupcakes. She would have been baking even without me there, I knew. Still, it made me feel better, especially when she decorated the cupcakes with quirky eyestalks and the occasional constellation-sprinkle of crushed pearls.

None of the emissaries knew what to make of me. Their histories spoke of my mother as a solitary guardian. The first set treated me as an interpreter, which was harmless enough, as my mother could understand everything they said without my help. At least they interacted with me, very politely at that. They seemed distressed that, along with their offerings for the museum, they had not brought gifts for me. I had to assure them that they had not caused offense, especially once I figured out that the offerings were holy instruments of torture. My moral convictions were diffuse in those days, yet still I had no great liking for pain unasked for, and no great animus for anyone either. I half-expected my mother to scorn the items set down before her, with their cunning barbed filaments and aberrant hooks. Instead, she thanked the emissaries graciously and placed the instruments in a case rimmed with gold. When I later tried to open the case, I couldn't, and felt reassured after all.

The second set pretended I didn't exist. At first I was baffled, then infuriated, and then I came to the conclusion, based on some of the cultural artifacts they shared with my mother, that they regarded me as a type of ambulatory furniture.

After that, I understood my place in the masque and did my best to play the part. Some of them hung their personal library-strands around my shoulders, spinning superstates of beaded condensates dark and dazzling. I drowsed to the strands' hum and daydreamed of exploring the mysterious interior of the palace-ship they had traveled here in.

The third set was preceded by what I first mistook for fireworks. My mother liked to mark the New Year and other anniversaries—both celebrations and mourning days; the color schemes were quite distinct—with spectacular displays of ghostly lights. She said that everyone grew a year older on the New Year, although there were other ways to reckon age. On this occasion, we walked along one of the promenades and I pressed my face up against the viewport, marveling that the glass felt neither cold nor hot but was simply smooth and kind against my skin.

My mother studied my face, then said, without the slightest trace of alarm, "This is something you must learn to recognize, eggling. We are under attack."

I began to shake. I'd had my disputes with my mother. As a child I had done my share of kicking and screaming and biting. (Biting a bonedrake, even one who is doing her best not to do you injury, is a bad idea. My jaw hurt for the next week. I never did it again.) But I had never been the target of serious hostility.

"These are merely temperamental chemical compounds," she added. "I have faced far worse."

"How often does this happen?" I asked.

She eyed me sideways. There was an odd odor, which I identified as that of smoke. But it was a smoke of pyres, rather than a smoke of pastries overbaked. (A rare occurrence. She was attentive to her craft.) "I could give you the percentages," she said. "About 47% of them come in with guns or missiles or something of the sort. It depends on how you define 'weapon,' and that's as difficult as you'd expect any semantic question to be."

"How do you know we're in no real danger?" I said, unable to hide my apprehension.

"The fortress has survived this long for a reason," my mother said, "and I'm not averse to putting in upgrades as they occur to me."

So my mother's fondness for redecorating had a purpose other than the aesthetic. "I suppose," I said, "this isn't the worst form of danger anyway." I was learning.

Her smile was bonier than usual. "Indeed."

The third set of emissaries eventually became satisfied that they couldn't crack the fortress unless it wanted to be cracked, and they asked to parlay. The parlay itself was aggressive, and quite enjoyable once I got into the spirit of it. The emissaries, from an alliance of several species with wildly differing homeworlds, spoke to us with endearing frankness. They told my mother she was a terrible cook, which by their standards she probably was. They also gave us suggestions on how to improve the suits she had provided for their use.

Their purpose, now that they had established that they could not defeat her, was to recruit her. Their logic confused me. Exactly what did they think they could offer her? As the conversation wore on and I nibbled on crackers—every so often I needed a break from cupcakes or fruits or porridge with mushrooms—it transpired that they thought my mother was *bored*.

Once they mentioned the idea, it bothered me more and more. She had been here so long that I could scarcely conceptualize the span of time. What if she was, indeed, bored? What if she was going to leave the fortress behind and—and what? I couldn't imagine what would happen to me.

• • • •

After surviving an attack, even one about which my mother was so unconcerned, I was certain that our next encounter with emissaries couldn't go any worse. At least, it would be no more than another assault. Just to prepare myself, however, I threw myself into the study of conflagrations.

The simulators left me with nightmares of coagulated fluids and unfoul vapors; I rarely smelled anything in my dreams. I emerged drenched with sweat and wracked by pains from the way I tensed up imagining the sounds of puncture, or ambush, or venom hisses.

My mother encouraged me to take sand baths and steam baths, or to meditate in the gardens. She was a great believer in sand baths. I chafed at being offered such mundane comforts. She only harrumphed and said that the young had no appreciation for the value of ordinary things. To please her, I lingered in the baths and the gardens. Neither helped much.

The fourth set of emissaries came five days before one of the anniversaries that my mother observed. Granted, she was not inflexible. If courtesy required, she would simply put off the observance until a better opportunity came along. This was one of the sadder ones, where she retreated to light incense in a plain dark shrine. In years past she had permitted me to help her, and the sweet, woody smell of the smoke would cling to my clothes and hair and follow me into my sleep. I never smelled the blend on my mother; no matter what she did, she had a curious odor of marrow and melting wax.

In any case, my mother made her preparations for the anniversary as usual. In retrospect, I should have apprehended that these next visitors were unusual even by my mother's standards. When the fleet showed up on the far-scryers, her status lights changed to a colder and more melancholy blue than I had ever seen before.

"What is it?" I asked, shifting the great facets this way and that so I could view the fleet from different angles. Besides the far-scryers, the fortress had a staggering array of early warning systems. I could work most of them well enough to satisfy my basic curiosity, although I was reliant upon my mother's experience and the fortress's tutorial systems to guide me through the more complex commands.

My mother was silent, statue-like. My heart stuttered. It was unlike her to deny me answers, even the infuriating riddling ones she sometimes gave to encourage me to figure out what she really meant.

When she answered, it was very literally. "It's quite a fleet," she said, "with a formation similar to one I knew in the past. The flagship is a work of art, isn't it? I wonder if that's what they want me to add to the collection."

I examined the flagship. As starships went, it had a certain grandeur. It was the fleet's largest ship by far. The golden armor was, incredibly, decorated with fantastical treasures: cameos of queens and knights carved from mirrorstones, rubies and spinels glimmering with the bloodlight of small sacrifices, knives in caskets welded in archaeological splendor to the hull.

"Are the weapons—"

My mother spoke over me, as though she had heard another question entirely. "That one, in the rear guard," she said. Her voice was becoming clipped, distant, like bones clacking together.

Obligingly, I viewed the ship she had indicated. At first I scarcely recognized it as such. The flagship, for all its gaudiness, was an ellipsoid, a solid shape. This other ship looked more like a seethe of insects beneath the surface of the night, elusively visible even with the far-scryer's customary adjustments for the limitations of human perception.

"That is the pleasure-wrecker *Five Hundred Stings and One Chalice*," my mother said. I was becoming increasingly unnerved, yet all I could do was look from her dimmed eyes to the ship, from the ship to her eyes. "Even here I have heard stories of its exploits. At full capacity, it carries over a million of its people. In the old days those would have been sculptors, calligraphers, perfumers, cooks. They designed ships to go to war for them—"

"Aren't these all warships?" I had gone on to examine the armaments on the others. Bombs, mines, putrescences (I wasn't sure what this meant, except that I didn't want to be hit by them), the occasional canister of apiarist's fire. No two were the same, which struck me as strange.

"They are indeed," my mother said. "Well, we will send out the welcome-banner, and see what they have for us. I hope we can accommodate them all." The fortress had its secrets of involute geometry, but so did the fleet we beheld.

The welcome-banner changed not at all with the calendar's groanings. My mother said that sometimes constancy was a virtue. It consisted of a pattern of particles, a display of dappled light. In it I often glimpsed the coalescence of stars, the alchemical nature of metals noble and otherwise, the asymmetry of yearning.

The flagship asked for permission to send a single visitor, using an old protocol. My mother granted it. I hadn't expected otherwise. The two of us went down to one of the fortress's many antechambers, this one hung about with violet-green fronds and filled with a dense, cloying steam. I wore the minimum of protection necessary, the usual mesh. The steam would not do me lasting damage, but there was no need to be reckless.

The visitor was a robot, darkly iridescent, with a shape not unlike my own. I envied it its sleek limbs, the precise joints, the sheen of its crested head. It and my mother rapidly agreed to switch to a different interlingua, one that better reflected the robot's needs. Then it introduced itself as Hauth of the Greater Choreographical Society.

By now I knew of dance, so I mistook Hauth for a form of artist. That wasn't entirely inaccurate, at that. But Hauth would, it emerged, be better described as a historian or propagandist.

At no point was Hauth's manner anything but polite. It had come, it said with its buzzing accent, because it wished to interview my mother personally and incorporate the results in its chronicle.

"If that is your wish," my mother said, still burning with that sad blue light. "My hospitality is yours."

Hauth explained its recording instruments and editing procedures and the musical conventions by which the final work would be scored. Then it looked at me. I had lost interest and was examining a fern's spores. It added, smoothly, "I would like permission to interview your ward as well."

"Eggling," my mother said when I didn't react; I hadn't been paying attention. "I advise against it—"

"Is she old enough to make this decision for herself?" Hauth interrupted.

My mother sighed. "She is."

"Then I wish to hear her answer."

"Mother?" I asked waveringly.

"I advise against it."

"Why?"

"Because you can't unknow things once you know them," she said. "Because you can't return to being a child once you become an adult."

I should have been paying attention to her phrasing here; I was not. Not that I was the first to make such a mistake, but I hope you will grow to be wiser than I was.

"I would prefer," Hauth said, even more crushingly polite, "that the decision be wholly her own."

"No decision is wholly anyone's own," my mother said, "but I take your point. It's up to you, eggling. I will not send our guest away. However, if you would rather not hear what it has to say, I must insist that you not be further involved in its investigations. I will handle them myself."

This made me stubborn. She gave me a warning look, which I ignored; I had gotten to that age. At the time, I thought only that Hauth might be able to tell me things about my mother that she hadn't wanted me to hear. I didn't realize my mother was more worried about the things that *I* would have difficulty facing.

"I will be available whenever you need me," my mother said, addressing Hauth. "Ask what you will of my child, if she consents to answer. Eggling, if you want this to stop at any time, you know how to find me."

I watched as she snaked around toward one of the two doors out, her status lights flaring bright, then dimming almost to black.

Hauth stood with its masked face, its edged patience. I stared at it, then said, "I can show you around the fortress."

It spoke. This time the buzzing accent sounded more harmonious, but that might have been my imagination. "I would be grateful if you would show me the places that make you think of your mother," it said.

*What a peculiar request,* I thought. Still, surely there was no harm. I glanced at the door where my mother had just left. "Come with me," I said.

• • • •

These were the places I showed Hauth, and which I hope to show you:

First was the kitchen. Well, one of the kitchens. There were multiples. For the purposes of baking cupcakes for me, my mother only used one kitchen, even if she occasionally strayed to the others if she thought I needed fish stew in my diet. I had to explain cupcakes to Hauth. It didn't eat. I worried about what to offer as refreshments.

I didn't know whether Hauth never laughed, or robots in general never did, but it said, gently, "You will have figured out that I don't metabolize the way you do. I am well-supplied for this visit. I appreciate that you are thinking of my needs, however."

Hauth asked me what cupcakes tasted like, perhaps because the chemical analysis was lacking in metaphor, or else because it was amused by how much I had to say about different flavors and textures. I believe its interest was genuine.

Next came one of the gardens. Not my favorite one, because that wasn't what Hauth had asked about, but the one where my mother spent the most time. I rarely went there unless specifically invited to. My mother had never forbidden my presence. Rather, the pillars of ice, the ashen winds, and the metallic light like bronze wearing thin, filled me with a tremulous unease. It was difficult to convince myself that I felt no physical chill, that my billowing mesh gave me plenty of protection. Yet this was where my mother came for the unnamed anniversaries that meant so much to her.

The floor was raked by claw-marks, which formed sinuous and self-intersecting trails. Ordinarily my mother sheathed her claws. Even on those occasions when some accident necessitated scratching up the fortress, she was assiduous about repairs. Here, however, she wanted to leave some trace of her agitation.

Hauth approached the shrine that formed the centerpiece of the garden and peered at the burnt-out stubs of incense sticks. Ash and sand stirred slightly, glimmered palely. It did not touch anything. "What does this mean to you?" it asked.

Not: *What does this mean to your mother?* I supposed it already knew the answer to that. I was seized with the simultaneous and contradictory desire to know and not to know. But Hauth had asked first. I explained about the anniversaries. "She comes here at such times," I said, irrationally convinced that I was betraying her. Surely, though, she would have told me if there was anything I should refuse to answer? For that matter, I couldn't imagine that she wasn't monitoring us anyway, or incapable of intervening if she needed to. "I don't often accompany her here."

Hauth walked around without fitting its footsteps to the claw-paths. I wasn't sure whether I liked that or not, for all its respectful demeanor. "You don't know why she comes here," it said.

"Do you?"

"She hasn't told you?"

"I've asked," I said. "Her answers are vague. I don't want to hurt her."

"I can tell you," Hauth said after a pause, "but I will keep it to myself if you prefer."

It was too much, especially combined with my mother's mysterious behavior earlier. "I want to know."

"Around now," it said, "she is remembering the deaths of her comrades."

*Comrades?* I wondered. Certainly my mother could defend herself, but I rejected the image of her fighting alongside others of her kind—if, indeed, they had also been bonedrakes.

"The most important one," it went on, as if it had not noticed the way I was shivering, "commemorates the day she deserted."

"I can't imagine—" I stopped. My mother, who loved cupcakes and carillons. I could see her as a deserter more easily than I could see her as a warfighter.

Hauth turned away from the shrine. "Many people died," it said.

"Let's go somewhere else," I said, before Hauth could tell me anything else. "I can show you the observatory."

Hauth was amenable. Doubtless it sensed that it had me trapped, and all it had to do to wait for me to succumb. The observatory didn't have much to offer someone who had, I presumed, traveled a great distance to visit the fortress. Still, Hauth admired the telescopes with their sphinx-stare lenses, and the way a particular view of a nebula complemented mobiles that spun this way and that, catching the light. It told me about sites it had visited in the past: symphony-bridges of tinted ice, to be ruined attractively whenever the universe exhaled; stars in the process of colliding and merging; moons turned into sculptures exalted by sgraffito depictions of elemental valences.

As the day wore on, I showed Hauth everything I could think of. Inevitably, I thought, it would demand to speak to my mother. But no: it listened to everything I had to say, however hollow it started to sound.

Finally I cracked, and asked what it had not volunteered to tell me. "Why are you really here?" I said.

"I came to find out more about your mother's past," Hauth said, "just as I told her. Since she still lives, it seemed appropriate to seek her out."

"Then why talk to me?"

"Aren't you a part of her life, too?"

I bit my lip. I hadn't seen her in all this time, showing Hauth around. We were sitting in the kitchen because I needed to be in comforting surroundings. For the first time, I didn't feel comforted at all. The kitchen had been designed, I saw now, so that it could accommodate both a bonedrake and a human, for all that my mother could compress herself astonishingly when she had to. When had she thought to do that? And when, for that matter, had she fixed on cupcakes as her hobby of choice, when she didn't eat them?

When had she decided to rear a human child?

"What are you going to do with your chronicle?" I said.

"Share it," it said. "With everyone."

"I want to see it," I said.

"Yes," it said. "Yes. When it's done. But it's not, yet."

I knew what it was asking. "I will take you to my mother now."

We found her in the shrine of ashes, naturally. There was no incense. The place was as ethereally cold as ever, a cold that sapped the place of color and settled over me in a gray pall even as my mesh kept me incongruously comfortable.

Hauth bowed to my mother. It looked both awkward and serious, because the length of its limbs weren't right for the gesture. "Guardian," it said, or an approximation thereof.

"Say it," she returned. "You know my old name as well as anyone." She was coiled around the shrine, eyes slitted. If possible, her status lights were bluer than ever, almost to the point of being shadow-silvered. The tip of her tail lashed back and forth like a clock's tongue. I could feel the seconds crumbling away.

"Unit Zhu-15 Jiemsin," Hauth said. "You haven't answered to that name in a long time, but I imagine even now you remember the imperatives programmed into you, and the importance of rank hierarchy."

I didn't know anything about imperatives. Military hierarchy, on the other hand, was a reasonably common concept. This intruder had come into our home and accused my mother of being a deserter, had made her sad and strange. If I had known that that was going to upset her like this, I would have begged her to turn it away, no matter how splendid the grave-offering of museum-ships it had brought.

"Mother," I said. She wouldn't look at me, and I spoke again, louder. "Mother. Tell it to leave."

She shook her head. "Ask your questions, Hauth," she said wearily.

I wanted to grab one of her legs and shake it. It was a wonder that I restrained myself.

"I will tell this side of the story too," it said, as though an entire conversation to which I had not been privy had passed between them already. "I know the rest already."

"The rest of what?" I asked.

Hauth turned its regard not on me, but on my mother.

"Go ahead," my mother said, "and tell her what you will tell the world,

248

if she wants to know. It is not, after all, any news to me."

Hauth's mask grew translucent. "Do you want to know?"

"I cannot fail to know forever," I said unsteadily.

"Your mother is one of the greatest war engines ever devised," Hauth said. "She was not the only one. The bonedrakes' creators slaughtered their way into an empire. But the creators had not been as careful with their imperatives as they thought, and eventually the bonedrakes turned on their masters. Then they fought over their masters' leavings."

"This means nothing to me," I said. It was almost true.

"There was one exception," Hauth said. "Unit Zhu-15 Jiemsin, who did not turn against her masters, and did not turn against her comrades, and did not do anything but run."

I opened my mouth, resenting the critique implied in Hauth's tone.

Hauth wasn't done. "Of course, she had few options, and all of them were bad. So she ran and hid and didn't emerge until nothing was left but the smoke of legends. And then she retreated to this fortress, to guard the fossils of history even though no one was left to put them in any context."

"Which is where you come in, I suppose," I said. I meant it to be savage. My voice betrayed me. "Mother, is this true?" *Do you want this to matter to me?*

All she had to do was say something calming, call me "eggling" the way she always did. She had raised me. I owed nothing to this robot and its stories of a world that I needed not involve myself with. Besides, it itself had described the past as the "smoke of legends"; what did it matter anymore?

"It's all true," my mother said. "I learned that there were things that mattered more than war. I did not want to fight anymore. So I left. But that can't be the sum of your purpose, Hauth."

"I want to ask you to add my chronicle," Hauth said. "To persuade your visitors of the futility of war. Which you know about better than anyone else."

My mother blinked at it. "Yes to the first, no to the second," she said, crisp, sharp, unfailingly kind. "The fortress is neutral in all matters. I will answer questions if asked. I will accept new artifacts for the collection. But I will not press any viewpoint on another. That is all."

"I must insist," Hauth said. "The Greater Choreographical Society, as an ally of the Everywhere Pact, feels strongly about this point. Already the

Pact would see you brought down. I was hoping to save a valuable historical repository by persuading you of the rightness of our cause."

My mother's only response to this was a snort.

"In that case," it said, "the Everywhere Pact will have no choice but to turn against you. And my chronicle will only rally more to their cause."

"And you came here looking for help finishing it?" I demanded incredulously. My heart was thumping horribly.

"Your fleet can't do anything to me," my mother said, "and nor can anything else that you care to throw at the fortress." She had not moved, except that her tail-tip continued to lash back and forth. "But you're right that I won't keep you from departing, or sharing your chronicle with everyone who wants to hear it. With people who want to think of us as a monument to war rather than a simple collection of things that happened, good or bad or indifferent."

"Don't be absurd," I said, appalled. "Stop it from leaving."

"Why?" she said. "It is my choice."

Her agitation was palpable, however. The tail lashing was one thing, but her claws came out with a snick and the gun mounts at her sides coruscated.

"I had originally thought you would have figured out this part of your mother's past," Hauth said. "In my interactions, however, it became clear that you had no idea. In all this time, then, you had no idea that your mother was a soldier, and that she had masters, and what kinds of orders they gave her."

My mother reared up to her full height. The ceiling was far above; nevertheless, her shadow fell over me like a shroud. "I don't take orders from children," she said to me, very quietly. "My masters were not that stupid. Adults are another matter. You were the last one. Your parents had put you in an ice-egg before they were obliterated; the other egglings didn't survive. You slept for eons while I deliberated and gathered my strength. I thought enough time had passed that we could start over."

I had no weapon on me, nothing that had any chance of harming an entity of metal and shielded circuits. But I launched myself at Hauth anyway, then choked back a shriek as something slammed into me and knocked me aside: my mother's tail.

My side hurt and I couldn't breathe. My mother stood between me and Hauth. She was crowned in blue fire, and she resembled nothing so much as a skeleton stitched together by sinew of shadows.

"It won't matter if you kill me," Hauth said. "I am not an entity like you or your mother. My experience-sum is copied to alter-selves at regular intervals. The same mechanism suffices to distribute the chronicle."

It said something about Hauth that it expected an appeal of pure reason to sway me, and more about me that the appeal moved me not at all. The irony was that my mother and Hauth fundamentally agreed on the value of peace; but she would not impose it, while Hauth would. And Hauth now returned her hospitality with a threat. I could not forgive that.

I did not know how to fight. I did not know how to use my fists or feet, or any of the guns or knives amenable to human hands. My teeth, as I had learned early in life, were practically useless. But Hauth's remarks, and my mother's hints, had given me to understand that I had one weapon after all: my mother.

"You were waiting for me to grow up all that time," I said to her. "To see if you had raised me true."

She gave a terrible cry. For all the defenses the fortress boasted, she was its greatest one. "If you kill it," she said in a tattered voice, "then we have nothing more in common. But I will not fight you either, weapon though I am."

"Then what will you do?" I said. I didn't recognize my own voice. I might have been crying.

"I stopped fighting so many years ago the number has no meaning to you," she said. "I am not going to start again now. It is always possible, of course, that my imperatives are stronger than my ability to resist them even after all my edits, and that I will do as you order anyway."

She did not say: *I thought I had taught you better than this.* We were beyond that now.

My hatred for Hauth was passionate and sharp-edged and did not hurt nearly so much as the grief in my mother's eyes. I whirled and fled as fast as I could, down the corridors I had grown up in. No one came after me.

• • • •

I could not go back to my mother after that. The fortress was closed to me now. I was given time to adjust to the idea that I was to leave. Only certain doors opened to me, for all that meals were provided, along with any other diversion I asked for.

Eventually I came to a small ship, as beautiful as a flowerbud. When I finally brought myself to enter it, knowing that I must then depart for good, I found waiting for me a single cupcake decorated with azalea-pink frosting. I made myself eat it, and never managed to remember how it tasted.

My exile was a centrifugal one. Any path was open to me except the one I wanted to take, curving back home. As you grow older, I will tell you of the times I almost died, and the lifetimes I spent in ancestral halls looking for mentions of my mother's origins, however thready, not already discussed in Hauth's chronicle. I took lovers who murmured poetry-of-absences into my dreams, and wept when I left them; I learned everything from surgery to cloud-gardening. One thing I never took up, however, was baking.

I have told you all this as we travel, as you curl your cilia inquisitively within the birthing sac, listening even unborn. I can only hope to be as good a mother to you as my mother was to me. It would have been preferable to return you to your people, had any remained, but by the time I passed by their system, they had destroyed themselves in an ecological collapse that left entire worlds pitted with corrosive seas. I salvaged what I could, alone. We carry with us their songs and histories and genealogy-braids, the possibility of future generations of your kind, so that you may decide what to do with them when you are older.

Long years have passed since I left the fortress behind, having broken the rules that my mother laid down. She had already forgiven me when I left; I needed all this time to forgive myself. In the meantime, I see the fortress's welcome-banner streaming out toward us, luminous like an effusion of flowers, and I imagine that your grandmother will be pleased to meet you.

---

Yoon Ha Lee's collection *Conservation of Shadows* came out from Prime Books in 2013 and was one of *Publisher Weekly*'s Best Books of 2013. His *Machineries of Empire* trilogy was recently acquired by Solaris Books, with the first volume, *Ninefox Gambit*, due out in June 2016. His short story "Effigy Nights" was a World Fantasy nominee in 2014. Other short fiction has appeared in *Tor.com*, *The Magazine of Fantasy & Science Fiction*, *Clarkesworld*, *Lightspeed*, *Beneath Ceaseless Skies*, and other venues, as well as being reprinted by various Year's Best anthologies.

# The Devil In America
## By Kai Ashante Wilson

*for my father*

*1955*

*Emmett Till, sure, I remember. Your great grandfather, sitting at the table with the paper spread out, looked up and said something to Grandma. She looked over my way and made me leave the room: Emmett Till. In high school I had a friend everybody called Underdog. One afternoon—1967?— Underdog was standing on some corner and the police came round and beat him with nightsticks. No reason. Underdog thought he might get some respect if he joined up for Vietnam, but a sergeant in basic training was calling him everything but his name—nigger this, nigger that—and Underdog went and complained. Got thrown in the brig, so he ended up going to Vietnam with just a couple weeks' training. Soon after he came home in a body bag. In Miami a bunch of white cops beat to death a man named Arthur McDuffie with heavy flashlights. You were six or seven: so, 1979. The cops banged up his motorcycle trying to make killing him look like a crash. Acquitted, of course. Then Amadou Diallo, 1999; Sean Bell, 2006. You must know more about all the New York murders than I do. Trayvon, this year. Every year it's one we hear about and God knows how many just the family mourns.*

*—Dad*

1877 August 23

"'Tis all right if I take a candle, Ma'am?" Easter said. Her mother bent over at the black iron stove, and lifted another smoking hot pan of cornbread from the oven. Ma'am just hummed—meaning, *Go 'head*. Easter came wide around her mother, wide around the sizzling skillet, and with the ramrod of

253

Brother's old rifle hooked up the front left burner. She left the ramrod behind the stove, plucked the candle from the fumbling, strengthless grip of her ruint hand, and dipped it wick-first into flame. Through the good glass window in the wall behind the stove, the night was dark. It was soot and shadows. Even the many-colored chilis and bright little pumpkins in Ma'am's back garden couldn't be made out.

A full supper plate in her good hand, lit candle in the other, Easter had a time getting the front door open, then out on the porch, and shutting back the door without dropping any food. Then, anyhow, the swinging of the door made the candle flame dance fearfully low, just as wind gusted up too, so her light flickered *way* down… and went out.

"Shoot!" Easter didn't say the curse word aloud. She mouthed it. "Light it back for me, angels," Easter whispered. "Please?" The wick flared bright again.

No moon, no stars—the night sky was clouded over. Easter hoped it wasn't trying to storm, with the church picnic tomorrow.

She crossed the yard to the edge of the woods where Brother waited. A big old dog, he crouched down, leapt up, down and up again, barking excitedly, just as though he were some little puppy dog.

"Well, hold your horses," Easter said. "I'm coming!" She met him at the yard's end and dumped the full plate over, all her supper falling to the ground. Brother's head went right down, tail just a-wagging. "Careful, Brother," Easter said. "You *watch* them chicken bones." Then, hearing the crack of bones, she knelt and snatched ragged shards right out of the huge dog's mouth. Brother whined and licked her hand—and dropped his head right back to buttered mashed yams.

Easter visited with him a while, telling her new secrets, her latest sins, and when he'd sniffed out the last morsels of supper Brother listened to her with what anybody would have agreed was deep love, full attention. "Well, let me get on," she said at last, and sighed. "Got to check on the Devil now." She'd left it til late, inside all evening with Ma'am, fixing their share of the big supper at church tomorrow. Brother whined when she stood up to leave.

Up the yard to the henhouse. Easter unlatched the heavy door and looked them over—chickens, on floor and shelf, huddling quietly in thick straw, and all asleep except for Sadie. Eldest and biggest, that one turned just her head and looked over Easter's way. Only reflected candlelight, of course, but Sadie's beady eyes looked *so* ancient and *so* crafty, blazing like embers. Easter backed on out, latched the coop up securely again, and made the trip around the henhouse, stooping and stooping and stooping, to check for gaps in the boards. Weasel holes, fox doors.

There weren't any. And the world would go on exactly as long as Easter kept up this nightly vigil.

Ma'am stood on the porch when Easter came back up to the house. "I don't *appreciate* my good suppers thrown in the dirt. You hear me, girl?" Ma'am put a hand on Easter's back, guiding her indoors. "That ole cotton-picking dog could just as well take hisself out to the deep woods and hunt." Ma'am took another tone altogether when she meant every word, and *then* she didn't stroke Easter's head, or gently brush her cheek with a knuckle. This was only complaining out of habit. Easter took only one tone with her mother. Meek.

"Yes, Ma'am," she said, and ducked her head in respect. Easter *didn't* think herself too womanish or grown to be slapped silly.

"Help me get this up on the table," Ma'am said—the deepest bucket, and brimful of water and greens. Ma'am was big and strong enough to have lifted *ten* such buckets. It was friendly, though, sharing the little jobs. At one side of the bucket, Easter bent over and worked her good hand under the bottom, the other just mostly ached now, the cut thickly scabbed over. She just sort of pressed it to the bucket's side, in support.

Easter and her mother set the bucket on the table.

Past time to see about the morning milk. Easter went back to the cellar and found the cream risen, though the tin felt a tad cool to her. The butter would come slow. "Pretty please, angels?" she whispered. "Could you help me out a little bit?" They could. They did. The milk tin warmed ever so slightly. Just right. Easter dipped the cream out and carried the churn back to the kitchen.

Ma'am had no wrinkles except at the corners of the eyes. Her back was unbowed, her arms and legs still mighty. But she was old now, wasn't she? Well nigh sixty, and maybe past it. But still with that upright back, such quick hands. *Pretty* was best said of the young—Soubrette Toussaint was very pretty, for instance—so what was the right word for Ma'am's severe cheekbones, sharp almond-shaped eyes, and pinched fullness of mouth? Working the churn, Easter felt the cream foam and then thicken, pudding-like. Any other such marriage, and you'd surely hear folks gossiping over the dead wrongness of it—the wife twenty-some years older than a mighty good-looking husband. *What in the world, I ask you, is that old lady doing with a handsome young man like that?* But any two eyes could see the answer here. Not pretty as she must once have been, with that first husband, whoever he'd been, dead and buried back east. And not pretty as when she'd had those first babies, all gone now too. But age hadn't only taken from Ma'am, it had given too. Some rare gift, and so much of it that Pa *had* to be pick of the litter—kindest, most handsome man in the world—just to stack up. Easter poured off the buttermilk into a jar for Pa, who liked that especially. Ma'am might be a challenge to love sometimes, but respect came easy.

"I *told* him, Easter." Ma'am wiped forefinger and thumb down each dandelion leaf, cleaning off grit and bugs, and then lay it aside in a basket. "Same as I told you. *Don't mess with it.* Didn't I say, girl?"

"Yes, Ma'am." Easter scooped the clumps of butter into the bowl.

Ma'am spun shouting from her work. "That's *right* I did! And I pray to God you *listen*, too. That fool out there *didn't*, but Good Lord knows I get on my knees and pray *every night* you got some little bit of sense in your head. Because, Easter, I ain't *got* no more children—you my last one!" Ma'am turned back and gripped the edge of the table.

Ma'am wanted no comfort, no acknowledgement of her pain at such moments—just let her be. Easter huddled in her chair, paddling the salt evenly through the butter, working all the water out. She worked with far more focus than the job truly needed.

Then, above the night's frogcroak and bugchatter, they heard Brother bark in front of the house, and heard Pa speak, his very voice. Wife and daughter both gave a happy little jump, looking together at the door in anticipation. Pa'd been three days over in Greenville selling the cigars. Ma'am snapped her fingers.

"Get the jug out the cellar," she said. "You know just getting in your Pa wants him a little tot of cider. Them white folks." As if Ma'am wouldn't have a whole big mug her ownself.

"Yes, Ma'am." Easter fetched out the jug.

Pa opened the door, crossed the kitchen—touching Easter's head in passing, he smelt of woodsmoke—and came to stand behind Ma'am. His hands cupped her breasts through her apron, her dress, and he kissed the back of her neck. She gasped aloud. "Wilbur! *the baby*...!" That's what they still called Easter, "the baby." Nobody had noticed she'd gotten tall, twelve years old now.

Pa whispered secrets in Ma'am's ear. He was a father who loved his daughter, but he was a husband first and foremost. *I'm a terrible thirsty man,* Pa had said once, *and your mama is my only cool glass of water in this world.* Ma'am turned and embraced him. "I know it, sweetheart," she said. "I know." Easter covered up the butter. She took over washing the greens while her parents whispered, intent only on each other. Matched for height, and Ma'am a little on the stout side, Pa on the slim, so they were about the same thickness too. The perfect fit of them made Easter feel a sharp pang, mostly happiness. Just where you could hear, Pa said, "And you *know* it ain't no coloreds round here but us living in Rosetree…"

Wrapped in blankets up in the loft, right over their bed, of course she heard things at night, on Sundays usually, when nobody was so tired.

An effortful noise from Pa, as if he were laboring some big rock heave-by-heave over to the edge of the tobacco field, and then before the quiet, sounding sort of worried, as if Pa were afraid Ma'am might accidently touch the blazing hot iron of the fired-up stove, Pa would say, "*Hazel!*"

"… so then Miss Anne claimed she seen some nigger run off from there, and *next thing* she knew—fire! Just *everywhere*. About the whole west side of Greenville, looked to me, burnt down. Oh yeah, and in the morning here come Miss Anne's husband talkmbout, 'Know what else, y'all? That nigger my wife seen last night—matterfact, he *violated* her.' Well, darling, here's what I wanna know…"

Ma'am would kind of sigh throughout, and from one point on keep saying—not loud—"Like *that*…" However much their bed creaked, Ma'am and Pa were pretty quiet when Easter was home. Probably they weren't, though, these nights when Pa came back from Greenville. That was why they sent her over the Toussaints'.

"…*where* this 'violated' come from all of a sudden? So last night Miss Anne said she maybe *might* of seen some nigger run off, and this morning that nigger jumped her show 'nough? And then it *wasn't* just the one nigger no more. No. It was two or three of 'em, maybe about five. *Ten* niggers—at least. Now Lord knows I ain't no lawyer, baby, I *ain't,* but it seem to me a fishy story done changed up even fishier…"

Ma'am and Pa took so much comfort in each other, and just plain *liked* each other. Easter was glad to see it. But she was old enough to wonder, a little worried and a little sad, who was ever going to love her in the way

Ma'am and Pa loved each other.

"What you still doing here!" Ma'am looked up suddenly from her embrace. "Girl, you should of *been* gone to Soubrette's. *Go.* And take your best dress and good Sunday shoes too. Tell Mrs. Toussaint I'll see her early out front of the church tomorrow. You hear me, Easter?"

"Yes, Ma'am," she said. And with shoes and neatly folded clothes, Easter hurried out into the dark wide-open night, the racket of crickets.

On the shadowed track through the woods, she called to Brother but he wouldn't come out of the trees, though Easter could hear him pacing her through the underbrush. Always out there in the dark. Brother wanted to keep watch whenever Easter went out at night, but he got shy sometimes too. Lonesome and blue.

• • • •

And this whole thing started over there, in old Africa land, where in olden days a certain kind of big yellow dog (*you* know the kind I'm talking about) used to run around. Now those dogs ain't nowhere in the world, except for . . . Anyway, the prince of the dogs was a sorcerer—about the biggest and best there was in the world. One day he says to hisself, *Let me get up off four feet for a while, and walk around on just two, so I can see what all these folk called 'people' are doing over in that town.* So the prince quit being his doggy self and got right up walking like anybody. While the prince was coming over to the peoples' town, he saw a pretty young girl washing clothes at the river. Now if he'd still been his doggy self, the prince probably would of just *ate* that girl up, but since he was a man now, the prince seen right off what a pretty young thing she was. So he walks over and says, Hey, gal. You want to lay down right here by the river in the soft grass with me? Well—and anybody *would*—the girl felt some kind of way, a strange man come talking to her so fresh all of a sudden. The girl says, Man, don't you see my hair braided up all nice like a married lady? (Because that's how they did over in Africa land. The married ladies, the girls still at home, plaited their hair up different.) So the dog prince said, Oh, I'm sorry. I come from a long way off, so I didn't know what your hair meant. And he *didn't*, either, cause dogs don't braid their hair like people do. *Hmph*, says the gal, all the while sort of taking a real good look over him. As a matter of fact, the dog prince made a *mighty* fine-looking young man, and the girl's mama and papa had married her off to just about the oldest, most dried-up, and granddaddy-looking fellow you ever saw. That old man was rich, sure, but he really couldn't do nothing in the married way for a young gal like that, who wasn't twenty years old yet. So, the gal says, *Hmph*, where you come from anyways? What you got to say for yourself? And it must of been pretty good too, whatever the prince had to say for hisself, because, come nine months later, that gal was mama to your great great—twenty greats— grandmama, first one of us with the old Africa magic.

• • • •

It wasn't but a hop, skip, and jump through the woods into Rosetree proper. Surrounding the town green were the church, Mrs. Toussaint's general store, and the dozen best houses, all two stories, with overgrown rosebushes in front. At the other side of the town green, Easter could see Soubrette sitting out on her front porch with a lamp, looking fretfully out into night.

It felt nice knowing somebody in this world would sit up for her, wondering where she was, was everything all right.

In her wretched accent, Easter called, "*J'arrive!*" from the middle of the green.

Soubrette leapt up. "Easter?" She peered into the blind dark. "I can't see a thing! Where are you, Easter?"

Curious that *she* could see so well, cutting across the grass toward the general store. Easter had told the angels not to without her asking, told them *many* times, but still she often found herself seeing with cat's eyes, hearing with dog's ears, when the angels took a notion. The problem being, folks *noticed* if you were all the time seeing and hearing what you shouldn't. But maybe there was no need to go blaming the angels. With no lamp or candle, your eyes naturally opened up something amazing, while lights could leave you stone-blind out past your bright spot.

They screamed, embraced, laughed. Anybody would have said three *years*, not days, since they'd last seen each other. "Ah, viens ici, toi!" said Soubrette, gently taking Easter's ruint hand to lead her indoors.

Knees drawn up on the bed, Easter hugged her legs tightly. She set her face and bit her lip, but tears came anyway. They always did. Soubrette sighed and closed the book in her lap. Very softly Easter murmured, "I like *Rebecca* most."

"Yes!" Soubrette abruptly leaned forward and tapped Easter's shin.

"Rowena is nice too—she *is*!—but I don't even *care* about old Ivanhoe. It just isn't *fair* about poor Rebecca…"

"He really don't deserve either one of 'em," Easter said, forgetting her tears in the pleasure of agreement. "That part when Ivanhoe up and changed his mind all of a sudden about Rebecca—do you remember that part? '… *an inferior race* …' No, I didn't care for him after that."

"Oh *yes*, Easter, I remember!" Soubrette flipped the book open and paged back through it. "At first he sees Rebecca's so beautiful, and he likes her, but then all his niceness is '… *exchanged at once for a manner cold, composed, and collected, and fraught with no deeper feeling than that which expressed a grateful sense of courtesy received from an unexpected quarter, and from one of an inferior race* …' Ivanhoe's just *hateful*!" Soubrette lay a hand on Easter's foot. "Rowena and Rebecca would have been better off *without* him!"

Soubrette touched you when she made her points, and she made them in the most hot-blooded way. Easter enjoyed such certainty and fire, but it made her feel bashful too. "You ain't taking it too far, Soubrette?" she asked softly. "Who would they love without Ivanhoe? It wouldn't be nobody to, well, *kiss*."

It made something happen in the room, that word *kiss*. Did the warm night heat up hotter, and the air buzz almost like yellowjackets in a log? One and one made two, so right there you'd seem to have a sufficiency for a kiss, with no lack of anything, anyone. From head to toe Easter knew right where she was, lightly sweating in a thin summer shift on this August night, and she knew right where Soubrette was too, so close that—

"Girls!" Mrs. Toussaint bumped the door open with her hip. "The iron's good and hot on the stove now, so…"

Easter and Soubrette gave an awful start. *Ivanhoe* fell to the floor.

"… why don't you come downstairs with your dresses…?" Mrs. Toussaint's words trailed away. She glanced back and forth between the girls while the hot thing still sizzled in the air, delicious and wrong. Whatever it was seemed entirely perceptible to Mrs. Toussaint. She said to her daughter, "Chérie, j'espère que tu te comportes bien. Tu es une femme de quatorze ans maintenant. Ton amie n'a que dix ans; elle est une toute jeune fille!"

She spoke these musical words softly and with mildness—nevertheless they struck Soubrette like a slap. The girl cast her gaze down, eyes shining with abrupt tears. High yellow, Soubrette's cheeks and neck darkened with rosy duskiness.

"Je me comporte toujours bien, Maman," she whispered, her lips trembling as if about to weep.

Mrs. Toussaint paused a moment longer, and said, "Well, fetch down your dresses, girls. Bedtime soon." She went out, closing the door behind her.

The tears *did* spill over now. Easter leaned forward suddenly, kissed Soubrette's cheek, and said, "J'ai *douze* ans."

Soubrette giggled. She wiped her eyes.

Much later, Easter sat up, looking around. Brother had barked, growling savagely, and woken her up. But seeing Soubrette asleep beside her, Easter knew that couldn't be so. And no strange sounds came to her ears from the night outside, only wind in the leaves, a whippoorwill. Brother never came into the middle of town anyway, not ever. The lamp Mrs. Toussaint had left burning in the hallway lit the gap under the bedroom door with orange glow. Easter's fast heart slowed as she watched her friend breathing easily. Soubrette never snored, never tossed and turned, never slept with her mouth gaping open. Black on the white pillow, her long hair spilled loose and curly.

"Angels?" Easter whispered. "Can you make my hair like Soubrette's?" This time the angels whispered, *Give us the licklest taste of her blood, and all Sunday long tomorrow your hair will be so nice. See that hatpin? Just stick Soubrette in the hand with it, and not even too deep. Prettiest curls anybody ever saw.* Easter only sighed. It was out of the question, of course. The angels sometimes asked for the most shocking crimes as if they were nothing at all. "Never mind," she said, and lay down to sleep.

While true that such profoundly sustaining traditions, hidden under the guise of the imposed religion, managed to survive centuries of slavery and subjugation, we should not therefore suppose that ancient African beliefs suffered no sea changes. Of course they did. 'The Devil' in Africa had been capricious, a trickster, and if cruel, only insomuch as bored young children, amoral and at loose ends, may be cruel: seeking merely to provoke an interesting event at any cost, to cause some disruption of the tedious status quo. For the Devil in America, however, malice itself was the end, and temptation a means only to destroy. Here, the Devil would pursue the righteous and the wicked, alike and implacably, to their everlasting doom . . .

*White Devils/Black Devils*, Luisa Valéria da Silva y Rodríguez

1871 August 2

The end begins after Providence loses all wiggle room, and the outcome becomes hopeless and fixed. That moment had already happened, Ma'am would have said. It had happened long before either one of them were born. Ma'am would have assured Easter that the end began way back in slavery times, and far across the ocean, when that great-grandfather got snatched from his home and the old wisdom was lost.

Easter knew better, though. A chance for grace and new wisdom had always persisted, and doom never been assured . . . right up until, six years old, Easter did what she did one August day out in the tobacco fields.

On that morning of bright skies, Pa headed out to pick more leaves and Easter wanted to come along. He said, Let's ask your mama.

"But he *said*, Wilbur." Ma'am looked surprised. "He told us, *You ain't to take the baby out there, no time, no way.*"

Pa hefted Easter up in his arms, and kissed her cheek, saying, "Well, it's going on three years now since he ain't been here to say *Bet not* or say *Yep, go 'head.* So I wonder how long we suppose to go on doing everything just the way he said, way back when. Forever? And the baby *wants* to go . . ." Pa set her down and she grabbed a handful of his pants leg and leaned against him. "But, darling, if you say not to, then we *won't.* Just that simple."

Most men hardly paid their wives much mind at all, but Pa would listen to any little thing Ma'am said. She, though, *hated* to tell a man what he could and couldn't do—some woman just snapping her fingers, and the man running lickety-split here and there. Ma'am said that wasn't right. So she crossed her arms and hugged herself, frowning unhappily. "Well . . ." Ma'am said. "Can you just wait a hot minute there with the mule, Wilbur? Let me say something to the baby." Ma'am unfolded her arms and reached out a hand. "Come here, girl."

Easter came up the porch steps and took the hand—swept along in Ma'am's powerful grip, through the open door, into the house. "*Set.*" Ma'am pointed to a chair. Easter climbed and sat down. Ma'am knelt on the floor. They were eye-to-eye. She grasped Easter's chin and pulled her close. "Tell me, Easter—what you do, if some lady in a red silk dress come trying to talk to you?"

"I shake my head *no*, Ma'am, and turn my back on her. Then the lady have to go away."

"That's *right*! But what if that strange lady in the red dress say, *Want me to open up St. Peter's door, and show you heaven? What if she say to you, See them birds flying there? Do me one itsy bitsy favor, and you could be in the sky flying too.* What then, Easter? Tell me what you do."

"Same thing, Ma'am." She knew her mother wasn't angry with her, but Ma'am's hot glare—the hard grip on her chin—made tears prick Easter's eyes. "I turn my back, Ma'am. She *have to* go, if I just turn my back away."

"Yes! And will you *promise*, Easter? Christ is your Savior, will you *swear* to turn your back, if that lady in the pretty red dress come talking to you?"

Easter swore up and down, and she meant every word too. Ma'am let her go back out to her father, and he set her up on the mule. They went round the house and down the other way, on the trail through woods behind Ma'am's back garden that led to the tobacco fields. Pa answered every question Easter asked about the work he had to do there.

That woman in the red dress was a sneaky liar. She was '*that old serpent, called the Devil, and Satan, which deceiveth the whole world . . .*' Warned by Ma'am, Easter guarded night and day against a glimpse of any such person. In her whole life, though, Easter never did see that lady dressed all in red silk. Easter knew nothing about her. She only knew about the angels.

She didn't *see* them, either, just felt touches like feathers in the air—two or three angels, rarely more—or heard sounds like birds taking off, a flutter of wings. The angels spoke to her, once in a while, in whispering soft harmony. They never said anything bad, just helpful little things. Watch out, Easter—gon' rain cats and dogs once that cloud there starts looking purplish. Your folks sure would appreciate a little while by theyself in the house. Why not be nice? Ma'am's worried sick about Pa over in Greenville, with those white folks, so you'd do best to keep your voice down, and tiptoe extra quiet, else you 'bout to get slapped into tomorrow. And, Easter, don't tell nobody, all right? Let's us just be secret friends.

All right, Easter said. The angels were nice, anyway, and it felt good keeping them to herself, having a secret. No need to tell anybody. Or just Brother, when he came out the woods to play with her in the front yard, or when Ma'am let her go walking in the deep woods with him. But in those days Brother used to wander far and wide, and was gone from home far more often than he was around.

The tobacco fields were *full* of angels.

Ever run, some time, straight through a flock of grounded birds, and ten thousand wings just rushed up flapping into the air all around you? In the tobacco fields it was like that. And every angel there *stayed* busy, so the tobacco leaves grew huge and whole, untroubled by flea-beetles or cutworms, weeds or weather. But the angels didn't do *all* the work.

Pa and a friend of his from St. Louis days, Señor, dug up the whole south field every spring, mounding up little knee-high hills all over it. Then they had to transplant each and every little tabacky plant from the flat dirt in the north field to a hill down south. It was back-breaking work, all May long, from sunup to sundown. Afterwards, Pa and Señor had only small jobs, until now—time to cut the leaves, hang and cure them in the barn. Señor had taught Pa everything there was to know about choosing which leaf when, and how to roll the excellent *criollito* tabacky into the world's best cigars. What they got out of one field sold plenty well enough to white folks over in Greenville to keep two families in good clothes, ample food, and some comforts.

A grandfather oaktree grew between the fields, south and north. Pa agreed with Easter. "That big ole thing *is* in the way, ain't it? But your brother always used to say, *Don't you never, never cut down that tree, Wilbur.* And it do make a nice shady spot to rest, anyway. Why don't you go set over there for a while, baby child?"

Easter knew Pa thought she must be worn out and sorry she'd come, just watching him stoop for leaves, whack them off the plant with his knife, and lay them out in the sun. But Easter loved watching him work, loved to follow and listen to him wisely going on about why this, why that.

Pa, though, put a hand on her back and kind of scootched her on her way over toward the tree, so Easter went. Pa and Señor began to chant some work song in Spanish. *Iyá oñió oñí abbé* . . .

Once in the oaktree's deep shade, there was a fascinating discovery round the north side of the big trunk. Not to see, or to touch—or know in any way Easter had a name for—but she could *feel* the exact shape of what hovered in the air. And this whirligig thing'um, right here, was exactly what kept all the angels hereabouts leashed, year after year, to chase away pests, bring up water from deep underground when too little rain fell, or dry the extra drops in thin air when it rained too much. And she could tell somebody had jiggered this thing together who hardly knew what they were doing. It wasn't but a blown breath or rough touch from being knocked down.

Seeing how rickety the little angel-engine was, Easter wondered if she couldn't do better. Pa and Señor did work *awful* hard every May shoveling dirt to make those hills, and now in August they had to come every day to cut whichever leaves had grown big enough. Seemed like the angels could just do *everything* . . .

"You all right over there, baby girl?" Pa called. Dripping sweat in the glare, he wiped a sleeve across his brow. "Need me to take you back to the house?"

"I'm all right," Easter shouted back. "I want to stay, Pa!" She waved, and he stooped down again, cutting leaves. See there? Working so hard! She could *help* if she just knocked this rickety old thing down, and put it back together better. Right on the point of doing so, she got one sharp pinch from her conscience.

Every time Easter got ready to do something bad there was a moment beforehand when a little bitty voice—one lonely angel, maybe—would whisper to her. *Aw, Easter. You know good and well you shouldn't.* Nearly always she listened to this voice. After today and much too late, she *always* would.

But sometimes you just do bad, anyhow.

Easter picked a scab off her knee and one fat drop welled from the pale tender scar underneath. She dabbed a finger in it, and touched the bloody tip to the ground.

The angel-engine fell to pieces. Screaming and wild, the angels scattered every which way. Easter called and begged, but she could no more get the angels back in order than she could have grabbed hold of a mighty river's gush.

*And the tobacco field . . . !*

Ice frosted the ground, the leaves, the plants, and then melted under sun beating down hotter than summer's worst. The blazing blue sky went cloudy and dark, and boiling low clouds spat frozen pellets, some so big they drew blood and raised knots. Millions of little noises, little motions, each by itself too small to see or hear, clumped into one thick sound like God's two hands rubbing together, and just as gusts of wind stroke the green forest top, making the leaves of the trees all flip and tremble, there was a unified rippling from one end of the tobacco field to the other. Not caused by hands, though, nor by the wind—by busy worms, a billion hungry worms. Grayish, from maggot-size to stubby snakes, these worms ate the tobacco leaves with savage appetite. While the worms feasted, dusty cloud after dusty cloud of moths fluttered up from the disappearing leaves, all hail-torn and frost-blackened, half and then wholly eaten.

In the twinkling of an eye, the lush north field was stripped bare. Nothing was left but naked leaf veins poking spinily from upright woody stems—not a shred of green leaf anywhere. But one year's crop was nothing to the angels' hunger. They were owed *much* more for so many years' hard labor. Amidst the starving angels, Pa and Señor stood dazed in the sudden wasteland of their tobacco field. All the sweet living blood of either this man or the other would just about top off the angels' thirsty cup.

Easter screamed. She called for some help to come—any help at all.

And help *did* come. A second of time split in half and someone came walking up the break.

• • • •

Like the way you and Soubrette work on all that book learning together. Same as that. You *gotta* know your letters, *gotta* know your numbers, for some things, or you just can't rightly take part. Say, for instance, you had some rich colored man, and say this fellow was *very* rich indeed. But let's say he didn't know his numbers at all. Couldn't even count his own fingers up to five. Now, he ain't a bad man, Easter, and he ain't stupid either, really. It's just that nobody ever taught numbering to him. So, one day this rich man takes a notion to head over to the bank, and put his money into markets and bonds, and what have you. Now let me ask you, Easter. What you think gon' happen to this colored man's big ole stack of money, once he walks up in that white man's bank, and gets to talking with the grinning fellow behind the counter? *You* tell me. I wanna hear what you say.

Ma'am. The white man's gonna see that colored man can't count, Ma'am, and cheat him out of all his money.

That's *right* he is, Easter! And I *promise you* it ain't no other outcome! Walk up in that bank just as rich as you please—but you gon' walk out with no shoes, and *owing* the shirt on your back! Old Africa magic's the same way, but *worse*, Easter, cause it ain't money we got, me and you—all my babies had—and my own mama, and the grandfather they brung over on the slave ship. It's *life*. It's life and death, not money. Not play-stuff. But, listen here—we don't know our numbers no more, Easter. See what I'm saying? That oldtime wisdom from over there, what we used to know in the Africa land, is all gone now. And, Easter, you just *can't* walk up into the spirits' bank not knowing your numbers. You *rich*, girl. You got gold in your pockets, and I *know* it's burning a hole. I know cause it burnt me, it burnt your brother. But I pray you listen to me, baby child, when I say— you walk up in that bank, they gon' take a *heap* whole lot more than just your money.

• • • •

Nothing moved. Pa and Señor stood frozen, the angels hovering just before the pounce. Birds in the sky hung there, mid-wingbeat, and even a blade of grass in the breath of the wind leaned motionless, without shivering. Nothing moved. Or just one thing did—a man some long way off, come walking this way toward Easter. He was *miles* off, or much farther than that, but every step of his approach crossed a strange distance. He bestrode the stillness of the world and stood before her in no time.

In the kindest voice, he said, "You need some help, baby child?"

Trembling, Easter nodded her head.

He sat right down. "Let us just set here for a while, then"—the man patted the ground beside him—"and make us a *deal*."

He was a white man tanned reddish from too much sun, or he could've had something in him maybe—been mixed up with colored or indian. Hair would've told the story, but that hid under the gray kepi of a Johnny Reb. He wore that whole uniform in fact, a filthy kerchief of Old Dixie tied around his neck.

Easter sat. "Can you help my Pa and Señor, Mister? The angels about to eat 'em up!"

"Oh, don't you *worry* none about that!" the man cried, warmly reassuring. "I can help you, Easter, I most certainly can. But"—he turned up a long forefinger, in gentle warning—"*not* for free."

Easter opened her mouth.

"*Ot!*" The man interrupted, waving the finger. "Easter, Easter, Easter . . ." He shook his head sadly. "Now why you wanna hurt my feelings and say you ain't got no money? Girl, you know I don't want no trifling little money. You know *just* what I want."

Easter closed her mouth. He wanted blood. He wanted life. And not a little drop or two, either—or the life of some chicken, mule, or cow. She glanced at the field of hovering angels. They were owed the precious life of one man, woman, or child. How much would *he* want to stop them?

The man held up two fingers. "That's all. And you get to pick the two. It don't have to be your Pa and Señor at all. It could be any old body." He waved a hand outwards to the world at large. "Couple folk you ain't even met, Easter, somewhere far away. That'd be just fine with me."

Easter hardly fixed her mouth to answer before that still small voice spoke up. *You can't do that. Everybody is somebody's friend, somebody's Pa, somebody's baby. It'd be plain dead wrong, Easter.* This voice never said one word she didn't already know, and never said anything but the God's honest truth. No matter what, Easter *wasn't* going against it, ever again.

The man made a sour little face to himself. "Tell you what then," he said. "Here's what we'll do. Right now, today, I'll call off the angels, how about that? And then you can pay me what you owe by-and-by. Do you know what the word '*currency*' means, Easter?"

Easter shook her head.

"It means the *way* you pay. Now, the *amount*, which is the worth of two lives, stays exactly the same. But you don't have to pay in blood, in life, if you just change the *currency*, see? There's a lot you don't know right now, Easter, but with some time, you might could learn something useful. So let me help out Señor and your Pa today, and then me and you, we'll settle up later on after while. Now when you wanna do the settling up?"

Mostly, Easter had understood the word "later"—a *sweet* word! She really wouldn't have minded some advice concerning the rest of what he'd said, but the little voice inside couldn't tell her things she didn't already know. Easter was six years old, and double that would make *twelve*. Surely that was an eternal postponement, nearabout. So far away it could hardly be expected to arrive. "When I'm twelve," Easter said, feeling tricky and sly.

"All right," the man said. He nodded once, sharply, as folks do when the deal is hard but fair. "Let's shake on it."

Though she was just a little girl, and the man all grown up, they shook hands. And the angels mellowed in the field, becoming like those she'd always known, mild and toothless, needing permission even to sweep a dusty floor, much less eat a man alive.

"I'll be going now, Easter." The man waved toward the field, where time stood still. "They'll all wake up just as soon as I'm gone." He began to get up.

Easter grabbed the man's sleeve. "Wait!" She pointed at the ruins of two families' livelihood. "What about the *tabacky*? We need it to live on!"

The man looked where Easter gestured, the field with no green whatsoever, and thoughtfully pursed his lips. "Well, as you can see, *this* year's tabacky is all dead and gone now. 'Tain't nothing to do about that. But I reckon I could set the angels back where they was, so as *next* year— and on after that—the tabacky will grow up fine. Want me to do that, Easter?"

"*Yes!*"

The man cocked his head and widened his eyes, taking an attitude of the greatest concern. "Now you *show*, Easter?" he asked. "Cause that's extry on what you already owe."

So cautioning was his tone, even a wildly desperate little girl must think twice. Easter chewed on her bottom lip. "How much extra?" she said at last.

The man's expression went flat and mean. "*Triple*," he said. "And triple that again, and might as well take that whole thing right there, and triple it about ten more times." Now the very nice face came back. "But what you gon' do, baby girl? You messed up your Pa's tabacky field. *Gotta* fix it." He shrugged in deepest sympathy. "*You* know how to do that?"

Easter had to shake her head.

"Want *me* to then?"

Easter hesitated . . . and then nodded. They shook on it.

The man snapped his fingers. From all directions came the sounds and sensations of angels flocking back to their old positions. The man stood and brushed off the seat of his gray wool trousers.

Easter looked up at him. "Who are you, Mister? Your name, I mean."

The man smiled down. "How 'bout you just call me the banker," he said. "Cause—*whew*, baby girl—you owe me a lot! Now I'll be seeing you after while, you hear?" The man became his own shadow, and in just the way that a lamp turned up bright makes the darkness sharpen and flee, his shadow thinned out along the ground, raced away, and vanished.

"*¡Madre de Díos!*" Señor said, looking around at the field that had been all lush and full-grown a moment ago. He and Pa awakened to a desolation, without one remnant of the season's crop. With winces, they felt at their heads, all cut and bruised from hailstones. Pa spun around then, to look at

Easter, and she burst into tears.

These tears lasted a while.

Pa gathered her up in his arms and rushed her back to the house, but neither could Ma'am get any sense from Easter. After many hours she fell asleep, still crying, and woke after nightfall on her mother's lap. In darkness, Ma'am sat on the porch, rocking in her chair. When she felt Easter move, Ma'am helped her sit up, and said, "Won't you tell me what happened, baby child?" Easter *tried* to answer, but horror filled up her mouth and came pouring out as sobs. Just to speak about meeting that strange man was to cry with all the strength in her body. God's grace had surely kept her safe in that man's presence, but the power and the glory no longer stood between her and the revelation of something unspeakable. Even the memory was too terrible. Easter had a kind of fit and threw up what little was in her belly. Once more she wept to passing out.

Ma'am didn't ask again. She and Pa left the matter alone. A hard, scuffling year followed, without the money from the cigars, and only the very last few coins from the St. Louis gold to get them through.

*He was the Devil,* Easter decided, and swallowed the wild tears. She decided to grow wise in her way as Pa was about tobacco, though there was nobody to teach her. The Devil wouldn't face a fool next time.

> *1908*
>
> *The mob went up and down Washington Street, breaking storefront windows, ransacking and setting all the black-owned business on fire. Bunch of white men shot up a barbershop and then dragged out the body of the owner, Scott Burton, to string up from a nearby tree. After that, they headed over to the residential neighborhood called the Badlands, where black folks paid high rent for slum housing. Some 12,000 whites gathered to watch the houses burn.*
>
> *—Dad*

1877 August 24

At the church, the Ladies' Missionary Society and their daughters began to gather early before service. The morning was gray and muggy, not hot at all, and the scent of roses, as sweet and spoiled as wine, soaked the soft air. "Easter, you go right ahead and cut some for the tables," Mrs. Toussaint said, while they walked over to the church. "Any that you see, still nice and red." She and Soubrette carried two big pans of *jambalaya rouge*. Easter carried the flower vases. Rosebushes taller than a man grew in front of every house on the Drive, and were all heavily blooming with summer's doomed roses. Yet Easter could only stop here and there and clip one with the scissors Mrs. Toussaint had given her, since most flowers had rotted deeply burgundy or darker, long past their prime.

With more effort than anybody could calculate, the earth every year brought forth these flowers, and then every year all the roses died. "What's wrong, Easter?" Soubrette said.

"Aw, it's nothing." Easter squeezed with her good hand, bracing the scissors against the heel of her ruint one. "I'm just thinking, is all." She put the thorny clipping into a vase and made herself smile.

At the church there were trestles to set up, wide boards to lay across them, tablecloths, flower vases, an immense supper and many desserts to arrange sensibly. *And my goodness, didn't anybody remember a lifter for the pie . . .? Girls—you run on back up to the house and bring both of mine . . .*

She and Soubrette were laying out the serving spoons when Easter saw her parents coming round Rosetree Drive in the wagon. Back when the Mack family had first come to Rosetree, before Easter's first birthday, all the white folks hadn't moved to Greenville yet. And in those days Ma'am, Pa, and her brother still had "six fat pocketfuls" of the gold from St. Louis, so they could have bought one of the best houses on the Drive. But they'd decided to live in the backwoods outside of town instead (on account of the old Africa magic, as Easter well knew, although telling the story Ma'am and Pa never gave the reason). Pa unloaded a big pot from the wagon bed, and a stack of cloth-covered bread. Ma'am anxiously checked Easter over head to toe—shoes blacked and spotless, dress pressed and stiffly starched, and she laid her palm very lightly against Easter's hair. "Not troubled at all, are you?"

"No, Ma'am."

"Don't really know *what's* got me so wrought up," Ma'am said. "I just felt like I needed to get my eyes on you—*see* you. But don't you look nice!" The worry left Ma'am's face. "And I declare, Octavia can do *better* by that head than your own mama." Ma'am fussed a little with the ribbon in Easter's hair, and then went to help Mrs. Toussaint, slicing the cakes.

Across the table, Mrs. Freeman said, "I do *not* care for the look of these clouds." And Mrs. Freeman frowned, shaking her head at the gray skies.

"No, I surely don't."

*Won't a drop fall today*, the angels whispered in Easter's ear. *Sure 'nough rain hard tomorrow, though.*

Easter smiled over the table. "Oh, don't you worry, Mrs. Freeman." And with supernatural confidence, she said, "It ain't gon' rain today."

The way the heavyset matron looked across the table at Easter, well, anybody would call that *scared,* and Mrs. Freeman shifted further on down the table to where other ladies lifted potlids to stir contents, and secured the bread baskets with linen napkins. It made Easter feel so bad. She felt like the last smudge of filth when everything else is just spic- and-span. Soubrette bumped her. "Take one of these, Easter, will you?" Three vases full of flowers were too many for one person to hold. "Maman said to put some water in them so the roses stay fresh." Together they went round the side of the church to the well.

When they'd come back, more and more men, old folks, and children were arriving. The Missionary ladies argued among themselves over who must miss service, and stay outside to watch over supper and shoo flies and what have you. Mrs. Turner said that she would, *just to hush up the rest of you.* Then somebody caught sight of the visiting preacher, Wandering Bishop Fitzgerald James, come down the steps of the mayor's house with his cane.

### 1863

*So that riot started off in protest of the draft, but it soon became a murder spree, with white men killing every black man, woman, or child who crossed their path. They burned down churches, businesses, the homes of abolitionists, and anywhere else black people were known to congregate, work, or live—even the Colored Orphan Asylum, for example, which was in Midtown back then. Altogether, at least a hundred people were killed by whites. And there's plenty more of these stories over the years, plenty more. Maybe you ought to consider Rosetree. That there's a story like you wouldn't believe.*

*—Dad*

Eyes closed, sitting in the big fancy chair, Wandering Bishop Fitzgerald James seemed to sleep while Pastor Daniels welcomed him and led the church to say *amen.* So skinny, so old, he looked barely there. But his suit was very fine indeed, and when the Wandering Bishop got up to preach, his voice was huge.

He began in measured tones, though soon he was calling on the church in a musical chant, one hard breath out—*huh!*—punctuating each four beat line. At last the Wandering Bishop sang, his baritone rich and beautiful, and his sermon, *this one,* a capstone experience of Easter's life. Men danced, women lifted up their hands and wept. Young girls cried out as loudly as their parents. When the plate came around, Pa put in a whole silver dollar, and then Ma'am nudged him, so he added another.

After the benediction, Ma'am and Pa joined the excited crowd going up front to shake hands with the visiting preacher. They'd known Wandering Bishop Fitzgerald James back before the war, when he sometimes came to Heavenly Home and preached for the coloreds—always a highlight! A white-haired mulatto, the Wandering Bishop moved with that insect-like stiffness peculiar to scrawny old men. Easter saw that his suit's plush lapels were velvet, his thin silk necktie cherry-red.

"Oh, I remember you—sure do. Such a pretty gal! Ole Marster MacDougal always used to say, *Now, Fitzy, you ain't to touch a hair on the head of that one, hear me, boy?*" The Wandering Bishop wheezed and cackled. Then he peered around, as if for small children running underfoot. "But where them little yeller babies at?" he said. "Had you a whole mess of 'em, as I recall."

Joy wrung from her face until Ma'am had only the weight of cares, and politeness, left. "A lovely sermon," she murmured. "Good day to you, Bishop." Pa's forearm came up under her trembling hand and Ma'am leaned on him. Easter followed her parents away, and they joined the spill of the congregation out onto the town green for supper. Pa had said that Easter just had a way with some onions, smoked hock and beans, and would she please fix up a big pot for him. Hearing Pa say so had felt very fine, and Easter had answered, "Yes, sir, I sure will!" Even offered a feast, half the time Pa only wanted some beans and bread, anyhow. He put nothing else on his plate this Sunday too.

The clouds had stayed up high, behaving themselves, and in fact the creamy white overcast, cool and not too bright, was more comfortable than a raw blue sky would have been. Men had gotten the green all spruced up nice, the animals pent away, all the patties and whatnot cleaned up. They'd also finally gotten around to chopping down the old lightning-split, half-rotten crabapple tree in the middle of the green. A big axe still stuck upright from the pale and naked stump. Close by there, Soubrette, Mrs.

Toussaint, and her longtime gentleman friend, Señor Tomás, had spread a couple blankets. They waved and called, *Hey, Macks!*, heavy plates of food in their laps. Easter followed Ma'am and Pa across the crowded green.

Pa made nice Frenchy noises at Miss and Mrs. Toussaint, and then took off lickety-split with Señor, gabbling in Spanish. Ma'am sat down next to Mrs. Toussaint and they leaned together, speaking softly. "What did you think of the Wandering Bishop?" Easter asked Soubrette. "Did you care for the sermon?"

"Well . . ." Soubrette dabbed a fingerful of biscuit in some gravy pooled on Easter's plate. "He had a *beautiful* way of preaching, sure enough." Soubrette looked right and left at the nearby grown-ups, then glanced meaningfully at Easter—who leaned in close enough for whispers.

Señor, the Macks, and the Toussaints always sat on the same pew at church, had dinner back and forth at one another's houses, and generally just hung together as thick as thieves. Scandal clung to them both, one family said to work roots and who knew what all kind of devilment. And the other family . . . well, back east Mrs. Toussaint had done *some* kind of work in La Nouvelle-Orléans, and Easter knew only that rumor of it made the good church ladies purse their lips, take their husbands' elbows, and hustle the men right along—*no* lingering near Mrs. Toussaint. These were the times Easter felt the missing spot in the Mack family worst. There was no one to ask, "What's a '*hussycat*'?" The question, she felt, would hurt Soubrette, earn a slap from Ma'am, and make Pa say, shocked, "Aw, Easter—what you asking *that* for? Let it alone!" His disappointment was always somehow worse than a slap.

Brother, she knew, would have just told her.

The youngest Crombie boy, William, came walking by slowly, carrying his grandmother's plate while she clutched his shoulder. The old lady shrieked.

"*Ha' mercy,*" cried Old Mrs. Crombie. "The sweet blessèd Jesus!" She let go of her grandson's shoulder, to flap a hand in the air. "Ain't *nothing* but a witch over here! I ain't smelt devilry this bad since slavery days, at that root-working Bob Allow's dirty cabin. Them old Africa demons just *nasty* in the air. Who is it?" Old Mrs. Crombie peered around with cloudy blue eyes as if a witch's wickedness could be seen even by the sightless. "Somebody *right* here been chatting with Ole Crook Foot, and I know it like I know my own name. Who?"

Easter about peed herself she was that scared. Rude and bossy, as she'd never spoken to the angels before, she whispered, "Y'all *get*," and the four or five hovering scattered away. Ma'am heard that whisper, though, and looked sharply at Easter.

"Who there, Willie?" Old Mrs. Crombie asked her grandson. "Is it them dadburn Macks?"

"Yes'm," said the boy. "But, Granny, don't you want your supper—?"

"Hush up!" Old Mrs. Crombie blindly pointed a finger at the Macks and Toussaints—catching Easter dead in its sights. "*All Saturday long* these Macks wanna dance with the Devil, and then come set up in the Lord's house on Sunday. Well, no! Might got the *rest* of you around here too scared to speak up, but *me*, I'ma go ahead say it. '*Be vigilant*,' says the Book! '*For your adversary walks about like a roaring lion*.' The King of Babylon! The Father of Lies!"

And what were they supposed to do? Knock an old lady down in front of everybody? Get up and run in their Sunday clothes, saying *excuse me, excuse me*, all the way to edge of the green, with the whole world sitting there watching? Better just to stay put, and hope like a sudden hard downpour this would all be over soon, no harm done. Ma'am grabbed Willie down beside her, said something to him, and sent the boy scurrying off for reinforcements.

"And Mister Light-Bright, with the red beard and spots on his face, always smirking—oh, I know *just* what that one was up to! Think folk around here don't know about St. Louis? Everybody know! *The Devil walked abroad in St. Louis*. And that bushwhacked Confederate gold, we all know just how you got it. Them devil-haunted tabacky fields *too*—growing all outta season, like this some doggone Virginia. This ain't no Virginia out here! Well, where he been at, all these last years? Reaped the whirlwind is what I'm guessing. Got himself strick down by the Lord, huh? *Bet* he did."

Preacherly and loud, Old Mrs. Crombie had the families within earshot anything but indifferent to her testimony. But no matter the eyes, the ears, and all the grownfolk, Easter didn't care to hear any evil said of Brother. She had to speak up. "Ma'am, my brother was good and kind. He was the *last* one to do anybody wrong."

"And here come the *daughter* now," shouted Old Mrs. Crombie. "Her brother blinded my eyes when I prayed the Holy Ghost against them. Well, let's see what *this* one gon' do! Strike me dumb? Ain't no matter—til then,

I'ma be steady testifying. I'ma keep *on* telling the Lord's truth. Hallelujah!"

At last the son showed up. "Mama?" Mr. Crombie took firm hold of his mother's arm. "You just come along now, Mama. Will you let hungry folk eat they dinner in peace?" He shot them a look, very sorry and all-run-ragged. Ma'am pursed her lips in sympathy and waved a hand, *it's all right.*

"Don't worry none about us," Pa said. "Just see to your Ma." He spoke in his voice for hurt animals and children.

"Charleston?" Old Mrs. Crombie said timidly, the fire and brimstone all gone. "That you?"

"Oh, Mama. Charlie *been* dead. White folk hung him back in Richmond, remember? This *Nathaniel.*"

Old Mrs. Crombie grunted as if taking a punch—denied the best child in favor of this least and unwanted. "Oh," she said, "Nathaniel."

"Now y'all know she old," Mr. Crombie raised his voice for the benefit of all those thereabouts. "Don't go setting too much store by every little thing some old lady just half in her right mind wanna say."

Old Mrs. Crombie, muttering, let herself be led away.

Ma'am stood up, and smiled around at Pa, Mrs. Toussaint, Señor, Soubrette. "Everybody excuse us, please? Me and Easter need to go have us a chat up at the church. No, Wilbur, that's all right." She waved Pa back down. "It ain't nothing but a little lady-business me and the baby need to see to, alone." When one Mack spoke with head tilted just so, kind of staring at the other one, carefully saying each word, whatever else was being said it really meant *old Africa magic.* Pa sat down. "And don't y'all wait, you hear? We might be a little while talking. *Girl.*" Ma'am held out a hand.

Hand-in-hand, Ma'am led Easter across the crowded green, across the rutted dirt of the Drive, and up the church steps.

"Baby child," Ma'am said. When Easter looked up from her feet, Ma'am's eyes weren't angry at all but sad. "If I *don't* speak, my babies die," she said. "And If I *do*, they catch a fever from what they learn, take up with it, and die anyhow." As if Jesus hid in some corner, Ma'am looked all around the empty church. The pews and sanctuary upfront, the winter stove in the middle, wood storage closet in back. "Oh, Lord, is there any right way to do this?" She sat Easter at the pew across from the wood-burning stove, and sat herself. "Well, I'm just gon' to *tell* you, Easter, and tell everything I know. It's plain to see that keeping you in the dark won't help nothing. This here's what *my* mama told me. When . . ."

• • • •

. . . they grabbed *her* pa, over across in Africa land, he got *bad* hurt. It was smooth on top of his head right here [*Ma'am lay a hand on the crown of her head, the left side*] and all down the middle of the bare spot was knotted up, nasty skin where they'd cut him terrible. And *there,* right in the worst of the scar was a—*notch?* Something like a deep dent in the bone. You could take the tip of your finger, rest it on the skin there, and feel it give, feel no bone, just softness underneath . . .

So, you knew him, Ma'am?

Oh, no. My mama had me old or older than I had *you,* child, so the grandfolk was dead and gone *quite* a ways before I showed up. Never did meet him. Well . . . not to meet in the flesh, I never did. Not alive, like you mean it. But that's a whole '*nother* story, and don't matter none for what I'm telling you now. The thing I want you to see is how the old knowing, from grandfolk to youngfolk, got broke up into pieces, so in these late days I got nothing left to teach my baby girl. Nothing except, *Let that old Africa magic alone.* Now *he,* your great-grandpa, used to oftentimes get down at night like a dog and run around in the dark, and then come on back from the woods before morning, a man again. Might of brought my grandmama a rabbit, some little deer, or just anything he might catch in the night. Anybody sick or lame, or haunted by spirits, *you* know the ones I mean—folk sunk down and sad all the time, or just always *angry,* or the people plain out they right mind—he could reach out his hand and brush the trouble off them, easy as I pick some lint out your hair. And a very fine-looking man he was too, tall as anything and just . . . sweet-natured, I guess you could say. *Pleasant.* So all the womenfolk loved him. But here's the thing of it. Because of that hurt on his head, Easter—because of *that*—he was simple. About the only English he ever spoke was *Yeah, mars.* And most of the time, things coming out his mouth in the old Africa talk didn't make no sense, either. But even hurt and simple and without his good sense, he *still* knew exactly what he was doing. Could get down a dog, and get right back up again being people, being a man, come morning—whenever he felt like it. *We can't, Easter.* Like I told you, like I told your brother. All us coming after, it's just the one way if we get down on four feet. Not *never* getting up no more. That's the way I lost *three* of mine! No. Hush. Set still there and leave me be a minute . . . So these little bits and pieces I'm telling you right now is every single thing I got from my mama. All *she* got out of your great grand and the old folk who knew him from back over there. Probably you want to know where the right roots at for this, for that, for everything. Which strong words to say? What's the best time of day, and proper season? Why the moon pull so funny, and the rain feel so sweet and mean some particular thing but you can't say what? *Teach me, Ma'am*, your heart must be saying. But I can't, Easter, cause it's gone. Gone for good. They drove us off the path into a wild night, and when morning came we were too turned around, too far from where we started, to *ever* find our way again. Do you think I was my mama's onliest? I wasn't, Easter. Far from it. Same as you ain't *my* only child. I'm just the one that *lived*. The one that didn't mess around. One older sister, and one younger, I saw them both die *awful*, Easter. And all your sisters, and your brothers . . .

• • • •

Easter stood looking through the open doors of the church on a view of cloudy sky and the town green. The creamy brightness of early afternoon had given way to ashen gray, and the supper crowd was thinning out though many still lingered. Arm dangling, Ma'am leaned over the back of the pew and watched the sky, allowing some peace and quiet for Easter to think.

And for her part Easter knew she'd learned plenty today from Ma'am about why and where and who, but that she herself certainly understood more about *how*. In fact Easter was sure of that. She didn't like having more knowledge than her mother. The thought frightened her. And yet, Ma'am had never faced down and tricked the Devil, had she?

"Oh, Easter . . ." Ma'am turned abruptly on the pew ". . . I clean forgot to tell you, and your Pa *asked* me to! A bear or mountain lion—*something*— was in the yard last night. The dog got scratched up pretty bad chasing it off. Durn dog wouldn't come close, and let me have a proper look-see . . ."

Sometimes Ma'am spoke so coldly of Brother that Easter couldn't *stand* it. Anxiously she said, "Is he hurt bad?"

"Well, not so bad he couldn't run and hide as good as always. But something took a mean swipe across the side of him, and them cuts weren't pretty to see. *Must of* been a bear. I can't see what else could of gave that dog, big as he is, such a hard time. The *barking* and *racket*, last night! You would of thought the Devil himself was out there in the yard! But, Easter, set down here. Your mama wants you to set down right here with me now for a minute."

Folks took this tone, so gently taking your hand, only when about to deliver the worst news. Easter tried to brace herself. Just now, she'd seen everybody out on the green. So who could have died?

"I know you loved that mean old bird," Ma'am said. "*Heaven* knows why. But the thing in the yard last night broke open the coop, and got in with the chickens. The funniest thing . . ." Ma'am shook her head in wonder. "It didn't touch *nah* bird except Sadie." Ma'am hugged Easter to her side, eyes full of concern. "But, Easter—I'm sorry—it tore old Sadie to *pieces.*"

Easter broke free of Ma'am's grasp, stood up, blind for one instant of panic. Then she sat down again, feeling nothing. She felt only tired. "You done told me this, that, and the other thing"—Easter hung her head sleepily, speaking in a dull voice—"but why didn't you never say the one thing I *really* wanted to know?"

"And what's that, baby child?"

Easter looked up, smiled, and said in a brand new voice, "Who slept on the pull-out cot?"

Her mother hunched over as if socked in the belly. "What?" Ma'am whispered. "What did you just ask me?"

Easter moved over on the pew close enough to lay a kiss in her mother's cheek or lips. This smile tasted richer than cake, and this confidence, just as rich. "Was it Brother Freddie slept on the pull-out cot, Hazel Mae? Was it him?" Easter said, and brushed Ma'am's cheek with gentle fingertips. "Or was it you? Or was it *sometimes* him, and *sometimes* you?"

At that touch, Ma'am had reared back so violently she'd lost her seat—fallen to the floor into the narrow gap between pews.

Feeling almighty, Easter leaned over her mother struggling dazed on the ground, wedged in narrow space. ". . . ooOOoo . . . "Easter whistled in nasty speculation. "Now *here's* what I really want to know. Was it ever *nobody* on that pull-out cot, Hazel Mae? Just nobody atall*?*"

Ma'am ignored her. She was reaching a hand down into the bosom of her dress, rooting around as if for a hidden dollarbill.

Easter extended middle and forefingers. She made a circle with thumb and index of the other hand, and then vigorously thrust the hoop up and down the upright fingers. "Two peckers and one cunt, Hazel Mae—did *that* ever happen?"

As soon as she saw the strands of old beads, though, yellow-brownish as ancient teeth, which Ma'am pulled up out of her dress, lifted off her neck, the wonderful sureness, this wonderful strength, left Easter. She'd have turned and fled in fact, but could hardly manage to scoot away on the pew, so feeble and stiff and cold her body felt. She spat out hot malice while she could, shouting.

"One, two, three, four!" Easter staggered up from the end of the pew as Ma'am gained her feet. "And we even tricked that clever Freddie of yours, too. Thinking he was *so* smart. Won't *never* do you any good swearing off the old Africa magic, Hazel Mae! Cause just you watch, we gon' get this last one too! *All of yours—*"

Ma'am slung the looped beads around Easter's neck, and falling to her knees she vomited up a vast supper with wrenching violence. When Easter opened her tightly clenched eyes, through blurry tears she saw, shiny and black in the middle of puddling pink mess, a snake thick as her own arm, *much* longer. She shrieked in terror, kicking backwards on the ground. Faster than anybody could run, the monstrous snake shot off down the aisle between the pews, and out into the gray brightness past the open church doors. Easter looked up and saw Ma'am standing just a few steps away. Her mother seemed more shaken than Easter had ever seen her. "Ma'am?" she said. "I'm scared. What's wrong? I don't feel good. What's this?" Easter began to lift off the strange beads looped so heavily round her neck.

At once Ma'am knelt on the ground beside her. "You just leave those right where they at," she said. "Your great grand brought these over with him. Don't you *never* take 'em off. Not even to wash up." Ma'am scooped hands under Easter's arms, helping her up to sit at the end of a pew. "Just wait here a minute. Let me go fill the wash bucket with water for this mess. *You* think on what all you got to tell me." Ma'am went out and came back. With a wet rag, she got down on her knees by the reeking puddle. "Well, go on, girl. Tell me. All this about Sadie. It's something do with the old Africa magic, ain't it?"

The last angel supped at Easter's hand, half-cut-off, and then lit away. Finally the blood began to gush forth and she swooned.*

*Weird, son. Definitely some disturbing writing in this section. But overarching theme = a people bereft, no? Dispossessed even of cultural *patrimony? Might consider then how to represent this in the narrative structure. Maybe just omit how Easter learns to trick the Devil into the chicken? Deny the reader that knowledge as Easter's been denied so much. If you do, leave a paragraph, or even just a sentence, literalizing the "Fragments of History." Terrible title, by the way; reconsider.*

*—Dad*

People presently dwelling in the path of hurricanes, those who lack the recourse of flight, hunker behind fortified windows and hope that this one too shall pass them lightly over. So, for centuries, were the options of the blacks vis-à-vis white rage. Either flee, or pray that the worst might strike elsewhere: once roused, such terror and rapine as whites could wreak would not otherwise be checked. But of course those living in the storm zones know that the big one always does hit sooner or later. And much worse for the blacks of that era, one bad element or many bad influences—'the Devil,' as it were—might attract to an individual, a family, or even an entire town, the landfall of a veritable hurricane.

*White Devils/Black Devils*, Luisa Valéria da Silva y Rodríguez

1877 August 24

There came to the ears of mother and daughter a great noise from out on the green, the people calling one to another in surprise, and then with many horses' hooves and crack upon crack of rifles, the thunder spoke, surely as the thunder had spoken before at Gettysburg or Shiloh. Calls of shock and wonder became now cries of terror and dying. They could hear those alive and afoot run away, and hear the horsemen who pursued them, with many smaller cracks of pistols. *There!* shouted white men to each other, *That one there running!* Some only made grunts of effort, as when a woodsman embeds his axe head and heaves it out of the wood again—such grunts. Phrases or wordless sound, the whiteness could be heard in the voices, essential and unmistakable.

Easter couldn't understand this noise at first, except that she should be afraid. It seemed that from the thunder's first rumble Ma'am grasped the whole of it, as if she had lived through precisely this before and perhaps many times. Clapping a hand over Easter's mouth, Ma'am said, "Hush," and got them both up and climbing over the pews from this one to the one behind, keeping always out-of-view of the doors. At the back of the church, to the right of the doors, was a closet where men stored the cut wood burned by the stove in winter. In dimness—that closet, *very* tight— they pressed themselves opposite the wall stacked with quartered logs, and squeezed back into the furthest corner. There, with speed and strength, Ma'am unstacked wood, palmed the top of Easter's head, and pressed her down to crouching in the dusty dark. Ma'am put the wood back again until Easter herself didn't know where she was. "You don't *move* from here," Ma'am said. "Don't come at nobody's call but mine." Easter was beyond thought by then, weeping silently since Ma'am had hissed, "*Shut your mouth!*" and shaken her once hard.

Easter nudged aside a log and clutched at the hem of her mother's skirt, but Ma'am pulled free and left her. From the first shot, not a single moment followed free of wails of desperation, or the shriller screams of those shot and bayoneted.

Footfalls, outside—some child running past the church, crying with terror. Easter heard a white man shout, *There go one!* and heard horse's hooves in heavy pursuit down the dirt of the Drive. She learned the noises peculiar to a horseman running down a child. Foreshortened last scream, pop of bones, pulped flesh, laughter from on high. To hear something clearly enough, if it was bad enough, was the same as seeing. Easter bit at her own arm as if that could blunt vision and hearing.

*Hey there, baby child,* whispered a familiar voice. *Won't you come out from there? I got something real nice for you just outside.* No longer the voice of the kindly spoken Johnny Reb, this was a serpentine lisp—and yet she knew them for one and the same and the Devil. *Yeah, come on out, Easter. Come see what all special I got for you.* Jump up flailing, run away screaming—Easter could think of nothing else, and the last strands of her tolerance and good sense began to fray and snap. That voice went on whispering and Easter choked on sobs, biting at her forearm.

Some girl screamed nearby. It could have been *any* girl in Rosetree, screaming, but the whisperer snickered, *Soubrette. I got her!*

Easter lunged up, and striking aside logs, she fought her way senselessly with scraped knuckles and stubbed toes from the closet, on out of the church into gray daylight.

If when the show has come and gone, not only paper refuse and cast-off food but the whole happy crowd, shot dead, remained behind and littered the grass, then Rosetree's green looked like some fairground, the day after.

Through the bushes next door to the church Easter saw Mr. Henry, woken tardily from a nap, thump with his cane out onto the porch, and from the far side of the house a white man walking shot him dead. Making not even a moan old Mr. Henry toppled over and his walking stick rolled to porch's edge and off into roses. About eight o'clock on the Drive, flames had engulfed the general store so it seemed a giant face of fire, the upstairs windows two dark eyes, and downstairs someone ran out of the flaming mouth. That shadow in the brightness had been Mrs. Toussaint, so slim and short in just such skirts, withering now under a fiery scourge that leapt around her, then up from her when she fell down burning. The Toussaints kept no animals in the lot beside the general store and it was all grown up with tall grass and wildflowers over there. Up from those weeds, a noise of hellish suffering poured from the ground, where some young woman lay unseen and screamed while one white man with dropped pants and white ass out stood afoot in the weeds and laughed, and some other, unseen on the ground, grunted piggishly in between shouted curses. People lay everywhere bloodied and fallen, so many dead, but Easter saw her father somehow alive out on the town green, right in the midst of the bodies just kneeling there in the grass, his head cocked to one side, chin down, as if puzzling over some problem. She ran to him calling *Pa Pa Pa* but up close she saw a red dribble down his face from the forehead where there was a deep ugly hole. Though they were sad and open his eyes slept no they were dead. To cry hard enough knocks a body down, and harder still needs both hands flat to the earth to get the grief out.

In the waist-high corn, horses took off galloping at the near end of the Parks' field. At the far end Mrs. Park ran with the baby Gideon Park, Jr. in her arms and the little girl Agnes following behind, head hardly above corn, shouting *Wait Mama wait*, going as fast as her legs could, but just a little girl, about four maybe five. Wholeheartedly wishing they'd make it to the backwood trees all right, Easter could see as plain as day those white men on horses would catch them first. So strenuous were her prayers for Mrs. Park and Agnes, she had to hush up weeping. Then a couple white men caught sight of Easter out on the green, just kneeling there—some strange survivor amidst such thorough and careful murder. With red bayonets, they trotted out on the grass toward her. Easter stood up meaning to say, or even beginning to, polite words about how the white men should leave Rosetree now, about the awful mistake they'd made. But the skinnier man got out in front of the other, *running*, and hauled back with such obvious intent on his rifle with that lengthy knife attached to it, Easter's legs wouldn't hold her. Suddenly kneeling again, she saw her mother standing right next to the crabapple stump. Dress torn, face sooty, in stocking feet, Ma'am got smack in the white men's way. That running man tried to change course but couldn't fast enough. He came full-on into the two-handed stroke of Ma'am's axe.

Swapt clean off, his head went flying, his body dropped straight down. The other one got a hand to his belt and scrabbled for a pistol while Ma'am stepped up and hauled back to come round for his head too. Which one first, then—pistol or axe? He got the gun out and up and shot. Missed, though, even that close, his hand useless as a drunk's, he was so scared. The axe knocked his chest in and him off his feet. Ma'am stomped the body twice getting her axe back out. With one hand she plucked Easter up off the ground to her feet. "*Run*, girl!"

They ran.

They should have gone straight into the woods, but their feet took them onto the familiar trail. Just in the trees' shadows, a big white man looked up grinning from a child small and dead on the ground. He must have caught some flash or glimpse of swinging wet iron because that white man's grin fell off, he loosed an ear-splitting screech, before Ma'am chopped that face and scream in half.

"Rawly?" Out of sight in the trees, some other white man called. "You all right over there, Rawly?" The fallen man, head in halves like the first red slice into a melon, made no answer. Nor was Ma'am's axe wedging out of his spine soon enough. Other white men took up the call of that name, and there was crash and movement in the trees.

Ma'am and Easter ran off the trail the other way. The wrong way again. They should have forgotten house and home and kept on forever into wilderness. Though probably it didn't matter anymore at that point. The others found the body—axe stuck in it—and cared not at all for the sight of a dead white man, or what had killed him. Ma'am and Easter thrashed past branches, crackled and snapped over twigs, and behind them in the tangled brush shouts of pursuit kept on doubling. What sounded like four men clearly had to be at least eight, and then just eight couldn't half account for such noise. Some men ahorse, some with dogs. Pistols and rifles firing blind.

They burst into the yard and ran up to the house. Ma'am slammed the bar onto the door. For a moment, they hunched over trying only to get air enough for life, and then Ma'am went to the wall and snatched off Brother's old Springfield from the war. *Where the durn cartridges at, and the caps, the doggone ramrod . . . ?* Curses and questions, both were plain on Ma'am's face as she looked round the house abruptly disordered and strange by the knock-knock of Death at the door. White men were already in the yard.

The glass fell out of the back window and shattered all over the iron stove. Brother, up on his back legs, barked in the open window, his forepaws on the windowsill.

"Go on, Easter." Ma'am let the rifle fall to the floor. "Never mind what I said before. Just go on with your brother now. I'm paying your way."

Easter was too afraid to say or do or think, and Brother at the back window was just barking and barking. *She was too scared.*

In her meanest voice, Ma'am said, "Take off that dress, Easter Sunday Mack!"

Sobbing breathlessly, Easter could only obey.

"All of it, Easter, take it off. And throw them old nasty beads on the floor!"

Easter did that too, Brother barking madly.

Ma'am said, "Now—"

Rifles stuttered thunderously and the dark wood door of the house lit up, splintering full of holes of daylight. In front of it Ma'am shuddered awfully and hot blood speckled Easter's naked body even where she stood across the room. Ma'am sighed one time, got down gently, and stretched out on the floor. White men stomped onto the porch.

Easter fell, caught herself on her hands, and the bad one went out under her so she smacked down flat on the floor. But effortlessly she bounded up and through the window. Brother was right there when Easter landed badly again. He kept himself to her swift limp as they tore away neck-and-neck through Ma'am's back garden and on into the woods.*

*\* Stop here, with the escape. Or no; I don't know. I wish there were some kind of way to offer the reader the epilogue, and yet warn them off too. I know it couldn't be otherwise, but it's just so grim.*

—*Dad*

## Epilogue

They were back! Right out there sniffing in the bushes where the rabbits were. Two great *big* ole dogs! About to shout for her husband, Anna Beth remembered he was lying down in the back with one of his headaches. So she took down the Whitworth and loaded it herself. Of course she knew how to fire a rifle, but back in the War Between the States they'd hand-picked Michael-Thomas to train the sharpshooters of his brigade, and then given him one of original Southern Crosses, too, for so many Yankees killed. Teary-eyed and squinting from his headaches, he still never missed what he meant to hit. Anna Beth crept back to the bedroom and opened the door a crack.

"You 'wake?" she whispered. "Michael-Thomas?"

Out of the shadows: "Annie?" His voice, breathy with pain. "What is it?"

"I *seen* 'em again! They're right out there in the creepers and bushes by the rabbit burrows."

"You sure, Annie? My head's real bad. Don't go making me get up and it ain't nothing out there again."

"I just now seen 'em, Michael-Thomas. *Big* ole nasty dogs like nothing you ever saw before." Better the little girl voice—that never failed: "Got your Whitworth right here, honey. All loaded up and ret' to go."

Michael-Thomas sighed. "Here I come, then."

The mattress creaked, his cane thumped the floor, and there was a grunt as his bad leg had to take some weight as he rose to standing. (Knee shot off at the Petersburg siege, and not just his knee, either . . .) Michael-Thomas pushed the door wide, his squinting eyes red, pouched under with violet bags. He'd taken off his half-mask, and so Anna Beth felt her stomach lurch and go funny, as usual. Friends at the church, and Mama, and just *everybody* had assured her she would—sooner or later—but Anna Beth never had gotten used to seeing what some chunk of Yankee artillery had done to Michael-Thomas' face. Supposed to still be up *in* there, that chip of metal, under the ruin and crater where his left cheek . . . "Here you go." Anna Beth passed off the Whitworth to him.

Rifle in hand, Michael-Thomas gimped himself over to where she pointed—the open window. There he stood his cane against the wall and laboriously got down kneeling. With practiced grace he lay the rifle across the window sash, nor did he even bother with the telescopic sight at this distance—just a couple hundred yards. He shot, muttering, "Damn! Just *look* at 'em," a moment before he did so. The kick liked to knock him over.

Anna Beth had fingertips jammed in her ears against the report, but it was loud anyhow. Through the window and down the yard she saw the bigger dog, dirty mustard color—had been nosing round in the honeysuckle near the rabbit warren—suddenly drop from view into deep weeds. Looked like the littler one didn't have the sense to dash off into the woods. All while Michael-Thomas reloaded, the other dog nudged its nose downward at the carcass unseen in the weeds, and just looked up and all around, whining— pitiful if it weren't so ugly. Michael-Thomas shot that one too.

"Ah," he said. "Oh." He swapped the Whitworth for his cane, leaving the rifle on the floor under the window. "My head's *killing* me." Michael-Thomas went right on back to the bedroom to lie down again.

He could be relied on to hit just what he aimed for, so Anna Beth didn't fear to see gore-soaked dogs yelping and kicking, only half-dead, out there in the untamed, overgrown end of the yard, should she take a notion to venture out that way for a look-see. Would them dogs be just as big, up close and stone dead, as they'd looked from far-off and alive?

But it weren't carcasses nor live dogs, either, back there where the weeds grew thickest. Two dead niggers, naked as sin. Gal with the back of her head blown off, and buck missing his forehead and half his brains too. Anna Beth come running back up to the house, hollering.

---

Kai Ashante Wilson's stories, "Super Bass" and "Kaiju maximus®," can be read, respectively, online at *Tor.com* and in the December 2015 issue of *Lightspeed* magazine. His novella *The Sorcerer of the Wildeeps* is available for purchase from all fine e-book purveyors. His novelette, *«Légendaire.»*, can be read in the anthology *Stories for Chip*, which celebrates the legacy of science fiction grandmaster Samuel R. Delany. Kai Ashante Wilson lives in New York City.

# The Litany Of Earth
## By Ruthanna Emrys

After a year in San Francisco, my legs grew strong again. A hill and a half lay between the bookstore where I found work and the apartment I shared with the Kotos. Every morning and evening I walked, breathing mist and rain into my desert-scarred lungs, and every morning the walk was a little easier. Even at the beginning, when my feet ached all day from the unaccustomed strain, it was a hill and a half that I hadn't been permitted for seventeen years.

In the evenings, the radio told what I had missed: an earth-spanning war, and atrocities in Europe to match and even exceed what had been done to both our peoples. We did not ask, the Kotos and I, whether our captors too would eventually be called to justice. The Japanese American community, for the most part, was trying to put the camps behind them. And it was not the way of my folk—who had grown resigned to the camps long before the Kotos' people were sent to join us, and who no longer had a community on land—to dwell on impossibilities.

That morning, I had received a letter from my brother. Caleb didn't write often, and hearing from him was equal parts relief and uncomfortable reminder. His grammar was good, but his handwriting and spelling revealed the paucity of his lessons. He had written:

*The town is a ruin, but not near enouff of one. Houses still stand; even a few windos are whole. It has all been looked over most carefully long ago, but I think forgotten or ignored since.*

And:

*I looked through our library, and those of other houses, but there is not a book or torn page left on the shelves. I have saugt permisson to look throuh the collecton at Miskatonic, but they are putting me off. I very much fear that the most important volumes were placed in some government warehouse to be forgotten—as we were.*

289

So, our family collections were still lost. I remembered the feel of the old pages, my father leaning over me, long fingers tracing a difficult passage as he explained its meaning—and my mother, breaking in with some simple suggestion that cut to the heart of it. Now, the only books I had to work with were the basic texts and a single children's spellbook in the store's backroom collection. The texts, in fact, belonged to Charlie—my boss—and I bartered my half-remembered childhood Enochian and R'lyehn for access.

Charlie looked up and frowned as the bells announced my arrival. He had done that from the first time I came in to apply, and so far as I knew gave all his customers the same glare.

"Miss Marsh."

I closed my eyes and breathed in the paper-sweet dust. "I'm not late, Mr. Day."

"We need to finish the inventory this morning. You can start with the westerns."

I stuck my purse behind the counter and headed back toward the piles of spine-creased Edgar Rice Burroughs and Zane Grey. "What I like about you," I said honestly, "is that you don't pretend to be civil."

"And dry off first." But no arguments, by now, that I ought to carry an umbrella or wear a jacket. No questions about why I liked the damp and chill, second only to the company of old books. Charlie wasn't unimaginative, but he kept his curiosity to himself.

I spent the rest of the morning shelving. Sometimes I would read a passage at random, drinking in the impossible luxury of ink organized into meaningful patterns. Very occasionally I would bring one forward and read a bit aloud to Charlie, who would harumph at me and continue with his work, or read me a paragraph of his own.

By midafternoon I was holding down the register while Charlie did something finicky and specific with the cookbooks. The bells jangled. A man poked his head in, sniffed cautiously, and made directly for me.

"Excuse me. I'm looking for books on the occult—for research." He smiled, a salesman's too-open expression, daring me to disapprove. I showed him to the shelf where we kept Crowley and other such nonsense, and returned to the counter frowning thoughtfully.

After a few minutes, he returned. "None of that is quite what I'm looking for. Do you keep anything more . . . esoteric?"

"I'm afraid not, sir. What you see is what we have."

He leaned across the counter. His scent, ordinary sweat and faint cologne, insinuated itself against me, and I stepped back out of reach. "Maybe something in a storage room? I'm sure you must have more than these turn-of-the-century fakers. Some Al-Hazred, say? Prinn's *Vermis*?"

I tried not to flinch. I knew the look of the old families, and he had none of it—tall and dark-haired and thin-faced, conventional attractiveness marred by nothing more than a somewhat square nose. Nor was he cautious in revealing his familiarity with the Aeonist canon, as Charlie had been. He was either stupid, or playing with me.

"I've never heard of either," I said. "We don't specialize in esoterica; I'm afraid you'd better try another store."

"I don't think that's necessary." He drew himself straighter, and I took another step back. He smiled again, in a way I thought was intended to be friendly, but seemed rather the bare-toothed threat of an ape. "Miss Aphra Marsh. I know you're familiar with these things, and I'm sure we can help each other."

I held my ground and gave my mother's best glare. "You have me mistaken, sir. If you are not in the store to purchase goods that we actually have, I strongly suggest that you look elsewhere."

He shrugged and held out his hands. "Perhaps later."

Charlie limped back to the counter as the door rang the man's departure. "Customer?"

"No." My hands were trembling, and I clasped them behind my back. "He wanted to know about your private shelf. Charlie, I don't like him. I don't trust him."

He frowned again and glanced toward the employees-only door. "Thief?"

That would have been best, certainly. My pulse fluttered in my throat. "Well informed, if so."

Charlie must have seen how hard I was holding myself. He found the metal thermos and offered it silently. I shook my head, and with a surge of dizziness found myself on the floor. I wrapped my arms around my knees and continued to shake my head at whatever else might be offered.

"He might be after the books," I forced out at last. "Or he might be after us."

He crouched next to me, moving slowly with his bad knee and the stiffness of joints beginning to admit mortality. "For having the books?"

I shook my head again. "Yes. Or for being the sort of people who would have them." I stared at my interlaced fingers, long and bony, as though they might be thinking about growing extra joints. There was no way to explain the idea I had, that the smiling man might come back with more men, and guns, and vans that locked in the back. And probably he was only a poorly spoken dabbler, harmless. "He knew my name."

Charlie pulled himself up and into a chair, settling with a grunt. "I don't suppose he could have been one of those Yith you told me about?"

I looked up, struck by the idea. I had always thought of the Great Race as solemn and wise, and meeting one was supposed to be very lucky. But they were also known to be arrogant and abrupt, when they wanted something. It was a nice thought. "I don't think so. They have phrases, secret ways of making themselves known to people who would recognize them. I'm afraid he was just a man."

"Well." Charlie got to his feet. "No help for it unless he comes back. Do you need to go home early?"

That was quite an offer, coming from Charlie, and I couldn't bear the thought that I looked like I needed it. I eased myself off the floor, the remaining edge of fear making me slow and clumsy. "Thank you. I'd rather stay here. Just warn me if you see him again."

• • • •

The first change in my new life, also heralded by a customer . . .

It is not yet a month since my return to the world. I am still weak, my skin sallow from malnourishment and dehydration. After my first look in a good mirror, I have shaved my brittle locks to the quick, and the new are growing in ragged, but thick and rich and dark like my mother's. My hair as an adult woman, which I have never seen 'til now.

I am shelving when a familiar phrase stings my ears. Hope and danger, tingling together as I drift forward, straining to hear more.

The blond man is trying to sell Charlie a copy of the *Book of the Grey People*, but it soon becomes apparent that he knows little but the title. I should be more cautious than I am next, should think more carefully about what I reveal. But I like Charlie, his gruffness and his honesty and the endless difference between him and everything I have hated or loved. I don't like to see him taken in.

The blond man startles when I appear by his shoulder, but when I pull the tome over to flip the pages, he tries to regroup. "Now just a minute here, young lady. This book is valuable."

I cannot imagine that I truly look less than my thirty years. "This book is a fake. Is this supposed to be Enochian?"

"Of course it's Enochian. Let me—"

"Ab-kar-rak al-laz-kar-nef—" I sound out the paragraph in front of me. "This was written by someone who had heard Enochian once, and vaguely recalled the sound of it. It's gibberish. And in the wrong alphabet, besides. And the binding . . ." I run my hand over it and shudder. "The binding is real skin. Which makes this a very expensive fake for *someone*, but the price has already been paid. Take this abomination away."

Charlie looks at me as the blond man leaves. I draw myself up, determined to make the best of it. I can always work at the laundromat with Anna.

"You know Enochian?" he asks. I'm startled by the gentleness—and the hope. I can hardly lie about it now, but I don't give more than the bare truth.

"I learned it as a child."

His eyes sweep over my face; I hold myself impassive against his judgment. "I believe you keep secrets, and keep them well," he says at last. "I don't plan to pry. But I want to show you one of mine, if you can keep that too."

This isn't what I was expecting. But he might learn more about me, someday, as much as I try to hide. And when that happens, I'll need a reason to trust him. "I promise."

"Come on back." He turns the door sign before leading me to the storage room that has been locked all the weeks I've worked here.

• • • •

I stayed as late as I could, until I realized that if someone was asking after me, the Kotos might be in danger as well. I didn't want to call, unsure if the phone lines would be safe. All the man had done was talk to me—I might never see him again. Even so, I would be twitching for weeks. You don't forget the things that can develop from other people's small suspicions.

The night air was brisk, chilly by most people's standards. The moon watched over the city, soft and gibbous, outlines blurred by San Francisco's ubiquitous mist. Sounds echoed closer than their objects. I might have been swimming, sensations carried effortlessly on ocean currents. I licked salt from my lips, and prayed. I wished I could break the habit, but I wished more, still, that just once it would work.

"Miss Marsh!" The words pierced the damp night. I breathed clean mist and kept walking. *Iä, Cthulhu . . .*

"Please, Miss Marsh, I just need a moment of your time." The words were polite enough, but the voice was too confident. I walked faster, and strained my ears for his approach. Soft soles would not tap, but a hissing squelch marked every step on the wet sidewalk. I could not look back; I could not run: either would be an admission of guilt. He would chase me, or put a bullet in my skull.

"You have me mistaken," I said loudly. The words came as a sort of croak.

I heard him speed up, and then he was in front of me, mist clinging to his tall form. Perforce, I stopped. I wanted to escape, or call for help, but I could not imagine either.

"What do you want, sir?" The stiff words came more easily this time. It occurred to me belatedly that if he did not know what I was, he might try to force himself on me, as the soldiers sometimes had with the Japanese girls in the camp. I couldn't bring myself to fear the possibility; he moved like a different kind of predator.

"I'm sorry," he said. "I'm afraid we may have gotten off to a bad start, earlier. I'm Ron Spector; I'm with the FBI—"

He started to offer a badge, but the confirmation of my worst fears released me from my paralysis. I lashed out with one newly strong leg and darted to the side. I had intended to race home and warn the Kotos, but instead he caught his balance and grabbed my arm. I turned and grappled, scratching and pulling, all the time aware that my papa had died fighting this way. I expected the deadly shot at any moment, and struggled while I could. But my arms were weaker than Papa's, and even my legs were not what they should have been.

Gradually, I realized that Spector was only trying to hold me off, not fighting for his life, nor even for mine. He kept repeating my name, and at last:

"Please, Miss Marsh! I'm not trained for this!" He pushed me back again, and grunted as my nails drew blood on his unprotected wrist.

"Please! I don't mean you any harm; I just want to talk for five minutes. Five minutes, I promise, and then you can stay or go as you please!"

My panic could not sustain itself, and I stilled at last. Even then, I was afraid that given the chance, he would clap me in irons. But we held our tableau, locked hand to wrist. His mortal pulse flickered mouse-like against my fingertips, and I was sure he could feel mine roaring like the tide.

"If I let you go, will you listen?"

I breathed in strength from the salt fog. "Five minutes, you said."

"Yes." He released me, and rubbed the skin below his wristwatch. "I'm sorry, I should have been more circumspect. I know what you've been through."

"Do you." I controlled my shaking with effort. I was a Marsh; I would not show weakness to an enemy. They had drunk deep of it already.

He looked around and took a careful seat on one of the stones bordering a nearby yard. It was too short for him, so that his knees bent upward when he sat. He leaned forward: a praying mantis in a black suit.

"Most religions consist largely of good people trying to get by. No matter what names they worship, or what church they go to, or what language they pray in. Will you agree with me on this much?"

I folded my arms and waited.

"And every religion has its fanatics, who are willing to do terrible things in the name of their god. No one is immune." His lips quirked. "It's a failing of humanity, not of any particular sect."

"I'll grant you that. What of it?" I counted seconds in drips of water. I could almost imagine the dew clinging to my skin as a shield.

He shrugged and smiled. I didn't like how easy he could be, with his wrist still stinking of blood. "If you grant me that, you're already several steps ahead of the U.S. government, just post–World War I. In the twenties, they had run-ins with a couple of nasty Aeonist groups. There was one cult down in Louisiana that had probably never seen an original bit of the canon, but they had their ideas. Sacrificial corpses hanging from trees, the whole nine yards." He glanced at me, checking for some reaction. I did not grant it.

"Not exactly representative, but we got the idea that was normal. In '26, the whole religion were declared enemies of the state, and we started looking out for anyone who said the wrong names on Sunday night, or had the wrong statues in their churches. You know where it goes from there."

I did, and wondered how much he really knew. It was strange, nauseating, to hear the justifications, even as he tried to hold them at a distance.

"It won't shock you," he continued, "to know that Innsmouth wasn't the only place that suffered. Eventually, it occurred to the government that they might have overgeneralized, but it took a long time for changes to go through. Now we're starting to have people like me, who actually study Aeonist culture and try to separate out the bad guys, but it's been a long time coming."

I held myself very still through his practiced speech. "If this is by way of an apology, Mr. Spector, you can drown in it. What you did was beyond the power of any apology."

"Doubtless we owe you one anyway, if we can find a decent way of making it. But I'm afraid I've been sent to speak with you for practical reasons." He cleared his throat and shifted his knees. "As you may imagine, when the government went hunting Aeonists, it was much easier to find good people, minding their own business in small towns, than cultists well-practiced in conspiracy and murder. The bad guys tend to be better at hiding, after all. And at the same time, we weren't trying to recruit people who knew anything useful about the subject—after a while, few would have been willing even if we went looking. So now, as with the Japanese American community, we find ourselves shorthanded, ignorant, and having angered the people least likely to be a danger to the country."

My eye sockets ached. "I cannot believe that you are trying to recruit me."

"I'm afraid that's exactly what I'm doing. I could offer—"

"Your five minutes are up, sir." I walked past him, biting back anything else I might say, or think. The anger worked its way into my shoulders, and my legs, and the rush of my blood.

"Miss Marsh!"

Against my better judgment, I stopped and turned back. I imagined what I must look like to him. Bulging eyes; wide mouth; long, bony legs and fingers. "The Innsmouth look," when there was an Innsmouth. Did it signal danger to him? Something more than human, or less? Perhaps he saw just an ugly woman, someone whose reactions he could dismiss until he heard what he wanted.

Then I would speak clearly.

"Mr. Spector, I have no interest in being an enemy of the state. The state is larger than I. But nor will I be any part of it. And if you insist, you will listen to why. *The state* stole nearly two decades of my life. *The state* killed my father, and locked the rest of my family away from anything they thought might give us strength. Salt water. Books. Knowledge. One by one, they destroyed us. My mother began her metamorphosis. Allowed the ocean, she might have lived until the sun burned to ashes. They took her away. We know they studied us at such times, to better know the process. To better know how to hurt us. You must imagine the details, as I have. They never returned the bodies. Nothing has been given back to us.

"Now, ask me again."

He bent his head at last. Not in shame, I thought, but listening. Then he spoke softly. "The state is not one entity. It is *changing*. And when it changes, it's good for everyone. The people you could help us stop are truly hurting others. And the ones being hurt know nothing of what was done to your family. Will you hold the actions of a few against them? Should more families suffer because yours did?"

I reminded myself that, after humanity faded and died, a great insectoid civilization would live in these hills. After that, the Sareeav, with their pseudopods and strange sculptures. Therefore, I could show patience. "I will do what I can for suffering on my own."

More quietly: "If you helped us, even on one matter, I might be able to find out what really happened to your mother."

The guilt showed plainly on his face as soon as he said it, but I still had to turn away. "I cannot believe that even after her death, you would dare hold my mother hostage for my good behavior. You can keep her body, and your secrets." And in R'lyehn, because we had been punished for using it in the camps, I added, "And if they hang your corpse from a tree, I will kiss the ground beneath it." Then, fearful that he might do more, or say more, I ran.

I kicked off my shoes, desperate for speed. My feet slapped the wet ground. I could not hear whether Spector followed me. I was still too weak, as weak as I had been as a child, but I was taller, and faster, and the fog wrapped me and hid me and sped me on my flight.

Some minutes later I ducked into a side drive. Peering out, I saw no one following me. Then I let myself gasp: deep, shuddering breaths. I wanted him dead. I wanted them all dead, as I had for seventeen years. Probably some of them were: they were only ordinary humans, with creaking joints and rivulet veins. I could be patient.

I came in barefoot to the Kotos. Mama Rei was in the kitchen. She put down her chopping knife, and held me while I shook. Then Anna took my hand and drew me over to the table. The others hovered nearby, Neko looking concerned and Kevin sucking his thumb. He reminded me so very much of Caleb.

"What happened?" asked Anna, and I told them everything, trying to be calm and clear. They had to know.

Mama Rei tossed a handful of onions into the pan and started on the peppers. She didn't look at me, but she didn't need to. "Aphra-chan—Kappa-sama—what do you think he wants?"

I started to rub my face, then winced. Spector's blood, still on my nails, cut through the clean smell of frying onion. "I don't know. Perhaps only what he said, but his masters will certainly be angry when he fails to recruit me. He might seek ways to put pressure on me. It's not safe. I'm sorry."

"I don't want to leave," said Neko. "We just got here." I closed my eyes hard against the sting.

"We won't leave," said Mama Rei. "We are trying to build a decent life here, and I won't be scared away from it. Neither will you, Aphra-chan. This government man can only do so much to us, without a law to say he can lock us up."

"There was no law countenancing the things done to my family," I said.

"Times have changed," she said firmly. "People are watching, now."

"They took your whole town," said Anna, almost gently. "They can't take all of San Francisco, can they, Mama?"

"Of course not. We will live our lives, and you will all go to work and school tomorrow, and we will be careful. That is all."

There was no arguing with Mama Rei, and I didn't really want to. I loved the life I had, and if I lost it again, well . . . the sun would burn to ash soon enough, and then it would make little difference whether I had a few months of happiness here, or a few years. I fell asleep praying.

• • • •

One expects the storage room of a bookstore to hold more books. And it does. Books in boxes, books on shelves, books piled on the floor and the birch table with uneven legs. And one bookshelf more solid than the others, leaves and vines carved into dark wood. The sort that one buys for too much money, to hold something that feels like it deserves the respect.

And on the shelves, my childhood mixed with dross. I hold up my hand, afraid to touch, to run it across the titles, a finger's breadth away. I fear that they too will change to gibberish. Some of them already are. Some are titles I know to have been written by charlatans, or fakes as obvious as the blond man's *Grey People*. And some are real.

"Where did you get these?"

"At auction. At estate sales. From people who come in offering to sell, or other stores that don't know what they have. To tell the truth, I don't entirely either, for some of them. You might have a better idea?"

I pull down a *Necronomicon* with shaking hands, the one of his three that looks real. The inside page is thankfully empty—no dedication, no list of family names. No chance of learning whether it ever belonged to someone I knew. I read the first page, enough to recognize the over-poetic Arabic, and put it back before my eyes can tear up. I take another, this one in true Enochian.

"Why buy them, if you can't read them?"

"Because I might be able to, someday. Because I might be able to learn something, even with a word or two. Because I want to learn magic, if you must know, and this is the closest I can come." His glare dares me to scoff.

I hold out the book I've been cradling. "You could learn from this one, you know. It's a child's introductory text. I learned a little from it, myself, before I . . . lost access to my library." My glare dares him to ask. He doesn't intrude on my privacy, no more than I laugh at what he's revealed. "I don't know enough to teach you properly. But if you let me share your books, I'll help you learn as best I can." He nods, and I turn my head aside so my tears don't fall on the text—or where he can see.

• • • •

I returned to work the next day, wearing shoes borrowed from neighbors. My feet were far too big for anything the Kotos could lend me. Anna walked me partway before turning off for the laundromat—her company more comfort than I cared to admit.

I had hovered by the sink before breakfast, considering what to do about the faint smudge of Spector's blood. In the end, I washed it off. A government agent, familiar with the Aeonist canons, might well know how to detect the signs if I used it against him.

Despite my fears, that day was a quiet one, full of customers asking for westerns and romances and textbooks. The next day was the same, and the day after that, and three weeks passed with the tension between my shoulder blades the only indication that something was amiss.

At the end of those three weeks, he came again. His body language had changed: a little hunched, a little less certain. I stiffened, but did not run. Charlie looked up from the stack of incoming books, and gave the requisite glare.

"That's him," I murmured.

"Ah." The glare deepened. "You're not welcome here. Get out of my store, and don't bother my employees again."

Spector straightened, recovering a bit of his old arrogance. "I have something for Miss Marsh. Then I'll go."

"Whatever you have to offer, I don't want it. You heard Mr. Day: you're trespassing."

He ducked his head. "I found your mother's records. I'm not offering them in exchange for anything. You were right, that wasn't . . . wasn't honorable. Once you've seen them—if you want to see them—I'll go."

I held out my hand. "Very well. I'll take them. And then you will leave."

He held on to the thick folder. "I'm sorry, Miss Marsh. I've got to stay with them. They aren't supposed to be out of the building, and I'm not supposed to have them right now. I'll be in serious trouble if I lose them."

I didn't care if he got in trouble, and I didn't want to see what was in the folder. But it was my mother's only grave. "Mr. Day," I said quietly. "I would like a few minutes of privacy, if you please."

Charlie took a box and headed away, but paused. "You just shout if this fellow gives you any trouble." He gave Spector another glare before heading into the stacks—I suspected not very far.

Spector handed me the folder. I opened it, cautiously, between the cash register and a short stack of Agatha Christie novels. For a moment I closed my eyes, fixing my mother's living image in my mind. I remembered her singing a sacred chanty in the kitchen, arguing with shopkeepers, kneeling in the wet sand at Solstice. I remembered one of our neighbors crying in our sitting room after her husband's boat was lost in a storm, telling her, "Your faith goes all the way to the depths. Some of us aren't so lucky."

"I'm sorry," Spector said quietly. "It's ugly."

They had taken her deeper into the desert, to an experimental station. They had caged her. They had given her weights to lift, testing her strength. They had starved her for days, testing her endurance. They had cut her, confusing their mythologies, with iron and silver, noting healing times. They had washed her once with seawater, then fresh, then scrubbed her with dry salt. After that, they had refused her all contact with water, save a minimum to drink. Then not even that. For the whole of sixty-seven days, they carefully recorded her pulse, her skin tone, and the distance between her eyes. Perhaps in some vague way also interested in our culture, they copied, faithfully, every word she spoke.

Not one sentence was a prayer.

There were photos, both from the experiments and the autopsy afterward. I did not cry. It seemed extravagant to waste salt water so freely.

"Thank you," I said quietly, closing the folder, bile burning the back of my throat. He bowed his head.

"My mother came to the states young." He spoke deliberately, neither rushing to share nor stumbling over his apparent honesty. Anything else, I would have felt justified interrupting. "Her sister stayed in Poland. She was a bit older, and she had a sweetheart. I have files on her, too. She survived. She's in a hospital in Israel, and sometimes she can feed herself." He stopped, took a deep breath, shook his head. "I can't think of anything that would convince me to work for the new German government—no matter how different it is from the old. I'm sorry I asked."

He took the folder and turned away.

"Wait." I should not have said it. He'd probably staged the whole thing. But it was a far more thoughtful manipulation than the threats I had expected—and I found myself afraid to go on ignoring my enemies. "I will not work for you. But tell me about these frightening new Aeonists."

Whatever—if anything—I eventually chose to pass on to Spector, I realized that I very much wanted to meet them. For all the Kotos' love and comfort, and for all Charlie's eager learning, I still missed Innsmouth. These mortals might be the closest I could come to home.

• • • •

"Why do you want to learn this?" Though I doubt Charlie knows, it's a ritual question. There is no ritual answer.

"I don't . . ." He glares, a habit my father would have demanded he break before pursuing the ancient scholarship. "Some things don't go into words easily, all right? It's . . . it feels like what *should* be in books, I suppose. They should all be able to change the world. At least a little."

I nod. "That's a good answer. Some people think that 'power' is a good answer, and it isn't. The power that can be found in magic is less than what you get from a gun, or a badge, or a bomb." I pause. "I'm trying to remember all the things I need to tell you, now, at the beginning. What magic is *for* is understanding. Knowledge. And it won't work until you know how little that gets you.

"*Sharhlyda*—Aeonism—is a bit like a religion. But this isn't the Bible— most of the things I'm going to tell you are things we have records of: histories older than man, and sometimes the testimony of those who lived them. The gods you can take or leave, but the history is real.

"All of man's other religions place him at the center of creation. But man is nothing—a fraction of the life that will walk the Earth. Earth is nothing—a tiny world that will die with its sun. The sun is one of trillions where life flowers, and wants to live, and dies. And between the suns is an endless vast darkness that dwarfs them, through which life can travel only by giving up that wanting, by losing itself. Even that darkness will eventually die. In such a universe, knowledge is the stub of a candle at dusk."

"You make it all sound so cheerful."

"It's honest. What our religion tells us, the part that is a religion, is that the gods created life to try and make meaning. It's ultimately hopeless, and even gods die, but the effort is real. Will always have been real, even when everything is over and no one remembers."

Charlie looks dubious. I didn't believe it, either, when I first started learning. And I was too young then to find it either frightening or comforting.

• • • •

I thought about what Mr. Spector had told me, and about what I might do with the information. Eventually I found myself, unofficially and entirely on my own recognizance, in a better part of the city, past sunset, at the door of a home rather nicer than the Kotos'. It was no mansion by any imagining, but it was long lived-in and well kept up: two stories of brick and Spanish tile roof, with juniper guarding the façade. The door was painted a cheerful yellow, but the knocker was a fantastical wrought-iron creature that reminded me painfully of home. I lifted the cold metal and rapped sharply. Then I waited, shivering.

The man who opened the door looked older than Charlie. His gray hair frizzed around the temples and ears, otherwise slick as a seal. Faint lines creased his cheeks. He frowned at me. I hoped I had the right address.

"My name is Aphra Marsh," I said. "Does that mean anything to you? I understand that some in this house still follow the old ways."

He started, enough to tell me that he recognized my family's name. He shuffled back a little, but then leaned forward. "Where did you hear such a thing?"

"My family have their ways. May I enter?"

He stepped aside to let me in, in too reluctant a fashion to be truly gallant. His pupils widened between narrowed eyelids, and he licked his lips.

"What do you want, my lady?"

Ignoring the question for the moment, I stepped inside. The foyer, and what I could see of the parlor, looked pedestrian but painfully familiar. Dark wood furniture, much of it bookshelves, contrasted with leaf-green walls. Yet it was all a bit shabby—not quite as recently dusted or mended as would have satisfied my mother's pride. A year ago, it might have been the front room of any of the better houses in Innsmouth. Now . . . I wondered what my family home had looked like, in the years after my mother was no longer there to take pride in it. I put the thought forcibly out of my mind.

". . . in the basement," he was saying. "Would you like to see?"

I ran my memory back through the last seconds, and discovered that he was, in fact, offering to show me where they practiced "the old ways." "I would. But an introduction might be in order first?"

"My apologies, my lady. I am Oswin Wilder. High priest here, although probably not a very traditional one by your standards."

"I make no judgment." And I smiled at him in a way that suggested I might well do so later. It was strange. In Innsmouth, non-Sharhlyd outsiders had looked on us with fear and revulsion—even the Sharhlyd who were not of our kind, mostly the nervously misanthropic academics at Miskatonic, treated us with suspicion. Respect was usually subordinated to rivalries over the proper use of ancient texts. The few mortal humans who shared both our town and our faith had deferred openly, but without this taint of resentment.

He led me down solid wooden steps. I half expected a hidden sub-basement or a dungeon—I think he must have wanted one—but he had worked with the home he already had. Beyond the bare flagstone at the foot of the stairs, he had merely added a raised level of dark tile, painted with sigils and patterns. I recognized a few, but suspected more of being his own improvisations. At the far end of the room, candles flickered on a cloth-covered table. I approached, moving carefully around the simple stone altar in the center.

On the table sat a devotional statue of Cthulhu. I hardly noticed the quality of the carving or the material, although my childhood priest would have had something to say about both. But my childhood was long discarded, and the display struck my adult doubts with forgotten force. Heedless of the man behind me, I knelt. The flickering light gave a wet sheen to tentacles and limbs, and I could almost imagine again that they were reaching to draw me in and keep me safe. Where the statue in Innsmouth's church had depicted the god with eyes closed, to represent the mysteries of the deep, this one's eyes were open, black and fathomless. I returned the gaze, refusing to bow my head.

*Have you been waiting for us? Do you regret what happened? With all your aeons, did you even notice that Innsmouth was gone? Or did you just wonder why fewer people came to the water?*

*Are you listening, now? Were you ever there to listen?*

More tears, I realized too late—not something I would have chosen for the priest to see. But I flicked a drop of my salt water onto the statue, and whispered the appropriate prayer. I found it oddly comforting. My mother, old-fashioned, had kept a jar of seawater on the counter for washing tear-streaked faces, and brought it to temple once a month. But I had still given my tears to the god when I didn't want her fussing, or was trying to hide a fight with my brother.

We were near the ocean now. Perhaps the Kotos could spare a jar.

My musings were interrupted by the creak of the basement door and a tremulous alto.

"Oz? I knocked, but no one answered—are you down here?"

"Mildred, yes. Come on down; we have a guest."

Full skirts, garnet red, descended, and as she came closer I saw a woman bearing all my mother's remembered dignity. She had the air of magnificence that fortunate mortals gained with age; her wrinkles and gray-streaked hair only gave the impression of deliberate artistic choices. I stood and ducked my head politely. She looked me over, thin-lipped.

"Mil—Miss Marsh," said Wilder. "Allow me to introduce Mildred Bergman. Mildred, this is Miss Aphra Marsh." He paused dramatically, and her frown deepened.

"And what is she doing in our sanctum?"

"Miss *Marsh*," he repeated.

"Anyone can claim a name. Even such an illustrious one." I winced, then lifted my chin. There was no reason for me to feel hurt: her doubt should be no worse a barrier than Wilder's nervous pride.

Taking a candle from the altar for light—and with a whisper of thanks to Cthulhu for the loan—I stepped toward her. She stood her ground. "Look at me."

She looked me up and down, making a show of it. Her eyes stayed narrow, and if I had studied long enough to hear thoughts, and done the appropriate rites, I was sure I would have heard it. *Anyone can be ugly.*

Wilder moved to intervene. "This is silly. We have no reason to doubt her. And she found us on her own. She must have some knowledge of the old arts: we don't exactly put our address in the classifieds. Let it go and give her a chance to prove herself."

Bergman sniffed and shrugged. Moving faster than I would have expected, she plucked the candle from my hand and replaced it on the table. "As high priest, it is of course at your discretion what newcomers must do to join the elect. The others will be here soon; we'll see what they think of your guest."

I blinked at her. "I'll wait, then." I turned my back and knelt again at the god's table. I would not let her see my rage at her dismissal, or the fear that the gesture of defiance cost me.

• • • •

The first and most basic exercise in magic is looking at oneself. Truly looking, truly seeing—and I am afraid. I cannot quite persuade myself that the years in the camp haven't stolen something vital. After doing this simple thing, I will know.

I sit opposite Charlie on the plain wood floor of the storage room. He has dragged over a rag rug and the cushion from a chair for his knees, but I welcome the cool solidity. Around us I have drawn a first-level seal in red chalk, and between us placed two bowls of salt water and two knives. I have walked him through this in the book, told him what to expect, as well as I am able. I remember my father, steady and patient as he explained the rite. I may be more like my mother—impatient with beginners' mistakes, even my own.

I lead him through a grounding: tell him to imagine the sea in his veins, his body as a torrent of blood and breath. I simplify the imagery I learned as a child. He has no metamorphosis to imagine, no ancestors to tell him how those things feel under the weight of the depths. But he closes his eyes and breathes, and I imagine it as wind on a hot day. He is a man of the air, after all. I must tell him the Litany so he will know what that means, and perhaps he will make a new grounding that fits.

Bodies and minds settled, we begin the chant. His pronunciation is poor, but this is a child's exercise and designed for a leader and a stumbling apprentice. The words rise, bearing the rhythm of wind and wave and the slow movement of the earth. Still chanting, I lift the knife, and watch Charlie follow my lead. I wash the blade in salt water and prick my finger. The sting is familiar, welcome. I let a drop of my blood fall into the bowl, swirling and spreading and fading into clarity. I have just enough time to see that Charlie has done the same before the room too fades, and my inward perceptions turn clear.

I am inside myself, seeing with my blood rather than my eyes. I am exquisitely aware of my body, and its power. My blood *is* a torrent. It is a river emptying into the ocean; it thunders through me, a cacophony of rapids and white water. I travel with it, checking paths I have not trod for eighteen years. I find them surprisingly in order. I should have known, watching mortals age while my hard-used joints still moved easily—but that river still carries its healing force, still sweeps illnesses and aches from the banks where they try to cling. Still reshapes what it touches, patiently and steadily. Still carries all the markers of a healthy child who will someday, still, go into the water. I remember my mother telling me, smiling, that my blood knew already the form I would someday wear.

I am basking in the feel of myself, loving my body for the first time in years, when everything changes. Just for a moment, I am aware of my skin, and a touch on my arm.

"Miss Marsh, are you okay?"

And now I remember that one learns to stay inside longer with practice, and that I entirely neglected to warn Charlie against touching me. And then I am cast out of my river, and into another.

I've never tried this with anyone outside my own people. Charlie's river is terribly weak—more like a stream, in truth. It has little power, and detritus has made it narrow and shallow. Where my body is yearning toward the ocean, his has already begun to dry out. His blood, too, knows the form he will someday wear.

He must now be seeing me as intimately.

I force the connection closed, saying the words that end the rite as quickly as I dare. I come to, a little dizzy, swaying.

Charlie looks far more shaken. "That . . . that was real. That was magic."

And I can only feel relief. Of course, the strangeness of his first spell must overwhelm any suspicion over the differences in our blood. At least for now.

• • • •

Wilder's congregation trickled in over the next hour. They were male and female, robed richly or simply, but all with an air of confidence that suggested old families used to mortal power. They murmured when Wilder introduced them to me; some whispered more with Bergman afterward.

It only seemed like an endless aeon until they at last gathered in a circle. Wilder stood before the table, facing the low altar, and raised his arms. The circle quieted, till only their breath and the rustling of skirts and robes moved the air.

"Iä, iä, Cthulhu thtagn . . ." His accent was beyond abominable, but the prayer was familiar. After the fourth smoothly spoken mispronunciation, I realized that he must have learned the language entirely from books. While I had been denied wisdom writ solid in ink, he had been denied a guiding voice. Knowing he would not appreciate it now, I kept my peace. Even the mangled words were sweet.

The congregants gave their responses at the appropriate points, though many of them stumbled, and a few muttered nonsense rather than the proper words. They had learned from Wilder, some more newly than others. Many leaned forward, pupils dilated and mouths gaping with pleasure. Bergman's shoulders held the tension of real fervor, but her lids were narrowed as she avidly watched the reactions she would not show herself. Her eyes met mine and her mouth twitched.

I remembered my mother, her self-contained faith a complement to my father's easy affections. Bergman had the start of such faith, though she still seemed too conscious of her self-control.

After several minutes of call and response, Wilder knelt and took a golden necklet from where it had been hidden under the folds of the tablecloth. It was none of the work of my people—only a simple set of linked squares, with some abstract tentacular pattern carved in each one. It was as like the ornate bas-relief and wirework necklace-crowns of the deep as the ritual was like my childhood church. Wilder lifted it so that all could see, and Bergman stood before him. He switched abruptly to English: no translation that I recognized, presumably his own invention.

"Lady, wilt thou accept the love of Shub-Nigaroth? Wilt thou shine forth the wonders of life eternal for our mortal eyes?"

Bergman lifted her chin. "I shall. I am her sworn daughter, and the beloved of the Gods: let all welcome and return their terrible and glorious love."

Wilder placed the chain around her neck. She turned to face the congregation, and he continued, now hidden behind her: "Behold the glory of the All-Mother!"

"Iä Cthulhu! Iä Shub-Nigaroth!"

"Behold the dance in darkness! Behold the life that knows not death!"

"Iä! Iä!"

"Behold the secret ever hidden from the sun! See it—breathe it—take it within you!"

At this the congregation fell silent, and I stumbled over a swallowed shout of joy. The words were half nonsense, but half closer to the spirit of my remembered services than anything Wilder had pulled from his books. Bergman took from the table a knife, and a chalice full of some dark liquid. As she turned to place it on the altar, the scent of plain red wine wafted to my nostrils. She pricked her finger and squeezed a drop of blood into the cup.

As we passed the chalice from hand to hand, the congregants each sipped reverently. They closed their eyes and sighed at private visions, or stared into the wine wondering before relinquishing it to the next. Yet when it came around to me, I tasted only wine. With time and space for my own art, I might have learned from it any secrets hidden in Bergman's blood—but there was no magic here, only its trappings.

They were awkward, and ignorant, yearning and desperate. Wilder sought power, and Bergman feared to lose it, and the others likely ran the same range of pleasant and obnoxious company that I remembered from my lost childhood congregation. But whatever else they might be, Spector had been wrong. The government had no more to fear from them than it had from Innsmouth eighteen years ago.

• • • •

As Charlie shuts the door to the back room, I can see his hands trembling. Outside this room he wears a cynical elder's mask, but in truth he is in his late thirties—close enough to my age to make little difference, were we both common mortals. And life has been kind to him. What I now offer has been his greatest frustration, and his eagerness is palpable.

As he moves to clear the floor, I hold up my hand. "Later, we'll try the Inner Sea again"—his unaccustomed smile blossoms—"but first I need to read you something. It may help you to better understand what you're seeing, when you look into your own blood."

What I seek can be found in at least three books on his shelf, but I take down the children's text, flipping carefully until I come to the well-remembered illustration: Earth and her moon, with thirteen forms arrayed around them. I trace the circle with one too-long finger.

"I told you that you can take or leave the gods, but the history is real. This is that history. We have evidence, and eyewitnesses, even for the parts that haven't happened yet. The Great Race of Yith travel through space and through time, and they are brutally honest with those who recognize them. The Litany of Earth was distilled over thousands of years of encounters: conversations that together have told us all the civilizations that came before the human one, and all the civilizations that will come after we're gone."

I wait, watching his face. He doesn't believe, but he's willing to listen. He lowers himself slowly into a chair, and rubs his knee absently.

I skip over the poetry of the original Enochian, but its prompting is sufficient to give me the English translation from memory.

"This is the litany of the peoples of Earth. Before the first, there was blackness, and there was fire. The Earth cooled and life arose, struggling against the unremembering emptiness.

"First were the five-winged eldermost of Earth, faces of the Yith. In the time of the elders, the archives came from the stars. The Yith raised up the Shoggoth to serve them in the archives, and the work of that aeon was to restore and order the archives on Earth.

"Second were the Shoggoth, who rebelled against their makers. The Yith fled forward, and the Earth belonged to the Shoggoth for an aeon."

The words come easily, the familiar verses echoing back through my own short life. In times of hardship or joy, when a child sickened or a fisherman drowned too young for metamorphosis, at the new year and every solstice, the Litany gave us comfort and humility. The people of the air, our priest said, phrased its message more briefly: *This too shall pass.*

"Sixth are humans, the wildest of races, who share the world in three parts. The people of the rock, the K'n-yan, build first and most beautifully, but grow cruel and frightened and become the Mad Ones Under the Earth. The people of the air spread far and breed freely, and build the foundation for those who will supplant them. The people of the water are born in shadow on the land, but what they make beneath the waves will live in glory till the dying sun burns away their last shelter.

"Seventh will be the Ck'chk'ck, born from the least infestation of the houses of man, faces of the Yith." Here, at last, I see Charlie inhale sharply. "The work of that aeon will be to read the Earth's memories, to analyze and annotate, and to make poetry of the Yith's own understanding."

On I count, through races of artists and warriors and lovers and barbarians. Each gets a few sentences for all their thousands or millions of years. Each paragraph must obscure uncountable lives like mine, like Charlie's . . . like my mother's.

"Thirteenth will be the Evening People. The Yith will walk openly among them, raising them from their race's infancy with the best knowledge of all peoples. The work of that aeon will be copying the archives, stone to stone, and building the ships that will carry the archives, and the Evening, to distant stars. After they leave, the Earth will burn and the sun fade to ashes.

"After the last race leaves, there will be fire and unremembering emptiness. Where the stories of Earth will survive, none have told us."

We sit for a minute in silence.

"You ever meet one of these Yith?" Charlie asks at last. He speaks urgently, braced against the answer. Everything else I've told him, he's *wanted* to believe.

"I never have," I say. "But my mother did, when she was a girl. She was out playing in the swamp, and he was catching mosquitoes. Normally you find them in libraries, or talking to scholars, but she isn't the only person to encounter one taking samples of one sort or another. She asked him if mosquitoes would ever be people, and he told her a story about some Ck'chk'ck general, she thought the equivalent of Alexander the Great. She said that everyone asked her so many questions when she got home that she couldn't remember the details properly afterward." I shrug. "This goes with the magic, Mr. Day. Take them both, or turn your back."

• • • •

The basement door creaked, and skirts whispered against the frame.

"Oz," came Bergman's voice. "I wanted to talk to you about . . . Ah. It's you." She completed her regal descent. "Oz, what is *she* doing here?"

I rose, matching her hard stare. If I was to learn—or perhaps even teach—anything here, I needed to put a stop to this. And I still had to play a role.

"What exactly is it that you hold against me? I've come here many times, now. The others can see easily enough—none of them doubt what I am."

She looked down at me. "You could be an imposter, I suppose. It would be easy enough. But it's hardly the only possible threat we should be concerned about. If you are truly of the Deep Ones' blood, why are you not with your noble kin? Why celebrate the rites here, among ordinary humans who want your secrets for themselves?"

*Why are you not with your kin?* I swallowed bitter answers. "My loneliness is no concern of yours."

"I think it is." She turned to Wilder, who had kept his place before the altar. "If she's *not* a charlatan . . . either she's a spy, sent to keep us from learning her people's powers, or she's in exile for crimes we cannot begin to imagine."

I hissed, and unthinkingly thrust myself into her space, breathing the stink of her sharply exhaled breath. "They. Are. Dead."

Bergman stepped back, pupils wide, breath coming too quickly. She drew herself up, straightened her skirts, and snorted. "Perhaps you are a charlatan after all. Everyone knows the Deep Ones cannot die."

Again without thinking, I lunged for her. She stumbled backward and I caught her collar, twisted, and pulled. She fell forward, and I held her weight easily as she scrabbled to push me away. I blinked (eyes too big, too tight in their sockets), anger almost washed away by surprise. It was the first time the strength had come upon me.

And I had used it on an old mortal woman whose only crimes were pride and suspicion. I released her and turned my back. The joints of my fingers ached where I had clenched them. "Never say that again. Or if you must, say it to the soldiers who shot my father. We do not age, no—not like you do." I could not resist the barb. "But there are many ways to die."

Oz finally spoke, and I turned to see him helping Bergman to her feet. "Peace, Mildred. She's no spy, and I think no criminal. She will not take your immortality from you."

I paused, anger not entirely overwhelmed, and searched her features carefully. She was slender, small-eyed, fine-fingered—and unquestionably aged. For all her dignity, it was impossible that she might share even a drop of blood with my family.

She caught my look and smiled. "Yes, we have that secret from the Deep Ones. Does it surprise you?"

"Exceedingly. I was not aware that there *was* a secret. Not one that could be shared, at least."

A broader, angrier smile. "Yes—you have tried to keep it from us. To keep us small and weak and dying. But we have it—and at the harvest moon, I will go into the water. I am beloved of the Elder Gods, and I will dwell in glory with Them under the waves forever."

"I see." I turned to Wilder. "Have you done this before?"

He nodded. "Mildred will be the third."

"Such a wonderful promise. Why don't you walk into the ocean yourself?"

"Oh, I shall—when I have trained a successor who can carry on in my place." And he looked at me with such confidence that I realized whom he must have chosen for that role.

Mildred Bergman—convinced that life could be hoarded like a fortune—would never believe me if I simply *told* her the truth. I held up my hand to forestall anything else the priest might have to say. "Wilder, get out of here. I'll speak with you later."

He went. If he had convinced himself I would be his priestess, I suppose he had to treat me as one.

I sat down, cross-legged, trying to clear the hissing tension that had grown between us. After a moment she also sat, cautiously and with wincing stiffness.

"I'm sorry," I said. "It doesn't work like that. We go into the water, and live long there, because we have the blood of the deep in us. The love of the gods is not so powerful. I wish I had more to offer you. There are magics that can heal, that can ease the pains of age, that can even extend life for a few decades. I will gladly teach them to you." And I would, too. She had been vile to me, but I could invite her to Charlie's back room to study with us, and learn the arts that would give her both time and acceptance. All but one spell, that I would not teach, and did not plan to ever learn.

"You're lying." Her voice was calm and even.

"I'm not. You're going to drown yourself—" I swallowed. "I'm trying to save your life. You haven't done a speck of real magic in this room, you don't know what it's like, how it's different."

She started to say something, and I raised a hand. "No. I know you won't listen to what I have to say. Please, let me show you."

"Show me." Not a demand—only an echo, full of doubt.

"Magic." I looked at her, with my bulging eyes and thick bones, willing her, if she couldn't yet believe, at least to look at me.

"What's involved in this . . . demonstration?" she finally asked, and I released a held breath.

"Not much. Chalk, a pair of bowls, and a drop of blood."

Between my purse and the altar, we managed to procure what was needed—fortunate, as I would have hated to go up and ask Wilder to borrow them. Having practiced this with Charlie, I still had the most basic of seals settled in my mind, at least clearly enough for this simple spell. I moved us away from the carefully laid tile to the raw flagstone behind the stairs. There was no reason to vandalize Wilder's stage.

Bergman did not know the Litany, nor the cosmic humility that was the core of Sharhlyda practice. And yet, in some ways, she was easier to work with than Charlie. I could tell her to feel her blood as a river, without worrying what she might guess of my nature.

As I guided her through the opening meditation, Bergman's expression relaxed into something calmer, more introspective. She had some potential for the art, I thought. More than Wilder, certainly, who was so focused on the theater of the thing, and on the idea of power. Bergman's shoulders loosened, and her breath evened, but she kept her eyes open, waiting.

I pricked my finger and let the blood fall into the bowl, holding myself back from the spell long enough to wipe the blade and pass it to Bergman. Then I let the current pull me down . . .

Submerging only briefly before forcing myself upward, out of the cool ocean and into the harsh dry air. I took a painful breath, and laid my hand on Bergman's arm.

A thin stream moved through a great ravine, slow and emaciated. Rivulets trickled past great sandy patches. And yet, where they ran, they ran sweet and cool. The lines they etched, the bars and branches, made a fine and delicate pattern. In it I saw not only the inevitable decay that she strove against, but the stronger shape that was once hers—and the subtler strength in the shape she wore now.

"You *are* one of them."

I returned, gasping, all my instincts clamoring for moisture. I wanted to race upstairs and throw the windows open to the evening fog. Instead I leaned forward.

"Then you must also see—"

She sniffed, half a laugh. "I see that at least some of the books Wilder found can be trusted. And none of them have claimed that the Deep Ones are a more honest race than we. They do claim that you know more of the ancient lore than most humans have access to. So no, I don't believe that your immortality is a mere accident of birth. It can be ours as well—if we don't let you frighten us away from it."

We argued long and late, and still I could not move her. That night I argued with myself, sleepless, over whether it was my place to do more.

• • • •

Of course Charlie asks, inevitably.

I have been teaching him the first, simplest healing spells. Even a mortal, familiar with his own blood, can heal small wounds, speed the passage of trivial illnesses and slow the terrible ones.

"How long can I live, if I practice this?" He looks at me thoughtfully.

"Longer. Perhaps an extra decade or three. Our natures catch up with us all, in the end." I cringe inwardly, imagining his resentment if he knew. And I am beginning to see that he must know, eventually, if I continue with these lessons.

"Except for the Yith?"

"Yes." I hesitate. Even were I ready to share my nature, this would be an unpleasant conversation, full of temptation and old shame. "What the Yith do . . . there *are* spells for that, or something similar. No one else has ever found the trick of moving through time, but to take a young body for your own . . . You would not find it in any of these books, but it wouldn't be hard to track down. I haven't, and I won't. It's not difficult, from what I've heard, just wrong."

Charlie swallows and looks away. I let him think about it a moment.

"We forgive the Yith for what they do, though they leave whole races abandoned around fading stars. Because their presence means that Earth is remembered, and our memory and our stories will last for as long as they can find younger stars and younger bodies to carry them to. They're as selfish as an old scholar wanting eighty more years to study and love and breathe the air. But we honor the Yith for sacrificing billions, and track down and destroy those who steal one life to preserve themselves."

He narrows his eyes. "That's very . . . practical of you."

I nod, but look away. "Yes. We say that they do more to hold back darkness and chaos than any other race, and it is worth the cost. And of course, we know that we aren't the ones to pay it."

"I wonder if the . . . what were they called, the Ck'chk'ck . . . had a Nuremberg."

I start to say that it's not the same—the Yith hate nobody, torture nothing. But I cannot find it in me to claim it makes a difference. Oblivion, after all, is oblivion, however it is forced on you.

• • • •

The day after my fourth meeting with Spector, I did not go to work. I walked, in the rain and the chill, in the open air, until my feet hurt, and then I kept walking, because I could. And eventually, because I could, I went home.

Mama Rei was mending, Kevin on the floor playing with fabric scraps. The *Chronicle* lay open on the table to page seven, where a single column reported the previous night's police raid on a few wealthy homes. No reason was given for the arrests, but I knew that if I read down far enough, there would be some tittering implication of debauchery. Mama Rei smiled at me sadly, and flicked her needle through a stocking. The seam would not look new, but would last a little longer with her careful stitching.

"You told him," she said. "And he listened."

"He promised me there would be no camps." Aloud, now, it sounded like a slender promise by which to decide a woman's fate.

Flick. "Does he seem like an honorable man?"

"I don't know. I think so. He says that the ones they can't just let go, they'll send to a sanitarium." Someplace clean, where their needs would be attended to, and where they would be well fed. "He says Wilder really does belong there. He believed what he was telling the others. What he was telling Bergman."

And she believed what he told her—but that faith would not have been enough to save her.

No one's faith ever was.

Flick. Flick. The needle did a little dance down and around, tying off one of her perfect tiny knots. Little copper scissors, a gift purchased with my earnings and Anna's, cut the dangling thread. "You should check on her."

"I don't think she'll want to see me."

Mama Rei looked at me. "Aphra-chan."

I ducked my head. "You're right. I'll make sure they're treating her well."

But they would, I knew. She would be confined in the best rooms and gardens that her money could pay for, all her physical needs attended to. Kind men would try to talk her back from the precipice where I had found her. And they would keep her from drowning herself until her blood, like that of all mortals, ran dry.

I wondered if, as she neared the end, she would still pray.

If she did, I would pray with her. If it was good for nothing else, at least the effort would be real.

***

Ruthanna Emrys lives in a mysterious manor house in the outskirts of Washington DC with her wife and their large, strange family. She makes home-made vanilla, obsesses about game design, gives unsolicited advice, occasionally attempts to save the world, and blogs sporadically about these things at http://ashnistrike.livejournal.com and http://twitter.com/r_emrys. Her stories have appeared in a number of venues, including *Tor.com*, *Strange Horizons*, and *Analog*.

# A Guide To The Fruits Of Hawai'i
## By Alaya Dawn Johnson

Key's favorite time of day is sunset, her least is sunrise. It should be the opposite, but every time she watches that bright red disk sinking into the water beneath Mauna Kea her heart bends like a wishbone, and she thinks, *He's awake now.*

Key is thirty-four. She is old for a human woman without any children. She has kept herself alive by being useful in other ways. For the past four years, Key has been the overseer of the Mauna Kea Grade Orange blood facility.

Is it a concentration camp if the inmates are well fed? If their beds are comfortable? If they are given an hour and a half of rigorous boxercise and yoga each morning in the recreational field?

It doesn't have to be Honouliui to be wrong.

When she's called in to deal with Jeb's body—bloody, not drained, in a feeding room—yoga doesn't make him any less dead.

Key helps vampires run a concentration camp for humans.

Key is a different kind of monster.

$$\bullet \bullet \bullet \bullet$$

Key's favorite food is umeboshi. Salty and tart and bright red, with that pit in the center to beware. She loves it in rice balls, the kind her Japanese grandmother made when she was little. She loves it by itself, the way she ate it at fifteen, after Obachan died. She hasn't had umeboshi in eighteen years, but sometimes she thinks that when she dies she'll taste one again.

This morning she eats the same thing she eats every meal: a nutritious brick patty, precisely five inches square and two inches deep, colored puce. Her raw scrubbed hands still have a pink tinge of Jeb's blood in the cuticles. She stares at them while she sips the accompanying beverage,

317

which is orange. She can't remember if it ever resembled the fruit.

She eats this because that is what every human eats in the Mauna Kea facility. Because the patty is easy to manufacture and soft enough to eat with plastic spoons. Key hasn't seen a fork in years, a knife in more than a decade. The vampires maintain tight control over all items with the potential to draw blood. Yet humans are tool-making creatures, and their desires, even nihilistic ones, have a creative power that no vampire has the imagination or agility to anticipate. How else to explain the shiv, handcrafted over secret months from the wood cover and glue-matted pages of *A Guide to the Fruits of Hawai'i*, the book that Jeb used to read in the hours after his feeding sessions, sometimes aloud, to whatever humans would listen? He took the only thing that gave him pleasure in the world, destroyed it—or recreated it—and slit his veins with it. Mr. Charles questioned her particularly; he knew that she and Jeb used to talk sometimes. Had she *known* that the *boy* was like this? He gestured with pallid hands at the splatter of arterial pulses from jaggedly slit wrists: oxidized brown, inedible, mocking.

No, she said, of course not, Mr. Charles. I report any suspected cases of self-waste immediately.

She reports any suspected cases. And so, for the weeks she has watched Jeb hardly eating across the mess hall, noticed how he staggered from the feeding rooms, recognized the frigid rebuff in his responses to her questions, she has very carefully refused to suspect.

Today, just before dawn, she choked on the fruits of her indifference. He slit his wrists and femoral arteries. He smeared the blood over his face and buttocks and genitals, and he waited to die before the vampire technician could arrive to drain him.

Not many humans self-waste. Most think about it, but Key never has, not since the invasion of the Big Island. Unlike other humans, she has someone she's waiting for. The one she loves, the one she prays will reward her patience. During her years as overseer, Key has successfully stopped three acts of self-waste. She has failed twice. Jeb is different; Mr. Charles sensed it somehow, but vampires can only read human minds through human blood. Mr. Charles hasn't drunk from Key in years. And what could he learn, even if he did? He can't drink thoughts she has spent most of her life refusing to have.

• • • •

Mr. Charles calls her to the main office the next night, between feeding shifts. She is terrified, like she always is, of what they might do. She is thinking of Jeb and wondering how Mr. Charles has taken the loss of an investment. She is wondering how fast she will die in the work camp on Lanai.

But Mr. Charles has an offer, not a death sentence.

"You know… of the facility on Oahu? Grade Gold?"

"Yes," Key says. Just that, because she learned early not to betray herself to them unnecessarily, and the man at Grade Gold has always been her greatest betrayer.

*No, not a man,* Key tells herself for the hundredth, the thousandth time. *He is one of them.*

Mr. Charles sits in a hanging chair shaped like an egg with plush red velvet cushions. He wears a black suit with steel gray pinstripes, sharply tailored. The cuffs are high and his feet are bare, white as talcum powder and long and bony like spiny fish. His veins are prominent and round and milky blue. Mr. Charles is vain about his feet.

He does not sit up to speak to Key. She can hardly see his face behind the shadow cast by the overhanging top of the egg. All vampires speak deliberately, but Mr. Charles drags out his tones until you feel you might tip over from waiting on the next syllable. It goes up and down like a calliope—

"…what do you *say* to heading down there and *sort*ing the matter… out?"

"I'm sorry, Mr. Charles," she says carefully, because she has lost the thread of his monologue. "What matter?"

He explains: a Grade Gold human girl has killed herself. It is a disaster that outshadows the loss of Jeb.

"You would not believe the expense taken to keep those humans Grade Gold standard."

"What would I do?"

"Take it in hand, *of* course. It seems our small… Grade Orange operation has gotten some notice. Tetsuo asked for you… particularly."

"Tetsuo?" She hasn't said the name out loud in years. Her voice catches on the second syllable.

"*Mr.* Tetsuo," Mr. Charles says, and waves a hand at her. He holds a sheet of paper, the same shade as his skin. "He wrote you a *letter.*"

Key can't move, doesn't reach out to take it, and so it flutters to the black marble floor a few feet away from Mr. Charles's egg.

He leans forward. "I think... I remember something... you and Tetsuo..."

"He recommended my promotion here," Key says, after a moment. It seems the safest phrasing. Mr. Charles would have remembered this eventually; vampires are slow, but inexorable.

The diffuse light from the paper lanterns catches the bottom half of his face, highlighting the deep cleft in his chin. It twitches in faint surprise. "You *were* his pet?"

Key winces. She remembers the years she spent at his side during and after the wars, catching scraps in his wake, despised by every human who saw her there. She waited for him to see how much she had sacrificed and give her the only reward that could matter after what she'd done. Instead he had her shunt removed and sent her to Grade Orange. She has not seen or heard from him in four years. His pet, yes, that's as good a name as any—but he never drank from her. Not once.

Mr. Charles's lips, just a shade of white darker than his skin, open like a hole in a cloud. "And he wants you back. How do you *feel?*"

Terrified. Awestruck. Confused. "Grateful," she says.

The hole smiles. "Grateful! How interesting. Come here, girl. I believe I shall *have a taste.*"

She grabs the letter with shaking fingers and folds it inside a pocket of her red uniform. She stands in front of Mr. Charles.

"Well?" he says.

She hasn't had a shunt in years, though she can still feel its ridged scar in the crook of her arm. Without it, feeding from her is messy, violent. Traditional, Mr. Charles might say. Her fingers hurt as she unzips the collar. Her muscles feel sore, the bones in her spine arthritic and old as she bows her head, leans closer to Mr. Charles. She waits for him to bare his fangs, to pierce her vein, to suck her blood.

He takes more than he should. He drinks until her fingers and toes twinge, until her neck throbs, until the red velvet of his seat fades to gray. When he finishes, he leaves her blood on his mouth.

"I forgive... you for the boy," he says.

Jeb cut his own arteries, left his good blood all over the floor. Mr. Charles abhors waste above all else.

• • • •

*Mr. Charles will explain the situation. I wish you to come. If you do well, I have been authorized to offer you the highest reward.*

• • • •

The following night, Key takes a boat to Oahu. Vampires don't like water, but they will cross it anyway—the sea has become a status symbol among them, an indication of strength. Hawai'i is still a resort destination, though most of its residents only go out at night. Grade Gold is the most expensive, most luxurious resort of them all.

Tetsuo travels between the islands often. Key saw him do it a dozen times during the war. She remembers one night, his face lit by the moon and the yellow lamps on the deck—the wide cheekbones, thick eyebrows, sharp widow's peak, all frozen in the perfection of a nineteen-year-old boy. Pale beneath the olive tones of his skin, he bares his fangs when the waves lurch beneath him.

"What does it feel like?" she asks him.

"Like frozen worms in my veins," he says, after a full, long minute of silence. Then he checks the guns and tells her to wait below, the humans are coming. She can't see anything, but Tetsuo can smell them like chum in the water. The Japanese have held out the longest, and the vampires of Hawai'i lead the assault against them.

Two nights later, in his quarters in the bunker at the base of Mauna Kea, Tetsuo brings back a sheet of paper, written in Japanese. The only characters she recognizes are "shi" and "ta"— "death" and "field." It looks like some kind of list.

"What is this?" she asks.

"Recent admissions to the Lanai human residential facility."

She looks up at him, devoted with terror. "My mother?" Her father died in the first offensive on the Big Island, a hero of the resistance. He never knew how his daughter had chosen to survive.

"Here," Tetsuo says, and runs a cold finger down the list without death. "Jen Isokawa."

"Alive?" She has been looking for her mother since the wars began. Tetsuo knows this, but she didn't know he was searching, too. She feels swollen with this indication of his regard.

"She's listed as a caretaker. They're treated well. You could…" He sits beside her on the bed that only she uses. His pause lapses into a stop. He strokes her hair absentmindedly; if she had a tail, it would beat his legs. She is seventeen and she is sure he will reward her soon.

"Tetsuo," she says, "you could drink from me, if you want. I've had a shunt for nearly a year. The others use it. I'd rather feed you."

Sometimes she has to repeat herself three times before he seems to hear her. This, she has said at least ten. But she is safe here in his bunker, on the bed he brought in for her, with his lukewarm body pressed against her warm one. Vampires do not have sex with humans; they feed. But if he doesn't want her that way, what else can she offer him?

"I've had you tested. You're fertile. If you bear three children you won't need a shunt and the residential facilities will care for you for the rest of your mortality. You can live with your mother. I will make sure you're safe."

She presses her face against his shoulder. "Don't make me leave."

"You wanted to see your mother."

Her mother had spent the weeks before the invasion in church, praying for God to intercede against the abominations. Better that she die than see Key like this.

"Only to know what happened to her," Key whispers. "Won't you feed from me, Tetsuo? I want to feel closer to you. I want you to know how much I love you."

A long pause. Then, "I don't need to taste you to know how you feel."

• • • •

Tetsuo meets her on shore.

Just like that, she is seventeen again.

"You look older," he says. Slowly, but with less affectation than Mr. Charles.

This is true; so inevitable she doesn't understand why he even bothers to say so. Is he surprised? Finally, she nods. The buoyed dock rocks beneath them—he makes no attempt to move, though the two vampires with him grip the denuded skin of their own elbows with pale fingers. They flare and retract their fangs.

"You are drained," he says. He does not mean this metaphorically.

She nods again, realizes further explanation is called for. "Mr. Charles," she says, her voice a painful rasp. This embarrasses her, though Tetsuo would never notice.

He nods, sharp and curt. She thinks he is angry, though perhaps no one else could read him as clearly. She knows that face, frozen in the countenance of a boy dead before the Second World War. A boy dead fifty years before she was born.

He is old enough to remember Pearl Harbor, the detention camps, the years when Maui's forests still had native birds. But she has never dared ask him about his human life.

"And what did Charles explain?"

"He said someone killed herself at Grade Gold."

Tetsuo flares his fangs. She flinches, which surprises her. She used to flush at the sight of his fangs, her blood pounding red just beneath the soft surface of her skin.

"I've been given dispensation," he says, and rests one finger against the hollow at the base of her throat.

She's learned a great deal about the rigid traditions that restrict vampire life since she first met Tetsuo. She understands why her teenage fantasies of morally liberated vampirism were improbable, if not impossible. For each human they bring over, vampires need a special dispensation that they only receive once or twice every decade. *The highest reward.* If Tetsuo has gotten a dispensation, then her first thought when she read his letter was correct. He didn't mean retirement. He didn't mean a peaceful life in some remote farm on the islands. He meant death. Un-death.

After all these years, Tetsuo means to turn her into a vampire.

• • • •

The trouble at Grade Gold started with a dead girl. Penelope cut her own throat five days ago (with a real knife, the kind they allow Grade Gold humans for cutting food). Her ghost haunts the eyes of those she left behind. One human resident in particular, with hair dyed the color of tea and blue lipstick to match the bruises under her red eyes, takes one look at Key and starts to scream.

Key glances at Tetsuo, but he has forgotten her. He stares at the girl as if he could burn her to ashes on the plush green carpet. The five others in the room look away, but Key can't tell if it's in embarrassment or fear. The luxury surrounding them chokes her. There's a bowl of fruit on a coffee table. Real fruit—fuzzy brown kiwis, mottled red-green mangos, dozens of tangerines. She takes an involuntary step forward and the girl's scream gets louder before cutting off with an abrupt squawk. Her labored breaths are the only sound in the room.

"This is a joke," the girl says. There's spittle on her blue lips. "What hole did you dig her out of?"

"Go to your room, Rachel," Tetsuo says.

Rachel flicks back her hair and rubs angrily under one eye. "What are you now, Daddy Vampire? You think you can just, what? Replace her? With this broke down fogie look-alike?"

"She is not—"

"Yeah? What is she?"

They are both silent, doubt and grief and fury scuttling between them like beetles in search of a meal. Tetsuo and the girl stare at each other with such deep familiarity that Key feels forgotten, alone—almost ashamed of the dreams that have kept her alive for a decade. They have never felt so hopeless, or so false.

"Her name is Key," Tetsuo says, in something like defeat. He turns away, though he makes no move to leave. "She will be your new caretaker."

"Key?" the girl says. "What kind of a name is that?"

Key doesn't answer for a long time, thinking of all the ways she could respond. Of Obachan Akiko and the affectionate nickname of lazy summers spent hiking in the mountains or pounding mochi in the kitchen. Of her half-Japanese mother and Hawai'ian father, of the ways history and identity and circumstance can shape a girl into half a woman, until someone—*not a man*—comes with a hundred thousand others like him and destroys anything that might have once had meaning. So she finds meaning in him. Who else was there?

And this girl, whose sneer reveals her bucked front teeth, has as much chance of understanding that world as Key does of understanding this one. Fresh fruit on the table. No uniforms. And a perfect, glittering shunt of plastic and metal nestled in the crook of her left arm.

"Mine," Key answers the girl.

Rachel spits; Tetsuo turns his head, just a little, as though he can only bear to see Key from the corner of his eye.

"You're nothing like her," she says.

"Like who?"

But the girl storms from the room, leaving her chief vampire without a dismissal. Key now understands this will not be punished. It's another one—a boy, with the same florid beauty as the girl but far less belligerence, who answers her.

"You look like Penelope," he says, tugging on a long lock of his asymmetrically cut black hair. "Just older."

When Tetsuo leaves the room, it's Key who cannot follow.

• • • •

Key remembers sixteen. Her obachan is dead and her mother has moved to an apartment in Hilo and it's just Key and her father in that old, quiet house at the end of the road. The vampires have annexed San Diego and Okinawa is besieged, but life doesn't feel very different in the mountains of the Big Island.

It is raining in the woods behind her house. Her father has told her to study, but all she's done since her mother left is read Mishima's *Sea of Fertility* novels. She sits on the porch, wondering if it's better to kill herself or wait for them to come, and just as she thinks she ought to have the courage to die, something rattles in the shed. A rat, she thinks.

But it's not rat she sees when she pulls open the door on its rusty hinges. It's a man, crouched between a stack of old appliance boxes and the rusted fender of the Buick her father always meant to fix one day. His hair is wet and slicked back, his white shirt is damp and ripped from shoulder to navel. The skin beneath it is pale as a corpse; bloodless, though the edges of a deep wound are still visible.

"They've already come?" Her voice breaks on a whisper. She wanted to finish *The Decay of the Angel*. She wanted to see her mother once more.

"Shut the door," he says, crouching in shadow, away from the bar of light streaming through the narrow opening.

"Don't kill me."

"We are equally at each other's mercy."

She likes the way he speaks. No one told her they could sound so proper. So human. Is there a monster in her shed, or is he something else?

"Why shouldn't I open it all the way?"

He is brave, whatever else. He takes his long hands from in front of his face and stands, a flower blooming after rain. He is beautiful, though she will not mark that until later. Now, she only notices the steady, patient way he regards her. *I could move faster than you*, his eyes say. *I could kill you first.*

She thinks of Mishima and says, "I'm not afraid of death."

Only when the words leave her mouth does she realize how deeply she has lied. Does he know? Her hands would shake if it weren't for their grip on the handle.

"I promise," he says. "I will save you, when the rest of us come."

What is it worth, a monster's promise?

She steps inside and shuts out the light.

• • • •

There are nineteen residents of Grade Gold; the twentieth is buried beneath the kukui tree in the communal garden. The thought of rotting in earth revolts Key. She prefers the bright, fierce heat of a crematorium fire, like the one that consumed Jeb the night before she left Mauna Kea. The ashes fly in the wind, into the ocean and up in the trees, where they lodge in bird nests and caterpillar silk and mud puddles after a storm. The return of flesh to the earth should be fast and final, not the slow mortification of worms and bacteria and carbon gases.

Tetsuo instructs her to keep close watch on unit three. "Rachel isn't very... steady right now," he says, as though unaware of the understatement.

The remaining nineteen residents are divided into four units, five kids in each, living together in sprawling ranch houses connected by walkways and gardens. There are walls, of course, but you have to climb a tree to see them. The kids at Grade Gold have more freedom than any human she's ever encountered since the war, but they're as bound to this paradise as she was to her mountain.

The vampires who come here stay in a high glass tower right by the beach. During the day, the black-tinted windows gleam like lasers. At night, the vampires come down to feed. There is a fifth house in the residential village, one reserved for clients and their meals. Testsuo orchestrates these encounters, planning each interaction in fine detail: this human with that performance for this distinguished client. Key has grown used to thinking of her fellow humans as food, but now she is forced to reconcile that indelible fact with another, stranger veneer. The vampires who pay so dearly for Grade Gold humans don't merely want to feed from a shunt. They want to be entertained, talked to, cajoled. The boy who explained about Key's uncanny resemblance juggles torches. Twin girls from unit three play guitar and sing songs by the Carpenters. Even Rachel, dressed in a gaudy purple mermaid dress with matching streaks in her hair, keeps up a one-way, laughing conversation with a vampire who seems too astonished—or too slow—to reply.

Key has never seen anything like this before. She thought that most vampires regarded humans as walking sacks of food. What pleasure could be derived from speaking with your meal first? From seeing it sing or dance? When she first went with Tetsuo, the other vampires talked about human emotions as if they were flavors of ice cream. But at Grade Orange she grew accustomed to more basic parameters: were the humans fed, were they fertile, did they sleep? Here, she must approve outfits; she must manage dietary preferences and erratic tempers and a dozen other details all crucial to keeping the kids Grade Gold standard. Their former caretaker has been shipped to the work camps, which leaves Key in sole charge of the operation. At least until Tetsuo decides how he will use his dispensation.

Key's thoughts skitter away from the possibility.

"I didn't know vampires liked music," she says, late in the evening, when some of the kids sprawl, exhausted, across couches and cushions. A girl no older than fifteen opens her eyes but hardly moves when a vampire in a gold suit lifts her arm for a nip. Key and Tetsuo are seated together at the far end of the main room, in the bay windows that overlook a cliff and the ocean.

"It's as interesting to us as any other human pastime."

"Does music have a taste?"

His wide mouth stretches at the edges; she recognizes it as a smile. "Music has some utility, given the right circumstances."

She doesn't quite understand him. The air is redolent with the sweat of human teenagers and the muggy, salty air that blows through the open doors and windows. Her eye catches on a half-eaten strawberry dropped carelessly on the carpet a few feet away. It was harvested too soon, a white, tasteless core surrounded by hard, red flesh.

She thinks there is nothing of "right" in these circumstances, and their utility is, at its bottom, merely that of parasite and host.

"The music enhances the—our—flavor?"

Tetsuo stares at her for a long time, long enough for him to take at least three of his shallow, erratically spaced breaths. To look at him is to taste copper and sea on her tongue; to wait for him is to hear the wind slide down a mountainside an hour before dawn.

It has been four years since she last saw him. She thought he had forgotten her, and now he speaks to her as if all those years haven't passed, as though the vampires hadn't long since won the war and turned the world to their slow, long-burning purpose.

"Emotions change your flavor," he says. "And food. And sex. And pleasure."

*And love?* she wonders, but Tetsuo has never drunk from her.

"Then why not treat all of us like you do the ones here? Why have con—Mauna Kea?"

She expects him to catch her slip, but his attention is focused on something beyond her right shoulder. She turns to look, and sees nothing but the hall and a closed feeding room door.

"Three years," he says, quietly. He doesn't look at her. She doesn't understand what he means, so she waits. "It takes three years for the complexity to fade. For the vitality of young blood to turn muddy and clogged with silt. Even among the new crops, only a few individuals are Gold standard. For three years, they produce the finest blood ever tasted, filled with regrets and ecstasy and dreams. And then…"

"Grade Orange?" Key asks, her voice dry and rasping. Had Tetsuo always talked of humans like this? With such little regard for their selfhood? Had she been too young to understand, or have the years of harvesting humans hardened him?

"If we have not burned too much out. Living at high elevation helps prolong your utility, but sometimes all that's left is Lanai and the work camps."

She remembers her terror before her final interview with Mr. Charles, her conviction that Jeb's death would prompt him to discard his uselessly old overseer to the work camps.

A boy from one of the other houses staggers to the one she recognizes from unit two and sprawls in his lap. Unit-two boy startles awake, smiles, and bends over to kiss the first. A pair of female vampires kneel in front of them and press their fangs with thick pink tongues.

"Touch him," one says, pointing to the boy from unit two. "Make him cry."

The boy from unit two doesn't even pause for breath; he reaches for the other boy's cock and squeezes. And as they both groan with something that makes Key feel like a voyeur, made helpless by her own desire, the pair of vampires pull the boys apart and dive for their respective shunts. The room goes quiet but for soft gurgles, like two minnows in a tide pool. Then a pair of clicks as the boys' shunts turn gray, forcing the vampires to stop feeding.

"Lovely, divine," the vampires say a few minutes later, when they pass on their way out. "We always appreciate the sexual displays."

The boys curl against each other, eyes shut. They breathe like old men: hard, through constricted tubes.

"Does that happen often?" she asks.

"This Grade Gold is known for its sexual flavors. My humans pick partners they enjoy."

Vampires might not have sex, but they crave its flavor. Will she, when she crosses to their side? Will she look at those two boys and command them to fuck each other just so she can taste?

"Do you ever care?" she says, her voice barely a whisper. "About what you've done to us?"

He looks away from her. Before she can blink he has crossed to the one closed feeding room door and wrenched it open. A thump of something thrown against a wall. A snarl, as human as a snake's hiss.

"Leave, Gregory!" Tetsuo says. A vampire Key recognizes from earlier in the night stumbles into the main room. He rubs his jaw, though the torn and mangled skin there has already begun to knit together.

"She is mine to have. I paid—"

"Not enough to kill her."

"I'll complain to the council," the vampire says. "You've been losing support. And everyone knows how *patiently* Charles has waited in his aerie."

She should be scared, but his words make her think of Jeb, of failures and consequences, and of the one human she has not seen for hours. She stands and sprints past both vampires to where Rachel lies insensate on a bed.

Her shunt has turned the opaque gray meant to prevent vampires from feeding humans to death. But the client has bitten her neck instead.

"Tell them whatever you wish, and I will tell them you circumvented the shunt of a fully-tapped human. We have our rules for a reason. You are no longer welcome here."

Rachel's pulse is soft, but steady. She stirs and moans beneath Key's hands. The relief is crushing; she wants to cradle the girl in her arms until she wakes. She wants to protect her so her blood will never have to smear the walls of a feeding room, so that Key will be able to say that at least she saved one.

Rachel's eyes flutter open, land with a butterfly's gentleness on Key's face.

"Pen," she says, "I told you. It makes them... they *eat* me."

Key doesn't understand, but she doesn't mind. She presses her hand to Rachel's warm forehead and sings lullabies her grandmother liked until Rachel falls back to sleep.

"How is she?" It is Tetsuo, come into the room after the client has finally left.

"Drained," Key says, as dispassionately as he. "She'll be fine in a few days."

"Key."

"Yes?"

She won't look at him.

"I do, you know."

She knows. "Then why support it?"

"You'll understand when your time comes."

She looks back down at Rachel, and all she can see are bruises blooming purple on her upper arms, blood dried brown on her neck. She looks like a human being: infinitely precious, fragile. Like prey.

• • • •

Five days later, Key sits in the garden in the shade of the kukui tree. She has reports to file on the last week's feedings, but the papers sit untouched beside her. The boy from unit two and his boyfriend are tending the tomatoes and Key slowly peels the skin from her fourth kiwi. The first time she bit into one she cried, but the boys pretended not to notice. She is getting better with practice. Her hands still tremble and her misted eyes refract rainbows in the hard, noon sunlight. She is learning to be human again.

Rachel sleeps on the ground beside her, curled on the packed dirt of Penelope's grave with her back against the tree trunk and her arms wrapped tightly around her belly. She's spent most of the last five days sleeping, and Key thinks she has mostly recovered. She's been eating voraciously, foods in wild combinations at all times of day and night. Key is glad. Without the distracting, angry makeup, Rachel's face looks vulnerable and haunted. Jeb had that look in the months before his death. He would sit quietly in the mess hall and stare at the food brick as though he had forgotten how to eat. Jeb had transferred to Mauna Kea within a week of Key becoming overseer. He liked watching the lights of the airplanes at night and he kept two books with him: *The Blind Watchmaker* and *A Guide to the Fruits of Hawai'i*. She talked to him about the latter—had he ever tasted breadfruit or kiwi or cherimoya? None, he said, in a voice so small and soft it sounded inversely proportional to his size. Only a peach, a canned peach, when he was four or five years old. Vampires don't waste fruit on Grade Orange humans.

The covers of both books were worn, the spines cracked, the pages yellowed and brittle at the edges. Why keep a book about fruit you had never tasted and never would eat? Why read at all, when they frowned upon literacy in humans and often banned books outright? She never asked him. Mr. Charles had seen their conversation, though she doubted he had heard it, and requested that she refrain from speaking unnecessarily to the *har*vest.

So when Jeb stared at her across the table with eyes like a snuffed candle, she turned away, she forced her patty into her mouth, she chewed, she reached for her orange drink.

His favorite book became his means of self-destruction. She let him do it. She doesn't know if she feels guilty for not having stopped him, or for being in the position to stop him in the first place. Not two weeks later she rests beneath a kukui tree, the flesh of a fruit she had never expected to taste again turning to green pulp between her teeth. She reaches for another one because she knows how little she deserves this.

But the skin of the fruit at the bottom of the bowl is too soft and fleshy for a kiwi. She pulls it into the light and drops it.

"Are you okay?" It's the boy from unit two—Kaipo. He kneels down and picks up the cherimoya.

"What?" she says, and struggles to control her breathing. She has to appear normal, in control. She's supposed to be their caretaker. But the boy just seems concerned, not judgmental. Rachel rolls onto her back and opens her eyes.

"You screamed," Rachel says, sleep-fogged and accusatory. "You woke me up."

"Who put this in the bowl?" Kaipo asks. "These things are poisonous! They grow on that tree down the hill, but you can't eat them."

Key takes the haunted fruit from him, holding it carefully so as to not bruise it further. "Who told you that?" she asks.

Rachel leans forward, so her chin rests on the edge of Key's lounge chair and the tips of her purple-streaked hair touch Key's thigh. "Tetsuo," she says. "What, did he lie?"

Key shakes her head slowly. "He probably only half-remembered. It's a cherimoya. The flesh is delicious, but the seeds are poisonous."

Rachel's eyes follow her hands. "Like, killing you poisonous?" she asks.

Key thinks back to her father's lessons. "Maybe if you eat them all or grind them up. The tree bark can paralyze your heart and lungs."

Kaipo whistles, and they all watch intently when she wedges her finger under the skin and splits it in half. The white, fleshy pulp looks stark, even a little disquieting against the scaly green exterior. She plucks out the hard, brown seeds and tosses them to the ground. Only then does she pull out a chunk of flesh and put it in her mouth.

Like strawberries and banana pudding and pineapple. Like the summer after Obachan died, when a box of them came to the house as a condolence gift.

"You look like you're fellating it," Rachel says. Key opens her eyes and swallows abruptly.

Kaipo pushes his tongue against his lips. "Can I try it, Key?" he asks, very politely. Did the vampires teach him that politeness? Did vampires teach Rachel a word like *fellate*, perhaps while instructing her to do it with a hopefully willing human partner?

"Do you guys know how to use condoms?" She has decided to ask Tetsuo to supply them. This last week has made it clear that "sexual flavors" are all too frequently on the menu at Grade Gold.

Kaipo looks at Rachel; Rachel shakes her head. "What's a condom?" he asks.

It's so easy to forget how little of the world they know. "You use it during sex, to stop you from catching diseases," she says, carefully. "Or getting pregnant."

Rachel laughs and stuffs the rest of the flesh into her wide mouth. Even a cherimoya can't fill her hollows. "Great, even more vampire sex," she says, her hatred clearer than her garbled words. "They never made Pen do it."

"They didn't?" Key asks.

Juice dribbles down her chin. "You know, Tetsuo's dispensation? Before she killed herself, she was his pick. Everyone knew it. That's why they left her alone."

Key feels light-headed. "But if she was his choice… why would she kill herself?"

"She didn't want to be a vampire," Kaipo says softly.

"She wanted a *baby*, like bringing a new food sack into the world is a good idea. But they wouldn't let her have sex and they wanted to make her one of them, so—now she's gone. But why he'd bring *you* here, when *any* of us would be a better choice—"

"Rachel, just shut up. Please." Kaipo takes her by the shoulder.

Rachel shrugs him off. "What? Like she can do anything."

"If she becomes one of *them*—"

"I wouldn't hurt you," Key says, too quickly. Rachel masks her pain with cruelty, but it is palpable. Key can't imagine any version of herself that would add to that.

Kaipo and Rachel stare at her. "But," Kaipo says, "that's what vampires do."

"I would eat you," Rachel says, and flops back under the tree. "I would make you cry and your tears would taste sweeter than a cherimoya."

· · · ·

"I will be back in four days," Testsuo tells her, late the next night. "There is one feeding scheduled. I hope you will be ready when I return."

"For the… reward?" she asks, stumbling over an appropriate euphemism. Their words for it are polysyllabic spikes: transmutation, transformation, metamorphosis. All vampires were once human, and immortal doesn't mean invulnerable. Some die each year, and so their ranks must be replenished with the flesh of worthy, willing humans.

He places a hand on her shoulder. It feels as chill and inert as a piece of damp wood. She thinks she must be dreaming.

"I have wanted this for a long time, Key," he says to her—like a stranger, like the person who knows her the best in the world.

"Why now?"

"Our thoughts can be... slow, sometimes. You will see. Orderly, but sometimes too orderly to see patterns clearly. I thought of you, but did not know it until Penelope died."

Penelope, who looked just like Key. Penelope, who would have been his pick. She shivers and steps away from his hand. "Did you love her?"

She can't believe that she is asking this question. She can't believe that he is offering her the dreams she would have murdered for ten, even five years ago.

"I loved that she made me think of you," he says, "when you were young and beautiful."

"It's been eighteen years, Tetsuo."

He looks over her shoulder. "You haven't lost much," he says. "I'm not too late. You'll see."

He is waiting for a response. She forces herself to nod. She wants to close her eyes and cover her mouth, keep all her love for him inside where it can be safe, because if she loses it, there will be nothing left but a girl in the rain who should have opened the door.

He looks like an alien when he smiles. He looks like nothing she could ever know when he walks down the hall, past the open door and the girl who has been watching them this whole time.

Rachel is young and beautiful, Key thinks, and Penelope is dead.

• • • •

Key's sixth feeding at Grade Gold is contained, quiet and without incident. The gazes of the clients slide over her as she greets them at the door of the feeding house, but she is used to that. To a vampire, a human without a shunt is like a book without pages: a useless absurdity. She has assigned all of unit one and a pair from unit four to the gathering. Seven humans for five vampires is a luxurious ratio—probably more than they paid for, but she's happy to let that be Tetsuo's problem. She shudders to remember how Rachel's blood soaked into the collar of her blouse when she lifted the girl from the bed. She has seen dozens of overdrained humans, including some who died from it, but what happened to Rachel feels worse. She doesn't understand why, but is overwhelmed by tenderness for her.

A half-hour before the clients are supposed to leave, Kaipo sprints through the front door, flushed and panting so hard he has to pause half a minute to catch his breath.

"Rachel," he manages, while humans and vampires alike pause to look. She stands up. "What did she do?"

"I'm not sure… she was shaking and screaming, waking everyone up, yelling about Penelope and Tetsuo and then she started vomiting."

"The clients have another half hour," she whispers. "I can't leave until then."

Kaipo tugs on the long lock of glossy black hair that he has blunt-cut over his left eye. "I'm scared for her, Key," he says. "She won't listen to anyone else."

She will blame herself if any of the kids here tonight die, and she will blame herself if something happens to Rachel. Her hands make the decision for her: she reaches for Kaipo's left arm. He lets her take it reflexively, and doesn't flinch when she lifts his shunt. She looks for and finds the small electrical chip which controls the inflow and outflow of blood and other fluids. She taps the Morse-like code, and Kaipo watches with his mouth open as the glittering plastic polymer changes from clear to gray. As though he's already been tapped out.

"I'm not supposed to show you that," she says, and smiles until she remembers Tetsuo and what he might think. "Stay here. Make sure nothing happens. I'll be back as soon as I can."

She stays only long enough to see his agreement, and then she's flying out the back door, through the garden, down the left-hand path that leads to unit two.

Rachel is on her hands and knees in the middle of the walkway. The other three kids in unit two watch her silently from the doorway, but Rachel is alone as she vomits in the grass.

"You!" Rachel says when she sees Key, and starts to cough.

Rachel looks like a war is being fought inside of her, as if the battlefield is her lungs and the hollows of her cheeks and the muscles of her neck. She trembles and can hardly raise her head.

"Go away!" Rachel screams, but she's not looking at Key, she's looking down at the ground.

"Rachel, what's happened?" Key doesn't get too close. Rachel's fury frightens her; she doesn't understand this kind of rage. Rachel raises her shaking hands and starts hitting herself, pounding her chest and rib cage and stomach with violence made even more frightening by her weakness. Key kneels in front of her, grabs both of the girl's tiny, bruised wrists and holds them away from her body. Her vomit smells of sour bile and the sickly-sweet of some half digested fruit. A suspicion nibbles at Key, and so she looks to the left, where Rachel has vomited.

Dozens and dozens of black seeds, half crushed. And a slime of green the precise shade of a cherimoya skin.

"Oh, God, Rachel… why would you…"

"You don't deserve him! He can make it go away and he won't! Who are you? A fogey, an ugly fogey, an ugly usurping fogey and she's gone and he is a dick, he is a screaming howler monkey and I hate him…"

Rachel collapses against Key's chest, her hands beating helplessly at the ground. Key takes her up and rocks her back and forth, crying while she thinks of how close she came to repeating the mistakes of Jeb. But she can still save Rachel. She can still be human.

• • • •

Tetsuo returns three days later with a guest.

She has never seen Mr. Charles wear shoes before, and he walks in them with the mincing confusion of a young girl forced to wear zori for a formal occasion. She bows her head when she sees him, hoping to hide her fear. Has he come to take her back to Mauna Kea? The thought of returning to those antiseptic feeding rooms and tasteless brick patties makes her hands shake. It makes her wonder if she would not be better off taking Penelope's way out rather than seeing the place where Jeb killed himself again.

But even as she thinks it, she knows she won't, any more than she would have eighteen years ago. She's too much a coward and she's too brave. If Mr. Charles asks her to go back she will say yes.

Rain on a mountainside and sexless, sweet touches with a man the same temperature as wet wood. Lanai City, overrun. Then Waimea, then Honoka'a. Then Hilo, where her mother had been living. For a year, until Tetsuo found that record of her existence in a work camp, Key fantasized about her mother escaping on a boat to an atoll, living in a group of refugee humans who survived the apocalypse.

Every thing Tetsuo asked of her, she did. She loved him from the moment they saved each other's lives. She has always said yes.

"*Key!*" Mr. Charles says to her, as though she is a friend he has run into unexpectedly. "I have some*thing*… you might *just* want."

"Yes, Mr. Charles?" she says.

The three of them are alone in the feeding house. Mr. Charles collapses dramatically against one of the divans and kicks off his tight, patent-leather shoes as if they are barnacles. He wears no socks.

"There," he says, and waves his hand at the door. "*In* the bag."

Tetsuo nods and so she walks back. The bag is black canvas, unmarked. Inside, there's a book. She recognizes it immediately, though she only saw it once. *The Blind Watchmaker.* There is a note on the cover. The handwriting is large and uneven and painstaking, that of someone familiar with words but unaccustomed to writing them down. She notes painfully that he writes his "a" the same way as a typeset font, with the half-c above the main body and a careful serif at the end.

*Dear Overseer Ki,*
    *I would like you to have this. I have loved it very much and you are the only one who ever seemed to care. I am angry but*
    *I don't blame you. You're just too good at living.*
    *Jeb*

She takes the bag and leaves both vampires without requesting permission. Mr. Charles's laugh follows her out the door.

Blood on the walls, on the floor, all over his body.

I am angry but. You're just too good at living. She has always said yes.

She is too much of a coward and she is too brave.

• • • •

She watches the sunset the next evening from the hill in the garden, her back against the cherimoya tree. She feels the sun's death like she always has, with quiet joy. Awareness floods her: the musk of wet grass crushed beneath her bare toes, salt-spray and algae blowing from the ocean, the love she has clung to so fiercely since she was a girl, lost and alone. Everything she has ever loved is bound in that sunset, the red and violet orb that could kill him as it sinks into the ocean.

Her favorite time of day is sunset, but it is not night. She has never quite been able to fit inside his darkness, no matter how hard she tried. She has been too good at living, but perhaps it's not too late to change.

She can't take the path of Penelope or Jeb, but that has never been the only way. She remembers stories that reached Grade Orange from the work camps, half-whispered reports of humans who sat at their assembly lines and refused to lift their hands. Harvesters who drained gasoline from their combine engines and waited for the vampires to find them. If every human refused to cooperate, vampire society would crumble in a week. Still, she has no illusions about this third path sparking a revolution. This is simply all she can do: sit under the cherimoya tree and refuse. They will kill her, but she will have chosen to be human.

The sun descends. She falls asleep against the tree and dreams of the girl who never was, the one who opened the door. In her dreams, the sun burns her skin and her obachan tells her how proud she is while they pick strawberries in the garden. She eats an umeboshi that tastes of blood and salt, and when she swallows, the flavors swarm out of her throat, bubbling into her neck and jaw and ears. Flavors become emotions become thoughts; peace in the nape of her neck, obligation in her back molars, and hope just behind her eyes, bitter as a watermelon rind.

She opens them and sees Tetsuo on his knees before her. Blood smears his mouth. She does not know what to think when he kisses her, except that she can't even feel the pinprick pain where his teeth broke her skin. He has never fed from her before. They have never kissed before. She feels like she is floating, but nothing else.

The blood is gone when he sits back. As though she imagined it.

"You should not have left like that yesterday," he says. "Charles can make this harder than I'd like."

"Why is he here?" she asks. She breathes shallowly.

"He will take over Grade Gold once your transmutation is finished."

"That's why you brought me here, isn't it? It had nothing to do with the kids."

He shrugs. "Regulations. So Charles couldn't refuse."

"And where will you go?"

"They want to send me to the mainland. Texas. To supervise the installation of a new Grade Gold facility near Austin."

She leans closer to him, and now she can see it: regret, and shame that he should be feeling so. "I'm sorry," she says.

"I have lived seventy years on these islands. I have an eternity to come back to them. So will you, Key. I have permission to bring you with me."

Everything that sixteen-year-old had ever dreamed. She can still feel the pull of him, of her desire for an eternity together, away from the hell her life has become. Her transmutation would be complete. Truly a monster, the regrets for her past actions would fall away like waves against a seawall.

With a fumbling hand, she picks a cherimoya from the ground beside her. "Do you remember what these taste like?"

She has never asked him about his human life. For a moment, he seems genuinely confused. "You don't understand. Taste to us is vastly more complex. Joy, dissatisfaction, confusion, humility—*those* are flavors. A custard apple?" He laughs. "It's sweet, right?"

Joy, dissatisfaction, loss, grief, she tastes all that just looking at him.

"Why didn't you ever feed from me before?"

"Because I promised. When we first met."

And as she stares at him, sick with loss and certainty, Rachel walks up behind him. She is holding a kitchen knife, the blade pointed toward her stomach.

"Charles knows," she says.

"How?" Tetsuo says. He stands, but Key can't coordinate her muscles enough for the effort. He must have drained a lot of blood.

"I told him," Rachel says. "So now you don't have a choice. You will transmute me and you will get rid of this fucking fetus or I will kill myself and you'll be blamed for losing *two* Grade Gold humans."

Rachel's wrists are still bruised from where Key had to hold her several nights ago. Her eyes are sunken, her skin sallow. *This fucking fetus.*

She wasn't trying to kill herself with the cherimoya seeds. She was trying to abort a pregnancy.

"The baby is still alive after all that?" Key says, surprisingly indifferent to the glittering metal in Rachel's unsteady hands. Does Rachel know how easily Tetsuo could disarm her? What advantage does she think she has? But then she looks back in the girl's eyes and realizes: none.

Rachel is young and desperate and she doesn't want to be eaten by the monsters anymore.

"Not again, Rachel," Tetsuo says. "I *can't* do what you want. A vampire can only transmute someone he's never fed from before."

Rachel gasps. Key flops against her tree. She hadn't known that, either. The knife trembles in Rachel's grip so violently that Tetsuo takes it from her, achingly gentle as he pries her fingers from the hilt.

"*That's* why you never drank from her? And I killed her anyway? Stupid fucking Penelope. She could have been forever, and now there's just this dumb fogie in her place. She thought you cared about her."

"Caring is a strange thing, for a vampire," Key says.

Rachel spits in her direction but it falls short. The moonlight is especially bright tonight; Key can see everything from the grass to the tips of Rachel's ears, flushed sunset pink.

"Tetsuo," Key says, "why can't I move?"

But they ignore her.

"Maybe Charles will do it if I tell him you're really the one who killed Penelope."

"Charles? I'm sure he knows exactly what you did."

"I didn't *mean* to kill her!" Rachel screams. "Penelope was going to tell about the baby. She was crazy about babies, it didn't make any sense, and you had *picked her* and she wanted to destroy my life… I was so angry, I just wanted to hurt her, but I didn't realize…"

"Rachel, I've tried to give you a chance, but I'm not allowed to get rid of it for you." Tetsuo's voice is as worn out as a leathery orange.

"I'll die before I go to one of those mommy farms, Tetsuo. I'll die and take my baby with me."

"Then you will have to do it yourself."

She gasps. "You'll really leave me here?"

"I've made my choice."

Rachel looks down at Key, radiating a withering contempt that does nothing to blunt Key's pity. "If you had picked Penelope, I would have understood. Penelope was beautiful and smart. She's the only one who ever made it through half of that fat Shakespeare book in unit four. She could sing. Her breasts were perfect. But *her*? She's not a choice. She's nothing at all."

The silence between them is strained. It's as if Key isn't there at all. And soon, she thinks, she won't be.

"I've made my choice," Key says.

"*Your* choice?" they say in unison.

When she finds the will to stand, it's as though her limbs are hardly there at all, as though she is swimming in mid-air. For the first time, she understands that something is wrong.

• • • •

Key floats for a long time. Eventually, she falls. Tetsuo catches her.

"What does it feel like?" Key asks. "The transmutation?"

Tetsuo takes the starlight in his hands. He feeds it to her through a glass shunt growing from a living branch. The tree's name is Rachel. The tree is very sad. Sadness is delicious.

"You already know," he says.

*You will understand*: he said this to her when she was human. *I wouldn't hurt you*: she said this to a girl who—a girl—she drinks.

"I meant to refuse."

"I made a promise."

She sees him for a moment crouched in the back of her father's shed, huddled away from the dangerous bar of light that stretches across the floor. She sees herself, terrified of death and so unsure. *Open the door*, she tells that girl, too late. *Let in the light.*

---

Alaya Dawn Johnson is a Nebula award-winning short story writer and the author of six novels for adults and young adults. Her novel *The Summer Prince* was longlisted for the National Book Award for Young People's Literature. Her most recent, *Love Is the Drug*, was awarded the Andre Norton Award. Her short stories have appeared in many magazines and anthologies, including *Asimov's*, *F&SF and Zombies vs. Unicorns*. She lives in Mexico City.

# A Year And A Day In Old Theradane
## By Scott Lynch


### 1. Wizard Weather

It was raining when Amarelle Parathis went out just after sunset to find a drink, and there was strange magic in the rain. It came down in pale lavenders and coppers and reds, soft lines like liquid dusk that turned to luminescent mist on the warm pavement. The air itself felt like champagne bubbles breaking against the skin. Over the dark shapes of distant rooftops, blue-white lightning blazed, and stuttering thunder chased it. Amarelle would have sworn she heard screams mixed in with the thunder.

The gods-damned wizards were at it again.

Well, she had a thirst, and an appointment, and odd rain wasn't even close to the worst thing that had ever fallen on her from the skies over Theradane. As she walked, Amarelle dripped flickering colors that had no names. She cut a ghostly trail through fog that drifted like the murk beneath a pink and orange sea. As usual when the wizards were particularly bad, she didn't have much company. The Street of Pale Savants was deserted. Shopkeepers stared forlornly from behind their windows on the Avenue of Seven Angles.

This had been her favorite sort of night, once. Heavy weather to drive witnesses from the streets. Thunder to cover the noise of feet creeping over rooftops. These days it was just lonely, unpredictable, and dangerous.

A double arc of silvery lights marked the Tanglewing Canal Bridge, the last between her and her destination. The lights burned within lamps held by rain-stained white marble statues of shackled, hooded figures. Amarelle kept her eyes fixed on her feet as she crossed the bridge. She knew the plaques beneath the statues by heart. The first two on the left, for example:

BOLAR KUSS
TRAITOR
NOW I SERVE THERADANE ALWAYS


CAMIRA THOLAR
MURDERESS
NOW I SERVE THERADANE ALWAYS


The statues themselves didn't trouble her, or even the lights. So what if the city lit some of its streets and bridges with the unshriven souls of convicts, bound forever into melodramatic sculptures with fatuous plaques? No, the trouble was how those unquiet spirits whispered to passers-by.

*Look upon me, beating heart, and witness the price of my broken oaths.*

"Fuck off, Bolar," muttered Amarelle. "I'm not plotting to overthrow the Parliament of Strife."

*Take warning, while your blood is still warm, and behold the eternal price of my greed and slaughter!*

"I don't have a family to poison, Camira."

*Amarelle,* whispered the last statue on the left. *It ought to be you up here, you faithless bitch.*

Amarelle stared at that last inscription, just as she promised herself she wouldn't every time she came this way.


SCAVIUS OF SHADOW STREET
THIEF
NOW I SERVE THERADANE ALWAYS


"I never turned my back on you," Amarelle whispered. "I paid for sanctuary. We all did. We begged you to get out of the game with us, but you didn't listen. You blew it."

*You bent your knees to my killers before my flesh was even cold.*

"We all bought ourselves a little piece of the city, Scav. That was the plan. You just did it the hard way."

*Some day you will share this vigil with me.*

"I'm done with all that now. Light your bridge and leave me alone."

There was no having a reasonable conversation with the dead. Amarelle kept moving. She only came this way when she wanted a drink, and by the time she got off the bridge she always needed at least two.

Thunder rolled through the canyons of the streets. A building was on fire somewhere to the east, smoldering unnatural purple. Flights of screeching bat-winged beasts filled the sky between the flames and the low, glowing clouds. Some of them tangled and fought, with naked claws and barbed spears and clay jars of explosive fog. The objectives the creatures contended for were known only to gods and sorcerers.

Gods-damned wizards and their stupid feuds. Too bad they ran the city. Too bad Amarelle needed their protection.

## 2. The Furnished Belly of the Beast

The Sign of the Fallen Fire lay on the west side of Tanglewing Street. Was, more accurately, the entire west side of Tanglewing Street. No room for anything else beside the cathedral of coiled bones knocked down fifteen centuries before, back when wild dragons occasionally took offense at the growing size of Theradane and paid it a visit. This one had settled so artistically in death, some long-forgotten entrepreneur had scraped out flesh and scales and roofed the steel-hard bones right where they lay.

Amarelle went in through the dragon's mouth, shook burnt orange rain from her hair and watched wisps of luminous steam curl up from the carpet where the droplets landed. The bouncers lounging against eight-foot serrated fangs all nodded to her.

The tavern had doors where the dragon had once had tonsils. Those doors smelled good credit and opened smoothly.

The Neck was for dining and the Tail was for gambling. The Arms offered rooms for sleeping or not sleeping, as the renters preferred. Amarelle's business was in the Gullet, the drinking cavern under the dead beast's ribs and spine, where one hundred thousand bottles gleamed on racks and shelves behind the central bar.

Goldclaw Grask, the floor manager, was an ebony-scaled goblin in a dapper suit woven from actual Bank of Theradane notes. He had one in a different denomination for every night of the week; tonight he wore fifties.

"Amarelle Parathis, the Duchess Unseen," he cried. "I see you just fine!"

"That one certainly never gets old, Grask."

"I'm counting glasses and silverware after you leave tonight."

"I'm retired and loving it," said Amarelle. She'd pulled three jobs at the Sign of the Fallen Fire in her working days. Certainly none for silverware. "Is Sophara on bar tonight?"

"Of course," said Grask. "It's the seventeenth. Same night of the month your little crew always gets together and pretends it's just an accident. Those of you that aren't lighting the streets, that is."

Amarelle glared. The goblin rustled over, reached up, took her left hand, and flicked his tongue contritely against her knuckles.

"I'm sorry," he said. "I didn't mean to be an asshole. I know, you paid the tithe, you're an honest sheep living under the bombardment like the rest of us. Look, Sophara's waving. Have one on me."

Sophara Miris had mismatched eyes and skin the color of rosewood, fine aquamarine hair and the hands of a streetside card sharp. When she'd paid her sanctuary tithe to the Parliament of Strife, she'd been wanted on three hundred and twelve distinct felony charges in eighteen cities. These days she was senior mage-mixologist at the Sign of the Fallen Fire, and she already had Amarelle's first drink half-finished.

"Evening, stranger." Sophara scrawled orders on a slate and handed it to one of the libationarians, whose encyclopedic knowledge of the contents and locations of all the bottles kept the bar running. "Do you remember when we used to be interesting people?"

"I think being alive and at liberty is pretty damn interesting," said Amarelle. "Your wife planning on dropping in tonight?"

"Any minute now," said Sophara, stirring equal parts liquor and illusion into a multi-layered concoction. "The self-made man's holding a booth for us. I'm mixing you a Rise and Fall of Empires, but I heard Grask. You want two of these? Or something else?"

"You feel like making me a Peril on the Sea?" said Amarelle.

"Yours to command. Why don't you take a seat? I'll be over when the drinks are ready."

Ten dozen booths and suspended balconies filled the Gullet, each carefully spaced and curtained to allow a sense of intimate privacy in the midst of grand spectacle. Lightning, visible through skylights between the ribs, crackled overhead as Amarelle crossed the floor. Her people had a usual place for their usual night, and Shraplin was holding the table.

Shraplin Self-Made, softly whirring concatenation of wires and gears, wore a tattered vermilion cloak embroidered with silver threads. His sculpted brass face had black gemstone eyes and a permanent ghost of a smile. A former foundry drudge, he'd taken advantage of the old Theradane law that a sentient automaton owned its own head and the thoughts therein. Over the course of fifteen years, he'd carefully stolen cogs and screws and bolts and wires and gradually replaced every inch of himself from the neck down until not a speck of his original body remained, and he was able to walk away from the perpetual magical indenture attached to it. Not long after that he'd found klepto-kindred spirits in Amarelle Parathis' crew.

"Looking wet, boss," he said. "What's coming down out there?"

"Weird water," said Amarelle, taking a place beside him. "Pretty, actually. And don't call me boss."

"Certain patterns engrave themselves on my ruminatory discs, boss." Shraplin poured a touch of viscous black slime from a glass into a port on his neck. "Parliament's really going at it tonight. When I got here purple fire was falling on the High Barrens."

"That's one advantage of living in our prosperous thaumatocracy," sighed Amarelle. "Always something interesting exploding nearby. Hey, here's our girls."

Sophara Miris had one hand under a tray of drinks and the other around Brandwin Miris' waist. Brandwin had frosted lavender skin that was no magical affectation and thick amber spectacles over golden eyes. Brandwin, armorer, artificer, and physician to automatons, had the death sentence in three principalities for supplying the devices that had so frequently allowed the Duchess Unseen's crew to evade boring entanglements in local judicial systems. The only object she'd ever personally stolen in her life was the heart of the crew's magician.

"Shraplin, my toy," said Brandwin. She touched fingertips with the automaton before sitting down. "Valves valving and pipes piping?"

"Fighting fit and free of rust," said Shraplin. "And your own metabolic processes and needs?"

"Well attended to," said Sophara with a smirk. "Shall we get this meeting of the Retired Folks' Commiseration and Inebriation Society rolling? Here's something phlegmatic and sanguine for you, Shraplin."

She handed over another tumbler of black ooze. The artificial man had no use for alcohol, so he kept a private reserve of human temperaments magically distilled into asphaltum lacquer behind the bar.

"A Black Lamps of Her Eyes for me," said Sophara. "A Tower of the Elephant for the gorgeous artificer. And for you, Your Grace, a Peril on the Sea and a Rise and Fall of Empires."

Amarelle hefted the latter, a thick glass containing nine horizontal layers of rose-tinted liquors, each layer inhabited by a moving landscape. These varied from fallow hills and fields at the bottom to great cities in the middle layers to a ruin-dotted waste on high, topped by clouds of foam.

"Anyone heard from Jade?" she said.

"Same as always," said Shraplin. "Regards, and don't wait up."

"Regards and don't wait up," muttered Amarelle. She looked around the table, saw mismatched eyes and shaded eyes and cold black stones fixed on her in expectation. As always. So be it. She raised her glass, and they did likewise.

"Here's a toast," she said. "We did it and lived. We put ourselves in prison to stay out of prison. To absent friends, gone where no words nor treasure of ours can restore amends. We did it and lived. To the chains we refused and the ones that snared us anyway. We did it and lived."

She slammed the drink back, poured layers of foaming history down her throat. She didn't usually do this sort of thing to herself without dinner to cushion the impact, but hell, it seemed that kind of night. Lightning flashed above the skylights.

"Did you have a few on your way over here, boss?" said Shraplin.

"The Duchess is dead." Amarelle set her empty glass down firmly. "Long live the Duchess. Now, do I have to go through the sham of pulling my cards out and dealing them, or would you all prefer to just pile your money neatly in the center of the table for me?"

"Oh, honey," said Brandwin. "We're not using your deck. It knows more tricks than a show dog."

"I'll handicap myself," said Amarelle. She lifted the Peril on the Sea, admired the aquamarine waves topped with vanilla whitecaps, and in two gulps added it to the ball of fast-spreading warmth in her stomach. "There's some magic I can appreciate. So, are we playing cards or having a staring contest? Next round's on me!"

## 3. Cheating Hands

"Next round's on me," said Amarelle an hour and a half later. The table was a mess of cards, bank notes, and empty glasses.

"Next round's IN you, boss," said Shraplin. "You're three ahead of the rest of us."

"Seems fair. What the hell did I just drink, anyway?"

"A little something I call the Amoral Instrument," said Sophara. Her eyes were shining. "I'm not allowed to make it for customers. Kind of curious to see what happens to you, in fact."

"Water off a duck's back," said Amarelle, though the room had more soft edges than she remembered and her cards were not entirely cooperating with her plan to hold them steady. "This is a mess. A mess! Shraplin, you're probably sober-esque. How many cards in a standard deck?"

"Sixty, boss."

"How many cards presently visible in our hands or on the table?"

"Seventy-eight."

"That's ridiculous," said Amarelle. "Who's not cheating? We should be pushing ninety. Who's not cheating?"

"I solemnly affirm that I haven't had an honest hand since we started," said Brandwin.

"Magician," said Sophara, tapping her cards against her breast. "Enough said."

"I'm wearing my cheating hands, boss," said Shraplin. He wiggled his fingers in blurry silver arcs.

"This is sad." Amarelle reached behind her left ear, conjured a seventy-ninth card out of her black ringlets, and added it to the pattern on the table. "We really are getting old and decrepit."

Fresh lightning tore the sky, painting the room in gray-white pulses. Thunder exploded just overhead; the skylights rattled in their frames and even the great bone-rafters seemed to shake. Some of the other drinkers stirred and muttered.

"Fucking wizards," said Amarelle. "Present company excepted, of course."

"Why would I except present company?" said Brandwin, tangling the fingers of one hand in Sophara's hair and gracefully palming an eightieth card onto the table with her other.

"It's been terrible all week," said Sophara. "I think it's Ivovandas, over in the High Barrens. Her and some rival I haven't identified, spitting fire and rain and flying things all over the damn place. The parasol sellers have

THE LONG LIST ANTHOLOGY

been making a killing with those new leather and chainmail models."

"Someone ought to stroll up there and politely ask them to give it a rest." Shraplin's gleaming head rotated slowly until he was peering at Amarelle. "Someone famous, maybe. Someone colorful and respected. Someone with a dangerous reputation."

"Better to say nothing and be thought a fool," said Amarelle, "than to interfere in the business of wizards and remove all doubt. Who needs a fresh round? Next one's still on me. I plan on having all your money when we call it a night, anyway."

## 4. The Trouble With Glass Ceilings

The thunder and lightning were continuous for the next hour. Flapping, howling things bounced off the roof at regular intervals. Half the patrons in the Gullet cleared out, pursued by the cajoling of Goldclaw Grask.

"The Sign of the Fallen Fire has stood for fifteen centuries!" he cried. "This is the safest place in all of Theradane! You really want to be out in the streets on a night like this? Have you considered our fine rooms in the Arms?"

There was a high-pitched sound of shattering glass. Something large and wet and dead hit the floor next to the bar, followed by a shower of skylight fragments and glowing rain. Grask squawked for a house magician to unmake the mess while the exodus quickened around him.

"Ahhh, nice to be off duty." Sophara sipped unsteadily from a tumbler of something blue and uncomplicated. The bar had cut her off from casting her own spells into drinks.

"You know," said Amarelle, slowly, "maybe someone really should go up there to the High Barrens and tell that old witchy bitch to put a leash on her pets."

The room, through her eyes, had grown softer and softer as the noisy night wore on, and had now moved into a decidedly impressionist phase. Goldclaw Grask was a bright smear chasing other bright smears across the floor, and even the cards on the table were no longer holding still long enough for Amarelle to track their value.

"Hey," she said, "Sophara, you're a citizen in good standing. Why don't we get you made a member of Parliament so you can make these idiots stop?"

"Oh, brilliant! Well, first I'd need to steal or invent a really good youth-binding," said the magician, "something better than the three-in-five I'm working now, so I can ripen my practice for a century or two. You might find this timeline inconvenient for your purposes."

"Then you'd need to find an external power locus to kick up your juice," said Brandwin.

"Yes," said Sophara, "and harness it without any other hazard-class sorcerers noticing. Oh, and I'd also need to go *completely out of my ever-fucking head!* You have to be a dead-eyed dirty-souled maniac to want to spend your extended life trading punches with other maniacs. Once you've seized that power, there's no getting off the merry-go-round. You fight like hell just to hold on or you get shoved off."

"Splat!" said Brandwin.

"Not my idea of a playground," said Sophara, finishing her drink and slamming the empty glass down emphatically.

An instant later there was a horrendous shattering crash. A half-ton of dark winged something, its matted fur rain-wet and reeking, plunged through the skylight directly overhead and obliterated their table. A confused blur of motion and noise attended the crash, and Amarelle found herself on the floor with a dull ache between her breasts.

Some dutiful, stubborn fraction of her awareness kicked its way to the surface of the alcoholic ocean in her mind, and there clutched at straws until it had pieced together the true sequence of events. Shraplin, of course— the nimble automaton had shoved her aside before diving across the table to get Sophara and Brandwin clear.

"Hey," said Amarelle, sitting up, "you're not drunk at all!"

"That was part of my cheating, boss." The automaton had been very nearly fast enough, very nearly. Sophara and Brandwin were safe, but his left leg was pinned under the fallen creature and the table.

"Oh, you best of all possible automatons! Your poor foot!" Brandwin crawled over to him and kissed the top of his brass head.

"I've got three spares at home," said Shraplin.

"That tears it," muttered Amarelle, wobbling and weaving back to her feet. "Nobody drops a gods-damned gargoyle on my friends!"

"I think it's a byakhee," said Brandwin, poking at the beast. It had membranous wings and a spear protruding from what might have been its neck. It smelled like old cheese washed in gangrene and graveyard dew.

"I think it's a vorpilax, love," said Sophara. She drunkenly assisted her wife in pulling Shraplin out from under the thing. "Consider the bilateral symmetry."

"I don't care what it is," said Amarelle, fumbling into her long black coat. "Nobody drops one on my card game or my crew. I'm going to find out where this Ivovandas lives and give her a piece of my mind."

"Haste makes corpses, boss," said Shraplin, shaking coils and widgets from the wreckage of his foot. "I was just having fun with you earlier."

"Stupid damn commerce-murdering wizards!" Goldclaw Grask arrived at last, with a gaggle of bartenders and waiters in train. "Sophara! Are you hurt? What about the rest of you? Shraplin! That looks expensive. Tell me it's not expensive!"

"I can soon be restored to prime functionality," said Shraplin. "But what if I suggested that tonight is an excellent night for you to tear up our bill?"

"I, uh, well, if that wouldn't get you in trouble," said the goblin, directing waiters with mops toward the growing puddle of pastel-colored rainwater and gray ichor under the beast.

"If you give it to us freely," said Sophara, "it's not theft, and none of us break our terms of sanctuary. And Shraplin is right, Amarelle. You can't just go berate a member of the Parliament of Strife! Even if you could safely cross the High Barrens in the middle of this mess—"

"Of course I can." Amarelle stood up nearly straight and, after a few false starts, approximately squared her shoulders. "I'm not some marshmallow-muscled tourist, I'm the Duchess Unseen! I stole the sound of the sunrise and the tears of a shark. I borrowed a book from the library of Hazar and didn't return it. I crossed the Labyrinth of the Death Spiders in Moraska TWICE—"

"I know," said Sophara. "I was there."

"...and then I went back and stole all the Death Spiders!"

"That was ten years and an awful lot of strong drinks ago," said Sophara. "Come on, darling, I mixed most of the drinks myself. Don't scare us like this, Amarelle. You're drunk and retired. Go home."

"This smelly thing could have killed all of us," said Amarelle.

"Well, thanks to a little luck and a lot of Shraplin, it didn't. Come on, Amarelle. Promise us you won't do anything stupid tonight. Will you *promise* us?"

## 5. Removing All Doubt

The High Barrens, east of Tanglewing Street, were empty of inhabitants and full of nasty surprises from the battle in progress. Amarelle kept out of the open, moving from shadowed arch to garden wall to darkened doorway, stumbling frequently. The world had a fragile liquid quality, running at the edges and spinning on previously unrevealed axes. She was not drunk enough to forget that she had to take extra care and still far too drunk to realize that she ought to be fleeing the way she'd come.

The High Barrens had once been a neighborhood of mansions and topiary wonders and public fountains, but the coming of the wizard Ivovandas has sent the former inhabitants packing. The arguments of the Parliament of Strife had blasted holes in the cobblestones, cracked and dried the fountains, and sundered the mansions like unloved toy houses. The purple fire from before was still smoldering in a tall ruined shell of wood and brick. Amarelle sidestepped the street-rivers of melted lead that had once been the building's roof.

It wasn't difficult to find the manse of Ivovandas, the only lit and tended structure in the neighborhood, guarded by smooth walls, glowing ideograms, and rustling red-green hedges with the skeletons of many birds and small animals scattered in their undergrowth. A path of interlocked alabaster stones, gleaming with internal light, led forty curving yards to a golden front door.

Convenient. That guaranteed a security gauntlet.

The screams of terrible flying things high above made concentration even more difficult, but Amarelle applied three decades of experience to the path and was not disappointed. Four trapped stones she avoided by intuition, two by dumb drunken luck. The gravity-orientation reversal was a trick she'd seen before; she cartwheeled (sloppily) over the dangerous patch and the magic pushed her headfirst back to the ground rather than helplessly into the sky. She never even felt the silvery call of the tasteful hypnotic toad sculptures on the lawn, as she was too inebriated to meet their eyes and trigger the effect.

When she reached the front door, the golden surface rippled like a molten pool and a sculpted arm emerged clutching a knocker ring. Amarelle flicked a collapsible baton out of her coat and used it to tap the ring against the door while she stood aside. There was a brief pause after the darts had hissed through empty air, and then a voice boomed:

"WHO COMES UNBIDDEN TO THE DOOR OF THE SUPREME SPELLWRIGHT IVOVANDAS OF THE HONORABLE PARLIAMENT OF THERADANE? SPEAK, WORM!"

"I don't take shit from doors," said Amarelle. "I'm flattering your mistress by knocking. Tell her a citizen of Theradane is here to give her a frank and unexpurgated opinion on how terrible her aim is."

"YOUR ATTITUDE IS UNDERSTANDABLE AND NONETHELESS THOROUGHLY OFFENSIVE. ARCS OF ELECTRODYNAMIC FORCE WILL NOW BE APPLIED TO THE LOBES OF YOUR BRAIN UNTIL THEY ARE SCALDED PULP. TO RECEIVE THIS PRONOUNCEMENT IN THE FORM OF UNIVERSAL PICTOGRAMS, SCREAM ONCE. TO REQUEST MORE RAPID SENSORY OBLIVION, SCREAM TWICE AND WAIT TO SEE WHAT HAPPENS."

"The name is Amarelle Parathis, also known as the Duchess Unseen. Your mistress' stupid feuds are turning a fine old town into a shitsack misery farm and ruining my card games. Are you going to open up, or do I find a window?"

"AMARELLE PARATHIS," said the door. A moment passed. "YOUR NAME IS NOT UNKNOWN. YOU PURCHASED SANCTUARY FROM THE PARLIAMENT OF THERADANE TWO YEARS AND FOUR MONTHS AGO."

"Attadoor," said Amarelle.

"THE MISTRESS WILL RECEIVE YOU."

The sculpted hand holding the knocker withdrew into the liquid surface of the door. A dozen others burst forth, grabbing Amarelle by the throat, arms, legs, and hair. They pulled her off her feet and into the rippling golden surface, which solidified an instant later and retained no trace of her passage.

## 6. The Cabinet of Golden Hands

Amarelle awoke, thoroughly comfortable but stripped of all her weapons and wearing someone else's silk nightgown.

She was in a doorless chamber, in a feather bed floating gently on a pool of liquid gold that covered the entire floor, or perhaps was the entire floor. Ruby shafts of illumination fell from etched glass skylights, and when

Amarelle threw back her covers they dissolved into wisps of aromatic steam.

Something bubbled and churned beneath the golden pool. A small hemisphere rose from the surface, continued rising, became a tall, narrow, humanoid shape. The liquid drained away smoothly, revealing a dove-pale albino woman with flawless auric eyes and hair composed of a thousand golden butterflies, all fluttering elegantly at random.

"Good afternoon, Amarelle," said the wizard Ivovandas. Her feet didn't quite touch the surface of the pool as she drifted toward the bed. "I trust you slept well. You were magnificent last night!"

"Was I? I don't remember... uh, that is, I remember some of it... am I wearing your clothes?"

"Yes."

"Shouldn't I have a hangover?"

"I took it while you slept," said Ivovandas. "I have a collection of bottled maladies. Your hangover was due to be the stuff of legends. Here be dragons! And by 'here,' I mean directly behind your eyeballs, probably for the rest of the week. I'll find another head to slip it into, someday. Possibly I'll let you have it back if you fail me."

"Fail you? What?" Amarelle leapt to her feet, which sank awkwardly into the mattress. "You have me confused with someone who knows what's going on. Start with how I was magnificent."

"I've never been so extensively insulted! In my own foyer, no less, before we even adjourned to the study. You offered penetratingly savage elucidation of all my character flaws, most of them imaginary, and then you gave me the firmest possible directions on how I and my peers were to order our affairs henceforth, for the convenience of you and your friends."

"I, uh, recall some of that, I think."

"I am curious about a crucial point, citizen Parathis. When you purchased sanctuary from the Parliament of Theradane, you were instructed that personal threats against the members of said parliament could be grounds for summary revocation of sanctuary privileges, were you not?"

"I... recall something with that flavor... in the paperwork... possibly on the back somewhere... maybe in the margins?"

"You will agree that your statements last night certainly qualified as personal threats?"

"My statements?"

Smiling, Ivovandas produced a humming blue crystal and used it to project a crisp, solid image into the air beside the bed. It was Amarelle, black-coated and soaked with steaming magic rain, gesturing with clutching hands as she raved:

"And another thing, you venomous milk-faced thundercunt! NOBODY drops a dead vorpilax on my friends, NOBODY! What you fling at the other members of your pointy-hatted circle jerk is your business, but the next time you trifle with the lives of uninvolved citizens, you'd better lock your doors, put on your thickest steel corset, and hire a food taster, you catch my meaning?"

The image vanished.

"Damn," said Amarelle. "I've always thought of myself as basically a happy drunk."

"I'm three hundred and ten years old," said Ivovandas, "and I learned some new words last night! Oh, we were having such fun, until I found myself personally threatened."

"Yes. So it would seem. And how were you thinking we might, ah, proceed in this matter?"

"Ordinarily," said Ivovandas, "I'd magically redirect the outflow of your lower intestine into your lungs, which would be my little way of saying that your sanctuary privileges had been revoked. However, those skills of yours, and that reputation... I have a contract suited to such a contractor. Why don't you get dressed and meet me in the study?"

A powerful force struck Amarelle from behind, knocking her off the bed, headfirst into the golden pool. Rather than swimming down she found herself floating up, rising directly through the floor of Ivovandas' study, a large room full of bookshelves, scrollcases, and lacquered basilisk-skin paneling. Amarelle was suddenly wearing her own clothes again.

On the wall was an oil painting of the bedroom Amarelle had just left, complete with a masterful rendering of Ivovandas floating above the golden pool. As Amarelle watched, the painted figure grew larger and larger within the frame, then pushed her arms and head out of it, and with a twist and a jump at last floated free in the middle of the study.

"Now," said Ivovandas. "To put it simply, there is an object within Theradane I expect you to secure. Whether or not your friends help you is of no concern to me. As an added incentive, if you deliver this thing to me quietly and successfully, you will calm a great deal of the, ah, public disagreement between myself and a certain parliamentary peer."

"But the terms of my sanctuary!" said Amarelle. "You got part of my tithe! You know how it works. I can't steal within the boundaries of Theradane."

"Well, you can't threaten me either," said Ivovandas. "And that's a moot point now, so what have you got to lose?"

"An eternity not spent as a street lamp."

"Admirable long-term thinking," said Ivovandas. "But I do believe if you scrutinize your situation you'll see that you're up a certain proverbial creek, and I am the only provisioner of paddles willing to sell you one."

Amarelle paced, hands shoved sullenly into her coat pockets. She and her crew needed the security of Theradane; they had grown too famous, blown too much cover, taken too many interesting keepsakes from the rich and powerful in too many other places. Theradane's system was simplicity itself. Pay a vast sum to the Parliament of Strife, retire to Theradane, and don't practice any of the habits that got you in trouble outside the city. Ever.

"Have some heart, Amarelle. It's not precisely *illegal* for me to coax a master criminal back into operations within the city limits, but I can't imagine my peers would let the matter pass unremarked if they ever found out about it. Do as I ask and I'll gladly smash my little blue crystal. We'll both walk away smiling, in harmonious equipoise."

"What do you want me to secure for you?"

Ivovandas opened a tall cabinet set against the right-hand wall. Inside was a blank tapestry surrounded on all sides by disembodied golden hands not unlike the ones that had hauled Amarelle across the threshold. The hands leapt to life, flicking across the tapestry with golden needles and black thread. Lines appeared on the surface, lines that rapidly became clear to Amarelle as the districts of Theradane and their landmarks: the High Barrens, the Sign of the Fallen Fire, the Deadlight Downs, and a hundred others, stitch by stitch.

When the map was complete, one hand stitched in a final thread of summer-fire crimson, glowing somewhere in the northeastern part of the city.

"Prosperity Street," said Ivovandas. "In Fortune's Gate, near the Old Parliament."

"I've been there," said Amarelle. "What do you want?"

"Prosperity Street. In Fortune's Gate. Near the Old Parliament."

"I heard you the first time," said Amarelle. "But what do you… oh, *no*. You did not. You did *not* just imply that implication!"

"I want you to steal Prosperity Street," said Ivovandas. "The whole street. The entire length of it. Every last brick and stone. It must cease to exist. It must be removed from Theradane."

"That street is three hundred yards long, at the heart of a district so important and money-soaked that even you lunatics don't blast it in your little wars, and it's trafficked at every hour of every day!"

"It would therefore be to your advantage to remove it without attracting notice," said Ivovandas. "But that's your business, one way or the other, and I won't presume to give you instruction in your own narrow specialty."

"It. Is. A. STREET."

"And you're Amarelle Parathis. Weren't you shouting something last night about how you'd stolen the sound of the sunrise?"

"On the right day of the year," said Amarelle, "on the peak of the proper mountain, and with a great deal of help from some dwarves and more copper pipe than I can— damn it, it was very complicated!"

"You stole tears from a shark."

"If you can figure out how to identify a melancholy shark, you're halfway home in that business."

"Incidentally, what *did* you do with the Death Spiders of Moraska once you'd taken them?"

"I mailed them back to the various temples of the spider-priests who'd been annoying me. Let's just say that confinement left the spiders agitated *and* hungry, and that the cult now has very firm rules concerning shipping crates with ventilation holes. Also, I mailed the crates postage *due*."

"Charming!" cried Ivovandas. "Well, you strike me as just the sort of woman to steal a street."

"I suppose my only other alternative is a pedestal engraved 'Now I Serve Theradane Always.'"

"That, or some more private and personal doom," said Ivovandas. "But you have, in the main, apprehended the salient features of your choices."

"Why a street?" said Amarelle. "Before I proceed, let's be candid, or something resembling it. Why do you want this street removed, and how will doing so calm down the fighting between you and your… oh. Oh, hell, it's a locus, isn't it?"

"Yes," said Ivovandas. Her predatory grin revealed teeth engraved with hair-fine lines of gold in arcane patterns. "Prosperity Street is the external power locus of the wizard Jarrow, my most unbeloved colleague. It's how he finds the wherewithal to prolong this tedious contest of summoned creatures and weather. Without it, I could flatten him in an afternoon and be home in time for tea."

"Forgive me if this is a touchy subject, but I thought the nature of these loci was about the most closely-guarded secret you and your... colleagues possess."

"Jarrow has been indiscreet," said Ivovandas. "But then, he understands the knowledge alone is useless if it can't be coupled to a course of action. A street is quite a thing to dispose of, and the question of how to do so absolutely *stymied* me until you came calling with your devious head so full of drunken outrage. Shall we go to contract?"

The cabinet of golden hands unstitched the map of Theradane, and in its place embroidered a number of paragraphs in neat, even script. Amarelle peered closely at them. They were surprisingly straightforward, describing a trade of one (1) street for one (1) blue crystal to be smashed, but then...

"What the hell's this?" she said. "A deadline? A year and a day?"

"It's the traditional span for this sort of arrangement," said Ivovandas. "And surely you can see the sense in it. I prefer Jarrow de-fanged fairly soon, not five or ten or some nebulous and ever-changing number of years from now. I require you working with determination and focus. And you require some incentive other than simple destruction for failure, so there it all is."

"A year and a day," said Amarelle, "and I deliver the street, or surrender my citizenship and worldly wealth to permanent indenture in your service."

"It would be a comfortable and exciting life," said Ivovandas. "But you can avoid it if you're as clever as I hope you are."

"And what if I were to quietly report this arrangement to the wizard Jarrow and see if he could do better for me?"

"A worthwhile contemplation of treacherous entanglement symmetrical to my own! I salute your spirit, but must remind you that Jarrow possesses no blue crystal, nor do you or he possess the faintest notion of where my external locus resides. You must decide for yourself which of us would make the easier target. If you wish to be ruled by wisdom, you'll reach into your pockets now."

Amarelle did, and found that a quill and an ink bottle had somehow appeared therein.

"One street," she said. "For one crystal. One year and one day."

"It's all there in plain black thread," said Ivovandas. "Will you sign?"

Amarelle stared at the contract and ground her teeth, a habit her mother had always sternly cautioned her against. At last, she uncapped the bottle of ink and wet the quill.

## 7. Another Unexpected Change of Clothing

The usual tumult of wizardly contention had abated. Even Ivovandas and Jarrow seemed to be taking a rest from their labors when Amarelle walked out of the High Barrens under a peach-colored afternoon haze. All the clocks in the city sounded three, refuting and echoing and interrupting one another, the actual ringing of the hour taking somewhere north of two and a half minutes due to the fact that clocks in Theradane were traditionally mis-synchronized to confuse malicious spirits.

Amarelle's thoughts were an electric whirl of anxiety and calculation. She hailed a mechanavipede and was soon speeding over the rooftops of the city in a swaying chair tethered beneath the straining wings of a flock of mechanical sparrows. There was simply nowhere else to go for help; she would have to heave herself before her friends like jetsam washed up on a beach.

Sophara and Brandwin lived in a narrow, crooked house on Shankvile Street, a house they'd secured at an excellent price due to the fact that it sometimes had five stories and sometimes six. Where the sixth occasionally wandered off to was unknown, but while it politely declined their questions about its business it also had the courtesy to ask none concerning theirs. Amarelle had the mechanavipede heave her off into a certain third-floor window which served as a friends-only portal for urgent business.

The ladies of the house were in, and by a welcome stroke of luck so was Shraplin. Brandwin was fussing with the pistons of his replacement left foot, while Sophara sprawled full-length on a velvet hammock wearing smoked glasses and an ice-white beret that exuded analgesic mist in a halo about her head.

"How is it that you're not covered in vomit and begging for death?"

said Sophara. "How is it that you consumed three times your own weight in liquor and I've got sole custody of the hangover?"

"I had an unexpected benefactor, Soph. Can you secure this chamber for sensitive conversation?"

"The whole house is reasonably safe," groaned the magician, rolling off the hammock with minimal grace and dignity. "Now, if you want me to weave a deeper silence, give me a minute to gather my marbles. Wait…"

She pulled her smoked glasses off and peered coldly at Amarelle. Stepping carefully around the mess of specialized tools and mechanical gewgaws littering the carpet, she approached, sniffing the air.

"Something wrong, dearest?" said Brandwin.

"Shhhh," said Sophara. She rubbed her eyes in the manner of the freshly-awake, then reached out, moved Amarelle's left coat lapel aside, and pulled a gleaming gold thread out of the black wool.

"You," she said, arching her aquamarine eyebrows at Amarelle, "have been seeing another wizard."

Sophara clapped her hands and an eerie hush fell upon the room. The faint sounds of the city outside were utterly banished.

"Ivovandas," said Amarelle. "I ran off and did something stupid last night. In my defense, I would just like to say that I was angry, and you were the one mixing the drinks."

"You unfailingly omni-bothersome bitch," said Sophara. "Well, this little thread would allow Ivovandas to eavesdrop, if not for my counterspell and certain fundamental confusions worked into the stones of this house. And where there's obvious chicanery, there's something lurking behind it. Take the rest of your clothes off."

"What?"

"Do it now, Amarelle!" Sophara retrieved a silver-engraved casket from a far corner of the room, clicked it open, and made urgent motions while Amarelle shed her coat.

"You see how direct she is?" Brandwin squeezed a tiny bellows to pressurize a tube of glowing green oil within Shraplin's leg. "We'd never have gotten anywhere if she'd waited for me to make the first move."

"You keep your eyes on your work," said Sophara. "I'll do the looking for both of us and give you details later."

"I sometimes think that 'friend' is just a word I use for all the people I haven't murdered yet," said Amarelle, hopping and twirling out of her boots, leggings, belts, vest, blouse, sharp implements, silk ropes, smoke capsules, and smallclothes. When the last stitch was discarded, Sophara slammed the casket shut and muttered spells over the lock.

As a decided afterthought, smiling and taking her time, she eventually fetched Amarelle a black silk dressing robe embroidered with blue-white astronomical charts.

"It seems to be my day to try on everyone else's clothes," she muttered.

"I'm sorry about your things," said Sophara. "I should be able to sweep them for further tricks, but Ivovandas is so far outside my weight class, it might take days."

"Never let a wizard get their hands on your clothes," said Brandwin. "At least not until she promises to move in with you. It ought to be safe to talk now."

"I'm not entirely sure how to say this," said Amarelle, "but the concise version is that I'm temporarily unretired."

She told the whole story, pausing only to answer Sophara's excited questions about the defenses and décor of Ivovandas' manse.

"That's a hell of a thing, boss," said Shraplin when Amarelle finished. The clocks within the house started chiming five, and didn't finish for some time. The city clocks were still sealed beyond Sophara's silence. "I thought we were up against it when that shark tears job landed on us. But a street!"

"I wonder how Jarrow figured out it was a locus." Sophara adjusted the analgesic hat, which had done her much good over the long course of Amarelle's story. "I wonder how he harnessed it without anyone interfering!"

"Keep it relevant, dreamer." Brandwin massaged her wife's legs. "The pertinent question is, how are we going to pull it off?"

"I only came for advice," said Amarelle hastily. "This is all my fault, and nobody else needs to risk their sanctuary because I got drunk and sassed a wizard."

"Let me enlighten you, boss," said Shraplin. "If you don't want me to follow you around being helpful, you must be planning to smash my head right now."

"Amarelle, you *can't* keep us out in the cold now! This mischief is too delicious," said Sophara. "And it's clearly not prudent to let you wander off on your own."

"I'm grateful," said Amarelle, "but I feel responsible for your safety."

"The Parliament of Strife craps destruction on its own city at random, boss." Shraplin spread his hands. "How much more unsafe can we get? Frankly, two and a half quiet years is adequate to my taste."

"Yes," said Sophara. "Hang your delicate feelings, Amarelle, you know we won't let you... oh, wait. You foxy bag of tits and sugar! You didn't come here just for advice! You put your noble face on so we'd pledge ourselves without the pleasure of seeing you beg!"

"And you fell for it." Amarelle grinned. "So it's agreed, we're all out of retirement and we're stealing a street. If anyone cares to let me know how the hell that's supposed to work, the suggestion box is open."

## 8. The Cheap Shot

They spent the first two days in measurement and surveillance. Prosperity Street was three hundred and seventeen yards long running north-south, an average of ten yards wide. Nine major avenues and fifteen alleys bisected it. One hundred and six businesses and residences opened onto it, one of which was a wine bar serving distillations of such quality that a third day was lost to hangovers and remonstrations.

They struck on the evening of the fourth day, as warm mist curled lazily from the sewers and streetlamps gleamed like pearls in folds of gray gauze. The clocks began chiming eleven, a process that often lasted until it was nearly time for them to begin striking twelve.

A purple-skinned woman in the coveralls of a municipal functionary calmly tinkered with the sign post at the intersection of Prosperity and Magdamar. She placed the wooden shingle marked PROSPERITY S in a sack and tipped her hat to a drunk, semi-curious goblin. Brandwin emptied three intersections of PROSPERITY S signs before the clocks settled down.

At the intersection of Prosperity and Ninefingers, a polite brass-headed drudge painted over every visible PROSPERITY S with an opaque black varnish. Two blocks north, a mechanavipede flying unusually low with a cargo of one dark-haired woman crashed into a signpost, an accident that would be repeated six times. At the legendarily confusing seven-way intersection where the various Goblin Markets joined Prosperity, a sorceress disguised as a cat's shadow muttered quiet spells of alphabetic nullification, wiping every relevant signpost like a slate.

They had to remove forty-six shingles or signposts and deface the placards of sixteen businesses that happened to be named after the street. Lastly, they arranged to tip a carboy of strong vitriol over a ceremonial spot in the pavement where PROSPERITY STREET was set in iron letters. When those had become PRCLGILV SLGFLL, they gave the mess a quick splash of water and hurried away to dispose of their coveralls, paints, and stolen city property.

The next day, Ivovandas was less than impressed.

"Nothing happened." Her gold eyes gleamed dangerously and her butterflies were still. "Not one femto-scintilla of deviation or dampening in the potency of Jarrow's locus. Though there were quite a few confused travelers and tourists. You need to steal the street, Amarelle, not vandalize its ornaments."

"I didn't expect it to be that easy," said Amarelle. "I just thought we ought to eliminate the simplest approach first. Never lay an Archduke on the table when a two will do."

"The map is not the territory." Ivovandas gestured and transported Amarelle to the front lawn of her manse, where the hypnotic toad sculptures nearly cost her even more lost time.

## 9. Brute Force

Their next approach took eleven days to plan and arrange, including two days lost to a battle between parliament wizards in the western sectors that collapsed the Temple-Bridge of the God of Hidden Names.

The street signs had been restored at the intersection of Prosperity and Languinar, the southernmost limit of Prosperity Street. The sunrise sky was just creeping over the edge of the city in orange and scarlet striations, and the clocks were or were not chiming seven. A caravan of reinforced cargo coaches drawn by armored horses halted on Languinar, preparing to turn north. The signs hanging from the coaches read:

NUSBARQ DESISKO AND SONS
HAZARDOUS ANIMAL TRANSPORT

As the caravan moved into traffic, a woman in a flaming red dress riding a mecharabbit hopped rudely into the path of the lead carriage, triggering an unlikely but picturesque chain of disasters. Carriage after carriage toppled, wheel after wheel flew from its hub, horse team after horse team ran neighing into traffic as their emergency releases snapped. The side of the first toppled carriage exploded outward, and a furry, snarling beast came bounding out of the wreckage.

"RUN," cried someone, who happened to be the woman in the red dress. "IT'S A SPRING-HEELED WEREJACKAL!"

A heartbeat later her damaged mecharabbit exploded, enveloping her in a cloud of steam and sparks. The red dress was reversible and Amarelle had practiced swapping it around by touch. Three seconds later she ran from the cloud of steam dressed in a black hooded robe. Shraplin, not at all encumbered by seventy-five pounds of fur, leather, and wooden claws, merrily activated the reinforced shock-absorbing leg coils Brandwin had cobbled together for him. He went leaping and howling across the crowd, turning alarm into panic and flight.

Twenty-two unplanned carriage or mechanavipede collisions took place in the next half-minute, locking traffic up for two blocks north of the initial accident. Amarelle didn't have time to count them as she hurried north in Shraplin's wake.

Another curiously defective carriage in the Nusbarq Desisko caravan cracked open, exposing its cargo of man-sized hives to the open air and noise. Thousands of Polychromatic Reek-Bees, scintillating in every color of the rainbow and fearful for the safety of their queens, flew forth to spew defensive stink-nectar on everything within buzzing distance. The faintest edge of that scent followed Amarelle north, and she regretted having eaten breakfast. Hundreds of people would be burning their clothes before the day was through.

All along the length of Prosperity Street, aural spells prepared in advance by Sophara began to erupt. Bold, authoritative voices ordered traffic to halt, passers-by to run, shops to close, citizens to pray for deliverance. They screamed about werejackals, basilisks, reek-bees, Cradlerobber Wasps, rabid vorpilax, and the plague. They ordered constables and able-bodied citizens to use barrels and carriages as makeshift riot-barricades at the major intersections, which some of them did.

Amarelle reached the alley after Ninefingers Way and found the package she'd stashed behind a rotten crate the night before. Soon she emerged from the alley in the uniform of a Theradane constable, captain's bars shining on her collar, steel truncheon gleaming. She issued useless and contradictory orders, fomented panic, pushed shopkeepers into their stores and ordered them to bar their doors. When she met actual constables, she jabbed them with the narcotic prong concealed on the end of her truncheon. Their unconscious bodies, easily mistaken for dead, added a piquant verisimilitude to the raging disquiet.

At the northern end of Prosperity Street, a constabulary riot wagon commanded by a pair of uniformed women experienced another improbable accident when it came into contact with the open fire of a careless street fondue vendor. Brandwin and Sophara threw their helmets aside and ran screaming, infecting dozens of citizens with disoriented panic even before the rockets and canisters inside the wagon began to explode. For nearly half an hour pinkish-white arcs of sneezing powder, soporific smoke, and eye-scalding pepper dust rained on Prosperity Street.

Eventually, two parliament wizards had to grudgingly intervene to help the constables and bucket brigades restore order. The offices of Nusbarq Desisko and Sons were found to be empty and their records missing, presumably carried with them when they fled the city. The spring-heeled werejackal was never located and was assumed taken as a pet by some wizard or another.

"What do you mean, nothing happened?" Amarelle paced furiously in Ivovandas' study the following day, having explained herself to the wizard, who had half-listened while consulting a grimoire that occasionally moaned and laughed to itself. "We closed the full length of Prosperity Street down for more than three hours! We stole the street from everyone on it in a very meaningful sense! The traffic didn't flow, the riot barriers were up, not a scrap of commerce took place anywhere—"

"Amarelle," said the wizard, not taking her eyes from her book, "I applaud your adoption of a more dynamic approach to the problem, but I'm afraid it simply didn't do anything. Not the merest hint of any diminishment to Jarrow's arcane resources. I do wish it were otherwise. Mind the hypnotic toads, as I've strengthened their enchantments substantially." She snapped her fingers, and Amarelle was back on the lawn.

## 10. The Typographic Method

Sophara directed the next phase of their operations, resigning her place as mage-mixologist indefinitely.

"It was mostly for easy access to the bar anyway," she said. "And they'd kiss my heels to have me back anytime."

A studious, eye-straining month and a half followed. Sophara labored over spell-board, abacus, grimoire, and journal, working in four languages and several forms of thaumaturgical notation that made Amarelle's eyes burn.

"I keep telling you not to look at them!" said Sophara as she adjusted the analgesic beret on Amarelle's head. "You haven't got the proper optical geometry! You and Brandwin! You're worse than cats."

Brandwin prowled libraries and civic archives. Amarelle broke into seventeen major private collections. Shraplin applied his tireless mechanical perception to the task of rapidly sifting thousands of pages in thousands of books. A vast pile of notes grew in Brandwin and Sophara's house, along with an inelegant but thorough master list of scrolls, pamphlets, tomes, and records.

"Any guide to the city," chanted Amarelle, for the formula had become a sort of mantra. "Any notes of any traveler, any records of tax or residence, any mentions of repairs, any journals or recollections. Have we ever done anything *less* sane? How can we possibly expect to locate every single written reference to Prosperity Street in every single document in existence?"

"We can't," said Sophara. "But if my calculations are anywhere near correct, and if this can work at all, we only need to change a certain critical percentage of those records, especially in the official municipal archives."

Shraplin and Brandwin cut panels of wood down to precise replicas of the forty-six street signs and the sixteen business placards they had previously tried to steal. They scraped, sanded, varnished, and engraved, making only one small change to each facsimile.

"I have the key," said Brandwin, emerging from her incense-filled workroom one night, bleary-eyed and cooing at a small white moth perched atop her left index finger. "I call it the Adjustment Moth. It's a very complex and efficient little spell I can cast on anything about this size."

"And what will they do?" said Amarelle.

"They'll become iterating work-enhancers," said Sophara. "It'd take us years to manually adjust all the records we're after. Enchanted with my spell to guide and empower them, we can send these little darlings out to do almost all of the work for us in one night."

"How many do we need?" said Shraplin.

Nine nights later, from carefully-selected points around the city, they loosed 3,449 of Sophara's Adjustment Moths, each of which fluttered into the darkness and thence into libraries, archives, shop cupboards, private studies, and bedside cabinets. The 2,625 Adjustment Moths that were not eaten by bats or appropriated as cat toys located a total of 617,451 references to the name 'Prosperity Street' and made one crucial change to each physical text. By sunrise they were all dead of exhaustion.

Amarelle and her crew replaced the forty-six street signs and sixteen business placards under cover of darkness, then pried up one of the (restored) ceremonial iron letters sunk into the pavement. PROSPERIT STREET, the survivors said. PROSPERIT, read the signs and placards. PROSPERIT STREET read the name of the place in every guidebook, private journal, lease, assize, and tax record in the city, save for a few in magically-guarded sanctums of the Parliament of Strife.

Overnight, Prosperity Street had been replaced by its very close cousin, Prosperit Street.

"Amarelle," said Ivovandas, sipping daintily at a cup of molten gold she'd heated in a desk-side crucible, "I sympathize with your agitation at the failure of so original and far-ranging a scheme, but I really must stress the necessity of abandoning these fruitlessly metaphysical approaches. Don't steal the street's name, or its business, or its final 'Y.' Steal the street, wholly and physically!"

Amarelle groaned. "Back to the lawn?"

"Back to the lawn, my dear!"

## 11. After Amarelle, the Deluge

Twenty-seven days later, one of the natural storms of summer blew in from the west, a churning shroud of dark clouds looking for a brawl. As usual, the wizards of parliament preserved their individual territories and let the rest of Theradane fend for itself. It was therefore theoretically plausible that the elevated aqueduct that crossed Prosperity Street just north of Limping Matron Lane would choose that night to break under the strain.

Prosperity Street was already contending with plugs of debris clogging its sewer grates (these plugs granted unusual thickness and persistence by the spells of Sophara Miris) and with its own valley-like position at the foot of several more elevated neighborhoods. The foaming rush from the broken aqueduct turned a boot-soaking stream into a rather more alarming waist-high river.

Amarelle and her crew lurked in artificial shadows on a high rooftop, dutifully watching to ensure that no one, particularly children and goblins, suffered more than a soaking from the flood. The city hydromancers would eventually show up to set things right, but they were no doubt having a busy night.

"This is still a touch metaphysical, if you ask me," said Sophara.

"It's something of a hybrid approach," said Amarelle. "After all, how can it be a street if it's been physically turned into a canal?"


## 12. No

"No," said Ivovandas. Amarelle was returned to the lawn.


## 13. Instructive Measures

Half a year gone. Despite vandalism, riot, werejackals, clerical errors, and flood, Prosperity Street was more worthy of its name than ever. Amarelle strolled the pavement, feeling the autumn sun on her face, admiring the pale bronze leaves of Prayer-trees as they tumbled about in little clouds, inscribed with calligraphic benedictions for anyone whose path they crossed.

There was a stir in the crowds around her, a new cacophony of shouting and muttering and horse-hooves and creaking wheels. Traffic parted to the north, making way for a rumbling coach, half again as high and wide as anything on the street. It was black as death's asshole, windowless, trimmed with engraved silver and inlaid nacre. It had no horses and no driver; each of its four wheels was a circular steel cage in which a slavering red-eyed ghoul ran on four limbs, creating a forward impetus.

The singular coach moaned on its suspension as it swerved and lurched to a halt beside Amarelle. The ghouls leered at her, unbreathing, their flesh crisply necrotic like rice paper pressed over old oozing wounds. The black door flew open and a footstep fell into place. A velvet curtain still fluttered in the entrance to the coach, concealing whatever lay inside. A voice called out, cold as chloroform and old shame.

"Don't you know an invitation when you see one, citizen Parathis?"

Running from wizards in broad daylight without preparation was not a skill Amarelle had ever cultivated, so she stepped boldly into the carriage, ducking her head.

She was startled to find herself in a warm gray space at least forty yards on a side, with a gently curving ceiling lit by floating silver lights. A vast mechanical apparatus was ticking and pulsing and shifting in the middle of the room, something along the lines of an orrery, but in place of moons and planets the thin arms held likenesses of men and women, likenesses carved with exaggerated features and comical flaws. Amarelle recognized one of them as Ivovandas by the gold eyes and butterfly hair.

There were thirteen figures, and they moved in complex interlocking patterns around a model of the city of Theradane.

The carriage door slammed shut behind her. There was no sensation of motion, other than the almost-hypnotic sway and swing of the wizard-orrery.

"My peers," said the cold voice, coming now from behind her. "Like celestial bodies, transiting in their orbits, exerting their influences. Like celestial bodies, not particularly difficult to track or predict in their motions."

Amarelle turned and gasped. The man was short and lithe, his skin like ebony, his hair scrapped down to a reddish stubble. There was a scar on his chin and another on his jawline, each of them familiar to her fingers and lips. Only the eyes were wrong; they were poisoner's eyes, dead as glass.

"You have no fucking right to that face," said Amarelle, fighting not to shout.

"Scavius of Shadow Street, isn't it? Or more like 'wasn't it?' Came with you to Theradane, but we never got his sanctuary money. Blew it in some dramatic gesture, I recall."

"He got drunk and lost it all on a dice throw," she said, wetting her lips and forcing herself to say: "Jarrow."

"Pleased to meet you, Amarelle Parathis." The man wore a simple black jacket and breeches. He extended a hand, which she didn't take. "Lost it all on one throw? That was stupid."

"I'm not unacquainted with drunken mistakes myself," said Amarelle.

"And then he went and did something even more stupid," said Jarrow. "Earned a criminal's apotheosis. Transfigured into a street lamp."

"Please… take some other form."

"No." Jarrow scratched his head, shook a finger at her. "That's a fine starting point for the discussion I really brought you here for, Amarelle. Let's talk about behavior that might get someone transfigured into a street decoration."

"I'm retired."

"Sure, kid. Look, there's a very old saying in my family: 'Once is happenstance. Twice is coincidence. Three times is another wizard fucking with you.' You never spent much time near Prosperity Street before, did you? Your apartments are on Hellendal. South of Tanglewing Street. Right?"

"About the location of my apartments, of course."

"You've got iron in your spine, Amarelle, and I'm not here to prolong this or embarrass you. I'm just suggesting, to the room, if you like, that it would be a shame if any more unusual phenomena befell a part of Theradane that is of particular sentimental value to me. This is what your sanctuary money gets you. This is me being kind. Are you pretending to listen, or are you listening?"

"I'm listening."

"Here's a little something to further sharpen your hearing." A burlap sack appeared in Jarrow's hands and he threw it to her. It weighed about ten pounds, and the contents rattled. "The usual verification that I'm serious. You know how it works. Anyhow, in the best of all possible worlds, we never have to have a conversation like this again. What world do you want to live in, Amarelle Parathis?"

The air grew cold. The lights dimmed and receded into the corners of the room, vanishing like stars behind clouds. Amarelle's stomach tumbled, and then her boots were on pavement, the sound of traffic was all around her, and Prayer-tree leaves brushed her face.

The sun was high and warm, and the black coach was nowhere in sight.

Amarelle shook the sack open and cursed as Shraplin's head tumbled out. The edges of the pipes running out of his neck were burnt and bent.

"I don't know what to say, boss." His voice was steady but weak. "I'm embarrassed. I got jumped last night."

"What the hell did they do?"

"Nothing technically illegal, boss. They left my head and the contents intact. As for the rest, let's just say I don't expect to see it again."

"I'm sorry, Shraplin. I'll get you to Brandwin. I'm so sorry."

"Quit apologizing, boss." Something whirred and clunked behind the automaton's eyes, and he gave a garbled moan. "But I have to say, my reverence for these high-level wizard types is speeding in what you might call a southerly direction."

"We need more help," whispered Amarelle. "If we're going to put the boot to this mess, I think it's high time we got the whole band back together."

## 14. The Unretirement of Jadetongue Squirn

She was tall for a goblin, not that that meant anything to most other species. Her scales were like black glass, her eyes like the sudden plunge to blue depths beyond a continental shelf. Her pointed ears were pierced with silver rings, some of which held writing quills she could reach up and seize at leisure.

They all went together to see her in her shadowed cloister at the Theradane Ministry of Finance and Provision, a place that stank of steady habits, respectability, and workers who'd died at their desks with empty in-boxes. She was not best pleased to receive them.

"We're not what we were!" Jade hissed when Amarelle had finished telling most of the story, safely inside the goblin's office and Sophara's sound-proof bubble. "Look at you! Look at the messes you've made! And look at me. How can I possibly help you? I'm an ink-stained functionary these days. I scribe ordinances and design engravings for bank notes."

Amarelle stared at her, biting her lip. Jadetongue Squirn had been jailed six times and escaped six times. You could walk nearly around the world by setting foot only in nations that still sought her for trial. Smuggler, negotiator, procurer of bizarre supplies, she was also the finest forger Amarelle had ever met, capable of memorizing signatures at a glance and reproducing them with either hand.

"We've missed you at our drinking nights," said Brandwin. "You were always welcome. You were always *wanted.*"

"I don't belong anymore." Amarelle's voice was flat and she clung to her desk as though it could be a wall between herself and her old comrades. "I'm like a hermit crab that's pulled an office over itself. Maybe the rest of you were only kidding yourselves about retiring, but I'm the real thing. I haven't been coming out to see you because you'd expect Jadetongue Squirn, not this timid little person who wears her clothes."

"We're like a hand with a missing finger," said Amarelle. "We've got half a year to make three hundred yards of street vanish and we need that slick green brain of yours. You said it yourself—look at what a mess we've made so far! Look what Jarrow did to Shraplin."

Amarelle reached into a leather satchel. The automaton's head bounced on Jadetongue's desk a moment later, and she made a rattling noise in her throat.

"Ha ha! The look on your face!" said Shraplin.

"How about the look on *yours*, duncebucket?" she growled. "I ought to stuff you in a drawer for scaring me like that!"

"You see now why we have to have you back," said Amarelle. "Shraplin's the warning. Our next shot has to be for keeps."

"Three funny bitches and a smart-ass automaton sans ass," said Jade. "You think you can just walk in here, tug on my heartstrings, and snatch me out of my sad retirement."

"Yes," said Amarelle.

"We're still not what we were." She put a scaly hand on Shraplin's face, then spun him like a top. "I'm definitely not what I was. But what the hell. Maybe you're right, about needing help, at least."

"So, are you going to take a leave of absence or something?" said Shraplin, when he'd stopped saying "Whaaaaargabaarrrrrgggh!"

"A leave of absence? Are you sure you didn't damage the contents of your head?" Jadetongue glanced around at all the members of the crew. "Sweethearts, softskins, thimblewits, if you're determined to see this thing through, the municipal bureaucracy of Theradane is the *last* asset you want to toss carelessly over your shoulder!"

## 15. Honest Business

"I haven't asked you for anything to assist us in this whole affair," said Amarelle. "Not once. Now that needs to change."

"I'm not averse in theory to small favors," said Ivovandas, "given that the potential reward for your ultimate success is so personally tantalizing. But do understand, most of my magical resources are currently committed. Nor will I do anything overt enough to harden Jarrow's suspicions. He has the same authority to kill you outright that I do, if he can prove your violation of your sanctuary terms to our peers."

"We're starting a business," Said Amarelle. "The High Barrens Reclamation Consortium. We need you to sign on as the principal stakeholder."

"Why?"

"Because nobody can sue you." Amarelle pulled a packet of paper out of her coat and set them on Ivovandas' desk. "We need a couple of wagons and about a dozen workers. We'll provide those. We're going to excavate wrecked mansions in the High Barrens on days when you and Jarrow aren't blasting at each other."

"Again, why?"

"There's some things we need to take," said Amarelle with a smile, "and some things we need to hide. If we do it in our names, the heirs of all the families that ran like hell when you settled here and started shooting at other wizards will line up in court to stop us. If you're the one in charge, they can't do a damned thing."

"I will examine these papers," said Ivovandas. "I will have them returned to you if I deem the arrangement suitable."

Amarelle found herself on the lawn. But three days later, the papers appeared in her apartments, signed and notarized. The High Barrens Reclamation Consortium went to work.

The Parliament of Strife ruled Theradane absolutely but were profoundly disinterested in the mundane business of cleaning the streets and sorting the paperwork. That much they left to their city's strangely feudal and secretive bureaucracy, who were essentially free to do as they pleased so long as the hedges were trimmed and the damage from the continual wizard feuding was repaired. Jade worked efficiently from within this edifice. She pushed through all the requisite paperwork, forged or purchased the essential permits, swept all the mandated delays and hearings under the rug, and then stepped on the rug.

Brandwin hired their crew, a dozen stout men and women. They were paid the going wage for their work, that much again for the occasional danger of proximity to Ivovandas' battles, and a triple portion for keeping their mouths shut. For a week or two they excavated carefully in the wreckage of once-mighty houses, concealing whatever they took from the ruins beneath tarps on their wagons.

Next, Brandwin and Shraplin spent a week refurbishing a trio of wagons as mobile vending carts. They extended wooden skirts around them to the ground, installed folding awnings and sturdy roofs, carved signs and painted them attractively. One of the wagons was kitted out as a book stall, the other two as food carts.

The labyrinth of bribes and permits needed to launch this sort of venture was even more daunting than the one that had preceded the excavation company. Jade outdid herself, weaving blackmail and intimidation into a tapestry of efficient palm-greasing. Whether the permit placards that hung from the vending carts were genuine articles or perfect copies was ultimately irrelevant. No procedural complication survived first contact with Jade's attention.

With four months remaining, Amarelle and Sophara went into legitimate business for themselves. Amarelle peddled books on Prosperity Street until noon, while Sophara plied her precision sorcery for appreciative breakfast crowds on Galban Street. She cooked frosted walnut cakes into the shape of unicorns and cockatrices, caused fresh fruit to squeeze itself into juice glasses, and made her figs and dates give rude speeches while her customers tried to eat them and laugh at the same time. In the afternoon, she and Amarelle switched places.

Some days, Brandwin would operate the third vending cart, offering sweets and beer, but for some time she was absorbed in a number of demanding modifications to Shraplin's body and limbs. These modifications remained hidden in the darkness of her workshop; Shraplin never went out in public wearing anything but one of his ordinary bodies.

One bright day on Prosperity Street, a stray breeze blew one of Amarelle's books open and fluttered its pages. She moved to close it and was startled to find a detailed grayscale engraving of Scavius' face staring up at her from the top page.

"Amarelle," said the illustration. "You seem to have an unexpected literary sideline."

"Can't practice my former trade," she said through gritted teeth. "Money's getting tight."

"So you're exploring new avenues, eh? New avenues? Not even a smile? Well, fine, have it your way. I ought to snuff you, you realize. I don't know who or what prompted the weirdness of the previous few months—"

Amarelle fanned the pages of the book vindictively. The illustration flashed past on each one, and continued talking smoothly when Amarelle gave up.

"…but the wisest and cleverest thing would be to turn your bones to molten glass and take no chances. Alas, I need evidence of wrongdoing. Can't just blast sanctuary tithers. People might stop giving us large piles of treasure for the privilege."

"My business partners and I are engaged in boring, legitimate commerce," said Amarelle.

"I know. I've been peeking up your skirts, as it were. Very boring. I thought we ought to have a final word, though. A little reminder that you should stay boring, or I can think of one story that won't have a happy ending."

The book slammed itself shut. Amarelle exhaled slowly, rubbed her eyes, and went back to work.

On the days wore, on the legitimate business went. The women began to move their vending carts more frequently, investing some of their profits in small mechanical equines to make this work easier.

With three months left in the contract, the carts that moved up and down Prosperity Street began to cross paths with carts from elsewhere in the city in a complicated dance that always ended with an unmarked High Barrens Reclamation Consortium wagon paying a quiet evening visit to one of the mansions they were excavating.

Another two months passed, and there was no spot on Prosperity Street that Amarelle or Sophara or Brandwin had not staked out at least temporarily, no merchant they hadn't come to know by name, no constable they hadn't thoroughly pacified with free food, good beer, and occasional gifts of books.

Three days before the contract was due to expire, a loud explosion shook the north end of Prosperity Street, breaking windows and knocking pedestrians to the curb. A mansion in a private court was found burning, already collapsing into itself. A huge black coach lay wrecked in the drive, its ghoul-cage wheels torn open, its roof smashed, its insides revealing nothing but well-upholstered seats and a carpeted floor.

The next day, Amarelle Parathis was politely summoned to the manse of the wizard Ivovandas.

## 16. Bottled Malady

"Am I satisfied? Satisfaction is a palliative," said Ivovandas, gold-threaded teeth blazing with reflected light, butterflies fluttering furiously. "Satisfaction is mild wine. Satisfaction is a tiny fraction of what I feel. Delight and fulfillment pounding in my breast like triumphant chords! Seventy years of unprofitable disdain from this face-changing reprobate, and now his misery is mine to contemplate at leisure."

"I'm so pleased you were able to crush him," said Amarelle. "Did you manage to get home in time for your tea afterward?"

The golden wizard ignored her and kept staring at the glass cylinder on her desk. It was six inches tall and half as wide, capped with a ground-glass stopper and sealed with wax the color of dried blood. Inside it was wretched Jarrow, shrunken to a suitable proportion and clad in rags. He had reverted (or been forced into) the shape of a cadaverous pale man with a silver-black beard.

"Jarrow," she sighed. "Jarrow. Oh, the laws of proportion and symmetry are restored to operation between us; my sustained pleasure balanced accurately against your lingering discomfort and demise."

"So obviously," said Amarelle, "you consider me to have stolen Prosperity Street in accordance with the contract?"

Jarrow pounded furiously against the glass.

"Oh, obviously, dear Amarelle, you've acquitted yourself splendidly! Yet the street is still there, is it not? Still carrying traffic, still hosting commerce. Before I retrieve your blue crystal, are you of a mind to indulge my former colleague and I with an explanation?"

"Delighted," said Amarelle. "After all our other approaches failed, we decided to try the painstakingly literal. Prosperity Street is roughly three thousand, one hundred and seventy square yards of brick and stone surface. The question we asked ourselves was: who *really* looks at each brick and each stone?"

"Certainly not poor Jarrow," said Ivovandas, "else he'd not find his bottle about to join my collection."

"We resolved to physically steal every single square yard of Prosperity

Street, every brick and stone," said Amarelle. "Which yielded three problems. First, how to do so without anyone noticing the noise and tumult of our work? Second, how to do so without anyone objecting to the stripped and uneven mess made of the street in our wake? Third, how to provide the physical labor to handle the sheer volume and tedium of the task?"

"To answer the second point first, we used the High Barrens Restoration Consortium. They carefully fished through the mansions you two have destroyed in your feud to provide us with all the bricks and stones we could ever need.

"A large hollow space was constructed beneath each of our vending carts, which we first plied up and down assorted city streets, not just Prosperity, for an *interminable* length of time to allay suspicion that they were directly aimed at Jarrow's locus."

Jarrow banged his head repeatedly against the inside of his prison.

"Eventually we felt it was safe to proceed with our real business. The rest you must surely have guessed by now. The labor was provided by Shraplin, an automaton, whose meeting with Jarrow left him very eager to bear any trouble or tedium in the cause of his revenge. Shraplin utilized tool-arms custom-forged for him by Brandwin Miris to dig up the bricks and stones of the actual street, and to lay in their place the bricks and stones taken from the High Barrens mansions. At night, the detritus he'd scraped up by day was dumped into the ruins of those same mansions. As for why nobody ever heard Shraplin scraping or pounding away beneath our carts, all I can say is that our magician is highly adept at the production of sound-proof barriers to fit any space or need.

"All that was left to do," said Amarelle, stretching and yawning, "was to spend the months necessary to carefully position our carts over every square foot of Prosperity Street. Nobody ever noticed that when we moved on, the patches of street beneath us had changed subtly from the hour or two before. Eventually, we pried up the last brick that was genuinely important, and Jarrow's locus became just another city lane."

"Help me!" Jarrow cried, his voice high and faint as a whisper in the wind. "Get me away from her! I can be him for you! I can be Scavius! I can be anyone you want!"

"Enough from you, I think." Ivovandas slid his prison lovingly into a desk drawer, still smiling. She curled her fingers, and a familiar blue crystal appeared within them.

"You have suffered quite tenaciously for this," said Ivovandas. "I give it to you now as my half of our bargain, fairly begun and fairly concluded."

Amarelle took the glowing crystal and crushed it beneath her heel.

"Is that the end of it?" she said. "All restored to harmonious equipoise? I go on my way and leave you to your next few years of conversation with Jarrow?"

"In a manner of speaking," said Ivovandas. "While I have dutifully disposed of the crystal recording from last year's intemperate drunken visitation, I have just now secured an even more entertaining one in which you confess at length to crimes carried out in Theradane and implicate several of your friends by name."

"Yes," said Amarelle. "I did rather expect something like this. I figured that since I was likely to eat more treachery, I might as well have an appreciative audience first."

"I am the *most* appreciative audience! Oh, we could be so good for one another! Consider, Amarelle, the very reasonable bounds of my desires and expectations. I fancy myself fairly adept at identifying the loci in use by my colleagues. With Jarrow removed, there will be a rebalancing of the alliances in our parliament. There will be new testing and new struggles. I shall be watching very, very carefully, and inevitably I expect to have another target for you and your friends to secure on my behalf."

"You want to use us to knock off the Parliament of Strife, locus by locus" said Amarelle. "Until it's something more like the Parliament of Ivovandas."

"It might not happen in your lifetime," said the wizard. "But substantial progress could be at hand! In the meantime, I'll be quite content to let you remain at liberty in the city, enjoying your sanctuary, doing as you please. So long as you and your friends come when I call. Doubt not that I shall call."

## 17. The Work Ahead

Amarelle met them afterward on the Tanglewing Bridge, in the pleasant purple light of fading sunset. The city was quiet, the High Barrens peaceful, no fires falling from the clouds or screeching things sinking claws into one another.

They gathered in an arc in front of Scavius' statue. Sophara muttered and gestured with her fingers.

"We're in the bubble," she said. "Nobody can hear us, or even see us unless I... shut *up*, Scavius, I know you can hear us. You're a special case. How did it go down, Amarelle?"

"It went down like we expected," said Amarelle. "*Exactly* like we expected."

"I told you those kinds of sorcerers are all reflexively treacherous bags of nuts," said Sophara. "What's her game?"

"She wants us on an unpaid retainer so she can dig up the loci of more of her colleagues and send us after them."

"Sounds like a good way to kill some time, boss." Shraplin wound a crank on his chest, re-synchronizing some mechanism that had picked up a slight rattle. "I could stand to knock over a few more of those assholes. She'd save us a lot of work if she identified the loci for us."

"Couldn't agree more," said Sophara. "Now hold still."

She ran her fingers through Amarelle's hair, and after a few moments of searching carefully plucked out a single curling black strand.

"There's my little spy," said Sophara. "I'm glad you brought me that one Ivovandas planted on you, Am. I never would have learned how to make these things so subtle if I hadn't been able to pry that one apart."

"Do you think it will tell you enough?" said Brandwin.

"I honestly doubt it." Sophara slipped the hair into a wallet and smiled. "But it'll give me a good look at everything Amarelle was allowed to see, and that's much better than nothing. If we can identify her patterns and her habits, the bitch will eventually start painting clues for us as to the location of her own locus."

"Splat!" said Brandwin.

"Yeah," said Sophara. "And that's definitely my idea of a playground."

"I should be able to get some messages out of the city," said Jadetongue. "Some of the people we've got howling for our blood hate the Parliament of Strife even more. If we could make arrangements with them before we knock those wizards down, I'd bet we could buy our way back into the world. Theradane sanctuary in reverse, at least in a few places."

"I like the way you people think," said Amarelle. "Ivovandas as a stalking horse, and once we've got the goods on her we dump her ass in the river. Her and all her friends. Who's got the wine?"

Jade held out the bottle, something carnelian and bioluminescent and expensive. They passed it around, and even Shraplin dashed a ceremonial swig against his chin. Amarelle turned with the half-empty bottle and faced Scavius' statue.

"Here it is, you asshole. I guess we're not as retired as we might have thought. Five thieves going to war against the Parliament of Strife. Insane. The kind of odds you always loved best. Will you try to think better of us? And if you can't, will you at least keep a few pedestals warm? We might have a future as street lamps after all. Have one on us."

She smashed the bottle against his plaque, and they watched the glowing, fizzing wine run down the marble. After a few moments, Sophara and Brandwin walked away arm in arm, north toward Tanglewing Street. Shraplin followed, then Jade.

Amarelle alone remained in the white light of whatever was left of Scavius. What he whispered to her then, she kept to herself.

She ran to catch up with the others.

"Hey," said Jade. "Glad you're back! You coming to the Sign of the Fallen Fire with us? We're going to have a game."

"Yeah," said Amarelle, and the air of Theradane tasted better than it had in months. "Hell *yeah* we're going to have a game!"

---

Scott Lynch is the author of four novels in the Gentleman Bastard sequence. *The Lies of Locke Lamora* (2007) was a World Fantasy, British Fantasy, Crawford, Compton Crook, and Locus first novel finalist; its sequels are *Red Seas Under Red Skies* (2007), the New York Times best-selling *The Republic of Thieves* (2013), and the forthcoming *The Thorn of Emberlain*. His short fiction has appeared in *Popular Science, Swords and Dark Magic, Tales of the Far West, Fearsome Journeys,* and *Rogues*. He was a Campbell Best New Writer finalist for 2006 and 2007, and won the British Fantasy Award for best newcomer in 2008. He currently lives in Wisconsin, where he has been a volunteer firefighter since 2005. He shares a commuting relationship with his Massachusetts-based partner, author Elizabeth Bear.

# The Regular
## By Ken Liu

"This is Jasmine," she says.

"It's Robert."

The voice on the phone is the same as the one she had spoken to earlier in the afternoon.

"Glad you made it, sweetie." She looks out the window. He's standing at the corner, in front of the convenience store as she asked. He looks clean and is dressed well, like he's going on a date. A good sign. He's also wearing a Red Sox cap pulled low over his brow, a rather amateurish attempt at anonymity. "I'm down the street from you, at 27 Moreland. It's the gray stone condo building converted from a church."

He turns to look. "You have a sense of humor."

They all make that joke, but she laughs anyway. "I'm in unit 24, on the second floor."

"Is it just you? I'm not going to see some linebacker type demanding that I pay him first?"

"I told you. I'm independent. Just have your donation ready and you'll have a good time."

She hangs up and takes a quick look in the mirror to be sure she's ready. The black stockings and garter belt are new, and the lace bustier accentuates her thin waist and makes her breasts seem larger. She's done her makeup lightly, but the eye shadow is heavy to emphasize her eyes. Most of her customers like that. Exotic.

The sheets on the king-size bed are fresh, and there's a small wicker basket of condoms on the nightstand, next to a clock that says "5:58." The date is for two hours, and afterwards she'll have enough time to clean up and shower and then sit in front of the TV to catch her favorite show. She thinks about calling her mom later that night to ask about how to cook porgy.

She opens the door before he can knock, and the look on his face tells her that she's done well. He slips in; she closes the door, leans against it, and smiles at him.

"You're even prettier than the picture in your ad," he says. He gazes into her eyes intently. "Especially the eyes."

"Thank you."

As she gets a good look at him in the hallway, she concentrates on her right eye and blinks rapidly twice. She doesn't think she'll ever need it, but a girl has to protect herself. If she ever stops doing this, she thinks she'll just have it taken out and thrown into the bottom of Boston Harbor, like the way she used to, as a little girl, write secrets down on bits of paper, wad them up, and flush them down the toilet.

He's good looking in a non-memorable way: over six feet, tanned skin, still has all his hair, and the body under that crisp shirt looks fit. The eyes are friendly and kind, and she's pretty sure he won't be too rough. She guesses that he's in his forties, and maybe works downtown in one of the law firms or financial services companies, where his long-sleeved shirt and dark pants make sense with the air conditioning always turned high. He has that entitled arrogance that many mistake for masculine attractiveness. She notices that there's a paler patch of skin around his ring finger. Even better. A married man is usually safer. A married man who doesn't want her to know he's married is the safest of all: he values what he has and doesn't want to lose it.

She hopes he'll be a regular.

"I'm glad we're doing this." He holds out a plain white envelope.

She takes it and counts the bills inside. Then she puts it on top of the stack of mail on a small table by the entrance without saying anything. She takes him by the hand and leads him towards the bedroom. He pauses to look in the bathroom and then the other bedroom at the end of the hall.

"Looking for your linebacker?" she teases.

"Just making sure. I'm a nice guy."

He takes out a scanner and holds it up, concentrating on the screen.

"Geez, you *are* paranoid," she says. "The only camera in here is the one on my phone. And it's definitely off."

He puts the scanner away and smiles. "I know. But I just wanted to have a machine confirm it."

They enter the bedroom. She watches him take in the bed, the bottles of lubricants and lotions on the dresser, and the long mirrors covering the closet doors next to the bed.

"Nervous?" she asks.

"A little," he concedes. "I don't do this often. Or, at all."

She comes up to him and embraces him, letting him breathe in her perfume, which is floral and light so that it won't linger on his skin. After a moment, he puts his arms around her, resting his hands against the naked skin on the small of her back.

"I've always believed that one should pay for experiences rather than things."

"A good philosophy," he whispers into her ear.

"What I give you is the girlfriend experience, old fashioned and sweet. And you'll remember this and relive it in your head as often as you want."

"You'll do whatever I want?"

"Within reason," she says. Then she lifts her head to look up at him. "You have to wear a condom. Other than that, I won't say no to most things. But like I told you on the phone, for some you'll have to pay extra."

"I'm pretty old-fashioned myself. Do you mind if I take charge?"

He's made her relaxed enough that she doesn't jump to the worst conclusion. "If you're thinking of tying me down, that will cost you. And I won't do that until I know you better."

"Nothing like that. Maybe hold you down a little."

"That's fine."

He comes up to her and they kiss. His tongue lingers in her mouth and she moans. He backs up, puts his hands on her waist, turning her away from him. "Would you lie down with your face in the pillows?"

"Of course." She climbs onto the bed. "Legs up under me or spread out to the corners?"

"Spread out, please." His voice is commanding. And he hasn't stripped yet, not even taken off his Red Sox cap. She's a little disappointed. Some clients enjoy the obedience more than the sex. There's not much for her to do. She just hopes he won't be too rough and leave marks.

He climbs onto the bed behind her and knee-walks up between her legs. He leans down and grabs a pillow from next to her head. "Very lovely," he says. "I'm going to hold you down now."

She sighs into the bed, the way she knows he'll like.

He lays the pillow over the back of her head and pushes down firmly to hold her in place. He takes the gun out from the small of his back, and in one swift motion, sticks the barrel, thick and long with the silencer, into the back of the bustier, and squeezes off two quick shots into her heart. She dies instantly.

He removes the pillow, stores the gun away. Then he takes a small steel surgical kit out of his jacket pocket, along with a pair of latex gloves. He works efficiently and quickly, cutting with precision and grace. He relaxes when he's found what he's looking for; sometimes he picks the wrong girl—not often, but it has happened. He's careful to wipe off any sweat on his face with his sleeves as he works, and the hat helps to prevent any hair from falling on her. Soon, the task is done.

He climbs off the bed, takes off the bloody gloves, and leaves them and the surgical kit on the body. He puts on a fresh pair of gloves and moves through the apartment, methodically searching for places where she hid cash: inside the toilet tank, the back of the freezer, the nook above the door of the closet.

He goes into the kitchen and returns with a large plastic trash bag. He picks up the bloody gloves and the surgical kit and throws them into the bag. Picking up her phone, he presses the button for her voicemail. He deletes all the messages, including the one he had left when he first called her number. There's not much he can do about the call logs at the phone company, but he can take advantage of that by leaving his prepaid phone somewhere for the police to find.

He looks at her again. He's not sad, not exactly, but he does feel a sense of waste. The girl was pretty and he would have liked to enjoy her first, but that would leave behind too many traces, even with a condom. And he can always pay for another, later. He likes paying for things. Power flows to *him* when he pays.

Reaching into the inner pocket of his jacket, he retrieves a sheet of paper, which he carefully unfolds and leaves by the girl's head.

He stuffs the trash bag and the money into a small gym bag he found in one of the closets. He leaves quietly, picking up the envelope of cash next to the entrance on the way out.

• • • •

Because she's meticulous, Ruth Law runs through the numbers on the spreadsheet one last time, a summary culled from credit card and bank statements, and compares them against the numbers on the tax return. There's no doubt. The client's husband has been hiding money from the IRS, and more importantly, from the client.

Summers in Boston can be brutally hot. But Ruth keeps the air conditioner off in her tiny office above a butcher shop in Chinatown. She's made a lot of people unhappy over the years, and there's no reason to make it any easier for them to sneak up on her with the extra noise.

She takes out her cell phone and starts to dial from memory. She never stores any numbers in the phone. She tells people it's for safety, but sometimes she wonders if it's a gesture, however small, of asserting her independence from machines.

She stops at the sound of someone coming up the stairs. The footfalls are crisp and dainty, probably a woman, probably one with sensible heels. The scanner in the stairway hasn't been set off by the presence of a weapon, but that doesn't mean anything—she can kill without a gun or knife, and so can many others.

Ruth deposits her phone noiselessly on the desk and reaches into her drawer to wrap the fingers of her right hand around the reassuring grip of the Glock 19. Only then does she turn slightly to the side to glance at the monitor showing the feed from the security camera mounted over the door.

She feels very calm. The Regulator is doing its job. There's no need to release any adrenaline yet.

The visitor, in her fifties, is in a blue short-sleeve cardigan and white pants. She's looking around the door for a button for the doorbell. Her hair is so black that it must be dyed. She looks Chinese, holding her thin, petite body in a tight, nervous posture.

Ruth relaxes and lets go of the gun to push the button to open the door. She stands up and holds out her hand. "What can I do for you?"

"Are you Ruth Law, the private investigator?" In the woman's accent Ruth hears traces of Mandarin rather than Cantonese or Fukienese. Probably not well-connected in Chinatown then.

"I am."

The woman looks surprised, as if Ruth isn't quite who she expected. "Sarah Ding. I thought you were Chinese."

As they shake hands Ruth looks Sarah level in the eyes: they're about the same height, five foot four. Sarah looks well maintained, but her fingers feel cold and thin, like a bird's claw.

"I'm half-Chinese," Ruth says. "My father was Cantonese, second generation; my mother was white. My Cantonese is barely passable, and I never learned Mandarin."

Sarah sits down in the armchair across from Ruth's desk. "But you have an office here."

She shrugs. "I've made my enemies. A lot of non-Chinese are uncomfortable moving around in Chinatown. They stick out. So it's safer for me to have my office here. Besides, you can't beat the rent."

Sarah nods wearily. "I need your help with my daughter." She slides a collapsible file across the desk towards her.

Ruth sits down but doesn't reach for the file. "Tell me about her."

"Mona was working as an escort. A month ago she was shot and killed in her apartment. The police think it's a robbery, maybe gang-related, and they have no leads."

"It's a dangerous profession," Ruth says. "Did you know she was doing it?"

"No. Mona had some difficulties after college, and we were never as close as … I would have liked. We thought she was doing better the last two years, and she told us she had a job in publishing. It's difficult to know your child when you can't be the kind of mother she wants or needs. This country has different rules."

Ruth nods. A familiar lament from immigrants. "I'm sorry for your loss. But it's unlikely I'll be able to do anything. Most of my cases now are about hidden assets, cheating spouses, insurance fraud, background checks—that sort of thing. Back when I was a member of the force, I did work in Homicide. I know the detectives are quite thorough in murder cases."

"They're not!" Fury and desperation strain and crack her voice. "They think she's just a Chinese whore, and she died because she was stupid or got involved with a Chinese gang who wouldn't bother regular people. My husband is so ashamed that he won't even mention her name. But she's my daughter, and she's worth everything I have, and more."

Ruth looks at her. She can feel the Regulator suppressing her pity. Pity can lead to bad business decisions.

"I keep on thinking there was some sign I should have seen, some way to tell her that I loved her that I didn't know. If only I had been a little less busy, a little more willing to pry and dig and to be hurt by her. I can't stand

THE LONG LIST ANTHOLOGY

the way the detectives talk to me, like I'm wasting their time but they don't want to show it."

Ruth refrains from explaining that the police detectives are all fitted with Regulators that should make the kind of prejudice she's implying impossible. The whole point of the Regulator is to make police work under pressure more regular, less dependent on hunches, emotional impulses, appeals to hidden prejudice. If the police are calling it a gang-related act of violence, there are likely good reasons for doing so.

She says nothing because the woman in front of her is in pain, and guilt and love are so mixed up in her that she thinks paying to find her daughter's killer will make her feel better about being the kind of mother whose daughter would take up prostitution.

Her angry, helpless posture reminds Ruth vaguely of something she tries to put out of her mind.

"Even if I find the killer," she says, "it won't make you feel better."

"I don't care." Sarah tries to shrug but the American gesture looks awkward and uncertain on her. "My husband thinks I've gone crazy. I know how hopeless this is; you're not the first investigator I've spoken to. But a few suggested you because you're a woman and Chinese, so maybe you care just enough to see something they can't."

She reaches into her purse and retrieves a check, sliding it across the table to put on top of the file. "Here's eighty thousand dollars. I'll pay double your daily rate and all expenses. If you use it up, I can get you more."

Ruth stares at the check. She thinks about the sorry state of her finances. At forty-nine, how many more chances will she have to set aside some money for when she'll be too old to do this?

She still feels calm and completely rational, and she knows that the Regulator is doing its job. She's sure that she's making her decision based on costs and benefits and a realistic evaluation of the case, and not because of the hunched over shoulders of Sarah Ding, looking like fragile twin dams holding back a flood of grief.

"Okay," she says. "Okay."

. . . .

The man's name isn't Robert. It's not Paul or Matt or Barry either. He never uses the name John because jokes like that will only make the girls nervous. A long time ago, before he had been to prison, they had called him the Watcher because he liked to observe and take in a scene, finding the best opportunities and escape routes. He still thinks of himself that way when he's alone.

In the room he's rented at the cheap motel along Route 128, he starts his day by taking a shower to wash off the night sweat.

This is the fifth motel he's stayed in during the last month. Any stay longer than a week tends to catch the attention of the people working at the motels. He watches; he does not get watched. Ideally, he supposes he should get away from Boston altogether, but he hasn't exhausted the city's possibilities. It doesn't feel right to leave before he's seen all he wants to see.

The Watcher got about sixty thousand dollars in cash from the girl's apartment, not bad for a day's work. The girls he picks are intensely aware of the brevity of their careers, and with no bad habits, they pack away money like squirrels preparing for the winter. Since they can't exactly put it into the bank without raising the suspicion of the IRS, they tuck the money away in stashes in their apartments, ready for him to come along and claim them like found treasure.

The money is a nice bonus, but not the main attraction.

He comes out of the shower, dries himself, and wrapped in a towel, sits down to work at the nut he's trying to crack. It's a small, silver half-sphere, like half of a walnut. When he had first gotten it, it had been covered in blood and gore, and he had wiped it again and again with paper towels moistened under the motel sink until it gleamed.

He pries open an access port on the back of the device. Opening his laptop, he plugs one end of a cable into it and the other end into the half-sphere. He starts a program he had paid a good sum of money for and lets it run. It would probably be more efficient for him to leave the program running all the time, but he likes to be there to see the moment the encryption is broken.

While the program runs, he browses the escort ads. Right now he's searching for pleasure, not business, so instead of looking for girls like Jasmine, he looks for girls he craves. They're expensive, but not too expensive, the kind that remind him of the girls he had wanted back in high school: loud, fun, curvaceous now but destined to put on too much weight in a few years, a careless beauty that was all the more desirable because it was fleeting.

The Watcher knows that only a poor man like he had been at seventeen would bother courting women, trying desperately to make them like him. A man with money, with power, like he is now, can buy what he wants. There's purity and cleanliness to his desire that he feels is nobler and less deceitful than the desire of poor men. They only wish they could have what he does.

The program beeps, and he switches back to it.

Success.

Images, videos, sound recordings are being downloaded onto the computer.

The Watcher browses through the pictures and video recordings. The pictures are face shots or shots of money being handed over—he immediately deletes the ones of him.

But the videos are the best. He settles back and watches the screen flicker, admiring Jasmine's camerawork.

He separates the videos and images by client and puts them into folders. It's tedious work, but he enjoys it.

• • • •

The first thing Ruth does with the money is to get some badly needed tune-ups. Going after a killer requires that she be in top condition.

She does not like to carry a gun when she's on the job. A man in a sport coat with a gun concealed under it can blend into almost any situation, but a woman wearing the kind of clothes that would hide a gun would often stick out like a sore thumb. Keeping a gun in a purse is a terrible idea. It creates a false sense of security, but a purse can be easily snatched away and then she would be disarmed.

She's fit and strong for her age, but her opponents are almost always taller and heavier and stronger. She's learned to compensate for these disadvantages by being more alert and by striking earlier.

But it's still not enough.

She goes to her doctor. Not the one on her HMO card.

Doctor B had earned his degree in another country and then had to leave home forever because he pissed off the wrong people. Instead of doing a second residency and becoming licensed here, which would have made him easily traceable, he had decided to simply keep on practicing medicine on his own. He would do things doctors who cared about their licenses wouldn't do. He would take patients they wouldn't touch.

"It's been a while," Doctor B says.

"Check over everything," she tells him. "And replace what needs replacement."

"Rich uncle die?"

"I'm going on a hunt."

Doctor B nods and puts her under.

He checks the pneumatic pistons in her legs, the replacement composite tendons in her shoulders and arms, the power cells and artificial muscles in her arms, the reinforced finger bones. He recharges what needs to be recharged. He examines the results of the calcium-deposition treatments (a counter to the fragility of her bones, an unfortunate side effect of her Asian heritage), and makes adjustments to her Regulator so that she can keep it on for longer.

"Like new," he tells her. And she pays.

• • • •

Next, Ruth looks through the file Sarah brought.

There are photographs: the prom, high school graduation, vacations with friends, college commencement. She notes the name of the school without surprise or sorrow even though Jess had dreamed of going there as well. The Regulator, as always, keeps her equanimous, receptive to information, only useful information.

The last family photo Sarah selected was taken at Mona's twenty-fourth birthday earlier in the year. Ruth examines it carefully. In the picture, Mona is seated between Sarah and her husband, her arms around her parents in a gesture of careless joy. There's no hint of the secret she was keeping from them, and no sign, as far as Ruth can tell, of bruises, drugs, or other indications that life was slipping out of her control.

Sarah had chosen the photos with care. The pictures are designed to fill in Mona's life, to make people care for her. But she didn't need to do that. Ruth would have given it the same amount of effort even if she knew nothing about the girl's life. She's a professional.

There's a copy of the police report and the autopsy results. The report mostly confirms what Ruth has already guessed: no sign of drugs in Mona's systems, no forced entry, no indication there was a struggle. There was pepper spray in the drawer of the nightstand, but it hadn't been used. Forensics had vacuumed the scene and the hair and skin cells of dozens, maybe hundreds, of men had turned up, guaranteeing that no useful leads will result.

Mona had been killed with two shots through the heart, and then her body had been mutilated, with her eyes removed. She hadn't been sexually assaulted. The apartment had been ransacked of cash and valuables.

Ruth sits up. The method of killing is odd. If the killer had intended to mutilate her face anyway, there was no reason to not shoot her in the back of the head, a cleaner, surer method of execution.

A note in Chinese was found at the scene, which declared that Mona had been punished for her sins. Ruth can't read Chinese but she assumes the police translation is accurate. The police had also pulled Mona's phone records. There were a few numbers whose cell tower data showed their owners had been to Mona's place that day. The only one without an alibi was a prepaid phone without a registered owner. The police had tracked it down in Chinatown, hidden in a dumpster. They hadn't been able to get any further.

A rather sloppy kill, Ruth thinks, *if the gangs did it*.

Sarah had also provided printouts of Mona's escort ads. Mona had used several aliases: Jasmine, Akiko, Sinn. Most of the pictures are of her in lingerie, a few in cocktail dresses. The shots are framed to emphasize her body: a side view of her breasts half-veiled in lace, a back view of her buttocks, lounging on the bed with her hand over her hip. Shots of her face have black bars over her eyes to provide some measure of anonymity.

Ruth boots up her computer and logs onto the sites to check out the other ads. She had never worked in vice, so she takes a while to familiarize herself with the lingo and acronyms. The Internet had apparently transformed the business, allowing women to get off the streets and become "independent providers" without pimps. The sites are organized to allow customers to pick out exactly what they want. They can sort and filter by price, age, services provided, ethnicity, hair and eye color, time of availability, and customer ratings. The business is competitive, and there's a brutal efficiency to the sites that Ruth might have found depressing without the Regulator: you can measure, if you apply statistical software to it, how much a girl depreciates with each passing year, how much value men place on each pound, each inch of deviation from the ideal they're seeking, how much more a blonde really is worth than a brunette, and how much more a girl who can pass as Japanese can charge than one who cannot.

Some of the ad sites charge a membership fee to see pictures of the girls' faces. Sarah had also printed these "premium" photographs of Mona. For a brief moment Ruth wonders what Sarah must have felt as she paid to unveil the seductive gaze of her daughter, the daughter who had seemed to have a trouble-free, promising future.

In these pictures Mona's face was made up lightly, her lips curved in a promising or innocent smile. She was extraordinarily pretty, even compared to the other girls in her price range. She dictated in-calls only, perhaps believing them to be safer, with her being more in control.

Compared to most of the other girls, Mona's ads can be described as "elegant." They're free of spelling errors and overtly crude language, hinting at the kind of sexual fantasies that men here harbor about Asian women while also promising an American wholesomeness, the contrast emphasizing the strategically placed bits of exoticism.

The anonymous customer reviews praised her attitude and willingness to "go the extra mile." Ruth supposes that Mona had earned good tips.

Ruth turns to the crime scene photos and the bloody, eyeless shots of Mona's face. Intellectually and dispassionately, she absorbs the details in Mona's room. She contemplates the contrast between them and the eroticism of the ad photos. This was a young woman who had been vain about her education, who had believed that she could construct, through careful words and images, a kind of filter to attract the right kind of clients. It was naïve and wise at the same time, and Ruth can almost feel, despite the Regulator, a kind of poignancy to her confident desperation.

Whatever caused her to go down this path, she had never hurt anyone, and now she was dead.

• • • •

Ruth meets Luo in a room reached through long underground tunnels and many locked doors. It smells of mold and sweat and spicy foods rotting in trash bags.

Along the way she saw a few other locked rooms behind which she guessed were human cargo, people who indentured themselves to the snakeheads for a chance to be smuggled into this country so they could work for a dream of wealth. She says nothing about them. Her deal with

Luo depends on her discretion, and Luo is kinder to his cargo than many others.

He pats her down perfunctorily. She offers to strip to show that she's not wired. He waves her off.

"Have you seen this woman?" she asks in Cantonese, holding up a picture of Mona.

Luo dangles the cigarette from his lips while he examines the picture closely. The dim light gives the tattoos on his bare shoulders and arms a greenish tint. After a moment, he hands it back. "I don't think so."

"She was a prostitute working out of Quincy. Someone killed her a month ago and left this behind." She brings out the photograph of the note left at the scene. "The police think the Chinese gangs did it."

Luo looks at the photo. He knits his brow in concentration and then barks out a dry laugh. "Yes, this is indeed a note left behind by a Chinese gang."

"Do you recognize the gang?"

"Sure." Luo looks at Ruth, a grin revealing the gaps in his teeth. "This note was left behind by the impetuous Tak-Kao, member of the Forever Peace Gang, after he killed the innocent Mai-Ying, the beautiful maid from the mainland, in a fit of jealousy. You can see the original in the third season of *My Hong Kong, Your Hong Kong*. You're lucky that I'm a fan."

"This is copied from a soap opera?"

"Yes. Your man either likes to make jokes or doesn't know Chinese well and got this from some Internet search. It might fool the police, but no, we wouldn't leave a note like that." He chuckles at the thought and then spits on the ground.

"Maybe it was just a fake to confuse the police." She chooses her words carefully. "Or maybe it was done by one gang to sic the police onto the others. The police also found a phone, probably used by the killer, in a Chinatown dumpster. I know there are several Asian massage parlors in Quincy, so maybe this girl was too much competition. Are you sure you don't know anything about this?"

Luo flips through the other photographs of Mona. Ruth watches him, getting ready to react to any sudden movements. She thinks she can trust Luo, but one can't always predict the reaction of a man who often has to kill to make his living.

She concentrates on the Regulator, priming it to release adrenaline to quicken her movements if necessary. The pneumatics in her legs are charged, and she braces her back against the damp wall in case she needs to kick out. The sudden release of pressure in the air canisters installed next to her tibia will straighten her legs in a fraction of a second, generating hundreds of pounds of force. If her feet connect with Luo's chest, she will almost certainly break a few ribs—though Ruth's back will ache for days afterwards, as well.

"I like you, Ruth," Luo says, noting her sudden stillness out of the corner of his eyes. "You don't have to be afraid. I haven't forgotten how you found that bookie who tried to steal from me. I'll always tell you the truth or tell you I can't answer. We have nothing to do with this girl. She's not really competition. The men who go to massage parlors for $60 an hour and a happy ending are not the kind who'd pay for a girl like this."

• • • •

The Watcher drives to Somerville, just over the border from Cambridge, north of Boston. He parks in the back of a grocery store parking lot, where his Toyota Corolla, bought off a lot with cash, doesn't stick out.

Then he goes into a coffee shop and emerges with an iced coffee. Sipping it, he walks around the sunny streets, gazing from time to time at the little gizmo attached to his keychain. The gizmo tells him when he's in range of some unsecured home wireless network. Lots of students from Harvard and MIT live here, where the rent is high but not astronomical. Addicted to good wireless access, they often get powerful routers for tiny apartments and leak the network onto the streets without bothering to secure them (after all, they have friends coming over all the time who need to remain connected). And since it's summer, when the population of students is in flux, there's even less likelihood that he can be traced from using one of their networks.

It's probably overkill, but he likes to be safe.

He sits down on a bench by the side of the street, takes out his laptop, and connects to a network called "INFORMATION_WANTS_TO_BE_FREE." He enjoys disproving the network owner's theory. Information doesn't want to be free. It's valuable and wants to earn. And its existence doesn't free anyone; possessing it, however, can do the opposite.

The Watcher carefully selects a segment of video and watches it one last time.

Jasmine had done a good job, intentionally or not, with the framing, and the man's sweaty grimace is featured prominently in the video. His movements—and as a result, Jasmine's—made the video jerky, and so he's had to apply software image stabilization. But now it looks quite professional.

The Watcher had tried to identify the man, who looks Chinese, by uploading a picture he got from Jasmine into a search engine. They are always making advancements in facial recognition software, and sometimes he gets hits this way. But it didn't seem to work this time. That's not a problem for the Watcher. He has other techniques.

The Watcher signs on to a forum where the expat Chinese congregate to reminisce and argue politics in their homeland. He posts the picture of the man in the video and writes below in English, "Anyone famous?" Then he sips his coffee and refreshes the screen from time to time to catch the new replies.

The Watcher doesn't read Chinese (or Russian, or Arabic, or Hindi, or any of the other languages where he plies his trade), but linguistic skills are hardly necessary for this task. Most of the expats speak English and can understand his question. He's just using these people as research tools, a human flesh-powered, crowdsourced search engine. It's almost funny how people are so willing to give perfect strangers over the Internet information, would even compete with each other to do it, to show how knowledgeable they are. He's pleased to make use of such petty vanities.

He simply needs a name and a measure of the prominence of the man, and for that, the crude translations offered by computers are sufficient.

From the almost-gibberish translations, he gathers that the man is a prominent official in the Chinese Transport Ministry, and like almost all Chinese officials, he's despised by his countrymen. The man is a bigger deal than the Watcher's usual targets, but that might make him a good demonstration.

The Watcher is thankful for Dagger, who had explained Chinese politics to him. One evening, after he had gotten out of jail the last time, the Watcher had hung back and watched a Chinese man rob a few Chinese tourists near San Francisco's Chinatown.

The tourists had managed to make a call to 911, and the robber had fled the scene on foot down an alley. But the Watcher had seen something in the man's direct, simple approach that he liked. He drove around the block, stopped by the other end of the alley, and when the man emerged, he swung open the passenger side door and offered him a chance to escape in his car. The man thanked him and told him his name was Dagger.

Dagger was talkative and told the Watcher how angry and envious people in China were of the Party officials, who lived an extravagant life on the money squeezed from the common people, took bribes, and funneled public funds to their relatives. He targeted those tourists who he thought were the officials' wives and children, and regarded himself as a modern-day Robin Hood.

Yet, the officials were not completely immune. All it took was a public scandal of some kind, usually involving young women who were not their wives. Talk of democracy didn't get people excited, but seeing an official rubbing their graft in their faces made them see red. And the Party apparatus would have no choice but to punish the disgraced officials, as the only thing the Party feared was public anger, which always threatened to boil out of control. If a revolution were to come to China, Dagger quipped, it would be triggered by mistresses, not speeches.

A light had gone on in the Watcher's head then. It was as if he could see the reins of power flowing from those who had secrets to those who knew secrets. He thanked Dagger and dropped him off, wishing him well.

The Watcher imagines what the official's visit to Boston had been like. He had probably come to learn about the city's experience with light rail, but it was likely in reality just another state-funded vacation, a chance to shop at the luxury stores on Newbury Street, to enjoy expensive foods without fear of poison or pollution, and to anonymously take delight in quality female companionship without the threat of recording devices in the hands of an interested populace.

He posts the video to the forum, and as an extra flourish, adds a link to the official's biography on the Transport Ministry's web site. For a second, he regrets the forgone revenue, but it's been a while since he's done a demonstration, and these are necessary to keep the business going.

He packs up his laptop. Now he has to wait.

• • • •

Ruth doesn't think there's much value in viewing Mona's apartment, but she's learned over the years to not leave any stone unturned. She gets the key from Sarah Ding and makes her way to the apartment around 6:00 in the evening. Viewing the site at approximately the time of day when the murder occurred can sometimes be helpful.

She passes through the living room. There's a small TV facing a futon, the kind of furniture that a young woman keeps from her college days when she doesn't have a reason to upgrade. It's a living room that was never meant for visitors.

She moves into the room in which the murder happened. The forensics team has cleaned it out. The room—it wasn't Mona's real bedroom, which was a tiny cubby down the hall, with just a twin bed and plain walls—is stripped bare, most of the loose items having been collected as evidence. The mattress is naked, as are the nightstands. The carpet has been vacuumed. The place smells like a hotel room: stale air and faint perfume.

Ruth notices the line of mirrors along the side of the bed, hanging over the closet doors. Watching arouses people.

She imagines how lonely Mona must have felt living here, touched and kissed and fucked by a stream of men who kept as much of themselves hidden from her as possible. She imagines her sitting in front of the small TV to relax, and dressing up to meet her parents so that she could lie some more.

Ruth imagines the way the murderer had shot Mona, and then cut her after. Was there more than one of them so that Mona thought a struggle was useless? Did they shoot her right away or did they ask her to tell them where she had hidden her money first? She can feel the Regulator starting up again, keeping her emotions in check. Evil has to be confronted dispassionately.

She decides she's seen all she needs to see. She leaves the apartment and pulls the door closed. As she heads for the stairs, she sees a man coming up, keys in hand. Their eyes briefly meet, and he turns to the door of the apartment across the hall.

Ruth is sure the police have interviewed the neighbor. But sometimes people will tell things to a nonthreatening woman that they are reluctant to tell the cops.

She walks over and introduces herself, explaining that she's a friend of Mona's family, here to tie up some loose ends. The man, whose name is Peter, is wary but shakes her hand.

"I didn't hear or see anything. We pretty much keep to ourselves in this building."

"I believe you. But it would be helpful if we can chat a bit anyway. The family didn't know much about her life here."

He nods reluctantly and opens the door. He steps in and waves his arms up and around in a complex sequence as though he's conducting an orchestra. The lights come on.

"That's pretty fancy," Ruth says. "You have the whole place wired up like that?"

His voice, cautious and guarded until now, grows animated. Talking about something other than the murder seems to relax him. "Yes. It's called EchoSense. They add an adapter to your wireless router and a few antennas around the room, and then it uses the Doppler shifts generated by your body's movements in the radio waves to detect gestures."

"You mean it can see you move with just the signals from your wifi bouncing around the room?"

"Something like that."

Ruth remembers seeing an infomercial about this. She notes how small the apartment is and how little space separates it from Mona's. They sit down and chat about what Peter remembers about Mona.

"Pretty girl. Way out of my league, but she was always pleasant."

"Did she get a lot of visitors?"

"I don't pry into other people's business. But yeah, I remember lots of visitors, mostly men. I did think she might have been an escort. But that didn't bother me. The men always seemed clean, business types. Not dangerous."

"No one who looked like a gangster, for example?"

"I wouldn't know what gangsters look like. But no, I don't think so."

They chat on inconsequentially for another fifteen minutes, and Ruth decides that she's wasted enough time.

"Can I buy the router from you?" she asks. "And the EchoSense thing."

"You can just order your own set online."

"I hate shopping online. You can never return things. I know this one works; so I want it. I'll offer you two thousand, cash."

He considers this.

"I bet you can buy a new one and get another adapter yourself from EchoSense for less than a quarter of that."

He nods and retrieves the router, and she pays him. The act feels somehow illicit, not unlike how she imagines Mona's transactions were.

• • • •

Ruth posts an ad to a local classifieds site describing in vague terms what she's looking for. Boston is blessed with many good colleges and lots of young men and women who would relish a technical challenge even more than the money she offers. She looks through the resumes until she finds the one she feels has the right skills: jailbreaking phones, reverse-engineering proprietary protocols, a healthy disrespect for acronyms like DMCA and CFAA.

She meets the young man at her office and explains what she wants. Daniel, dark-skinned, lanky, and shy, slouches in the chair across from hers as he listens without interrupting.

"Can you do it?" she asks.

"Maybe," he says. "Companies like this one will usually send customer data back to the mothership anonymously to help improve their technology. Sometimes the data is cached locally for a while. It's possible I'll find logs on there a month old. If it's there, I'll get it for you. But I'll have to figure out how they're encoding the data and then make sense of it."

"Do you think my theory is plausible?"

"I'm impressed you even came up with it. Wireless signals can go through walls, so it's certainly possible that this adapter has captured the movements of people in neighboring apartments. It's a privacy nightmare, and I'm sure the company doesn't publicize that."

"How long will it take?"

"As little as a day or as much as a month. I won't know until I start. It will help if you can draw me a map of the apartments and what's inside."

Ruth does as he asked. Then she tells him, "I'll pay you three hundred dollars a day, with a five thousand dollar bonus if you succeed this week."

"Deal." He grins and picks up the router, getting ready to leave.

Because it never hurts to tell people what they're doing is meaningful, she adds, "You're helping to catch the killer of a young woman who's not much older than you."

Then she goes home because she's run out of things to try.

• • • •

The first hour after waking up is always the worst part of the day for Ruth.

As usual, she wakes from a nightmare. She lies still, disoriented, the images from her dream superimposed over the sight of the water stains on the ceiling. Her body is drenched in sweat.

*The man holds Jessica in front of him with his left hand while the gun in his right hand is pointed at her head. She's terrified, but not of him. He ducks so that her body shields his, and he whispers something into her ear.*

*"Mom! Mom!" she screams. "Don't shoot. Please don't shoot!"*

Ruth rolls over, nauseated. She sits up at the edge of the bed, hating the smell of the hot room, the dust that she never has time to clean filling the air pierced by bright rays coming in from the east-facing window. She shoves the sheets off of her and stands up quickly, her breath coming too fast. She's fighting the rising panic without any help, alone, her Regulator off.

The clock on the nightstand says 6:00.

*She's crouching behind the opened driver's side door of her car. Her hands shake as she struggles to keep the man's head, bobbing besides her daughter's, in the sight of her gun. If she turns on her Regulator, she thinks her hands may grow steady and give her a clear shot at him.*

*What are her chances of hitting him instead of her? Ninety-five percent? Ninety-nine?*

*"Mom! Mom! No!"*

She gets up and stumbles into the kitchen to turn on the coffeemaker. She curses when she finds the can empty and throws it clattering into the sink. The noise shocks her and she cringes.

Then she struggles into the shower, sluggishly, painfully, as though the muscles that she conditions daily through hard exercise were not there. She turns on the hot water but it brings no warmth to her shivering body.

Grief descends on her like a heavy weight. She sits down in the shower, curling her body into itself. Water streams down her face so she does not know if there are tears as her body heaves.

She fights the impulse to turn on the Regulator. It's not time yet. She has to give her body the necessary rest.

The Regulator, a collection of chips and circuitry embedded at the top of her spine, is tied into the limbic system and the major blood vessels into the brain. Like its namesake from mechanical and electrical engineering, it maintains the levels of dopamine, noradrenaline, serotonin and other chemicals in the brain and in her blood stream. It filters out the chemicals when there's an excess, and releases them when there's a deficit.

And it obeys her will.

The implant allows a person control over her basic emotions: fear, disgust, joy, excitement, love. It's mandatory for law enforcement officers, a way to minimize the effects of emotions on life-or-death decisions, a way to eliminate prejudice and irrationality.

*"You have clearance to shoot," the voice in her headset tells her. It's the voice of her husband, Scott, the head of her department. His voice is completely calm. His Regulator is on.*

*She sees the head of the man bobbing up and down as he retreats with Jessica. He's heading for the van parked by the side of the road.*

*"He's got other hostages in there," her husband continues to speak in her ear. "If you don't shoot, you put the lives of those three other girls and who knows how many other people in danger. This is our best chance."*

*The sound of sirens, her backup, is still faint. Too far away.*

After what seems an eternity, she manages to stand up in the shower and turn off the water. She towels herself dry and dresses slowly. She tries to think of something, anything, to take her mind off its current track. But nothing works.

She despises the raw state of her mind. Without the Regulator, she feels weak, confused, angry. Waves of despair wash over her and everything appears in hopeless shades of grey. She wonders why she's still alive.

*It will pass,* she thinks. *Just a few more minutes.*

Back when she had been on the force, she had adhered to the regulation requirement not to leave the Regulator on for more than two hours at a time. There are physiological and psychological risks associated with prolonged use. Some of her fellow officers had also complained about the way the Regulator made them feel robotic, deadened. No excitement from seeing a pretty woman; no thrill at the potential for a car chase; no righteous anger when faced with an act of abuse. Everything had to be deliberate: you decided when to let the adrenaline flow, and just enough to get the job done and not too much to interfere with judgment. But sometimes, they argued, you needed emotions, instinct, intuition.

Her Regulator had been off when she came home that day and recognized the man hiding from the city-wide manhunt.

*Have I been working too much? she thinks. I don't know any of her friends. When did Jess meet him? Why didn't I ask her more questions when she was coming home late every night? Why did I stop for lunch instead of coming home half an hour earlier? There are a thousand things I could have done and should have done and would have done.*

*Fear and anger and regret are mixed up in her until she cannot tell which is which.*

*"Engage your Regulator," her husband's voice tells her. "You can make the shot."*

*Why do I care about the lives of the other girls? she thinks. All I care about is Jess. Even the smallest chance of hurting her is too much.*

*Can she trust a machine to save her daughter? Should she rely on a machine to steady her shaking hands, to clear her blurry vision, to make a shot without missing?*

*"Mom, he's going to let me go later. He won't hurt me. He just wants to get away from here. Put the gun down!"*

*Maybe Scott can make a calculus about lives saved and lives put at risk. She won't. She will not trust a machine.*

*"It's okay, baby," she croaks out. "It's all going to be okay."*

*She does not turn on the Regulator. She does not shoot.*

Later, after she had identified the body of Jess—the bodies of all four of the girls had been badly burnt when the bomb went off—after she had been disciplined and discharged, after Scott and she had split up, after she had found no solace in alcohol and pills, she did finally find the help she needed: she could leave the Regulator on all the time.

The Regulator deadened the pain, stifled grief and numbed the ache of loss. It held down the regret, made it possible to pretend to forget. She craved the calmness it brought, the blameless, serene clarity.

She had been wrong to distrust it. That distrust had cost her Jess. She would not make the same mistake again.

Sometimes she thinks of the Regulator as a dependable lover, a comforting presence to lean on. Sometimes she thinks she's addicted. She does not probe deeply behind these thoughts.

She would have preferred to never have to turn off the Regulator, to never be in a position to repeat her mistake. But even Doctor B balked at that ("Your brain will turn into mush."). The illegal modifications he did agree to make allow the Regulator to remain on for a maximum of twenty-three hours at a stretch. Then she must take an hour-long break during which she must remain conscious.

And so there's always this hour in the morning, right as she wakes, when she's naked and alone with her memories, unshielded from the rush of red-hot hatred (for the man? for herself?) and white-cold rage, and the black, bottomless abyss that she endures as her punishment.

The alarm beeps. She concentrates like a monk in meditation and feels the hum of the Regulator starting up. Relief spreads out from the center of her mind to the very tips of her fingers, the soothing, numbing serenity of a regulated, disciplined mind. To be regulated is to be a regular person.

She stands up, limber, graceful, powerful, ready to hunt.

• • • •

The Watcher has identified more of the men in the pictures. He's now in a new motel room, this one more expensive than usual because he feels like he deserves a treat after all he's been through. Hunching over all day to edit video is hard work.

He pans the cropping rectangle over the video to give it a sense of dynamism and movement. There's an artistry to this.

He's amazed how so few people seem to know about the eye implants. There's something about eyes, so vulnerable, so essential to the way people see the world and themselves, that makes people feel protective and reluctant to invade them. The laws regarding eye modifications are the most stringent, and after a while, people begin to mistake "not permitted" with "not possible."

They don't know what they don't want to know.

All his life, he's felt that he's missed some key piece of information, some secret that everyone else seemed to know. He's intelligent, diligent, but somehow things have not worked out.

He never knew his father, and when he was eleven, his mother had left him one day at home with twenty dollars and never came back. A string of foster homes had followed, and *nobody*, nobody could tell him what he was missing, why he was always at the mercy of judges and bureaucrats, why he had so little control over his life, not where he would sleep, not when he would eat, not who would have power over him next.

He made it his subject to study men, to watch and try to understand what made them tick. Much of what he learned had disappointed him. Men were vain, proud, ignorant. They let their desires carry them away, ignored risks that were obvious. They did not think, did not plan. They did not know what they really wanted. They let the TV tell them what they should have and hoped that working at their pathetic jobs would make those wishes come true.

He craved control. He wanted to see them dance to his tune the way he had been made to dance to the tune of everyone else.

So he had honed himself to be pure and purposeful, like a sharp knife in a drawer full of ridiculous, ornate, fussy kitchen gadgets. He knew what he wanted and he worked at getting it with singular purpose.

He adjusts the colors and the dynamic range to compensate for the dim light in the video. He wants there to be no mistake in identifying the man.

He stretches his tired arms and sore neck. For a moment he wonders if he'll be better off if he pays to have parts of his body enhanced so he can work for longer, without pain and fatigue. But the momentary fancy passes.

Most people don't like medically unnecessary enhancements and would only accept them if they're required for a job. No such sentimental considerations for bodily integrity or "naturalness" constrain the Watcher. He does not like enhancements because he views reliance on them as a sign of weakness. He would defeat his enemies with his mind, and with the aid of planning and foresight. He does not need to depend on machines.

He had learned to steal, and then rob, and eventually how to kill for money. But the money was really secondary, just a means to an end. It was control that he desired. The only man he had killed was a lawyer, someone who lied for a living. Lying had brought him money, and that gave him power, made people bow down to him and smile at him and speak in respectful voices. The Watcher had loved that moment when the man begged him for mercy, when he would have done anything the Watcher wanted. The Watcher had taken what he wanted from the man rightfully, by superiority of intellect and strength. Yet, the Watcher had been caught and gone to jail for it. A system that rewarded liars and punished the Watcher could not in any sense be called just.

He presses "Save." He's done with this video.

Knowledge of the truth gave him power, and he would make others acknowledge it.

• • • •

Before Ruth is about to make her next move, Daniel calls, and they meet in her office again.

"I have what you wanted."

He takes out his laptop and shows her an animation, like a movie.

"They stored videos on the adapter?"

Daniel laughs. "No. The device can't really 'see' and that would be far too much data. No, the adapter just stored readings, numbers. I made the animation so it's easier to understand."

She's impressed. The young man knows how to give a good presentation.

"The wifi echoes aren't captured with enough resolution to give you much detail. But you can get a rough sense of people's sizes and heights and their movements. This is what I got from the day and hour you specified."

They watch as a bigger, vaguely humanoid shape appears at Mona's apartment door, precisely at 6:00, meeting a smaller, vaguely humanoid shape.

"Seems they had an appointment," Daniel says.

They watch as the smaller shape leads the bigger shape into the bedroom, and then the two embrace. They watch the smaller shape climb into space—presumably onto the bed. They watch the bigger shape climb up after it. They watch the shooting, and then the smaller shape collapses and disappears. They watch the bigger shape lean over, and the smaller shape flickers into existence as it's moved from time to time.

*So there was only one killer*, Ruth thinks. *And he was a client.*

"How tall is he?"

"There's a scale to the side."

Ruth watches the animation over and over. The man is six foot two or six foot three, maybe 180 to 200 pounds. She notices that he has a bit of a limp as he walks.

She's now convinced that Luo was telling the truth. Not many Chinese men are six foot two, and such a man would stick out too much to be a killer for a gang. Every witness would remember him. Mona's killer had been a client, maybe even a regular. It wasn't a random robbery but carefully planned.

The man is still out there, and killers that meticulous rarely kill only once.

"Thank you," she says. "You might be saving another young woman's life."

• • • •

Ruth dials the number for the police department.

"Captain Brennan, please."

She gives her name and her call is transferred, and then she hears the gruff, weary voice of her ex-husband. "What can I do for you?"

Once again, she's glad she has the Regulator. His voice dredges up memories of his raspy morning mumbles, his stentorian laughter, his tender whispers when they were alone, the soundtrack of twenty years of a life spent together, a life that they had both thought would last until one of them died.

"I need a favor."

He doesn't answer right away. She wonders if she's too abrupt—a side effect of leaving the Regulator on all the time. Maybe she should have started with "How've you been?"

Finally, he speaks. "What is it?" The voice is restrained, but laced with exhausted, desiccated pain.

"I'd like to use your NCIC access."

Another pause. "Why?"

"I'm working on the Mona Ding case. I think this is a man who's killed before and will kill again. He's got a method. I want to see if there are related cases in other cities."

"That's out of the question, Ruth. You know that. Besides, there's no point. We've run all the searches we can, and there's nothing similar. This was a Chinese gang protecting their business, simple as that. Until we have the resources in the Gang Unit to deal with it, I'm sorry, this will have to go cold for a while."

Ruth hears the unspoken. *The Chinese gangs have always preyed on their own. Until they bother the tourists, let's just leave them alone.* She'd heard similar sentiments often enough back when she was on the force. The Regulator could do nothing about certain kinds of prejudice. It's perfectly rational. And also perfectly wrong.

"I don't think so. I have an informant who says that the Chinese gangs have nothing to do with it."

Scott snorts. "Yes, of course you can trust the word of a Chinese snakehead. But there's also the note and the phone."

"The note is most likely a forgery. And do you really think this Chinese gang member would be smart enough to realize that the phone records would give him away and then decide that the best place to hide it was around his place of business?"

"Who knows? Criminals are stupid."

"The man is far too methodical for that. It's a red herring."

"You have no evidence."

"I have a good reconstruction of the crime and a description of the suspect. He's too tall to be the kind a Chinese gang would use."

This gets his attention. "From where?"

"A neighbor had a home motion-sensing system that captured wireless echoes into Mona's apartment. I paid someone to reconstruct it."

"Will that stand up in court?"

"I doubt it. It will take expert testimony and you'll have to get the company to admit that they capture that information. They'll fight it tooth and nail."

"Then it's not much use to me."

"If you give me a chance to look in the database, maybe I can turn it into something you *can* use." She waits a second and presses on, hoping that he'll be sentimental. "I've never asked you for much."

"This is the first time you've ever asked me for something like this."

"I don't usually take on cases like this."

"What is it about this girl?"

Ruth considers the question. There are two ways to answer it. She can try to explain the fee she's being paid and why she feels she's adding value. Or she can give what she suspects is the real reason. Sometimes the Regulator makes it hard to tell what's true. "Sometimes people think the police don't look as hard when the victim is a sex worker. I know your resources are constrained, but maybe I can help."

"It's the mother, isn't it? You feel bad for her."

Ruth does not answer. She can feel the Regulator kicking in again. Without it, perhaps she would be enraged.

"She's not Jess, Ruth. Finding her killer won't make you feel better."

"I'm asking for a favor. You can just say no."

Scott does not sigh, and he does not mumble. He's simply quiet. Then, a few seconds later: "Come to the office around 8:00. You can use the terminal in my office."

• • • •

The Watcher thinks of himself as a good client. He makes sure he gets his money's worth, but he leaves a generous tip. He likes the clarity of money, the way it makes the flow of power obvious. The girl he just left was certainly appreciative.

He drives faster. He feels he's been too self-indulgent the last few weeks, working too slowly. He needs to make sure the last round of targets have paid. If not, he needs to carry through. Action. Reaction. It's all very simple once you understand the rules.

He rubs the bandage around his ring finger, which allows him to maintain the pale patch of skin that girls like to see. The lingering, sickly sweet perfume from the last girl—Melody, Mandy, he's already forgetting her name—reminds him of Tara, who he will never forget.

Tara may have been the only girl he's really loved. She was blonde, petite, and very expensive. But she had liked him for some reason. Perhaps because they were both broken, and the jagged pieces happened to fit.

She had stopped charging him and told him her real name. He was a kind of boyfriend. Because he was curious, she explained her business to him. How certain words and turns of phrase and tones on the phone were warning signs. What she looked for in a desired regular. What signs on a man probably meant he was safe. He enjoyed learning about this. It seemed to require careful watching by the girl, and he respected those who looked and studied and made the information useful.

He had looked into her eyes as he fucked her, and then said, "Is something wrong with your right eye?"

She had stopped moving. "What?"

"I wasn't sure at first. But yes, it's like you have something behind your eye."

She wriggled under him. He was annoyed and thought about holding her down. But he decided not to. She seemed about to tell him something important. He rolled off of her.

"You're very observant."

"I try. What is it?"

She told him about the implant.

"You've been recording your clients having sex with you?"

"Yes."

"I want to see the ones you have of us."

She laughed. "I'll have to go under the knife for that. Not going to happen until I retire. Having your skull opened up once was enough."

She explained how the recordings made her feel safe, gave her a sense of power, like having bank accounts whose balances only she knew and kept growing. If she were ever threatened, she would be able to call on the powerful men she knew for aid. And after retirement, if things didn't work out and she got desperate, perhaps she could use them to get her regulars to help her out a little.

He had liked the way she thought. So devious. So like him.

He had been sorry when he killed her. Removing her head was more difficult and messy than he had imagined. Figuring out what to do with the little silver half-sphere had taken months. He would learn to do better over time.

But Tara had been blind to the implications of what she had done. What she had wasn't just insurance, wasn't just a rainy-day fund. She had revealed to him that she had what it took to make his dream come true, and he had to take it from her.

He pulls into the parking lot of the hotel and finds himself seized by an unfamiliar sensation: sorrow. He misses Tara, like missing a mirror you've broken.

• • • •

Ruth is working with the assumption that the man she's looking for targets independent prostitutes. There's an efficiency and a method to the way Mona was killed that suggested practice.

She begins by searching the NCIC database for prostitutes who had been killed by a suspect matching the EchoSense description. As she expects, she comes up with nothing that seems remotely similar. The man hadn't left obvious trails.

The focus on Mona's eyes may be a clue. Maybe the killer has a fetish for Asian women. Ruth changes her search to concentrate on body mutilations of Asian prostitutes similar to what Mona had suffered. Again, nothing.

Ruth sits back and thinks over the situation. It's common for serial killers to concentrate on victims of a specific ethnicity. But that may be a red herring here.

She expands her search to include all independent prostitutes who had been killed in the last year or so, and now there are too many hits. Dozens and dozens of killings of prostitutes of every description pop up. Most were sexually assaulted. Some were tortured. Many had their bodies mutilated. Almost all were robbed. Gangs were suspected in several cases. She sifts through them, looking for similarities. Nothing jumps out at her.

She needs more information.

She logs onto the escort sites in the various cities and looks up the ads of the murdered women. Not all of them remain online, as some sites deactivate ads when enough patrons complain about unavailability. She prints out what she can, laying them out side by side to compare.

Then she sees it. It's in the ads.

A subset of the ads triggers a sense of familiarity in Ruth's mind. They were all carefully written, free of spelling and grammar mistakes. They were frank but not explicit, seductive without verging on parody. The johns who posted reviews described them as "classy."

It's a signal, Ruth realizes. The ads are written to give off the air of being careful, selective, *discreet*. There is in them, for lack of a better word, a sense of *taste*.

All of the women in these ads were extraordinarily beautiful, with smooth skin and thick, long flowing hair. All of them were between twenty-two and thirty, not so young as to be careless or supporting themselves through school, and not old enough to lose the ability to pass for younger. All of them were independent, with no pimp or evidence of being on drugs.

Luo's words come back to her: *The men who go to massage parlors for $60 an hour and a happy ending are not the kind who'd pay for a girl like this.*

There's a certain kind of client who would be attracted to the signs given out by these girls, Ruth thinks: men who care very much about the risk of discovery and who believe that they deserve something special, suitable for their distinguished tastes.

She prints out the NCIC entries for the women.

All the women she's identified were killed in their homes. No sign of struggle—possibly because they were meeting a client. One was strangled, the others shot in the heart through the back, like Mona. In all the cases except one—the woman who was strangled—the police had found record of a suspicious call on the day of the murder from a prepaid phone that was later found somewhere in the city. The killer had taken all the women's money.

Ruth knows she's on the right track. Now she needs to examine the case reports in more detail to see if she can find more patterns to identify the killer.

The door to the office opens. It's Scott.

"Still here?" The scowl on his face shows that he does not have his Regulator on. "It's after midnight."

She notes, not for the first time, how the men in the department have often resisted the Regulator unless absolutely necessary, claiming that it dulled their instincts and hunches. But they had also asked her whether she had hers on whenever she dared to disagree with them. They would laugh when they asked.

"I think I'm onto something," she says, calmly.

"You working with the goddamned Feds now?"

"What are you talking about?"

"You haven't seen the news?"

"I've been here all evening."

He takes out his tablet, opens a bookmark, and hands it to her. It's an article in the international section of the *Globe*, which she rarely reads. "Scandal Unseats Chinese Transport Minister," says the headline.

She scans the article quickly. A video has surfaced on the Chinese microblogs showing an important official in the Transport Ministry having sex with a prostitute. Moreover, it seems that he had been paying her out of public funds. He's already been removed from his post due to the public outcry.

Accompanying the article is a grainy photo, a still capture from the video. Before the Regulator kicks in, Ruth feels her heart skip a beat. The image shows a man on top of a woman. Her head is turned to the side, directly facing the camera.

"That's your girl, isn't it?"

Ruth nods. She recognizes the bed and the nightstand with the clock and wicker basket from the crime scene photos.

"The Chinese are hopping mad. They think we had the man under surveillance when he was in Boston and released this video deliberately to mess with them. They're protesting through the backchannels, threatening retaliation. The Feds want us to look into it and see what we can find out about how the video was made. They don't know that she's already dead, but I recognized her as soon as I saw her. If you ask me, it's probably something the Chinese cooked up themselves to try to get rid of the guy in an internal purge. Maybe they even paid the girl to do it and then they killed her. That or our own spies decided to get rid of her after using her as bait, in which case I expect this investigation to be shut down pretty quickly.

Either way, I'm not looking forward to this mess. And I advise you to back off as well."

Ruth feels a moment of resentment before the Regulator whisks it away. If Mona's death was part of a political plot, then Scott is right, she really is way out of her depth. The police had been wrong to conclude that it was a gang killing. But she's wrong, too. Mona was an unfortunate pawn in some political game, and the trend she thought she had noticed was illusory, just a set of coincidences.

The rational thing to do is to let the police take over. She'll have to tell Sarah Ding that there's nothing she can do for her now.

"We'll have to sweep the apartment again for recording devices. And you better let me know the name of your informant. We'll need to question him thoroughly to see which gangs are involved. This could be a national security matter."

"You know I can't do that. I have no evidence he has anything to do with this."

"Ruth, we're picking this up now. If you want to find the girl's killer, help me."

"Feel free to round up all the usual suspects in Chinatown. It's what you want to do, anyway."

He stares at her, his face weary and angry, a look she's very familiar with. Then his face relaxes. He has decided to engage his Regulator, and he no longer wants to argue or talk about what couldn't be said between them.

Her Regulator kicks in automatically.

"Thank you for letting me use your office," she says placidly. "You have a good night."

• • • •

The scandal had gone off exactly as the Watcher planned. He's pleased but not yet ready to celebrate. That was only the first step, a demonstration of his power. Next, he has to actually make sure it pays.

He goes through the recordings and pictures he's extracted from the dead girl and picks out a few more promising targets based on his research. Two are prominent Chinese businessmen connected with top Party bosses; one is the brother of an Indian diplomatic attaché; two more are sons of the House of Saud studying in Boston. It's remarkable how similar the dynamics between the powerful and the people they ruled over were around the world. He also finds a prominent CEO and a Justice of the Massachusetts Supreme Judicial Court, but these he sets aside. It's not that he's particularly patriotic, but he instinctively senses that if one of his victims decides to turn him in instead of paying up, he'll be in much less trouble if the victim isn't an American. Besides, American public figures also have a harder time moving money around anonymously, as evidenced by his experience with those two Senators in DC, which almost unraveled his whole scheme. Finally, it never hurts to have a judge or someone famous that can be leaned on in case the Watcher is caught.

Patience, and an eye for details.

He sends off his emails. Each references the article about the Chinese Transport Minister ("see, this could be you!") and then includes two files. One is the full video of the minister and the girl (to show that he was the originator) and the second is a carefully curated video of the recipient coupling with her. Each email contains a demand for payment and directions to make deposits to a numbered Swiss bank account or to transfer anonymous electronic cryptocurrency.

He browses the escort sites again. He's narrowed down the girls he suspects to just a few. Now he just has to look at them more closely to pick out the right one. He grows excited at the prospect.

He glances up at the people walking past him in the streets. All these foolish men and women moving around as if dreaming. They do not understand that the world is full of secrets, accessible only to those patient enough, observant enough to locate them and dig them out of their warm, bloody hiding places, like retrieving pearls from the soft flesh inside an oyster. And then, armed with those secrets, you could make men half a world away tremble and dance.

He closes his laptop and gets up to leave. He thinks about packing up the mess in his motel room, setting out the surgical kit, the baseball cap, the gun and a few other surprises he's learned to take with him when he's hunting.

Time to dig for more treasure.

• • • •

Ruth wakes up. The old nightmares have been joined by new ones. She stays curled up in bed fighting waves of despair. She wants to lie here forever.

Days of work and she has nothing to show for it.

She'll have to call Sarah Ding later, after she turns on the Regulator. She can tell her that Mona was probably not killed by a gang, but somehow had been caught up in events bigger than she could handle. How would that make Sarah feel better?

The image from yesterday's news will not leave her mind, no matter how hard she tries to push it away.

Ruth struggles up and pulls up the article. She can't explain it, but the image just *looks* wrong. Not having the Regulator on makes it hard to think.

She finds the crime scene photo of Mona's bedroom and compares it with the image from the article. She looks back and forth.

*Isn't the basket of condoms on the wrong side of the bed?*

The shot is taken from the left side of the bed. So the closet doors, with the mirrors on them, should be on the far side of the shot, behind the couple. But there's only a blank wall behind them in the shot. Ruth's heart is beating so fast that she feels faint.

The alarm beeps. Ruth glances up at the red numbers and turns the Regulator on.

The clock.

She looks back at the image. The alarm clock in the shot is tiny and fuzzy, but she can just make the numbers out. They're backwards.

Ruth walks steadily over to her laptop and begins to search online for the video. She finds it without much trouble and presses play.

Despite the video stabilization and the careful cropping, she can see that Mona's eyes are always looking directly into the camera.

There's only one explanation: the camera was aimed at the mirrors, and it was located in Mona's eye.

The eyes.

She goes through the NCIC entries of the other women she printed out yesterday, and now the pattern that had proven elusive seems obvious.

There was a blonde in Los Angeles whose head had been removed after death and never found; there was a brunette, also in LA, whose skull had been cracked open and her brains mashed; there was a Mexican woman and a black woman in DC whose faces had been subjected to post-mortem trauma in more restrained ways, with the cheekbones crushed and broken. Then finally, there was Mona, whose eyes had been carefully removed.

The killer has been improving his technique.

The Regulator holds her excitement in check. She needs more data.

She looks through all of Mona's photographs again. Nothing out of place shows up in the earlier pictures, but in the photo from her birthday with her parents, a flash was used, and there's an odd glint in her left eye.

Most cameras can automatically compensate for red-eye, which is caused by the light from the flash reflecting off the blood-rich choroid in the back of the eye. But the glint in Mona's picture is not red; it's bluish.

Calmly, Ruth flips through the photographs of the other girls who have been killed. And in each, she finds the tell-tale glint. This must be how the killer identified his targets.

She picks up the phone and dials the number for her friend. She and Gail had gone to college together, and she's now working as a researcher for an advanced medical devices company.

"Hello?"

She hears the chatter of other people in the background. "Gail, it's Ruth. Can you talk?"

"Just a minute." She hears the background conversation grow muffled and then abruptly shut off. "You never call unless you're asking about another enhancement. We're not getting any younger, you know? You have to stop at some point."

Gail had been the one to suggest the various enhancements Ruth has obtained over the years. She had even found Doctor B for her because she didn't want Ruth to end up crippled. But she had done it reluctantly, conflicted about the idea of turning Ruth into a cyborg.

"This feels wrong," she would say. "You don't need these things done to you. They're not medically necessary."

"This can save my life the next time someone is trying to choke me," Ruth would say.

"It's not the same thing," she would say. And the conversations would always end with Gail giving in, but with stern warnings about no further enhancements.

Sometimes you help a friend even when you disapprove of their decisions. It's complicated.

Ruth answers Gail on the phone, "No. I'm just fine. But I want to know if you know about a new kind of enhancement. I'm sending you some pictures now. Hold on." She sends over the images of the girls where she can see the strange glint in their eyes. "Take a look. Can you see that flash in their eyes? Do you know anything like this?" She doesn't tell Gail her suspicion so that Gail's answer would not be affected.

Gail is silent for a while. "I see what you mean. These are not great pictures. But let me talk to some people and call you back."

"Don't send the full pictures around. I'm in the middle of an investigation. Just crop out the eyes if you can."

Ruth hangs up. The Regulator is working extra hard. Something about what she said—cropping out the girls' eyes—triggered a bodily response of disgust that the Regulator is suppressing. She's not sure why. With the Regulator, sometimes it's hard for her to see the connections between things.

While waiting for Gail to call her back, she looks through the active online ads in Boston once more. The killer has a pattern of killing a few girls in each city before moving on. He must be on the hunt for a second victim here. The best way to catch him is to find her before he does.

She clicks through ad after ad, the parade of flesh a meaningless blur, focusing only on the eyes. Finally, she sees what she's looking for. The girl uses the name Carrie, and she has dirty-blond hair and green eyes. Her ad is clean, clear, well-written, like a tasteful sign amidst the parade of flashing neon. The timestamp on the ad shows that she last modified it twelve hours ago. She's likely still alive.

Ruth calls the number listed.

"This is Carrie. Please leave a message."

As expected, Carrie screens her calls.

"Hello. My name is Ruth Law, and I saw your ad. I'd like to make an appointment with you." She hesitates, and then adds, "This is not a joke. I really want to see you." She leaves her number and hangs up.

The phone rings almost immediately. Ruth picks up. But it's Gail, not Carrie.

"I asked around, and people who ought to know tell me the girls are probably wearing a new kind of retinal implant. It's not FDA-approved. But of course you can go overseas and get them installed if you pay enough."

"What do they do?"

"They're hidden cameras."

"How do you get the pictures and videos out?"

"You don't. They have no wireless connections to the outside world. In fact, they're shielded to emit as little RF emissions as possible so that they're undetectable to camera scanners, and a wireless connection would just mean another way to hack into them. All the storage is inside the device. To retrieve them you have to have surgery again. Not the kind of thing most people would be interested in unless you're trying to record people who *really* don't want you to be recording them."

*When you're so desperate for safety that you think this provides insurance*, Ruth thinks. *Some future leverage.*

And there's no way to get the recordings out except to cut the girl open. "Thanks."

"I don't know what you're involved in, Ruth, but you really are getting too old for this. Are you still leaving the Regulator on all the time? It's not healthy."

"Don't I know it." She changes the subject to Gail's children. The Regulator allows her to have this conversation without pain. After a suitable amount of time, she says goodbye and hangs up.

The phone rings again.

"This is Carrie. You called me."

"Yes." Ruth makes her voice sound light, carefree.

Carrie's voice is flirtatious but cautious. "Is this for you and your boyfriend or husband?"

"No, just me."

She grips the phone, counting the seconds. She tries to will Carrie not to hang up.

"I found your web site. You're a private detective?"

Ruth already knew that she would. "Yes, I am."

"I can't tell you anything about any of my clients. My business depends on discretion."

"I'm not going to ask you about your clients. I just want to see you." She thinks hard about how to gain her trust. The Regulator makes this difficult, as she has become unused to the emotive quality of judgments and impressions. She thinks the truth is too abrupt and strange to convince her. So she tries something else. "I'm interested in a new experience. I guess it's something I've always wanted to try and haven't."

"Are you working for the cops? I am stating now for the record that you're paying me only for companionship, and anything that happens beyond that is a decision between consenting adults."

"Look, the cops wouldn't use a woman to trap you. It's too suspicious."

The silence tells Ruth that Carrie is intrigued. "What time are you thinking of?"

"As soon as you're free. How about now?"

"It's not even noon yet. I don't start work until 6:00."

Ruth doesn't want to push too hard and scare her off. "Then I'd like to have you all night."

She laughs. "Why don't we start with two hours for a first date?"

"That will be fine."

"You saw my prices?"

"Yes. Of course."

"Take a picture of yourself holding your ID and text it to me first so I know you're for real. If that checks out, you can go to the corner of Victory and Beech in Back Bay at 6:00 and call me again. Put the cash in a plain envelope."

"I will."

"See you, my dear." She hangs up.

· · · ·

Ruth looks into the girl's eyes. Now that she knows what to look for, she thinks she can see the barest hint of a glint in her left eye.

She hands her the cash and watches her count it. She's very pretty, and so young. The ways she leans against the wall reminds her of Jess. The Regulator kicks in.

She's in a lace nightie, black stockings and garters. High-heeled fluffy bedroom slippers that seem more funny than erotic.

Carrie puts the money aside and smiles at her. "Do you want to take the lead or have me do it? I'm fine either way."

"I'd rather just talk for a bit first."

Carrie frowns. "I told you I can't talk about my clients."

"I know. But I want to show you something."

Carrie shrugs and leads her to the bedroom. It's a lot like Mona's room: king-size bed, cream-colored sheets, a glass bowl of condoms, a clock discreetly on the nightstand. The mirror is mounted on the ceiling.

They sit down on the bed. Ruth takes out a file, and hands Carrie a stack of photographs.

"All of these girls have been killed in the last year. All of them have the

420

same implants you do."

Carrie looks up, shocked. Her eyes blink twice, rapidly.

"I know what you have behind your eye. I know you think it makes you safer. Maybe you even think someday the information in there can be a second source of income, when you're too old to do this. But there's a man who wants to cut that out of you. He's been doing the same to the other girls."

She shows her the pictures of dead Mona, with the bloody, mutilated face.

Carrie drops the pictures. "Get out. I'm calling the police." She stands up and grabs her phone.

Ruth doesn't move. "You can. Ask to speak to Captain Scott Brennan. He knows who I am, and he'll confirm what I've told you. I think you're the next target."

She hesitates.

Ruth continues, "Or you can just look at these pictures. You know what to look for. They were all just like you."

Carrie sits down and examines the pictures. "Oh God. Oh God."

"I know you probably have a set of regulars. At your prices you don't need and won't get many new clients. But have you taken on anyone new lately?"

"Just you and one other. He's coming at 8:00."

Ruth's Regulator kicks in.

"Do you know what he looks like?"

"No. But I asked him to call me when he gets to the street corner, just like you, so I can get a look at him first before having him come up."

Ruth takes out her phone. "I need to call the police."

"No! You'll get me arrested. Please!"

Ruth thinks about this. She's only guessing that this man might be the killer. If she involves the police now and he turns out to be just a customer, Carrie's life will be ruined.

"Then I'll need to see him myself, in case he's the one."

"Shouldn't I just call it off?"

Ruth hears the fear in the girl's voice, and it reminds her of Jess, too, when she used to ask her to stay in her bedroom after watching a scary movie. She can feel the Regulator kicking into action again. She cannot let her emotions get in the way. "That would probably be safer for you, but we'd lose the chance to catch him if he *is* the one. Please, I need you to go through with it so I can get a close look at him. This may be our best chance of stopping him from hurting others."

Carrie bites her bottom lip. "All right. Where will you hide?"

Ruth wishes she had thought to bring her gun, but she hadn't wanted to spook Carrie and she didn't anticipate having to fight. She'll need to be close enough to stop the man if he turns out to be the killer, and yet not so close as to make it easy for him to discover her.

"I can't hide inside here at all. He'll look around before going into the bedroom with you." She walks into the living room, which faces the back of the building, away from the street, and lifts the window open. "I can hide out here, hanging from the ledge. If he turns out to be the killer, I have to wait till the last possible minute to come in to cut off his escape. If he's not the killer, I'll drop down and leave."

Carrie is clearly uncomfortable with this plan, but she nods, trying to be brave.

"Act as normal as you can. Don't make him think something is wrong."

Carrie's phone rings. She swallows and clicks the phone on. She walks over to the bedroom window. Ruth follows.

"This is Carrie."

Ruth looks out the window. The man standing at the corner appears to be the right height, but that's not enough to be sure. She has to catch him and interrogate him.

"I'm in the four-story building about a hundred feet behind you. Come up to apartment 303. I'm so glad you came, dear. We'll have a great time, I promise." She hangs up.

The man starts walking this way. Ruth thinks there's a limp to his walk, but again, she can't be sure.

"Is it him?" Carrie asks.

"I don't know. We have to let him in and see."

Ruth can feel the Regulator humming. She knows that the idea of using Carrie as bait frightens her, is repugnant even. But it's the logical thing to do. She'll never get a chance like this again. She has to trust that she can protect the girl.

"I'm going outside the window. You're doing great. Just keep him talking and do what he wants. Get him relaxed and focused on you. I'll come in before he can hurt you. I promise."

Carrie smiles. "I'm good at acting."

Ruth goes to the living room window and deftly climbs out. She lets her body down, hanging onto the window ledge with her fingers so that she's invisible from inside the apartment. "Okay, close the window. Leave just a slit open so I can hear what happens inside."

"How long can you hang like this?"

"Long enough."

Carrie closes the window. Ruth is glad for the artificial tendons and tensors in her shoulders and arms and the reinforced fingers, holding her up. The idea had been to make her more effective in close combat, but they're coming in handy now, too.

She counts off the seconds. The man should be at the building … he should now be coming up the stairs … he should now be at the door.

She hears the door to the apartment open.

"You're even prettier than your pictures." The voice is rich, deep, satisfied.

"Thank you."

She hears more conversation, the exchange of money. Then the sound of more walking.

They're heading towards the bedroom. She can hear the man stopping to look into the other rooms. She almost can feel his gaze pass over the top of her head, out the window.

Ruth pulls herself up slowly, quietly, and looks in. She sees the man disappear into the hallway. There's a distinct limp.

She waits a few more seconds so that the man cannot rush back past her before she can reach the hallway to block it, and then she takes a deep breath and wills the Regulator to pump her blood full of adrenaline. The world seems to grow brighter and time slows down as she flexes her arms and pulls herself onto the window ledge.

She squats down and pulls the window up in one swift motion. She knows that the grinding noise will alert the man, and she has only a few seconds to get to him. She ducks, rolls through the open window onto the floor inside. Then she continues to roll until her feet are under her and activates the pistons in her legs to leap towards the hallway.

She lands and rolls again to not give him a clear target, and jumps again from her crouch into the bedroom.

The man shoots and the bullet strikes her left shoulder. She tackles him as her arms, held in front of her, slam into his midsection. He falls and the gun clatters away.

Now the pain from the bullet hits. She wills the Regulator to pump up the adrenaline and the endorphins to numb the pain. She pants and concentrates on the fight for her life.

He tries to flip her over with his superior mass, to pin her down, but she clamps her hands around his neck and squeezes hard. Men have always underestimated her at the beginning of a fight, and she has to take advantage of it. She knows that her grip feels like iron clamps around him, with all the implanted energy cells in her arms and hands activated and on full power. He winces, grabs her hands to try to pry them off. After a few seconds, realizing the futility of it, he ceases to struggle.

He's trying to talk but can't get any air into his lungs. Ruth lets up a little, and he chokes out, "You got me."

Ruth increases the pressure again, choking off his supply of air. She turns to Carrie, who's at the foot of the bed, frozen. "Call the police. Now."

She complies. As she continues to hold the phone against her ear as the 911 dispatcher has instructed her to do, she tells Ruth, "They're on their way."

The man goes limp with his eyes closed. Ruth lets go of his neck. She doesn't want to kill him, so she clamps her hands around his wrists while she sits on his legs, holding him still on the floor.

He revives and starts to moan. "You're breaking my fucking arms!"

Ruth lets up the pressure a bit to conserve her power. The man's nose is bleeding from the fall against the floor when she tackled him. He inhales loudly, swallows, and says, "I'm going to drown if you don't let me sit up."

Ruth considers this. She lets up the pressure further and pulls him into a sitting position.

She can feel the energy cells in her arms depleting. She won't have the physical upper hand much longer if she has to keep on restraining him this way.

She calls out to Carrie. "Come over here and tie his hands together."

Carrie puts down the phone and comes over gingerly. "What do I use?"

"Don't you have any rope? You know, for your clients?"

"I don't do that kind of thing."

Ruth thinks. "You can use stockings."

As Carrie ties the man's hands and feet together in front of him, he coughs. Some of the blood has gone down the wrong pipe. Ruth is unmoved and doesn't ease up on the pressure, and he winces. "Goddamn it. You're one psycho robo bitch."

Ruth ignores him. The stockings are too stretchy and won't hold him for long. But it should last long enough for her to get the gun and point it at him.

Carrie retreats to the other side of the room. Ruth lets the man go and backs away from him towards the gun on the floor a few yards away, keeping her eyes on him. If he makes any sudden movements, she'll be back on him in a flash.

He stays limp and unmoving as she steps backwards. She begins to relax. The Regulator is trying to calm her down now, to filter the adrenalin out of her system.

When she's about half way to the gun, the man suddenly reaches into his jacket with his hands, still tied together. Ruth hesitates for only a second before pushing out with her legs to jump backwards to the gun.

As she lands, the man locates something inside his jacket, and suddenly Ruth feels her legs and arms go limp and she falls to the ground, stunned.

Carrie is screaming. "My eye! Oh God I can't see out of my left eye!"

Ruth can't seem to feel her legs at all, and her arms feel like rubber. Worst of all, she's panicking. It seems she's never been this scared or in this much pain. She tries to feel the presence of the Regulator and there's nothing, just emptiness. She can smell the sweet, sickly smell of burnt electronics in the air. The clock on the nightstand is dark.

She's the one who had underestimated *him*. Despair floods through her and there's nothing to hold it back.

Ruth can hear the man stagger up off the floor. She wills herself to turn over, to move, to reach for the gun. She crawls. One foot, another foot. She seems to be moving through molasses because she's so weak. She can feel every one of her forty-nine years. She feels every sharp stab of pain in her shoulder.

She reaches the gun, grabs it, and sits up against the wall, pointing it back into the center of the room.

The man has gotten out of Carrie's ineffective knots. He's now holding Carrie, blind in one eye, shielding his body with hers. He holds a scalpel against her throat. He's already broken the skin and a thin stream of blood flows down her neck.

He backs towards the bedroom door, dragging Carrie with him. Ruth knows that if he gets to the bedroom door and disappears around the corner, she'll never be able to catch him. Her legs are simply useless.

Carrie sees Ruth's gun and screams. "I don't want to die! Oh God. Oh God."

"I'll let her go once I'm safe," he says, keeping his head hidden behind hers.

Ruth's hands are shaking as she holds the gun. Through the waves of nausea and the pounding of her pulse in her ears, she struggles to think through what will happen next. The police are on their way and will probably be here in five minutes. Isn't it likely that he'll let her go as soon as possible to give himself some extra time to escape?

The man backs up another two steps; Carrie is no longer kicking or struggling, but trying to find purchase on the smooth floor in her stockinged feet, trying to cooperate with him. But she can't stop crying.

*Mom, don't shoot! Please don't shoot!*

Or is it more likely that once the man has left the room, he will slit Carrie's throat and cut out her implant? He knows there's a recording of him inside, and he can't afford to leave that behind.

Ruth's hands are shaking too much. She wants to curse at herself. She cannot get a clear shot at the man with Carrie in front of him. She cannot.

Ruth wants to evaluate the chances rationally, to make a decision, but regret and grief and rage, hidden and held down by the Regulator until they could be endured, rise now all the sharper, kept fresh by the effort at forgetting. The universe has shrunken down to the wavering spot at the end of the barrel of the gun: a young woman, a killer, and time slipping irrevocably away.

She has nothing to turn to, to trust, to lean on, but herself, her angry, frightened, trembling self. She is naked and alone, as she has always known she is, as we all are.

The man is almost at the door. Carrie's cries are now incoherent sobs.

It has always been the regular state of things. There is no clarity, no relief. At the end of all rationality there is simply the need to decide and the faith to live through, to endure.

Ruth's first shot slams into Carrie's thigh. The bullet plunges through skin, muscle, and fat, and exits out the back, shattering the man's knee.

The man screams and drops the scalpel. Carrie falls, a spray of blood blossoming from her wounded leg.

Ruth's second shot catches the man in the chest. He collapses to the floor.

*Mom, Mom!*

She drops the gun and crawls over to Carrie, cradling her and tending to her wound. She's crying, but she'll be fine.

A deep pain floods through her like forgiveness, like hard rain after a long drought. She does not know if she will be granted relief, but she experiences this moment fully, and she's thankful.

"It's okay," she says, stroking Carrie as she lies in her lap. "It's okay."

• • • •

[Author's Note: the EchoSense technology described in this story is a loose and liberal extrapolation of the principles behind the technology described in Qifan Pu et. al., "Whole-Home Gesture Recognition Using Wireless Signals," *The 19th Annual International Conference on Mobile Computing and Networking (Mobicom'13)* (available at http://wisee.cs.washington.edu/wisee_paper.pdf). There is no intent to suggest that the technology described in the paper resembles the fictional one portrayed here.]

Ken Liu (http://kenliu.name) is an author and translator of speculative fiction, as well as a lawyer and programmer. A winner of the Nebula, Hugo, and World Fantasy Awards, he has been published in *The Magazine of Fantasy & Science Fiction*, *Asimov's*, *Analog*, *Clarkesworld*, *Lightspeed*, and *Strange Horizons*, among other places. He also translated the Hugo-winning novel, *The Three-Body Problem*, by Liu Cixin, which is the first translated novel to win that award.

Ken's debut novel, *The Grace of Kings*, the first in a silkpunk epic fantasy series, was published by Saga Press in April 2015. Saga will also publish a collection of his short stories, *The Paper Menagerie and Other Stories*, in March 2016. He lives with his family near Boston, Massachusetts.

# Grand Jeté (The Great Leap)
## By Rachel Swirsky

ACT I: Mara
*Tombé*
(Fall)

As dawn approached, the snow outside Mara's window slowed, spiky white stars melting into streaks on the pane. Her abba stood in the doorway, unaware that she was already awake. Mara watched his silhouette in the gloom. Shadows hung in the folds of his jowls where he'd shaved his beard in solidarity after she'd lost her hair. Although it had been months, his face still looked pink and plucked.

Some nights, Mara woke four or five times to find him watching from the doorway. She didn't want him to know how poorly she slept and so she pretended to be dreaming until he eventually departed.

This morning, he didn't leave. He stepped into the room. "Marale," he said softly. His fingers worried the edges of the green apron that he wore in his workshop. A layer of sawdust obscured older scorch marks and grease stains. "Mara, please wake up. I've made you a gift."

Mara tried to sit. Her stomach reeled. Abba rushed to her bedside. "I'm fine," she said, pushing him away as she waited for the pain to recede.

He drew back, hands disappearing into his apron pockets. The corners of his mouth tugged down, wrinkling his face like a bulldog's. He was a big man with broad shoulders and disproportionately large hands. Everything he did looked comical when wrought on such a large scale. When he felt jovial, he played into the foolishness with broad, dramatic gestures that would have made an actor proud. In sadness, his gestures became reticent, hesitating, miniature.

"Are you cold?" he asked.

In deep winter, their house was always cold. Icy wind curled through cracks in the insulation. Even the heater that abba had installed at the foot of Mara's bed couldn't keep her from dreaming of snow.

Abba pulled a lace shawl that had once belonged to Mara's ima from the back of her little wooden chair. He draped it across her shoulders. Fringe covered her ragged fingernails.

As Mara rose from her bed, he tried to help with her crutches, but Mara fended him off. He gave her a worried look. "The gift is in my workshop," he said. With a concerned backward glance, he moved ahead, allowing her the privacy to make her own way.

Their white German Shepherd, Abel, met Mara as she shifted her weight onto her crutches. She paused to let him nuzzle her hand, tongue rough against her knuckles. At thirteen, all his other senses were fading, and so he tasted everything he could. He walked by her side until they reached the stairs, and then followed her down, tail thumping against the railing with every step.

The door to abba's workshop was painted red and stenciled with white flowers that Mara had helped ima paint when she was five. Inside, half-finished apparatuses sprawled across workbenches covered in sawdust and disassembled electronics. Hanging from the ceiling, a marionette stared blankly at Mara and Abel as they passed, the glint on its pupils moving back and forth as its strings swayed. A mechanical hand sprang to life, its motion sensor triggered by Abel's tail. Abel whuffed at its palm and then hid behind Mara. The thing's fingers grasped at Mara's sleeve, leaving an impression of dusty, concentric whorls.

Abba stood at the back of the workshop, next to a child-sized doll that sat on a metal stool. Its limbs fell in slack, uncomfortable positions. Its face looked like the one Mara still expected to see in the mirror: a broad forehead over flushed cheeks scattered with freckles. Skin peeled away in places, revealing wire streams.

Mara moved to stand in front of the doll. It seemed even eerier, examined face to face, its expression a lifeless twin of hers. She reached out to touch its soft, brown hair. Her bald scalp tingled.

Gently, Abba took Mara's hand and pressed her right palm against the doll's. Apart from how thin Mara's fingers had become over the past few months, they matched perfectly.

Abba made a triumphant noise. "The shape is right."

Mara pulled her hand out of abba's. She squinted at the doll's imitation flesh. Horrifyingly, its palm shared each of the creases on hers, as if it, too, had spent twelve years dancing and reading books and learning to cook.

Abel circled the doll. He sniffed its feet and ankles and then paused at the back of its knees, whuffing as if he'd expected to smell something that wasn't there. After completing his circuit, he collapsed on the floor, equidistant from the three human-shaped figures.

"What do you think of her?" abba asked.

Goosebumps prickled Mara's neck. "What is she?"

Abba cradled the doll's head in his hands. Its eyes rolled back, and the light highlighted its lashes, fair and short, just like Mara's own. "She's a prototype. Empty-headed. A friend of mine is working on new technology for the government—"

"A prototype?" repeated Mara. "Of what?"

"The body is simple mechanics. Anyone could build it. The technology in the mind is new. It takes pictures of the brain in motion, all three dimensions, and then creates schematics for artificial neural clusters that will function like the original biological matter—"

Mara's head ached. Her mouth was sore and her stomach hurt and she wanted to go back to bed even if she couldn't sleep. She eyed the doll. The wires under its skin were vivid red and blue as if they were veins and arteries connecting to viscera.

"The military will make use of the technology," Abba continued. "They wish to recreate soldiers with advanced training. They are not ready for human tests, not yet. They are still experimenting with animals. They've made rats with mechanical brains that can solve mazes the original rats were trained to run. Now they are working with chimpanzees."

Abba's accent deepened as he continued, his gestures increasingly emphatic.

"But I am better. I can make it work in humans now, without more experiments." Urgently, he lowered his voice. "My friend was not supposed to send me the schematics. I paid him much money, but his reason for helping is that I have promised him that when I fix the problems, I will show him the solution and he can take the credit. This technology is not for civilians. No one else will be able to do this. We are very fortunate."

Abba touched the doll's shoulder so lightly that only his fingertips brushed her.

"I will need you to sit for some scans so that I can make the images that will preserve you. They will be painless. I can set up when you sleep." Quietly, he added, "She is my gift to you. She will hold you and keep you...if the worst..." His voice faded, and he swallowed twice, three times, before beginning again. "She will protect you."

Mara's voice came out hoarse. "Why didn't you tell me?"

"You needed to see her when she was complete."

Her throat constricted. "I wish I'd never seen her at all!"

From the cradle, Mara had been even-tempered. Now, at twelve, she shouted and cried. Abba said it was only what happened to children as they grew older, but they both knew that wasn't why.

Neither was used to her new temper. The lash of her shout startled them both. Abba's expression turned stricken.

"I don't understand," he said.

"You made a new daughter!"

"No, no." Abba held up his hands to protect himself from her accusation. "She is made *for* you."

"I'm sure she'll be a better daughter than I am," Mara said bitterly.

She grabbed a hank of the doll's hair. Its head tilted toward her in a parody of curiosity. She pushed it away. The thing tumbled to the floor, limbs awkwardly splayed.

Abba glanced toward the doll, but did not move to see if it was broken. "I— No, Marale— You don't—" His face grew drawn with sudden resolution. He pulled a hammer off of one of the work benches. "Then I will smash her to pieces."

There had been a time when, with the hammer in his hand and a determined expression on his face, he'd have looked like a smith from old legends. Now he'd lost so much weight that his skin hung loosely from his enormous frame as if he were a giant coat suspended from a hanger. Tears sprang to Mara's eyes.

She slapped at his hands and the hammer in them. "Stop it!"

"If you want her to—"

"Stop it! Stop it!" she shouted.

Abba released the hammer. It fell against the cement with a hollow, mournful sound.

Guilt shot through her, at his confusion, at his fear. What should she do, let him destroy this thing he'd made? What should she do, let the hammer blow strike, watch herself be shattered?

Sawdust billowed where the hammer hit. Abel whined and fled the room, tail between his legs.

Softly, abba said, "I don't know what else to give."

Abba had always been the emotional heart of the family, even when ima was alive. His anger flared; his tears flowed; his laughter roared from his gut. Mara rested her head on his chest until his tears slowed, and then walked with him upstairs.

· · · ·

The house was too small for Mara to fight with abba for long, especially during winters when they both spent every hour together in the house, Mara home-schooling via her attic space program while abba tinkered in his workshop. Even on good days, the house felt claustrophobic with two people trapped inside. Sometimes one of them would tug on a coat and ski cap and trudge across the hard-packed snow, but even the outdoors provided minimal escape. Their house sat alone at the end of a mile-long driveway that wound through bare-branched woods before reaching the lonely road that eventually led to their neighbors. Weather permitting, in winter it took an hour and a half to get the truck running and drive into town.

It was dawn by the time they had made their way upstairs, still drained from the scene in the basement. Mara went to lie down on her bed so she could try for the illusion of privacy. Through the closed door, she heard her father venting his frustration on the cabinets. Pans clanged. Drawers slammed. She thought she could hear the quiet, gulping sound of him beginning to weep again under the cacophony.

She waited until he was engrossed in his cooking and then crept out of her bedroom. She made her way down the hallway, taking each step slowly and carefully so as to minimize the clicking of her crutches.

Ima's dance studio was the only room in the house where abba never went. It faced east; at dawn, rose- and peach-colored light shimmered across the full-length mirrors and polished hardwood. An old television hung on the southern wall, its antiquated technology jury-rigged to connect with the household AI.

Mara closed the door most of the way, enough to muffle any sound but not enough to make the telltale thump that would attract her father's attention. She walked up to the television so that she could speak softly and still be heard by its implanted AI sensors. She'd long ago mastered the trick of enunciating clearly enough for the AI to understand her even when she was whispering. "I'd like to access a DVD of ima's performances."

The AI whirred. "Okay, Mara," said its genial, masculine voice. "Which one would you like to view?"

"Giselle."

More clicks and whirs. The television blinked on, showing the backs of several rows of red velvet seats. Well-dressed figures navigated the aisles, careful not to wrinkle expensive suits and dresses. Before them, a curtain hid the stage from view, the house lights emphasizing its sumptuous folds.

Mara sat carefully on the floor near the ballet barre so that she would be able to use it a lever when she wanted to stand again. She crossed the crutches at her feet. On the television screen, the lights dimmed as the overture began.

Sitting alone in this place where no one else went, watching things that no one else watched, she felt as if she were somewhere safe. A mouse in its hole, a bird in its nest—a shelter built precisely for her body, neither too large nor too small.

The curtain fluttered. The overture began. Mara felt her breath flowing more easily as the tension eased from her shoulders. She could forget about abba and his weeping for a moment, just allow herself to enter the ballet.

Even as an infant, Mara had adored the rich, satiny colors on ima's old DVDs. She watched the tragedies, but her heart belonged to the comedies. Gilbert and Sullivan's *Pineapple Poll*. Ashton's choreography of Prokofiev's *Cinderella*. Madcap *Coppélia* in which a peasant boy lost his heart to a clockwork doll.

When Mara was small, ima would sit with her while she watched the dancers, her expression half-wistful and half-jaded. When the dancers had sketched their bows, ima would stand, shaking her head, and say, "Ballet is not a good life."

At first, ima did not want to give Mara ballet lessons, but Mara insisted at the age of two, three, four, until ima finally gave in. During the afternoons while abba was in his workshop, Mara and ima would dance togher in the studio until ima grew tired and sat with her back against the mirror, hands wrapped around her knees, watching Mara spin and spin.

After ima died, Mara had wanted to ask her father to sign her up for dance school. But she hated the melancholia that overtook him whenever they discussed ballet. Before getting sick, she'd danced on her own instead, accompanying the dancers on ima's tapes. She didn't dance every afternoon as she had when ima was alive. She was older; she had other things to do—books to read, study hours with the AI, lessons and play dates in attic space. She danced just enough to maintain her flexibility and retain what ima had taught her, and even sometimes managed to learn new things from watching the dancers on film.

Then last year, while dancing with the Mouse King to *The Nutcracker*, the pain she'd been feeling for months in her right knee suddenly intensified. She heard the snap of bone before she felt it. She collapsed suddenly to the floor, confused and in pain, her head ringing with the echoes of the household's alarms. As the AI wailed for help, Mara found a single thought repeating in her head. *Legs don't shatter just because you're dancing. Something is very wrong.*

On the television screen, the filmed version of Mara's mother entered, dancing a coy *Giselle* in blue tulle. Her gaze slanted shyly downward as she flirted with the dancers playing Albrecht and Hilarion. One by one, she plucked petals from a prop daisy. *He loves me, he loves me not.*

Mara heard footsteps starting down the hall. She rushed to speak before abba could make it into the room—"AI, switch off—"

Abba arrived before she could finish. He stood in the doorway with his shoulders hunched, his eyes averted from the image of his dead wife. "Breakfast is ready," he said. He lingered for a moment before turning away.

• • • •

After breakfast, abba went outside to scrape ice off of the truck.

They drove into town once a week for supplies. Until last year, they'd always gone on Sundays, after Shabbat. Now they went on Fridays before Mara's appointments and then hurried to get home before sunset.

Outside, snowflakes whispered onto the hard-pack. Mara pulled her knit hat over her ears, but her cheeks still smarted from the cold. She rubbed her gloved hands together for warmth before attaching Abel's leash. The old dog seemed to understand what her crutches were. Since she'd started using them, he'd broken his lifelong habit of yanking on the strap and learned to walk daintily instead, placing each paw with care.

Abba opened the passenger door so that Abel could clamor into the back of the cab. He fretted while Mara leaned her crutches on the side of the truck and pulled herself into the seat. He wanted to help, she knew, but he was stopping himself. He knew she hated being reminded of her helplessness.

He collected her crutches when she was done and slung them into the back with Abel before taking his place in the driver's seat. Mara stared silently forward as he turned the truck around and started down the narrow driveway. The four-wheel-drive jolted over uneven snow, shooting pain through Mara's bad leg.

"Need to fix the suspension," abba grumbled.

Because abba was a tinkerer, everything was always broken. Before Mara was born, he'd worked for the government. These days, he consulted on refining manufacturing processes. He felt that commercial products were shoddily designed and so he was constantly trying to improve their household electronics, leaving his dozens of half-finished home projects disassembled for months while all the time swearing to take on new ones.

The pavement smoothed out as they turned onto a county-maintained road. Piles of dirty snow lined its sides. Bony trees dotted the landscape, interspersed with pines still wearing red bows from Christmas.

Mara felt as though the world were caught in a frozen moment, preserved beneath the snow. Nothing would ever change. No ice would melt. No birds would return to the branches. There would be nothing but blizzards and long, dark nights and snow-covered pines.

Mara wasn't sure she believed in G-d, but on her better days, she felt at peace with the idea of pausing, as if she were one of the dancers on ima's DVDs, halted mid-leap.

Except she wouldn't pause. She'd be replaced by that thing. That doll.

She glanced at her father. He stared fixedly at the road, grumbling under his breath in a blend of languages. He hadn't bought new clothes since losing so much weight, and the fabric of his coat fell in voluminous folds across the seat.

He glanced sideways at Mara watching him. "What's wrong?"

"Nothing," Mara muttered, looking away.

Abel pushed his nose into her shoulder. She turned in her seat to scratch between his ears. His tail thumped, tick, tock, like a metronome.

• • • •

They parked beside the grocery. The small building's densely packed shelves were reassuringly the same year in and year out except for the special display mounted at the front of the store. This week it showcased red-wrapped sausages, marked with a cheerful, handwritten sign.

Gerry stood on a ladder in the center aisle, restocking cereals. He beamed as they walked in.

"Ten-thirty to the minute!" he called. "Good morning, my punctual Jewish friends!"

Gerry had been slipping down the slope called being hard of hearing for years now. He pitched his voice as if he were shouting across a football field.

"How is my little adult?" he asked Mara. "Are you forty today, or is it fifty?"

"Sixty-five," Mara said. "Seventy tomorrow."

"Such an old child," Gerry said, shaking his head. "Are you sure you didn't steal that body?"

Abba didn't like those kinds of jokes. He used to worry that they would make her self-conscious; now he hated them for bringing up the subject of aging. Flatly, he replied, "Children in our family are like that. There is nothing wrong with her."

Mara shared an eye roll with the grocer.

"Never said there was," Gerry said. Changing the subject, he gestured at Mara's crutches with a box of cornflakes. "You're an athlete on those. I bet there's nothing you can't do with them."

Mara forced a smile. "They're no good for dancing."

He shrugged. "I used to know a guy in a wheelchair. Out-danced everyone."

"Not ballet, though."

"True," Gerry admitted, descending the ladder. "Come to the counter. I've got something for you."

Gerry had hardly finished speaking before Abel forgot about being gentle with Mara's crutches. He knew what Gerry's gifts meant. The lead wrenched out of Mara's hand. She chased after him, crutches clicking, but even with his aging joints, the dog reached the front counter before Mara was halfway across the store.

"Wicked dog," Gerry said in a teasing tone as he caught Abel's leash. He scratched the dog between the ears and then bent to grab a package from under the counter. "Sit," he said. "Beg." The old dog rushed to do both. Gerry unwrapped a sausage and tossed it. Abel snapped and swallowed.

Mara finished crossing the aisle. She leaned against the front counter. She tried to conceal her heavy breathing, but she knew that her face must be flushed. Abba waited at the edges of her peripheral vision, his arms stretched in Mara's direction as if he expected her to collapse.

Gerry glanced between Mara and her father, assessing the situation. Settling on Mara, he tapped a stool behind the counter. "You look wiped. Take a load off. Your dad and I can handle ourselves."

"Yes, Mara," abba said quickly. "Perhaps you should sit."

Mara glared. "Abba."

"I'm sorry," abba said, looking away. He added to Gerry, "She doesn't like help."

"No help being offered. I just want some free work. You up for manning the register?" Gerry tapped the stool again. "I put aside one of those strawberry things you like. It's under the counter. Wrapped in pink paper."

"Thanks," Mara said, not wanting to hurt Gerry's feelings by mentioning that she couldn't eat before appointments. She went behind the counter and let Gerry hold her crutches while she pulled herself onto the stool. She hated how good it felt to sit.

Gerry nodded decisively. "Come on," he said, leading abba toward the fresh fruit.

Abba and Gerry made unlikely friends. Gerry made no bones about being a charismatic evangelical. During the last election, he'd put up posters saying that Democratic voters were headed to hell. In return, abba had suggested that Republican voters might need a punch in the jaw, especially any Republican voters who happened to be standing in front of him. Gerry responded that he supported free speech as much as any other patriotic American, but speech like that could get the H-E-double-hockey-sticks out of his store. They shouted. Gerry told abba not to come back. Abba said he wouldn't even buy dog food from fascists.

The next week, Gerry was waiting on the sidewalk with news about a kosher supplier, and Mara and abba went in as if nothing had ever happened.

Before getting sick, Mara had always followed the men through the aisles, joining in their arguments about pesticides and free-range chickens. Gerry liked to joke that he wished his children were as interested in the business as Mara was. *Maybe I'll leave the store to you instead of them*, he'd say, jostling her shoulder. He had stopped saying that.

Mara slipped the wrapped pastry out from under the counter. She broke it into halves and hid one in each pocket, hoping Gerry wouldn't see the lumps when they left. She left the empty paper on the counter, dusted with the crumbs.

An activity book lay next to where the pastry had been. It was for little kids, but Mara pulled it out anyway. Gerry's children were too old to play with things like that now, but he still kept an array of diversions under the counter for when customers' kids needed to be kept busy. It was better to do something than nothing. Armed with the felt-tip pen that was clipped to the cover, she began to flip through pages of half-colored drawings and connect-the-dots.

A few aisles over, near the butcher counter, she heard her father grumbling. She looked up and saw Gerry grab abba's shoulder. As always, he was speaking too loudly. His voice boomed over the hum of the freezers. "I got in the best sausages on Wednesday," he said. "They're kosher. Try them. Make them for your, what do you call it, sadbath."

By then, Gerry knew the word, but it was part of their banter.

"Shabbat," Abba corrected.

Gerry's tone grew more serious. "You're losing too much weight. A man needs meat."

Abba's voice went flat. "I eat when I am hungry. I am not hungry so much lately."

Gerry's grip tightened on abba's shoulder. His voice dropped. "Jakub, you need to take care of yourself."

He looked back furtively at Mara. Flushing with shame, she dropped her gaze to the activity book. She clutched the pen tightly, pretending to draw circles in a word search.

"You have to think about the future," said Gerry. His voice lowered even further. Though he was finally speaking at a normal volume, she still heard every word. "You aren't the one who's dying."

Mara's flush went crimson. She couldn't tell if it was shame or anger—all she felt was cold, rigid shock. She couldn't stop herself from sneaking a glance at abba. He, too, stood frozen. Neither of them ever said it. It was a game of avoidance they played together.

Abba pulled away from Gerry and started down the aisle. His face looked numb rather than angry. He stopped at the counter, looking at everything but Mara. He took Abel's leash and gestured for Mara to get off of the stool. "We'll be late for your appointment," he said, even though it wasn't even eleven o'clock. In a louder voice, he added, "Ring up our cart, would you, Gerry? We'll pick up our bags on our way out of town."

• • • •

Mara didn't like Doctor Pinsky. Abba liked him because he was Jewish even though he was American-born reform with a degree from Queens. He wore his hair close-cut but it looked like it would Jew 'fro if he grew it out.

He kept his nails manicured. His teeth shone perfectly white. He never looked directly at Mara when he spoke. Mara suspected he didn't like children much. Maybe you needed to be that way if you were going to watch the sick ones get worse.

The nurses were all right. Grace and Nicole, both blonde and a bit fat. They didn't understand Mara since she didn't fit their idea of what kids were supposed to be like. She didn't talk about pop or interactives. When there were other child patients in the waiting room, she ignored them.

When the nurses tried to introduce her to the other children anyway, Mara said she preferred to talk to adults, which made them hmm and flutter. *Don't you have any friends, honey?* Nicole had asked her once, and Mara answered that she had some, but they were all on attic space. A year ago, if Mara had been upset, she'd have gone into a-space to talk to her best friend, Collin, but more and more as she got sick, she'd hated seeing him react to her withering body, hated seeing the fright and pity in his eyes. The thought of going back into attic space made her nauseous.

Grace and Nicole gave Mara extra attention because they felt sorry for her. Modern cancer treatments had failed to help and now Mara was the only child patient in the clinic taking chemotherapy. *It's hard on little bodies,* said Grace. *Heck, it's hard on big bodies, too.*

Today it was Grace who came to meet Mara in the waiting room, pushing a wheelchair. Assuming it was for another patient, Mara started to gather her crutches, but Grace motioned for her to stay put. "Let me treat you like a princess."

"I'm not much of a princess," Mara answered, immediately realizing from the pitying look on Grace's face that it was the wrong thing to say. To Grace, that would mean she didn't feel like a princess because she was sick, rather than that she wasn't interested in princesses.

"I can walk," Mara protested, but Grace insisted on helping her into the wheelchair anyway. She hadn't realized how tightly abba was holding her hand until she pulled it free.

Abba stood to follow them. Grace turned back. "Would you mind staying? Doctor Pinsky wants to talk to you."

"I like to go with Mara," abba said.

"We'll take good care of her." Grace patted Mara's shoulder. "You don't mind, do you, princess?"

Mara shrugged. Her father shifted uncertainly. "What does Doctor Pinsky want?"

"He'll be out in a few minutes," said Grace, deflecting. "I'm sorry, Mr. Morawski. You won't have to wait long."

Frowning, abba sat again, fingers worrying the collar of his shirt. Mara saw his conflicting optimism and fear, all inscribed plainly in his eyes, his face, the way he sat. She didn't understand why he kept hoping. Even before they'd tried the targeted immersion therapy and the QTRC regression, she'd known that they wouldn't work. She'd known from the moment when she saw the almost imperceptible frown cross the diagnostician's face when he asked about the pain she'd been experiencing in her knee for months before the break. Yes, she'd said, it had been worse at night, and his brow had darkened, just for an instant. Maybe she'd known even earlier than that, in the moment just after she fell in ima's studio, when she realized with strange, cold clarity that something was very wrong.

Bad news didn't come all at once. It came in successions. Cancer is present. Metastasis has occurred. The tumors are unresponsive. The patient's vitals have taken a turn for the worse. We're sorry to say, we're sorry to say, we're sorry to say.

Grace wheeled Mara toward the back, maintaining a stream of banal, cheerful chatter, remarks about the weather and questions about the holidays and jokes about boys. Mara deflected. She wasn't ever going to have a boyfriend, not the way Grace was teasing her about. Adolescence was like spring, one more thing buried in endless snow.

• • • •

Mara felt exhausted as they pulled into the driveway. She didn't have the energy to push abba away when he came around the truck to help her down. Mara leaned heavily on her father's arm as they crunched their way to the front door.

She vomited in the entryway. Abel came to investigate. She pushed his nose away while abba went to get the mop. The smell made her even more nauseated and so when abba returned, she left him to clean up. It made her feel guilty, but she was too tired to care.

She went to the bathroom to wash out her mouth. She tried not to catch her eye in the mirror, but she saw her reflection anyway. She felt a shock of alienation from the thin, sallow face. It couldn't be hers.

She heard abba in the hallway, grumbling at Abel in Yiddish. Wan, late afternoon light filtered through the windows, foreshadowing sunset. A few months ago, she and abba would have been rushing to cook and clean before Shabbat. Now no one cleaned and Mara left abba to cook alone as she went into ima's studio.

She paused by the barre before sitting, already worried about how difficult it would be to get up again. "I want to watch *Coppélia*," she said. The AI whirred.

*Coppélia* began with a young woman reading on a balcony—except she wasn't really a young woman, she was actually an automaton constructed by the mad scientist, Dr. Coppélius. The dancer playing Coppélia pretended to read from a red leather book. Mara told the AI to fast-forward to ima's entrance.

Mara's mother was dancing the part of the peasant girl, Swanhilde. She looked nothing like the dancer playing Coppélia. Ima was strong, but also short and compact, where Coppélia was tall with visible muscle definition in her arms and legs.

Yet later in the ballet, none of the other characters would be able to tell them apart. Mara wanted to shake them into sense. Why couldn't they tell the difference between a person and a doll?

• • • •

Abba lit the candles and began the prayer, waving his hands through the smoke. They didn't have an adult woman to read the prayers and abba wouldn't let Mara do it while she was still a child. *Soon*, he used to say, *after your bat mitzvah*. Now he said nothing.

They didn't celebrate Shabbat properly. They followed some traditions—tonight they'd leave the lights on, and tomorrow they'd eat cold food instead of cooking—but they did not attend services. If they needed to work then they worked. As a family, they had always been observant in some ways and relaxed in others; they were not the kind who took well to following rules. Abba sometimes seemed to believe in Hashem and at other times not, though he believed in rituals and tradition. Still, before Mara had become ill, they'd taken more care with *halakha*.

As abba often reminded her, Judaism taught that survival was more important than dogma. *Pikuach nefesh* meant that a hospital could run electricity that powered a machine that kept a man alive. A family could work to keep a woman who had just given birth comfortable and healthy.

Perhaps other people wouldn't recognize the exceptions that Mara and her father made from Shabbat as being matters of survival, but they were. They were using all they had just by living. Not much remained for G-d.

The long window over the kitchen counters let through the dimming light as violet and ultramarine seeped across the horizon. The tangerine sun lingered above the trees, preparing to descend into scratching, black branches. Mara's attention drifted as he said Kiddush over the wine.

They washed their hands. Abba tore the challah. He gave a portion to Mara. She let it sit.

"The fish is made with ginger," abba said. "Would you like some string beans?"

"My mouth hurts," Mara said.

Abba paused, the serving plate still in his hands.

She knew that he wouldn't eat unless she did. "I'll have a little," she added softly.

She let him set the food on her plate. She speared a single green bean and stared at it for a moment before biting. Everything tasted like metal after the drugs.

"I used turmeric," he said.

"It's good."

Mara's stomach roiled. She set the fork on her plate.

Her father ate a few bites of fish and then set his fork down, too. A maudlin expression crossed his face. "Family is Hashem's best gift," he said.

Mara nodded. There was little to say.

Abba picked up his wine glass. He twisted the stem as he stared into red. "Family is what the *goyim* tried to take from us with pogroms and ghettoes and the *shoah*. On Shabbat, we find our families, wherever we are."

Abba paused again, sloshing wine gently from side to side.

"Perhaps I should have gone to Israel before you were born."

Mara looked up with surprise. "You think Israel is a corrupt theocracy."

"There are politics, like opposing a government, and then there is needing to be with your people." He shrugged. "I thought about going. I had money then, but no roots. I could have gone wherever I wanted. But I thought, I will go to America instead. There are more Jews in America than Israel. I did not want to live in the shadow of the *shoah*. I wanted to make a family in a place where we could rebuild everything they stole. *Der mensch trakht un Gatt lahkt.*"

He had been speaking rapidly, his accent deepening with every word. Now he stopped.

His voice was hoarse when it returned.

"Your mother...you...I would not trade it, but..." His gaze became diffuse as if the red of the wine were a telescope showing him another world. "It's all so fragile. Your mother is taken and you...*tsuris, tsuris*...and then there is nothing."

• • • •

It was dark when they left the table. Abba piled dishes by the sink so that they could be washed after Shabbat and then retired to his bedroom. Abel came to Mara, tail thumping, begging for scraps. She was too tired to make him beg or shake hands. She rescued her plate from the pile of dishes and laid it on the floor for him to lick clean.

She started toward her bed and then changed her mind. She headed downstairs instead, Abel following after. She paused with her hand on the knob of the red-painted door before entering abba's workshop.

Mara hadn't seen abba go downstairs since their argument that morning but he must have managed to do it without her noticing. The doll sat primly on her stool, dignity restored, her head tilted down as if she were reading a book that Mara couldn't see.

Mara wove between worktables until she reached the doll's side. She lifted its hand and pressed their palms together as abba had done. It was strange to see the shape of her fingers so perfectly copied, down to the fine lines across her knuckles.

She pulled the thing forward. It lolled. Abel ducked its flailing right hand and ran a few steps away, watching warily.

Mara took hold of the thing's head. She pressed the tip of her nose against the tip of its nose, trying to match their faces as she had their palms. With their faces so close together, it looked like a Cyclops, staring back at her with one enormous, blank eye.

"I hate you," Mara said, lips pressed against its mute mouth.

It was true, but not the same way that it had been that morning. She had been furious then. Betrayed. Now the blaze of anger had burned down and she saw what lay in the ashes that remained.

It was jealousy. That this doll would be the one to take abba's hand at Shabbat five years from then, ten years, twenty. That it would take and give the comfort she could not. That it would balm the wounds that she had no choice but to inflict.

Would Mara have wanted a clockwork doll if it meant that she could keep ima?

She imagined lying down for the scans. She imagined a machine studying her brain, replicating her dreams neuron by neuron, rendering her as mathematical patterns. She'd read enough biology and psychology to know that, whatever else she was, she was also an epiphenomenon that arose from chemicals and meat and electricity.

It was sideways immortality. She would be gone, and she would remain. There and not there. A quantum mechanical soul.

Love could hurt, she knew. Love was what made you hurt when your ima died. Love was what made it hurt when abba came to you gentle and solicitous, every kindness a reminder of how much pain you'd leave behind.

She would do this painful thing because she loved him, as he had made this doll because he loved her. She thought, with a sudden clenching of her stomach, that it was a good thing most people never lived to see what people planned to make of them when they were gone.

What Gerry had said was as true as it was cutting. Abba was not the one who would die.

• • • •

Abba slept among twisted blankets, clutching his pillow as if afraid to let it go.

Mara watched from the doorway. "Abba."

He grumbled in his sleep as he shifted position.

"Abba," she repeated. "Please wake up, abba."

She waited while he put on his robe. Then, she led him down.

She made her way swiftly through the workshop, passing the newly painted marionette and the lonely mechanical hand. She halted near the doll, avoiding its empty gaze.

"I'm ready now," she said.

Abba's face shifted from confusion to wariness. With guarded hope, he asked, "Are you certain?"

"I'm sure," she said.

"Please, Mara. You do not have to."

"I know," she answered. She pressed herself against his chest, as if she were a much smaller child looking for comfort. She felt the tension in his body seep into relief as he wept with silent gratitude. She was filled with tears, too, from a dozen emotions blended into one. They were tears of relief, and regret, and pain, and love, and mourning, and more.

He wrapped his arms around her. She closed her eyes and savored the comfort of his woody scent, his warmth, the stubble scratching her arm. She could feel how thin he'd become, but he was still strong enough to hold her so tightly that his embrace was simultaneously joyful and almost too much to bear.

<br>

Act II: Jakub<br>
Tour en l'air<br>
(Turn in the Air)

Jakub was careful to make the scans as unobtrusive as possible. If he could have, he'd have recorded a dozen sessions, twenty-five, fifty, more. He'd have examined every obscure angle; he'd have recorded a hundred redundancies.

Mara was so fragile, though; not just physically, but mentally. He did not want to tax her. He found a way to consolidate what he needed into six nighttime sessions, monitoring her with portable equipment that he could bring into her bedroom which broadcast its data to the larger machinery in the basement.

When the scans were complete, Jakub spent his nights in the workshop, laboring over the new child while Mara slept. It had been a long time since he'd worked with technology like this, streamlined for its potential as a weapon. He had to gentle it, soothe it, coax it into being as careful about preserving memories of rainy mornings as it was about retaining reflexes and fighting skills.

He spent long hours poring over images of Mara's brain. He navigated three-dimensional renderings with the AI's help, puzzling over the strangeness of becoming so intimate with his daughter's mind in such an unexpected way. After he had finished converting the images into a neural map, he looked at Mara's mind with yet new astonishment. The visual representation showed associational clusters as if they were stars: elliptical galaxies of thought.

It was a truism that there were many ways to describe a river—from the action of its molecules to the map of its progress from tributaries to ocean. A mind was such a thing as well. On one end there was thought, personality, individual...and on the other...It was impossible to recognize Mara in the points of light, but he was in the midst of her most basic elements, and there was as much awe in that as there was in puzzling out the origin of the universe. He was the first person ever to see another human being in this way. He knew Mara now as no one else had ever known anyone.

His daughter, his beloved, his *sheineh maideleh*. There were so many others that he'd failed to protect. But Mara would always be safe; he would hold her forever.

Once Jakub had created the foundational schematics for manufacturing analogues to Mara's brain structures, the remainder of the process was automated. Jakub needed only to oversee it, occasionally inputting his approval to the machine.

Jakub found it unbearable to leave the machinery unsupervised, but nevertheless, he could not spend all of his time in the basement. During the mornings when Mara was awake, he paced the house, grumbling at the dog who followed him up and down the hallways as if expecting him to throw a stick. What if the process stalled? What if a catastrophic failure destroyed the images of Mara's mind now when her health was even more fragile and there might be no way to replace them?

He forced himself to disguise his obsession while Mara was awake. It was important to maintain the illusion that their life was the same as it had been before. He knew that Mara remained uneasy with the automaton. Its very presence said so many things that they had been trying to keep silent.

Mara's days were growing even harder. He'd thought the end of chemotherapy would give her some relief, but cancer pain worsened every day. Constant suffering and exhaustion made her alternately sullen and sharp. She snapped at him when he brought her meals, when he tried to help her across the house, when she woke to find him lingering in the doorway while she slept. Part of it was the simple result of pain displacing patience, but it was more, too. Once, when he had touched her shoulder, she'd flinched; then, upon seeing him withdraw, her expression had turned from annoyance to guilt. She'd said, softly, "You won't always be able to do that." A pause, a swallow, and then even more quietly, "It reminds me."

That was what love and comfort had become now. Promises that couldn't be kept.

Most nights, she did not sleep at all, only lay awake, staring out of her window at the snow.

Jakub searched for activities that might console her. He asked her if she'd like him to read to her. He offered to buy her immersive games. He suggested that she log into a spare room with other sick children where they could discuss their troubles. She told him that she wanted to be alone.

She had always been an unusual child, precocious and content to be her own companion. Meryem had said it was natural for a daughter of theirs, who had been raised among adults, and was descended from people who were also talented and solitary. Jakub and Meryem had been similar as children, remote from others their own age as they pursued their obsessions. Now Jakub wished she had not inherited these traits so completely, that she was more easily able to seek solace.

When Mara didn't think he was watching, she gathered her crutches and went into Meryem's studio to watch ballets. She did not like it when he came too close, and so he watched from the hallway. He could see her profile reflected in the mirrors on the opposite wall. She cried as she watched, soundless tears beading her cheeks.

One morning when she put on *A Midsummer Night's Dream*, Jakub ventured into the studio. For so long, he had stayed away, but that had not made things better. He had to try what he could.

He found Mara sitting on the floor, her crutches leaning against the ballet barre. Abel lay a few feet away with his head on his paws. Without speaking, Jakub sat beside them.

Mara wiped her cheeks, streaking her tears. She looked resentfully at Jakub, but he ignored her, hoping he could reach the part of her that still wanted his company even if she had buried it.

They sat stoically for the remainder of act one, holding themselves with care so that they did not accidentally shift closer to one another. Mara pretended to ignore him, though her darting glances told another story. Jakub let her maintain the pretense, trying to allow her some personal space within the studio since he had already intruded so far. He hoped she would be like a scared rabbit, slowly adjusting to his presence and coming to him when she saw that he was safe.

Jakub had expected to spend the time watching Mara and not the video, but he was surprised to find himself drawn into the dancing. The pain of seeing Meryem leap and spin had become almost a dull note, unnoticeable in the concert of his other sorrows. Meryem made a luminous Titania, a ginger wig cascading in curls down her back, her limbs wrapped in flowers, leaves and gossamer. He'd forgotten the way she moved onstage, as careful and precise as a doe, each agile maneuver employing precisely as much strength as she needed and no more.

As Act II began, Mara asked the AI to stop. Exhaustion, she said. Jakub tried to help her back to her room, but she protested, and he let her go.

She was in her own world now, closing down. She had no room left for him.

*What can I do for you, Marale?* he wanted to ask. *I will do anything. You will not let me hold you so I must find another way. I will change the laws of life and death. I will give you as much forever as I can,* sheineh maideleh. *See? I am doing it now.*

He knew that she hated it when he stood outside her door, watching, but when he heard her breath find the steady rhythm of sleep, he went to the threshold anyway. While she slept, Mara looked peaceful for a while, her chest gently rising and falling underneath her snow-colored quilt.

He lingered a long time. Eventually, he left her and returned downstairs to check the machines.

The new child was ready to be born.

• • • •

For years, Jakub had dreamed of the numbers. They flickered in and out of focus as if displayed on old film. Sometimes they looked ashen and faded.

At other times, they were darker than any real black. Always, they were written on palettes of human flesh.

Sometimes the dreams included fragmentary memories. Jakub would be back in the rooms his grandparents had rented when he was a child, watching bubbe prepare to clean the kitchen, pulling her left arm free from one long cotton sleeve, her tattoo a shock on the inside of her forearm. The skin there had gone papery with age, the ink bleached and distorted, but time and sun had not made the mark less portentous. She scoured cookware with steel wool and caustic chemicals that made her hands red and raw when they emerged from the bubbling water. No matter how often Jakub watched, he never stopped expecting her to abandon the ancient pots and turn that furious, unrelenting scrubbing onto herself.

Zayde's tattoo remained more mysterious. It had not been inflicted in Auschwitz and so it hid in the more discreet location they'd used on the trains, needled onto the underside of his upper arm. Occasionally on hot days when Jakub was small, zayde would roll up his sleeves while he worked outside in the sun. If Jakub or one of the other boys found him, zayde would shout at them to get back inside and then finish the work in his long sleeves, dripping with sweat.

Jakub's grandparents never spoke of the camps. Both had been young in those years, but even though they were not much older when they were released, the few pictures of them from that time showed figures that were already brittle and dessicated in both physique and expression. Survivors took many paths away from the devastation, but bubbe and zayde were among those who always afterward walked with their heads down.

Being mutually bitter and taciturn, they resisted marriage until long after their contemporaries had sought comfort in each other's arms. They raised their children with asperity, and sent them into the world as adults with small gifts of money and few displays of emotion.

One of those children was Jakub's mother, who immigrated to the United States where she married. Some years later, she died in childbirth, bearing what would have been Jakub's fifth brother had the child not been stillborn. Jakub's father, grieving, could not take care of his four living sons. Instead, he wrote to his father-in-law in Poland and requested that he come to the United States and take them home with him.

Even then, when he arrived on foreign shores to fetch boys he'd never met and take them back with him to a land they'd never known; even then when the moment should have been grief and gathering; even then zayde's face was hard-lined with resignation. Or so Jakub's elder brothers had told him, for he was the youngest of the surviving four, having learned to speak a few words by then but not yet able to stand on his own.

When the boys were children, it was a mystery to them how such harsh people could have spent long enough together to marry, let alone have children. Surely, they would have been happier with others who were kinder, less astringent, who could bring comfort into a marriage.

One afternoon, when Jakub was four years old, and too naïve to yet understand that some things that were discussed in private should not be shared with everyone, he was sitting with bubbe while she sewed shirts for the boys (too expensive to buy, and shouldn't she know how to sew, having done it all her life?). He asked, "If you don't like zayde, why did you marry him?"

She stopped suddenly. Her hands were still on the machine, her mouth open, her gaze fastened on the seam. For a moment, the breath did not rise in her chest. The needle stuttered to a stop as her foot eased its pressure on the pedal.

She did not deny it or ask *What do you mean?* Neither did she answer any of the other questions that might have been enfolded in that one, like *Why don't you like him?* or *Why did you marry at all?*

Instead, she heard Jakub's true question: *Why zayde and not someone else?*

"How could it be another?" she asked. "We're the same."

And then she began sewing again, making no further mention of it. It was what zayde would have done, too, if Jakub had taken his question to where his grandfather worked at replacing the wiring in their old, old walls.

As important as it was for the two of them that they shared a history, it also meant that they were like knives to each other, constantly reopening each other's old wounds and salting them with tears and anger. Their frequent, bitter arguments could continue for days upon days.

The days of arguing were better than those when bitter silence descended, and each member of the family was left in their own, isolated coldness.

It was not that there were no virtues to how the boys were raised. Their bodies were kept robust on good food, and their minds strengthened with the exercise of solving problems both practical and intellectual. Zayde concocted new projects for them weekly. One week they'd learn to build cabinets, and the next they'd read old books of philosophy, debating free will versus determinism. Jakub took Leibniz's part against zayde's Spinoza. They studied the Torah as an academic text, though zayde was an atheist of the bitter stripe after his time in the camps.

When Jakub was nine, bubbe decided that it was time to cultivate their spirits as well as their minds and bodies. She revealed that she had been having dreams about G-d for decades, ever since the day she left the camp. The hours of her rescue haunted her; as she watched them replay, she said, the world seemed to shimmer with awe and renewal. Over the years, she had come to believe that was the presence of G-d. Knowing zayde's feelings about G-d, bubbe had kept her silence in the name of peace for decades, but that year, some indefinable thing had shifted her conscience and she could do so no longer.

As she'd predicted, zayde was furious. "I am supposed to worship a G-d that would make *this* world?" he demanded. "A G-d like that is no G-d. A G-d like that is evil."

But despite the hours of shouting, slammed doors, and smashed crockery, bubbe remained resolute. She became a *frum* woman, dressing carefully, observing prayers and rituals. On Fridays, the kitchen became the locus of urgent energy as bubbe rushed to prepare for Shabbat, directing Jakub and his brothers to help with the chores. All of them worked tensely, preparing for the moment when zayde would return home and throw the simmering cholent out of the window, or—if they were lucky—turn heel and walk back out, going who-knew-where until he came home on Sunday.

After a particularly vicious argument, zayde proclaimed that while he apparently could not stop his wife from doing as she pleased, he would absolutely no longer permit his grandsons to attend *shul*. It was a final decision; otherwise, one of them would have to leave and never come back. After that, bubbe slipped out alone each week, into the chilly morning.

From zayde and bubbe, Jakub learned that love was both balm and nettle. They taught him from an early age that nothing could hurt so much as family.

· · · ·

Somehow, Jakub had expected the new child to be clumsy and vacant as if she were an infant, but the moment she initialized, her blank look vanished. Some parts of her face tensed and others relaxed. She blinked. She looked just like Mara.

She prickled under Jakub's scrutiny. "What are you staring at? Is something wrong?"

Jakub's mouth worked silently as he sought the words. "I thought you would need more time to adjust."

The child smiled Mara's cynical, lopsided smile, which had been absent for months. "I think you're going to need more time to adjust than I do."

She pulled herself to her feet. It wasn't just her face that had taken on Mara's habits of expression. Without pause, she moved into one of the stretches that Meryem had taught her, elongating her spine. When she relaxed, her posture was exactly like Mara's would have been, a preadolescent slouch ameliorated by a hint of dancer's grace.

"Can we go upstairs?" she asked.

"Not yet," Jakub said. "There are tests to perform."

Tests which she passed. Every single one. She knew Mara's favorite colors and the names of the children she had studied with in attic space. She knew the color and weight of the apples that would grow on their trees next fall and perfectly recited the recipe for baking them with cinnamon. In the gruff tone that Mara used when she was guarding against pain, she related the story of Meryem's death—how Meryem had woken with complaints of feeling dizzy, how she had slipped in the bath later that morning, how her head had cracked against the porcelain and spilled red into the bathwater.

She ran like Mara and caught a ball like Mara and bent to touch her toes like Mara. She was precisely as fleet and as nimble and as flexible as Mara. She performed neither worse nor better. She was Mara's twin in every way that Jakub could measure.

"You will need to stay here for a few more days," he told her, bringing down blankets and pillows so that he could make her a bed in the workshop. "There are still more tests. You will be safer if you remain close to the machines."

The new child's face creased with doubt. He was lying to spare her feelings, but she was no more deceived than Mara would have been. She said, "My room is upstairs."

For so many months, Jakub and Mara had taken refuge in mutual silence when the subject turned uncomfortable. He did not like to speak so bluntly. But if she would force him—"No," he said gently. "That is Mara's room."

"Can't I at least see it?"

Wheedling thinned her voice. Her body language occupied a strange lacuna between aggression and vulnerability. She faced him full-on, one foot advancing, with her hands clenched tightly at her sides. Yet at the same time, she could not quite meet his eyes, and her head was tilted slightly downward, protecting her neck.

Jakub had seen that strange combination before. It was not so unusual a posture for teenagers to wear when they were trying to assert their agency through rebellion and yet simultaneously still hoping for their parents' approval.

Mara had never reached that stage. Before she became ill, she had been calm, abiding. Jakub began to worry that he'd erred in his calculations, that the metrics he'd used had been inadequate to measure the essence of a girl. Could she have aged so much, simply being slipped into an artificial skin?

"Mara is sleeping now."

"But I *am* Mara!" The new child's voice broke on her exclamation.

Her lips parted uncertainly. Her fingers trembled. Her glance flashed upward for a moment and he saw such pain in it. No, she was still his Mara. Not defiant, only afraid that he would decide that he had not wanted a mechanical daughter after all, that he would reject her like a broken radio and never love her again.

Gently, he laid his hand on her shoulder. Softly, he said, "You are Mara, but you need a new name, too. Let us call you Ruth."

He had not known until he spoke that he was going to choose that name, but it was a good one. In the Torah, Ruth had given Mara *hesed*. His Mara needed loving kindness, too.

The new child's gaze flickered upward as if she could see through the ceiling and into Mara's room. "Mara is the name ima gave me," she protested.

Jakub answered, "It would be confusing otherwise."

He hoped that this time the new child would understand what he meant without his having to speak outright. The other Mara had such a short time. It would be cruel to make her days harder than they must be.

• • • •

On the day when Jakub gave the automaton her name, he found himself recalling the story of Ruth. It had been a long time since he had given the

Torah any serious study, but though he had forgotten its minutiae, he remembered its rhythm.

*It began when a famine descended on Judah.*

*A man, Elimelech, decided that he was not going to let his wife and sons starve to death, and so he packed his household and brought them to Moab. It was good that he had decided to do so, because once they reached Moab, he died, and left his wife and sons alone.*

*His wife was named Naomi and her name meant pleasant. The times were not pleasant.*

*Naomi's sons married women from Moab, one named Orpah and the other named Ruth. Despite their father's untimely death, the boys spent ten happy years with their new wives. But the men of that family had very poor luck. Both sons died.*

*There was nothing left for Naomi in Moab and so she packed up her house and prepared to return to Judah. She told her daughters-in-law, "Go home to your mothers. You were always kind to my sons and you've always been kind to me. May Hashem be kind to you in return."*

*She kissed them goodbye, but the girls wept.*

*They said, "Can't we return to Judah with you?"*

*"Go back to your mothers," Naomi repeated. "I have no more sons for you to marry. What can I give if you stay with me?"*

*The girls continued to weep, but at last sensible Orpah kissed her mother-in-law and left for home.*

*Ruth, who was less sensible; Ruth, who was more loving; Ruth, who was more kind; Ruth, she would not go.*

*"Don't make me leave you," Ruth said. "Wherever you go, I will go. Wherever you lodge, I will lodge. Your people will be my people and your G-d my G-d."*

*When Naomi saw that Ruth was committed to staying with her, she abandoned her arguing and let her come.*

*They traveled together to Bethlehem. When they arrived, they found that the whole city had gathered to see them. Everyone was curious about the two women traveling from Moab. One woman asked, "Naomi! Is that you?"*

*Naomi shook her head. "Don't call me Naomi. There is no pleasantness in my life. Call me Mara, which means bitterness, for the Almighty has dealt very bitterly with me."*

*Through the bitterness, Ruth stayed. While Naomi became Mara, Ruth stayed. Ruth gave her kindness, and Ruth stayed.*

• • • •

Jakub met Meryem while he was in Cleveland for a robotics conference. He'd attended dozens, but somehow this one made him feel particularly self-conscious in his cheap suit and tie among all the wealthy *goyim*.

By then he was living in the United States, but although he'd been born there, he rarely felt at home among its people. Between talks, he escaped from the hotel to go walking. That afternoon, he found his way to a path that wound through a park, making its way through dark-branched trees that waved their remaining leaves like flags of ginger, orange and gold.

Meryem sat on an ironwork bench beside a man-made lake, its water silvered with dusk. She wore a black felt coat that made her look pallid even though her cheeks were pink with cold. A wind rose as Jakub approached, rippling through Meryem's hair. Crows took off from the trees, disappearing into black marks on the horizon.

Neither of them was ever able to remember how they began to converse. Their courtship seemed to rise naturally from the lake and the crows and the fallen leaves, as if it were another inevitable element of nature. It was *bashert*.

Meryem was younger than Jakub, but even so, already ballet had begun taking its toll on her body. Ballet was created by trading pain for beauty, she used to say. Eventually, beauty vanished and left only the pain.

Like Jakub, Meryem was an immigrant. Her grandparents had been born in Baghdad where they lived through the *farhud* instead of the *shoah*. They stayed in Iraq despite the pogroms until the founding of Israel made it too dangerous to remain. They abandoned their family home and fled to the U.S.S.R.

When Meryem was small, the Soviet government identified her talent for dance and took her into training. Ballet became her new family. It was her blood and bone, her sacred and her profane.

Her older brother sometimes sent letters, but with the accretion of time and distance, Meryem came to think of her family as if they were not so much people as they were the words spelled out in Yusuf's spidery handwriting.

Communism fell, and Meryem's family was given the opportunity to reclaim her, but even a few years away is so much of a child's lifetime. She begged them not to force her to return. They no longer felt like her home. More, ballet had become the gravitational center of her life, and while she still resented it—how it had taken her unwillingly, how it bruised her feet and sometimes made them bleed—she also could not bear to leave its orbit. When Yusuf's letters stopped coming some time later, she hardly noticed.

She danced well. She was a lyrical ballerina, performing her roles with tender, affecting beauty that could make audiences weep or smile. She rapidly moved from corps to soloist to principal. The troupe traveled overseas to perform Stravinsky's *Firebird*, and when they reached the United States, Meryem decided to emigrate, which she accomplished with a combination of bribes and behind-the-scenes dealings.

Jakub and Meryem recognized themselves in each other's stories. Like his grandparents, they were drawn together by their similarities. Unlike them, they built a refuge together instead of a battlefield.

After Meryem died, Jakub began dreaming that the numbers were inscribed into the skins of people who'd never been near the camps. His skin. His daughter's. His wife's. They were all marked, as Cain was marked, as the Christians believed the devil would mark his followers at the end of time. Marked for diaspora, to blow away from each other and disappear.

• • • •

"Is the doll awake?" Mara asked one morning.

Jakub looked up from his breakfast to see her leaning against the doorway that led into the kitchen. She wore a large t-shirt from Yellowstone that came to her knees, covering a pair of blue jeans that had not been baggy when he'd bought them for her. Her skin was wan and her eyes shadowed and sunken. Traces of inflammation from the drugs lingered, painfully red, on her face and hands. The orange knit cap pulled over her ears was incongruously bright.

Jakub could not remember the last time she'd worn something other than pajamas.

"She is down in the workshop," Jakub said.

"She's awake, though?"

"She is awake."

"Bring her up."

Jakub set his spoon beside his leftover bowl of *chlodnik*. Mara's mouth was turned down at the corners, hard and resolute. She lifted her chin at a defiant angle.

"She has a bed in the workshop," Jakub said. "There are still tests I

457

must run. It's best she stay close to the machines."

Mara shook her head. It was clear from her face that she was no more taken in by his lie than the new child had been. "It's not fair to keep someone stuck down there."

Jakub began to protest that the workshop was not such a bad place, but then he caught the flintiness in Mara's eyes and realized that she was not asking out of worry. She had dressed as best she could and come to confront him because she wanted her first encounter with the new child to be on her terms. There was much he could not give her, but he could give her that.

"I will bring her for dinner," he said. "Tomorrow, for Shabbat."

Mara nodded. She began the arduous process of departing the kitchen, but then stopped and turned back. "Abba," she said hesitantly. "If ima hated the ballet, why did you build her a studio?"

"She asked for one," Jakub said.

Mara waited.

At last, he continued, "Ballet was part of her. She could not simply stop."

Mara nodded once more. This time, she departed.

Jakub finished his *chlodnik* and spent the rest of the day cooking. He meted out ingredients for familiar dishes. A pinch, a dash, a dab. Chopping, grating, boiling, sampling. Salt and sweet, bitter and savory.

As he went downstairs to fetch Ruth, he found himself considering how strange it must be for her to remember these rooms and yet never to have entered them. Jakub and Meryem had drawn the plans for the house together. She'd told him that she was content to leave a world of beauty that was made by pain, in exchange for a plain world made by joy.

He'd said he could give her that.

They painted the outside walls yellow to remind them of the sun during the winter, and painted blue inside to remind them of the sky. By the time they had finished, Mara was waiting inside Meryem's womb. The three of them had lived in the house for seven years before Meryem died.

These past few weeks had been precious. Precious because he had, in some ways, finally begun to recover the daughter that he had lost on the day her leg shattered—Ruth, once again curious and strong and insightful, like the Mara he had always known. But precious, too, because these were his last days with the daughter he'd made with Meryem.

Precious days, but hardly bearable, even as he also could not bear that they would pass. Precious, but more salt and bitter than savory and sweet.

The next night, when Jakub entered the workshop, he found Ruth on the stool where she'd sat so long when she was empty. Her shoulders slumped; her head hung down. He began to worry that something was wrong, but then he saw that she was only reading the book of poetry that she held in her lap.

"Would you like to come upstairs for dinner?" Jakub asked.

Setting the poems aside, Ruth rose to join him.

• • • •

Long before Jakub met Meryem—back in those days when he still traveled the country on commissions from the American government—Jakub had become friends with a rabbi from Minneapolis. The two still exchanged letters through the postal mail, rarefied and expensive as it was.

After Jakub sent the news from Doctor Pinsky, the rabbi wrote back, "First your wife and now your daughter...*es vert mir finster in di oygen.* You must not let yourself be devoured by *agmes-nefesh.* Even in the camps, people kept hope. *Yashir koyech,* my friend. You must keep hope, too."

Jakub had not written to the rabbi about the new child. Even if it had not been vital for him to keep the work secret, he would not have written about it. He could not be sure what the rabbi would say. Would he call the new child a golem instead of a girl? Would he declare the work unseemly or unwise?

But truly, Jakub was only following the rabbi's advice. The new child was his strength and hope. She would prevent him from being devoured by sorrow.

• • • •

When Jakub and Ruth arrived in the kitchen for Shabbat, Mara had not yet come.

They stood alone together in the empty room. Jakub had mopped the floors and scrubbed the counters and set the table with good dishes. The table was laid with challah, apricot chicken with farfel, and almond and raisin salad. *Cholent* simmered in a crock pot on the counter, waiting for Shabbat lunch.

Ruth started toward Mara's chair on the left. Jakub caught her arm, more roughly than he'd meant to. He pulled back, contrite. "No," he said softly. "Not there." He gestured to the chair on the right. Resentment crossed the new child's face, but she went to sit.

It was only as Jakub watched Ruth lower herself into the right-hand chair that he realized his mistake. "No! Wait. Not in Meryem's chair. Take mine. I'll switch with you—"

Mara's crutches clicked down the hallway. It was too late.

She paused in the doorway. She wore the blonde wig Jakub had bought for her after the targeted immersion therapy failed. Last year's green Pesach dress hung off of her shoulders. The cap sleeves neared her elbows.

Jakub moved to help with her crutches. She stayed stoic while he helped her sit, but he could see how much it cost her to accept assistance while she was trying to maintain her dignity in front of the new child. It would be worse because the new child possessed her memories and knew precisely how she felt.

Jakub leaned the crutches against the wall. Ruth looked away, embarrassed.

Mara gave her a corrosive stare. "Don't pity me."

Ruth looked back. "What do you want me to do?"

"Turn yourself off," said Mara. "You're *muktzeh*."

Jakub wasn't sure he'd ever before heard Mara use the Hebrew word for objects forbidden on the Sabbath. Now, she enunciated it with crisp cruelty.

Ruth remained calm. "One may work on the Sabbath if it saves a life."

Mara scoffed. "If you call yours a life."

Jakub wrung his hands. "Please, Mara," he said. "You asked her to come."

Mara held her tongue for a lingering moment. Eventually, she nodded formally toward Ruth. "I apologize."

Ruth returned the nod. She sat quietly, hands folded in her lap. She didn't take nutrition from food, but Jakub had given her a hollow stomach that she could empty after meals so she would be able to eat socially. He waited to see if she would return Mara's insults, but she was the old Mara, the one who wasn't speared with pain and fear, the one who let aggressors wind themselves up if that was what they wanted to do.

Jakub looked between the girls. "Good," he said. "We should have peace for the Sabbath."

He went to the head of the table. It was late for the blessing, the sun skimming the horizon behind bare, black trees. He lit the candles and waved his hands over the flames to welcome Shabbat. He covered his eyes as he recited the blessing. "*Barukh atah Adonai, Elohaynu, melekh ha-olam…*"

Every time he said the words that should have been Meryem's, he remembered the way she had looked when she said them. Sometimes she peeked out from behind her fingers so that she could watch Mara. They were small, her hands, delicate like bird wings. His were large and blunt.

The girls stared at each other as Jakub said kaddish. After they washed their hands and tore the challah, Jakub served the chicken and the salad. Both children ate almost nothing and said even less.

"It's been a long time since we've had three for Shabbat," Jakub said. "Perhaps we can have a good *vikuekh*. Mara, I saw you reading my Simic? Ruth has been reading poetry, too. Haven't you, Ruth?"

Ruth shifted the napkin in her lap. "Yehuda Amichai," she said. "*Even a Fist Was once an Open Palm with Fingers.*"

"I love the first poem in that book," Jakub said. "I was reading it when—"

Mara's voice broke in, so quietly that he almost didn't hear. "Ruth?"

Jakub looked to Ruth. The new child stared silently down at her hands. Jakub cleared his throat, but she did not look up.

Jakub answered for her. "Yes?"

Mara's expression was slack, somewhere between stunned and lifeless. "You named her Ruth."

"She is here for you. As Ruth was there for Mara."

Mara began to cry. It was a tiny, pathetic sound. She pushed away her plate and tossed her napkin onto the table. "How could you?"

"Ruth gives *hesed* to Mara," Jakub said. "When everyone else left, Ruth stayed by her side. She expected nothing from her loving, from her kindness."

"*Du kannst nicht auf meinem rucken pishen unt mir sagen class es regen ist,*" Mara said bitterly.

Jakub had never heard Mara say that before either. The crass proverb sounded wrong in her mouth. "Please, I am telling you the truth," he said. "I wanted her name to be part of you. To come from your story. The story of Mara."

"Is that what I am to you?" Mara asked. "Bitterness?"

"No, no. Please, no. We never thought you were bitterness. Mara was the name Meryem chose. Like Maruska, the Russian friend she left behind." Jakub paused. "Please. I did not mean to hurt you. I thought the story would help you see. I wanted you to understand. The new child will not harm you. She'll show you *hesed.*"

Mara flailed for her crutches.

Jakub stood to help. Mara was so weak that she accepted his assistance. Tears flowed down her face. She left the room as quickly as she could, refusing to look at either Jakub or the new child.

Jakub looked between her retreating form and Ruth's silent one. The new child's expression was almost as unsure as Jakub's.

"Did you know?" Jakub asked. "Did you know how she'd feel?"

Ruth turned her head as if turning away from the question. "Talk to her," she said quietly. "I'll go back down to the basement."

• • • •

Mara sat on her bed, facing the snow. Jakub stood at the threshold. She spoke without turning. "*Hesed* is a hard thing," she said. "Hard to take when you can't give it back."

Jakub crossed the room, past the chair he'd made her when she was little, with Meryem's shawl hung over the back; past the hanging marionette dressed as Giselle; past the cube Mara used for her lessons in attic space. He sat beside her on her white quilt and looked at her silhouetted form against the white snow.

She leaned back toward him. Her body was brittle and delicate against his chest. He remembered sitting on that bed with Mara and Meryem, reading stories, playing with toys. *Tsuris, tsuris.* Life was all so fragile. He was not graceful enough to keep it from breaking.

Mara wept. He held her in his large, blunt hands.

## Act III: Ruth
### *Échappé*
### (Escape)

At first, Ruth couldn't figure out why she didn't want to switch herself off. Mara had reconciled herself to Ruth's existence, but in her gut, she still wanted Ruth to be gone. And Ruth was Mara, so she should have felt the same.

But no, her experiences were diverging. Mara wanted the false daughter to vanish. Mara thought Ruth was the false daughter, but Ruth knew she wasn't false at all. She *was* Mara. Or had been.

Coming into existence was not so strange. She felt no peculiar doubling, no sensation that her hands weren't hers, no impression that she had been pulled out of time and was supposed to be sleeping upstairs with her face turned toward the window.

She felt more secure in the new body than she had in Mara's. This body was healthy, even round in places. Her balance was steady; her fingernails were pink and intact.

After abba left her the first night, Ruth found a pane of glass that he'd set aside for one of his projects. She stared at her blurred reflection. The glass showed soft, smooth cheeks. She ran her fingers over them and they confirmed that her skin was downy now instead of sunken. Clear eyes stared back at her.

Over the past few months, Mara had grown used to experiencing a new alienation every time she looked in the mirror. She'd seen a parade of strangers' faces, each dimmer and hollower than the last.

Her face was her own again.

• • • •

She spent her first days doing tests. Abba watched her jump and stretch and run on a treadmill. For hours upon hours, he recorded her answers to his questions.

It was tedious for her, but abba was fascinated by her every word and movement. Sometimes he watched as a father. Sometimes he watched as a scientist. At first Ruth chafed under his experimental gaze, but then she remembered that he had treated Mara like that, too. He'd liked to set up simple experiments to compare her progress to child development manuals. She remembered ima complaining that he'd been even worse when Mara was an infant. Ruth supposed this was the same. She'd been born again.

While he observed her, she observed him. Abba forgot that some experiments could look back.

The abba she saw was a different man than the one she remembered sitting with Mara. He'd become brooding with Mara as she grew sicker. His grief had become a deep anger with G-d. He slammed doors and cabinets, and grimaced with bitter fury when he thought she wasn't looking. He wanted to break the world.

He still came down into the basement with that fury on his face, but as he talked to Ruth, he began to calm. The muscles in his forehead relaxed. He smiled now and then. He reached out to touch her hand, gently, as if she were a soap bubble that might break if he pressed too hard.

Then he went upstairs, back to that other Mara.

"Don't go yet," Ruth would beg. "We're almost done. It won't take much longer."

He'd linger.

She knew he thought she was just bored and wanted attention. But that wasn't why she asked. She hated the rain that silvered his eyes when he went up to see the dying girl.

After a few minutes, he always said the same thing, resolute and loyal to his still-living child. "I must go, *nu?*"

He sent Abel down in his place. The dog thumped down and waited for her to greet him at the foot of the stairs. He whuffed hello, breath humid and smelly.

Ruth had been convinced—when she was Mara—that a dog would never show affection for a robot. Maybe Abel only liked Ruth because his sense of smell, like the rest of him, was in decline. Whatever the reason, she was Mara enough for him.

Ruth ran the treadmill while Abel watched, tail wagging. She thought about chasing him across the snowy yard, about breaking sticks off of the bare-branched trees to throw for him. She could do anything. She could run; she could dance; she could swim; she could ride. She could almost forgive abba for treating her like a prototype instead of a daughter, but she couldn't forgive him for keeping her penned. The real Mara was stuck in the house, but Ruth didn't have to be. It wasn't fair to have spent so long static, waiting to die, and then suddenly be free—and still remain as trapped as she'd ever been.

After the disastrous Shabbat, she went back down to the basement and sat on one of abba's workbenches. Abel came down after her. He leaned against her knees, warm and heavy. She patted his head.

She hadn't known how Mara was going to react.

She should have known. She would have known if she'd thought about it. But she hadn't considered the story of Mara and Ruth. All she'd been thinking about was that Ruth wasn't her name.

Their experiences had branched off. They were like twins who'd shared the womb only to be delivered into a world where each new event was a small alienation, until their individual experiences separated them like a chasm.

One heard a name and wanted her own back. One heard a name and saw herself as bitterness.

One was living. One was dying.

She was still Mara enough to feel the loneliness of it.

The dog's tongue left a trail of slobber across the back of her hand. He pushed his head against her. He was warm and solid, and she felt tears threatening, and wasn't sure why. It might have been grief for Mara. Perhaps it was just the unreasonable relief that someone still cared about her. Even though it was miserly to crave attention when Mara was dying, she still felt the gnaw of wondering whether abba would still love her when Mara was gone, or whether she'd become just a machine to him, one more painful reminder.

She jumped off of the table and went to sit in the dark, sheltered place beneath it. There was security in small places—in closets, under beds, beneath the desk in her room. Abel joined her, pushing his side against hers. She curled around him and switched her brain to sleep.

• • • •

After Shabbat, there was no point in separating Ruth and Mara anymore. Abba told Ruth she could go wherever she wanted. He asked where she wanted to sleep. "We can put a mattress in the parlor," he said. When she didn't react, he added, "Or the studio…?"

She knew he didn't want her in the studio. Mara was mostly too tired to leave her room now, but abba would want to believe that she was still sneaking into the studio to watch ima's videos.

Ruth wanted freedom, but it didn't matter where she slept.

"I'll stay in the basement," she said.

When she'd had no choice but to stay in the basement, she'd felt like a compressed coil that might spring uncontrollably up the stairs at any moment. Now that she was free to move around, it didn't seem so urgent. She could take her time a little, choose those moments when going upstairs wouldn't make things worse, such as when abba and Mara were both asleep, or when abba was sitting with Mara in her room.

Once she'd started exploring, she realized it was better that she was on her own anyway. Moving through the house was dreamlike, a strange blend of familiarity and alienation. These were rooms she knew like her skin, and yet she, as Ruth, had never entered them. The handprint impressed into the clay tablet on the wall wasn't hers; it was Mara's. She could remember the texture of the clay as she pushed in her palm, but it hadn't been her palm. She had never sat at the foot of the plush, red chair in the parlor while ima brushed her hair. The scuff marks on the hardwood in the hallway were from someone else's shoes.

As she wandered from room to room, she realized that on some unconscious level, when she'd been Mara, she'd believed that moving into a robotic body would clear the haze of memories that hung in the house. She'd imagined a robot would be a mechanical, sterile thing. In reality, ima still haunted the kitchen where she'd cooked, and the studio where she'd danced, and the bathroom where she'd died. Change wasn't exorcism.

• • • •

Ruth remained restless. She wanted more than the house. For the first time in months, she found herself wanting to visit attic space, even though her flock was even worse about handling cancer than adults, who were bad enough. The pity in Collin's eyes, especially, had made her want to puke so much that she hadn't even let herself think about him. Mara had closed the door on her best friend early in the process of closing the doors on her entire life.

She knew abba would be skeptical, though, so she wanted to bring it up in a way that seemed casual. She waited for him to come down to the workshop for her daily exam, and tried to broach the subject as if it were an afterthought.

"I think I should go back to the attic," she ventured. "I'm falling behind. My flock is moving on without me."

Abba looked up from the screen, frowning. He worried his hands in a way that had become troublingly familiar. "They know Mara is sick."

"I'll pretend to be sick," Ruth said. "I can fake it."

She'd meant to sound detached, as if her interest in returning to school was purely pragmatic, but she couldn't keep the anticipation out of her tone.

"I should go back now before it's been too long," she said. "I can pretend I'm starting to feel better. We don't want my recovery to look too sudden."

"It is not a good idea," abba said. "It would only add another complication. If you did not pretend correctly? If people noticed? You are still new-made. Another few weeks and you will know better how to control your body."

"I'm bored," Ruth said. Making another appeal to his scholarly side, she added, "I miss studying."

"You can study. You've been enjoying the poetry, yes? There is so much for you to read."

"It's not the same." Ruth knew she was on the verge of whining, but she couldn't make her voice behave.

Abba paused, trepidation playing over his features as he considered his response. "Ruth, I have thought on this…I do not think it is good for you to go back to attic space. They will know you. They might see that something is wrong. We will find you another program for home learning."

Ruth stared. "You want me to leave attic space?" Almost everyone she knew, apart from abba and a few people in town, was from the attic. After a moment's thought, the implications were suddenly leaden in her mind. "You don't just want me to stop going for school, do you? You want me to stop seeing them at all."

Abba's mouth pursed around words he didn't want to say.

"Everyone?" asked Ruth. "Collin? Everyone?"

Abba wrung his hands. "I am sorry, Mara. I only want to protect you."

"Ruth!" Ruth said.

"Ruth," abba murmured. "Please. I am sorry, Ruthele."

Ruth swallowed hard, trying to push down sudden desperation. She hadn't wanted the name. She didn't want the name. But she didn't want to be confused for the Mara upstairs either. She wanted him to be there with *her*, talking to *her*.

"You can't keep me stuck here just because she is!" she said, meaning the words to bite. "She's the one who's dying. Not me."

Abba flinched. "You are so angry," he said quietly. "I thought, now that you were well—You did not used to be so angry."

"You mean *Mara* didn't used to be so angry," Ruth said. A horrible thought struck her and she felt cold that she hadn't thought of it before. "How am I going to grow up? Am I going to be stuck like this? Eleven, like she is, forever?"

"No, Ruth, I will build you new bodies," said abba. "Bodies are easy. It is the mind that is difficult."

"You just want me to be like her," Ruth said.

Abba fumbled for words. "I want you to be yourself."

"Then let me go do things! You can't hide me here forever."

"Please, Ruth. A little patience."

Patience!

Ruth swung off of the stool. The connectors in her wrist and neck tore loose and she threw them to the floor. She ran for the stairs, crashing into one of the diagnostic machines and knocking it over before making it to the bottom step.

Abba said nothing. Behind her, she heard the small noise of effort that he made as he lowered himself to the floor to retrieve the equipment.

It was strange to feel such bright-hot anger again. Like abba, she'd thought that the transfer had restored her even temper. But apparently the anger she'd learned while she was Mara couldn't just be forgotten.

She spent an hour pacing the parlor, occasionally grabbing books off of a shelf, flipping through them as she walked, and then tossing them down in random locations. The anger's brightness faded, although the sense of injustice remained.

Later, abba came up to see her. He stood with mute pleading, not wanting to reopen the argument but obviously unable to bear continuing to fight.

Even though Ruth hadn't given in yet, even though she was still burning from the unfairness, she couldn't look into his sad eyes without feeling thickness in her throat.

He gestured helplessly. "I just want to keep you safe, Ruthele."

They sat together on the couch without speaking. They were both entrenched in their positions. It seemed to Ruth that they were both trying to figure out how to make things right without giving in, how to keep fighting without wounding.

Abel paced between them, shoving his head into Ruth's lap, and then into abba's, back and forth. Ruth patted his head and he lingered with her a moment, gazing up with rheumy but devoted eyes.

Arguing with abba wasn't going to work. He hadn't liked her taking risks before she'd gotten sick, but afterward, keeping her safe had become obsession, which was why Ruth even existed. He was a scientist, though; he liked evidence. She'd just have to show him it was safe.

Ruth didn't like to lie, but she'd do it. In a tone of grudging acceptance, she said, "You're right. It's too risky for me to go back."

"We will find you new friends," abba said. "We will be together. That's what is important."

• • • •

Ruth bided her time for a few days. Abba might have been watching her more closely if he hadn't been distracted with Mara. Instead, when he wasn't at Mara's bedside or examining Ruth, he drifted mechanically through the house, registering little.

Ruth had learned a lot about engineering from watching her father. Attic space wasn't complicated technology. The program came on its own cube which meant it was entirely isolated from the household AI and its notification protocols. It also came with standard parental access points that had been designed to favor ease of use over security—which meant there were lots of back-end entryways.

Abba didn't believe in restricting access to knowledge so he'd made it even easier by deactivating the nanny settings on Mara's box as soon as she was old enough to navigate attic space on her own.

Ruth waited until nighttime when Mara was drifting in and out of her fractured, painful sleep, and abba had finally succumbed to exhaustion. Abba had left a light on in the kitchen, but it didn't reach the hallway to Mara's room, which fell in stark shadow. Ruth felt her way to Mara's threshold and put her ear to the door. She could hear the steady, sleeping rhythm of Mara's breath inside.

She cracked the door. Moonlight spilled from the window over the bed, allowing her to see inside. It was the first time she'd seen the room in her new body. It looked the same as it had. Mara was too sick to fuss over books or possessions so the objects sat in their places, ordered but dusty. Apart from the lump that Mara's body made beneath the quilt, the room looked as if it could have been abandoned for days.

The attic space box sat on a low shelf near the door. It fit in the palm of Ruth's hand. The fading image on its exterior showed the outline of a house with people inside, rendered in a style that was supposed to look like a child's drawing. It was the version they put out for five-year-olds. Abba had never replaced it. A waste of money, he said, when he could upgrade it himself.

Ruth looked up at the sound of blankets shifting. One of Mara's hands slipped free from the quilt. Her fingers dangled over the side of the bed, the knuckles exaggerated on thin bones. Inflamed cuticles surrounded her ragged nails.

Ruth felt a sting of revulsion and chastised herself. Those hands had been hers. She had no right to be repulsed.

The feeling faded to an ache. She wanted to kneel by the bed and take Mara's hand into her own. She wanted to give Mara the shelter and empathy that abba had built her to give. But she knew how Mara felt about her. Taking Mara's hand would not be *hesed*. The only loving kindness she could offer now was to leave.

As Ruth sat in ima's studio, carefully disassembling the box's hardware so that she could jury-rig it to interact with the television, it occurred to her that abba would have loved helping her with this project. He loved scavenging old technology. He liked to prove that cleverness could make tools of anything.

The complicated VR equipment that made it possible to immerse in attic space was far too bulky for Ruth to steal from Mara's room without being caught. She thought she could recreate a sketchy, winnowed down version of the experience using low technology replacements from the television and other scavenged equipment. Touch, smell and taste weren't going to happen, but an old stereo microphone allowed her to transmit on the voice channel. She found a way to instruct the box to send short bursts of visuals to the television, although the limited scope and speed would make it like walking down a hallway illuminated by a strobe light.

She sat cross-legged on the studio floor and logged in. It was the middle of the night, but usually at least someone from the flock was around. She was glad to see it was Collin this time, tweaking an experiment with crystal growth. Before she'd gotten sick, Ruth probably would have been there with him. They liked going in at night when there weren't many other people around.

She saw a still of Collin's hand over a delicate formation, and then another of him looking up, startled. "Mara?" he asked. "Is that you?"

His voice cracked when he spoke, sliding from low to high. It hadn't been doing that before.

"Hi, Collin," she said.

"Your avatar looks weird." She could imagine Collin squinting to investigate her image, but the television continued to show his initial look of surprise.

She was using a video skin capture from the last time Mara had logged in, months ago. Without a motion reader, it was probably just standing there, breathing and blinking occasionally, with no expression on its face.

"I'm on a weird connection," Ruth said.

"Is it because you're sick?" Collin's worried expression flashed onscreen. "Can I see what you really like? It's okay. I've seen videos. I won't be grossed out or anything. I missed you. I thought—we weren't sure you were coming back. We were working on a video to say goodbye."

Ruth shifted uncomfortably. She'd wanted to go the attic so she could get on with living, not to be bogged down in dying. "I don't want to talk about that."

The next visual showed a flash of Colin's hand, blurred with motion as he raised it to his face. "We did some stuff with non-Newtonian fluids," he said tentatively. "You'd have liked it. We got all gross."

"Did you throw them around?" she asked.

"Goo fight," Collin agreed. He hesitated. "Are you coming back? Are you better?"

"Well—" Ruth began.

"Everyone will want to know you're here. Let me ping them."

"No. I just want to talk to you."

A new picture: Collin moving closer to her avatar, his face now crowding the narrow rectangle of her vision.

"I looked up osteosarcoma. They said you had lung nodules. Mara, are you really better? Are you really coming back?"

"I said I don't want to talk about it."

"But everyone will want to know."

Suddenly, Ruth wanted to be anywhere but attic space. Abba was right. She couldn't go back. Not because someone might find out but because everyone was going to want to know, what about Mara? They were going to want to know about Mara all the time. They were going to want to drag Ruth back into that sick bed, with her world narrowing toward death, when all she wanted was to move on.

And it was even worse now than it would have been half an hour ago, before she'd gone into Mara's room and seen her raw, tender hand, and thought about what it would be like to grasp it.

"I have to go," Ruth said.

"At least let me ping Violet," Collin said.

"I'll be back," Ruth answered. "I'll see you later."

On the television: Collin's skeptical face, brows drawn, the shine in his eyes that showed he thought she was lying.

"I promise," she said, hesitating only a moment before she tore the attic space box out of her jury-rigged web of wires.

Tears were filling her eyes and she couldn't help the sob. She threw the box. It skittered across the wooden floor until it smacked into the mirror. The thing was so old and knocked about that any hard collision might kill it, but what did that matter now? She wasn't going back.

She heard a sound from the doorway and looked up. She saw abba, standing behind the cracked door.

Ruth's anger flashed to a new target. "Why are you spying on me?"

"I came to check on Mara," abba said.

He didn't have to finish for his meaning to be clear. He'd heard someone in the studio and hoped it could still be his Marale.

He made a small gesture toward the attic space box. "It did not go well," he said quietly, statement rather than question.

Ruth turned her head away. He'd been right, about everything he'd said, all the explicit things she'd heard, and all the implicit things she hadn't wanted to.

She pulled her knees toward her chest. "I can't go back," she said.

Abba stroked her hair. "I know."

• • • •

The loss of attic space hurt less than she'd thought it would. Mara had sealed off those tender spaces, and those farewells had a final ring. She'd said goodbye to Collin a long time ago.

What bothered her more was the lesson it forced; her life was never going to be the same, and there was no way to deny it. Mara would die and be gone, and Ruth had to learn to be Ruth, whoever Ruth was. That was what had scared Mara about Ruth in the first place.

The restlessness that had driven her into attic space still itched her. She started taking walks in the snow with Abel. Abba didn't try to stop her.

She stopped reading Jewish poetry and started picking up books on music theory. She practiced sight reading and toe-tapped the beats, imagining choreographies.

Wednesdays, when abba planned the menu for Shabbat, Ruth sat with him as he wrote out the list he would take to Gerry's on Thursday. As he imagined dishes, he talked about how Mara would like the honey he planned to infuse in the carrots, or the raisins and figs he would cook with the rice. He wondered what they should talk about—poetry, physics, international politics—changing his mind as new topics occurred to him.

Ruth wondered how he kept hoping. As Mara, she'd always known her boundaries before abba realized them. As Ruth, she knew, as clearly as Mara must, that Mara would not eat with them.

Perhaps it was cruel not to tell him, but to say it felt even crueler.

On a Thursday while abba was taking the truck to town, Ruth was looking through ima's collection of sheet music in the parlor when she heard the click of crutches down the hall. She turned to find Mara was behind her, breathing heavily.

"Oh," said Ruth. She tried to hide the surprise in her voice but failed.

Mara's voice was thin. "You didn't think I could get up on my own."

"I…" Ruth began before catching the angry look of resolution on Mara's face. "No. I didn't."

"Of course not," Mara said bitterly. She began another sentence, but was interrupted by a ragged exhalation as she started to collapse against the wall. Ruth rushed to support her. Mara accepted her assistance without acknowledging it, as if it were beneath notice.

"Are you going to throw up?" Ruth asked quietly.

"I'm off the chemo."

Mara's weight fell heavily on Ruth's shoulder. She shifted her balance, determined not to let Mara slip.

"Let me take you back to bed," Ruth said.

Mara answered, "I wanted to see you again."

"I'll take you. We can talk in there."

Ruth took Mara's silence as assent. Abandoning the crutches, she supported Mara's weight as they headed back into the bedroom. In daylight, the room looked too bright, its creams and whites unsullied.

Mara's heaving eased as Ruth helped her into the bed, but her lungs were still working hard. Ruth waited until her breathing came evenly.

Ruth knelt by the bed, the way abba always had, and then wondered if that was a mistake. Mara might see Ruth as trying to act like she was the one in charge. She ducked her gaze for a moment, the way Abel might if he were ashamed, hoping Mara would see she didn't mean to challenge her.

"What did you want to say to me?" Ruth asked. "It's okay if you want to yell."

"Be glad," Mara said, "That you didn't have to go this far."

Mara's gaze slid down Ruth's face. It slowly took in her smooth skin and pink cheeks.

Ruth opened her mouth to respond, but Mara continued.

"It's a black hole. It takes everything in. You can see yourself falling. Nothing looks like it used to. Everything's blacker. So much blacker. And you know when you've hit the moment when you can't escape. You'll never do anything but fall."

Ruth extended her hand toward Mara's, the way she'd wanted to the other night, but stopped before touching her. She fumbled for something to say.

Flatly, Mara said, "I am glad at least someone will get away."

With great effort, she turned toward the window.

"Go away now."

• • • •

She shouldn't have, but Ruth stood at the door that night when abba went in to check on Mara. She watched him kneel by the bed and take her hand. Mara barely moved in response, still staring out the window, but her fingers tensed around his, clutching him. Ruth remembered the way abba's hand had felt when she was sleepless and in pain, a solid anchor in a fading world.

She thought of what abba had said to her when she was still Mara, and made silent promises to the other girl. *I will keep you and hold you. I will protect you. I will always have your hand in mine.*

• • • •

In the morning, when Ruth came back upstairs, she peeked through the open door to see abba still there beside Mara, lying down instead of kneeling, his head pillowed on the side of her mattress.

She walked back down the hallway and to the head of the stairs. Drumming on her knees, she called for Abel. He lumbered toward her, the thump of his tail reassuringly familiar. She ruffled his fur and led him into the parlor where she slipped on his leash.

Wind chill took the outside temperature substantially below freezing, but she hesitated before putting on her coat. She ran her hand across the "skin" of her arm. It was robotic skin, not human skin. She'd looked at some of the schematics that abba had left around downstairs and started to wonder about how different she really was from a human. He'd programmed her to feel vulnerable to cold, but was she really?

She put the coat back on its hook and led Abel out the door. Immediately, she started shivering, but she ignored the bite. She wanted to know what she could do.

She trudged across the yard to the big, bony oak. She snapped off a branch, made Abel sit while she unhooked his leash, and threw the branch as far as she could. Abel's dash left dents in the snow. He came back to her, breath a warm relief on her hand, the branch slippery with slobber.

She threw it again and wondered what she could achieve if abba hadn't programmed her body to think it was Mara's. He'd given her all of Mara's limits. She could run as fast as Mara, but not faster. Calculate as accurately as Mara, but no moreso.

Someday, she and abba would have to talk about that.

She tossed the stick again, and Abel ran, and again, and again, until he was too tired to continue. He watched the branch fly away as he leaned against Mara's leg for support.

She gave his head a deep scratch. He shivered and he bit at the air near her hand. She realized her cold fingers were hurting him. For her, the cold had ceased to be painful, though she was still shivering now and then.

"Sorry, boy, sorry," she said. She reattached his leash, and watched how, despite the temperature, her fingers moved without any stiffness at all.

She headed back to the house, Abel making pleased whuffing noises to indicate that he approved of their direction. She stopped on the porch to stamp the snow off of her feet. Abel shook himself, likewise, and Ruth quickly dusted off what he'd missed.

She opened the door and Abel bounded in first, Ruth laughing and trying to keep her footing as he yanked on the leash. He was old and much weaker than he had been, but an excited burst of doggy energy could still make her rock. She stumbled in after him, the house dim after her cold hour outside.

Abba was in the parlor, standing by the window from which he'd have been able to see them play. He must have heard them come in, but he didn't look toward her until she tentatively called his name.

He turned and looked her over, surveying her bare arms and hands, but he gave no reaction. She could see from his face that it was over.

• • • •

He wanted to bury her alone. She didn't argue.

He would plant Mara in the yard, perhaps under the bony tree, but more likely somewhere else in the lonely acreage, unmarked. She didn't know how he planned to dig in the frozen ground, but he was a man of many contraptions. Mara would always be out there, lost in the snow.

When he came back, he clutched her hand as he had clutched Mara's. It was her turn to be what abba had been for Mara, the anchor that kept him away from the lip of the black hole, the one steady thing in a dissolving world.

• • • •

They packed the house without discussing it. Ruth understood what was happening as soon as she saw abba filling the first box with books. Probably she'd known for some time, on the fringe of her consciousness, that they would have to do this. As they wrapped dishes in tissue paper, and sorted through old papers, they shared silent grief at leaving the yellow house that abba had built with Meryem, and that both Mara and Ruth had lived in all their lives.

Abba had enough money that he didn't need to sell the property. The house would remain owned and abandoned in the coming years.

It was terrible to go, but it also felt like a necessary marker, a border bisecting her life. It was one more way in which she was becoming Ruth.

They stayed in town for one last Shabbat. The process of packing the house had altered their sense of time, making the hours seem foreshortened and stretched at turns.

Thursday passed without their noticing, leaving them to buy their groceries on Friday. Abba wanted to drive into town on his own, but Ruth

THE LONG LIST ANTHOLOGY

didn't want him to be alone yet.

Reluctantly, she agreed to stay in the truck when they got there. Though abba had begun to tell people that she was recovering, it would be best if no one got a chance to look at her up close. They might realize something was wrong. It would be easier wherever they moved next; strangers wouldn't always be comparing her to a ghost.

Abba was barely out of the truck before Gerry caught sight of them through the window and came barreling out of the door. Abba tried to get in his way. Rapidly, he stumbled out the excuse that he and Ruth had agreed on, that it was good for her to get out of the house, but she was still too tired to see anyone.

"A minute won't hurt," said Gerry. He pushed past abba. With a huge grin, he knocked on Ruth's window.

Hesitantly, she rolled it down. Gerry crossed his arms on the sill, leaning his head into the vehicle. "Look at you!" he exclaimed. "Your daddy said you were getting better, but just *look* at you!"

Ruth couldn't help but grin. Abel's tail began to thump as he pushed himself into the front seat to get a better look at his favorite snack provider.

"I have to say, after you didn't come the last few weeks..." Gerry wiped his eyes with the back of his hand. "I'm just glad to see you, Mara, I really am."

At the sound of the name, Ruth looked with involuntary shock at abba, who gave a sad little smile that Gerry couldn't see. He took a step forward. "Please, Gerry. She needs to rest."

Gerry looked back at him, opened his mouth to argue, and then looked back at Ruth and nodded. "Okay then. But next week, I expect some free cashier work!" He leaned in to kiss her cheek. He smelled of beef and rosemary. "You get yourself back here, Mara. And you keep kicking that cancer in the rear end."

With a glance back at the truck to check that Mara was okay, abba followed Gerry into the store. Twenty minutes later, he returned with two bags of groceries, which he put in the bed of the truck. As he started the engine, he said, "Gerry is a good man. I will miss him." He paused. "But it is better to have you, Mara."

Ruth looked at him with icy surprise, breath caught in her throat.

Her name was her own again. She wasn't sure how she felt about that.

• • • •

The sky was bronzing when they arrived home.

On the stove, *cholent* simmered, filling the house with its scent. Abba went to check on it before the sun set, and Ruth followed him into the kitchen, preparing to pull out the dishes and the silverware and the table cloth.

He waved her away. "Next time. This week, let me."

Ruth went into ima's studio. She'd hadn't gone inside since the disaster in attic space, and her gaze lingered on the attic box, still lying dead on the floor.

"I'd like to access a DVD of ima's performances," she told the AI. "Coppelia, please."

It whirred.

The audience's rumblings began and she instructed the AI to fast-forward until Coppelia was onstage. She held her eyes closed and tipped her head down until it was the moment to snap into life, to let her body flow, fluid and graceful, mimicking the dancer on the screen.

She'd thought it would be cathartic to dance the part of the doll, and in a way it was, but once the moment was over, she surprised herself by selecting another disc instead of continuing. She tried to think of a comedy that she wanted to dance, and surprised herself further by realizing that she wanted to dance a tragedy instead. Mara had needed the comedies, but Ruth needed to feel the ache of grace and sorrow; she needed to feel the pull of the black hole even as she defied its gravity and danced, en pointe, on its edge.

• • • •

When the light turned violet, abba came to the door, and she followed him into the kitchen. Abba lit the candles, and she waited for him to begin the prayers, but instead he stood aside.

It took her a moment to understand what he wanted.

"Are you sure?" she asked.

"Please, Marale," he answered.

Slowly, she moved into the space where he should have been standing. The candles burned on the table beneath her. She waved her hands through the heat and thickness of the smoke, and then lifted them to cover her eyes.

She said, "*Barukh atah Adonai, Elohaynu, melekh ha-olam, asher kid'shanu b'mitzvotav, v'tzivanu, l'had'lik neir shel Shabbat.*"

She breathed deeply, inhaling the scents of honey and figs and smoke.

"*Amein.*"

She opened her eyes again. Behind her, she heard abba's breathing, and somewhere in the dark of the house, Abel's snoring as he napped in preparation for after-dinner begging. The candles filled her vision as if she'd never seen them before. Bright white and gold flames trembled, shining against the black of the outside sky, so fragile they could be extinguished by a breath.

---

Rachel Swirsky holds an MFA from the Iowa Writers Workshop and graduated from Clarion West in 2005. She's published seventy short stories in markets varying from *Tor.com* to *The New Haven Review*. Her work has been nominated for the Hugo, the Locus Award, the World Fantasy Award, the Sturgeon Award, and others, and twice won the Nebula Award. Her included work, "Grand Jete," was originally printed in Subterranean Online's final issue, has been reprinted in year's best anthologies from Dozois, Strahan, and Horton, and was nominated for the Nebula and World Fantasy Awards. She wrote it in the winter while she was working on her MFA and outside it was very cold and lonely.

# Acknowledgments

I would not have been able to put this project together without the grace of the authors who allowed me permission to reprint their work. Skyboat Media has been a delight to work with in the production of the audiobook. Galen Dara for her wonderful art, Polgarus Studios for their work on the interior layotus, and Pat R. Steiner for the cover layout.

Alex Shvartsman was invaluable in the planning of the logistics of the Kickstarter project and the selfpublishing details. Tasha Turner Lennhoff shared valuable insight from her experience with Kickstarter. Others, including Christie Yant, John Joseph Adams, and Andi O'Connor were willing to field questions to help my first time at this go as smoothly as possible.

My writer friends, especially those of Codex and of Dire Turtle, I could not have done this without your feedback and your support and most of all your enthusiasm. With a big project like this outside of my past experience, it would have been easy to be daunted and decide to just find something else to do with my time, but when I shared my ideas, that enthusiasm sustained me and drove me to make the project as big and as great as I could.

There are so many who helped make the Kickstarter for this anthology a success. 416 backers who gave enough to not only produce the ebook and print edition, but also to fund the audiobook edition produced by Skyboat Media.

Many wonderful and talented people offered rewards for the Kickstarter as well: Rachael K. Jones, Sam J. Miller, Ruthanna Emrys, Rachel Swirsky, Stefan Rudnicki, Gabrielle de Cuir, Sylvia Spruck Wrigley, Galen Dara, Wilson Fowlie, Graeme Dunlop, Anaea Lay, Cassie Alexander, Yoon Ha

Lee, and Usman T. Malik.

Many people helped spread the word, including Mike Glyer at File770, Andrew Liptak at IO9, Cory Doctorow at BoingBoing, James Aquilone at SF Signal, and Alasdair Stuart at Escape Artists.

Thank you all, so much.
—David Steffen—

# Backer Appreciation

This is a partial list of those who backed the Kickstarter campaign. There were many others, and they all made this project possible.

Aaron Feldman
Aaron Pound
Abital and Daryl
Alain Fournier
Allen Sale
Alyssa Hillary
Amanda N. H. Jacobson
Andreas Matern
Andrew Griffin
Andrew Hatchell
Andrew Neil Gray
Andrew Scott
Awn Elming
Becky Punch
Ben Weiss
Bonnie Warford
Brady Emmett
Bran Heatherby
Brian Vander Veen
Brooks Moses
C. C. S. Ryan
C J Cabourne
Callum D Barber
Cathi Falconwing
Chad Bowden
Chad Haefele
Chad Peck
Chan Ka Chun Patrick
Chris Brant
Chris Jones
Chris Loeffler

Chris McCartney
Christian Brunschen
Coral Moore
D Franklin
D. S. Gardner
Dani Daly
Daniel Ryan
Danielle M. LeFevre
Dave Miller
David Bell
David Zurek
Doire
Doug Engstrom
Dreamer Bast
The Drs Link
Dusty Rittenbach
Elizabeth A. Janes
Elizabeth Kite
Elyse Grasso
Emma R. Anderson
Elizabeth Ridgway
Erin C.
Evergreen Lee
Ghoti Watson
Glen Han
Graeme W
Greysen Colbert
Hampus Eckerman
Heather Rose Jones
Ian Chung
Ian Stockdale

Janice Mars
Jeff Soesbe
Jennifer M. Brown
Joi Tribble
Jon Lasser
Jonathan Woodward
Joshua O'Hara
Joshuah Trocchi
Kat "CiaraCat" Jones
Kayliealien
Kelly Jennings
Ken Josenhans
KendallPB
Kevin Wine
Lance Calhoun
Lee Ann Rucker
Lennhoff Family
Lexi B.
Liz Boschee Nagahara
Loren Rhoads
Lorin Grieve
Lucy_k_p
M. Darusha Wehm
Maddie Jirasek
Mark Whyte
Mary Kay Kare
Mary Ratliff
Matthew McVickar
Maurice Forrester
Mel
@ofeenah
Jim MacLachlan
Michael McNertney
Michael Monette
Michael Scott Shappe
Michelle Kurrle
Mick Green
Mikayla Micomonaco
Mike Griffith
Morris Keesan
Nate Bird
Pablo Garcia
Pamela A Crews

Patrick J. Ropp
Patrick King
Patti Short
Paul Bowtle
Paul Willett
Peter Moore
Peter Ransom
Rachael K. Jones
Rachel Swirsky
RKBookman
Rukesh Patel (Lallipolaza)
Ruth Sochard Pitt
Sandy Swirsky
Sarah Elkins
Sean Vanbergen
Serena Tibbitt
Sergey Storchay
Shara S White
Shauna Roberts
Shawn Marier
Stephen Burridge
Steve Barnett
Steve Gere
Susan Hanfield
Tatiana J. Bohush
Ted Logan
Terry Weyna
Tim Sharrock
Tomas Burgos-Caez
Tony Cullen
Wilson Fowlie
Zach Weinberg

# About the Editor

David Steffen is an editor, writer, publisher, and software engineer. He has edited and written for the *Diabolical Plots* zine since its launch in 2008, and which started publishing new fiction in 2015. He is most well-known for co-founding and administering The Submission Grinder, a free web tool that helps writers find markets for their fiction and to find response time statistics about those markets. His fiction has been published in many great venues, including *Escape Pod, Daily Science Fiction, Drabblecast, Podcastle, AE,* and *Podcastle*.

*The Long List* is his first anthology project.

28509702R00314

Made in the USA
Middletown, DE
17 January 2016